Ray Irish Occult Suspense Mysteries Omnibus

WORKS BY GORDON BREWER

Ray Irish Occult Mystery
A Shot of Irish
(Ray Irish Occult Suspense Mystery Book 1)
Die If You Want Praise
(Ray Irish Occult Suspense Mystery Book 2)
Drink with The Devil at Midnight
(Ray Irish Occult Suspense Mystery Book 3)
No Remedy Against Death:
(Ray Irish Occult Suspense Mystery Book 4)
Ray Irish Occult Suspense Mysteries Omnibus
Death Stalks the Runway: Ray Irish Mystery Case File #1
Reaper Walks the Garden: Ray Irish Mystery Case File #2

Paranormal and Fantasy
Beowulf: Curse of The Dreygurs
Infinite Loop
The Curse of Blackbane

Clovel Sword Chronicles Series

Shield of Skool (Book 1)
Battle for Three Realms (Book 2)
Downfall of the Gods (Book 3)
Clovel Sword Chronicles: Omnibus Edition

Clovel Sword Saga Series

Clovel Sword Saga: Volumes 1 - 2
Skeletons of Nilgava: Clovel Sword Saga 3
The Bleeding Mountains: A Clovel Sword Saga 4

Ray Irish Occult Suspense Mysteries Omnibus

GORDON BREWER

Brewer Internet Publishing LLC
2023

Dedication

To my family and friends, thank you. Without your support and patience, none of my books would be possible.

Special thanks to Breonna for her invaluable help as my beta reader.

Contents

Ray Irish Occult Suspense Mystery Book 1

Chapter 1: Welcome to the City

A slumped figure moved along with several hundred souls on the cold sidewalks of Oyster City that morning. A gray sky hid the sun, making the buildings' colors appear muted. Raymond Irish moved slowly, unlike the surrounding people. His head was down and his fedora pushed low. The man with his hands stuffed in his worn brown pants scanned the pavement for anything useful. His left pocket had a hole that he kept putting his finger through. While probing the hole would not return his last quarter, it kept him from overthinking. When left alone with his thoughts, his worst memories crept into full view.

No, the hole in his pocket reminded him of his current situation.

Ray was out of cash—road stake, as the hobos called it. Never a good idea to be in a hobo situation, let alone in the dead of winter and stuck in some city where nobody knew your name. Oyster City looked like many of the other medium-sized towns he recalled before the war. But it still wasn't home, and he was sure that he hated the place's name. He wasn't a fan of oysters, anyway. Sure, the town had some elements that Irish might consider his city. The dim neon lights and signs hanging in front of the diners, bars, and different stores along Broadway where he wandered.

On the street next to him, noisy vehicles belched fumes and smoke as they rushed every few feet in a line to the next busy intersection. Red, yellow, and green-colored lights, along with the occasional traffic cop, all tried to keep the downtown chaos from becoming full anarchy.

While Irish walked next to multistory buildings lining the street, Ray thought about the lost souls who walked inside, ready to fulfill another day in return for a few bits of cabbage. He could picture the throngs herding into elevators which lifted them into the sky, where they remained chained to a desk, toiling amid paperwork while silently urging the weekend to arrive faster. He had been there, enduring a soul-crushing job trying to sell trinkets to another person in a similar building somewhere in another part of the country. It was a rat race of collective struggle for the multitudes who watched the clocks on the walls before returning to their homes, sitting among the laid-out grids where the street names all had a familiar look, like Maple or Oak. Shivering, Ray suddenly felt his belly growl angrily. His last breakfast came from spending yesterday's dime on an orange in a nameless town before he hopped a train. He might not envy their downtrodden life, but at least those pushing past him had money to stave off hunger and keep warm at night.

The hole in his pants now forgotten, Ray mentally counted the number of places he'd been through since returning to civilian life. This gray town where he woke that morning made it stop number seven in the last year.

Good ol' lucky seven!

Irish ruefully tried to remember some of his travel. Mostly, one town appeared the same as another, especially for a guy who lived hand to mouth as he drifted across the states. Spending nearly three years of hell in the Pacific, jumping from one island and the next, the man followed a shiftless pattern. However, his wandering was something he controlled. Even cold and hungry, Ray Irish believed he was in charge of his destiny, not waiting for some damned moron to order him around.

As he stooped to pick up a cigar stub lying next to a lamp pole, Ray could not shake the unease drifting through him about his entrance into this particular town. The entire last year remained unsettled in his mind. Since he did not smoke, he placed the cigar into his jacket pocket that did not have a hole. It would be useful later for trading with other hobos.

Ray pushed away thoughts about his recent past hardships, which bothered him more than he liked to admit. Irish did not return to the appreciative and adoring crowds he read about in *Stars and Stripes*. The thongs who lined the docks after VJ Day never saw him. Instead, Ray Irish arrived weeks later and carried on a stretcher to a truck that took him to another hospital. It was the start of his tedious existence, which required a guy to forget thoughts of a future.

Well, that isn't the whole truth.

Haunting memories of the Canal and Okinawa remained. Some of it contained patches of images muddled in his mind, but one date stood out. Easter Sunday in 1945 etched into his memory like blasted concrete. He did not hear the explosion, but Ray remembered the winds he floated upon as his mind came in and out of a fog of pain and nothingness. Dragged through rocks for what seemed like miles, he remembered a tent where he watched a man with intense blue eyes and wearing bloody white clothes. The nurse said something, but they glanced at each other with knowing looks. He saw in their expressions that he would not survive. The eyes he saw pissed him off.

I'll live just to shove it in your faces!

Ray was never sure if he said it out loud. But he'd proved them wrong. Days of endless boredom came that went along with intense agony from multiple surgeries. Then, another round of countless days involving rehab when he got to a hospital near San Francisco. Weeks went by before they took his casts off, and they taught him to walk again, primarily by a big man in white who barked orders like a Marine. Still, he kept his recent past locked up, buried deep like his friends buried on those cursed islands.

In many ways, Ray Irish woke up to his new reality somewhere between Kansas and Missouri inside a smelly cattle car on a train heading east. That morning, he stared at the back of a wristwatch. Engraved on the watch were the words, *To Ray from Amy, '42*. In that cattle car, he decided he had to hock the once treasured heirloom. For the first time, Ray realized that all the booze might have given Irish liquid forgetfulness, but he put himself into the bottom of a barrel. There would be no returning to a sold ranch in Wyoming. His girl, Amy, had other plans. She was already married to someone who had returned from the war earlier. He sold the watch on the streets of Chillicothe for a grubstake to the next town.

Now Ray stood on the street of a place he couldn't find on a map. Oyster City might be a fair-sized town along the Chesapeake Bay coast, but the area looked to be on its last legs. Just north of the Mason Dixon Line, the port used to carry rust-red iron ore and lumber from Maryland out of the small harbor to places worldwide. The city took on a weary resignation, with the war ended like it expected to dry up and blow away with the next recession.

Ray came by this information from a thin, black man who called himself Pappy, running a newsstand on the corner a couple of blocks back. Being a drifter meant learning to get information from those who knew the area. A barrelful of information, the newsy kept his smile despite the hobo's questions. Pappy continued selling his newspapers to those passing by while telling Irish to look for jobs down at the docks. Encouraged by the tip from the only friendly person he had met, Irish followed the sidewalk on his way down to the port. He kept his eyes down to get hobo valuables along the street.

The chill of the air pressed on his clothes as another shiver shook him like a malaria fever. He just could not get warm. Hell, it remained a surprise to him that Ray had woken up at all that morning.

Irish heard yells and screams from below him as the railroad police rousted the hobos out of a nearby freight car on another line. Ray lay behind the observatory windows of an empty Pullman car. It was the only place he could grab when the Capitol Limited came to a stop in a small town called Garrett, back in Indiana. Somehow, during the night, Ray rode through Pennsylvania and nearly all of Maryland on the moving train.

While Irish ached to his core, barely able to move, the icy wind failed to kill him during the journey. Nobody noticed his prone form as he slept on a moving train, even after it stopped to discharge all the passengers. Ray always guessed he could sleep through anything, and now he had proved it. Irish caulked it up to his Irish luck. It took him some time to leave the car and slip into the town to dodge the railroad police.

Poking his index finger in the pocket hole again reminded him to keep moving. As Ray walked along, he mostly kept his eyes on the sidewalk. Bitter experience focused him on finding loose change that occasionally showed up on the concrete. More valuable were the cigarette butts or matches used for trading with others like him who were down on their luck. Unconsciously, he followed the traffic flow of legs, trying to avoid running into those who hurried past him. Each person trying to get out of the frosty morning air helped move the crowd along briskly.

"I don't have enough for a damn flophouse," Ray told himself.

In his difficult position, he needed to find a mission and battle the other tramps for a place to eat and sleep after hearing sermons against alcohol and drugs.

Well, at least I might get a bath and a shave, he thought while rubbing the few days' growth of beard on his face.

A gust of wind made Irish reconsider the possibility of a warm place, although he wasn't sure what was worse, the flophouse or the cold freight cars. Either way, he hoped lady fortune would come back to him soon enough.

Suddenly, the drifter noticed the tired, brown luster of a penny lying on the pavement. Even better, there were a couple of half-smoked butts near it as well. Ray made a beeline to the money and abruptly stopped, bending to get the coin. He felt a weight strike into his side when the woman fell over him, sending them both to the rough pavement.

"Watch where the hell you're going," Ray fumed, talking to the back of a stylish, tan wool coat while he grabbed his injured knee.

Quickly, he checked his trouser pant leg to ensure there were no rips.

"Skin can regrow, but not my pants," he grumbled to himself.

"Put on a stop sign next time," a woman's flustered voice replied indignantly. Ray looked over and saw her striking hazel eyes dancing with annoyance. The attractive woman sitting on the ground then gave him an uncertain grin, causing her slightly upturned nose to wiggle. Irish immediately liked her face, and her gesture reminded him of a rabbit-a cute little rabbit.

"Touché," he told her, as he smiled.

They burst out laughing at how silly they both appeared.

Ray let out a startled cry as a hand grabbed his collar and lifted him from the pavement. The tight grip on his coat and shirt began choking him as he scrambled to keep up with his elevating body. Soon he stood face to face with a bulky man wearing a too-small, gray wool suit. The undersized ape sported a chauffeur's hat on his head.

"I'll teach you to hurt a lady," the driver snarled as he twisted hard on Ray's collar. Ray's face turned a couple of shades of blue as he tried to breathe. He slammed one fist into his attacker's arm and thought he struck a steel column.

"Quincannon, let him go. It was an accident," the lady ordered the man in gray. The goon in the suit eyed her, cocking his massive head to one side skeptically, then released the drifter.

As he fell back among the gawking onlookers who gathered to witness the spectacle, Ray coughed and hacked for air. He noticed the disappointed crowd quickly broke up, returning to their monotonous routine.

Between gasping breaths, Irish listened as the lady told the brute to leave. She stepped over him, offering her apologies.

"Thanks, I guess." He forced out the words with another cough.

"Quincannon's pretty defensive about my welfare," the lady explained.

Her concerned expression helped Ray stop an upcoming sarcastic comment. He heard the almost abandoned tone in the woman's husky voice that caught his attention as well. He joined her when she glanced over at her ape protector, who continued to stare at Ray.

"Here, open your hand." Ray held out his fist, and she hesitated, then opened her palm. "It was supposed to be a lucky coin. The first one I found today. You take it."

He dropped a penny into her hand, and her puzzled look made him smile.

"I only appear like a bum in times like these. Good luck to you," Ray said before he kneeled to retrieve the cigarette butts.

They're worth more anyway.

Just as the drifter started to depart, the lady stepped in front of him with an outstretched hand.

"Here, this might bring you some luck as well." She smiled with perfect teeth. Irish instinctively held out his hand, and the lady placed two items into his palm before she spun back to the large vehicle at the curb. Ray liked the look of her long legs as she slid into the open door of a black Packard Clipper. He felt the staring eyes of the gray ape as the driver shut the heavy steel door before racing around the car to the driver's seat on the other side.

The large car drove away, leaving Ray inspecting the five dollar token and business card in his hand. The coin showed the emblem of a flower and the words *Stanley Rose,* while the business card revealed her husband's name.

"I guess Mrs. Henry La Spina of Terrace Court must take in strays for a hobby," Irish thought aloud as he caught the last glimpse of the car as it disappeared into traffic.

~~~

Greye La Spina pulled out her compact mirror, then glanced back through the window to catch another glimpse of the stranger staring at her car. His manner was unlike most of the drunks and vagrants she occasionally saw inside the mission. Despite his outward appearance as a bum with a scruffy beard and dirty face, he carried rugged self-confidence. The intense gaze of his brown eyes
~~~

reminded her of someone in her past. She liked his look. The woman also noticed the button on his lapel. An Honorable Service pin given to discharged veterans, just like the one her brother wore, made Greye smile at the coincidence. The stranger's size appeared a good fit as well. She remembered her soft spot for big men in uniform and briefly wondered what the drifter looked like without his stubble.

"He's a bum," a gruff voice brought her out of her thoughts.

"Maybe so, but he could have prospects for the future," she said, holding on to a spark of an idea.

"You don't need no more boyfriends," Quincannon growled.

"I wasn't considering that," she told him flatly, although his suggestion intrigued her. Quincannon stared at her through the rearview mirror. She gazed back. "He's an ex-serviceman, like my brother, just needing some help. You didn't need to strangle him."

"Your brother," the driver scoffed. "Nothing but a two-bit gunsel. Anyway, I do the thinking around here in this racket."

"Hugh is not that way!" she raised her voice. "You need to remember you're a handyman around here. Henry would fire you if he saw you beating up tramps on the street."

"Your husband might stomp around some, but he wouldn't do anything. We both know that. He's just another puppet on the strings controlled by what's prim and proper in this city." Quincannon continued glancing into the rearview mirror. "What'd ya give the bum?"

"You're the chauffeur. Keep your attention on the road," she reminded him.

"I asked, what did you hand him?" The chauffeur's voice boomed.

Greye took a deep breath.

"Don't talk to me that way. I swear to God that I'll go to Henry and get rid of you."

"Sweetie, you ain't doing any such thing. We both know it, so get off your high horse. Remember, this is Quincannon. Now, what did you give him?" His tone turned to a snarl.

She stared at the back of his head, contemplating her options. They were not good.

"All right, if you must know, I gave him a card for the mission. Just like Henry asked us, remember?"

The chauffeur snorted.

"Best that you remember as well. Don't make things any more complicated. We're too close to the end of this, and I'm not losing out on a fortune here. You're walking on a tight line along with the rest of us, and don't you forget it. You were supposed to keep that damn bishop happy, and now he's suspicious about Guy Young getting his meat hooks into you."

"That was your stinking fault," she replied hotly. "You and your bright ideas got me into this, damn you!"

Quincannon grunted his chuckle.

"Yeah, I didn't hear you complain at the time, sister. You jumped on this whole setup like a dog goes for a bone. Just remember that any slip up now could spoil that pot at the end of the rainbow. If this falls through, them butches running the state pen will trade cigarettes to play with that pretty little body of yours."

Greye La Spina went silent; her face turned angry as she stuffed the compact back in her purse. The guy driving the car held the cards, and that made it worse. She retreated to stare at the gray, wintry morning outside while Quincannon glared in the mirror.

~~~

Late in the afternoon, Irish walked along Bridge Street, leaving the dock area. Making his way back to the Salvation Mission House, Ray felt tired and frustrated. His feet hurt, and his stomach grumbled for nourishment. The day made the drifter yearn for three squares and a rack somewhere, and it could be anywhere, including hanging with the do-gooders.

After leaving his encounter with Mrs. La Spina, Ray found the mission just in time to grab a lecture and a bowl of soup served with a slice of day-old bread. It was heaven for the moment. The ladies and men running the vagrant facility were efficient. The director running the show gave Irish a quick look over before sending him on his way after the meal, advising him against liquor's evils. Irish scowled at his host, saying he could find better attitudes at a bar. The director's insinuation left Ray with a foul taste in his mouth as he went to the docks. Sure, Irish played a drunk for a while, but that was the past. At this point, Irish hoped he might pull a job just long enough to get some cash before hopping the next train out of Oyster City. In time, he'd find his place to land somewhere.

However, Ray's initial optimism quickly waned after he stuck his head into one office door after another along the waterfront buildings. He realized he needed to shave and to get better clothes. However, the way managers and supervisors responded to him reminded Ray why he didn't like people who held even a little power over others.

Too many of the bosses turned into crumbs, nothing but petty losers, he thought bitterly.

Worse for him, without the right contacts, Ray was out of luck. A drifter without a union card meant there were no jobs in town. The competition remained tough since many folks got laid off when the bustling wartime economy slowed.

Twilight hovered over the buildings, as Ray felt his frustration build with each step on the cold sidewalk. He remembered a saying that a little suffering might be good for the soul, but it made him damn mad as well. He'd seen enough sorrow for a lifetime. His existence over the last few years consisted of cleaning
~~~

up after human cruelty. Ray couldn't count the number of crappy, little islands where he cut open slit trenches for Graves Registration people to dump the bodies of the stinking dead. When he finished, his bulldozer covered the open wound, leaving the landscape flat and barren. Ray could handle all sorts of jobs, but want ads in the papers were not crying for men with his lousy attitude to do nasty work that nobody else wanted.

Engrossed in his thoughts, Ray almost didn't hear the scuffle coming from an alleyway. A familiar sound of knuckles striking flesh forced him to stop. Turning back to the alley, he looked around the corner. In the dim light of creeping night, Irish could make out the outlines of three men clustered together. One man in a dark fedora held a smaller person from behind while a big goon with a light-colored hat kept slamming his fist into the prisoner's belly, muttering words Irish couldn't hear. The thin captive, doubled over in pain, just shook his head. The scene swept across Ray like the rotting smell of a jungle. It reminded him of sadistic Shore Patrol goons beating up drunken sailors on leave. It made him angry.

Irish let the fury overwhelm him, and he charged full speed into the fray. He tackled the goon throwing punches at the prisoner. They fell back toward the building. Ray felt a satisfying, painful cry released by his opponent as they struck the brick wall. Stunned, the big thug fell away, slowly sliding down the rough surface. Springing off the man that he used as a tackling dummy, the drifter bounced to his feet. He went after the hoodlum in the dark hat, who threw his little prisoner out of the way. The criminal's hand went inside his coat, but Ray struck the guy before he could grab his weapon. A rock-hard fist hit the hood right between the eyes, sending the thug's dark fedora tumbling away. Another quick slam from Ray's right fist landed on the goon's temple, and the guy dropped to his knees. Ray finished him with a kick to the ribs. The big man lay on his side, curled up in a fetal position, coughing and retching.

"Come on," the prisoner's voice cried out.

Irish felt a tug on his jacket. Reluctantly, he followed the skinny man, who ran with a limp out of the alley. Ray glanced back to see the thugs pulling themselves from the ground when he turned the corner. Then, the man did a double-take. In the blink of an eye, the drifter swore he saw a clown mask watching them from a dark window across the alley. When he glanced back, the shadowy figure in the black robe no longer remained, only a gentle sway of curtains still moving. Irish sped up to catch the stranger running in front of him. The man jumped into a new, black Hudson car. Impatiently, the driver yelled for Irish to get inside. The vehicle sped away just as the goons exited the alley.

"Damn, that was close. Thanks for the assist, buddy." The thin man in glasses coughed and then gave a nervous laugh.

His face flush with excitement and terror, he kept glancing at Ray.

"That's okay; I don't like bullies. Just keep your eyes on the road," the drifter replied as his foot felt for the non-existent brake pedal.

The car crossed the center line each time the driver looked at him, caused Ray to press down hard on the floorboard.

"Well, mister, if that's the case, you're in the wrong town," the man smirked before taking another glance at his passenger. "The criminals fill this place with them. Anyway, I owe you."

"Forget it. It looks like you lost your hat," Irish said. "Did those hoods get your money?"

Another chuckle came out.

"Nah, they weren't after that. They're some of Young's toughs, trying to give me a warning." The driver rubbed his abdomen. "I can replace the hat."

"Heading to the police station?" Ray asked.

The driver grunted.

"It's a waste of time; those hoodlums already have an alibi. Even if I knew their names, which I don't, they'd have a whole bunch of witnesses saying they were nowhere around that alley."

"So, that's how it works around here!"

Ray went quiet when the other man nodded. Instinctively, the drifter felt curious, but then again, he didn't need any trouble.

The driver turned the Hudson into another alley by the street sign that told Ray they had just left Broadway. The car came to a stop next to a white door with splotches of dark rust. With full darkness covering the city, only a yellow bulb lit the area around the door.

"It's safe here. Come inside and let's talk," the man in glasses told Ray as he got out of the car.

Suspicion filled Irish as he watched the driver exit the vehicle. He watched him walk around the front of the car, pulling keys from his trousers. Ray slid out, carefully inspecting the area while his driver fumbled at the door's lock.

"Damn thing needs some oil," he complained before the door finally yielded.

Inside, his host flipped on another switch, filling the room with light while Ray slowly followed.

"No need to be so nervous," the man said, extending his right hand. "J. Allan Dunn is the name, and this old place is an office and storage building. The building was a gift to the city a few years back, and we rented it out to some companies who took most of it over for storage."

"Ray Irish." The drifter shook his hand. The firm grip of Dunn's hand remained wet with sweat.

J. Allan Dunn took a seat behind the cluttered desk, his green eyes darting between the window and the drifter. Overall, J. Allan carried the appearance of a skinny owl. The guy had a touch of gray to the remaining hair that still clung around the edges of his sizeable, balding head. His narrow face and hook nose, along with the balding, suggested he could have been anywhere from thirty to fifty years old, Ray guessed. Dunn wore a tailored, dark gray suit with a colorful, red tie, nearly pulled off during the fight. His intense eyes appeared extra large behind the black-framed glasses he wore.

"I take it you are someone who knows how things work around this city," Irish noted as he looked around the room. Dusty shelves on one wall behind the desk held black binders, while various blue charts covered the walls on either side.

"I'm the Director of Public Works for Oyster City." J. Allan leaned back; his wooden chair gave a tired squeak. His face beamed proudly. "I have a direct line to the mayor."

"Then why is a city director getting beaten up in an alley?" Ray looked down at him. "And why bring me here to tell me?"

"Grab a seat, and I'll explain." Dunn pointed to two wood chairs, each filled with binders. He waited until Irish removed the files from one chair and pulled it closer to the desk.

"You see, the city is a pretty quiet place, or at least it used to be. People got along just fine, knew their places, and didn't make trouble. Since the war ended, there have been a few rotten eggs pushing in with their money and influence. It's kind of tug of war, if you will, between the good and bad sides. One of the bad ones is a racketeer named Guy Young, who's not even a local person. You just met with some of his hired hands."

The balding director leaned forward in his chair while readjusting his tie.

"On the other side, you have Mayor Hopley and his people trying to do good things for this city. They always have since their family has been here since the founding of the town. I'm local as well. My sister is married to a Hopley. Right in between, you have honest folk like me who are getting squeezed."

"Not a pleasant situation for you," Ray conceded. "Now, what's this got to do with me?"

Dunn pulled his chair close to the oak desk.

"Well, let me ask you a question. I noticed the ruptured duck on your lapel. I couldn't go myself, but I respect those who did. Are you a bindlestiff, or are you looking for a job?"

The drifter's eyes grew dark. "I'm not a bum, just got into town. I've been looking for a job. Nothing available without a union card, so they tell me."

"That's what I thought, probably down to your last dime at this point." J. Allan absently nodded while adjusting his glasses.

Irish hesitated.

"This morning, I came in with the overnight train." He passed on explaining his accommodations.

"Yeah, I understand. The problem is you got here about six months too late. They shut down the munitions plant outside of town. Mayor's trying to fix the problem, working with people to bring in jobs. Still, he's getting a lot of heat from the dockworkers and their union boss who can't see reality. Add to that mix is this Guy Young and his illegal operations; this city is at a crossroads. It grew up too fast during the war, quicker than the District Attorney or the police can handle. And they need help. You saw that yourself." The director smiled, apparently happy in his description of his fair city.

Irish listened patiently, waiting for the other shoe to drop. He instinctively liked the little guy, but he didn't trust him. Ray did not trust most people.

"Yeah, I'm sure there are lots of places like that. Lots of people come into a place and that upsets the apple cart," he agreed carefully.

Dunn's pale face looked over Irish again.

"Obviously, you can handle yourself in tough situations. But you'll need to clean up and get some clothes," he continued. "Then, get you in front of Cat."

"What are you talking about?" Ray's tone changed to suspicion.

J. Allan smiled again.

"I'm offering you one hundred and fifty a week to come work for me!"

Irish went silent. The offer seemed too much for a regular job, and something was wrong with how the man presented it to him.

"That's a lot of salad for an honest city director to pay a guy," Ray thought aloud. "What's the job?"

Dunn's eyes hardened at the comment.

"Some of us in the city help fix the problems I just laid out for you. I need someone who can keep in the shadows and figure out what is happening, particularly with this Young and his goons. You know, help get the dope on dirty laundry that doesn't get into the papers, kind of snoop, if you will," he said. "Plus, if things get tough, I want a guy who can get in and out without losing his head."

Ray stared at the Director of Public Works; for a moment, he was speechless. "Let's slow down, so I understand. Are you talking about a guy who sticks his nose in the wrong places? What makes you think I'm this guy? You've only known me a couple of minutes," he replied.

"Well, you're a stranger, yet you jumped in to help me, so I think I owe you a chance. Plus, you're a veteran, which means you can take an order when it needs to happen. And you are working on our side for a good cause," Dunn told him as he stood from his chair, leaning over the desk with his thin arms propping him up. "As I said, I go all the way up to the mayor. I've been thinking about this idea for a while. When the thugs are threatening businesses and those with money, some of us must step up. You know, help get the right people so they can fix the problems. What's your answer? Are you in or not?"

Ray kept looking at Dunn's face, searching for a clue about his sanity. Crazy plan or not, the drifter quickly mulled over his options.

"I stay on the right side of the law at all times," Irish finally replied.

"Not a problem. You just get information and relay it back to me. Occasionally, you take care of a few odds and ends that might come up," Dunn explained. "You know, help keep people in line who forget who they work for, and I'll make sure you aren't crossing the line. I have the ear of the mayor, and that means the police. Good enough?"

"Listen; despite the way I reacted back there, I'm not a heavy." Ray Irish tried to resist the offer. "You're not looking for some thug to go around knocking heads just for your entertainment? I don't think the mayor would go along with that idea."

"No, no, nothing like that," J. Allan assured him. "I'm talking about entirely legal work here. You're a troubleshooter, so to speak, trying to sniff out where the bad guys are heading. That means you can help head them off. Also, you'll be hanging out with them as you need to." He gave Ray a half-smile. "That means some of the fancy places they visit. There will be benefits in it for you beyond the pay that way."

"You know you could just pay a local snitch to keep you in the know? It would be a lot cheaper for you," Irish said with a nod as he rose from his chair.

J. Allan frowned. "Yeah, I know all about that. Cops can't trust them, so what makes you think I can? Besides, Young has more money than God right now. He owns the snitches," the director said. "Now, can you get me reliable information to weed out these folks?"

"I'm broke, so I can't look a gift horse in the mouth," Ray said, then took a deep breath before reaching out his hand to seal the offer with a handshake. "As long as what you tell me stays legit, then I guess I'm your man. How does this go now? Am I working for the city?"

"Not exactly," Dunn replied, pausing when he saw Ray's expression while he dropped his extended hand.

"It's not what you think. I can't put you on the payroll. There would be too many questions. The wrong people might notice. Besides, you would stand out like a sore thumb," the man explained to Ray.

"One of my trash men doesn't make enough money to go around some of these places to ask the questions and get answers."

He glanced away, and the director retook his seat.

"My idea is you will work as an independent agent for the paper here. The *Morning Beacon* would use you as kind of a legman for them. That way, you're working for the 4th estate with eyes and ears on reporters inside the building who can help get you the latest news. Plus, we can get the information before the paper prints it. You know, keep ahead of the muckrakers. I need someone to keep their mouth shut and their eyes and ears open. The last man couldn't handle the job."

"How's the paper involved with this scheme? I don't see their benefit," Ray said as his suspicions remained. He was suddenly curious about the last guy.

"That's not your affair," the director told him as he pulled his wallet from his jacket. "I'll get you lawfully tied into them with a small paycheck, which keeps everything on the up and up. But you can't forget who brought you to the dance. Is that understood?"

A few minutes later, the former drifter left his new office with three sawbucks in his coat pocket and a key to the office door. Ray made his way down to Cherry Street, following Dunn's directions to a hotel while he racked his brain to soothe his doubts. Irish knew that he should have asked more questions. Ray's insides told him to remain suspicious of Allan, but he convinced himself that it was better to take the cash that the director waved in front of him.

Several blocks later, the drifter found the Hotel Alexander. After the clerk behind the desk cast him a suspicious glance, insisting they had a full hotel, Irish pulled a ten spot. He told the clerk to book him into the place for a couple of nights. Suddenly, as Ray expected, a room became available.

The next morning, an oppressive fog covered the city's larger buildings' tops, leaving the air cold and damp. Ray walked along Chandler Avenue, sporting a new blue suit, along with a new black fedora. Before he stepped into the office, Irish took a quick walk around the outside of the rundown building. As he strolled along, inspecting the front facing the street, only boarded-up windows and a locked door greeted him. The old sign above the door spelled out *Swede's Fine Clothes*. Making his way back to the alley, he thought about his change in luck. A few bucks in his pocket and a hot meal for breakfast gave Irish a renewed sense of identity. He even wondered if a steady job like this might help him bury some demons he carried. For the first time in a while, Ray could almost believe in the future. He didn't realize he was smiling as he entered the dusty office.

Waiting around for his boss, Ray inspected every inch of the room, first out of curiosity and then from genuine interest. Nearly everything he found related to the municipal codes and legal documents needed for construction. Most of the material contained plans and contracts about the new buildings and key public works within the city. However, he discovered several items of interest. Ray might not be a private dick, but it didn't take a genius to figure out his new boss. Irish decided if J. Allan Dunn was an honest city official, then he was the pope. A couple of documents revealed his boss took money off the top of several lucrative city contracts. Also, he confirmed Dunn's name on several blueprints as the owner of the land before construction. Then, he remembered Mayor Hopley's name, which he noticed on some of the other plots and charts he looked through. Digging deeper, it became apparent that his boss, and probably the Mayor, owned several parcels of land where major construction happened. He would bet that they bought the land cheap, long before the construction began.

"My, my, my new benefactor is a busy man trying to get wealthy on the back of John Q. Public," Ray whistled as he leaned back in the squeaking chair. "No wonder he needs information." Then he heard a car pull down the alley. After the vehicle stopped, Irish listened to a car door open, then slam shut, followed by footsteps.

J. Allan entered the office a few minutes before eleven in the morning. At first, the Oyster City Director of Public Works didn't recognize the person sitting behind the desk, causing his owl-like eyes to widen in fear.

Irish slid his feet off the desk. "You didn't say what time, so I got here a while ago."

Dunn gave a quick, sheepish grin. "Well, you'll stay busy from now on." He closed the door, glancing outside before he turned back to the desk.

"Worried about Young's men?" Ray asked.

"No, it's just a habit. You'll pick it up quick enough if you plan on staying in this city." J. Allan's thin face grew hard. "Now, let's get to your work. You will go over to the *Beacon* and meet with Catherine Bennett. Just remember that she likes to be called Cat."

"Why her, and what am I talking about?" Ray rose from the seat and picked up his fedora from the desk.

"She's a photographer down at the paper and a pretty darn good one," Dunn stated with an air of pride. "Cat gets paid for special events photos when she's not trying to become a reporter. That means she gets paid only for the pictures. The good news is that she knows a lot of the town gossip and hangs out with the lady that handles the society pages." The boss nervously began pacing the floor as he laid out his thoughts.

"It may give you a headache listening to the girl, but find the latest news on Guy Young and any of his associates. You can learn more by hanging around the reporters there. Keep an eye open for anything that involves Young and another bad guy called Johnny Jacobi."

"Who is this Jacobi?" Ray interrupted.

"He's some Jew hoodlum from the capital upstate. It seems he's got some business down here, but nobody knows if he's tied in with Guy or not. It's probably nothing, so keep your focus on Young. Your job is to find out his rackets along the dock and any other places he's been muscling in. You can't fight a battle without knowing who the soldiers are."

Ray didn't like the reference to action from some damn civilian, but he held his tongue.

"All right, I just show up to the paper asking for this woman and go from there. How do I get paid?"

"I'll leave cash here each week. The first drawer on your right, the key is on the top of the shelf there." Dunn pointed at the spot.

"There's no phone here. What if I need to get in touch with you?" Ray asked.

"You won't," J. Allan told him flatly. "We aren't socializing. And don't come looking for me. Our meeting place will be here. Only a few know about this office, since the businesses use the rest of the building upstairs as a storage area for their records and other junk. I'll leave a message at your hotel when we meet again."

Ray nodded.

"You're telling me I'm strictly a guy working for the paper who's not associated with you."

"You got it. I don't know you from Adam. Now, get your ass over to 4th and Broadway. Cat knows you'll be looking for her. I'll be in touch in a day or two. I want to see progress. There's a lot on the line here." Dunn went to the entrance, checking carefully outside when he opened the door before he walked to his car.

Irish left the building a few minutes later. He exited the alley and found a taxi near the corner. Fifteen minutes later, Ray climbed out of the cab stopped in front of a gray, squat building flashing the Morning Beacon's name on the rooftop. Inside the lobby, he took the marble steps to the first office he found. Opening a door marked *Press*, Irish passed several cluttered desks. He came to a counter stacked with paper next to a water cooler, where several men stood. They were gabbing about a poker game from the night before.

"Hey, can any of you tell me where a girl called Cat hangs out?" Ray interrupted.

"Yeah, I might," a red-haired man with a kid's face told Irish as the stranger gave him the once over. His brown coat looked new and expensive, but the remains of breakfast showed on his black tie. "Who wants to know?"

"A guy she's expecting," Ray told him emphatically.

"Cat didn't say anything to me," the young man replied while moving closer. "What did you say your name was?"

Ray scowled at the person trying to intimidate him.

"I didn't know you were her secretary." Snickering broke out among the group as Irish continued. "Now, do you have any idea where she is, or do I have to find her boss?"

The red-haired kid blinked at the threat.

"She's up on the second floor, photography," he said before sullenly turning away. Ray listened to the men around the counter, making wisecracks about the exchange.

Ray Irish found Catherine Bennett standing by a messy desk, contemplating a line of photographs hanging by clips. The black and white images covered a portion of the wall between a file cabinet and the desk. The young woman with short, strawberry-blond hair wore a blue sweater and gray trousers. Ray took a double-take at the woman's nicely compact figure.

"Are you Cat?"

He moved to get a better view after closing the door. She wasn't a stunner, but darn cute.

Nodding, she remained focused on the photos in front of her. Finally, she pulled a single black-and-white picture from the clip.

"You must be Irish," she replied, not bothering to look up.

Ray remained quiet, looking around the empty room. A long table ran along the back wall. He could smell the chemical stench coming from containers running along the shelves above the table. A black curtain covered the entrance to another room near the chemicals.

Laying the photo on the desk, she turned her attention to Ray. She gave him a smug grin, her slight freckles showing beneath thin makeup.

"From the description of the encounter last night, I expected some big, rough-looking guy with a broken nose."

Irish smiled.

"I mend pretty quickly."

They heard the door open, and Ray looked around as the young man he left in the office downstairs was standing at the entrance. An uncomfortable pause filled the air while the red-haired man looked like he wanted to hide. The photographer saved him.

"George, come on in; I want you to meet someone." Cat waved him inside.

"Irish, this is George Hopley. He's a legman here, chasing down whatever stories he hears about on the streets."

Ray stared. Aside from George's deliberate intrusion, he didn't like the extra company.

"Yeah, we met. I thought he was your clerk."

The kid scowled, but he didn't take the bait.

"Listen, sorry about the third degree, but you're a stranger around here. How long have you been in town?"

"Hopley, eh," Irish changed the subject. "Same as the last name of the mayor. I'm betting you're local."

"Yeah, the mayor's my uncle." George's attention followed Cat as she picked up a brown camera in its case. She stepped next to Ray.

"You guys can catch up when we get back. I've got an assignment with Irish." She slid her arm inside his, pulling them toward the door. Ray couldn't help but give George a satisfied wink as they left the room.

"Well, sister, where are we heading?" Irish tried to keep up as the girl trotted down the stairs while she slipped the homemade leather camera strap over her arm.

"Keep up," she ordered. "Sam's Cafe is just around the corner."

They crossed the busy street, avoiding a couple of angry drivers who honked and blasted a few curses through closed car windows. Turning the corner, Ray glanced back. Shaking his head, he scolded himself for acting like his new boss. The couple went another block before entering a small diner holding a pair of customers at either end of the counter. They didn't bother to look up. Still taking the lead, Cat pulled into a booth, giving herself a view of the outside street through the large front window.

Ray slid in across from her, suddenly noticing how young she looked. Barely out of high school, if he had to guess. Her blue eyes twinkled with amusement as she watched him.

"I've been out of college for a couple of years," she told him, grinning at his expression. "Everyone thinks I'm younger than I am."

"You read minds as well?" Ray replied, and she laughed.

"Won't your boyfriend track us down here?" he asked lightly.

"He's not my boyfriend, just a bit too protective at times. Besides, the food here is too expensive for a reporter," Cat told him as the waitress came to the booth.

"Two coffees," she ordered.

She watched the server step back to the lunch counter.

"Yeah, it's the Ritz, with their prices. It must be a penny more," he told her, but his mocking comment went past the girl. "Anyway, George acted more than curious when I asked about you."

"George is a good egg, but he's not for me. Besides, I didn't bring you here to talk about him. Dunn says you're the new guy working for him." A determined look replaced the grin on her face.

"So I hear. I spoke with Dunn this morning, and he said to meet with you since you had the lay of the land."

Cat cocked her head.

"Funny, I never heard of him going into work before noon. You must be high on his list of to-dos since Young's men tried to pound on him. The crooks down at City Hall must be getting nervous if they grab a stranger for help. Do you have any idea of what you're up against?"

"Okay, how did you know about the thugs working over Dunn? Are you a reporter as well?" Irish noticed the cynical comments from those used to the city.

"No, but I will be," she told him enthusiastically. "Dunn called me last night to give me the scoop about you. He wanted me to size you up and give you the layout of things. Right now, I'm a photographer for the paper, mostly taking pictures of the women's club events or the political things going on in town." She patted the camera case next to her.

"Then what's the dope on Dunn and you? He tells me he's just an honest city official." Ray noticed Cat glance away before answering.

"Do you believe him?"

"Let's just say I have ideas against that. But I work for this director now, so I'm not sure how much I care," Irish told her.

"Good," she replied, seeming relieved at his statement. "Nobody is honest inside City Hall. Heck, there's no one honest in Oyster City. J. Allan Dunn pays me to do things for him, like keeping my ears open to news about the mayor and such. I let him in on things that the newspaper knows. He talks big, but he's only a minor cog in the political machine who owes his position to his wife's relations. But he knows who runs things, so he's good at getting things for the mayor. From what I've heard, he's the old boy's handyman."

"Then, who's the big guy in town, the mayor?" he asked. Ray believed the first hour in a town told you a lot about its character.

She stared at him for a moment. "Horace Hopley acts the part, that's for sure." Cat leaned forward. "But I wouldn't put my money on that, if you know what I mean."

"Kind of a puppet on the strings of someone else, is that it?" Irish raised an eyebrow at the comment.

She nodded.

"Yeah, Dunn likes to tell me he's part of the right side, keeping Oyster City good for all of us. But that's just Mayor Hopley's speech. I mean, I grew up here, and there's always someone either trying to knock off another person or some type of graft that people are involved in." She gave a slight frown at the thought, pausing to take a sip of her coffee. "First thing you have to know is to watch your back. You never know who you're dealing with, and people can get real mean."

Ray thought about J. Allan's edgy looks out the window.

"I'll keep your warning in mind. Any ideas on who pulls strings in this city?"

Cat glanced away briefly before she shook her head. Irish took a drink.

"What about you? Dunn acts like you are working on their side. Taking pics of events for the mayor and staying up on things."

Cat nodded. "Nearly every time a shovel hits the ground, I'm there. I never understood why the public works department thinks they need pictures before they build something. I mean, the paper never runs the photos. Then again, I get paid either way."

"Yeah, I get it." Ray nodded, wondering at Dunn's interest in keeping her employed. "What about this Young character?"

"Guy Young is unknown. He is a good-looking devil who came into the city right before the end of the war. Pretty soon after that, he brought in that large gambling boat. It's out in the bay, so the city can't shut it down. Otherwise, he's got his thugs running around making sure business owners pay him for fire insurance, so their places don't go up in smoke. All it took was a couple of warehouses burned out, and now people pay his thugs and keep quiet. District Attorney can't prove anything, of course."

"That makes him another textbook racketeer. Why don't the state cops take down gambling on the ship?" Ray wondered aloud.

Cat looked at him oddly.

"Why would they? Guy has paid off a bunch of people in the capital, so they don't bother him. I've seen some of the crooked politicians who bring down their lovers for parties out on the *Stanley Rose*. I even got some pictures of a couple of local bigwigs with their whores." Her voice conveyed proud satisfaction in her work.

Ray thought about the five-dollar token in his pocket, but he returned his focus to Cat.

"You have pictures of these corrupt politicians? You said you wanted to be a reporter. Don't you news hawks want to spill the beans on that type of stuff?"

"Are you kidding me? I ought to be a reporter, but I like the money these shysters will pay for the pics a lot more. The big newspapers won't spend money on those pics. And they don't care about political crooks running Oyster City. Those local newspapers that might have an interest would have an accidental fire, so they don't bother," she told him, giving a knowing nod. "Anyway, I have George contact the guy and see if the dope wants the negatives, which they do, of course. You see, George makes sure they know the guy's wife might take them to court with the pictures. Most of the time, they come through. Then we split the money." The smug look she gave him caused Ray to remain quiet for a moment.

Irish took a sip of coffee, suddenly wishing it had a shot of whiskey in it. The cute young kid across the table had the corrupt soul of a grifter. She acted like a person who would happily kick you into your grave if convenient, and the action brought her some cash.

"I get it. No wonder you work part time."

"It pays the bills," she said with a grin, while Ray's face remained unmoved.

"Get back to Young. He's got a racket going along with gambling and extortion. If nobody is pestering him, what does he want? Beating up Dunn doesn't accomplish much. It seems like this Young character already has it pretty good."

She shrugged her shoulders, looking down at her cup.

"Word is he'd like to become the owner of Oyster City. Maybe he's trying to build an empire. Either way, he's been going after some of those on the city payroll who can help him. Those related to the mayor like Dunn can't pay off when he threatens. Some coppers are taking his money, so it's not clear who those in City Hall can trust anymore. It's obvious that Dunn wants you to find out."

"Really? You seem to know a lot about what J. Allan wants," Ray observed.

Cat's face hardened.

"I'm smarter than you might think. I can figure things out. You are unknown, so if you ask questions, nobody gets wise to who pays you. I don't know how he does it, but getting attached to the paper means you can check things out. I'm guessing people will assume you're just another reporter sticking his nose in the wrong place. It's not like some reporters are taking sides depending on who's paying them. You're just like the last guy Dunn hired."

"Okay, you're smart," he told her. "Now, what about Jacobi?"

Her eyes widened at the name, but she quickly replied she knew little about the gang leader. The lie was obvious, but Ray let it go, sure that Cat wouldn't tell him anything useful. Already, Irish had difficulty figuring out the right pieces in this puzzle.

She looked at him when Ray grew quiet, wondering what he thought. She noticed how much his demeanor toward her changed during the conversation.

"Listen, I've got to get back to work. I'll check around and keep my eyes open."

Ray took a sip of coffee and frowned.

"Damn, coffee's cold." He looked at her, confident he could not trust his new partner. "Tell me something. Are you paid to keep an eye on me or just feed information?"

She smiled brightly.

"I'm not paid to be a private dick. From what you've told me, it seems you're on your own around here. I'm just the messenger."

Nodding, Ray stood and pulled a couple of dimes from his pocket.

"Well, you're honest about that. I'll see you around." He quickly turned and left the café, not bothering to wait for her. Irish paid no attention to her stunned gaze as he walked past the front diner window.

A few blocks away, Irish came to the newsstand on Main Street, where Pappy ran his business. Unexpectedly, the older man recognized Ray in his new clothes. Irish purchased the morning paper and started jawing with a wiry man sitting on a stool. It didn't take long to get him warmed up, and Pappy eventually spilled the news about the rough and tumble world inside Oyster City. The newsy's version also connected with Cat's understanding of the world. However, Pappy also explained more about the constant turmoil over the years.

"Been here most of my life," Pappy told Ray as he took a nickel from a passing customer. "Can't say it's changed in how things get done. Oh, there are new buildings and roads, and all those at the top seem to have their fingers in everybody's pie. Those that say too much against the progress appear to end up missing. I noticed you aren't leaving."

"Yeah, got a job," Ray told him before he asked Pappy about what he meant about missing people, but his new contact shook his head.

"You'll see it soon enough," Pappy told him stubbornly.

Irish changed the subject and asked about the Jacobi gang. The newsstand owner explained that Johnny Jacobi owned most pawnshops around the state. The gangster had his sights set on moving his game into Oyster City before the war broke out. Then, Guy Young showed up to put his stamp on the town. According to Pappy, recently, a couple of Young's thugs went missing after Jacobi's men spotted them. Irish tipped him a buck for the information, causing the old newsy's brown eyes to light up.

"Say, what side are you working for?" Pappy asked with a hint of suspicion.

"Just for me, keep your ears open, and some more of the green can come your way," Irish told him.

Pappy gave a friendly smile as Ray walked away.

The rest of the afternoon found Irish in the library. His attempts at flirting with the stiff blonde behind the book counter went nowhere, but he found a book about the local history. The man was curious about the suspicion he had witnessed in his short time there. Reading about the founders who established the city, Irish combed through a large stack of old newspapers. Stories from the *Beacon* and their rival newspaper, the *Star*, made him him feel like he was back in school. Still, he went through news clips from the last year, bypassing the war articles and concentrating on the police reports and political events.

When Irish finished, he believed he understood the city and its people. On its own, Oyster City carried a tragic history with floods and fires that nearly destroyed the early settlement in the 18th century. An early immigrant pioneer named Henry Andras founded the town, setting up his shipping and fishing company along the bay. Growing wealthy on the backs of slaves and Far East trade before the Civil War, the family ran the town like their fiefdom. According to one book, only in the last century had other wealthy families, like the Hopley's and La Spina's, earned powerful positions over the city.

Irish spotted something unusual in all of his reading. For such a small city, the number of murders, disappearances, and other violent crimes appeared to make Chicago look like a citadel of virtue. There was also a string of corruption stories that seemed to go nowhere. It appeared his employers were just as crooked as those trying to push into the town. At least Young and Jacobi were upfront about their corruption. The disappointing confirmation made Irish seriously reconsider his new line of work.

Not long after six, Ray stepped into the lobby tavern at the Alexander hotel. He watched the few patrons with casual glances at the large mirror across the bar counter. A salesman pitched his line of wares to a bald gentleman at one end of the room. The bored businessman kept his attention on a cute redhead across the room. After a couple of shots of Irish whiskey, the new troubleshooter ordered a grinder sandwich. Observing those in the bar again, he noticed the redhead was waiting for someone.

A few moments later, Ray got his food and glanced at a young married blonde lady passing behind him to join the redhead woman. Recognizing their forced discreteness as he covertly observed them, he knew a deeper relationship was going on between the two ladies.

At times, the world is pretty damn screwy!

He smiled to himself. Spending several months in bed with little to do, but watching people and their interactions gave him insight. Ray noticed the small things that showed something deeper in a person's expressions and mannerisms. Deducing the reasons behind the clues he viewed became a game to kill the time.

Irish reached into his pocket to pay the check, finding the five-spot token that Mrs. Greye La Spina gave him. He flipped the golden-colored coin in his hand. It came up heads in his palm.

"Say, how does a guy get out to the *Stanley Rose*?" he asked the bartender named Frank.

"There's an exclusive water taxi down at the docks, over on the last piers. Signs should show you." The burly man smiled, lifting his pencil mustache. "Say, if you're looking to lose your money, I can put you into a great Acey Deucey game that's closer."

Ray shook his head.

"Nah, I'm thinking of a gal with hazel eyes!"

His first view of the *Stanley Rose* gave Ray a quick flashback. A former cargo ship that sat low in the water had a passing similarity to the thousands of Liberty ships he saw filling the seas around Japan a few years before. However, the *Rose* carried a white paint coat and strings of flashing lights, making sure people knew its location. While the ship was not exceptionally large, Ray quickly noticed the loud music coming from a live band on board. It came to him over the sound of his taxi boat's motor and props churning through the water.

On the *Stanley Rose*, Irish milled around the deck after handing his hat to a young girl wearing too much makeup. The main deck held a dance floor with a small band playing some of the latest tunes. Several gaming tables in the corners of the sizeable area kept the focus of the small crowds. The deck below his floor had more tables placed inside smaller rooms. He assumed the quieter places held the poker cheats who played their loaded games against their marks. Ray saw enough crooked card games over the years in the Pacific.

I wish I had half of all the dough I lost!

It appeared half those hanging around the dance floor were drunken women in their best dresses while men, young and old, kept buying more of the cheap booze. Curious, Ray watched a staggering couple heading up and began following them as they took a flight of stairs above the main level. Trailing discreetly behind, he reached a passageway and then waited as they snuggled near a partially open door. Before they entered the room, he saw the woman expertly slip her hand into her client's suit pocket, quickly retrieving his wallet.

Passing by the now-closed door, Ray shook his head at the stupidity of the drunken sap inside. At least the prostitutes were nice looking around here, he thought cynically. Irish walked to the other end of the passageway, where he came to another stairway leading back to the main deck. Pushing his way through the crowd, Ray found the bar and got a whiskey on the rocks. Leaning against the counter, he noticed a closed door with a sign spelling out *Management* in stenciled letters on the other end of the room. He thought nothing of it until the door opened and he saw her.

Greye La Spina walked into the room wearing a tight, pale yellow dress, which accented her knockout figure. Just behind her walked a tall, sophisticated man wearing a tuxedo. Ray noticed her escort's self-possessed features, his blue eyes, sharp nose over thin lips, and jet black hair slicked back.

Guy Young made quite an entrance as well. Irish grinned when he saw the large goons in matching brown suits trailing behind Young. The only difference between the two bald men was one thug had a scar across his nose. Tweedledee and Tweedledum's cartoon picture immediately came to mind as he watched them follow their boss.

When Greye walked by Irish, and he got a close-up view. Her pale face carried the emotion of a porcelain doll. Her smudged lipstick and her hair were slightly out-of-place. The hallmarks of her fun behind closed doors. Guy guided her to the stairs leading to the deck below. Her racketeer escort beamed a ludicrous smile of satisfaction at her public humiliation.

"It looks like the bishop's wife is still coming up short on the tables."

The contemptuous whispered comment came from a half-drunk woman standing behind Ray. Short and overweight, the lady looked close to middle age. Wearing a tight pink dress made for a younger woman, the caustic lady kept trying to get her husband to dance. The gray-haired man obviously wanted to be elsewhere. Slugging back the last of his whiskey, Ray stepped in front of the woman, holding out an arm.

"Come on, I need a partner," Ray told the cheerful lady. As he led her to the dance floor, Irish noticed the gray-haired man wander away. Unspoken thanks appeared from the released prisoner's eyes.

Dance moves slowly came back to Ray as he tried to make his best impression of Fred Astaire, which needed a lot of work. Luckily, she remained happily unconcerned, sloshing her words during their conversation.

"So, young lady, what's your name?" he asked.

The woman giggled. "Just call me Pearl. You dance well."

"As do you," he smiled gamely. "I'm a stranger here. Have you been to this place before?"

"Yes, dear, we…I mean, I come here quite often. It's such a blast. You stick with me, and I'll show you around." Pearl stepped in closer as the tempo slowed during the next song. The overabundance of her perfume reminded Irish of the sickly sweet smell of flowers on the Solomon Islands.

"What about your husband? I don't want to make enemies."

Pearl smiled, giving him a wink. "He'll wear himself out at the poker tables downstairs. We have plenty of time."

After several drinks, the chubby woman became more talkative. She and her husband, a banker, knew the social circles of the city. Most of what she knew was second hand or idle gossip. However, he gathered some details about Greye La Spina.

"You know the bishop comes from a long line of La Spina's in this city." The married woman pushed in close to him. "But that thing he married, nobody's ever heard of her. I understand his wife hangs around this boat most of the time."

Pearl made it clear that Greye carried a low reputation as the wife of a respected bishop. The drunk woman considered Henry La Spina for sainthood for dealing with such a situation.

"What about Guy Young? Why does he let her hang around? From some women looking at him, he has plenty of opportunities," Ray mused.

Pearl shook her head, nearly stumbling as he helped her recover.

"He's a collector of things. I hear he likes to use her to show off he can do anything he wants. Now, let's get another drink." She batted her eyes; the thick mascara left little lines around her eyelids. "I want to show you some of the cozy hideaway places they have here."

Ray decided he wasn't drunk enough for a turn with Pearl, so he took her to the bar before breaking away to find the restroom. The information gave him the idea for a quick exit from the ship with hat in hand. Irish made his way back to the small dock where the water taxis dropped off the passengers. Intrigued by Greye La Spina's relationship with Guy Young, he decided she could be a way into the racketeer's inner circle.

Stepping down a metal stairway, Irish went over the stories he heard as he exited the ship. Then Ray saw Greye standing alone on the dock; her attention focused on the dark water just a few steps away.

"Ma'am, you forgot something," Ray told her, coming up behind her while holding out his closed hand.

She jumped at his words before turning to him and instinctively holding out her hand. Ray placed the five-dollar token in her palm, and Greye looked at the item. Confusion filled her face.

"You gave it to me yesterday morning after I knocked you down," he explained with a grin.

Her hazel eyes lit up, the porcelain mask gone. "My, you clean up well." Greye glanced him over. "And a new suit. You must have hit the jackpot here."

"No, just got a job," Ray told her with a bemused smile. "You look fantastic."

He meant every word.

"Thank you. And you look better without the beard." Her smile appeared relaxed and genuine.

"Yeah, I know. A bath helps as well." He intentionally looked her over. "Mmm, there's something else about you." He paused again, then snapped his fingers. "I know! I don't see a great ape hanging around."

Greye chuckled at the comment.

"Well, that can happen with the right people."

"That's good to know. Perhaps you can get a drink with me to finish out the evening?"

Her nose gave that cute twitch again, and her smile fell away.

"Unlikely. You read the card that came with the chip I gave you. I'm unavailable."

Ray went for broke when he saw two boats approaching. One boat looked to be a private one for the bishop's wife since he saw Quincannon in his gray suit driving it.

"I remember every second, along with the smell of your perfume. You're not the type that a guy forgets. I figured I could repay you with a drink. It's a shame you're not into fun."

"Then you give a call to Oscar 2525. You can ask for Bishop La Spina. He's known to take in strays." Her snicker caused Ray to smile at her jab.

"Ray Irish is the name. Now you know me, so I'm not a stray to you. When I call, it'll be for that lovely lady who likes more entertainment than just throwing down tokens on a table. Anyway, there's good Irish whiskey at the Alexander Hotel." Ray tipped his hat, and he jumped on the water taxi, which arrived first at the dock.

He smiled at the ape-man when his taxi pulled away, allowing the chauffeur to guide his smaller boat next to the ramp. Ray nodded to Greye as his craft left the dock.

<center>~~~</center>

A wheelchair's wooden wheels gave off a hideous squeaking noise as a tall man in black pushed the mechanism along the hallway. The attendant's face remained impassive, drawn, and wrinkled tightly like dry leather. The man's suit carried the lost style from generations before. At a distance, he could have passed for an eerie copy of Abraham Lincoln with the tall hat he wore. In the wheelchair, an elderly lady stared ahead at the open door where a rotund man nervously stood. The old woman's eyes were dark, unlike the colorful gypsy outfit she wore. An incredible display of bright yellow and red flowers covered her dress. A golden headscarf, wrapped tight around her skull, covered much of the woman's white and gray hair.

When the wheelchair reached the nervous man standing at the door marked with the title of mayor. Mayor Hopley hastily stepped aside while he nodded his welcome.

"You are looking well. It's been such a long time since you have come to my office."

"Bah, don't bother with the platitudes, Horace. I'm here because the spirits are restless. You've been weak." The gypsy directed her companion to stop the wheelchair next to a large oak desk. She shoved aside a small stack of papers that were in her way, sending several files to the floor. Mayor Hopley kneeled to retrieve them. He was visibly upset, but he said nothing.

She pulled a pack of cards from her lap and quickly placed several of them face-up on his desk while the mayor of Oyster City sat in his chair. Carefully, watching the tarot cards she laid out, the potbelly man's blue eyes glanced back and forth between the woman and her companion.

"There, the cards tell me everything," the gypsy said as she leaned back. "The Knight of Swords enters this world; he is a foolish one. Carried in by The Card with No Name." The woman tapped her finger on the card.

"Look well at the card, Horace. The spirits came to me, and they know. The outsiders will seek your overthrow."

Horace stared at the depiction of a corpse wielding a sickle. His eyes widened at the rest of the cards he recognized.

"Your vision cannot be correct. Over many years since the last cycle, nothing puts the elders at risk. Many came here during the war, but they leave with the munitions plant gone. What does this mean?"

The gypsy gave a nearly toothless grin as she pointed to the ancient, cursed symbol closest to him. The thick paper held a picture of a demon. It rested on top of the Emperor's card.

"You see the cloven one," the woman's finger tapped on the image. "He stands in judgment of people who cannot stop the outsiders who come close to the throne. The strangers grew strong from the war years, leaving our rule at risk. Horace, you have been weak!"

"It will be up to the Shadows to fix this. With the coming blood moon, the great one's spirit must arise and bring order to the chaos. Like times of old, the Shadows will bring forth a new cycle, so justice against these outsiders comes."

Chapter 2: A Trail of Death

Two nights later, a bored and frustrated Irish stared at the banana leaf wallpaper in his room. He decided it was ugly, which went along with his mood. He still knew little about the operations of Young and his band of merry thugs. Despite the money laid out around town, everyone seemed to clam up when Ray asked for details. Also, he had scant information about any connections with Jacobi. Cat gave him nothing from her contacts when Ray looked her up. However, he considered the possibility she might go directly to Dunn to get some extra green. Irish wouldn't put it past the cute little picture taker. Worse, J. Allan Dunn already expected miracles, upset that Ray gave him nothing to show for his money so far. His initial confidence changed, and Irish strongly considered taking the next week's pay and skipping town. Such thoughts made him even angrier, since he hated the idea of quitting. Like a dog with a bone, once he got started working on something, he finished it.

The phone rang, and Ray picked it up, about to bark at the caller. However, the soft voice asking for him changed his mind.

"The Irish whiskey is better at the Six Jolly Squires. There's a dark booth in the back," Greye's voice purred.

"I'll be there," he replied without a second thought. He heard the phone click, and Ray put the receiver down while he scanned his room for pants.

Taking a taxi to the city's outskirts, Irish found the tavern just off Route 67, which led to the state capital. The Six Jolly Squires stood like the last building on the way out of town, its squat adobe-style architecture out of place among the surrounding farmland. Pulling into a nearly empty parking lot, Ray got out and noticed a rundown motel with most of the lights missing on the flashing sign across the street. Otherwise, the area around the highway remained undeveloped woodland. Walking to the front door, he noticed a new red Packard convertible parked on the dark side of the building. The flashy vehicle had difficulty trying to hide between two older black cars parked on either side.

Inside, Ray found a quaint bar with a row of red cloth-covered booths running along the front windows. A young couple ate dinner while two men sat at the bar, working types, judging by their overalls. Both men stared at their mugs of beer, quietly listening to a song by the King Cole Trio coming from the radio behind the bar. In the back, off to his right, Ray noticed another booth, partially concealed by a thick, dark curtain. The red glow of a cigarette appeared to float inside the dark and secluded spot. As he walked closer, he noticed a definite feminine figure nearly hidden in the shadows. He slid into the booth.

"Nice and quiet." Ray looked Greye over; he wasn't disappointed. The seductive woman wore a low-cut, dark red dress, with a mink stool lying across her shoulders. A stylish black hat sat on the table beside her. She held a whiskey tumbler in her hand.

"Give me an Irish straight and another drink for the woman," Ray ordered after a bored-looking waitress arrived. He kept his eyes on the quiet woman, who finished her cigarette and took another drink.

"Do you always take charge when you arrive?" Her words sloshed a bit.

He smiled and replied, "Bad habit, I guess. I'll try to fix it."

"I don't like wimps," she said simply, her eyes watched him like a cat staring at a mouse.

"Then we'll get along famously," he said, sliding closer as the waitress brought their drinks. Ray raised his glass. "So, what do we toast to?"

Greye smiled.

"To our health, of course, and to no men in gray suits following us." She lifted her glass before taking another sip. "I noticed the pin on your lapel. You must be ex-army, like my brother."

"Seabee," he corrected her as he took a drink, "one of the thousands."

"But you walk stiff, were you wounded?" Greye didn't appear to hear him. His face turned dark.

"Yeah, you could say that. But my parts still work just fine."

She smiled.

"I'm sorry. I was just trying to know your background. You come into this city like a tramp, now you're wearing new clothes, and you say you have a job. It appears you move fast."

"I get it, looking for the flaws." Irish took a sip of his whiskey. "Good luck to you with that idea; I'm just an average Joe."

The cheap fake whiskey made him frown. In Greye's expression, he observed a vulnerable and caring quality. But he was cynical enough to believe that she knew all the tricks to keep his attention.

"Everyone has secrets. You're not quite the lady that you project, are you?"

"I'm not sure what you mean?" Her hazel eyes lit up with a quick flare.

"Mrs. Henry La Spina, age twenty-nine, married to an older man for about two years. Before that, you were unknown in Oyster City, which helps fill the streets with many rumors about you. Now, you frequent the home of an infamous man named Guy Young, the *Stanley Rose* owner, and other assorted rackets. Not quite the demure preacher's wife that many in your social class expect." He leaned back in the seat, taking a sip of his drink while observing her. Her reaction slightly surprised him.

"You act like a private detective. I'm flattered that you've been checking up on me." Her tone was even, not hostile like he expected.

"I like the package, and curiosity just got the best of me," he told her. "Plus, I had time to think. Most pretty ladies don't hand their card to a bum to get acquainted. That makes you a smart woman."

Greye beamed.

"I'm glad because few men can figure out the clues they receive." She set her tumbler down, staring at it. "Tell me the truth. With all the rumors and innuendo, why are you here?"

"I guessed you must be lonely living among those who resent your presence. Why else would you give me the card?" Her nod confirmed his thoughts.

"It's not what you think about the *Stanley Rose*," she told him, her eyes remained fixed on the nearly empty glass. "I like to gamble. Henry doesn't think it proper for the bishop's wife to be there. But he tolerates it because he loves me."

"Yeah, I saw how proper you were the other night as you came out of his office. Anyway, it's none of my business what you do with your spare time."

She didn't look at him.

"I know what people say. I'm a gold digger who married Henry because his family has money. They don't realize he's not that wealthy. Then, some say I enjoy being a whore outsider who shacks up with Young to rub my husband's face in my misery. Is that why you're here? You need another notch in your belt with a lonely wife?"

"I told you why I'm here. I've got a lot of faults, but lying ain't one of them. People make all sorts of accusations when a person doesn't fit the mold, been there myself. I know what it's like to be an outsider."

"Do you?" Her eyes widened, disbelief cascaded down her face as she looked up. "Have you attended social functions where you stand alone the entire night while the people mock you? They're oh so silent, but the glances are there. Life among those with money isn't what people dream about."

"No," Ray told her, finishing the drink. "I can't say I've been there or that I understand."

"Stay around long enough, and you'll see the evil this place tries to hide." She shook her head bitterly, taking another drink. "They hate anybody who wasn't born here."

"Well, then we have something in common; I'm not from here either," he told her. "Maybe we will find out more."

"Are you married?" she asked suddenly.

"No, and it's probably best," he told her with a shrug. "Some say I have a chip on my shoulder, but mostly, I haven't found a place I like enough to stay around."

"Don't get married," Greye warned him. "You learn all sorts of things you don't want to find out."

"What's your story?" He glanced over at the bar, but no one appeared to pay them any attention.

"I needed stability. Henry gave that to me." Her reply seemed rehearsed, but he let it go.

Ray remained quiet for a moment, knowing she wasn't telling him the whole story. "I guess I can see that. Doesn't make for a pleasant thought about the future." He changed the direction of the conversation.

"Why don't we go for a drive?" he suggested. "I'm a stranger, and you can show me around,"

Greye smiled at the thought and nodded, moving closer to him. And he liked the smell of her perfume when she leaned on his arm.

"I don't have to be back for a while," she whispered in his ear. "Let's find a nice, quiet spot."

They walked out to her red car. Greye climbed into the driver's side. When Irish was about to get into the Packard, he noticed a dark car parked behind them with someone inside in the driver's seat. Something in the way the person sat, leaning against the door, bothered him.

"Just a second." He glanced inside at Greye, leaving his door open.

"What is it?" La Spina turned to look out of the rear window.

Ray did not reply as he wandered toward the dark vehicle. The pale light coming from a sign hanging on the back of the tavern made it difficult for him to see. He heard Greye open her car door, and Irish glanced back. When he reached the front of the car, he thought the person inside the vehicle must have passed out.

"Hey there, are you okay?" He paused.

The figure inside did not move, and silence filled the air. Irish stepped along the driver's side; the crunch of his footsteps sounded loud in the still night. He stopped and heard Greye's footsteps coming closer. Shadows filled the inside of the car, making it difficult to see.

"Hey there, wake up!"

A car turned out of the motel parking lot across the street. Its bright lights outlined the scene for Irish. In the brief flash, he saw a large man's head lulling eerily to the side. A long line ran across the guy's throat with dark red blood covering the upper half of the body. While he stood momentarily frozen by the ghastly sight, Ray Irish heard a woman's muffled scream. By the time he turned around, Greye had reached her car and was frantically climbing inside. As he shuffled after her, her Packard spun around the parking lot, the passenger side door swinging wildly as the vehicle reached the highway. Watching the red taillight disappear down the lonely road, Ray Irish stood in the dark lot as the dust settled around him.

~~~

Catherine Bennett confidently strode through the hallway to Room 402. She knocked on the varnished door, but no response came from inside. Scowling, Cat pounded on the wood forcefully. Finally, a gruff voice told her to hang on, and she heard the heavy footsteps come to the thick, wooden door. As soon as the door opened, Cat pushed her way past the surprised man.
~~~

"What the hell are you doing? I don't need no hotel peeper knocking down my door," Irish growled, taking a quick scan around the hallway before shutting the door.

She laughed at him, going to the unmade bed where she sat, picking up his blue suit jacket from the brass footboard. "Don't worry; I know my way around here. By the way, Dunn is looking for you. You realize it's nearly noon. Most of us begin work in the morning." She looked at Ray in his underwear, his legs showing jagged, thick scars along his thighs and calves. Her smile faded momentarily. "You might want to put on your pants around a lady."

"And you might want to get the hell out of my room," he replied crossly, pulling his pants off the back.

"Don't be like that. I'm a friend, remember?" Her eyes danced at his discomfort. "I came up with George, and he's already talked to the hotel cop. The newspaper got George a room on the third floor. We're keeping a watch on the restaurant across the street."

"Should I care?" he inquired as he finished buttoning his pants.

"You might; it's got something to do with Guy Young."

Ray stared at her.

"All right, give!"

"They say Guy is coming off his boat to meet with someone at the restaurant. That's mighty rare since City Hall has the word out to arrest Young if he ever comes into town. But, since some cops take his money, that's not happening. George brought along some binoculars, and he's going to be heading down when he spots Young. He wants to find out who shows up to meet with Guy. I'm here for any pictures I can get."

"Thanks for the news. Now, you can beat it," Irish told her as he pulled a white shirt from the dresser.

Cat frowned.

"I thought you liked me."

Ray took a deep breath before glancing at her.

"Sure, I like you. You've got spunk, that's for sure." He refused to say more while he went back to buttoning his shirt.

"Who's the girl?"

"What do you mean?" Ray continued his work.

"I told you I was smart. I can smell expensive lady's perfume on this jacket, and the doorman told me he saw you pull up in a taxi late last night." Cat smiled smugly at him.

"Then you can figure out that it's none of your business," Irish told her point-blank. "Besides, I don't need you checking on me. I had a long night, and I'm tired."

The girl slid off the end of the bed, handing him his jacket before stepping to the door.

"I bet so," she cooed. "If I had to guess, you're barking up the wrong tree. Gold diggers don't like coming down from their society perches."

"What a minute. You said Dunn wanted me." Ray took a seat to put on his shoes. "I didn't get any message."

"You just did. Get to that office nobody knows about," she told him, her voice dripping with sarcasm as she closed the door.

As Cat walked down the hall, she felt her annoyance still growing. Ray Irish was a chump, she decided. She knew he had been with Greye La Spina; the scent coming from his jacket gave him away. The one time Cat met Greye, and she remembered the same expensive and exclusive smell from Paris. That meant the haughty bitch played the newcomer for a fool. The woman was walking trouble, according to everything she knew. She heard about the wife of the bishop acting like Guy Young's hot little mole. And she hated how Greye rubbed her husband's face in her escapades with other men out on the gambling boat. Henry La Spina deserved better. It wasn't fair how the Greye woman grabbed a good guy like the bishop. Cat knew from personal experience the decent things Henry La Spina did for the poor families of Oyster City. The kind, big man who ran the large Episcopal Church set up the foundation that helped her family many times. The young woman understood only too well that her single mom would have given up had it not been for Henry's help. It was one of the few positive memories growing up in the tenements along the docks. Catherine Bennett never trusted men, but Bishop Henry La Spina always came through for her family.

Coming to a stop at the end of the stairs, the would-be reporter looked across the lobby. Despite her annoyance with the guy, she liked Irish. Not particularly handsome, he still had a rugged, honest, square face and penetrating brown eyes. She saw through the gruff way he spoke. Ray carried a chip on his shoulder, but she noticed something else in his demeanor that he kept well hidden. She guessed it had something to do with his injuries and his distinctive walk. Curiosity got the best of her as Cat went to a line of phone booths to make a call.

~~~

Ray walked to the dingy little office, his mind still on the events from the night before. He'd seen enough death that the thought of the body failed to bother him that much. After his experience in the Pacific, another corpse would be a minor annoyance, just another grisly image to recall in his nightmares. However, he remained upset at being left behind by Greye. Irish briefly considered calling the police about his discovery after she left. However, the headlines would not help his plans to keep quiet and remain in the background. Ray decided to walk across the highway and phone for a taxi from the motel. With reservations screaming inside his head, Irish left the body for others to discover.

As Ray rounded the corner into the alley, he noticed the black car by the door. Dunn was unhappy, sitting behind the desk and tapping with the gold ring on his left hand as Irish walked into the room. When Irish spoke, the director interrupted.
~~~

"I expect results. You haven't shown me anything, and the word is coming back to me about you hanging around Henry La Spina's wife. You can play with floozies on your dime."

Irish held his gaze on Dunn for a long moment.

"Well, if you have a better idea of how to get closer to Young, you let me know. It's not like I can walk up to Guy and ask him questions about his latest racket. So far, I've learned that big-shot wrapped some people like Greye La Spina around his finger. I noticed several city bigshots hanging out at that gambling boat, so it's clear everything ties back to there." Ray tried to remain calm despite his rising fury.

"Everyone knows about Greye La Spina and Young. What makes you think she'll tell you anything?" J. Allan remained unimpressed.

"Well, if she's a girlfriend, they are not a happy couple. From what I heard last night, this Young character has something on her. Enough to get a woman to act like the racketeer's moll in public. I watched Young, and I could tell he liked her humiliation." Ray sat down on the chair, tipping back his fedora as he leaned against the chair back.

"Add to that fact, your little girl photographer told me she and George Hopley are hanging out at the hotel. They're checking on something about Young," Irish continued. "It might be something, or it might not, but I'll keep looking into that meeting. Either way, Greye seems to be a path into Guy Young's motives, or at least into his world."

Dunn leaned back in the squeaking chair, putting his foot on the desk.

"All right, maybe I get what you're telling me. Who says she can get you that?"

"Listen, I never claimed to be an expert here," Ray refused to back off. "You told me to get information; I'm doing that. It's still your call; you want me to get more dope on the racket or not?"

J. Allan slapped at his pants, knocking off the dust from leaning against the desk. "Do you think your angle will work?"

"Your guess is as good as mine, but I'm telling you, that bishop's wife is the way to get inside. I'm willing to bet my money on that. So, unless you get someone talking or you have some way to shut down that boat out there, you can bet Guy Young keeps making trouble for your boss."

The city director looked at Irish for a moment.

"All right, keep it going. I guess I'm asking for a lot, and you're making sense. By the way, you heard that Henry La Spina's chauffeur got knocked off last night?" Dunn misread the surprised expression on Ray's face. "Yeah, state police found him in a car by a tavern out on 67. It was a bloody mess; somebody slit the guy's throat."

"Christ, what is the name of the bar?" Ray asked, putting on his best poker face. J. Allan replied with the name Irish already knew, *The Six Jolly Squires*.

"Any ideas on who did it?" Irish shifted in his chair, thinking of Greye, who left him at the tavern.

"Hell, do I look like a newspaper? For all I know, it could be Greye La Spina. Unless this murder gets that rat Guy Young out of this town, I don't care. I have enough pressure coming to me about other things." J. Allan suddenly stopped. "That's an idea. Maybe you can find something that might tie in Guy Young with the murder. Get something like that, and the police could ride him out-of-town right into the big house. See what you can find out."

Dunn walked to the door, putting on his hat. Ray's voice grew tense.

"All right, I'll see what happened. If it smells like Young is involved, I'll let you know. Just need my pay soon, or else I'm back on the street. These people don't play cheap, and I'm nearly busted."

Dunn opened the door and turned back.

"Just don't bring Cat into this conversation." He paused at the look on Irish's face. "She might decide to run with it in the paper, just to become a big-shot reporter. We don't need too many people involved. You can leave a message on that desk. The money will be there tomorrow."

~~~

When he heard the first two shots, Irish instantaneously reacted by sprinting to the closest building corner. He peered around the corner of Cherry and 8th, watching people scatter while two men pumped several more rounds into a man lying on the sidewalk across the street. Ray recognized the familiar sound of gunfire. The killer ran toward a nearby car. Ray was close enough to see that one assassin looked about his size.

The killer wore a blue suit and black hat while his face beamed a smile from under a pencil mustache. As he ran, the assassin tried to shove a semi-automatic pistol into his jacket as he ran. The other killer looked like an ex-boxer, overweight, with heavy jowls, his brown suit shaking with his fat. The two assassins jumped into a black DeSoto coupe before they sped away.

Irish noted the numbers on the automobile's plate as he followed the crowd over to the person lying on the pavement. Slowly, the victim rolled over, his hands trying to stop the bleeding. It was a useless endeavor. By the time Ray pushed through the thin line of people who stood in his way, the man in the tweed coat had died. The dead man's one good eye stared helplessly while a dark socket remained open on the other side of the face where a glass eye once resided. Irish noticed an older lady bent over to retrieve the fake eyeball and then pocketed the macabre item in her handbag. No one moved to stop her.

As the thickening blood pool drifted from beneath the corpse, Ray overheard someone's voice identify the dead man as One-Eye Cornell. Just then, he felt a presence next to him. Catherine stared at the body for a few seconds before quickly bringing her Watson camera into operation. She pulled the film holder out of the bulky box with experienced ease and promptly placed a new holder inside. After a couple of pictures of the scene, the photographer moved away for
~~~

another angle. Irish observed her as she pushed through some bystanders, yelling at them to move for the press.

A few feet away, George already had a distinguished older gentleman in his clutches, trying to get the white-haired man's view of the killing. Something in the way the interviewer kept talking bothered him. The reporter attempted to lead the witness into confirming details about the men. George appeared to know more about the appearance of the killers than the witness.

Curious, Irish looked back at the Hotel Alexander, trying to understand how someone could have observed such a minute detail. The third room overlooked the scene from half a block away.

As he stepped away from the crowd, something gave under the leather sole of his shoe, and he looked down to find a shell casing left on the sidewalk. Crouching down, he carefully picked up a half-crushed shell casing using his fingernails. The troubleshooter looked closely to verify the engraving.

Wow, a .38 Super Auto.

Now he understood why the gun looked familiar to him. It was an unusual caliber explicitly designed for a model 1911 semi-automatic pistol. Irish carried a different caliber version of the gun during the war. Dropping the casing back on the sidewalk, Ray stood and slid his way out of the crowd just as the police arrived. The black, four-door car with a single, flashing, red light mounted on the driver's side window came to a stop along the curb. Two uniformed policemen got out and pushed through the crowd. Ray worked his way across the street to the hotel, trying to confirm his suspicions. Reaching the entrance, he looked back at the group of people. Irish looked at the *Beacon*'s legman, now talking with another witness. He could make out George's face, but he could not make out enough details to say for sure if the killer had a mustache or not.

While Ray watched the scene, the meat wagon arrived, parking behind the police car. The crowd was now being moved away from the body by another policeman, who hurried over on foot. The troubleshooter observed Cat take more pictures of the scene, including the ambulance drivers loading the body onto a stretcher. When a plainclothes detective, wearing an old-fashioned derby hat, arrived in another squad car, Irish waited for a few cars to pass, then he drew closer. He watched the events unfold as he kept glancing at George Hopley. Cat joined the silent man.

"You'll never guess who that is," she whispered to Ray, bringing him out of his trance.

"They called him One-Eyed Cornell," Irish replied. "I overheard your pal talking to a witness."

"Yeah, but did you know he's Young's number two man?" she asked.

Irish glanced at her.

"That's right," she said with a smile. "And guess who I saw leaving like a bat out of hell down the alley?"

"Are you going to tell me or spill it to your boyfriend over there?" He took a deep breath, expecting he already knew the answer.

Cat gave him a frown.

"Well, I noticed Guy Young's car leaving down an alley. I guessed you might care."

Irish nodded absently. "Thanks. I guess that means George had the information on Young all right. Your boyfriend seems to know a lot for a legman."

"Quit saying that. George is not my boyfriend," she insisted. "He's a talented reporter."

Ray stared at her. "You told me he is normally chasing down crime news after it happened. As I understand it, a legman finds the story at the time, then heads to a payphone to unload his notes to rewrite men back at your paper. So how did he get the tip ahead of time? Who'd spill the news like that unless it cost money?"

Cat went silent, looking at George while her partner nodded to his last interview and started toward them.

"Tell me this, were you waiting in the hotel room when the murder happened?" Ray kept his voice to a near whisper.

"Sure, I got bored, but George wouldn't leave the window. Suddenly he gets excited, and he looked back at me, waving me to the window. Then we heard the shots," she explained.

"Did you see either of the guys who killed Cornell?" Irish whispered to Cat.

She shook her head as George came up to them.

"Cat, I've got a great story here. How were the camera shots? Do you think you got enough?" The reporter beamed at the girl, who gave him a hesitant smile back. "We need to get back and get them developed. This story is page one stuff." George took her by the arm, and they hurried away. Cat glanced back at Ray several times before the partners walked out of sight.

Irish noticed the thinning crowd and walked over to the detective, who stood by his police car. The large man looked bored as he listened to the conversation between a uniformed officer and a witness.

"Officer, did anyone give you the license number from the killer's car?" Ray looked at the detective.

The detective's icy blue eyes widened, and he stopped chewing on an unlit cigar.

"You have that? Where the hell have you been?"

Irish pointed to the curb where he stood with Cat.

"Watching you guys work. I figured you might want to look over the area where they parked their getaway car."

The cop clamped his cigar back into his mouth, then pulled off his bowler hat, running his hand through his sandy hair.

"Let me guess; you're a damn private dick going to tell me how to do my job. What's your name?"

Ray just smiled.

"Hell no, I ain't no shamus. I just was standing on the corner as they ran to their car." Irish then gave the cop the information on the car and the tag numbers.

The lieutenant turned, interrupting the uniformed policeman.

"Willy, take this gentleman's information. Then get word back to headquarters immediately from his description. I want the information out to state patrol as well. You can bet they will head upstate."

As Irish stepped near the policemen, the big, sandy-haired man stopped him. "You didn't say your name."

"Ray Irish. I work for the *Morning Beacon*."

"Like hell," the detective told him. "Since when do reporters give us something before it's in your damn paper?"

"I didn't say I was a reporter," Ray told him. "Just don't like seeing folks murdered as they walk down the street."

The cop held out his right hand; his smile revealed yellow, stained teeth. "Lieutenant Campbell is the name. Irish, if your information is solid, I think we'll get along just fine."

Ray accepted the handshake and recounted the events he had witnessed earlier.

~~~

That evening, Irish got a message at the lobby desk with a number and the initials he recognized. He made the call from his room, and a couple of rings later, the sultry voice of Greye La Spina answered.

"I have some time this evening and an unopened bottle of Macphail's if you're still interested."

Suspicious but intrigued, Ray took up the offer.

"Where at?" he asked.

"Meet me at the corner of Peach and 8th; I'll pick you up," she told him before hanging up.

The red car carrying the quiet couple came to a stop on a bluff overlooking Oyster City. The moonlit night gave them a splendid view of the bay from the secluded parking area. Greye turned off the car and looked at the moon low on the horizon.

"You left me holding the bag," he told her flatly when they came to a stop. He noticed she was wearing a black dress and wondered how much was a put-on show about her driver's death.

"I'm sorry, but I couldn't get involved in that. You know that." She sniffed, pulling a handkerchief from her purse. She dabbed at her nose. "Quincannon worked for my husband for years. They were close."

"Yeah, it's terrible. Any ideas on who might have killed your driver?" Irish kept watching her.

Greye shook her head.

"No, he didn't have an enemy."
~~~

"Remember, I met the guy," he reminded her, trying not to laugh. "The loud gorilla had plenty of people who would have hated him. The question is, how many people fought for a spot to bump him off? But that's not why we're here, is it?"

Greye said nothing for a moment, then she shook her head and pulled a bottle from next to the seat.

"I saw nothing so horrible like last night. I was up all night, thinking about the blood," she said while slowly turning the bottle in her hands. "This is my way of making up for leaving you. I stole it from the liquor cabinet. There are two tumblers in the glove box."

Her vulnerability came through with a tired sigh, and Ray reached into the compartment for the glasses.

"You can pour," he told her as he held out a glass.

While it wasn't Irish whiskey, the drink went down smooth, and the warmth did Ray some good. It also brought Mrs. La Spina sliding her body close to him.

"It'll get pretty cold soon." She settled in next to him. After another drink, Greye placed his arm over her shoulder.

"Well, I think we can work on warming things up." He smiled before pulling her close and planting a kiss on her full lips.

She reached for him, instantly reacting to the kiss by pressing closer. Then she pushed away from the kiss, telling him, "I'm not like this with other men."

"I understand."

However, his mind sarcastically wondered how many times she'd told such a lie as he pulled her close again, his lips pressed to hers. His hand quickly slid behind her back, his rough hands feeling the goosebumps on her delicate skin. A quick move with his fingers unhooked the lace bra while his other hand smoothly slid up to cradle her left breast. Her response, along with a nearly silent moan, told him they would be there for a while.

Yeah, she's not like this! His inner voice smirked at the thought.

~~~

It was late afternoon two days later when Cat left Irish a message at his hotel's front desk. Using one of the several payphones lined up in the lobby, Ray dialed the unknown number. Several rings later, Cat's deadpan voice answered. It took a slight pause for him to recognize the voice.

"What's up?"

"George is dead." The lifeless answer came from Cat. He heard a sniffle before she continued. "They found him behind Levine Pawn Shop on 8th. I'm in the shop right now."

"Sorry kid, I'll be right down," Ray replied before hanging up.

It took about twenty minutes for Irish to get to the alley, and the taxi stopped behind a police cruiser blocking the alleyway. Catherine stood halfway down the narrow and isolated lane behind the row of buildings. When he walked up, he
~~~

noticed how her camera still hung from her shoulder, uncased. A *Beacon* reporter, with notes in hand, walked past Ray, looking at him strangely. Irish stood next to Cat, noticing her vacant stare at several trash cans and a pool of blood on the ground.

"Shot in the back last night," she told him, after coming out of her thoughts. "I overheard the police say it was two shots from a .38. One bullet while he ran away, and the other finished him. They just carried his body away."

"When did you hear about it?" he asked while he watched as the police finished their investigation. He guessed the hit came from a professional by the way the men were talking. There were few clues and no witnesses.

"Dice, one of our other legmen, called me. A garbage man found the body." The girl leaned against the dark red brick wall. "Why would someone do that to George?"

Irish expected tears, but she refused to cry. He guessed that would come later, in private.

"Come on, let's go. No reason to hang around here."

Ray led them away, taking Peach Avenue toward the Alexander. Irish remained quiet, remembering his suspicions about George. A couple of blocks later, Cat finally began to talk.

"You didn't trust George, did you?"

Irish paused before telling her the truth. "Not since the Cornell killing. At first, I thought he was just an eager beaver, like you."

"You were trying to tell me something that day," she said, glancing at him. "You asked a lot of questions about where George and I were when One-Eye got shot."

"No, not really; I was trying to work it out in my mind. Something about the way he interviewed the first witness bothered me," Ray explained. "He had a description of the two assassins down like he watched the whole thing, more detail than the witness remembered."

"That doesn't mean anything. I told you George had binoculars," Cat objected.

"All right, but explain how he would know what they looked like unless he tracked them going to Cornell and watched the whole thing? You told me he called you to the window. That must mean that he had to spot the two men closing on Cornell. But you told me you were looking for Guy Young. Isn't that right?"

She stopped, thinking back to that day. "Well, maybe he saw the killers when he got downstairs. He ran to the sidewalk when I was just getting to the lobby. He must have got a look when they drove away."

Ray shook his head.

"Even if George left the room just after the first two shots, like you said, he couldn't have made it down to the street soon enough to see the men getting into the car. Remember, I stood near where they parked the getaway car. It drove away from the hotel. Now I stood close enough to see the killers. But there's no way he could have spotted a small mustache from that distance. That means he could have only seen him with the binoculars, or he knew the guy."

"But why?" she stated, mostly to herself.

"He took a payoff. Somebody doesn't want anyone to know the reason," Irish finished the sentence with a curse.

Another block of silence followed before Ray asked another question. "Are you sure the cops said it was a .38 that killed George?"

"Yeah, they found two cases in the alley. They don't expect prints," the woman nodded. "Why do you ask?"

"It means the weapon was a semi-automatic like the other day. Most people using a .38 have a revolver which won't leave the cases," he explained. "If George was too close to something after they paid him, it stands to reason that it's the same killers."

Cat visibility deflated at the thought, and he cursed himself for mentioning it. They continued along the street, taking a turn on Cherry Street to his hotel. Inside the lobby, they went to the bar. He ordered two drinks.

"If George took a payoff, I need to find out who set him up," Catherine spoke after staring into the mirror behind the bar.

"Why? It won't bring him back," Irish reminded her. "And it might get people coming after you."

Her blue eyes flashed as she glanced at him. "I'm not afraid."

"You should be," Ray told her. "Even if you find out, who's going to do something about it? The police might if you can get to one who isn't paid off by the same folks. Otherwise, you'd be risking your neck for nothing."

Cat gulped down the drink, slamming the glass down on the counter.

"I don't want to drink with a coward," she fumed. She slid off the stool and walked out of the bar. Irish watched her through the glass doors. He smelled trouble, and he guessed someone would need to keep an eye on her. Ray decided it would not be him.

<center>~~~</center>

After finishing several drinks, a very high Irish found a message waiting for him at the counter in the lobby. The familiar initials asked him to come to the *Stanley Rose*. Walking away from the large marble counter, Ray passed by LeRoy, the hotel dick, who eyed him suspiciously. Cat told him once that the retired cop distrusted almost everyone who came into the hotel. Ray gave him a grin, then went out of the lobby doors to the street.

As he rode in the water taxi across the bay, Ray kept thinking about Greye. Curious why she wanted to meet on the gambling ship, he reminisced about their last time together. Irish decided the wife must be getting lonely again. Not that he minded, since she reminded him of an Australian whore. He considered Greye to be a bit more refined and generous than the prostitute. Ray liked her company more than he would admit.

On the *Stanley Rose*, Ray checked in his fedora with the pretty little thing still wearing too much makeup when he heard a gruff voice next to him.

"The boss wants to talk with you."

Ray turned toward the thug, still wearing the same brown suit. As Irish considered making a smart comeback to Tweedledum, he felt someone walk up behind him. He glanced back at another goon, not liking where the conversation was going.

"Come with us," said the brawler.

"And if I don't?" Irish asked while knowing the answer.

"Then we get to hurt you," Tweedledum told him with a gleam in his eye.

Ray nodded.

"Then, I guess I'm coming with you." He didn't like the invite, but his other option was less appealing. He wasn't drunk enough to take on two thugs bigger than he was.

Following the first Twiddle in the brown suit, the trio walked across the nearly empty dance floor. Ray glanced around for any familiar faces, but he didn't recognize anyone. They went through a door by the bar, which led them into a small hallway. The lead thug knocked before opening another door.

The room they entered looked like a gilded bedroom with a large, circular bed in the middle. Several large mirrors hung over the bed and along the walls. Occasional chairs, overly ornate and painted in gilt, sat along one wall along with a couch with gold-colored fabric. However, in one corner of the room sat a large, blond colored desk facing them. Guy Young stood next to the desk, his blue eyes staring daggers at Irish.

"I'm glad you accepted my invitation," Young said. Dressed in most of a black tux, he picked up a white bow tie from his desk and expertly began putting it on.

"I didn't have much choice with Tweedledee and Tweedledum here. So, what do you want?" Ray felt a growing distaste for the black-haired man.

Suddenly, Irish took a powerful punch to the lower back, and he dropped to his knees. Ray wondered if he still had kidneys as he tried to recover from the blow.

"You need to learn manners. A stranger who comes into Oyster City with a terrible habit of asking questions about me and my business." Ray's host stepped to a large mirror on the wall, where he adjusted his bow tie.

Before Ray replied, he took a vicious punch to the side of the head. The blow sent him over to his side, the thick carpet doing little to protect his head when he hit the steel deck. He tried to shake his head to stop the multiple images of Young he saw as he looked up. One thug yanked Irish from the floor. Ray swung his fist, but it glanced off Tweedledee's broad shoulder. The air escaped from his lungs as a fist buried itself in his abdomen. Irish folded over, and Tweedledum pinned Ray's arms behind his back. The other goon lifted their victim's head, slapping him several times across the face. Blood flowed from his swollen lip while Ray tried to get his wind back.

"My men are impatient to get back to their work." Young stepped away from the mirror. "Now that I have your attention, why are you so interested in my affairs?"

Ray hesitated, his muddled brain trying to think of a story. "I'm not sure what you mean." The next sentence didn't make it out of his mouth as he caught another strike in his mid-section.

Pulling up one of the gilt chairs, Guy sat down.

"You will tell me the truth, or you will continue to suffer a beating which will probably kill you. In the end, I will get what I want." There was nothing in Young's cold voice that hinted at compassion. "The way the tide runs, your body will wash up on Mile Cove Beach. There will be no link back to this ship. What's your choice?"

"Okay, okay, I get it. I work for the *Beacon*," Ray confessed, desperately trying to think of a cover story.

"That's better, but I don't believe you. You're an unknown in this town. Now you're suddenly working for the local rag and asking about me. Next, you're making all dizzy with one of my girls. It doesn't make sense." The thug leader nodded, and his men used Ray's face and body as a punching bag for several more minutes. The battered prisoner's left eye quickly swelled shut, and his nose leaked blood like a sieve. Crumpling to his knees, he felt Young's hoodlum lift him to a standing position.

"I swear that's the god's honest truth. You can check," Irish insisted, trying to think of anything to survive. Tweedledee pressed the prisoner's arms behind his back while his partner pulled Ray's head up.

"All right, prove it to me," Guy demanded.

"I worked with that legman that got killed last night." Ray went cold at his mistaken cover story since George was spying on Guy Young. He tensed, expecting more punches. Instead, the racketeer put his hand to his chin.

"Yeah, I heard about that reporter getting gunned down. I would have liked a chat with him, considering all the lies the punk put into the paper about me. What about Greye La Spina? You were with her the other night, the same night that Quincannon got knocked off. Did you bump him off for her?"

"No. I didn't know that her driver was dead until the next day. I first met Greye downtown after I got off the train in Oyster City, and she gave me a five-dollar token from your ship, so I came to thank her," Irish told him.

Laughter exploded in the room from the two thugs, and the gangster smiled. "Yeah, she likes it when men thank her, the epitome of virtue that share crop is. Quincannon used to keep her occupied before she got too greedy and needed my help." Guy's face grew dark again. "What else did she want?"

Ray shook his head.

"I swear I only met her a couple of times. We never talked about you. She was upset over their driver's death. I didn't even know she was with you until I saw her on this ship the other night."

"You're telling me you were working with that dead reporter, and you just happened to meet one of my girls on my ship? That's mighty thin."

The prisoner turned his battered head to stare at Young.

"I know it sounds crazy, but I've got no reason to take anything to the grave. I'm on the level. Even the police can verify I was working for the paper. I even told them what I saw the day Cornell died."

The statement struck a chord with the gangster.

"Hmmm, that's interesting. I heard a reporter talked to the cops, giving them the dope on One-Eye's killers. But that might mean you were hanging around there, and you're involved with this scheme. Since I was late getting there, they only took out my friend," Young observed icily. Ray instantly understood more than a few policemen were on Guy's payroll.

"No, I swear I was just coming up the street when I heard the first shots. I got there when they put a couple of more bullets into your guy, then watched them run across the street to their car," the prisoner on the floor explained. "I gave the cops all I know."

The black-haired man appeared to be considering Ray's words before he replied.

"Then you're not worth anything to me. Why should I let you live?"

Irish jumped at a desperate gamble.

"Because I am the one that got the best look at the men who killed your number one guy. The police have the description, but you know they aren't going to turn over this city to look for them, are they? Like you, I'm putting my money that someone is gunning for you. Since I saw the killers, I can be the one to help you find the guys. Knocking me off won't help you."

The boss's blue eyes stared at Ray for a long minute, the longest minute of his life since the Pacific.

"Why would you want to help me?"

"It beats a watery grave," Irish told him honestly. "The way I see it, you can run the town. I don't owe this city anything."

"You have my attention," Young nodded. "Tell me what you told the cops."

As the battered man described the scene he witnessed, Guy suddenly rose from his chair. He put on his tux jacket, smiling.

"Tonight, fortune smiles on you, Irish. Your bet is right that I didn't kill my friend. One-Eye and I went way back, and I want those sons of bitches that put lead into him." The racketeer stared down at the prisoner. "You've got a job now, legman. You're going to find the killers and let me know where they are so I can take care of them. Is that understood?"

Ray nodded slowly.

"Yeah, I get it. What about Jacobi's gang? Do you think they are in the middle of this hit?"

Moving back to the mirror, Young picked at his jacket, finding invisible lint on the black cloth.

"You've been checking up already. Good for you." He paused, considering the idea.

"Johnny, putting a hit out on me? We have an arrangement, but I don't trust him," he told Ray.

"You have your work cut out for you, shamus. I expect something soon from you, or the next conversation will not end well."

As Young left the room, he nodded to his two men. Tweedledee dragged the beaten man out of a side door while Tweedledum followed his boss.

~~~

Irish finally reached the Hotel Alexander as the light of the morning sun broke over the horizon. Tied by his wrists from a pipe inside a makeshift cell on the ship for several hours, Ray finally heard someone enter the room to release him. Most patrons had left the vessel, so Young's men dragged Ray to the main deck before dropping him into a skiff with a small outboard motor. The thugs took their beaten guest to the city dock, where they kicked him a couple of times with a reminder to find Cornell's assassins. From there, Ray staggered to his feet and walked to the hotel, determining that taxis were nearly impossible to find that early in the morning in Oyster City.

Battered and exhausted, Irish refused to acknowledge the horrified look he got from the hotel clerk while he walked to the elevator. The operator inside, who leaned dozing against the wall, suddenly jerked awake when Ray closed the elevator doors. A blonde teen with acne, dressed in a red uniform, started apologizing.

"Jeez, mister." The kid scrambled from his stool. "Are you all right? I can get a doc if you need it."

"Never mind, just get this thing to the 4th floor," he told him gruffly. Ray could only think of sleep.

After he got to his room, Ray removed his coat and went into the bathroom. He stood in front of the mirror, trying to clean off the blood while inspecting the damage. Irish heard his hotel door suddenly open. A man in a dark brown suit walked in as Irish looked out the bathroom door.

"You're in the wrong damn room. Beat it," Ray growled as he held a wet washcloth on his injured eye.

"Lieutenant Howard." The cop didn't bother to pull out his badge. Instead, the stone face flatfoot pointed to his chest pocket as he closed the door and sat in the chair by the entrance.

"Looks like you made some friends," the detective told him snidely.

"Yeah, maybe you coppers should be on the streets taking care of those friends instead of hanging around my room," Irish replied.
~~~

He instantly disliked Howard, who glared at him.

"From the way you look, you have enough problems with Guy Young and his group," the cop continued. "I wouldn't make it worse by pissing me off. We have a witness who states you were down at the *Six Jolly Squires* a couple of nights back. The same night that a chauffeur for Bishop La Spina got bumped off."

"I heard about it, but don't know anything," Ray told him, dabbing at his fat lip to clean up the dried blood. "I went in for a drink and left."

"Did you leave alone?" The way the detective asked, Irish knew better than to lie.

"No, I left with someone. But your witness saw that."

The cop nodded as he got up from the chair. He walked over to a bureau and opened the drawer. As he rummaged through the clothes, he asked what Ray did for a living.

"I work for the *Beacon*," Irish was already tired of telling people the lie.

Howard grunted. "Who was the dish you left with?"

"Not your type," Ray told him, taking the chair. The sidelong glance from Howard caused Irish to realize he was close to heading to the police station. He changed tactics as the cop went through another drawer.

"Listen, she's a married woman, so there's no need to get her involved. We had a drink and left together. Drove around the city, and I didn't get back to the hotel until late. I have witnesses for that if you need it."

"All right, then save me some time and give me your knife," Howard told him.

"I don't have one, not even a penknife. Reporters don't need to carry them." Irish carefully leaned against the chair back. His head still hurt from the beating, and now he felt dizzy with the exhaustion.

"Yeah, you're a reporter like I'm the Duke of Wellington," Howard's reply came as he searched the last drawer. The grimace on the cop's face revealed a couple of missing teeth. Ray also noticed he had several scars along the temple line of his brown hair. Irish would have made a bet the mark came from a bottle breaking across the flatfoot's head. No wonder the guy carried a lousy attitude.

"Satisfied I don't have a knife? Say, what gives? You don't think I cut the guy's throat?" Ray's curiosity started to get to him.

The cop finished his search, stepping closer to Irish; his brown eyes showed a growing irritation with Irish. "How did you know about his throat? That wasn't in the papers.

"I'm with the *Beacon*, remember? I hear things." Irish dabbed at his face with the towel.

"Alright, wise guy, since you know. Some crazy nearly decapitated the victim. Nobody heard anything, or so they say," Howard growled out the words.

"Well, as I said, I don't know anything beyond what the papers say. And I don't have a knife. It seems like you are fishing in the wrong hole, lieutenant. I'm new to this city and have no reason to knock off some chauffeur." Ray tried to keep his smugness out of his tone. He failed.

The cop stepped closer, nearly hovering over Irish.

"You might if the married dame was Greye La Spina. She's known to be keeping Quincannon wrapped around her finger. Could be you might have done her a favor."

"I'd laugh, but my ribs hurt too much. Listen, I'm not dumb enough to kill someone over a dame. Are you going to book me or something? Your net has sizeable holes in it, I mean with no weapon and no real motive. Since the bishop's name is bound to come up, do you want the heat from City Hall accusing his wife of involvement in this murder?" Ray slowly stood, his ribs aching. He walked by the cop, going to the bathroom again. "You can let yourself out."

The detective followed Irish, forcing him to turn around.

"Listen, smart man; you better watch your step around me. Young's men are weak sisters compared to the grilling I'll do on you."

"Thanks, I'll remember that. But you just told me something already. Since nobody knew about Guy's thugs using me for a punching bag, I take it your inside information came along with a little cabbage from his side."

Ray couldn't say more when his breath left him again. The wicked punch coming from the cop struck him square in the belly, sending Ray into the bathroom doorframe. He slid to the floor, his arms folded around his abdomen.

"Your smart mouth will get you a tomb. Don't leave town, wise guy, unless you want a cell as a material witness. I'll put the screws to you and have you singing like a bird about you and that La Spina dame." The cop stood up and straightened his tie before he left the room, slamming the door on the way out.

When Irish finally recovered his breath, he crawled to the bed.

Damn rough night, he thought as he sank into unconsciousness.

~~~

A harsh ring kept going and going, finally pulling Irish out of his dreamless sleep. His hand fumbled around in the general direction of the sound, finding the phone handset.

"Yeah, what do you want?"

"Ray, it's Cat. I've got something, but I'm not coming to your hotel. Where can we meet?" Her tone was a mix of fear and excitement. It forced him awake.

"Your coffee shop," he told her, trying to shake the fog. "Give me twenty minutes."

"I'll be there. And make sure you're not getting tailed. I caught sight of one of Young's paid off coppers watching the Alexander." She hung up, and Ray winced as he tried to get out of bed.

Irish made it to Sam's nearly thirty minutes later, avoiding the front lobby and taking a couple of alleys to his destination. He loosened up some seriously stiff muscles during his walk. The man groaned at his efforts while he wondered about what Cat might have. He also carried suspicions about the little woman.
~~~

When the troubleshooter sat down at the booth, Ray felt someone step from the back of the room.

"You look like hell. Who did that to you?" Cat quickly slid into the booth across from him, her eyes betraying the concern about his battered face. The pair waited to talk after a gray-haired waitress brought them a cup of coffee.

"Guy Young and his friends asked me some questions," he told her, pulling his handkerchief to wipe his sweating face carefully. The long walk took a lot out of him. "So, why did you call in a coward?"

She was about to say something, then halted. Her face betrayed a mix of emotions.

"I'm sorry for what I said. George's murder got to me. I mean, it wasn't like I loved him or anything, but he was always there."

She looked at him, but his face remained emotionless. "You probably can't understand," she finally said.

"No, I probably can't understand a friend dying," he replied sarcastically. "What a crock. If you're looking for sympathy about George, I'm plum out. He got killed because he was a crook, on the take, or both. Just like everyone else I know in this damn city."

Her face darkened.

"Like me, that's what you're saying."

Ray nodded.

"Listen carefully. When I say crooked, I'm talking about everyone, including myself. Since I took this damn job, I'm as dirty as the next guy. But I'm not taking beatings for lies and deceit."

"What do you mean? Are you leaving?" Cat's eyes flared.

"No!" Ray growled at her, then looked around and lowering his voice. "It means if you come to me for help, then I have to trust you. What's more, you need to trust me. It's as simple as that."

Ray paused, rubbing his sore left side.

"I'll start first and lay it on the line with you. As of last night, I'm stuck in between that favorite racketeer, Guy Young, and our mutual friend, J. Allan Dunn. No man can have two masters and survive, especially not in this damn town. Now, if I'm rough on you as we go along, that's the reason. There can be no ulterior motives between us. I know you're smart and ambitious. However, I can't trust you any more than I trust Dunn. You've been putting your hand in a dirty cookie jar too many times. In my mind, all the filth in this place is rubbing off on you. Prove me wrong if you want my help."

Irish waited for her to think about what he said. He saw her blue eyes searching his face, looking for a sign. Ray tried not to think about how attractive he found her at the moment.

Cat sighed.

"All right, I guess I deserve that. I called you for help. But I also realized I was wrong about what happened at the bar. I know you aren't a coward, even when I said it." She gave a glance around, leaning forward. "I know a little bit about you. I had a friend check on you."

"Was that your idea?" Ray's mocking smile hurt his face as he stuffed his handkerchief back in his coat pocket.

"Dunn asked me to check up, since nobody knows you. But I didn't give him everything," Cat pointed out. "Your war record is only so-so with all the time you spent in the brig for things like striking an officer and insubordination. I decided not to pass that stuff on."

"Yeah, I have a problem with people ordering me around. I'm not sure I should thank you for that. Might have been a favor had he fired me the next day." The irony of what she told him forced a smirk.

"Are you working for only Dunn?"

"He's been good to me since I can remember," she told him. "Even though he was just a clerk working for the city, he helped my mom and me out. I owe him a lot."

"Then you're not taking a little cabbage from anyone else? Something you might just kind of forget about?" Ray wanted to see her reaction. Cat passed his test when her eyes flashed at him.

"I swear, I'm not. Whatever else you think about me, my word is good, damn it," the woman boiled.

Irish held up his hand. "Okay, I'll accept your word."

Ray finished his coffee and waved over the waitress for more. When the older lady arrived, he told her to bring him a sandwich.

Cat waited until the waitress left.

"I have a lead on one of the assassins, the guy with the mustache. But I can't take him and his partner alone. I need your help."

"Keep it down and explain," Irish cautioned her.

She leaned in close.

"Jack Ripley had a hot tip today down at the *Beacon*. He told me the police believe one of the Cornhill's killers is a known convict. The guy's name is Hugh Pendexter, and he did time in the pen after a couple of holdups. He's been lucky since they can't pin any killings on him. Jack says the kid is crazy as a loon. Even Johnny Jacobi's gang doesn't want him."

"The last time we met, you didn't know much about Jacobi." Irish raised an eyebrow.

"Yeah, well, that was Dunn's idea." Her face reddened. "He only cares about Guy Young and his gang, so he told me to keep anything I learned between him and me."

"From now on, you tell me when Dunn wants to filter things," Ray told her. "You and I can figure out what's useful, not him."

Cat nodded.

"All right, I'll accept that, but what about my information on this Pendexter hood?"

Irish shrugged.

"I'm not sure. Do you know if someone tipped off the police?" She shook her head.

"Alright, let's start with the idea that your lead is probably correct. But I think there's more to it. Call it a gut feeling," Ray told her.

"Then you think Ripley's working for Young?" Cat's face turned angry. "Not everyone is on the take!"

"Calm down," he warned her as the waitress brought his sandwich. He gulped down a couple of bites while she waited impatiently.

"It could be legit, but I'm careful now! Somebody tried to put a hit on Young. He did not know who killed his friend. I could tell when I gave him the full rundown of what happened."

Irish wondered if at least one cop wasn't on Young's payroll, but he kept that thought in the back of his mind.

"Now Young wants me to track down the assassin," he explained.

"But why would you tell him?" Cat insisted and then stopped when Ray cocked his head, food still in his open mouth.

Cat quickly went on, her face reddened again, "Sorry, I forgot you didn't have much choice. What I mean is, why you? He's got a bunch of thugs who take orders from him."

"Hell, I can only guess. If the police know something, that means Young knows this as well. All I understand at this point is that I'm a useful stooge for him since I'm a witness to the killers. If the cops grab the murderers first, then the case will take weeks. Young might just wait for the right opportunity; have prisoners knock the killers off in jail. Hell, around here, he'll probably have a cop do it."

Ray told her before finishing off his sandwich.

"Something else just came to me. Young can't be sure about everyone in this city. He's probably covering all his bases to make sure he gets the killers. And if I were him, I would try to finger what person put the hit on me. Who else could have known that the mobster left the *Stanley Rose*? When I asked the guy about Johnny Jacobi, he said they had some arrangement, but he indicated he was going to be more cautious." He shrugged his shoulders. "Your guess is as good as mine on where this leads to."

"It'll be back to Greye La Spina; I'm willing to lay my last buck on that," Cat told him emphatically.

Irish noticed the flash of dislike in her eyes.

"Why? Young chases her around the bed. Hell, everyone in town knows that. The mobster even told me a little about her and Quincannon, her driver. She's probably been in bed with half the city, if the rumors are right. Greye may be no saint, but how does this hit on a racketeer involve her?"

Cat shook her head.

"As you said, call it a gut feeling! I found out that Quincannon spent time at the state penitentiary. He was the strong arm for grifters before becoming a driver for La Spina. Seems like a pretty strange pairing, if you ask me."

Ray Irish let out a low whistle as he carefully leaned back on the bench seat. His mind raced with thoughts, and none of them was good about Greye. Deep inside, she seemed to play a game, and he wasn't sure of the rules. After a moment, Irish pulled himself out of his thoughts. He did not like the self-satisfied expression on her face.

He gave Cat a sour look.

"Well, we have another twist in this puzzle. I guess I need to talk with J. Allan Dunn. Arrange some time with your boss as soon as you can and give me a call. I'll be around."

Chapter 3: The Gumshoe

The morning air had the same chilly dampness that went through the coat and right into the bones. Irish came to expect the clammy atmosphere in Oyster City. It seemed as natural to the town as the stink coming off the wastewater, spilling into the bay. However, Irish had other thoughts on his mind as he walked to the dingy office in the alley behind Chandler Avenue.

"You're late. Cat says you have something important." The boss scowled at Ray, in an unhappy mood as usual.

"Good to see you again as well," Irish told him, the handle of the still opened door in his hand. He swung the door shut and pulled a chair next to the desk. Ray glanced at Cat as he leaned his large frame on the back of the chair. "Did she give you the latest?"

"Yeah, I know all about your run-in with Young," Dunn told him, drumming his fingers on the desk.

"Then, first things first," Ray told him. "I stopped by the *Morning Beacon* and found out something fascinating. When I spoke with Max Brand, he said he had never heard of me. Nearly had me thrown out when I asked about my employment with his paper. Since he's the publisher and editor, I suspect he knows what he's talking about." Ray observed J. Allan, expecting a reaction.

"So, boss, what am I missing?" he asked.

Dunn blinked his eyes quickly.

"Yeah, you're not with them. The *Beacon* knows nothing about you."

"Really? That's all you can say." He paused. "Well, it got me to thinking. You screwed up, and you made me a marked man, just like the first so-called troubleshooter you hired."

Irish noticed Cat's surprise at the news, but he centered his attention on Dunn.

"I've already told that damn lie to the cops and Guy Young. That means the word is out on the street. They aren't going to take too kindly to me when they find out. And I can guarantee you. Somebody will check on me, just like you had Cat look into my past."

Dunn's fingers paused their drumbeat on the desk, and his face twisted into a grimace, looking like he needed to find the bathroom.

"Okay, what do you want? If it's an apology, it's not going to happen. You're a drifter, and you're getting paid well. Besides, I haven't seen much for all of the money I've spent."

"I don't want a damn apology, you son of a bitch," Ray growled as he leaned over the desk above the balding man. "I want the damn truth. Your lie has me exposed to the wrong people. Cat pegged you; you're nobody in this town. I say you're full of shit. I want honest answers quick, or, by God, I'm going to throw your ass out of that window behind me."

His owl eyes widened at the thought, but J. Allan quickly regained his composure in front of Ray. Slowly, he nodded.

"All right, all right, I guess I owe you an explanation."

The boss glanced at Cat.

"I don't have the pull over at the paper by myself. I swear that a little pressure from the right people would have it worked out before it came to this. It's a good idea, but they wouldn't go for it."

"Who are they? If you don't have the pull, then tell me who you think does," Irish told him as he hovered over the desk.

"People I know," Dunn replied. "You won't know them, but I'm telling you they run the show. They run around like fools, but they don't understand the danger this Young and his gang represent. But they do now, by God."

"I don't care about that crap. You've been filling my head with all sorts of malarkey. But the buck stops here, tonight. I have a cop who's making it clear I can't leave town, and he's probably working for Young and his hoodlums. And that damn racketeer is telling me I'm hunting down Cornwall's killers like some cursed shamus." Irish pushed away from the desk.

"You've gotten paid well." Dunn gave a grim smile.

"To hell with you and the dirty money." Irish glared at him. "You can delude yourself all you want about your honesty. Hell, you don't even cover your tracks. Look around this office. It's filled with the documents about your game, so don't give me the business. You son of a bitch, you saw how Young worked when his men went after you the other night. Do you think your friends will do anything about that? They'll let you hang."

Ray noticed how Dunn's expression changed. His boss finally recognized his whole corrupt lifestyle was at risk.

"I'm standing out like a sore thumb now. According to Young, if he doesn't like my answers, you'll find my body out at Mile Cove Beach." Irish turned from the desk, disgust on his face.

"Remember that you can wind up there just as well."

"Just like the last guy," Cat spoke up with a stunned expression on her face. "That's why the last guy Dunn hired is missing."

"What do you mean?" Ray asked, seeing a grimace in the director's expression.

She stood up, stepping closer to the desk.

"What you just said reminded me of someone. A guy named Pulaski started poking around just like you."

She turned her stare to the fidgeting, thin man behind the desk.

"You probably did the same thing to Irish, didn't you? You promised Pulaski this cover that didn't come through. But he didn't leave the job suddenly. What really happened?"

"Listen, I don't know where Pulaski went." J. Allan stood up, his eyes darting back and forth between Cat and Irish. "He just didn't show up one day after I paid him." Their boss started pacing behind the desk. "He told me about some cop he was following around; then he just quit showing up. I checked at the hotel. But he never checked out and his room was empty."

"And you never assumed something went wrong with your scheme?" The sarcasm dripped while Ray walked back to the desk.

"I followed up," Dunn glared back. "Everything pointed to Pulaski taking off. Damn fool acted like a bull in the china closet. Someone might have paid him to leave town. Who says the guy didn't just leave?"

"I say so," Cat snapped. "You know as well as I do that the state police found several bodies on that beach across the bay over the last year. Everybody knows people come up missing when they go to that gambling ship. The local cops would not bother with something out of their jurisdiction."

"And maybe you're reaching, assuming Pulaski got knocked off. Each time the state folks found those bodies, they could not identify them since they were in the water for so long. You have no proof," J. Allan told them defiantly.

Ray Irish slammed his fist into a pile of papers sitting on the desk.

"Enough! Dunn, you wanted someone to do your dirty work with no ties back to your office. Well, unless you find me some cover, I'll make sure you get the heat. Just remember, the police won't need to use some rubber hoses on me to get me to talk, and Young's thugs will be happy to beat it out of me."

Irish paused, seeing his words sink in.

"I'll put money that your cronies will leave you to the wolves if word spreads that the Oyster City Director of Public Works is spying on racketeers. Plus, he's acting like the District Attorney. You think you will last very long?"

J. Allan Dunn grimaced at the thought. The director fully understood his idea might backfire. He did not want a scandal to upset his applecart. Then his eyes lit up.

"I just figured out how I can make this happen. Those cronies, as you call them, will now see the light."

"What do you mean?" Ray's curiosity got the best of him.

"It's another angle I should have thought of before. With Fordham stepping into the ring to go against our mayor, nobody will argue with me." The boss leaned back as the chair squeaked in protest.

"What are you talking about?" Cat asked. "What's that low life got to do with it?"

"You haven't heard that Mark Henry Fordham is getting in the upcoming election?" J. Allan looked at both, surprised at their blank stares. "It just came out today that he's holding a rally down at the union hall tomorrow." He gazed at Cat. "And you know that means he's running to take over. He could win the damn thing with so many workers down on the unemployment lines."

"Remember, there's a stranger in this office. Who the hell is this guy, and what does this have to do with me?" Exasperation flowed with Ray's words.

Cat smiled sympathetically.

"Fordham is a union boss who controls a lot of what happens along the docks. He's got a squeaky-clean reputation with the public. But I've heard that he has a lot of dirty ties with Jacobi and Young. Rumor is Fordham makes Mayor Hopley and City Hall look like cheap chisels with their graft."

J. Allan frowned at her description of him and his cronies. Irish couldn't help but give a smug grin at the reaction.

"Anyway," Dunn interrupted, "I have a way to get you the cover you need. It'll be entirely legal, and you won't have to act the part. Even better, Oyster City is your employer. I'll have the backing of the mayor for you. Just give me a day since I have to get the right paperwork in place. I'll call you when I've got everything ready."

Ray stared at Dunn for a long while, then glanced at Cat. She gave him a shrug. Ray picked up his fedora from the floor, where he dropped it.

"I don't like it, but I guess I don't have much choice. You let me know what you got, and I'll keep my head low. Don't let me down on this, or I might just walk over to Fordham and see what he can do to help me out." Irish walked out of the office, walked out of the alley, and turned onto Chandler Avenue. He heard running footsteps.

"Hey, slow down." Catherine pulled next to him, trying to catch her breath. "Where are you going now?"

"I have an appointment with a hazel-eyed bitch who set me up," he replied severely. "And you're not welcome to join me."

"I wasn't planning on coming along," Cat huffed. "I just wanted to tell you I'm sorry about all the lies. You know Dunn lied to me as well."

The sound of their footsteps was the only noise for a block as Ray remained silent. The chill of the night air blanketed them while a few cars passed them.

"Cat, I'm not blaming you for Dunn. I'm a big boy, and I should have told him to jump in the bay when he offered me this mess." Ray shoved his icy hands into his pockets.

"That's all right. Like I told you before, J. Allan has been good to me, and I never paid much attention to some of his double-dealings. It comes with the territory; you know what I mean?" She tried to sound confident. "By the way, you mentioned something about a cop who might be on Young's payroll. What did you mean by that?"

As they walked along, Irish explained his run-in with Detective Howard and his hotel room search. She listened without interruption. When he finished, Cat waved down a taxi.

"You go find your girlfriend," she told him when the cab stopped at the curb beside them. "I've got a couple of errands of my own."

Ray stood with the taxi door open, his face wearing a puzzled expression while watching Cat walk away.

In front of the *Six Jolly Squires*, his taxi stopped, and Ray climbed out while feeling a sense of déjà vu. The nearly empty parking lot looked the same as he remembered. The only difference was that the traffic on the highway was busier on this night. Ray made his way to the bar inside, sitting at the end after a glance at the empty booth where he met Greye a week before. The bartender, he recognized, but there was no waitress that evening.

Ray ordered an Irish on the rocks and thought about his situation and his options. He couldn't leave town without cops sending out flyers about him, and he was not sure when Guy Young's thugs might suddenly come up looking for answers. Tired of playing defense, Irish decided he would play offense now.

The second round came, and he asked the bartender if he recalled seeing Greye La Spina in the booth the other night. The bartender looked him over carefully before shaking his head. Irish pulled a Lincoln from his wallet and laid it on the bar with his hand remaining on the bill.

"Stunner with hazel eyes, wearing a tight, red dress along with a mink stool and black hat last week," Irish told him. "She drinks whiskey straight and comes here with a big guy occasionally. Now, do you remember?"

The beefy man smiled, his teeth showing noticeable dentures. "Yeah, you two were drinking over in the corner there. You had a drink and left; you're a good tipper."

Irish inched the five spot closer to him. "What's your name?"

"They call me Ralphie?" Misgivings filled the bartender's features.

"Don't worry; I'm only looking for information. Do you know the woman's name?"

The bartender looked at Ray. "Why are you asking? Don't you know her name?"

He pulled back his hand with the money. "That wasn't the question."

"Oh, I get you," the bartender said. "No, mister, she's never said but a couple of words the times I've seen her. At first, I thought she was just a lonely wife type, ya know, with the ring and all. Just comes in for a drink, and then a man will show up. She acts all prim and proper, but the way she acts after the joe shows, I'd guess she's a high-class whore. Boy, she's hanging in the wrong place. We don't get high-class guys in here much."

"So, who are the guys coming to see her? Can you describe them?" Greye's real motives for coming to the bar grabbed his attention.

"Most of the time, a big brute of a guy dressed as a chauffeur came for her. That's why I thought she pulled the tricks at the place across the street. Occasionally, other joes pulled into the bar looking for her."

"The driver, you mean the one killed outside?" Ray watched Ralphie staring at the bill on the counter. "Do you know where they went?"

"Nah, I don't know. You know I found the chauffeur guy in his car after I closed up the place. Like I told the cops, I never saw him come inside that night. I thought the guy just fell asleep, but then I saw the guy's throat. It was gruesome."

"Yeah, I bet." Ray took another drink. "Give me more about the people who meet her. What do they look like?"

From the bartender's description, it was clear Guy Young came by the tavern on one occasion. While that wasn't a surprise, the last description forced Ray to ask another question.

"You're sure the young guy who met with her had a pencil mustache? Did he keep glancing around a lot, like a guy not wanting to be seen in public?"

The tavern keeper grinned as he watched Ray remove his hand from the bill from the counter. "You described him to a tee. He's about your size and acted like he didn't want to see no cops hanging around."

~~~

After one more drink and a long drive from the bar, Irish got out of a taxi stopped in front of a large, stone mansion of Henry and Greye La Spina. With its sizable front façade and large windows appearing like two eyes on either side of the front entrance, the bishop's home gave the creepy impression of a haunted house. However, the dwelling looked minuscule next to its neighboring building—a massive stone church. A bell tower, soaring into the night sky, rang out the final peal of notes from the hour chime. Before he left the tavern, Ray called the house asking for Greye, but the butler told him Mrs. La Spina was not home. He did not believe it. Irish took the marble steps two at a time to the twin doors of the house. A weathered-looking, thin man in a black suit opened it.

The butler again told Irish that Mrs. La Spina was not available. When Ray asked for the bishop, the thin man let out a resigned sigh, informing him that the La Spina would return soon from a benefit.

"Then, I suggest you tell the lady of the house that she will meet with me right now, or I might need to speak with her husband instead. That will light a fire under her." Irish growled out.
~~~

He noticed the gentleman raise an eyebrow at the implied threat and asked Ray to wait. A few moments later, the butler returned to escort Irish into a large room, which Ray guessed was the study. Antiques filled the room while rows of books covered the walls. A large oak desk sat on one side, near the windows covered in red curtains. Behind the desk was a large shield with the family coat of arms, the elaborate display surrounded by rows of ancient, ceremonial daggers. On the other side of the massive fireplace, an ornate couch sat with several baroque tables and chairs clustered around.

In a few minutes, Greye walked into the room, her eyes betraying her surprised shock. Ray nearly forgot that his bruised and swollen face would make most people do a double-take. However, her expression turned frosty.

"Why are you here?" Greye asked, smoothing her one-piece jumper nervously.

"I got a message to meet you on the *Stanley Rose* two nights ago. You didn't show up. I'm trying to figure out why you set me up for my beating?" he told her gruffly as he came closer, catching a whiff of her perfume. It didn't soothe him.

Greye stared at him for a moment.

"I don't know what you're talking about, Ray. My husband and I attended a concert that night."

"Really, and who else was there?" he asked snidely.

"Well, Mayor Hopley and the rest of the town's upper crust were at the concert. Trust me; you wouldn't have fit in." Her eyes flashed before she turned away.

"Yeah, like you fit in with the upper crust. But as you noticed, your boyfriend, Guy Young, entertained me for a while, before his men took me home after their fists got sore. Now you're telling me they were using your name to get me out to the Rose." He drew close to her. "Can you explain why they would decide to use that rouse?"

"I have no idea. You must have upset someone." Greye continued, staring at the bookcase.

Ray noticed the titles were mostly in Latin, and it reminded him of the woman's husband. He kept his focus on her reflection coming from the gold wall mirror.

"Yeah, they told me more about you. You have quite a partner there with Guy Young. He thinks so highly of you he said you were one of his girls. Quite the romantic guy. I guess you don't mind that as much as me showing up here." His words dripped with scorn. Greye La Spina remained quiet, her face emotionless.

"It got even better when I got to my hotel; a cop named Howard came by my room. He was very interested in the death of your chauffeur. He gave me some powerful hints that I was a suspect." Ray saw a sudden flash of concern on the porcelain face.

"Did he ask about me?"

Irish gave her a grim smile.

"No, fortunately for you, he didn't ask me for an alibi, at least not yet. But you'll be there for me when I need you, won't you, sweetie?"

Greye glanced at him.

"I don't know what you're talking about."

"Yeah, I'm sure of that." His frustration with her came out with a growl. "But, so that you know, I gave a fiver to the tavern owner, and it jogged his memory. Lady, I'm not sure of your game here, but should I send the copper over to the bar for information?"

Her eyes widened.

"What do you want? You know where things stand. Are you looking for money? I don't have much."

"Yeah, when I look around the room, I see how poor you and your husband are. It's amusing to see how well the charities do." He came around to face her, and their eyes met. "Unlike you and the rest of the people in this city, I'm not here to shake you down. All I want is the truth, and I'm not leaving without it."

Her face went a shade paler at his demand. She shook her head. "I can't right now, especially not here," she told him. "I'll meet you somewhere tomorrow."

Irish scowled at her. "I'm not dumb enough to fall for another one of your games. If not here, we can leave now, and you can tell me."

Fear filled her face.

"I swear I can't. My husband's due to arrive anytime. He can't see you with me."

Ray stopped, deciding he had pushed his luck enough.

"All right, I'll call you tomorrow at noon, and we'll meet. You'll have plenty of time to explain what's going on. And I mean to know the truth about this."

Irish turned to leave when Greye stopped him.

Muffled voices came from outside the door.

"That's my husband," Greye told him as she tugged on his arm. "Come with me. Hurry!"

Irish pulled free of Greye and opened the door. Inside the foyer, a large, older man dressed in a black suit was just taking off his wool topcoat. As Ray entered the lobby, the weathered Jeeves quietly exited with the bishop's hat and coat. The fat face of Bishop Henry La Spina showed his shock at the stranger in his home. Henry's eyes narrowed, darting back and forth between Ray and Greye, who came in behind Irish. Her face betrayed the growing anger at Ray.

"Sorry to bother you, bishop, but my name is Ray Irish, and I'm trying to follow up on some leads for the *Beacon* concerning the death of your driver.

Would you have a moment to talk?" Ray extended his right while giving the gentlemen his cheesiest smile.

Momentarily stunned at the display, the gray-haired man slowly shook Ray's hand. The bishop's hand was large and cold. Irish noticed La Spina's brown eyes scrutinizing him.

"At this time of night? I say this is most irregular." Henry suddenly turned firm as Irish continued smiling. He stood taller than Ray, but his hefty form showed soft and overweight from the years of quiet living. Henry appeared quite a bit older than his wife, despite knowing that he was in his mid-forties.

"Well, you're a tough person to get a hold of." Irish glanced back at Greye, who stood like a marble statue. Ray wondered if she was holding her breath. "Your wife was gracious enough to chat with me while I waited. I promise I won't take up but a couple of minutes."

Henry walked past his horrified wife, going toward the study.

"Oh, very well, please come inside. I don't know what more I can tell you."

As Ray walked past the frozen statue, he gave her a wink, amused at the panic he saw in her. Irish made sure he closed the doors to the room. Taking a chair across from the bishop, who sat on the couch, he tried to imitate a reporter.

"I understand it's a difficult time for you and those in your household right now. I'll only bother you with a couple of questions. How long did you employ Quincannon?"

The fake reporter noticed the bishop's calculating attitude. The change surprise Ray; he expected a meek cleric.

"Your people have already asked this question," Henry told him. "Judging by your battered condition, I don't believe you are a reporter. Why are you here, Mr. Irish?"

Undaunted, Ray continued.

"Well, the reality is that I'm more of a troubleshooter for them. I'm focused on the reporter that got bumped off the other day. It's bad for the newspaper business."

"What's that got to do with my chauffeur?" La Spina asked.

"Well, similar crimes with both men killed in an isolated location and no witnesses. We're trying to determine if there might be any connection," Irish replied.

The bishop's expression turned friendlier to Ray. "Really? How interesting. I understood the murders occurred in two different ways. Well, Quincannon had been with me for...let me see now, at least five years."

"Before you married?" Ray asked, wondering if Greye was discretely listening from a nearby room.

"Yes, a few years before, he came to work for me as a handyman while I was the parish priest. You see, he had some trouble with the law and made every sign of trying to reform. He made good on that and took on additional duties as my responsibilities increased." Henry leaned back on the couch, pulling a cigar from an Asian style box. The bishop failed to offer Ray one of the cigars.

"Do you know why he might need to be at that particular tavern? Can you think of someone he might have been waiting for?"

La Spina froze, his hand half-extended toward his silver lighter.

"Absolutely not," Henry said too quickly before he paused. "What I mean to say is there was no reason for him to be there. I certainly did not order him to go there. I had gone to my room early that evening to finish some of the diocese paperwork. He had the evening off, so his time was his own."

"What about Mrs. La Spina?" Irish decided to do a test of the water. The instant harsh reaction didn't surprise him.

The large man's eyes narrowed, and his face soured.

"What has my wife to do with this? You were discussing my servant."

Smiling again, Irish forced himself away from a sarcastic comment about his wife.

"I'm not saying anything, bishop. I was just wondering if you or your wife might have asked him to go there for some reason. By the way, did you happen to know George Hopley, the reporter? I'm sure you know he was a distant relation to the mayor."

"Neither of us knew this person. Now, I'm a busy man." The bishop rose from the couch; the cigar remained unlit in his hand.

Ray rose from the chair.

"Yeah, I get the hint. I appreciate your time, and I'll see myself out."

When the large wooden door closed behind him, Irish stopped at the bottom of the steps, tightening up his coat as the chill enveloped him. He felt a pair of eyes, glanced up at the light coming from an upstairs window, and caught the outline of Greye as she stepped away from the curtains. Irish didn't notice the other pair of eyes watching him from a dark window on the first floor.

~~~

The sun slowly sank as Cat tried to stay warm inside her frigid car. She wondered if she was a fool. Ray's story about Lieutenant Howard gave her an idea. At the corner of the street and alley, Cat watched Howard while shivering from the cold outside the abandoned warehouse.

After leaving Ray, Cat followed the cop from the police station based on her hunch. She recognized Howard's name, remembering rumors of the cop on the take. She wanted proof about who was paying the cop. An excellent photograph might be a scoop for the paper or a quick way for some cash. Either idea was good with her.

However, she didn't enjoy waiting for something to happen, her hand resting on her camera case. She looked down at the box. In her hurry to track down
~~~

Howard, Cat forgot to bring a smaller camera. Oh well, she would improvise, she decided, as she glanced at Howard. Covered by the smog of his cigarette, the cop showed his impatience as he paced around in a circle. Then he recognized the long, black Cadillac coming closer. Cat noticed his change and began rolling down her window.

Quietly cursing at the poor angle of her shot, she took the picture anyway before sliding in a new negative. Sliding across the front seat, she silently exited her gray vehicle on the passenger side. Trying to appear as casual as someone could while holding a large reporter's camera, she worked her way over to the side of a nearby building. She lined up another shot. Then she caught her breath.

His large head leaning out of the window, Mark J. Fordham barked orders at the detective. From the anger in his tone and the few words she could make out, the union boss was upset with the policeman. The growled response from Howard was unclear. He flicked away his cigarette, and the smoke around Howard cleared, and she got her photograph. Just after that, she saw Fordham disappear from the window, tossing a package out. As the vehicle drove away, the policeman kneeled to pick up the small bag.

I guess City Hall doesn't pay enough!

Moving quickly, Cat walked to her car, glancing to ensure Howard was not looking in her direction. When she got to the vehicle, she noticed the cop heading to his old Ford. Hurrying, she threw the camera into the seat next to her and started the car. Cat drove up next to the detective as he was about to get into his vehicle. She stopped and opened her door, standing on the running board to see over the top of the car.

"Lieutenant Plug Howard, you remember me, don't you? Cat Bennett, do you have any updates about the murder of George Hopley?"

The detective turned, recognizing her. He glanced inside her car while pulling a cigarette from his coat pocket. "I've got a couple of leads I'm following up on," he told her gruffly. "You're off the beaten path. Why are you down here?"

Cat frowned. "I want someone to catch the bastard that killed George. When I saw you, I was hoping you might have some news."

The cop stared at her for a long moment, glancing at the large truck driving up behind the girl's car.

"Is that right? Well, maybe your friend poked his nose into someone's business, and it came back to bite him." His scarred face remained impassive as she slid back inside her vehicle.

As Cat drove away, she didn't like how the corrupt cop stared at her.

~~~

Late afternoon of the next day, Irish paced his room, still unable to meet with Greye. Despite his threats about exposing her, every time he called the house, Greye was not there. He left a message, but over four hours later, he remained in
~~~

his room, trying to figure out his next move. When the phone did ring, it was J. Allan Dunn at the other end of the line.

"Get your butt over to the second floor of the Mayflower Building. Go to the office past the District Attorney and ask for Hobart. Just sign the forms and get your license; everything is in order. You're a private detective working for my office. You're looking into graft with some of our contracts." Dunn hung up before Ray responded.

Fifteen minutes later, Irish entered an odd-looking, dark gray structure that resembled a small castle with Grecian columns on the front. Above the fortress-like doors, *Oyster City Courthouse* showed him he was at the correct building. Ray remained uneasy as he climbed the white marble steps to the second floor. He debated the wisdom of trusting Dunn. The troubleshooter walked past the open double doors of the Oyster City District Attorney's office. A glance inside showed him a mix of people in suits and police uniforms. When he arrived at the end of the hall, a door marked *Records* greeted him. Inside, Ray found a small vestibule with a gray-haired clerk sitting behind a caged window.

"J. Allan Dunn told me to ask for Hobart about signing some forms," Irish explained to the old employee standing behind the counter.

"That'd be me. You must be Ray Irish. Let me see some identification." Hobart squinted as he looked out of his cage, his spectacles dangling at the end of his long nose.

Ray pulled out his wallet and showed the clerk his old military ID card. Since he left the service, Irish never bothered to get a driver's license. Drifters seldom had the opportunity to drive a car. The old man behind the counter hardly glanced at the trifold document before he pushed two pieces of paper under the bars.

"That's the paid-up surety bond, so you sign both copies and give me back one of them," the clerk told him.

He quickly began pecking on a typewriter, which looked like it came from the 19th century. Irish skimmed through the document, still debating the idea of becoming a private detective. Becoming a shamus was the last job Ray might have thought about when he drifted into town. He shrugged his shoulders.

"Why not?" he said aloud.

"Huh, something wrong, mister?" the ancient man asked as he pulled a wallet-sized card from the typewriter.

"No, I guess not. Just wonder how that little piece of paper will stop bullets," Ray joked with the baffled clerk.

Irish stepped into the lobby with an official license in his breast pocket when he noticed Lieutenant Campbell leaning against the wall, apparently waiting on him.

"I thought I recognized you when you passed the DA's office," the policeman observed. Ray noticed his unfriendly tone. "I thought you were working for the *Beacon*? Were you lying to me?"

"Somebody lied to me about my employer. I'm getting it cleared up," Irish told him.

Campbell nodded. His eyes were like a vulture looking at a dying animal.

"I can guess," he said. "Being a working shamus gives you an out if someone like me or the District Attorney asks too many questions, is that it?"

"More like it might help prolong my time here with some rats who messed up my face. You got time for coffee or do you have something against a new private flatfoot?"

Campbell's face brightened at the offer.

"As long as you're buying, I can risk it."

The two men took the detective's car to *Sam's*. They conversed long enough for Ray to find out his driver's full name.

"Lieutenant Arizona Charlie Campbell." Irish grinned as he spoke the name aloud. "Your parents must have hated you."

The driver gave him a sidelong glance.

"Nah, they liked me well enough, but Mom loved the cowboys in the Wild West show that came through town. Arizona Charlie was the major attraction. According to her, he did some amazing trick shots while riding his horse."

"Let me guess, like your namesake; you're a hell of a shot as well," Irish inquired as he watched the people walking by on the sidewalk.

"I hit what I aim at," Arizona told him lightly. "Army did their share of training to help. What about you? I saw the ruptured duck; what service?"

"Seabees," Ray replied. "Three years on God knows how many crappy little islands."

The detective nodded approvingly. "Yeah, European theater myself, following around some bastard who kept trying to get us killed. Got back early in '45."

Irish remained quiet as his thoughts went back to the Pacific. He scraped a lot of sand and dirt while working a bulldozer while he toasted brown under the tropical sun. Ray remembered the stench of destruction and mayhem. That came after the mind-numbing terror when the shells flew in close.

"Yeah, well, at least now we're getting paid better when they try to kill us," Ray finally said as they pulled up to the curb in front of the café.

"Speak for yourself, Shamus. You aren't a cop," Arizona replied as he got out of the automobile. "By the way, how'd you get your face busted up? You get sideways with a girl?"

Ray's expression grew serious.

"Young and his two mugs didn't like the look, so they helped me understand things."

Arizona slowed by the front door of the building. "Did that have anything to do with Cornwall's killing?"

"Not really," Irish told him. "They had a beef about my interest in things about this city. I was asking too many questions since I'm unknown around here."

"Yeah, that probably put you between them and the deep blue sea," the cop told him, his expression turning grave. "Watch out for that group. People end up missing after they get around Guy Young."

"Yeah, so I hear. That's part of the reason we're here." Ray opened the door to the café with a smirk on his face.

After getting their coffee served, Irish asked the cop about the recent murders. "I'm curious about the .38 slugs that killed George Hopley and One-Eye Cornwall. Do you know if the bullets match? The papers never revealed that information."

The cop gave him a funny look.

"You have been reading those magazines on becoming a detective."

"Yeah, page forty-three, under how to find the murderer. Listen, I don't want to get under the skin of a local copper," Irish told him before burning his tongue on the scalding coffee. "If it's sensitive information, I'm only curious."

Arizona shrugged.

"I guess it's fair to discuss since nobody but you and I see the possibility," he said. "I asked Ron Howard about getting it checked, but that never happened."

"Are you talking about Detective Howard, the big guy with a scar on his face?" Ray asked.

"Yeah, he's one of the other lieutenants on the force," he told him. "Do you know him?" Arizona glanced at Ray as they turned the corner.

"Just met him recently," Irish replied. "He stopped by to rearrange my furniture at the hotel, looking for that knife which killed Quincannon, the La Spina's chauffeur." Campbell's right eyebrow rose slightly at the news.

"Why you?" the cop asked.

Ray blasted himself for digging a hole, but he gave him a quick rundown of his stop at the *Six Jolly Squires*, making sure not to bring in Greye La Spina's name. "Apparently, going to a tavern for a drink gets you on his bad side."

Arizona remained noncommittal.

"Yeah, that can happen when a guy gets bumped off in the parking lot, and nobody saw it," he said thoughtfully. "It's funny how he tracked you down if you only had a drink there. Did you have an alibi for Howard?

"His sucker punch over my attitude must have caused it to slip his mind." Irish dodged the question, noticing the detective gave a slight umm sound as he took another sip of coffee. "So, what's the motive behind Quincannon's death? I mean, coming after a stranger in town doesn't make a lot of sense. It's not like he owed me money or anything."

The cop shrugged his shoulders. "Howard's just checking all the leads. I doubt there's much to go on since nobody heard anything or saw anything. Now, why did you ask about the slugs on those other killings?" Curiosity mixed with suspicion in Arizona's tone.

"No particular reason. I thought it was odd that both guns were semi-automatics of the same caliber. The shell casing I saw on the sidewalk near One-Eyed Cornell was a .38 Super. Since the war, many guys came back with their 1911s, but those are .45 caliber. I figured there wouldn't be too many of those .38 autos. But what do I know? I'm not a cop."

"Well, there's some sense in your thinking. The .38 Super out guns most cop weapons, so the gang types like it," Arizona told him as he glanced at the waitress. He turned back to Ray. "But you're thinking like me. That's why I went to the coroner and had the bullets sent out to the state lab to see if there's a match. I'm waiting on word from them," the policeman told him.

"I wonder why Howard didn't think about doing this." Ray waved over the waitress for a refill.

"Some of us flatfoots are better than others. If Howard found just a penknife on you, then you'd be sitting in the slammer." Arizona watched Ray nod in agreement while they waited until the lady pouring the scalding sludge left them.

"You can bet Howard hasn't forgotten about you," Campbell continued. "Now, tell me something. Why are you sniffing around these murders and hanging out with Guy Young?"

Irish went silent for a moment.

"Well, let me put it this way: a client thinks it's Guy Young who committed the killings. But I'm not biting on that. When I met Young, I was pretty convinced that he wanted One-Eye's killer. Something makes me think there's a link, but I'm not sure where. I guess you cops would call it a gut feeling."

Campbell laughed.

"Yeah, you could call it that. Guy Young knocking off his right-hand hoodlum." The cop mulled over the idea for a moment before he shook his head.

"No, I'm not buying it either. The description of the two guys you gave isn't any of his people; I know that. Plus, I haven't heard of any hired guns in town. Young is a son of a bitch, but I don't think he'll be going to such trouble to take out one of his own. He'd just make them disappear."

Ray looked out the window at the nearly empty street outside.

"Yeah, that's my thinking as well. Heard anything about Jacobi pushing into this city? It seems pretty obvious that knocking off number one and number two in Young's gang would make it easier."

The cop gave a grim smile.

"Yeah, and the Jacobi group would be the type to set up a hit. But I haven't heard anything like that. Before you get involved with Jacobi, you might want to rethink your career. Being a lion tamer is safer than snooping around Jacobi."

"Luck of the Irish," Ray said lightly. "Are they in the city?"

"Yeah, his mob controls a couple of pawnshops in town. Nothing major we know about since they like to stay upstate in the capital. Johnny is an ex-booze runner who stays quiet. You know, keep out of the limelight. There's supposed to be a truce going on with Johnny Jacobi and Guy Young."

"Yeah, Guy mentioned that when he left." Ray finished his cup.

Arizona stared at him.

"You know you're damn fortunate that Guy let you walk away from that boat of his."

"I know, but it was only because my great charm persuaded him I can identify the guys who killed his man. Guy says he wants the assassins for himself."

"You better find them before we do." Arizona pushed back his cup. "And a free piece of advice. You better have an alibi for Howard when he comes back looking for it. He's known to work people over until he gets the confession he wants." The tone of the cop's voice made Irish look at him.

"Good thing I don't own a knife, especially one with blood on it," Ray made a thin joke.

Campbell slid out of the booth, standing as he put on his hat.

"That won't make any difference if the weapon somehow shows up in your room or inside your coat after you take a beating. Just something to consider when dealing with Howard, especially since you're a stranger in town." Arizona threw a dime down on the table. "Anyway, we're square."

"Yeah, thanks for the advice," Irish told him. "Let me know if those bullets match, and I'll owe you another coffee."

Arizona replied with a mocking half-laugh, nodding at the waitress when he left.

~~~

Irish stopped by Pappy's newsstand on his way back to the hotel. The energetic newsy was just closing up the wooden shack as Ray approached.

"Been a few days since I heard from the Irish," the black man told him, giving a self-satisfied grin. "The Young boys did a pretty good job on you."

"So, you heard," Ray replied, mildly surprised the newsy already knew his name. He helped Pappy lift down the thick, wood panel which covered the front of the stand.

"Word gets around here pretty quick when people want it to." Pappy pulled a few copies of the late paper and tucked them under his arm. "My wife uses them
~~~

to wrap things at the meat market each week. There's an advantage to having these stands," he explained.

"Any other items about me I should know," Ray tried to make a joke about it, but he wasn't surprised when the newsy continued.

"Aside from that missing Bird girl, not much news is coming out right now. However, I heard one of the detectives seems interested in you. You might be at the top of the list with some killings." Pappy gave Ray a curious look at the idea.

"Yeah, I can bet who that is," Irish replied with a curse. "That son of a bitch Howard acts like the shore patrol goons I remember a few years back. Tell me about this mayor race I just heard about. Anything unusual?"

"Nah, Mark Fordham has wanted to get control of the city for a while now. Lost the last election by a landslide against Hopley, but times are tough now for some folks. I guess Fordham likes his chances." The newsy gave Ray a toothy smile before lowering his voice. "But I wouldn't take his odds."

"What do you mean? Are you saying they already fixed the election?" It did not surprise Irish, but he was curious.

"Well, some would say that's impossible. Then again, accidents have been known to happen. A few years back, Bob Marlow, a shoo-in for the local council seat, shot himself in the head the day before the election." There was an air of conspiracy in his voice as the streetlights turned on down the street. Pappy lit himself a cigarette as he leaned against the building.

Ray looked around the clearing streets, watching the cars slowly make their way home. He noticed the night was coming fast as the air took on a chill. "People do strange things when they feel the pressure."

His companion smiled thoughtfully.

"That's what I hear. Still, it's hard to explain how such things happen in a locked room, and no gun found at the scene. Reporters never could square up that angle. Oyster City seems to have strange cases like that."

Irish guessed Pappy was hinting at something.

"What do you mean?"

"Well, I'm a bit like you," he explained. "I grew up here but left with my parents until coming back in '29 with my new bride, Emma. We both waited a while before we took the plunge. The first job I found when I got back into the city was over at the *Beacon*, delivering the bundles all over the city's black district and out to some of the rural areas. Long-time residents were not happy with changes made by outsiders."

Not seeing any links to his problems, Ray changed the subject as the two men started walking along Main Street.

"What did you think of George Hopley?"

The gray-haired man shrugged his shoulders as he lit another cigarette. "Just like most of the legmen I've dealt with, had some good traits and some not so good."

Ray's attention perked up.

"What is not so good?"

"I don't want to speak ill of the dead, but he lived pretty high on the hog, if you know what I mean?" Pappy replied as the two men turned the corner, heading along 13th Street.

Irish nodded as he remembered the reporter's expensive suit. "Yeah, I see what you mean. Do you have any ideas where a guy like that pulls extra cabbage?"

"Oh, there's tons of ways. It depends on what team you play for," the old man said stoically. "Either tip-off folks about the crooks or help keep things buried when people ask. There's no end of larceny in some folk's hearts."

"Yeah, it goes with this city," Irish told him sarcastically.

There was a snort from his new friend, who remained quiet for a while.

"Any feel for what team George might have been playing for?" Ray asked.

"Nah, but if I were a gambling man, I would lay my bets on his uncle, the mayor," Pappy told him as he flicked his finished butt away into the street. "Those folks have been here forever. The families have a lot of money, and they stay real tight. Those in charge don't like outsiders mixing close to them from what I hear, almost as bad as the Andras family treated newcomers."

"Wait, you mean like Henry Andras?" The name of the original town founder surprised Irish.

Pappy gave him a surprised look.

"You have been reading your history. Me too; I like to hang out at the library, reading all about the past. Yeah, Andras is the same family who has been living up on the hill since the founding. The old lady runs the place. I've only seen her once. She looked old as the hills and wearing some gypsy clothing when I saw her. I guess the rich folk get pretty eccentric at times."

Ray chuckled at the comment before fishing for additional information about the La Spinas. Giving him five bucks, Ray listened to Pappy and his views about the La Spina family. The newsy believed the bishop was a decent person with a lousy wife. He pointed out that a lot of the gossip came from the gray-haired ladies' club who disapproved of the younger woman. Pappy even recalled a previous encounter with Quincannon, the driver and handyman, who threatened the newsy early one morning. It seemed the chauffeur walked away with one of his papers without paying. As Pappy told Irish, a lot of folks hated the giant thug.

Pappy stopped as they arrived in front of the building on the corner of 13th and Federal.

"Say, my wife told me to bring you over for dinner sometime. Why don't you come on up? I can show you some of my books."

Ray hesitated. "I don't want to intrude on your wife at the last minute."

The black man eyed him skeptically. "You sure that's the reason, Irish?"

Irish understood.

"Well, if you insist. It's not like my dinner card is full, so all right by me. I tell you what, let me grab a bottle of wine from that liquor store down the street. I'll come over in a few minutes."

"Wine, eh? That's a first." Pappy rubbed his chin. "Make it snappy. We have smothered pork chops, and I'm hungry. Our apartment is 3A."

"Sounds great. Just give me a few minutes." Ray turned toward the liquor store they had passed a half a block away. It was a quick walk back to the building, where he found Pappy waiting on him in the lobby.

"I went to the manager's apartment to drop off a paper, and we got to talking. He's been a loyal friend to my wife and me," the newsy explained as he led them to the small elevator.

Ray found a spotless living room inside the apartment with a comfortable couch and sitting chair, both with a matching green and yellow floral pattern on the cloth. Along one wall was a set of bookshelves filled with books and various knickknacks on the shelves' top. A telephone chair sat next to the radio.

"Hello, Emma," the older man called out. "I brought Ray Irish over like you asked." Pappy turned back to Ray after closing the door. "I'll take the wine, and you find a seat. The pork chops will just need some warming."

Pappy walked past the radio, stopping to turn it on as he went into the kitchen. Ray went over to the bookshelves and browsed through his host's reading material. The scope and breadth of the books on history impressed him. He picked up *Caesar's Conquest of Gaul* and decided his Latin remained too rusty to read the book.

Irish heard the sounds of pots clanging inside the kitchen. "Say, Pappy, where did you go to college?" he asked.

The wiry man stuck his head out of the doorway, smiling when he recognized the substantial book Ray held. "I didn't, but my momma was a teaching assistant at a private school. Since it was a white school, they couldn't let her be a full teacher, being colored and all, so she made darn sure her boys could read Latin. It helped whenever we ran into the headmaster. He didn't like us colored folk that much."

"Sounds like your momma was a hell of a woman," Irish told him.

"That she was," he told Ray as Pappy walked out of the kitchen carrying plates, which he placed on the table. A couple of trips back to the kitchen and the table had three plates with silverware and glasses. Ray offered to help, but Pappy told Irish he would handle it.

"Go listen to the radio, and I'll call you when everything is ready," his host insisted. "Jack Benny should be on pretty soon."

As Irish half-listened to the radio, he wondered about his host's wife. He had heard no one but Pappy moving around inside the apartment. When he was about to ask, the newsy stepped from the kitchen with the plates holding the main course.

"Find yourself a seat while I get the potatoes and okra," he told Ray.

Taking a seat, he waited as Pappy placed the fine china bowls on the table and took a seat. Unexpectedly, Ray's host grew uncomfortable, glancing at the empty chair across from him.

"You're probably wondering where Emma's at," he said sadly. "So you understand, she's here with us. You see, most people think that my wife died a couple of years ago." He continued staring at the empty chair next to him. "But my Emma's still with me. We talk every night once I come home. And every morning, she's there telling me to have a great day. That's why I'm always happy at my work, knowing my Emma is waiting for me."

Stunned, Irish could not think of anything to say at first.

"Well, can you tell me what happened?" he finally asked.

Pappy frowned, then nodded.

"A young punk stole a car and ran over my wife as she crossed the street downstairs," he explained. "She was going to the butcher for pork chops. When I got there, the policeman told me she never knew what hit her. It's funny because I know what he said was true. Emma said she just woke up in our bed when I saw her the next day. It's kind of comforting to know that's she still here, watching over things. Helps get me through the days, if you see what I mean?"

Irish stared at the wine on the table, then he looked at the empty chair, almost seeing the image of a woman in his mind. Ray recalled a Marine corporal who survived a mortar round striking his foxhole in Guadalcanal. The red-haired kid swore his dead father warned him to get out of the trench just moments before the explosion.

If it happened there, then it could be the same here, Ray reminded himself. He reached over and picked up the wine bottle.

"Do you have a corkscrew?" He asked. "I would like to try this wine with those pork chops. I'm hungry, and I can't wait to hear more about Emma."

~~~

Deep in thought as he walked back from Pappy's apartment, Ray stepped off the curb when he heard his name called. Looking over, he recognized the red Packard and the lady inside. He walked to the driver's side window, which was open.
~~~

"I'm sorry for the delay, but it took a while for me to work my way free of my husband. He's getting suspicious of me recently. I can't get a moment's peace."

"I can't imagine why," Irish said evenly. Greye's eyes flashed with anger.

"Do you still want to talk or not? If so, get in," Greye told him, her manner cold. "I know someplace quiet."

Irish looked around, then went to the other side of the vehicle and got in. As Greye pulled into the street, he looked her over, noticing her black dress and hat.

"Where are we going?" He turned around to make sure no one was tailing them on the nearly deserted street.

"There's a place just outside the city where no one will bother us." Greye's expression changed, and she gave him a sultry glance. "That's what you wanted. I even got some whiskey to make the evening a little more pleasant."

Ray leaned back in the seat. "You think of everything."

~~~

Catherine spent most of the day searching for answers about George Hopley and receiving only more questions. Much of what she learned agreed with Ray Irish about her friend. George was heavily on the take, at least by inference. Worse, she could find nothing to pin down which single person her friend might have done favors for in return for cash. The legman worked all over the city, searching for the latest story, which made her work difficult.

One lead sent her to a tavern along the waterfront, a place called Anthony's. She did not have a handle on who owned the joint. When she walked in, Cat immediately did not like the place. Several tables held men who looked like they recently escaped from prison. They eyed her suspiciously. After taking a deep breath, she walked to the back of the room, where she spoke with the bartender despite her initial disgust. The man was an ex-fighter named Joe Knapp. He wore black pants and a white undershirt that could not cover his hairy back or enormous belly. It was hard to tell the primary color of his shirt from all the food and sweat stains.

When Cat stepped up to the tall wooden bar, the slob behind the counter leered at her. He smiled, listening to her questions while his eyes remained transfixed on her breasts. Despite the unpleasant experience, the photographer discovered George came to the place often, and he arrived at the bar on the day of his murder. It took a five-dollar bill to get the information out of him, but she only discovered that George left with a fat guy wearing a brown suit and gray hat.

"I don't know who the guy was," Knapp told her. "Maybe my memory is failing. You come back to my office, and maybe I'll remember. It won't cost you any more cash. I'll have you work it off."
~~~

Cat forced herself not to punch the leering man's face, but she made sure to knock an empty bar glass from the counter when she turned away and left the bar. She dealt with such treatment her entire life while living around the docks with a single mom. Pigs like Knapp were one reason Cat did not trust men.

After getting in her car, she drove to the *Beacon* to finish her pictures from the morning. A couple of times, she felt like a black sedan was following her. After taking a couple of quick turns around corners, Cat decided it was her nerves getting the best of her. When she arrived at the home of the paper, Cat was already mulling over the information she had got. Taking the steps two at a time, the photographer nearly ran into Tom Brand, son of the editors and one reporter she trusted.

"Hey, next time, look up as you come up the stairs," the thin man scolded her with a grin.

"Sorry, Tom, I was thinking about something." Cat stopped with a sudden thought. "Would you know anything about some characters hanging out at Anthony's?"

The reporter gave her a frown. "You mean that dive along Waterfront Drive?" His face remained grave when she nodded. "I wouldn't hang around that place, especially if I was a woman."

"I was checking out a lead," she confessed lightly. "Who owns the tavern?"

Tom shook his head. "Nobody knows, so I would guess it's a front. My suspicion is Fordham has his money in there. I hear that's where his people recruit their heavies to keep some of his business partners in line. What are you checking out?"

Cat gave Brand the description of the person seen leaving with George Hopley.

"I'm trying to figure out who might have killed George. This guy left that bar with him on the day of his murder. The bartender claimed he didn't know the guy, but I'm suspicious."

"Yeah, I would be as well," the reporter paused. "Your description seems to match up with a new guy in the city. Nobody knows much about him, but he's been showing up all over the place recently."

She looked at him. "Are you sure? Any idea what his racket is?"

He shrugged. "No, I'm just telling you what I've heard."

"Okay, thanks for the tip." Cat walked away.

"You still have a bee in your bonnet about Greye La Spina?" Brand asked.

Cat nearly tripped over the step in her haste to find out more.

"Sure, what do you have?"

"Well, I overheard part of a telephone conversation that Gladys was having. From what I can tell, someone thinks they need money to reveal something in Mrs. La Spina's past. You need to speak with Gladys for more of the scoop. I know the paper will print nothing about the bishop's wife, but it sounded kind of interesting. I figured you'd want to know."

Thanking him for the information, Cat immediately jockeyed past a couple of men who were jawing in front of the building entrance. She made her way to the office where Gladys sat, working on her latest Mrs. Purvey article.

"All right, spill it," Cat told her as she slid into an uncomfortable chair next to the desk.

The woman behind the typewriter looked up, her dainty glasses perched precariously at the end of her bulbous nose. Her green eyes twinkled as she gave a mischievous grin.

"Mrs. Purvey is unsure of what you are talking about, my little reader." Gladys returned to her typing. Cat sighed impatiently. Mrs. Purvey was the pen name of Gladys Peer, who wrote the weekly society column. While the work was famous throughout the northeast part of the U.S., it came from the entire persona Gladys took on when she worked. She was successful, but more than a few of those in the building considered Miss Peer a leading candidate for the nuthouse.

"Enough, it's been a long day, Gladys. You know, I only come in for the juicy tidbits. I hear you have something on Greye La Spina." Cat moved around in her seat, trying to find a comfortable position.

Mrs. Purvey stopped typing again.

"Dearie, you shouldn't be eavesdropping on my conversations." The social reporter saw the stare from Cat and changed her persona again. "It's an innuendo to a dead end," Gladys told her. "I got a letter from a gentleman named John Robertson a couple of months back."

Gladys informed her that John Robertson claimed that Greye La Spina had a relative who was a criminal out of Boston.

"The person who wrote the letter wanted money from the paper for the proof. I called out to a friend at a Boston paper to check on the guy, and they called me back today. They told me this Robertson chap died during a bank robbery in Brockton a couple of months back. He was a clerk in the bank."

~~~

Late that evening, as Ray Irish drove away with Greye La Spina, Catherine Bennett sat alone at her small table inside her apartment. She half-heard the song by the Ink Spots on her radio. In her hand, there was a small glass of Irish whiskey and ice. She paid little attention to the hazy smoke from the charred remains of a cigarette drifting up from the ashtray. Instead, Cat was trying to put the pieces into place from her long day of snooping around the city.

Like her friend, Gladys, Cat believed the information about Greye La Spina meant nothing. The description of the fat man who left with George was too vague for her to go much further. The only real traction she had for the day was her photos of Fordham stretched across the table. She picked up one picture showing
~~~

Detective Howard taking something from the union boss. She smiled, wondering how much the photo and negative might be worth to the mayoral candidate and the crooked cop.

Stretching her arms above her head, she yawned, thinking about her next steps. Cat's lips turned to a frown at the realization that she would have to find out more about Fordham and his goons. She didn't want to step in with the sharks without some backup on her side. With another yawn, she got up and dropped the photo as she set the tumbler down. The photographer turned off the light as she went to her bedroom.

The distant chime of a mantle clock struck its third note, which went unheard as Cat slept. Suddenly, she woke to the pressure of a rough hand over her mouth. The dark figure pulled his legs over the top half of her body, pinning her arms inside the blanket as she futilely tried to struggle. Then, cold steel pressed against her cheek, and she froze.

"Don't scream, bitch, or I'll start slicing you," the ominous male voice told her as the figure leaned on her. "Now, nod your head if you understand."

The woman followed the instructions, trying to see who was above her in the pale moonlight that filled the room.

"Good, now I'm gonna let go of your mouth." She felt the blade slid from her cheek and press on her neck. "Try an' scream, and I'll cut your throat. Understand?"

Cat nodded again, and she felt the pressure over her mouth relax and move away.

"You were asking a lot of questions at Anthony's today. Why?" His foul breath crossed her face.

"Please, don't hurt me. I…I was trying to find out about who killed George Hopley." She felt the sting when he slapped her, then put his hand over her mouth. She did not cry out.

"Why were you at Anthony's?" The man pressed the side of his knife blade hard on her windpipe before he let her talk.

"George went there on the day someone murdered him." Cat prayed silently.

"All right, you little tomato. Who are you working for?" The threatening voice hovered near her ear.

"For me," she replied, but swiftly got another slap across her face for the effort. Then, the creep struck her with a backhand.

"Am I gonna have to cut the answer out of you? Who are you working for?"

Panic overwhelmed her as her voice grew shrill.

"I swear to God; I'm telling you the truth. He was a friend of mine. I just want the bastards that killed him."

The rough hand went over her mouth again. "Then why the camera?"

The intruder let her speak again. "I'm a photographer for the *Beacon*. It's my job," she said as he shifted his body. The goon slid over to the side of the bed. His hand remained over her mouth, and the knife still pressed on her throat.

"You're gonna get up and give me the negatives and pictures you took," he told her.

She tried to shake her head, wanting to say she did not have them, but the goon gave her several hard backhands across her face. Cat felt the taste of blood coming from a swollen lip.

"Don't lie to me, twit. I followed you to that fleabag building where you work, so I know you have the developed pictures. Plus, you didn't leave any negatives there. Now give them to me, and you have nothing to worry about."

He grabbed her hair, painfully pulling her from the bed. Cat gave a quiet cry from the pain.

"Keep quiet," the thug warned her, pulling in close behind her.

They plodded into the next room, the man only pausing to let her turn on the switch to light the room. Cat glanced back, but she could only see a black mask over the intruder's face. However, he caught her glimpse.

"If you want to stay alive, get the pictures, bitch," he growled as he pushed her across the small living room.

She led the intruder to the table. After forcing her to gather them into a small pile, the man quickly pocketed the articles inside his black jacket. After a quick scan around the room, he asked if that was all the pictures. She nodded.

"It better be. Now back to your bedroom." He forced his prisoner across the apartment.

When they arrived next to the nightstand, he forced her to turn around. Panic filled Catherine as she saw his dark brown eyes meet hers. He pushed her down to a sitting position on the edge of the bed. "Too bad. I have my orders, or we could have some fun."

The intruder dangled the long switchblade in her face. Holding the weapon in front of her eye, he placed his hand on her throat. Then, he pushed her to lie back on the bed. Slowly, the creep sliced through the silk cloth of her pajama top as he gave her another warning not to move. Reaching the top of her garment, her attacker pulled back the pajamas, exposing her breasts. She felt the tears welling up in her eyes as he roughly groped her breasts with a calloused hand. He leaned in close to her face, his intense breaths compelling her to expect the worse.

"Now that I have your attention, this is your only warning, bitch. Everybody knows your racket, taking pictures and getting men to pay off for them. If you go anywhere near Fordham, I'm coming back to enjoy you like a whore for the night. Then I'll cut you up into small pieces for the cops to find."

The creep suddenly slid off of her bed. Cat did not move as she watched his dark figure cross the room to her bedroom window, silently climbing out into the night. After the soft creaking sounds of his steps going down the fire escape receded. The only sound in the room was Cat's sobbing as she curled up under her sheets.

Chapter 4: Sucker Punch

"Your face is healing up," Greye said, glancing at Ray. They passed through the open gate leading into the abandoned ammunition plant. The words sounded stiff and rehearsed.

"Well, my insides are mostly in the same place," Ray replied. He tried to remain aloof, doubting her motives. But he told himself that she might be a patsy as well.

Greye La Spina pulled her car between two silent buildings after passing through an open gate, which led into an abandoned ammunition plant. The yellow light of a single bulb coming from the corner of the wooden structure created a romantic atmosphere.

"This is the perfect place for us to talk," she told him as she turned off the engine. "I understand no one comes out to this place so that we will have it to ourselves. It's amazing how quiet this factory is since it closed down."

"That's not what you want to talk about, is it?" Ray asked.

Greye shook her head, her soft eyes appealing to him. "What did you tell my husband?"

His scowl darkened at her question. "You think I'm enough of a rat to tell your husband about you and me dancing in the back seat? I didn't say a damn thing about you. I asked why Quincannon was hanging around that tavern when you and I were there," he said. "But you figured it out already, or your husband told you. I don't think you realize this game you're playing could blow up in your face. That means it could do the same to me. You need to tell me what you're involved in," Irish told her.

"I don't have to tell you anything," she replied, her voice rising. "I'm tired of people telling me what to do."

"Really?" He raised an eyebrow. "Babe, you better explain and get me to believe you so that I can help both of us. That might keep your name away from the cops and the papers. If they get wise, we'll need each other as an alibi. Otherwise, you can play your little charade for them by yourself."

"You're a rat," she said, refusing to look at him.

"Lady, I'm getting squeezed from two sides here, so I'm not helping unless I know the rules." Irish tried to keep his voice calm.

She remained quiet for a moment, then nodded. "All right, if that's how it has to be." She reached into her purse and pulled out a silver flask. "You can have the truth." Greye took a swig from the small vessel, making a show of shivering before she handed it to Ray. He tipped it back.

"Not bad whiskey," Ray told her approvingly. "Well, since we have some time, start with your husband. How does he fit into this mess?"

"I met Henry in New York when he was out there for a conference with a bunch of religious leaders. I was working behind the cigarette counter, and he started talking to me. He was lonely. Anyway, it wasn't anything to me, but he was nice enough. I overheard one of the bishops there say he was a man on the rise…well, I got interested in him. Like I told you, I married Henry because he had prestige and I wanted something stable. I just didn't know he was a eunuch." Ray noticed her tears in the dim light. She pulled a handkerchief from her purse and dabbed her nose.

"Then, how does Quincannon come into this? You said he was acting like your husband. Did he come to your rescue at night when hubby is gone?"

"No." She paused, watching him take another drink. "Well, not a first. I'll admit I was lonely, but I had no interest in him. He's crude and a slob; I mean, he was. Then, something happened, and he helped me find a temporary solution to the problem."

Ray glanced at her. "You're not saying what something is, but it sounds like his fix cost you more than you thought. How did he help you?

Greye shook her head. "Let's just say he came up with enough money to help me avoid legal issues," she told him. "After that, he acted like I was his property. He even treated Henry differently. My husband became furious."

"Quincannon must have decided you owed him enough to do as he pleased." Ray leaned back, tipping the flask.

"The jerk told me he was in love with me. He would get jealous if I went someplace without him. He complained about me going out to the ship." She gave a scoffing laugh. "Damn fool is the one who came up with the idea."

"Are you saying that you're not quite the gambling addict you pretend to be?" Irish sounded pleased with himself.

The lady in black shook her head.

"I seldom go to that place to gamble. Guy Young treats me all right as long as I do what he wants. Gambling is the cover story for my husband."

"I think I can figure it out," he said drolly.

The wife refused to give Ray the stern glare for his statement.

"Is that why Quincannon was hanging outside the tavern where we met?" He was interested in her story, but still skeptical about how much of it was true.

She looked at him, her face showing a range of emotions. "I'm not sure, but I guess he followed me that night. He was always trying to find out what I was doing. It was like he had me on a leash. You got a taste of it. You know how he reacted when you accidentally knocked me over, and I gave you that card."

"Yeah, that whole thing makes me a suspect to the cops if they figure out I was with you that night," he told her offhand. "I don't get it, a classy dame like you hanging with a racketeer. If it's about the money you owe Young, your husband could find a few wealthy friends and pay it off. You wouldn't have to be the guy's…" Ray stopped himself.

"His whore, that's what you meant to say." Her face grew dark. "It's not that simple, and I'm not explaining it to you."

"That's fine," he replied. "Just remember you, and I are the only alibi for each other the night that Quincannon got knocked off. Nothing good would come from going to the cops. We should keep it under wraps, but that doesn't mean they won't show up looking for answers. The police might find out your driver followed you around."

Greye stared at her hands and nodded.

"That's why nobody can know. Quincannon came to my room the night before and told me we would quit the charade soon. He said that he figured out a way to leave town, and we would have everything to ourselves. Nobody would be the wiser, and he had it all worked out. Difficult to believe, isn't it?"

Ray took another swig from the flask. He kept his voice even, although he was thinking of his first night with her.

"I don't know. A guy gets ideas about the woman he chases around the mattress." His thoughts drifted a bit before he came back to her dead chauffeur, and he shook his head again, suddenly feeling an unusual calm settle inside him.

"Yeah, he was a fool," she replied bitterly.

"I don't know. Either your chauffeur was lying to himself, or..." Ray slid down the seat, feeling the effects of the drink. "Was your husband home the night Quincannon told you to stop?"

He slurred his words, and Greye looked at him strangely. "Yes, Henry was downstairs. Are you okay?"

Ray nodded sleepily.

"So, you and Quincannon were in deep into something. That might explain what happened. What's this charade and the favor you owe him?"

Irish saw the world spinning around him, and he caught a glint of disdain in Greye's eyes as she studied him. He lifted his arm to open the car door, and his hand fumbled with the handle, unable to grab it. Then the door opened, and he fell out of the vehicle. Landing hard on his shoulder, Ray found his face only a few inches away from a dark pair of leather shoes. He rolled over to look at two faces peering down. In his blurring vision, the vaguely familiar images of a fat guy and a thin man with a small pencil mustache leaned over him.

"Take him to your place, and I'll be there in the morning. Don't do anything until I get there." Greye's voice faded in and out. "We have to make this look perfect."

The stranger with the pencil mustache gave Ray a foul grin, then kicked him in the head. Ray Irish fell into the deep cavity of unconsciousness.

~~~
~~~

A small, circular room held a five-sided table with chairs for each person walking through the entrance's black door. The night sky, filled with stars, sent in a trickle of light through the glass cupola ceiling. As each masked person took their assigned seat, while an attendant, dressed in a flowing black robe, lit a small red candle. The servant placed the burning tallow on the table in front of each seat. The masks, which thoroughly covered each of the participants' faces, had large openings looking like smiles while exposing the wearer's lips. A deck of ancient tarot cards lying near the head of the table revealed the cast of disguised characters. An empty gold cup with five sides, each engraved with symbols, sat on top of the cards.

The Magician, The High Priestess, The Empress, and The Emperor took their respective seats. Two other masked people moved to their positions by the entrance. Standing next to the door were two figures wearing the faces of Death and Judgment. All the characters wore black robes.

The last person slowly entered the room, the tiny figure using hands wrinkled by age to keep the horned mask from sliding down. The face bore the image of a demon-like creature, and the frail body underneath wore a flowing red robe. Taking the seat in front of the door, the person under the mask cursed at the sight of a drugged rabbit lying on the large plate.

"What is this? Animal blood has little power and only whets the appetites of our protectors," the frail voice complained.

The masks exchanged glances around the table. No one volunteered information.

"Must my servant find human victims for us each full moon?" She pounded the table. "Well, no more. It's time the Shadows brought their own. Empress, you'll work with the High Priest to give us our next sacrifice. Since he could not join us this evening, the task becomes his."

The woman across the table let out an audible huff, but she nodded.

The masked demon picked up a jewel-encrusted dagger that was lying on the plate.

"A human sacrifice when the blood moon rises, or we'll select a member of the Shadows to volunteer their blood. Is that understood?"

Sliding the blade from the sheath, a shaking hand brought the engraved knife above the sacrifice. With a quick strike, the blade cut the throat of the unfortunate animal. It lay there, silently dying, while the human creatures chanted a series of words over and over.

Death stepped forward, picking up the plate and carefully pouring the blood into the golden cup. The demon wiped the dagger clean with a cloth, reinserting it into the engraved gold-covered sheath. Death placed the half-filled cup in front of the devil, who took the first foul drink. Each creature around the table shared in the blood sacrifice. The High Priestess giggled nervously before tasting the blood, while the Empress told the person to remain quiet. Death took the last drink before returning to the entrance. Only Judgment stayed away from the table, carefully watching but remaining aloof from the proceedings.

The demon flipped over the cards, mumbling incoherent phrases. Following the exposure of seven cards from the deck, the old woman in the red robe spoke.

"The dreams you have troubled each of you. The nightmares tell you that the souls of our ancestors are distressed. Those around this table know this truth and the time to act is upon us. We will take action against the people who threaten our city."

The faces around the table turned their heads to glance at the others. Slowly, the group nodded in agreement. The Magician asked for guidance, and the demon held up a hand, now devoid of wrinkles and age spots. The frail voice grew more robust, while her tone remained grave.

"Nightmares will scare some of those against the Order, but some of our opponents are brutal remnants of philistines who value nothing but power. I've seen the spirit who will stop those people who work against our families. Death and Judgment will ensure that our Empress finds our next sacrifice for the master. When you receive the word, follow their instructions. If you fail, the master will have your blood."

The demon gazed around the table. "As a reminder, the laws of our society remain inviolable since our founding over two centuries ago. Death will come to rip your soul from its shell, and Judgment will cast you to Andras for your failure."

~~~

A dark and quiet world greeted Irish when he came out of his stupor. The rag stuffed inside his mouth threatened to choke him, and Ray panicked. Turning his cheek, he saw a thin line of light coming from underneath the door. The peek calmed him after a moment, and he tried to focus his thoughts. Discovering his feet remained unbound, Ray twisted and turned, his numb wrists behind him, unable to help his struggle.

Through his turns inside the confined space, he gradually determined he lay inside a small closet. Working his body around, Ray lifted his feet, trying to find the door handle; his movement's noise seemed loud. He stopped, intently listening, but silence remained outside the door. Unable to turn the round knob with his polished leather shoes, Ray twisted his body around, his legs causing him to groan as the muscles cramped. Finally, Irish turned over, and he got to his knees. A fog came over him again, but he shook it off as he stood. Ray's head struck a shelf, causing him to curse silently. Using his bound hands to feel around the door, he finally found the handle. He found the door latch and pushed with his back to open the door. However, the latch popped open, sending Irish falling
~~~

to the floor when the door swung open. Landing hard on his shoulder, he shook his head while he rolled over.

Ray Irish stared into the open eyes of a dead man. The pencil mustache was dark against the pale skin, his face still showing the combined expression of horror and disbelief. Irish pulled his face away from the corpse, his dazed mind reeling at the pool of blood he fell into while his body twisted away. The throat of the dead man held the same extended red cut across, just like Quincannon. A horrified shriek began, then instantly cut off from the other side of the room.

Greye La Spina stood by the doorway, her fists clutched to her mouth while her wide eyes remained focused on the corpse. He watched her back into the opened door, her head shaking back and forth.

"No, no, no…" The words were a whisper, barely audible past her clutched hands.

Cat pushed past Greye before coming to a complete stop as the bloody scene came into full view. Her expression went from shock to relief. She came to him, kneeling beside Ray.

"Are you all right?" she asked, reaching around his head to unbind his gag.

The man nodded, trying to spit out the rag. He coughed out his thanks to her while his mind continued to shake off the effects of his spiked drink. Finally, he told her to help remove the bindings on his wrists.

Cat helped him over and saw the rope tightly cutting into his skin. She noticed the dagger lying in the blood, and she paused. Cat steeled herself to the uncomfortable dampness and picked up the weapon to cut through the rope.

Freed, Irish tried to get to his feet before he fell again. His head still swimming, Ray noticed Greye tearfully leave the room.

"I'll call the sheriff," Cat told him, dropping the dagger in front of Irish. He stared at the weapon briefly, trying to remember where he had seen it before.

Carefully, Ray stumbled while trying to get up, his legs refusing his attempts to walk. He finally made it to the door, leaning against the wall. He looked down the hall, but Greye was gone. Pushing away from the wall, his still numb hands clumsily closed the door.

"Put the phone down," Irish heard himself tell Cat. She looked at him, about to say something to the hotel operator. He gestured for her to hang up while he held her gaze. Cat put down the phone.

"Why don't you want the police?" she asked.

"I'm saving us from questions that we can't answer. Now wash your hands. We have to get out of here," Ray told her as his brain slowly pulled things together.

Glancing at the dagger on the floor again, he suddenly felt an icy chill fill him, along with a boost of adrenaline. He carefully picked up the murder weapon, taking it to the bathroom. After he washed the blood from the dagger and his hands, Ray dried both using a white hand towel hanging by the sink.

Cat stared at him as he left the small bathroom. Irish walked across the room while he wiped the weapon thoroughly clean of any fingerprints before throwing it down by the body. He noticed she remained standing by the bathroom door, watching him.

"Damn it, wash your hands. We have to get out of here. I think this might be a setup that went wrong." He went to the phone, wiped the receiver's black handle, then went to the closet and wiped off the closet handles. Ray glanced at Cat, who finished with her hands. He told her to wipe down the sink and faucets with the hand towel. Irish quickly scanned the room for any obvious clues.

"All right, I think I've got everything. Did you wipe everyplace you touched?"

Cat nodded as she stepped around the floor's bloodstained areas, and Ray cautiously opened the door. After he cleaned the door handle, Irish motioned for Cat to leave ahead of him. The troubleshooter took the hand towel she carried and stuffed it into one pocket of his coat. Then he used his towel to close the door. The pair rushed down the hallway while Ray used the wet cloth on the bloodstains on his coat.

"I'm a mess; let's find the back stairs out of here," he jammed the wet and bloody cloth into his other coat pocket.

The photographer led them along the passageway to a narrow door that opened to stairs. A minute later, the couple exited the building's back, stepping out onto a gravel path. An old rock fence with a large, open field on the other side informed Ray they were no longer in the city.

"My car's out front," she told him. "You go to the side of the building, and I'll meet you there." Before he could reply, Cat stepped back into the building. Irish looked over his clothes with a scowl, trying to wipe the worst of the blood away after pulling out one towel again. Then Ray cautiously followed the wall until he reached the corner of the structure. Soon, Cat drove up in her gray Olds coupe. He slid in on the bench seat, and the pair drove away. Not long after pulling out of the parking lot, they passed a black and white sedan blaring sirens as the county sheriff sped to the crime scene. Ray watched the car running through the parking lot and saw the sign to the Sleeping Acre Inn by the road.

"Well, you saved my hide. Thanks," Irish opened the window to ward off his drowsiness. "Now, the next question: how in the hell did you find me?"

Cat glanced at him.

"I followed your girlfriend." Irish waited for a moment. "Give me more than that."

"La Spina came out of her house this morning in a big hurry." His driver kept glancing in the rearview mirror. "I knew something was going on, so I tailed her to that hotel."

"Wait, are you saying you were staking out her place? I'm not complaining, but where the hell did you come up with that?" He looked behind again, breathing a sigh of relief that no one followed them.

"Yeah, I couldn't sleep," Cat replied. The clipped tone of her voice got Ray's attention. She changed the subject.

"Will that cleaning we did to the room work?" she asked.

Irish glanced back again.

"Yeah, any fingerprints they find will come out too smudged for the detectives to make anything out of," he replied. "As long as nobody saw us, I think we'll be fine. What happened at La Spina's house?"

"Greye made a beeline to this place. I thought she might have another boyfriend up here, so I figured I would check out what room and come back to take a private photo of her and this person." She glanced at Ray. "You know, to get her to talk. That's when I found you. What happened?"

"The bitch gave me a mickey, and when I fell out of the car, that dead guy decided to kick my face in for fun. That's the last thing I remember until I woke up in the closet."

Ray stuck his head partially out of the window. The breeze felt wonderful. Then he turned back to her.

"Next thing I know, I'm lying in the blood, staring at a dead man. I'm sure that's Pendexter. The other guy's face was hazy to me, but I'm betting the other killer was involved. I remember two of them staring down at me."

"You have any idea what they took you out there for?"

"I think that bitch and her hoodlum friends were trying damn hard to leave me for a big fall. But I have no idea what their plan was. You didn't see Greye's face, but that dead guy had to mean something to her. She was behind this, and now I have to figure it out. That's why I didn't want to explain to the cops. They will never believe my story; she's the bishop's wife."

"I was there, and I would have backed you," Cat told him empathically, then her voice softened as she thought about the situation. "But La Spina could have paid off someone, forcing them to go after you and me."

"Exactly my point." Ray looked at the drying blood stains covering his clothes. "I don't plan on waiting in jail to figure out the score. We need to find someplace where I can get cleaned up and ditch these clothes."

"I've got that covered; we'll go to my place," she told him.

It took a while before the pair could get into Cat's apartment after the drive. She ran into an elderly male neighbor at the front door of the building. The friend began telling her about his recent trip to California. Ray felt very exposed by the back corner of the building in the alleyway as he waited near foul-smelling trash cans. Irish could almost imagine a police car suddenly turning into the alley to find him.

Finally able to free herself from the gray-haired man, Cat let Ray into the building through the back door. They made their way up the staircase, each person expecting the worst. Fortunately, their luck held, and the unlikely couple went inside.

"Remember to keep it down," she warned him. "I can't have any male visitors here."

Irish gave her a cheesy grin. "You weren't too worried about that back at my hotel."

Cat's face remained serious.

"Get that jacket and shirt off, and I'll dispose of them down the incinerator. The landlord has the boiler running all the time for the hot water."

A few minutes later, Cat threw the garments and towels into the incinerator on her way out of the building. With only his pants on, Ray waited for her to return. While she went to the Hotel Alexander for his clothes, the man helped himself to a cheese sandwich. Then he wandered around the apartment. The place's décor was stylish and straightforward, with a small couch and a matching chair in white, along with an art déco chrome end table. The kitchen was tidy; however, the tiny dining table had two nearly empty folders on the top, which looked out of place. On top of one folder sat a bottle of Irish whiskey and an almost full ashtray with ashes covering part of the tabletop. He moved around one folder and saw a picture underneath.

Irish recognized the dead detective in the photo. Ray guessed Cat was still working on some blackmail to bring in some extra cabbage. He frowned as he tossed the picture back on the table, taking the bottle of whiskey to the sink. The troubleshooter pulled a tumbler from the cabinet and poured himself half a glass. Irish took a sip as he went to the couch in the living room.

For some reason, the photo bothered him. Not the picture itself, but the larceny which seemed to fill Cat's heart. Somehow, Ray liked to believe in the initial wholesome picture of her he created in his mind when they first met. He did not like the reality which came out the more he knew about her. She was playing a dangerous game that had already killed her partner, George Hopley. He questioned why he felt the need to protect her. There was something about Cat that he liked. She was strong, willing to help him, even though she knew little about him. He downed the whiskey in the tumbler.

I need another drink!

When Cat arrived back at her apartment, she found Irish sitting on the couch. She barely recognized him. Ray's usual calm changed into an embittered rage. Cat noticed the nearly empty bottle next to him. Silently, he took the clothes and disappeared into her bedroom. She talked through the door, happily explaining all the strange looks received when she smuggled the clothes out of the hotel. Cat heard no reply from Ray. He walked out of her bedroom wearing a clean blue suit. There was a slight wobble in his walk, and his eyes carried a murderous look that scared her.

"Where are you going?" Cat asked him, heading to the door as she cut him off.

"I have business with someone," Irish told her, his voice low, nearly inaudible.

"You can't kill her." Cat recognized his murderous intentions.

Ray stopped when she placed her hand on his chest. He looked at the small woman with a raised eyebrow.

"Why the hell not? The whore has it coming," he told her viciously. "Get out of my way!"

She remained in front of him. Cat knew drunken rage, and she hated it, considering such actions as pathetic. Still, she tried to reason with Ray.

"Listen to me. You're not a murderer; I know your record. If you kill her, you will die. Those who are friends of the bishop will be happy to send you to the electric chair. As far as the people that run this city are concerned, two more dead outsiders are a good thing."

"It doesn't matter as long as she gets it in the end," he fumed at her. Unexpectedly, she smacked him hard across the face. Fear crossed her eyes, then anger, but her action worked. His bruised face hurt from the strike.

"Don't be a stupid drunk. Some of us are on your side. Now, sit down and relax for a minute. I'll get us a drink. You can wallow in your anger, but just stay here." Cat took a step over to the end table and picked up the empty glass.

Shocked by the slap, Ray's eyes narrowed as he felt his nose bleed. Grudgingly, he pulled a handkerchief from his pocket and dabbed at his nose. His murderous glare subsiding, the man went to the couch, his expression remaining cold. He took a seat and watched her.

Cat went to the kitchen and pulled another tumbler from the shelf. She filled the glasses, making sure one glass had water only. The woman talked while she worked, trying to forge a plan.

"Greye La Spina isn't in a good position. You're still alive and her partner is dead. Let's use that to our advantage. She can't be sure what happens next."

Handing Ray a glass of water when she came to the couch, she sat next to him.

"You have a bad temper, and it gets worse when you drink," she told him as calmly as she could. However, there was an intensity in her eyes when she turned to him. "I don't like drunks, and I don't like self-pity. I've seen enough of that stuff in the past."

"Yeah, maybe so, but save the analyzing for someone else," he told her gruffly, staring at the glass. "Now you've got my attention. Do you have something like a plan, or do you just like hitting me?"

Cat gave an unexpected grin.

"Well, mostly the hitting part, but you know I'm right."

Irish grunted, still staring at the glass before he set it on the table, untouched.

"The way I see it, Greye wanted me out of the way. She worked me into her trap, but I can't figure out her angle. The bitch has two male partners who could have killed me at that old military base. That's where she gave me the mickey. Nobody would have found my body for days, so why drag me out to the motel?"

He leaned back in the chair.

"Maybe they didn't want to kill you, might have wanted to find out something from you," she suggested.

"It's possible," he agreed as he let out a deep breath. "I remember she told the guys not to do anything until she got there. After that, it's all black." Ray shook his head. "No, there's something else going on here. You don't take a guy out to a motel. There are too many people around to hear things if they planned on beating the information out of me."

"Then, what?" she asked.

Irish shrugged.

"It was a setup, but I guess I'm going to have to ask her."

Cat glared at him.

"Forget that idea. Do you think La Spina will leave that lovely mansion of hers now? If I'm standing in her shoes, I wait until you show up and have the cops haul you away. Greye could claim you raped her. In this state, you get the death penalty for that. Besides, we still have to worry about her accomplice." She leaned back, taking a large sip of her drink, and sighed.

"That's assuming the cops don't trace you and me back to the Camelot somehow. You know, it would only take an anonymous call from her partner to have the heat come down on us."

Ray nodded, remembering the scene at the motel room. "Yeah, that means we put the heat on Greye."

Cat remained silent, a sudden weariness creeping over her. She didn't like the implications of his idea. She yawned, and it reminded Irish of an unasked question.

"What's with the picture on your table?"

"What do you mean?" Her surprise showed when she asked. Cat looked at the table, getting up from the couch to see. Walking toward the table, she picked up the photo carefully.

"There's something you're not telling me." He wondered at her dramatic reaction to his question. There was a hint of dread in her eyes when she turned back to him.

"Where did you get this?" she asked, trying to keep the rising anxiety from overcoming her.

Irish went to her. "It was under the folder with the bottle sitting on it. Why, what's going on?"

Cat remained quiet as she stepped back to the couch and fell into the soft foam. Irish took a seat on the chair across from her. The room remained quiet, like a tomb. Finally, Cat told him what had happened after the intruder came into her room. She kept the story brief and avoided the part about the assailant groping her.

"I'm sorry it happened," he said. "You said Fordham played dirty. And now we know he has at least one cop on his payroll. I don't like it. Detective Howard must have tipped off Fordham, who sent that thug after you."

She nodded, then drank down the rest of her glass.

"Yeah, I'm not going to lie to you. I can be tough, but that bastard scared me. He followed me from Anthony's. It could have been that bartender who tipped him off. Knapp wasn't telling me something, even though he admitted some guy left with George." She explained what the bartender told her.

Irish got up from the seat and walked to the table in the kitchen. He looked at the picture again.

"That doesn't tell me why you decided to be a shamus and stake out the La Spina's house this morning."

Cat rose, going into the kitchen as well.

"I was too afraid to fall back asleep. I couldn't stop thinking about everything that was going on," the woman confessed. "The more I thought about it, the worse it seemed. Howard appears to be working for both Young and Fordham. Remember when I said that it all went back to Greye La Spina?"

Ray absently nodded as he held the picture.

"Well, maybe Fordham and Young are working together if they are using the same cop. I wondered how much your girlfriend might know. I can't ask questions about Hopley's death anymore, since Howard might have tipped off Fordham about me. Since I couldn't sleep, I followed Greye. I figure if I was lucky, I might confront her about Fordham and John Robertson."

Irish put the picture on the table.

"Who the hell is Robertson?"

Cat explained what she had discovered from Gladys at the *Beacon*.

"Someone needs to do some snooping into that bitch's mysterious background," she told him as she walked into the living room with a tired sigh. "I need some sleep," she confessed.

"No time for that; you need to pack," Ray told her.

"What are you talking about?" She turned to him, surprised.

"It sounds like you need to get away for a few days. You're going to Boston to track down that lead," Irish told her with a smile.

"Are you saying I should let that bastard scare me away? That's not going to happen." She crossed her arms defiantly.

"No, I'm not saying they are scaring you away. But let's be smart about this," Ray explained. "You have a substantial lead; I don't care what Gladys says. Nobody from Boston writes a letter to a small city paper about the illustrious bishop's wife unless they have something."

"I'm not running away," she said again.

"Damn it; it's your turn to listen! Let them think they ran you off. You're not a cop, and you've got a big target on you. There's no reason to get killed. I can't leave town, but I can follow up with that bartender who you said knows more. We'll just swap the assignments."

"What if nothing pans out?" she asked.

"Well, then we know. But let's see if we can get something on Greye that every big shot in this town will have trouble handling. If she has a secret, we can use it. It might explain something she mentioned about her debt to Quincannon. While you're gone, I'm checking out the bar. Plus, I'll go talk to a friendly cop about the match or not on the slugs that killed George and One-Eye Cornell." His mind raced with questions.

"You be careful," she warned. "That creep who came into my apartment had a knife."

Ray appreciated the concern in her eyes, but he remained stoic.

"I'll be okay. You just worry about yourself."

Cat frowned. "What about Dunn?"

"What about him?" Irish asked with a chuckle. "Just tell him you're looking up some background on Guy Young, and he'll pay for your trip. He can stew on it if he doesn't like what you come back with."

"You like to control things, don't you? I mean, you dislike people telling you what to do."

She grinned.

"You're the second person to say that since I got to this place," Ray replied as he took her arm and turned her to the bedroom.

"Now get yourself packed. You're heading to Boston on the next train. You can get some shuteye on the way."

~~~

Ray Irish pulled up to Anthony's in Cat's gray Olds about thirty minutes after dropping her off at the station. While he waited for Cat to pack, he called the station to get her ticket. After watching her enter the train station building, the
~~~

man felt a slight sense of loss, which the shamus quickly buried. He knew he had to keep his focus on finding who attacked Cat. Ray looked around the busy street when he got out of the car, trying to steer clear of any potential trouble.

A simple tin sign identified the tavern among the line of weathered, two-story weather buildings along the street. Walking inside, a blast of stale beer and body odor greeted Irish as he pushed past the door. Most of the regular's attention followed the stranger as he walked past them, before going back to their whispered conversations. Ray stepped to the end of the bar, where the hulking bartender stood, leaning against the counter. He noticed Knapp straighten for a moment to give him the once-over before returning to leaning on his elbows against the wooden top of the bar.

"You must be Knapp. Remember a good-looking girl who came in here the other day asking about George Hopley?" Irish went straight to the point.

The scarred face of the ex-fighter gave no hint he heard the question. Instead, he pulled a mug from the tray below his belly, sitting it on the counter.

"I only talk with customers."

"Then fill it with a decent beer," Ray told him.

Still leaning against the bar, Knapp pulled a bottle and opened it. He placed the warm bottle across from Ray, who stepped to the counter and threw a dime on the bar. He picked up the mug.

"The name of the guy who left with George Hopley the other day. You know the name, and I'm asking for it."

Knapp snorted.

"What makes you think I'll give it to you?"

Irish continued to look at his beer.

"You look like a person who wouldn't mind a little cabbage for the name."

Knapp scowled at the shamus, leaning closer to his customer. "Well, you might have it wrong."

Ray glanced at the boxer's large hands gripping the edge of the dirty counter. A disfigured right knuckle showed him the ex-fighter's primary weapon. Irish felt the weight of the hefty glass in his hand, and he sensed a growing dislike for the slob behind the bar.

"I'll tell you what I'll do," Knapp continued. "You send that sweet little dish back to my office, and she can do me a favor for the name." The bartender gave an evil grin as he licked his lips. "She looks the type."

Irish reached across the bar, grabbing the ex-fighter by his hair. He slammed the off-balanced man's face into the bar counter. Still holding Knapp's greasy hair, Ray smashed the mug into the bar and pushed the half-broken glass in front of Knapp's wide, watery eyes.

"You tell me the name, or you get accidentally blinded, that's my offer." A deep growl of rage came from Irish.

Less than a minute later, Ray left the bar with the name of Fat Louie. Hands still shaking with his receding fury, he got into the car. As the shamus drove away, he didn't notice another vehicle pull away from the curb behind him.

Ray found Arizona Campbell sitting at his desk, having a late lunch. The pastrami and rye sandwich sat half-finished on the man's desk with a cup of coffee. The shamus knocked and stuck his head in the door.

"Got time for me?" Irish asked after he saw the detective's grimace.

"No, but get in here since it saves me the trouble of tracking you down," Arizona told him.

After he entered, Ray closed the door, taking the wooden chair across from the policeman who tried to finish his lunch.

"Something I need to know about?"

"You might say that. It appears Bishop La Spina has called the DA about you." The cop took a large bite of his meal.

"And?" Ray asked, expecting the worse.

"According to the bishop, you misrepresented yourself to him, posing as a reporter. He claims you pushed past his butler to harass his wife. He also states on another occasion that you threatened his wife. At this point, he says he is seriously considering the idea of pressing charges against you." Arizona glared at Irish.

"What do you think?" Ray asked.

The policeman wolfed down the rest of his sandwich.

"Listen, I don't care if you play footsy with his wife. Hell, a lot of guys already have. But I can tell you this: go anywhere near that woman now, and the DA will slap you in the slammer and put you in front of a grand jury. After that, there will be enough charges against you to send you to the pen for several years. You got that?"

"I get it." Irish smiled unexpectedly. "With her husband suddenly involved, Greye is afraid of her shadow now."

"What do you mean?" Arizona became intrigued.

"You'll be the first to know when I have it," Ray assured him. "Anyway, I'm not seeing that woman, especially not by myself. I just stopped by to see if you got a match on the bullets that killed George and One-Eye."

Campbell stared at him for a long moment.

"Yes, there's a match. The same gun used in both murders."

"You have any suspects?" Ray forced himself not to say more when the detective shook his head.

"When we get the gun, we'll have our guy. But I've got other things going on right now. You still interested in Guy Young's work?" Arizona asked as he grimaced at the foul police coffee. Irish nodded carefully.

"We got a call from the county sheriff, who told us they found a stiff at the Camelot Motel this morning. Young owns that place under another name, and the sheriff is sure there is a prostitution ring going on there." The cop noticed Ray's reaction to the mention of a corpse. Arizona paused, then took a drink of his coffee.

"You been out there recently?" he asked.

"No, never heard of the place." Irish realized the conversation was getting dangerous. "Is that it?"

"Yeah, and remember to stay away from the La Spina's, or a ton of trouble will fall on you," the policeman warned again before Ray left the office.

~~~

The winter darkness settled early under the gray sky while Henry La Spina looked out the window at the large mansion of the Hopley's across the street. The fortress-like building stood tall, complete with gray stones, tall windows, turrets, and even gargoyles on the eves. Shadows from the nearby lights fell across the grotesque figureheads, briefly reminding him of his childhood fear of nighttime monsters. A dark limousine pulled out of the driveway, turning into the street for the mayor's nightly trip to the house of his sister. The large man turned to his desk when he saw his wife. Greye's eyes were red, and she sniffed, wiping her nose with a tissue.

"My dear, you look terrible. You should go to bed." Henry's voice carried a natural soothing tone from years of practice.

Greye shook her head. "I'll be all right; it's just, I'm having a difficult time. So many bad things are happening."

He remained in his place by the window.

"Quincannon and his associate were not of our class, so you shouldn't dwell on such things." When La Spina turned back to look out of the window, he didn't see his wife's contorted expression at his comment. "Be thankful for the things we have together. Remember, I took care of that imbecile Irish fellow who threatened you."

"I'm grateful for that. Are you expecting someone?" She noticed how unusually tense he appeared.

Henry remained silent for a moment, nodding absently.

"Yes, I received a phone call today and am expecting them to arrive anytime. Why don't you go to our bedroom and rest for a while? I'll be quite busy this evening."

She knew the tone of his voice meant for her to leave. She sighed, feeling tired and confused. Greye silently left, leaving the door open.

A few minutes later, the bishop saw his visitor pull up in a black car about half a block away. Henry watched as the person got out of the car, looking carefully around the area before walking along the sideway to the fence
~~~

surrounding the house. The bishop left the window and walked to his front door. Hearing footsteps on the front steps, the cleric opened the door as the surprised visitor reached for the doorbell.

"Were you waiting for me?" Detective Howard asked as he entered the residence.

"Let's just say we have sensitive issues we must discuss," the bishop replied; his dull face showed no emotion which bothered his visitor.

Henry led the corrupt policemen to his study, closing and locking the door. Ron Howard looked around the plush room, pushing back his fedora while unconsciously licking his lips at the thoughts running through his head. He put his hand in his wool coat, pulling out something wrapped in a white cloth.

"Here's the sensitive issue, bishop," Howard stated as he confidently crossed the room, placing the object on the desktop. The lieutenant unwrapped the white handkerchief he held while Henry walked over. He displayed a gold dagger with precious embedded stones on the scabbard and handle.

"Friend of mine at the sheriff's office found this in a motel today. It appears this weapon cut a man's throat. It looks like it'll fit nicely back in your display case," he told the bishop. "However, it will come at a cost."

The bishop glanced at his collection of similar-looking daggers behind his desk. He stared at the weapon on the bureau. "It appears to be a Holbein dagger, also known as a *basler.* By the shape and design, I would estimate the late 1500s. You can see the dance of death design engraved into the gold sheath of the dagger."

"It's specific to the Swiss maker," he continued with a scholarly air. "The Nazi's copied the style, as you can see from the hilt. It is an expensive collectible, no doubt. However, I'm not sure why you have contacted me about this. It would seem to be evidence of a murder, would it not?"

The detective gave him a sidelong glance, then a smug laugh.

"All right, I'll play along, professor." He stepped to the displays on the wall, pulling a half-used cigar from his pocket and jamming it in his mouth. "Let's talk about the evidence. You collect fancy knives like these. Your so-called chauffer, Quincannon, has his throat slit wide open by a similar knife, perhaps the very one on your desk. And today, a known associate of your chauffeur, a guy named Pendexter, winds up with his throat slit in the same manner."

The bishop stepped around to sit in his leather chair, leaning back with his hands pressed together.

"Lieutenant, I'm still not sure why this should concern me. At best, your links appear to be an interesting coincidence."

Ron Howard glared at him.

"Let's just see if I can concern you, then. Just so happens, your wife frequently met with the two murdered men at a local tavern. The place is out of the way and designed for women like her. Maybe you got a little jealous and fixed the problem. You understand what I'm telling you. If I take this to the grand jury, either you or your little whore wife could wind up sitting in an electric chair. Should I go on?"

Henry La Spina's eyes narrowed, but he gave Howard a friendly smile.

"Your manners are quite undignified. Do you believe the District Attorney would bring my family name into such a dastardly scheme with such little evidence? You realize, of course, the Smyth family is close friends with the La Spina family."

Howard began chewing on his cigar, his face revealing the corrupt man's quandary.

"Of course, I know all about the District Attorney's ties with your family. What if I said I have fingerprints on the weapon to prove my theory?"

The bishop's eyebrow rose slightly.

"Then, by all means, you should place your opinion in front of the District Attorney for his review. I would suggest you have such fingerprints before you meet with him. Having grown up with Peter Smyth, I know he is not a forgiving person."

Detective Howard silently stared for a long moment at his intended victim, his chomping mouth threatening to eat through the cigar. Finally, he went to the desk and picked up the weapon with his open hand. The cop slid the knife into his pocket while putting the white handkerchief into his shirt pocket. As he turned to leave, Henry spoke up.

"If that dagger is no longer evidence, perhaps we can come to an arrangement. Since it is such a rare piece, I might be interested in purchasing it from you."

The cop stopped, somewhat confused by the offer. Howard pulled the weapon out of his pocket and looked at Henry. "How much is it worth?"

"Oh, in the right hands, about a thousand dollars," the bishop replied with a smile. "I believe the foundation would like to add that weapon to our collection; you see some of our collection on the wall behind me."

Howard grinned.

"Funny how you religious types can collect such things. But it'll take fifteen hundred for me to forget about this thing. Cash!"

"I don't carry much money in the house. Let us say, tomorrow evening at the end of Andras Lane. I have an appointment there at about ten o'clock. Let's make it eleven," La Spina offered.

Howard frowned slightly. He didn't like the place, but the isolated area worked.

"All right, I'll be there, and I'll see myself out." The corrupt cop unlocked the door and left the room. Henry La Spina slowly turned the revolving chair around to look at his collection as he lightly whistled a hymnal.

~~~

After leaving Cat's car just down the street, Irish walked to his hotel when he heard the gruff voice address him.

"Hey, mister, you got a light?"

When Ray turned around, a large man, dressed in dark coveralls and wearing a heavy wool jacket, stepped from the shadows. He heard footsteps behind him and glanced back to see another similarly attired goon walk up close behind him.

"I take it you don't need a match." Irish slowly slid his hand into his suit pocket.

"You're a right smart cookie," the thug in front of him growled. "Come with us."

Irish slowly pulled to the side while turning his body. Suddenly, he pointed his finger, pushing his pocket out. In the dark, he hoped it was a reasonable impression of a gun.

"Before you make a mistake, I don't miss from this distance," he lied.

"You're bluffing, flatfoot," the leader growled.

"You want to bet your life on it?" Irish gave him a cocky grin. "I can show you my new gun permit after I plug you."

The two large men paused, apparently unsure, then the leader laughed.

"I'll think we'll chance it."

Ray did not wait for their next move. He turned and ran straight into the thug behind him, running over the surprised brute using a stiff arm that would make a football coach proud. His rebuilt legs pounded along the sidewalk as he raced across the street while the two men came after him. Irish turned the corner, finding the block filled with closed stores. The sounds of his pursuer's footsteps drew closer. Ray knew he wasn't going to outrun them, and his mind raced for a solution. Then he saw a neon sign flashing toward the end of the block. Becoming winded, the man pushed himself, just reaching the door as it opened. He almost ran into a uniformed beat cop leaving 13th Street Tavern.

"Whoa there, you looking to have me run you in? Say, what's your hurry?" The policemen barred the way as he looked at Ray.

"Sorry, I…I was looking for a phone," Irish lied as he looked back at his pursuers. The two men were standing a few feet away, trying to catch their wind.

The cop looked over at the men.

"Are you two planning on joining us?" he asked sharply. The leader in coveralls shook his head and walked away.
~~~

"Mister, I'd suggest you hang inside and find that phone. It looks like the rats are out tonight," the policemen told Ray as he slowly followed the thugs who had started across the street.

Irish watched the uniformed man walk away, swinging his baton while whistling. He had a sudden chill come over him. It was the uncanny feeling that someone was watching him. Then he saw a figure standing in the shadows of an alley by a nearby building. For a moment, Ray caught sight of a pale face staring at him. He blinked a couple of times and watched the figure slowly back into the dark shadow. The skeleton image he saw froze like ice, with the hairs on the back of his neck standing up. Ray hesitated, debating whether to enter the tavern. Then curiosity got the best of him, and Irish walked toward the alley, looking away as he crossed the street. When Irish reached the other side of the road, he cautiously entered the alley entrance, letting his eyes adjust to the darkness. The mysterious shadow figure was gone.

Chapter 5: Backtrack

Detective Plug Howard's rugged face flashed into the light when he struck a match inside the shadows of his black sedan. The large man scowled, flicked the stub of dying flame out the open window of his car. He let out a long stream of cigarette smoke while he looked over the desolate scenery around him. It was a moonlit night. His car sat at the end of the narrow-paved road where he faced a quiet-looking mansion. In his eyes, the house looked like a haunted chateau with absurdly ornamented towers, spires, and a steeply pitched roof overlooking the road. Even more ominous, the spacious yard came, complete with white headstones and ancient trees. Andres Hill held the numerous graves and tombs of the family and their relatives.

Howard was a rookie cop on the beat when he first discovered the lonely road in the middle of Oyster City. A narrow driveway pushed through two giant oaks at the end of the road, leading to the house. He never liked the graveyard look of the area around the mansion.

The soft sounds of a whistled tune came through the vehicle's window. Opening the car door, Howard got out and cautiously looked around his motor vehicle. He noticed a person standing underneath the ancient oaks in the middle of the driveway. The cop saw the large figure wave to him.

"Damn rich people," Howard grumbled as he closed the car door and walked up the road. When he reached the start of the driveway, Howard heard nearby footsteps stealthily moving on his right side. He paused, scanning in the direction of the sound, but he didn't see anything.

"All right, La Spina, I'm here." He thundered, but only silence greeted him. Then he heard the crunching steps in front of him in the shadows. The sound came from the shadows near a large crypt that lay next to the driveway ahead. The dark figure stopped in a patch of moonlight and waved him forward before retreating into the shadows.

"All right, damn it, I'm not going any further, and you better have the money," Howard snapped, disturbed by the strange atmosphere.

He considered increasing the dagger's price when he came next to the rectangular, stone-gray crypt. The stone appeared eerily white under the moonlight.

"Get your ass out here so we can settle this, La Spina," Lieutenant Howard growled. Then he froze as the figure emerged from the tree's shadow.

Only a few paces away stood a masked man in a black robe. The smiling mask of death over the figure's face sent an icy fear through the detective as he backed up several steps. He became irritated.

"You better think twice about playing games with me," Howard growled as his hand started for the pistol inside his jacket. Intent on the figure in front of him, the policeman failed to recognize the faint sound of footsteps behind him.

Before he could turn around, Howard took a massive slap across the back of his head, which stunned him. The thick, weighted leather billy club hit him again, sending the policeman to the ground.

Almost instantly, a group of masked people fell on their quarry, binding Howard's hands and gagging him. As he pulled out of his shocked state, the large man tried to fight, but he was too late. Strong hands held fast to his legs, as the detective felt a rope twist around one ankle. Then, within a few seconds, he found himself upside down, swinging above the tomb among the shadows. Howard's struggles slowed as he tried to understand why the costumed figures gathered around him.

The figure of Death laid the golden dagger on the slab after pulling it from the lieutenant's jacket. Masked Judgment placed a gold cup next to the knife. The High Priestess giggled as she started to spin the hanging man.

"It's a perfect night for the blue moon. The master will be pleased," she stated, followed by a shrill laugh at the thought. Leaving the sluggishly spinning cop, the masked woman lit two candles and placed them next to the cup.

Judgment grunted as he replied. "Worthless foreigner will be no loss. It's about time someone from our group finally brought us a sacrifice."

The Demon picked up the dagger.

"It's a fitting end and a much better sacrifice."

With a steady hand, the person grabbed the struggling detective by his thinning hair as he wriggled around like a worm on a hook. The smiling Demon slid the sharp blade across the victim's throat, and the High Priest held the cup under the sacrifice's head. He struggled to collect the stream of blood spurting from their twisting prey's throat. Judgment dipped his finger into the cup and then drew a Goetic seal below their sacrifice as tribute to their raven-head master. While the dying man's struggles slowed, the masked figures began their chants to the ancient, banished one. Plug Howard gave one final death spasm while trying to remember a prayer from childhood.

Each member drank from the cup of human blood that passed between them while the Demon laid out cards next to hastily placed candles around the seal. While reciting an incantation passed down by generations of elders, the masked creature's trembling voice suddenly grew stronger. Those around the slab looked at each other; their eyes widen with a mixture of wonder and dread. The surrounding air abruptly grew cold, and the faint noises of the night went silent. Almost imperceptibly at first, a dark shadow rose from the marble tomb. Quickly, the mist enveloped the hanging body before it slid like a waterfall into the Demon holding the tarot cards. The demon mask figure began to shudder and tremble;

then, the body became a wooden statue. An ominous poem from the depths of hell addressed the followers.

"More blood must flow, for the nights still yearn, bringing great prosperity through the power of the one greater.

"In the early night on the large bay, water will burn, fed by bodies of flames coming from the outsider.

"Sacrifice and blood from one family put into the urn; the gift of your fortune by your great provider."

The figure of the demon rose in the air as the fiend spoke. When the dark shadow wrapped around the robed person's body finished, a hideous wail came from the floating shade. Wretched howls erupted from dogs in the distance; their pitiful pleas echoed into the night. Then, the rigid statue of the hovering person suddenly fell to the ground.

After a momentary pause, the figure wearing the mask of death walked next to the unconscious body. Death stood and looked around the tomb at the followers. "You've heard the master's demands. We must decide which family will bear the coming sacrifice."

~~~

As the train from Boston rolled into the Oyster City station on a cold, overcast morning the next day, Catherine Bennett remained lost in thought. Her trip revealed much more than she anticipated, giving her additional reasons to dislike Greye La Spina. The conversations with two reporters at the *Boston Post* revealed the dark past of the bishop's wife. It was something she intended to confront Greye about. Cat vowed she would ensure the wretched woman released her grip on Henry La Spina.

Cat stood and waited when the train lurched to a stop while an older couple moved through the aisle. Finally, she could retrieve her travel case from an overhead rack. She made her way through the nearly empty train car. Before stepping off the train, the petite woman put on a long, blue wool coat, then worked her way through the small crowd milling about the station platform.

"You going my way, sister?"

The familiar voice caught her by surprise. Standing by a water fountain was Ray Irish, his blue suit covered by a green trench coat. He smiled, taking off his hat as he stepped toward her. His face was still black and blue from his beating, but her eyes brightened.

"Well, look at you. When did you decide to play a chauffeur?"

Ray took her small case. "I just needed to make sure you got your car back. It's been kind of quiet with you out of the city." He took her by the arm and guided them to the exit. When they reached the car, both went to the driver's side. Ray grinned self-consciously before grabbing the handle and opening the door for her.
~~~

"I guess my days as chauffeur are already over," he joked as he bowed slightly. After the grinning woman slid in, he threw the leather case into the back seat, then hurried to the other side of the car.

As the couple drove through the city, an awkward silence hung around them as each person waited on the other to start the conversation. Finally, Cat broke the ice.

"Did anything happen while I was gone?"

Irish leaned against the door, looking at her, then tipped back his fedora. "Only the name Fat Louie came out. Have you heard of him?"

"Yeah, that rings a bell, but I can't remember from where. You know who he is?" She glanced at him.

"I'm not sure, but Louie walked out of that bar with George on the day your friend got killed. If I guessed correctly, Louie took him to the partner, and they murdered George that day. Either way, I would find out more about the name when I spoke with Arizona the other day, but he wasn't in a good mood. It seems Bishop La Spina made it clear to the cops that I am not welcome near him or his wife."

Cat's eyes narrowed as she took the corner, coming to a stop behind a line of cars held up in a traffic jam on Waterfront Street. She turned to look at him.

"I don't know who this Arizona is, but it's obvious Greye had her husband talk to his friends in City Hall."

"Arizona Campbell is a detective that I know. He seems like a good egg," Ray explained.

"Yeah, I've heard that last name before, but don't know much about him," Cat replied, tapping her hand on the steering wheel. "Anyway, back to your girlfriend. She must be getting nervous if she went to her husband about you. It's evil how the woman has the bishop wrapped around her finger, but not for long. You won't believe what I found out in Boston."

"I wondered when you would get to that." He gave her a sly grin. "And enough with the girlfriend routine. She's everyone's girlfriend."

Cat's eyes remained dark.

"Well, you can sure pick them. Greye La Spina is nothing more than a two-bit grifter. According to the people I spoke with, she has a history of scams and cons. They told me she worked with a guy named Sydney Green. The two of them traveled along the coast, convincing people they can bring in enormous fortunes to religious charities."

"Somehow, that doesn't surprise me," Ray conceded as he thought about the news. "I take it you think she must have married the bishop to help get her foot in the door with their scam. I wonder what she's after?"

"It's your girlfriend. You tell me." Cat gave him a scornful look.

He returned her look with a glare.

"All right, you win the point. What else did you get on Greye?"

She gave him a wicked smile, putting the car into gear as the line slowly moved. "Something even better. I got her maiden name. It's Pendexter."

Irish sat up at the news.

"Wait, you mean she's related to the dead killer at the Camelot?"

"Yeah, I couldn't find out anything more than that. The reporters I spoke with said Greye used many aliases as she ran with Green before he died. There has to be something there, like a family connection."

Irish whistled at the news. "I wonder how many people know…"

He stopped mid-sentence as several police cars and a white ambulance came into view. He assumed a wreck must have occurred, and then he returned to Catherine's information.

"Well, that blows several holes into my thoughts about Guy Young. He must have known about some of this." He shook his head. "Anyway, I have some news for you. I got word that the gun that killed George was the same as the one used on One-Eye. That means we know Pendexter murdered your friend. I remember the bastard carried the same automatic."

Cat went silent after she nodded at the information. After a moment, she sighed, then spoke. "Well, I'm glad we know who did it. Now, let's make sure that this Fat Louie gets what's coming to him."

"I'm with you, sister. But what's bothering me is the question of the mastermind trying to kill Young?" he asked.

"Does that matter? Shouldn't we focus on Greye?" she asked as she eased the vehicle by one police car which partially blocking a lane. A small army of police and reporters grouped around a black car parked on the edge of the street.

"You forget Dunn pays me for information on Young. Since I can't go near the bishop and his wife, I need to have another way to find out," Ray told her absently as he observed the group of policemen. He knew something big was happening, but one of the uniformed men came toward their slowing vehicle and waved them on. Cat pushed on the gas pedal, and they turned on Cherry Street, heading to downtown.

"Well, I still say we need to follow your girlfriend," Cat insisted. "We can bet she has a connection with the murders. It can't be a coincidence she has the same last name as one killer."

With a sign, Irish nodded.

"All right, we'll risk it," he agreed. "She's the key to getting Guy Young, and I want bitch put away." He smiled to himself. "Arizona didn't say anything about tailing her. Do me a favor, and let's stop by the newsstand. I want to get the latest from Pappy."

~~~
~~~

Later that day, J. Allan Dunn paced behind the desk inside the dingy office as he mulled over the information coming from Ray and Cat. His scowling face enhanced the number of wrinkles on his forehead after listening to the past few events.

"You're telling me that the wife of the bishop, one of the most highly regarded men in the city, is involved with a large graft scheme. But you have no evidence to back it up?" He scowled as he questioned the pair. "Is that what I'm paying you for, to find out rumors like that?"

Ray stood from his chair, leaning over the desk.

"Listen, Cat discovered a lot about Greye La Spina, who is the single tie into your racketeer on the boat," he insisted. "We know Greye has some relationship to that hood, Hugh Pendexter, who got killed last week. And I know the damn woman tried to kill me."

"What are you talking about?" J. Allan interrupted.

Irish grimaced.

"Just a slight case of my getting kidnapped by Hugh and his partner, Fat Louie. Mrs. La Spina set it up. But that doesn't matter for the moment, since it just muddies the water. But it means there are high stakes here. This morning, Pappy told us that the sheriff assumed Pendexter got killed by the Young gang in retaliation for the hit against One-Eye Cornell."

"I'll agree. It sounds like the bishop's wife has some evil seed in the family, but I don't see the connection," the director replied as he sat down in the chair. The squeaking noise from the movement filled the room.

"I told you this was a spider web, but we have enough information for the papers to ride Greye La Spina out of town," Ray told him. "And I'll bet your good bishop won't be far behind her if the papers run with it."

Dunn's eyes narrowed. "What you have are rumors and guesses, so don't go too far with your assumptions. I agree your information could cause some families with problems. But that can't get out. It would cause the mayor a major headache."

He turned to Cat, his voice turning almost fatherly in its tone.

"What else have you got on your trip?"

The young woman pulled a small notepad from her purse. Irish noticed how she acted like the reporters she watched at the *Beacon*.

"Well, I found out that Hugh Pendexter probably killed the clerk who wrote the letter to the *Beacon* about Greye La Spina. There was a holdup, but the reporters who covered the story told me the whole affair seemed rather suspicious. The masked robbers only went to the window where Robertson stood, and they took his cash, then shot him before running out of the bank. Cops picked up Hugh a few days later on another charge. Before the cops could make the case against him, Pendexter posted bond and skipped town." She looked up from her notes. "Nobody could figure out how he came up with the dough."

"Could be his criminal friends helped him out," Dunn reasoned.

Cat shook her head.

"No, I agree with Ray on this. That La Spina woman had something to do with springing the killer in Boston. You didn't see how she reacted when she saw the dead killer at the motel."

Their boss, leaning back in the chair, nearly tipped over at the news.

"Wait a minute; you were at the motel where this guy got killed? How could you be so foolish?" His anger caught Cat off guard.

"I was following Greye, and she drove straight to the motel and walked right into the room," she explained. "When I got there, she was in a panic. I don't think she even saw me when she took off as I helped get Ray out of there."

Cat glanced at Ray.

Dunn shook his head. "I can't believe you did such a thing." He looked at Irish, his eyes flashing hatred when he spoke. "Are you trying to get her killed? Cat is just a kid."

Ray held Dunn's gaze.

"Listen, Cat saved my hide, and you're missing what she's telling you. We have shady people involved in the murder of Cat's friend. We also have some scheme going apparently involves Guy Young. Maybe it affects the Mayor, who you want to protect. I'm going to figure this out using Greye La Spina, who tried to kill me."

The director leaned back in his chair. "Are you telling me or asking?"

"I'm telling you where the evidence leads," Irish stated, refusing to back down.

"Dunn, you need to listen to us," Cat interjected. "Do you want to know what's happening or not? There are several people dead, and we tied most of them back to that woman. I don't think Henry is anything but a victim. But his name carries a lot of weight in this city, including the mayor. You know the mayor will need to keep this tamped down, or he'll get roasted by Townsend. Your job is on the line as well."

After a long silence, the thin man behind the desk slowly leaned back.

"All right, but you let me know if anything starts to come back anywhere near the bishop or anyone else near him. Do you understand that?"

"I understand," Ray agreed. He started for the door as Cat scrambled to her feet. Irish stopped and turned back to the desk.

"One other thing, I need a gun permit."

"I'm not your secretary." Dunn's scowl returned.

"Yeah, but you can get things done when you want," Irish responded. "Your city has some dark roads which get uglier each time we take another step. The other night, I had two toughs trying to take me for a ride. I don't know who their boss is, but I'm pretty sure it wasn't Guy Young's people. That means I'm stepping on someone's toes. Anyway, the cops will ask why I need a gun in this fair city. I don't think you want me to try that route."

The sarcasm was clear in Ray's voice.

"You said you went to that bar for information." Dunn grew interested. "That's one of Mark Fordham's places. I don't know what you did, but it must have got his attention."

"Well, you can see why a gat comes into the picture," Ray replied.

"No promises, but I'll see what I can do," Dunn reluctantly told him. "Fordham's getting pretty outspoken about how he's going to change this city. There are some rumors about police looking the other way at things going on down along the docks, which will protect him. I think the mayor is getting nervous."

"He's not the only one," Ray told him as he opened the door, then stepped outside.

<p style="text-align:center">~~~</p>

The sunlight quickly drifted into the night under the dull sky as Cat pulled into her regular parking spot beside her apartment building. She shut off the motor and waited for a moment while her partner seemed lost in thought.

"Why don't you come up for dinner?" she broke the silence.

"You must have heard my stomach." His jest was halfhearted, but he got out of the car. Irish remained quiet as he followed her inside the building. She didn't like his silence. It reminded her of the calm before the storm with his temper. She unlocked the door and entered.

"Why the silent treatment?" she asked, while taking off her coat. Ray's rugged face went blank for a moment.

"Sorry, I was thinking about my time since I woke up in this city." He walked to the couch, still wearing his trench coat, as he sat down. He watched her hang her coat and hat on the arms of a hat tree. When Cat turned around, she noticed how weary Ray looked.

"And what have you decided?" She sat next to him.

"Why do you stay here?" He leaned back.

Cat paused at the surprising question. Her face took on a bit of a pout as she considered it. Finally, she answered.

"I'm not sure, to be honest. I've lived here most of my life, so it's familiar to me. Why do you ask?"

Ray let out a deep breath.

"I don't know. Something is gnawing at me. When I first got here, I did some reading at the library about the city with all the violence and strange things that happen here. At first, I couldn't believe it, but now everything seems to fit with this damn town." He looked at her with a tired smile. "I guess I'm just trying to put things into place. It seems to be bigger than just a few hoodlums. Then again, maybe I'm just adding pieces that shouldn't be there."

Cat rose from the couch.

"You must be hungry; I'll get dinner started," she told him quickly. In the kitchen, she pulled out a pan, the clanging noise filling the apartment. "You can fix us some drinks if you want one. The bottle's still on the table."

Irish liked the idea and took off his coat before he walked to the small dining area to retrieve the nearly empty bottle of whiskey. He watched the woman pulling meat wrapped in butcher paper from the refrigerator. Despite his empty stomach, Ray's eyes followed her body's curves, accented by her white and blue dress. Ray squeezed past her along the narrow aisle between the cabinets and the stove to get the glasses.

"I hope you like steak," she moved over when he passed.

"Anything you make will be great," he told her as he poured the drinks.

She laughed.

"You've never tasted my cooking."

"I'll risk it," Ray amicably replied as he handed her the glass. She took the tumbler, and they lofted their drinks in a silent toast. He slid past her again, enjoying the scent of her perfume. He went to sit at the dining table.

"To answer your earlier question, I have always wondered if this city has a curse," Cat told him. "I heard about all the horrible history growing up, which is fascinating in a strange way. But the war started, and I was just out of high school when my mother died. I needed work, so when the job at the *Beacon* came up, I jumped at it. I guess I never decided to leave Oyster City."

"I guess I can understand that," Irish told her after a sip of his drink. "I've been drifting from place to place for a while now. When I woke in this city, well, it was just a distinct feeling. I mean, every city has something you immediately notice about its atmosphere. It's kind of hard to describe."

He paused as he tried to form the right words.

"Let me put it this way. This city was the first spot where you can feel everything pressing down on you, kind of cloudy all the time," he finally declared. "It's almost like the feeling you get when a shell lands close but doesn't explode. You wait and wait, just hoping it doesn't kill you."

Cat remained quiet, seemingly focused on the meal as she went back and forth between the cabinets and the refrigerator. After an untenable silence, she finally spoke.

"I'm worried about Henry La Spina. We need to get him away from his wife."

Irish didn't look up from staring at his glass.

"I don't think he'll be so willing to walk away. He knows something about her; nobody's that blind. I'm more interested in his daggers."

"You can't believe the bishop would have something to do with those murders." She turned down the flame of one burner.

"Why are you so sure? If I remember my scriptures correctly, he's a man, which means he can sin just like anybody else." Ray leaned back in the comfortable chair. "How do you know him?"

"That's a long story," she said, walking out of the kitchen. "Let's just say the man would be a saint if I had a vote in the matter."

As they ate, Cat opened up about some of her past to Irish. She explained how the bishop, at the time just a simple pastor, provided support to her mother, who kept finding drunken losers who often beat Cat's mom. Even though Cat was born of out wedlock, Henry La Spina always treated her family with respect. By the time they finished dinner, Ray knew much more about Catherine Bennett. The man congratulated himself on one part of his initial assessment of her; the lady was a tough spitfire. She was growing on him.

"Why the grin?" Cat asked him.

"Oh, I don't know. Just enjoying the conversation, I guess. By the way, you're not a half-bad cook. I'm getting the real husband's treatment tonight." His grin turned into a smile.

Her bright eyes faded at his comment, and a decidedly icy chill fell across the room. "Well, don't get used to it, partner. There's a lot of work to do, and I can't have you over here all the time. Now, what can we do about the bishop?"

Ray's smile dropped.

"Yeah, well, I can see your loyalty to him, but I'm not sure what we can do. Even if we tell him about what we know, what will happen? Nothing! He can't afford the scandal of it." His demeanor grew hard. "That reminds me, I just remembered where I saw that dagger before, the one on the floor in the motel where Pendexter died."

"What, you mean that fancy knife with the blood on it?" She shivered involuntarily. "I don't want to think about it."

He leaned forward.

"Yeah, there are several of those daggers on display in the bishop's house. I got a glance at them on the wall behind his desk. At least, they looked similar."

Cat's eyes grew wide. "Do you think there's a link?"

"I can't imagine there are many people collecting those things," Ray said as he latched onto the idea.

"Probably part of something that woman's involved with," she told him.

"Her reaction to her brother getting killed makes me doubt that," he replied. "You saw it yourself; Greye didn't know Pendexter was dead. If those weapons match, it changes my ideas. Those daggers look expensive, so maybe they are part of the bitch's scheme. It would do my soul good to know she's spending time behind bars if the weapons were part of their graft scheme. It all seems to come back to your idea about becoming her shadow."

Cat thought about it and finally agreed.

"I'll drop by your hotel early in the morning and pick you up. I don't believe that it will do much good to wait there overnight. Mayor Hopley's banquet at his home will go late. All the big shots in the city are there."

Ray rose from his chair, walking to the couch for his hat and coat. "Yeah, I agree. Let's start at sunrise. Since you're the one with the car, I don't have any choice in this." He put on the coat and went to the door. "Thanks for the meal." He didn't bother to look back as he closed the door behind him.

Cat watched the door for a long time, half expecting him to return and somewhat hoping he might. When it was clear Ray would not return, she cleared the table while berating herself for her reaction. She knew her frosty response to his joke about a husband sent their enjoyable evening into a tailspin. But that was all right; the woman reminded herself. No matter how awkward, she would not allow a man to break through to control her life. Cat learned from her mother about love and the perils of trusting a man to do the right thing. Catherine Bennett would be the one who decided her future, not a drunken drifter.

~~~

"My dear, I'm sorry I can't attend the reception this evening. I know it's most inconvenient, but I can't let my friend down." Greye strolled seductively in her tight-fitting dress to the desk of her husband. Henry always liked the way his wife looked in green. She came around the desk, leaning down to kiss his cheek while he remained passive.

"Are you sure? I know you've been upset for some reason," he said, his dark eyes turning sympathetic.

"Yes, I'll be all right," she promised, patting him lightly on the shoulder. "It's just a difficult time for me with all of the events going on and such." Greye had difficulty trying not to tear up.

"Which friend are you taking care of this time?" His tone remained even, almost distracted.

"Why, Mary Bird, of course!" She feigned astonishment, then explained. "I told you this morning at breakfast. You know she's been in such a state since her daughter ran away with that terrible man. She still doesn't understand why the police claim her daughter is missing."

Henry nodded.

"Of course, I'm sure it's a challenging time for her. You know I could skip this event the mayor is holding. I really should come along since I'm the bishop," he stated, knowing her reply.
~~~

"No, my dear, you have more important matters to attend. I'll pop by and make sure Mary is doing well. Hopefully, I'll be home early, but you know how she can be." Greye gave the man another peck on the cheek. "I'll be home as soon as I can."

The bishop watched her stroll across the room, and a grim look fell across his face. "I'm sure you will. Give my condolences to Mary."

Greye's car reached a parking area by the docks about an hour later. She stopped by Mary Bird's home on the way to the pier to make a quick courtesy call to the distraught woman who would probably not even remember Greye showing up. Mrs. La Spina knew Mary would turn into an incoherent lush within an hour after dinner, drowning her sorrow with sedatives and alcohol. Greye's expression turned rigid as she considered Mrs. Bird's reaction to her daughter running away. She disliked weak people.

Greye, in green, stepped from her car, suddenly finding a large man standing next to her. He wore a black, wool trench coat, and his face remained partially hidden by the shadows of his wide brim Fedora. He took her by the arm, his grip painfully tight.

"What are you doing?" She futilely tried to pull away.

The giant goon looked down at her. "Come on; the boss is waiting."

Greye was about to complain when Tweedledum stepped next to her.

"Lady, just keep your mouth shut, and you won't get hurt. Come on!" A second thug led the trio to a car that came to a stop next to them. The men pushed her inside.

While the large Cadillac drove away, Greye sat between the two silent men. The unusual and sinister way the thugs treated her filled Greye with growing apprehension. A few minutes later, the car turned into an alley, where they got out and entered the back of an unfamiliar building. Her escorts remained quiet, taking her past an open door. Fear gripped her as Greye walked with her guards to an office inside the narrow confines of a long hallway. The room was empty, and the goon pointed her to a single chair in front of a worn-out desk. Visibly nervous at the unexpected treatment, she quietly sat on the edge of the chair while her escort took a position by the door. She fumbled with her purse, looking inside before she clipped it shut.

A few minutes later, her host arrived. Guy Young watched her reactions as he whispered something to his henchmen before he approached. His lips were a cruel, thin line, nearly a smirk. His eyes were cold and dark.

"My dear Mrs. La Spina, you've been keeping important information from me."

She gave him a puzzled look, trying to force a smile.

"I'm not sure I understand."

He sat next to her.

"Oh, you're quite the grifter. It appears you've been running this scam on your husband and me. And you try to act like you don't know. I'll tell you what; I'll help your memory by bringing in a friend of yours."

Young waved to his bodyguard, who opened the door.

A rotund man in a black suit burst through the entrance, falling to the floor face-first. At first, Greye believed the man was dead. The large thug who came into the room stepped close and rolled the figure in the black suit over on his back. The beaten man looked up at her through a massively swollen and bruised head. Greye recognized him through the dried blood and sweat.

"My contacts finally found one man who tried to knock me off. You can see how upset that makes me. At first, I thought about a nice and slow death, but Fat Louie talked. It was an interesting conversation, as you probably realize by now. You see, this worthless piece of trash tells me your brother helped to kill my friend. Worse, he claims you knew about it before the hit happened."

The racketeer placed his chilly hand on her shoulder. He smiled at the shiver he felt running through her flesh.

"But it's your lucky night, baby. Louie traded all he had for his life. He told me all about the scam you've been running. Now, let's talk about those bearer bonds you have stashed away. Then, maybe you can convince me why you shouldn't be floating in the bay as fish food."

~~~

As Irish walked along the dark street a block away from Cat's apartment, he had the nagging suspicion someone was following him. The street lamp's yellow glow made it difficult to see far on the empty sidewalk. He kept a steady pace, his ears trying to decipher every sound reaching him. Passing along a row of dark townhomes, he heard the rhythmic sound of leather footsteps striking concrete behind him. The noise picked up speed as his tail tried to close in.

Ray reached the corner at 8th and turned left, his glance behind revealing just a shadow of a movement about half a block away. The shamus continued along before he took across the quiet street, heading into an alleyway behind several buildings where he entered. Despite his racing heart, Irish tried to appear casual while walking into the alley, and worked through his limited options. Still unarmed, he decided the dark shadows would be his best defense for the moment.

There was a single light shining above the first building's back door, which Irish quickly passed. Ray slowed his pace, picking his way through the maze of containers and old equipment that dotted the confined area between buildings. The troubleshooter paused for a moment, and then Irish heard the footsteps coming into the alley, confirming his fear. Deciding the end of the lane was too far away, Ray quietly eased his body along the brick wall. He quietly followed along until he reached the closed door, where the darkest shadow swallowed his image.
~~~

The footsteps following him slowed, and Irish saw the person following him. A guy in a leather jacket and wearing a longshoreman's cap passed underneath the backdoor light before coming to a stop. Ray's follower walked a few steps into the gloom by the next building.

"Come on out, shamus, I know you're in here. I've got a message for you."

Ray remained covered inside the shadowed doorway.

"Then give it," he replied before sliding along the wall until he pulled behind the concrete steps leading to the door.

"You're not very sociable." The figure walked toward the sound of Ray's voice. There was the indistinct sound of a flashlight click, and a light beam focused toward the shadowed doorway.

Crouching down, Ray saw the faint outline of a trash bin just a few steps away, and he quietly moved to a position behind the container. He felt around the ground, looking for anything to defend himself, and all he found was a tin can.

The flashlight beam slowly scanned the area around the back door where Irish was hiding just seconds before. He could hear footsteps growing closer and giving a hollow whistle.

"Why are you hiding? I thought you carried a gun. Maybe I should tell you what I plan on doing to your little girlfriend. Yeah, I've been watching that dish." The stranger's mocking voice echoed slightly in the alley.

As the beam of light grew stronger, coming closer to his position, Ray heard a soft metal click. The flashlight beam moved toward a new sound from across the alley, and Ray took a glance at his opponent. The silver gleam of a long switchblade caught his eye.

Nearly upon the large container where Irish hid, the hoodlum in the leather coat edged carefully around the side. Fortunately, the light allowed Ray to see his hand still holding the can. Just as Irish felt his attacker getting close to the back of the steel trashcan, he flicked the tin can to the other side of the container. As the beam of light swept away to the sound source, Irish sprang up from his position. The sweeping blow from his fist glanced across his opponent's face. But the punch wasn't enough, and the goon whipped around. Ray instantly felt a sharp pain in his upper arm. Still, he struck his attacker with another blow, this time punching the man's head. Irish grabbed the forearm of his opponent's knife hand, holding off the deadly weapon while pressing hard into his opponent's flesh.

A strike from the flashlight came across Ray's forehead. The blow caused him to release his attacker's arm, but Ray pressed his weight advantage to get to his attacker's side. He pushed the thug into the wall a few steps away.

Just as the two men struck the wall, Irish felt a hot, burning pain slice across his ribs. Grabbing his opponent's hair, Irish pulled back as hard as he could, hearing the man yell in agony. Ray twisted his body around, locking his arm around his opponent's neck. With his attacker's head enclosed in the crook of his arm, he darted toward the trash container.

With the goon in tow, Irish slammed his opponent into the steel wall. He heard a sickening crunch under his arm. Ray grabbed the edge of the crate, trying to remain upright. While feeling his chest, his hand came across the sticky blood from his wound. Lightheaded dizziness washed over him as he tried to walk, only to grasp the edge of the trash bin again. Seconds later, he slid down to the ground next to his dead assailant.

~~~

Cat heard a banging noise at her apartment door just as she was getting ready for bed. Silently, she opened the table drawer by her bed, retrieving a revolver and double-checking her already locked windows. Cat slipped into the living room, easing to the front entrance of her apartment. There was another bump appearing to come from the lower part of the wooden door. She crept to the door, cautiously placing her ear close. Another hammer blow against the wood caused her to jump back. After a long moment, curiosity got the best of her. Keeping her gun pointed at the door, she turned the handle. Unexpectedly, the door pushed open, and the upper body of a man fell into the room. The woman backed away in fright, nervously pointing the gun at the man. Finally, she drew closer and looked closer at the man illuminated by the pale light streaming in from the hallway. It was Ray Irish.

~~~

The sound of voices invaded the strange dreams of Ray as he woke. Immediately, Irish noticed a dull pain in his shoulder and ribcage with each breath he took. He opened his eyes and focused on two people sitting at a dining room table. Arizona and Cat were chatting amicably, each holding a cup of coffee.

"Who let the cop in?" Irish growled at the pair, and they turned to look at him. As he got his bearings, Ray realized he was lying on Cat's couch in her apartment. He remembered her helping him to the stuffed chair after he fell into the apartment. Irish also recalled her quick thinking to help stop his bleeding. His shirt was missing, and he was lying on a towel. Ray tried to sit up, but a wave of pain shot through his shoulder and ribcage.

"Lay still, Irish. Doc says you'll survive," the lieutenant replied airily before turning serious. "We need to talk."

Irish didn't like the expression on Arizona's face.

"Yeah, I guessed as much. I remember most of it until I got here." Ray let out a sigh. "Did you find the guy who attacked me?"

Arizona nodded as he pulled out a notebook from his coat pocket. "Right where you said he was. You did a hell of a job on his face. Is he the one that cut you up?"

"Damn, I would have thought that's obvious." Ray glared at him.

"If I hadn't found that knife in the dead man's hands, you might be lying in a medical cell with charges on you. Arizona raised an eyebrow. I could have considered it manslaughter. You get it?"

Ray grimaced as he tried to sit up again, then gave up the idea. "Yeah, I understand." He paused to collect his thoughts. "Here's the condensed version. I'm walking to my hotel when I discover someone following me. I try to lose him by ducking into the alley, but he tries to hunt me with that flashlight and knife you found. A fight breaks out, and he loses."

The policeman scribbled on his notepad, then looked up at the shamus. "Is that it?"

"Well, other than bleeding all over the street as I walked a couple of blocks back here, I don't have much after that. I recall talking with Cat for a bit. Also, somebody in a dark coat kept poking me, but a lot of that is a blur," he said as he shook his head.

"You were pretty out of it," Cat spoke up. "You kept telling me not to take you to the hospital. Just find a doctor. I called a physician I know and convinced him to come over. He stitched you up and left here not too long ago. He said you needed a transfusion at the clinic since you lost a lot of blood."

"Why would you ask her to keep from the hospital?" Arizona acted indifferent when he asked, but Irish wasn't buying the sham.

"Maybe because I'm an outsider who doesn't trust anyone," Ray told him directly. "Ever since I arrived in this city, only a few people have proven they aren't on the take of somebody else."

He waited for a response, but Arizona just nodded.

"Or maybe I was out of my head from blood loss," the injured man gave a half-laugh.

Arizona's face screwed up with a wry grin.

"That's more official and makes sense to me. Your story matches what my men found, so it's self-defense," he told Ray. "I doubt the District Attorney will bother you about it. But might use it to keep you away from the bishop's wife. You'll need to come down to the station to fill out an official statement."

"You mind if I give it a day or two?" Irish asked, feeling his eyelids getting heavy.

"Sure, I've got enough things on my desk. I don't need more work just because you knocked off some low life." Arizona turned serious again.

"Did you know the guy?"

"Never saw him before, but he must have been watching this building for a dupe like me to rob," Ray shook his head as he recalled what the assailant told him about Cat.

Irish looked at her as she silently walked around the apartment. She stopped to re-arrange the various knickknacks on a shelf.

"Well, that fits what we know. The guy you killed was an ex-con by the name of Woolrich, who got to Oyster City about a month or so back. Hung around a place called Anthony's," the lieutenant told them.

He didn't notice the reaction from Cat, who stopped in her tracks. Irish saw the look on her face, and he wanted to ask more, but he felt his mind drifting.

"Either you police are a damn efficient lot, or you had something on him already." Ray closed his eyes, trying to fight off a wave of nausea.

"Yeah, we're efficient in keeping tabs on ex-cons who hang out at that place. This guy was a thief and maybe a rapist, but never proved," Arizona told him, noticing something unspoken in the long glance from Ray to Cat. He disregarded his curiosity. "Anyway, I have to get going. I have bigger things to work on."

"Are you working on the death of that policeman?" Cat asked.

The detective nodded as he put his notebook into his jacket.

"Do you know who killed Detective Howard?" Her question caught the cop's interest.

"Not yet, but why are you interested?" Arizona focused on how she clasped her hands.

"I thought there was something familiar about the car when we drove past the spot where all of the police were. I saw Howard about the murder of George Hopley, who was a friend of mine," Cat replied, fighting to keep her dislike of the dead cop from showing.

"Yeah, I know all about that from your friend on the couch. The good news is we solved Hopley's case." Arizona stared at her carefully.

"What do you mean, solved?" Ray asked sleepily.

Arizona glanced over.

"Just like I said. You remember when I told you about that stiff that they found at the Camelot Motel? His gun matched up with bullets found in Hopley and Cornell."

"Not to tell you about your business, but you have the second guy who pumped slugs into Cornell. He's still running around," Irish reminded him.

Campbell scowled at him. "Yeah, shamus, we got that figured out. The partner killed Pendexter and left. The sheriff has witnesses saying there was an argument early in the morning. He probably took the money for the hit. I guess he didn't want to share."

"Do you have a name on the partner?" Cat asked.

"I doubt we'll get anything else." Arizona shook his head. "Out of our jurisdiction, anyway, it's just one crook killing another."

"Well, I've got a name for you. Fat Louie seems to match the description of the guy I saw shooting One-Eye. Cat and I found out that Louie left *Anthony's* with George Hopley. It happened on the day they killed the reporter. You might want to check if he's still hanging around," Ray told the policemen as Arizona turned to leave.

"Wait a minute," the detective growled. "Are you still working on this case?"

"Not anymore," Irish told him. "I can't say I'm sorry about that either. Remember, you just said it's closed. Word will get back to Guy Young. That will square it with him and me in my books."

"All right, but I wouldn't bet on it. Young isn't the type to let his marks payoff. Anyway, I'll let my guys know to keep an eye out for Louie. In the meantime, you call me if you hear anything related to Howard's murder. Trouble seems to follow you around."

"Yeah, you'll be my first call. I'm sorry a policeman got killed. What happened?"

"That's under wraps right now, but it was a damn bad way to go. Life of a cop, I guess," Arizona told him. He turned to Cat, who walked to the door. "Young lady, you need some sleep. I'll see you later."

Arizona tipped his derby cap as he walked past Cat. She closed the door after him and remained for a moment before turning away. The woman saw Irish struggling to rise from his resting place again.

"Where do you think you're going?" she demanded as he raced to the couch.

Straining, Ray nearly got to a sitting position.

"I've been too much of a burden on you already, so I'll go to my hotel room."

"Like hell you will," Cat flared at him, forcing him back down. "Doc told me you needed to rest, and you will do exactly that. Quit trying to be a hero. Now, lay back before I get angry!"

He stopped his effort and gave her a tired grin as he closed his eyes.

"All right, you win. Come sit down. You look about out on your feet."

Cat nodded and took a seat in the chair across from him. She stared at him for a moment. Ray felt her stare, but he kept his eyes closed.

"I guess I owe you twice now," Irish said quietly. "I'm sorry I turned up on your doorstep."

Cat leaned back in her chair.

"You are darn right you owe me." There was nothing spiteful in her voice, just a tired jest.

"I don't like how this whole thing is turning," she confessed. "I saw your expression when you spoke about the ex-con who attacked you. You think he was the one who broke into my apartment? Maybe I should thank you."

"No need. The ass told me he was planning on coming back for you after he took me out." Ray started feeling his body drifting again. "It got me mad."

She looked at him on her sofa. His long frame filled the cushions, and his feet dangled off the arm of the chair. "Get some rest. Doc told me you lost quite a bit of blood. He says those stitches will have to come out in a few days."

Irish wasn't listening.

"You know, whoever hired Woolrich to keep an eye on you might send another? That con didn't work for free. Any ideas about who the money man might be?" He couldn't turn off the questions.

Cat nodded.

"Yeah, I have an idea, but we'll talk about it later. Just get some rest, Ray."

~~~

Greye La Spina walked into her luxurious home late that Saturday morning, about the time Arizona was leaving Cat's apartment. She did not acknowledge the butler, who passed by her as she hastened through the lobby and into the dining room. Greye went directly to the small alcove behind a vertical bar. The first tumbler she took from the overhead cabinet spilled from her hand, shattering loudly on the floor. She did not look at the glass fragments all around her feet. Instead, the red-eyed woman grabbed another glass and rapidly filled it with the first bottle she found under the counter. Greye's face screwed up at the bitter taste of gin, but she finished the glass. Then she forced another drink down before she stepped around the bar to a stool on the other side. She did not hear the grating noise of the glass that she ground into the wood floor with her shoes.

Her mind remained on the last terrible hours of watching Young order his men to kill Louie in front of her. Greye stared at the mirror across from her, but all she could see was the open mouth and eyes of her partner as he gasped his last breath. He was the last of the group of ex-cons brought in by Quincannon. Now she was alone. But at least she was alive, for the moment. Greye was still shaking as she slugged down the drink, feeling the effects of the alcohol on her empty stomach. She hoped it would dull the searing memories.

Greye believed herself to be as hard as the next grifter, male or female, who came out of Boston's North End tenements. However, she was not an executioner, a butcher who enjoyed the slow killing of another person. That was what she witnessed as a human devil called Guy Young had Louie tortured to death. He forced her to hear each scream and endure the suffering of her partner, even after she told the racketeer everything concerning the scam on the church trust. The devil gave her the show to reinforce his obvious message.

"Lady, your ass and soul belong to me," Guy's voice etched into her brain. "You give me the bonds, and you live; it's as simple as that."

Visibly shaking, Mrs. La Spina reached across the bar, pulling the bottle over to refill her glass. Her future lay shattered like the glass on the floor. Her sudden laugh caught her by surprise. She could still hear Quincannon's voice when he gathered their small group to outline the scam. He told her and the others how easy it would be in this Podunk city.

The bishop and the church funds that Henry controlled would be easy pickings. Greye would use her feminine charms just like all the other times, and
~~~

her husband would never be the wiser until they left town. All of them would roll in cabbage, laughing at the suckers holding the bag when they left the state.

The first feelings of lightheaded dizziness crowded into her thoughts. On Monday, when the bonds went to Young, Greye no longer carried a death sentence. The distraught woman in the mirror chuckled at the idea. Her reflection returned a grim smile, her mind telling her to be honest. She would still die a slow, painful death.

"Don't worry; your husband will forgive you since that's his business. You just do as I tell you, and he can keep that bright cathedral. And you will continue to play his loving wife. I believe your husband will cooperate with me as his new business partner. Otherwise, it'll be jail time for you and, probably, for him as well."

Young unbuttoned her dress while she watched his men drag away the body of her dead associate. Guy explained how her new world was before forcing her to lie back on the top of the filthy desk.

"Of course, I don't hold grudges. In fact, your scam has given me even more ideas. But I'll keep some of those bonds as evidence against your husband. I don't want you forgetting who is running the show."

The smile of the devil filled his face as he savagely ripped off her panties. He pushed into her without remorse. As he continued to rape her, Young told her his plans.

"Mark Fordham is going to be the next mayor. Since I have an agreement with the new mayor, I'll soon control the foundation and other such lucrative enterprises. Once we control the DA and the coppers, my legal businesses will hide the illegal stuff. I owe it all to you. Who knows what things I'll dream up for you?"

The cruel man's words echoed in her mind while Greye staggered up the stairs. There was no way to escape; Young told her that.

Near the top of the stairs, the bishop's wife looked over the railing, debating for a moment about letting herself fall over. She shook her head, knowing she was too much of a coward for suicide. Greye noticed the concerned expression on her maid's face, who stood nearby. Suddenly, maniacal laughter exploded from her as she wobbled over to the full double doors leading into her bedroom. When Greye closed the doors, the sound suddenly stopped. Mrs. La Spina walked several feet, falling on top of her bed, while silently crying.

~~~

Monday morning, the sunlight crept into the room just as a heavy knocking came from the hotel door. Irish was still painfully sore, but managed to get out of bed and slide on his pants while the next round of heavy blows hammered his door. J. Allan Dunn stood at the entrance, then stepped past the surprised shamus.
~~~

"There's no other way to put this, Ray, but you're through with all of this. I want you out of town by the end of the day." The thin man fidgeted with the brim of his hat, glancing up at Irish.

"Who the hell do you think you are?" His hand still on the half-closed door, Ray's temper flashed. "You're not big enough to make me do anything. If you want to quit paying for me to do your dirty work, that's fine; we'll call it quits. But don't you threaten me."

Dunn gave Irish a long, icy stare.

"I told you there are no other options," he said. "I've got folks screaming about you already. Then Cat tells me about the guy hanging out around her apartment who tried to kill you. They might have killed her. You've got to go."

"Dunn, there's something you are not telling me about Cat, Ray scowled at him. "Remember, I'm the one who's taken the hits, but this is the second time you mentioned the threat to her. She's not your responsibility."

He looked down at his hat again.

"She's a kid; you get paid for taking the risk."

Irish knew something else was there.

"Cat told me you helped her family out since she was a child. Most people aren't so generous with strangers."

The edgy look from Dunn was telling.

"It's none of your business. Now, are you leaving?"

Irish shook his head.

"You can go to hell. I told you I want that grifting bishop's wife in prison or dead. I've been around you enough to know you didn't make the call. Someone must be telling you to do this. Who is it?"

"I don't know what you're talking about," Dunn told him. "Now you get out of this city."

Irish placed his palm in the middle of Dunn's chest, stopping him in his tracks.

"Listen, you damn grafter," he stated, trying to ignore the pain from his injured chest. "I've had enough. You're the one who wanted to know what was happening in this damn place. Now somebody's running scared because I've found out more than you and your boss bargained for."

"Get your hand off me; you're fired," J. Allan told him. "That means stay away from Cat."

"All right, bub, we'll play it your way. But remember, I'll leave when I decide to." Irish opened the door wide for his ex-boss to leave. When he closed it, Ray stuck his hand in his pocket and retrieved a small roll of bills. A glance told him he would be looking for another place to stay by the end of the day.

About an hour later, Irish stood in the Hotel Alexander's lobby, reading the *Beacon* with a small case at his side. All of his worldly possessions, comprising two new suits and some underwear, were inside the case.

At least, it's more than I had when I arrived in Oyster City, Ray thought.

He leaned against one column, scanning through the want ads while he looked for a place he could afford. The pickings were sparse. But he was thankful since his injured ribs and shoulder were still pretty sore, so he would not be doing much walking.

"Are you heading somewhere, sailor?" Cat stepped next to him, looking down at his case.

He did not look up from his paper.

"Yeah, I'm trying to find someplace that won't bankrupt me before a week's out. Your buddy Dunn came by to fire me."

Cat went silent for a moment at the news.

"Damn, I shouldn't have told him about the bastard who broke into my apartment."

Ray glanced at her, debating on how much she realized J. Allan was shielding her.

"It was an excuse on top of a few other items," he told her. "He made it clear I was to leave town."

"What did you tell him?" She tried to remain indifferent.

"I believe, go to hell was the main point of the conversation." He gave a brief grin as he turned the page. "But it might not take long before I'm hanging out at the mission from what I see in this rag you work for."

"What about your case? Are you going to let Greye La Spina get away with what's she done?" Cat's voice was even, but Ray sensed her resolve to clear the bishop.

Ray folded the paper, turning to her.

"I have no case. We both know that I'm not a private detective, just a drifter who lived on some dirty cash for a while. I plan on getting her, but not the way we discussed. Those plans are gone. I've got to find a regular job somewhere and bide my time until she slips up. Maybe I can monitor her when I'm not working."

She suddenly hooked her arm with his, causing him to wince.

"No, we're not waiting for something that might not happen. Grab your suitcase, mister," she told him. "We've got to get over to keep an eye on La Spina's house."

As Cat drove, Ray kept looking at the black, feathered hat in the shape of a bird that she wore. While it matched her white and black polka dot blouse and black trousers, it was hardly undercover. He just smiled as she updated him on her latest news. Somehow Cat convinced one reporter, a guy name Berkley, to stake out the bishop's house over the weekend. Apparently, Greye La Spina arrived home on Saturday and had not left the house, even on Sunday morning. It forced the bishop to attend his church services alone. The reporter told her how upset the cleric appeared when Henry La Spina left the house.

"What do you owe this guy for the favor?" Ray asked as he held onto the door handle when her car took a turn. His tender ribs hurt at the effort to keep from sliding on the bench seat. He wondered if Cat secretly wanted to drive a race car.

"Oh, nothing much, just a dinner," she replied, with her attention focused on beating another car to an intersection. "Men like to do favors for me. By the way, I thought of something, so I think I'll do a favor for you."

"Let's start by not getting me killed," he told her as she sped away from a stop sign.

"Oh, you're a funny man," she frowned. "Do you want my idea or not?"

"Sure, let's hear it."

"You've still got a private investigator license. Dunn won't pull that away from you; too much trouble to bother. You just open your own business. I can see it now, Ray Irish Agency," she glanced over with a self-satisfied smile.

"Yeah, I can see it now, clients lining up by my cot inside the mission to discuss their problems." His grumpy sarcasm did not change her enthusiasm.

"I got that covered as well. What if I told you there's a Mrs. Purvey? I know who has a place that might work for you? It's on the second floor of a building on Broadway across from the *Beacon*."

Her excitement got under Ray's skin.

"Why are you so damn sure I want to stay in this place?" he asked. "Maybe I want to hightail it out of here and let the place rot to the ground?"

"Listen, Ray. I know you better than you realize," she said. "You're not going anywhere because you're stubborn as a mule. You're still on the case, but just not getting paid for the moment. Now, quit you're beefing and get with the program."

"All right, I'm with you. Just get us there alive." Irish decided Cat sounded a lot like one of his drill instructors in boot camp.

As the couple sat in Cat's car three houses down from the La Spina's, Irish focused on a dark gray Studebaker. Parked at the alley entrance across the street from the bishop's house, Ray watched the man who sat on the driver's side. The cigarette smoke exiting from the car window showed them that the stranger had no intention of leaving soon.

"We have someone else very interested in the bishop's house," Ray pointed out. "You know him?"

"No, and he doesn't look friendly," Cat squinted in the early morning sun. "What do you think is going on?"

Ray grimaced as he slid down low in the seat, trying to keep his large bulk out of sight.

"Maybe Greye's past is catching up with her. We'll just have to watch and find out. As long as the guy doesn't have a heater, we will be all right. Otherwise..." He let the thought drift.

"Are you going to be all right? You're still not healed." Cat slumped down in the seat, but she didn't remove her hat. With a smile, Irish told her he would be fine. Then he reminded her that the stranger in the car might notice a blackbird bouncing around in the driver's seat. Cat glared at him but finally removed the offending article

"Well, smart mouth, if you open my glove compartment, you'll find we're not defenseless," she told Ray, who popped open the small door in front of him. Inside, he discovered a .38 snub-nosed revolver and a box of cartridges. He flicked open the cylinder; it revealed she had loaded the weapon.

"That's a smart move; let's hope we don't need it," he told her.

"Well, your little scene in the alley the other night got me to thinking about the dangers. I drove out to a small town south of here and picked it up. Call it a present. It beats a knife." She watched him handle the weapon nonchalantly.

"Thanks, now I'm illegal as hell if I use it." Ray grimly smiled as he stuffed the items into his suit pockets. "But it makes the odds better."

"You know, I would like to see the bishop's knife collection again," he said out of nowhere.

"You keep talking about that. Why?" Cat asked as she stopped chewing on a fingernail.

"Something keeps bothering me about those guys getting their throats cut. It doesn't fit. It seems to me that a guy who helped kill Cornell using a gun would do the same with his partner. And, even weirder, why was Quincannon sitting in the parking lot at the same tavern where I met Greye? Even if he's following her, who killed him and why?"

While staring at the other car down the street, the shamus didn't see his partner's reaction to the news.

"What are you talking about?"

Ray quickly told her about the night he found Quincannon's body in the Six Jolly Squires tavern where Greye left him. He could see she grew upset, but he wasn't sure why.

"Why didn't you go to the police?" she asked.

"And tell them what? She would have left me hanging, and her husband would have protected her. Anyway, that's beside the point right now. My question is whether someone used one of those daggers on the wall in those killings." He stared at the stately manor house.

"I can't understand why you remain interested. What is it with you?" Cat shook her head in disbelief. "You like unraveling puzzles or something?"

Irish smiled at her.

"I hate puzzles; used to drive me nuts as a kid. I do like logical thinking, and we have two murders that don't fit the bill. First, the chauffeur was a big and strong guy who was in prison. You would think he would know how to defend himself. Someone nearly decapitated the guy, according to Howard. From the quick view of the murder scene I got, someone must have slipped up behind him. Second, you have a hoodlum who carries a gun, and somehow, he gets killed by a partner who is using a knife. I don't buy it. You and I both saw the dagger on the floor. A professional doesn't leave evidence like that. But Arizona told me they didn't find the weapon. How did the knife disappear, and why was it dropped?"

She was silent for a moment.

"All right, they're not logical. What does it mean?"

"I'm not sure, but it says someone went back for the dagger after we left the room. Someone wanted the weapon to remain hidden," he concluded. "The fact that both men get killed the same way makes me think they're linked."

Cat looked at the house. "One dagger used to kill Quincannon and Pendexter; then the evidence could be on the wall. But they would be clean by now."

"Exactly," he told her. "But you see why that display bothers me. Hopefully, we can find out from Greye when she decides to leave her house. Otherwise, we check with the servants. They would notice something missing."

Cat nodded, frowning at the implications.

It was close to ten in the morning when Greye La Spina exited her home. Dressed in a pair of slacks and a white top, she looked almost drab as she took the back steps to the garage. Sliding into the roadster, Greye tied a red scarf around her head to hide the undone hair, and she put on a pair of dark sunglasses to obscure the puffy, red eyes. Pulling out of the drive, the woman did not even look as she shot into the street.

The dark gray vehicle pulled into the street and followed her. Surprised by the sudden movement of the cars, Cat scrambled to get her coupe moving. She caught up with the others before Ray warned her to back off. Reluctantly, Cat complied.

"What if we lose them?" She frowned.

"Then we get to entertain each other until Greye goes back home, and we do it all over again," Irish told her casually, but he didn't believe it. The stranger in the gray car in front of them might have other plans for Mrs. La Spina.

They followed the two vehicles down Pine Street until Greye turned onto 12th and pulled up to the street's first parking spot. The gray Studebaker tailing Greye passed her Packard and stopped in a parking spot several car lengths ahead. Cat drove past both cars and turned into the alley.

"You'll need to go around the block so we can keep an eye on them," Ray grumbled when Cat brought her car to a stop.

"No, you get to go around the block." The woman opened the car door while her blue eyes danced with excitement. "I'm going to walk back and monitor things from the corner. We only met once so I can follow her. When La Spina leaves, you can come to pick me up."

While Irish winced in pain, sliding over to the driver's side, Cat made her way back to the corner of the building. After a glance, she quickly disappeared. Ray had to admit he liked Cat's idea as he drove around to 13th Street before getting back on Pine.

He pulled into a parking spot near the corner just as Greye appeared. As she stepped out in front of his car, Ray held his breath for a long moment. However, Greye remained oblivious to him. The woman hurried across the sidewalk, entering the building. Ray gingerly worked across the seat and looked up at the Morris Bank sign above the double doors. Just a few seconds later, Cat came around the corner, and Ray pointed to the building. She crossed in front of the car and went to the front window of the bank. His partner watched inside while pretending to dab at her face as she looked into a small pocket mirror.

"Well, hello there. I thought I recognized you. What a small world." Irish turned back to the passenger side to find a woman's face nearly inside the window. Initially surprised, he finally recognized the visitor.

"Hello, Pearl." He remained polite, although the chubby woman blocked his view. Pearl's low cut, bright green dress exposed her cleavage. "Have you been out to the *Stanley Rose* recently?"

The platinum blonde smiled, her cherry lipstick showing on a couple of front teeth. "Yes, and I haven't seen you out there. I've needed a dance partner."

There was a cough behind Pearl, and she pulled away from the car, turning to see Cat.

Smiling brightly, Cat slid past her. "I'm sorry, but he's waiting for me."

There was a long, pregnant pause as Cat opened the door and got into her vehicle.

"Well, aren't you going to introduce me?" Pearl came back to the open window. She asked with a tight-lipped smile.

Irish gave her a thin grin.

"Sorry, this is Catherine Bennett; she's a photographer with the *Beacon*. We're working on something."

"My husband, James, is the president and owner of the Morris Bank." Pearl gave Cat an indifferent glance. "I'm sure you've heard of him. The Morris Bank is one of the biggest banks in the city."

Cat shook her head. "I can't say that I have, but it's nice to meet you."

Pearl kept her attention on the shamus.

"I want a turn with you at the Masquerade ball. The *Stanley Rose* will be hopping this Saturday." She noticed the couple in the car looked confused.

"Oh, come now, Mr. Irish, you need to read the society pages. A man with your talent would do well with the right contacts." She leaned in the window again. "That nice Mr. Fordham is having a costume ball on the ship. There'll be lots of drinks and dancing. Everyone will be going."

Before Ray could reply, Pearl glanced at her watch.

"I'm late for the Manfred Circle meeting. Don't forget this weekend. I'll have a flapper custom on." She started walking away at a brisk clip, her purse flapping as Pearl held her green hat with the other hand. After a moment, both the driver and the passenger started laughing.

"Where did you come up with that girlfriend?" Cat's smug response caused Irish to frown.

"I needed information, and she needed a dance partner," Ray observed the heavyset woman turn the corner. "At least we know where Fordham will be that night. Now, what did you see inside the bank?"

"Greye went straight to the vault. I didn't get a good look, but it appears she's getting into a safe deposit box. Something's not right with her," she said, looking uneasy. "I wonder what she's up to?"

Irish quickly looked down, tipping his fedora low across his face.

"We'll know soon enough. She's leaving now."

After Greye left the building, she walked behind Cat's car and across the street. They waited until she turned the corner. Ray commented on the small attaché case Greye was now carrying. He pulled the car forward slowly, turning the corner at a snail's pace until they could see her get into her vehicle. Fortunately, traffic remained light that morning, and Ray stopped for a moment, waiting for the red Packard to pull into the street. As they expected, the man following Greye pulled in behind her while Irish backed off, keeping both vehicles in his sight. Soon, La Spina's car took a right on 9th, and her followers continued their pursuit.

Gradually, the buildings thinned out, replaced by two-story Victorian homes covered in gingerbread. The Packard picked up speed as the traffic lessened when the trio of vehicles turned onto State Road 66.

"I don't like this," the shamus grumbled. "I think she might be skipping town." He glanced at the fuel gauge. "I hope she doesn't have a full tank of gas."

As the cars reached the city limits, the gray coupe suddenly sped up, getting close to Greye's rear bumper. The driver attempted to whip around to pass, but Greye pushed her accelerator, cutting the gray vehicle off by using the oncoming traffic. It was apparent; the stranger following La Spina had orders to keep her from leaving town.

"Better hang on, because we're going to play this game as well," Irish warned his passenger as he gunned her coupe.

The flathead V6 screamed as they gained on the two vehicles in front of them. Greye kept speeding up, then slowing as she cut off the gray coupe trying to get past. The stranger in the coupe wasn't paying attention to the car behind him. When the thug swung into the other lane to cut off La Spina's car, Ray pressed the gas pedal to the floor. He steered directly at the back bumper of the gray coupe. The collision forced the coupe into the broad ditch next to the road. As they flew past the stranger's car, Irish glimpsed the goon trying to steer back to the road. It was a mistake. Cat turned to watch the gray car flip over several times, landing on its top at the edge of a cornfield before dust obscured the view. Glancing at her driver, she realized the deadly look in Ray's eyes had returned. He would move heaven and earth to make sure Greye would not leave the city.

As they closed on Greye's convertible, she took a sudden turn onto a dirt road, forcing Ray to slam on the brakes, nearly missing the turn. While the Packard had more power under the hood, the driver kept over-steering on the loose gravel road. While the vehicles made their way through the hills overlooking the nearby bay, Irish kept closing after each turn. Greye's car pulled away from them on the straight section of the road.

Finally, Ray decided to bump the Packard with a determined clamp of his jaw when he caught up on a curved section of the road. He let off the gas too soon, and the cars barely touched. However, Greye panicked when she saw the vehicle so close behind her. Gunning the engine, the car's rear end slid away into the soft soil by the edge of the road. La Spina over-corrected, then slammed her brakes, and turned into an open field while Ray shot past her.

By the time Irish came to a stop on the dirt road, he could see only dust flying up from the nearby field. The man slammed Cat's car into reverse and reached the small path leading into the cultivated land. Following the trail of dust, he and Cat soon came upon the stopped convertible. The driver's door hung wide open while one rear tire looked nearly shredded. Scanning the area, they noticed Greye running away, the brown portfolio case she carried flapping in one hand.

With a stone face, Ray pressed on the gas, passing the woman's disabled car and quickly coming up behind her. Greye's terrified face kept looking back at the oncoming coupe. For a moment, Cat wondered if Irish would run the woman over. Finally, he stopped as she came near the edge of a deep ravine.

"That bitch is mine," he stated in a growling whisper as he threw the car out of gear and pulled back on the handbrake.

Ray jumped out of the car, leaving the door open as he followed the bishop's wife. Greye slowed as she reached the steep drop off by an old stone fence covered with thorn bushes. Looking back, she recognized Ray steadily coming toward her.

Sprinting several feet to the wall, she broke a heel, causing her to lose the shoe. Greye looked down at the rocky face of the ravine below; tears filled her eyes. Kicking off her other shoe, she started running parallel with the fence. A glance back revealed her pursuer steadily closing on her with the look of death on his face. Desperation overcame her fear, and Greye tried to push through the small hole in the fence line. Thorns cut into her body, and she heard her blouse ripping. The tangle of roots tripped her, and she landed hard on the ledge overlooking the steep ravine.

Searching for an escape, she suddenly felt a hand grasp her collar and lift her from the ground. Immediately, Mrs. La Spina screamed in terror. Irish dragged her back through the brush and threw her to the ground. His bruised face showed the hatred as her screams for help quickly turned into uncontrollable sobs.

"Mrs. La Spina, you have a lot to answer for," Cat told Greye as she stepped next to Irish. She could see he had his hand on the gun in his pocket, but Ray had his other hand pressed against his injured chest. The pain of the recent stabbing showed through the anger.

"Don't kill me, please, I'm begging you. I can pay you," Greye sobbed. There was a slight trail of blood coming down her cheek. "It's in this case; just let me go." She hurriedly opened the attaché she carried, showing the green and white paper. "Look, see? Plenty of money. They're as good as cash."

When Ray spoke, his voice was tight and controlled.

"Lady, I don't give a damn about those things. I want to know why you tried to kill me. Then I plan on taking you back to the cops so you can explain to them about your brother and Fat Louie. Your husband can't protect you from this. I like to think that putting you into prison will make me feel better, but I doubt it."

"You can't take me back. I'm a dead woman." The distraught woman's eyes widened.

"You think I care about that? I figured you were skipping town," Ray shot back.

"Did you wear out your welcome?" Cat asked smugly. "I suppose the car following you was one of Guy Young's thugs, keeping an eye on you."

Greye buckled, her upper body leaning forward and shaking as she tried to control herself.

"He knows about the bonds, he knows everything about the grift, the setup, and now he'll take over everything."

She halted, then whispered.

"He'll kill me!"

"Sister, slow down and start making some sense. What are you talking about?" Irish glanced at Cat, who shrugged in response.

Taking a deep breath, Greye looked up, covered in streaks of dirt and tears.

"Quincannon set up this whole hoax. But now everything has spiraled out of control. Guy Young has taken over, and I have to get out of Oyster City."

"No, you're going to lay it out for us. I want the whole truth, or by God, I'll take you to Young myself. I haven't forgotten about the motel, you bitch." His venom caused Greye to stop. She stared at him for a moment before she dropped her head.

"All right, I'll tell you everything." La Spina's shoulders slumped.

"When Quincannon got out of prison, he came to Oyster City and found a job with Henry La Spina. After a while, he figured out there was a fortune tied up in the United Church Foundation that Henry runs. The foundation got all types of donations, so nobody realized how many were rare antiques and other items." She told the story like it was customary to be a crook.

"Quincannon contacted his friend in Boston, Fat Louie. They hatched this scheme to sell off the stuff and pocket the money."

"So, you're innocent in this entire scheme?" Ray's voice dripped with scorn.

"I didn't say that." Greye glared at him. "Louie decided we needed someone on the inside since they couldn't just steal it and fence the stuff locally. They had to get it out of state. Quincannon knew the bishop was going to New York for a week, so I met him and kept him occupied, making sure he didn't go back to Oyster City early. My partners hauled the most expensive stuff away from a warehouse in town." Greye paused when she saw the look of hate on Cat's face.

"Go on," the photographer told her bitterly.

"Well, Henry got serious and asked me to marry him before he left New York. I went along with the idea, thinking that I would just leave him before any wedding bells." She paused. The bishop's wife looked at Ray and Cat.

"That's when the scam went wrong. I swear to you that the guys told me the complete plan was to grab the stuff and let La Spina think Quincannon took off with them. Henry wouldn't do anything about it since it meant bad press, and the foundation could afford the loss. We would meet up in Boston and split the dough."

"What happened?" Cat asked.

"The damn Quincannon and Louie got greedy. They came up with the bright idea to go for everything. They forged a letter from the bishop's stationery to keep it all legal like for the accountant. Even better, they found some firm in New York to issue bearer bonds so there would be no questions. It would look like all the profit was going towards the construction of a new church. It was all part of their brilliant scheme. They would sell everything and turn it into these bonds. Good as gold and easier to carry was the idea."

"Let me guess; you had to marry Henry to keep the scam going for a while longer?" Cat fumed. "God, you're a worthless tramp."

Greye shook her head.

"You've never starved, looking at everything from the outside. All the money was there for the taking. So what if one guy takes the fall? It's not like the La Spinas can't afford it. Henry's family owns a good part of the city."

Irish grabbed Cat before she could pounce on her, but he lost some skin from the back of his hand during the commotion.

"Enough!" he yelled as he pulled her away from Greye. La Spina avoided the photographer's wild swings. After a couple of minutes, Ray released Cat, who continued to stare daggers at the bishop's wife.

"You two can have it out later," Irish told them.

He stepped over to Greye and crouched in front of her, his voice cold.

"Now, get back to the truth. You and your partners planned on taking the bearer bonds and skipping the state, leaving the bishop holding the bag. What happened? You could have left a while ago."

"We were going to do just that. Then, everything went south. Quincannon found out about how much my husband's weapons collection was worth, and he decided to go after that as well. Henry started getting suspicious of him when his driver started asking all these questions about the daggers. He hadn't spoken with the accounting firm yet, but I knew that was coming soon. When he did, the whole thing would blow up in our faces."

Ray stood up, his legs aching at the effort.

"Explain how Hugh Pendexter gets into this. Cat found out he killed someone back in the Boston area and somehow got out of the state. Then, he guns down One-Eye Cornell along with this Fat Louie, as you know."

"I heard all about you in Boston," Cat told her. "You ran the coast, grifting people. I suspect you had something to do with getting him out of jail there. He didn't come up with the bail on his own."

Greye looked back at Ray, teary eyes pleading. "I had to; Hugh was my baby brother. I couldn't leave him there. He'd get the chair."

"I can't imagine you could go to your husband for the cash. And it was too dangerous to sell any of the bonds you had." Irish paced around her as he worked through her motives.

He stopped and looked down.

"My guess is you got the cash from your favorite racketeer."

"It was Quincannon's idea," She nodded. "He noticed how Guy looked at me when I went to the ship occasionally. Quincannon said it was the perfect setup, and we figured we could skip town before I needed to repay him."

"Yeah, you sound like a grifter, that's for sure. What happened? Young decided you needed to make good on the money? When you couldn't pay up, he started using you as his whore, is that it?"

She barely nodded; her tears started flowing again.

"One night, out of the blue, I got a call saying I had one day to pay up. I went out to the ship that evening to ask for more time. That son of a bitch just laughed and said he'd go to my husband for the money. I couldn't let that happen, so I begged him. Then he told me he knew about my past in Boston."

"What kind of deal did you work out?" Cat asked.

"I went to work for Young. Important people came to the *Stanley Rose*. You know, the political types out of the capital that came down for a woman. I was to help him with those clients, to make sure they left happy. After I entertained them, he would make deals with them. You used that to influence those back at the capital." Greye La Spina looked up at the shamus. "I didn't have any choice."

Ray nodded, but his face remained unsympathetic.

"I bet not. What about your Boston partners? Did they go along with it?"

"Damn, Quincannon was all right with it. Bastard told Hugh that I was the perfect person. Said he should have thought of the idea first. My brother went out to *Stanley Rose* one night with Louie. At first, they promised to work a deal with Guy Young to get me out of his grip. Then, they saw all the marks coming aboard, and they came up with their crazy idea, a plan to knock Young off and take over his racket. They tried to get Quincannon to go along, but he wanted nothing to do with it. He told them it was too risky and said they were nuts. Hugh talked me into it. I wanted Young to get what was coming to him."

Ray shook his head at the news.

"God, I thought you had some brains at first. You went from the frying pan to the fire with that stupid move."

She dropped her head, going quiet for a moment.

"We were past the point of no return. I had to keep everything under wraps. I fed everything I could find out about Guy to my brother and Louie. We were so close to the jackpot, Quincannon started pushing to get the hell out of the city. Then you showed up…" She looked up at him, her eyes pleading.

"I wasn't lying about how things were that night I betrayed you. But now they're all dead, and I don't want to die." Greye's head fell into her hands, and she was sobbing. Irish glanced at Cat, and her face remained unmoved.

"My, aren't you a dutiful little woman, staying so busy with so many men? Enough of the tears, lady. Let's go." He reached down, touching her shoulder, and the bishop's wife flinched.

"Where are you taking me?" The panic in her voice was authentic.

"We'll talk about it in the car," he told her, gripping her shoulder hard.

Cat drove while Ray sat in the back seat with Greye. The bishop's wife clutched the small brown case holding the bearer bonds.

As they retraced their path back to Oyster City, the woman told them more about her past with Fat Louie. He pulled her out of the tenements of North Boston. She also talked about her brother's time in prison, where he met Quincannon.

Greye spoke quietly, almost in a trance, her accent growing thicker while she explained her experience the night Young killed Fat Louie. The bishop's wife told them about the gruesome death and Young's plans after Mark Fordham took over. She mentioned the leader of the union dockworkers had a stake in the *Stanley Rose*. Irish listened while he tried to piece together a plan which didn't involve someone dying as a result. When the bishop's wife finished, Cat brought up her friend.

"Explain why your kid brother killed my friend, George Hopley." Cat's voice remained like ice.

"I didn't know about that. You must understand that I'm not a killer, I'm not," Greye told her as she looked down at the case. "George took some money from my brother to help arrange things. Fat Louie confessed to Guy Young that he and my brother used this reporter to get to him. Then Louie told him about my part of trying to knock him off."

Irish glanced at Greye as she stared at the case in her lap.

"You cold-hearted bitch, you just said your partner got tortured to death. Of course, he told them all he knew," Ray said. "Now explain why you knocked me out and left me with your brother in that damn motel? And don't say that it was your partner's idea! I remember enough to know that plan came from you."

Greye said nothing for a moment; Ray could tell she was desperately trying to think up some fiction. He grabbed her by her hair and pulled her head back.

"I told you I want the truth. Otherwise, I'll have my partner drive us out to a lonely place, and I'll beat it out of you. I'm tired of you and your damned lies."

"Stop it, I swear I'll tell you the truth," she cried out in pain. "After my brother and Louie missed out on killing Young, they knew the gangster would be after them. Then you told me that Guy Young was putting the squeeze on you. I had to do something."

Ray released her, pulling his hand away like he was touching something dead.

"Give the rest to me straight," he growled.

"You forced me to do this," Greye pleaded. "Since you were about the same size as my brother, the idea was we would leave you in the motel. I would send a message to Guy saying it was you that set up the plan to knock him and Cornell off. When they came after you, we would get out of this place for good." Greye paused when she realized how badly her statement appeared. "I swear I was going to give you a head start; that's why I came to the motel," she quickly added, expecting a violent reaction.

Instead, he slid away from her.

"You're a worthless piece of garbage. Not too concerned about other people dying for what you're holding in your lap. By the way, who do you think killed your brother? Was it one of Young's thugs?"

She shook her head.

"I know it wasn't Guy Young or Louie. At first, I thought it was you, but I remembered they tied you up after I thought about it. But someone must have known about the place and where my brother was."

"That doesn't matter," Cat spoke up from the front seat. "We need to take this bitch to the police. She can explain all she wants. Let them sort it out."

Greye's eyes widened as she jerked up from the seat. She pleaded with Irish, grabbing his arm.

"You can't. Guy knows everything, and he's in this with Fordham. They have cops on their payroll. He had Fat Louie killed in front of me, and that bastard Young laughed. I won't last a day in jail. Give me a chance to get out of town. I was going to do that for you."

"You're pathetic," he told her as he looked back at the road. Irish noticed the city limits were getting close. Ray looked at Cat through the rearview mirror.

"Turn off the road up here, and let's find a place to park."

When the car came to a stop, Ray opened the door and nearly pushed Greye out of the backseat after taking the small portfolio she held. They parked in a sheltered, isolated area with trees all around.

"You can't just kill me and take the money?" Greye stared at her captor, expecting the worst.

"Lady, I thought mighty hard about what you did. And you deserve worse. But no, I'm not killing you, and I'm not taking this blood money. Now shut your pie hole and go sit down over there while I talk to my partner about this." Ray got in the front seat next to Cat and closed the door. He watched Greye look around the secluded area before dropping her head and slowly stepping away.

"We really should take her to the cops," Cat told him as he looked out the window.

"She's right about what will happen if we do that," he shook his head. "They'll kill her in there. Young's got too much pull with the police; we both know that. Greye is a witness to a murder, and she knows too much about Young. Plus, the story will come out about their scam to bilk the foundation, and you know that won't help your bishop. He married a witch, and he'll be paying for it. You want that on your conscience?"

"I could live with her death," she told him coldly.

"Yeah, so could I, but it's still wrong," he gave a grim smile. "Besides, I met Henry, and I don't think her husband deserves a corpse for a wife," he said as he patted the case in his lap. "However, these bonds give me an idea. Can we hide her out somewhere and make a deal with Guy Young?"

"What kind of deal?" Cat's jaw nearly dropped in amazement at the suggestion.

"Guy Young came off his ship to kill Louie. If he wants these damn bonds so bad, I'm willing to bet that he'll come ashore for these things, especially if we use Mrs. La Spina as bait. Remember, she's a witness, and Guy can't keep her alive now. He'll know pretty soon that his thug who was following her got dumped. Young will guess that she hightailed it out of the state. If we can hide her out for a day or so, he'll start getting worried. I think we can convince him to risk a meeting for the bonds. Otherwise, she'll go to the cops." Irish laid the idea out as he thought of it.

Cat stared out the window at the bishop's wife. She sat on the ground, looking off into the horizon. "All right, so he comes ashore to meet us. What then? His goons will be all over us."

"We set it up to give Young and his thugs to the police. The honest ones will jump at the chance to throw him in jail. We have a witness to the killing." Ray looked out at Greye in the field.

"I don't like it," Cat shook her head. "Greye will get off scot-free. I thought you wanted her in prison?"

"I do, but everything else I've come up with involves people getting killed," Ray replied. "Think of it this way. If I'm right, your friend the bishop gets to clean up the mess left by his wife. Don't you think the important people associated with Henry La Spina will help fix the problem? Plus, we have someone who can help us."

"Who would that be?" Cat turned to him.

"J. Allan Dunn." There was a foul grin on his face when he spoke.

"Why would he help us?"

Ray looked at her, surprised.

"He wouldn't unless we give him something he can't refuse; Mayor Hopley's re-election. You have that in your apartment."

Cat paused, transfixed at the idea forming.

"I think I understand. Once Young is in jail, Dunn takes the bonds and fixes the books with the foundation. In return, he gets the photo I have along with what we think we know about Young and Fordham."

"And they'll ship the good, little wife is out of town after a quiet divorce," Irish nodded. "Someone will probably warn her about the threat of prison if she opens her mouth. I don't like it any more than you do, but I like the other options even less."

"You could just put a bullet in her and give the bonds back to the bishop. It would be simpler and cleaner," Cat suggested coldly.

"Have you killed someone?" he glared at her.

Cat looked away and shook her head. After a moment, she finally spoke.

"I've never hated someone like that. I guess I couldn't do it."

"Once you pull the trigger, you'll always remember the face," he said. "I've seen enough death to last me a lifetime."

"Still, I'm not sure about the plan, but I can't think of anything better." Cat gazed out of the car window. "You're the one who got the worst of this so far. I guess you're looking for something more than killing someone."

"Well, I would like a little payback against Young and some others working for him." Ray agreed. "Plus, if Greye leaves town, I don't think she'll have the smarts to pull off more graft. She follows what others want her to do."

She gave him a smirk.

"By the way, you're beginning to think like everyone else in Oyster City."

His face went dark at the thought.

"I hope the hell not!"

~~~

Cat stopped by the home of Gladys Peer, telling Ray that she was picking up keys to a hideout for their passenger. He stayed with Greye in the car, watching as she tried to clean the worst of the dirt from her face using Cat's pocket mirror.

"Ray, those bonds are my ticket to staying alive. Guy knows everything. A cop will tip him off, and we'll be dead; he'll kill anyone who tries to stop him. Just let me go, and I'll be so far away, Young will never find me," Greye pleaded with him.

"No dice, lady. So far, your thinking has got your partners killed. I suggest you better line up the story you plan on giving your husband. If he's as good as
~~~

everyone says, you might come out of this without going to prison," Irish told her, refusing to lay out everything he and Cat planned. She gave him a poisonous glance but went quiet. He noticed how Greye had recovered her composure, but she was correct about one thing. Young would be gunning for him. The idea he planned was risky, and there was always a chance he might miss an angle in his complex web of a plan.

"I don't know what Henry will do, or even if he can do anything," Greye leaned back in the seat. "I'm not sure how I can tell him what happened."

"You're a liar and a tramp, so using the truth might be a refreshing change." Cat slid into the driver's side, overhearing the conversation coming from the open car window. She did not bother to look at the bishop's wife.

When they arrived in front of the building at Chandler and Peach Street's corner, Greye remained sullen. Ray wondered how much of the drama he witnessed in the field was real or just an act. She had an unusual ability to work on a guy's emotions, even when they had reason to kill her.

The trio entered a doorway between a restaurant and a dry cleaner, taking the stairs to the second floor. There were two doors at the top of the stairs. Cat unlocked the door on the left to find a nearly empty office. A single dust-covered desk and antique wood chair sat in the middle of the room. An open door in the back revealed another room with a bed.

"This will be your home until we get things set up," Cat told Greye, placing the light-colored folder holding the bonds on the desktop. "It's not the luxury, but Young won't be able to find you here. Nobody knows about the place. There's nothing to tie you to this office."

There was a frown on Greye's face as she inspected the room. She walked to the bedroom, her torn blouse barely hanging from her scratched shoulder. After a quick look around, she came back into the office. "I've seen worse," she told them, her Boston accent gone and her poise returning. She looked at her dirty clothes.

"What about clothes and food?"

"We'll come up with something," Ray told her. "Cat and I will be around to keep an eye on you." His eyes narrowed. "Don't make me bring a cop."

Slowly, Greye nodded as she looked away.

"I understand. You're running the show."

"Well, for the moment, anyway. Get cleaned up, and we'll go out and make a call to your husband. You can tell him you're staying with some friends for a couple of days. That's as close to the truth as you ever give him."

Greye looked out of the dusty window to the street. "I...I think that will work. He's very understanding."

"Yeah, with you, he'd have to be." Cat's bitter tone showed no truce. "I'll stay here with her," she turned to Ray. "You can call a mechanic about having her car towed to their house. There's nothing that Guy Young can do but watch her home."

Ray pulled the bonds from the desk, noticing Greye's eyes follow his movement. "I'll take these with me just in case our new partner forgets her agreement. When I get back, we'll get some food and make the phone call." As she stepped out of the office, he glanced back at Cat.

"Don't beat her up; we'll need her to make this thing work." There was a grin on his face.

"No promises," Cat replied.

~~~

It was the next morning when Irish walked along Main Street, heading for Pappy's newsstand. His mind remained muddled from lack of sleep and a whirlwind of thoughts. Ray spent an uncomfortable night sleeping in the old chair at the empty office, while Greye slept in a bed behind a closed door only a few paces away.

Early in the evening, after Greye got a bath and put on the clothes Cat came up with, her demeanor returned to a confident crook. Around him, Greye attempted her same sexy illusion. The trio took a ride to an isolated gas station, and Greye called her husband while Cat listened as she stood nearby. Ray could see the young woman's murderous stare as he filled up the car, and he recognized how much the photographer hated Greye. Irish shook his head, realizing his anger at the bishop's wife transformed into disgust. At least, he was not thinking of the best way to dispose of her body. Instead, he kept fine-tuning a plan which might keep all of them alive.

When they arrived back at the hideout, Cat stayed for the evening while Ray went out for their food. When he returned, Ray could feel the tension in the air. The man suspected the two women had a bitter argument while he was gone. Ray decided he would stay overnight and let Cat get some rest.

However, during the long evening with Greye, he had learned a lot about her. If he was honest with himself, Ray could understand how a pretty woman, growing up on the rough streets of North Boston, learned to use her sex to get out of poverty. Still, Greye's lack of conscience reminded him that behind her attractive smile was a heartless snake. In some ways, he felt sorry for the man married to her. Others might take her to bed, but Henry La Spina would have to pick up the pieces from his wife's pursuit of the easy buck. He gave a grim smile.

Yeah, the easy way to an early grave!

He stepped next to the wooden structure holding magazines and newspapers.

"Well, shamus, you look out of sorts." Pappy sat on a stool, handing out the latest paper. A pork-pie hat covered his head, and he wore a brown sweater over his black vest.
~~~

"Yeah, rough night," Ray told him, pulling a Lincoln from his pocket. "Say, can you let me know if you hear anything about Greye La Spina going around? It appears she might have left town."

"Funny thing, you asking me something like that." Pappy handed him the morning paper. "I heard this morning that a lot of folks are interested in her Packard."

Ray had to force a smile away as he scanned the paper. "I'll bet, maybe like Guy Young's folks."

"Those are the ones, all right. They were interested. You have something to do with it?"

"I don't know a thing." Irish shook his head.

Then he noticed a headline about a corpse found out at the abandoned military base. From the description, he guessed it was Fat Louie. He folded up the paper, sliding it under his arm.

"Got any other good stories?"

"Nah, it's been pretty quiet around here. You got the Soviets making noises overseas in Iran. That guy Churchill is talking about some Iron Curtain falling across Europe. Oh, and Mrs. Purvey's latest article claims that dinner dresses with just one shoulder strap are a very flattering look to the female figure."

Irish gave him a sour glance at the last bit of news. Pappy returned a big grin. "You should keep up with everything in the newspaper, my mother always told me. You might learn something."

"And how will that help me?" Ray asked.

"Well, there's a big party out on the *Stanley Rose* this weekend. Find you a girl to go out there, and she'll want that dinner dress. It seems like Fordham is going all out to get the very wealthy and very corrupt to pay his way to the top."

"Yeah, I heard about that," Irish told him. "I might have to check it out. Did you go to those places with your wife? I'll bet she liked to dance."

His friend suddenly frowned and chuckled at the idea.

"Not hardly. The colored class doesn't get that type of invitation. But my Emma danced better than Ginger Rogers."

"Yeah, I always said the world's a crazy place, with people filling their heads with crap. I saw enough of that malarkey in the Navy. Well, I've got to get going. I'll see you later."

"Irish, Emma told me to thank you for coming by the other day for dinner. She said that it was really sweet of you."

"I never turn down a free meal," he said with a wink. "Besides, those were the best pork chops I've ever had. We'll do it again soon."

Heading across the street, Ray stepped to the sidewalk. A white Hudson pulled close to the curb and honked. Inside was Lieutenant Arizona Campbell, who waved him into the car.

"Irish, how are you doing? You get healed yet?"

Ray nodded. "I'll survive once I get those stitches out if I don't scratch them out first," he said. "What's a police detective picking me up for?"

"It beats hauling you into the office for a chat. Have you been staying away from the La Spina gal?" The cop's tone was light, but Irish figured he was fishing.

"Haven't been around her place, if that's what you're asking. Is something up?" Irish stared ahead as the car took the turn down 6th Avenue.

"Well, the sheriff found her in a field before the tow truck picked it up. Plus, one of Young's thugs died in an auto accident out on the highway near there," Arizona glanced at his passenger. "I thought you might know more about it. The sheriff thinks another car was involved."

"Sounds like one of those gangsters making a play," Ray replied carefully. "Maybe you should ask Guy Young?"

"You're going to play it close to the vest?" the policeman grunted. "All right, you get Young to come ashore, and I'll be happy to talk with him. I've got several unexplained deaths he and I could chat about."

"I just read in the paper about the body they found. It sure seems like an excellent description of Fat Louie. You get a positive ID on it?" Ray told him, noticing the policeman turn by the courthouse.

Arizona remained quiet as he drove along. Ray glanced at him, and he could tell the cop was debating something. Finally, the man came to a decision.

"Listen, Irish, you realize you're playing with fire here? Word is out that we're supposed to be looking for Greye La Spina, but they're keeping everything very low-key. If something is going on between you and her, it would be wise to spill the beans. The DA is already looking to knock you down about her."

Irish watched as the vehicle drove past the District Attorney's office and turned on Patriot Street.

"Arizona, I'll tell you what. Find out if you have the body of Fat Louie. Then, I'll offer you a gift? Fair enough?"

Arizona pulled next to the sidewalk in front of the police station.

"You've got something up your sleeve." He turned the car off. "I don't like this one-man show you're running here. If you have something, turn it over."

Ray looked at him, pointing his thumb at the building.

"Do you trust everyone in there with information someone might have about Young and his operation?"

Arizona let out a deep breath and shook his head.

"No, I don't." He paused, glaring at the shamus. "I'll play along. You were right about the body; we got it tagged down at the morgue. Now, what is this gift?"

Irish opened the door and got out of the vehicle.

"I'll call you tonight at your office with the time and place. Have your best men with you, and I'll give you Guy Young on a silver platter."

~~~

The note arrived at the *Stanley Rose* when a young messenger handed the small envelope to the club manager. The short, balding man named Pauly frowned at the interruption to his overbearing flirtations with the hat-check girl who he brought in early that day. Addressed to Guy Young, the small letter held no other information as he debated whether to disturb his boss, who seldom rose before noon. Deciding to risk it, Pauly walked across the ship to the office where his boss had made his home. Just as the manager was about to knock on the door, he felt someone behind him.

"What are you doing? Nobody wakes the boss unless he tells them," Tweedledee grumbled at the short man.

Pauly turned, looking at the chest of the bodyguard. His beady eyes blinked several times, and he held up the envelope. "You can give this to him when he wakes up. This message just came in, and I figured it might be important."

The scarred man took the paper.

"Just get out of here, you little twerp. I'll take care of it."

The manager quickly walked away, cursing the guard under his breath. Tweedledee looked at the envelope again before depositing the message into his suit pocket.

An hour later, Guy Young sat behind his pretentious desk, drinking his coffee from a delicate cup while going through his daily ritual of reading his mail. As he scanned the terse letter from Greye La Spina, a cold fury slowly filled the racketeer's face. The bitch was making a play to double-cross him. He'd already assumed she left the state, but she remained close. After his henchman's death, the mobster sent out telegrams to friends throughout the country, offering a large reward for her death. Young believed in a few months; she would turn up in a morgue. The bonds would eventually make their way back to him, no doubt minus a recovery charge from his friends.

Instead, that whore wife was telling him what to do. The letter gave instructions for the racketeer to be waiting on her call to meet. Unless he agreed to split the bonds and allow her to leave town, Greye was going to the cops to become a witness to his murder of Fat Louie. She also said she would tell the police he killed her brother and One-Eye Cornell.

He flung the letter away, then took a massive swipe with his arm across the top of the desk, scattering the dishes from his breakfast. The breaking crash of glass and pottery woke the sleeping woman in the round bed. She immediately sat up, pulling the gold cover around her naked breasts. Guy noticed the movement and glared at the lovely girl.

"Get the hell out of here before I get mad," he fumed.
~~~

~~~

J. Allan Dunn walked into the administration building just after the church bells stopped ringing across the street. It was a few minutes after twelve. The thin man remained lost in thoughts while climbing the six sets of stairs leading to his office. His wife kept harping at him for another radio in the house, like one wasn't sufficient. The argument after breakfast left him with a headache. Helen enjoyed spending money, something he should have realized, considering her family ties. However, even after all the special deals J. Allan worked out to bring in the extra cash from city contracts. He was no further ahead than when he got the job. The thought depressed him as he turned down the hallway to an office with the sign on the door: Director of Public Works. The sound of his footsteps filled the empty hall since most of the employees had already left for lunch. He went into the office, paying no attention to Madge, who was not at her desk. His secretary was a virtual time clock, entering the office precisely at nine each morning. Dunn guessed Madge was just sitting down across the street at the diner where her beau worked. Opening the next door, he halted.

"Mr. Dunn, please shut the door. We have important business to discuss," Ray Irish told him as he sat behind the desk with his feet up on the desktop. Catherine Bennett stood by the window, turning around at the sound of the door opening.

"What the hell do you think you're doing? Get out of my office before I call the police," Dunn raised his voice, his eyes ablaze.

"Well, your secretary is on a long lunch hour so that we can have a chat. That's not a friendly welcome considering all we've been through together," Ray said as he lifted his feet, placing them on the floor. He leaned forward in the chair.

"I once saved you from being pounded by Young's thugs. But that's the past, and I'm not going to hold a grudge. However, I don't think you want to miss out on the opportunity that Cat and I have come up with for you."

Dunn slid off the cashmere coat he wore, hanging it up on the wooden coat rack behind the door. He placed his derby hat on the stand.

"You don't have anything I want, Irish. Now get out of here."

"Dunn, you want to hand your buddy the mayor his re-election on a platter or not? That's what Ray's offering you," Cat stated when she stepped to the desk and laid her photo of Mark Fordham with the dead policeman.

Glaring at her, J. Allan stepped over, looking at the picture.

"It's Fordham, so what?"

"He just happens to be with a corrupt cop by the name of Plug Howard, the murdered cop," she said. "Do I need to draw you a picture?"

Immediately, J. Allan shook his head.
~~~

"No, I get it. Get the dirty boys out, implying a policeman got killed because of his association with Howard." His eyes darted between the two people. "It might work, but I don't see the silver platter."

"Well, this is a two-part deal. You also get to save your boss the embarrassment of his close friend spending time behind bars. If Fordham gets this information, he'll have the election," Ray told him, observing Dunn's eyes widen, and the shamus smiled.

"No, I'm not talking about you," Irish said as he pulled out the small parcel holding the bearer bonds. He opened the case and removed one.

"One of our illustrious citizens is involved in a scam that's worth about fifty thousand dollars. If the information comes out and your boss loses the election, just think of the heads that will roll. Like rats from a sinking ship, it's about to get real messy when Fordham takes it over. Not to mention the fact that Young's gang has a deal with the union boss." Ray paused, holding out the paper. "I can always go to the mayor or the DA myself. Here's one of the bearer bonds issued for the construction of a non-existent church."

"I don't trust you, Irish. You're getting too bright." Grudgingly, Dunn looked over the paper in his hand. The bond showed the name United Church Foundation, and he greedily licked his lips. Then his eyes grew wide.

"Are you telling me Henry La Spina's involved in this?"

"His name's all over it, whether he's involved or not." Ray nodded. "I'm just trying to clean up all the loose ends of the web you stuck on me. Now, I'm driving you to the end of the rainbow, so it's your choice if you want the pot of gold or not."

Irish stood.

He stepped close to Dunn, pulling the bond from his hands.

"We're going to give your mayor both Guy Young and Mark Fordham," Cat told him with a smile as she picked up her photo. "But it's going to cost you."

"How much are you talking about?" Dunn asked as he eyed them suspiciously.

"First, you'll give me and Cat two thousand each for doing your dirty work. The money will be in our hands by the end of the day," Ray stated as he stuffed the bond back into the folder, then put it inside his coat. His grim smile showed his enjoyment as his former boss nearly choked on the price.

"What the hell are you talking about? I can't come up with that kind of cash so quickly," J. Allan stammered, staring at the coat pocket holding the bonds.

"Then you need to get with your boss and come up with enough money. No cash, then no photo and no bonds," Cat replied. "Think what Fordham might pay for it."

There was a long pause as Dunn's narrowed eyes kept darting between them.

"All right, I'll have it by tonight."

"Meet us at that out of the way office you use at five o'clock. By the way, I'm telling you not to let your friends in City Hall know about this. Otherwise, you can kiss the deal goodbye," Ray warned Dunn. "Any tidbits back to Fordham or Young will throw a wrench into the whole thing. That'll make it dangerous for Cat and you." Ray started for the door while Dunn's scowl followed him.

"Don't worry, we've got this worked out," Cat told the thin director. She patted him on the shoulder as she went to the door.

"Irish, it appears this city is rubbing off on you." J. Allan Dunn's mocking tone came as the troubleshooter opened the door.

Ray refused to look back.

"Don't ever say that to me again if you want to keep your teeth."

~~~

Ray was silent as Cat drove them back to Greye's hideout. She took many turns and a couple of back alleys to ensure no one was following them. After a while, she glanced at the silent man.

"Why did you tell Dunn this setup is dangerous for me?" she asked. "You're in as deep as I am."

Ray tipped back his hat, coming out of his thoughts.

"In his eyes, I'm expendable; you're not. I was making sure he would keep his mouth shut until I figure out who his partners are."

She turned into another alley, looking back in her mirror. "Dunn wouldn't sell us out. He's greedy, but not a fool."

"Yeah, but he'll be more careful since you're involved with this," he replied.

Cat frowned. "What are you saying?"

"Nothing," Ray told her firmly as they came to a stop close to the building. "I'm trying to keep this plan on track. Now, let's figure out how to tell Greye that she'll be the bait for Guy Young tonight."

Several minutes after the couple entered the room, they laid out the plan to the bishop's wife. It surprised Irish at Greye's calmness when she reluctantly accepted her role as the carrot to bring Guy Young into Oyster City. He told her that.

"I've been around cons all my life," she explained. "It didn't take a genius to figure out your plan when you asked me to write that note." Her strained face scowled. "You don't belong in this place if you're too honest to run with the money. What about my husband?"

"Once we get Young taken care of, then sort that out with him on your own," he replied. "We'll point out you've been cooperating with the authorities."

"Ray's already gave you an out since some people will clean up your mess with the foundation," Cat interrupted. "You might take it as a path for you to get the hell out of the city."

Panic filled Greye's hazel eyes at the news.
~~~

"You mean Henry already knows?"

"Maybe not yet, but that doesn't matter at the moment," Irish told her. He didn't understand why she appeared so upset.

"The cops will be there tonight, so you should be safe," his confident claim made Greye turn and walked to the back of the room as she considered the plan. Cat looked at her watch and stepped close to Irish.

"I'll get us some lunch. Don't let the damn woman out of your sight," Cat warned him. Ray absently nodded as he watched her standing in the sparse bedroom.

Not long after Cat left the building, Greye wandered back into the office. She quietly watched Irish for a long moment. He acted like he didn't notice as he leaned back in the chair. With his feet propped on top of the windowsill, Ray stared at the building across the street.

"You won't admit it, will you?" Greye said, interrupting his thoughts.

"Admit what?" he asked.

"You know there's something good between us. You've known it since the first time we met. I'm not the devil; I'm a survivor."

Irish remained quiet, continuing to stare out the window.

"That little girl isn't your type," she came closer to Ray, taking a seat on the edge of the desk. "Cat's still young and naïve. I could tell by the way she worships my husband. Your girlfriend can't see the forest for the trees." Greye shook her head.

"I pity her."

"I don't know about that; she's pretty sharp and tough. Grew up in this rotten place." Ray almost explained how the young woman saved his hide.

"You might be right. It is a corrupt city; I hate it here." She shivered.

"The problem is your little girlfriend worships icons, and there are no such things. Henry's a pretty good guy, but behind those puppy dog eyes, he has his secrets, like the rest of those in control of this town. But nobody gets behind the masks they put on."

"Well, Cat's someone I can trust. That's something you'll never know. Such ideas won't get past your greed." Irish looked at her finally. "You're only loyal to the cash you have."

Greye dropped her head.

"Greed isn't all I'm about." She paused, then looked at him. "But I can bet she'll never make you happy the way I can. Will you be content knowing that?"

Ray went quiet again. In the afternoon sun, she wasn't quite as attractive as he recalled the morning they met. Without the eyeshadow, the false lashes, and makeup covering the few emerging wrinkles, she would look like a thousand other everyday girls. But her eyes held a hypnotic fire, which drew him in for a moment. Full lips smiled as she leaned closer to him.

"Think about what's in that attaché you have. Fifty thousand could take you a long way. You could go anywhere and do anything. You and I could be happy together," she said, a mixture of hope and anxiety in her words.

He looked down at his suit, pulling the small portfolio from his jacket, his mind mildly entranced by the idea. Then Ray glanced at Greye, whose eyes followed the package in his hand.

"You told me you don't want to die," he said. "You think nobody hunts down this fifty thousand in blood money?"

"We could cash those in New York and disappear. No one could find us," she insisted. "I know people who can make it happen, new papers and a new life. That little girl will be a distant memory I'll make you forget. What do you say?" She licked her lips, eyes following the folder he placed on the desk near her.

Irish let out a long sigh as he let his feet fall to the floor. He stood, picking up the portfolio and putting it back in his pocket. When he opened the office door, Ray looked back.

"You didn't answer my question," she replied, gracefully sliding off the desk and stepping toward him.

"Yes, I gave you the answer."

He walked into the hall and closed the door.

With his trap in place, Ray Irish walked out of Dunn's anonymous storage office. The day was too cold for spring, but the sunlight felt good. All he needed now was the timing to fall into place, as expected.

Cat and Greye were still inside the office, where J. Allan had begrudgingly handed his photographer four thousand dollars. He got the incriminating picture of Fordham and the dead cop. Ray noticed the smirk directed at him from the bishop's wife while she witnessed the exchange. Ray glared at her for a moment, then nodded to the phone on the desk. Greye frowned and hesitated before she went to the desk and lifted the handset from the cradle. After taking a deep breath, she called the number to a diner by the docks where Young would be waiting.

As Irish slid into the coupe's passenger side, he considered the timing of their plan again. He had already called Arizona with the layout and timing, but he kept Greye's role a secret. The detective was less than thrilled with Ray's idea.

"You're taking a big gamble," Arizona warned him. "If you get someone killed, they'll throw away the key after you go to prison."

"Just make sure you arrive on time. We'll be in a gray coupe, getting there ahead of everyone. Any car that's coming into the place after that won't be on our side. When you hear the full story, you'll see that I don't have much choice. I can't have any police seen; otherwise, he'll never show up." Irish grimly smiled when he remembered Arizona's grunted disapproval, followed by a curse before he hung up.

Cat came out of the building, her brown wool coat covering her white blouse and tan slacks. Greye walked close behind, trying to keep warm in her thin red jacket, which covered her gray dress suit. Both women were silent, each person dealing with their concerns behind worried expressions. Ray guessed if he looked in a mirror, his face would show the same anxiety. In his pocket was the .45 auto he purchased that day, insisting Cat keep the snub-nose revolver she gave him.

"You better have the police there; Young is on his way," Greye told Ray as she climbed into the back seat. "The bastard had his man take my message, said he wouldn't talk to a person like me."

"I expect he didn't use those words." Irish flipped the seat back as she got comfortable.

"No, he didn't, but I don't care what they call me as long as I don't get killed by your brilliant idea," she replied to his sad smile.

Cat drove them out of the alley and followed the street toward the outskirts of the city. They were heading to the abandoned military base to make the swap. With the head start, they would be there twenty minutes before Young and his thugs. Arizona and his men would follow Guy right into the trap, cutting off any escape.

While Ray thought about any flaws in the plan, Cat interrupted his thoughts.

"What do you think our odds are coming out clean on this? Dunn tried hard to get me to stay there, even offered me more money."

"Why didn't you take him up on it?" Irish asked, staring at the nearly empty sidewalks as they drove.

Cat glanced at him, surprised.

"Are you kidding me? I want to see the look on their faces when the cops show up," she said. "Why do you think I have my camera case in the back seat? The *Beacon* will pay me a mint for the pics."

Irish groaned as he looked at her. "I'd say the odds of a picture aren't that high even when Arizona shows up. Just don't get yourself killed in the process. That camera won't stop a bullet."

"Ah, you do care." She gave him a light laugh and a wink, but he knew it was for show.

"I still don't like it," Greye complained. "You're relying on too many people who can sell us out."

"Shut up!" Cat countered before Irish could reply. "It was your scam that put all of us behind the eight ball."

After the outburst, they went silent until the car reached the abandoned base. Ray looked around when the vehicle passed by the abandoned guard shack and the gate which stood open. As expected, he did not see the hint of police. They slowly drove past the area where Greye had given the mickey to Irish. The eerily abandoned buildings on either side of the road looked ominous in the dusky evening light.

"Well, it looks like Arizona is following the plan. We'll have a few minutes, so let's head to the end of the road and turn around to face Young's men when they show up," Irish told Cat, who nodded. "The cops will follow them in, and we'll have Young in the trap."

A moment later, Cat suddenly slowed the vehicle when she noticed a car ahead, blocking their way. Almost immediately after, Greye let out a shriek as she saw two black cars speeding toward them after they emerged from between two buildings on their right.

"Gun it," Ray yelled at Cat, pulling his .45 auto while he started rolling down the passenger side window.

He didn't hear the shots, but the window next to him shattered as two bullets narrowly missed him. Cat pressed on the accelerator, pushing her car forward. She headed for a narrow opening between the blocking vehicle and a cement dock leading to a large building. Just as she reached the incline ramp, a car struck her gray coupe in the rear. Before they realized what had happened, their coupe flipped over on the driver's side.

Metal on the vehicle screeched loudly while the passengers slid down into the doors of the car. The two speeding vehicles attempting to ram Cat's car futilely tried to stop, but they crashed hard into the larger blockade car. The wrecks sent pieces of metal and glass across the area, as Cat's coupe stopped against the side of the raised dock.

Irish landed on Cat in the crash, and his survival instinct took over. He immediately pulled himself up to the passenger door and pushed the heavy steel door upward until it fell open. Greye scrambled forward, trying to get out of the car, but Irish stood in her way. Gun in hand, Ray climbed on top of the vehicle, quickly sending two bullets into the stunned driver of the blockade vehicle, only a few paces away. The driver died while he clutched the steering wheel of the car.

"Come on," Irish yelled down into the coupe, catching a glance of Greye's pale face, bleeding from a cut on her forehead.

He slid down to the ground, keeping the vehicle between himself and the thugs who scrambled out of their cars. Bullets peppered the bottom of the gray coupe as Greye struggled to haul herself out. She pulled herself from the car, tumbling headfirst onto the ground.

Firing another couple of rounds at one thug trying to move in closer, Irish felt something pushing into his ankle. Cat's feet hammered at the partially detached front windshield. He leaned down and grabbed the window's edge, helping her rip it away from the car. As Cat slid her body out of the vehicle, more rounds struck the bottom of her car. She scrambled through the window, yelling out in pain as the shattered glass pieces in the window frame cut into her leg. Cat pulled her revolver from her coat and crouched next to Ray.

While the trio remained protected on one side by the concrete dock and the car on their side, there was an open area on their right. Two men in long trench coats came toward them, using abandoned construction equipment for protection as they tried to cut Irish and Greye off. Irish fired at them, forcing the attackers behind the steel gear.

"You think the cops will protect you, Irish?" Guy Young's shout came from behind the blockading car. "Hell, I own them. Now let me have the bonds and that Greye bitch, and I'll let you and that photographer live."

"I'll tell you what. You can kiss my ass, and I'll still put a bullet in your brain," Irish yelled, looking over the car and seeing the racketeer's face. He quickly sent two bullets in Young's direction, forcing Guy to crouch.

Ray looked at the two women, his mind racing.

"We've got to play for time while we get the hell out of here."

Cat directed his attention to the building. "There's a dock door going into the building behind," she said. "We could try that."

Ray gave her a thin smile. "I hope you brought plenty of shells."

A torrent of bullets peppered the surrounding metal, forcing the trio to huddle close together. Cat took several shots toward the men, trying to flank them, and the men scrambled back.

"All right, we'll get inside and work our way through the building. They won't be able to rush us so easily." He saw Greye's tentative agreement as he quickly reloaded his gun's magazine.

"Alright, when I open up, you two run like hell."

Ray lifted himself and began firing at those thugs he saw. Cat took off first. Greye hesitated, then followed her to the dock door. Bullets peppered the ground near them as the women sprinted along. Fortunately, Cat pushed through with little effort, still holding the door open. Greye flung Cat away from the door when a massive chorus of lead peppered the entrance. The bullets ricocheted off the door and the concrete block wall. Falling to her knees, the bishop's wife let out a moan and grabbed her upper arm.

Cat ran back to the entrance.

"Irish, come on!"

She pushed the door wider while trying to watch the action outside. Ray let loose with a couple of rounds and started toward the building. A man in a yellow fedora stepped out from behind a green trailer holding a Tommy gun. Cat shot at the guy, but she missed. Fortunately, the thug ducked out of sight. Ray's clumsy gait slowed him, but his adrenalin tried to make up for it. Several shots struck the wall as he passed through the door, nearly tackling a large dusty crate a few paces inside the door. Cat slammed the door closed behind him.

Ray tried to push the crate by himself, but it barely moved. Cat and Greye quickly joined him, and, together, the small group moved the screeching heavy container. He noticed the grimace on Greye's face while she used only one arm to assist them.

"Where did you get hit?" he asked before he noticed the bloodstain.

Irish stood next to her and carefully pulled back the shoulder of her coat, and she took a quick breath.

Irish did a quick inspection of the wound; he glanced over at Cat, who was using the crate top as a workbench to reload her revolver.

"You'll be all right," Ray assured Greye. "It's not bleeding badly, and the bullet just went through the meat."

"It hurts like hell." Her eyes revealed the pain. However, the same expression showed her toughness.

"I'll buy an Irish whiskey for you when we're through." Ray winked as he made a field bandage by ripping her sleeve apart and tying off the strip around the wound. When he finished, he turned back to Cat, who had just completed reloading her weapon.

"By the time we're through with this, you will be an expert," he told her with a sly grin.

"You and your bright ideas. Now what's the plan?" the woman shot back.

Ray looked around the large room, heading toward an office along one side. The walls were cinderblock and the large windows high above, near the roof. A few small, grim-covered windows dotted the walls closer to the ground.

"It's the same plan. We have to stay alive. They'll be splitting up now, trying to find a way inside this place. We can look at the other entrances and block them off."

"How can you be sure the police will come?" Cat asked. "You heard Young. Someone tipped him off."

Irish stopped, his rugged face wrinkled at the thought.

"I still trust Arizona," he replied firmly. "Either way, I'm not going down without giving Guy Young a bloody nose. If you have a better idea, let me know."

Ray's attention focused on exits and windows. The cinderblock walls were a comfort, but he noticed too many windows for them to cover from one spot. Walking over to a wooden door marked with an Army acronym he could not decipher, he heard glass breaking behind the door.

"Damn," he cursed as he scanned around for anything to barricade the entrance. Seeing nothing available, he cautiously cracked open the door. Inside, one of Young's thugs was trying to enter the room through a narrow window, his leg already inside. Ray's gun rang out twice, and the hoodlum gave a shocked grunt as he fell back outside. However, another goon poked out a Tommy gun barrel, sending a hot lead trail at Irish. He barely got his head out of the way as the .45 caliber bullets struck the door, bursting through while leaving large holes. Backing away, he met the two women behind a large container filled with rusting metal parts.

"That machine gun gives him the advantage, and we can't bar the door. Let's find another place," Irish told them.

"I noticed that the overhead door on the other wall." Greye pointed across the room. "It might lead to another part of the building."

Ray quickly nodded, his attention preoccupied with the pounding sound coming from the front entrance, blocked by the large crate.

"All right, let's head to that door," Irish said, then hurried along the concrete floor. Moving past a row of warehouse forklifts, each covered in military green paint and dust, they reached the large entry to another part of the building. Ray lifted on the bottom handle before the door suddenly stopped with a creaking protest. The opening along the floor was only a couple of feet high.

Bullets ricocheted after them when a Thompson submachine gun open up after Young's triggerman finally got through the office. After scampering under the overhead door on all fours, the trio entered a dim room filled with fifty-five-gallon drums, marked *Waste Oil*. While Greye and Cat went into the room, Ray jumped on the overhead door's bottom edge and forced the reluctant metal to the floor. He looked around the area, finding a grime-covered screwdriver on the top of one barrel. The shamus pushed the tool between the frame and the roller.

"They're coming in from over there," Cat whispered in a pant as she pointed at another large door leading to the front dock.

Outside the entrance, the trio heard Young barking orders to his men.

"Well, let's give them a nasty welcome." He moved closer, taking up a position in the middle of the room with a clear view. Next to the large overhead door for equipment was a smaller exit leading to the outside. Cat took a spot behind another barrel near him while Greye crouched down behind Ray.

There was the sound of kicks striking the door, which finally burst open. Two men stormed through the door; one immediately cut down by Ray's .45. Cat shot the other hoodlum. The thug cried out in pain as he grabbed his belly, doubling up into a fetal position. However, another hoodlum stuck his gun into the opening and started blasting away, forcing Ray and Cat to keep down.

"It won't be much longer, shamus. You should have taken my offer," Guy Young yelled into the room.

Ray responded with two shots just to make himself feel better. The thug inside the room fired again, hitting the steel drum above Ray's head.

Irish waved to Cat, pantomiming to retreat. She nodded and slowly backed away. Reaching out, he gripped Greye by her uninjured shoulder and led her down the line of barrels while Cat went down another aisle. They met up near the wall at the back of the building. The only door opened into a narrow electrical room with a large diesel motor-generator. The massive equipment nearly filled the area with various sized crates and barrels scattered along the back wall. Above them was a line of grimy windows.

"Damn it; we're cut off!" Ray glanced around. "We're not going to last long without an escape route."

"Here, you're better at this," Cat handed her gun to Ray. "Greye and I will find a way we can get up to those windows."

Ray hesitated, looking back and forth at the women. Then he moved aside for the women to enter. Irish took up a position behind a concrete pillar while glancing around for their enemies. He did not have to wait long. A big thug dressed in a familiar tight-fitting suit ran to the right of Irish. He got off a hurried shot and missed. But he knew it had to be either Tweedledee or Tweedledum. Either way, Ray looked for the others he knew were coming.

Abruptly, a machine gun spat bullets, striking the concrete next to him. The ricocheting lead hit several barrels across from Ray. Waste oil started spilling from the green cans like black blood from a wound. Irish took a quick look around the corner of the pillar, glimpsing Guy Young moving forward with two of his men in front of him. He waited until one thug, a guy in a dark blue coat, made the mistake of moving away from cover. Ray's bullet found its mark, sending the mobster to the concrete.

Damn it!

He saw one of Young's henchman grabbed the hoodlum's machine gun.

While Irish held off the men trying to kill them, Cat and Greye stacked the empty barrels on top of a large wooden box crate. The sounds of gunfire grew closer, and each woman forced themselves to keep working despite the pain of their injuries. Even though it was cold inside the room, sweat started dripping from their faces from their frantic re-arranging of the metal containers. Finally, their haphazard-looking pyramid completed, Cat went to the room entrance. A large thug turned the corner, only a few paces from Irish. Then she realized the shamus was reloading his gun.

"Ray, look out on your right!"

Irish dropped his pistol and swung around with Cat's revolver. Near-simultaneous shots rang out, but Ray's bullet struck first, causing the thug to flinch. The two men stared blankly at each other for a moment. Then Tweedledum fell over face first, while Irish hurriedly searched for a bullet hole in him. Ray grabbed his .45 auto and scrambled back into the room while gunshots from Young's men peppered the wooden walls. He pulled next to Cat, his face ashen as he tried to catch his breath.

"Thanks for the save. Tweedledum had me dead to rights," he told her between breaths.

"Luck of the Irish," Cat smirked, then she went to the wall. Ray gave a smile while he watched her help Greye up their makeshift ladder. He turned his attention back to the outside of the room, where Young's men continued to close in. He shot when they broke from cover to keep their heads down, but he knew they would soon overwhelm the small room.

Greye reached the top of the stack first and attempted to pull open the sash in the center of a sizeable steel-framed window about two stories above the floor. Her injured arm shook at the painful effort, but grudgingly, the frame creaked open toward her. Cat climbed next to her and helped widen the opening enough for Greye to crawl out on the roof edge.

"Come on," Cat whistled down before she scrambled over the top of the window edge.

Irish shot off with two more rounds, slamming the door closed before he hurried to the stack of barrels. Pocketing his guns, he hurriedly climbed the rickety pile of drums, which wobbled beneath him. Trying to balance with each step to the window, Ray slipped near the top and threw his arms up to catch the window's metal edge. The containers beneath him suddenly let go, falling to the concrete and crashing into the door. Hanging from the window, Irish struggled to pull himself over the top of the sash. A machine gun spewed bullets into the door below him, the ricocheting noise deafening inside the narrow room.

As Ray finally pulled his body through the opening, one of their attackers pushed into the area. Irish looked down at the roof of a long steel shed below him. The women waited for him on top of the shed. He was still hanging on to the metal frame when the thug pointed his machine gun up. Ray released his grip just as the gangster let loose with bullets, shattering the glass.

Landing on his shoulder and striking his head, Ray let out a loud groan, then felt dizziness envelop his vision. The roaring pain in his hand reached him. Rolling onto his back, Irish gripped his wounded hand as blood flowed from where he used to have a pinky finger. He did not notice Greye crouch next to him.

"We have to keep moving."

She shook him on his shoulder after picking up his dropped weapon. Her desperate words forced Irish to come out of his stupor. He swung his body over the edge of the shed, falling to the ground. Ray landed on his feet, staggering back into the metal wall of the shed. He helped the bishop's wife slide off the shed while he tried to get his bearings.

The trio landed behind the building in an open area with a few abandoned equipment pieces next to the shed. About a hundred paces across from the building, more structures had the familiar hallmarks of barracks. Cat had already jumped down from the hut, moving ahead to find a place to go. Soon she was racing back to them.

"Someone is coming from a door over there," she breathlessly huffed while he staunched the flow of blood from his finger using a handkerchief,

"Get your revolver from my pocket." Ray nodded at his coat. He finished binding his wound and took his .45 from Greye.

"Come on, Arizona," Irish whispered to himself before he looked at the women.

"Well, we go the other way."

Irish began a slow trot, following grass and weed-covered ground along the back of the shop building and moving away from the immediate danger. As he got close to the end of the building, Ray peered around the corner of the shop. He froze.

Guy Young and two of his men were cautiously working their way along the side of the building and coming toward them. Trying to back up around the corner, Ray took a quick shot, which went wide of the mark. However, the enemy bullets came flying back his way.

"We've got problems!"

"Damn it, think of something," Greye shot back.

He tried to remain calm as his mind raced for an answer. If the trio tried to run across the open ground, the hoodlums would cut them down before they got to the barracks. All they could do was try to hold out behind the steel trash bin. He gingerly pulled the box of cartridges from his pocket, then asked Greye to help him open the small package.

"Get down," Ray whispered, crouching down as he pulled Greye down with him. One of Young's men took up a position behind the shed. Irish fumbled for his cartridges, his hand shaking as he tried to reload the gun's magazine.

"Cat, you focus on keeping those goon's heads down," he said, as he slid the magazine into the gun's handle. "I'll try to hold off that clown with the Thompson behind us."

The lull in the gun battle left a deathly quiet over the area. Irish recalled a similar calm during fighting in the south Pacific. But now, he felt even more like the odds were against him. The setting sun was leaving long shadows that covered their position. But they were still sitting ducks. Like the two women next to him, Irish prayed for any help that might be available.

He noticed the goon carrying the Tommy gun decided to make a move. He dashed behind several large rusting engines on a crate about a dozen paces away. Ray fired three shots that missed. Seeing Young and his two men still approaching, Cat stuck her hand around the building's corner and shot several times. When she peeked back around, the enemy had ducked out of sight.

The huddled group of intended targets could not hear the distinct wail of sirens approaching while Young's hitman peppered the heavy metal bin. The bullets striking the steel forced them to press close together, each praying for the loud noise to stop. Then, the hoodlum heard the police sirens and took off after he emptied the round magazine. Irish glanced up to see him running away and put two slugs into his back, sending the goon tumbling on the ground.

Cat looked around the corner, seeing Young running for the building's front with his massive bodyguard right behind him. The last thug, quicker and smaller, soon passed the two men, getting to the building's front first. Soon, their enemies were out of sight.

"Are they leaving?" she asked her comrades, her tone a mixture of hope and disbelief.

Irish carefully scanned the area around them and drifted to the corner of the structure. The echoes coming from the front of the building told him someone was attempting to start a car. The sound of sirens grew closer to the trio. Staying close to the wall, Ray edged along, as Greye and Cat followed him. When they reached the front of the building, the trio peered over the top of the concrete, which extended into the road. They witnessed the aftermath.

Two police cars raced toward the crashed vehicles near the dock. Before the first police cruiser could stop, Young's black car spun away, trying to avoid the cop's vehicle. The second squad car intentionally struck the front fender of Young's larger car, sending it into a row of the abandoned army carts lined along the road. When both vehicles came to a sudden stop, a firefight broke out between the police and the remaining hoodlums. Irish forced his interested partners to remain crouched behind the concrete with him. He glimpsed one policeman's brutal death from a hail of bullets. The large man in the brown suit tried to point the Tommy gun at another cop, only to succumb to the rapid-fire shots coming from the allies spilling out of their cars. His dying body spun around from the bullets striking him, a grotesque half-dance before he flopped to the ground. Inside the large vehicle, the driver hesitated about surrendering, and his delay cost him. One policeman shattered the windshield with his shot, and the driver lost half of his face in a few milliseconds.

Inside the back of the large black car, they heard the cries of Young yelling out his surrender. Carefully, the men in uniform, along with Lieutenant Arizona Campbell, closed around the vehicle. In less than a minute, Guy Young cautiously stepped from the car with his hands held up. While the gore covered his finely tailored suit, the racketeer who terrorized Oyster City stood unscathed.

Irish and the women walked toward the cops with their hands in the air as two more cars of uniformed men arrived. Arizona directed his men to handcuff Guy Young and then sped him away to jail.

In the back of the squad car, the racketeer gave Irish a smug grin. Ray suddenly wondered if the gangster could bond himself out of jail and back to his ship. It was something he never considered. Before he could condemn himself further, Arizona came toward Ray, and his face was red with anger.

"Damn, I'm sorry we're late," he told him. "Are any more of Young's gang around?"

"I think a few are in there; they might still be alive, so be careful," Ray nodded to the building where the first battle started. "One out behind the building is probably dead."

The man felt the shakes coming over his body while he recovered from the adrenalin surge. He leaned against Cat's overturned car, watching the detective yelled out the information to his men. Then he ordered a man to call in for an ambulance. After Arizona finished, the cop asked for Ray's gun, and Ray held it out for him. Cat came next to the policeman and handed her revolver over as well. She noticed Arizona raised an eyebrow.

"I made a lot of noise, but I'm not sure what I hit," she confided.

Her shaky hand released the weapon, and the policeman nodded. He waved over a young uniformed policeman when he noticed bloody bandages and dried bloodstains on the women.

"You take these ladies to the hospital now," Arizona ordered.

Irish put his hand on Cat's shoulder.

"Thanks for the backup. You missed getting your pictures."

"Yeah, it was a little too close for that." She gave him a tired grin, then followed Greye and the policeman to a squad car.

After the women got in the vehicle, Arizona turned to Ray. "You can go with me. That way, we can talk."

Several minutes later, the two men were sitting in the back of a police car while a uniformed cop drove them to the hospital. Arizona cop asked about Ray's injury.

"Hurts like hell," he replied with a grimace. "I'm missing a good part of a finger, so call me stubby." He leaned back in the seat, carefully placing his bandaged hand on his lap.

"You were late."

The cop looked away for a moment.

"Why in the hell didn't you tell me that Greye La Spina was in the middle of this? You almost got her killed."

"You'll find out when you talk to her at the hospital. There are a lot of twists to this story. By the way, it wasn't supposed to be a shootout with us against Young's men." Irish leaned back in the seat, tired and emotionally drained.

"I feel like a damn fool about that. Somebody jimmied the motors in the police cruisers we were using, so we only got partway there. It took a while for me to hijack a couple of squad cars."

Ray noticed Arizona left something major unsaid, but he let it go. Young paid off someone inside to hold up the cops coming to arrest the racketeer. They both knew it, and there was no reason for Ray to rub Arizona's nose in it.

Half an hour later, Irish sat inside a room at the Oyster City hospital. Arizona had the full story and the bearer bonds by the time they arrived. Irish told him about Greye's scam and the United Church Foundation books. Ray also explained someone from City Hall would smooth over the financials to keep the bishop's name out of any potential scandal.

Arizona did not appear surprised at the news, although he reminded Ray that the police should have handled the problem. Irish nodded with tired politeness.

"Maybe so, but in a less corrupt city," he said.

A uniformed policeman stood outside the hospital room, but Irish was unsure whether the cop was for protection or keeping him from leaving. He knew he broke a few laws in his scheme to trap Young. Private detective license or not, Ray considered his situation tenuous. A doctor had already patched him up, sticking a needle in his finger before cleaning and stitching up the wound. The needle hurt worse than the bullet, but it left most of his hand numbed. He was looking at his wrapped appendage when the door opened. Henry La Spina stepped inside the room.

"Mr. Irish, could you spare a moment of your time?" The big man was cordial as Ray eyed him carefully.

"I'm not going anywhere. What would you like to discuss?" Ray extended his right hand, and the bishop gave him a firm handshake.

"My wife," Henry told him quietly.

"How is she doing?" Ray asked, trying to keep the conversation from going the wrong direction.

The bishop gave a thin smile.

"The wound is painful but not of major concern, according to the doctor. But I believe you already surmised that."

"I've seen worse wounds," Irish admitted.

"Yes, I'm sure. Greye told me you fought in the war. You must be a brave man. However, your idea of handling this situation in this manner seems poorly conceived and executed." The tone from the bishop was not overly friendly.

Irish looked at Henry for a moment. "That could be. Then again, I'm new at handling another person's problem. Did your wife give you all the details?"

Henry nodded and gave him a quick summary of Greye's story, which Ray backed up at times. He noticed how the man's wife worked herself into the role of a victim with her story. It was also clear that Henry La Spina didn't believe the tale.

"So, what do you think?" Ray asked when he finished.

La Spina took a deep breath.

"I'm afraid my wife can be rash in her judgment, especially regarding her male friends. However, her scandalous exploits have come to my attention before. This entire scheme is a delicate matter, given what has occurred. You can see my problem."

"From what I heard, she got in over her head," Irish attempted to defend her. "It's not the first time in history such a thing has happened."

"I appreciate your tact, even if misplaced," the bishop gave him a half-smile. "I've heard many of the stories concerning Mrs. La Spina."

"Yeah, but you know very well that not every rumor is true," Ray reminded him. "Despite what people might say, your wife showed real grit in the battle with Young's thugs. I've seen guys take off running in the same type of fight. You're lucky that she's the kind of woman who won't fall apart on you."

Henry La Spina looked at him, his dark eyes sympathetic.

"I can tell you value bravery, Mr. Irish. However, I believe that loyalty and trust are missing in your description. The whole incident came about because of her relationship with…well, those with less breeding, shall we say." The bishop looked down at Ray's hand. "Still, despite my misgivings, it appears your efforts paid off. The police lieutenant gave me the bearer bonds, and they have put a notorious criminal behind bars. The foundation should survive, provided that I keep the newspapers from the story."

Ray shrugged his shoulders.

"I don't think anyone will talk about that. Guy Young and the shootout will be good headlines for a day or two, then, on to the next big item in Oyster City." An awkward silence filled the room.

"Thank you for your explanation and for keeping my wife alive. Good evening to you, sir." With that, the bishop shook Ray's hand again and left the room.

~~~

The man with the mask of the Emperor stared across the five-sided table at the large person wearing the guise of the High Priest. On the other side of the table sat Death and Judgment.

"You heard the commandment of the Master. The rest of the circle decided your family must make the sacrifice. When will this happen?" The Emperor's voice revealed the person's concern.

The High Priest looked around the table.

"You made that decision without my vote. Other candidates bleed just as easily."

"Are you forgetting your duties to the circle and the city? Judgment spoke with a deep, gravelly voice, pausing for a moment. Yes, we chose the creature, but you should have offered the sacrifice. Certainly, this pathetic person is of no importance."

"Besides, as an outsider, it's the only real option," Death's voice interjected, melodic and persuasive. The masked man continued, thoroughly convinced of the righteousness of his ideas. "The other people of which you speak are distant relations to the founding members. While their sacrifice may be necessary in the future, it's certainly not needed at the moment. Our Master will display his power soon; your sacrifice is a fitting tribute."

The Emperor gazed at the High Priest.

"We will work on the arrangements for your compliment to the Master. Do you agree?"

The room was silent for a moment, each masked person watching the Priest. Finally, the person nodded slowly, and the thin figure with the Demon mask entered the room.

"You have done well, my friends. Because of this delay, we will find a substitute to bring forth the Master and rid the city of its menace. It is a fitting irony that the perfect person waits for the Emperor and Death to dispense justice."

~~~

Two days later, Irish was back in Detective Campbell's office. The door was open, and the two men talked while drinking the bitter coffee, which might have been in the pot for the week. Arizona pulled out Ray's .45 auto from the desk drawer, sliding it over to the shamus.

"You might as well have this back," the cop told him as he flicked a thin card across the desk. "It appears you already had a concealed weapons permit."

Ray raised an eyebrow at the news, then picked up the permit with his name on it.

"Interesting how things work in this town."

"Yeah, it's just great how a person can have a license suddenly show up that's backdated. You're a lucky man," he said. "By the way, I heard the District Attorney is still upset with you for withholding evidence about Young. But it seems you have someone in a prominent place who backs you. It must be nice, but don't let it go to your head."

Campbell sighed as he leaned back in the chair.

"Don't worry; I'm sure it's only temporary. I'm not from this city," Ray reminded him as he put the gun in his pocket. "Did you figure out who nearly gummed up the works the other day? I'm guessing someone must have been listening in on our phone call."

"It could have been anyone. The policeman shook his head. The garage is open on two sides, and I checked. No fresh faces were poking around that day."

"Then someone listened on the phone call, keeping an eye on what you're doing, and relayed the information to someone else, maybe a cop or maybe just inside. Is that it?" Irish showed his surprise at the tentacles that Young held around the place.

"No other way around it," Arizona told him. "Don't be calling me anymore. We'll just have coffee."

"I'll make sure of it; just find a place that makes better java," Ray replied with a grin. "What about your famous prisoner? How's he taking the news?"

Arizona just shook his head.

"He made a big stink for a lawyer who is driving down from upstate," he said. "A judge will probably set bond tomorrow."

"You don't think they'll let him out?" Irish wasn't surprised, just angry.

"Who knows?" Arizona told him. "All I know is if he gets back on that ship, we can kiss any trial goodbye. Governor won't touch him. Welcome to the wonderful world of law in Oyster City."

Ray thought about another drink of coffee and decided against it. He stood, grabbing his hat from the desk.

"Well, let me know if I need to get nervous about Young getting out of jail. And, just so you don't think I've forgotten, thanks for the rescue the other day."

"Just don't keep doing things alone next time," the cop nodded.

Putting on his fedora, Ray walked to the door.

"What do you mean alone? I had help from two lovely women." Irish gave him a wink as he walked out.

~~~
~~~

Saturday morning, Irish sat inside his new office across from the building housing the *Beacon*. It was the same mostly barren room, but it looked a bit more complete with a recently wiped down desk and two used chairs, which Cat stole from J. Allan Dunn's office. She even found an old picture of Franklin Roosevelt for him to hang on the wall. The biggest difference was the sign on the outside of the office door saying Ray Irish Agency. He used some of Dunn's cash to pay for six months' rent and a painter to do the signage. Next week, he had a phone coming, making the newest private detective agency in Oyster City complete. The room in the back held a lumpy twin mattress on a squeaky bed frame. A small closet contained one of his two suits, while an old dresser that he found at the second-hand store over by the mission sat next to the bed.

The new business owner had his feet propped up on the windowsill as he looked across to the windows of the newspaper building. Despite the shop activity below, it remained relatively quiet during the weekdays. However, on the weekend, the dead silence would make a crypt owner proud.

On the nearly empty desk next to him, a copy of the morning paper lay open. The screaming headline blazed in bold type; *RACKETEER GIVES IT UP*. Irish already read the article several times, so he knew it nearly by heart. Guy Young committed suicide overnight inside the jail. Found hanging at the twisted end of a sheet inside the most secure facility in the city, the notorious gangster somehow staged a suicide. On top of that, it went undiscovered for over eight hours. Those might have been the facts reported by officials, but he believed little in the article. Guy Young had money and power, along with friends in the capital.

Plus, Young had a ruthless survivor streak. In his heart, Irish knew the gangster didn't kill himself. Ray would bet his last penny something else happened inside the cell.

However, as Ray's foot tapped unconsciously on the edge of the window, his mind left such speculation behind. Instead, he thought about daggers, particularly a wall of ceremonial knives hanging inside Bishop La Spina's house. The weapons continued to bother him, so much so that they invaded his dreams. When he woke, the shamus held had no memories other than a wall of blades and a vague, ominous feeling. The same sense he got when entering a dark, musty basement of an ancient building where the flesh on his arm went cold and prickly. It bothered him the same way the gangster's suicide did. It made little sense.

The sound of footsteps racing up the staircase outside of his office brought Ray out of his trance. He turned his head at the noise of his door handle turning. J. Allan Dunn entered the room, his thin face looking paler than usual.

"Have you seen Cat?" he asked.

Irish dropped his feet and turned in the chair. "No, not since yesterday," he told him. "Why?"

"Damn it; it can't be true." Dunn's voice cracked, and his blue eyes widened in fear.

Ray instantly stood up; he felt his panic from across the room.

"What's going on, Dunn?"

"I…I got a call this morning at home." Dunn began pacing in front of the desk, pulling off his hat, his hands slowly crushing it between his fingers. "Some guy said that Cat had a photograph they wanted back. He told me she's a guest on the *Stanley Rose* until I get the picture to them."

While he was pretty sure of the answer, Ray asked his question.

"Let's slow down here. How did they know you had it, and who wants it back?"

"It's Mark Fordham; he's kidnapped Cat. I just went over to Cat's apartment after the phone call, and she wasn't there. The landlord told me she left with a couple of men yesterday. From the description he gave me, it must have been a couple of Fordham's guys. Now the bastard wants to trade her for the photo she gave me, the one with Howard in it. The son of a bitch found out everything. I need your help." Dunn's watery eyes were pleading.

Irish felt a knot in his stomach at the news, remembering the thug with the knife who was staking out Cat's place. "I'll help, but how could they know about you getting the picture?"

Dunn's shoulders sagged as his pacing slowed. "I'm not sure, but someone knows about Cat and me. He told me that on the phone."

"What are you talking about?" Ray asked.

J. Allan stammered under his breath for a moment, unable to say anything intelligent. Finally, he turned and faced the shamus. "Catherine is my little girl. Her mother and I were nearly married. It's a long story, but Cat doesn't even know about this. The bastard on the phone just said if I wanted my daughter back, I needed to come through with the picture of Fordham. He warned me that if I didn't come through, she would end up a drowned cat, feeding the fish."

"Have you still got the photograph they want?" Irish turned to look out the window, trying to understand their options.

"Yes, I still have it," Dunn told him as he started pacing again.

Ray came back to his desk. "All right, what else did they tell you?"

"Not much," he admitted. "The guy said that Cat would wait by the podium on the *Stanley Rose* tonight. I bring the picture, and Cat can leave."

The air was thick and still for a moment. "Do you believe Fordham will let you and Cat off that ship?" Ray asked.

J. Allan stopped pacing.

"I don't know what they will do, but I know I don't have a choice."

Chapter 8: Death on the Bay

J. Allan Dunn, unrecognizable under his gold mask and red robe, remained silent as he and Irish sat in the water taxi heading to the *Stanley Rose*. Irish sat next to the city director, uncomfortable behind a grinning black mask. The entire get-up reminded him too much of the mysterious shadow figures he'd seen a few times in the alleys of Oyster City. At least the long, white robe covered him; he thought as he felt the .45 auto strapped to the inside of his ankle with some duct tape. He hated the improvised solution, but an ankle holster for his weapon was hard to find. Ray might lose some leg hair, but he felt safer if the thugs working for Fordham decided to remove Dunn and him permanently.

The rest of the partygoers heading to the gambling ship were an elaborately adorned collection of drunken men and women. Most of the women looked like they came out of a French painting with flashy and colorful hoop dresses and tight-fitting corsets, their masks delicately narrow to cover their eyes. Some husbands looked like terrible copies of the Founding Fathers, complete with powder wigs, which the men took off occasionally to scratch their balding heads. There was the sprinkling of traditional military uniforms among the rest of the men, while Ray's eyes landed on one lady. She had a knockout body and showed it with her tight buckskin custom. Unfortunately, Pocahontas looked nearly green from seasickness. The masquerade ball would be quite the event if she got sick in the middle of the dance floor. Irish turned his attention back to Dunn.

"Maria refused to marry me; she was in love with some bum who worked on the docks. The son of a bitch got himself killed not long after Maria sent me packing. But when I tried to do the right thing, she would have nothing to do with me. Still, I've helped them when they needed it. Her mom never turned down cash."

For some reason that Ray did not understand, Dunn suddenly appeared happy to unload his secret about Cat.

"I know I've not been a real father to her. But I didn't try to take Cat away from her mom. Maybe I should have. Maria was cute, but a high jumper. She liked to have everything if a guy didn't tie her down. I was just a clerk, going nowhere in her eyes." J. Allan sighed as he reminisced. "Of course, that meant she hooked onto every greaseball or crumb with a five-spot that came along."

"Why doesn't Cat know about you?" Ray tried to keep his voice down.

He did not need to worry with a burst of sudden croaking laughter from a fat guy looking like Ben Franklin.

J. Allan shrugged.

"I was just married when Cat started asking questions about her dad. You know, the kids at school got to her about not having a father and all. When Maria suggested letting her know the truth, I was still in a beef about it. I told Cat's mom that she made her bed. I might pay under the table, but I told Maria to leave me out of it. It was a dumb move. Don't think I don't regret it every time I see Cat."

"Nobody I know can tell the future. At least you tried; some people wouldn't." Irish failed to know why he was so sympathetic to the guy; it just seemed the right thing to do.

"But let's keep our heads here. Cat is tough; she'll be fine."

"You think they'll let us walk away?" J. Allan could have read Ray's mind.

"I'm not sure," he replied. "Fordham might be as ruthless as Young. I'm new here, if you remember?"

Dunn pulled off his mask to wipe his sweating face. "From what I know, he's not one to cross," he said. "Maybe he's just less public about what he does with those who cross him."

Irish realized their boat was closing fast on the *Stanley Rose,* and he stood.

"We'll know soon enough," he told him. "I bet Fordham will be easy to find since he's giving a speech for all these drunks."

J. Allan took a cursory look at the loud crowd behind them.

"He's using the ship to pad his pockets and win the election."

"Free food and booze are good ways to win your voters. Do your friends have a backup plan without your photo?" Ray noticed the fake Pocahontas now leaned over the edge of the water taxi. The girl puked up her guts as the little craft rocked back and forth in the deeper water.

"The mayor and his people always have a plan," Dunn assured the shamus with confidence. "But that won't help us here. I'm on my own. I couldn't even tell them about this thing."

The boat pulled up to the floating dock alongside the *Stanley Rose.* The passengers quickly spilled out to join with other revelers already taking part in the festivities. Two robed men held back, slowly following the group, which headed to the main deck where a small stage stood. Campaign posters and painted canvas banners covered the ship. Above the crowd, hundreds of red, white, and blue silk streamers flickered in the light breeze. Large theater lights flooded the open deck at the top of the vessel, giving a surreal daylight effect to the colorful display of customs.

Irish noticed a line forming at the side of the stage and soon saw the unmasked Mark Fordham, who stood like an emperor receiving his subjects' accolades. The guests slowly filed past the party host, giving their thanks and compliments. Electric and celebratory, the atmosphere felt like the night of the election. And the union boss stroked the egos of those passing by.

Dressed in a black tuxedo, Fordham displayed a powerful broad chest and shoulders from his years as a dock worker. His ample girth made him look like a professional wrestler. The host had gray around the temples of his thick, black hair, while his sunken gray eyes gave him a sleepy appearance. But Ray perceived an underlying menace behind the unassuming expression.

Irish and Dunn joined the line and soon noticed Cat nearby. The young woman, dressed as a flapper with a little mask covering her eyes, stood behind the stage. The clothes Cat wore, low cut and tight-fitting, highlighted her body. In another setting, the shamus would have liked the look. However, his attention quickly focused on the thug holding her arm. The lean gunman next to Cat sported a cowboy costume, and his gun belt displayed two revolvers.

"What do you want to bet those guns are real and loaded?" Ray whispered to J. Allan. "How about I pull back and start moving over to cover Cat? You can make the trade."

"That bastard acts like he's already won," Dunn replied bitterly, then nodded to Irish. "All right, I'll show my face to that union bum and make him go back to the stage. That way, you can cover both of us."

Ray started to leave the line when he felt a gun barrel pushing against his spine.

"Don't be stupid, shamus. We saw you coming with Dunn. You should have put on your costumes before you got to the dock. Just head to the stage, and we'll take you to the boss." The ominous growl was next to Ray's ear. Irish glanced behind to see two large men wearing military outfits from the First World War. The thugs didn't bother with masks.

At the same time, J. Allan Dunn felt a heavy hand on his shoulder, looking back to see one of Fordham's thugs who pushed him forward. Ray followed along, a gun poking into his back until they reached the end of the stage. Telling the two robed men not to move, one of the soldier goons went over to his boss. The cowboy escorted Cat until she stood across from Dunn. Soon, Fordham came to the back of the stage. Nodding to the man standing by Cat, the cowboy left and took up a position near the front of the stage to keep any onlookers away. Out of sight from most of the party-goers, Mark Fordham's manner changed. A spiteful gaze replaced the sleepy expression.

"I'm glad you could make it out to my victory party tonight," he addressed Dunn after the director took off his mask. "Now, let's just get this transaction completed so I can get back to my guests."

Dunn reached inside his robe, and one soldier quickly pointed his gun at them. The director froze.

"You want the damn picture or not?" he asked.

Fordham grunted, and his gray eyes remained cold.

"Go ahead."

Still in his mask, Ray walked next to Cat, taking her by the arm.

"Are you all right?"

"I'm fine," she told him, her stare remained on Fordham.

Fordham's eyes grew dark when he looked over.

"I don't like what you're implying, shamus. We treated her just fine. They just don't like people with bad attitudes. You might remember that when my boys come by to pick you up next time."

"Yeah, I have a problem with invitations like that. Next time, send a letter," Ray told him.

"You're a lucky wise guy," the wide man smirked. "I thought about having my men take you down below to teach you some manners. But I'm in a forgiving mood tonight. Once the election is over, I'm sure we'll talk again unless you get smart and leave town." The boss turned back to Dunn. "Now give me that damn picture. I've already got the negative."

Dunn pulled an envelope from his robe and handed the letter to the union boss.

"Don't think you've got it won yet, Fordham. It's known that strangers in this town get the short straw."

"Yeah, keep telling yourself that when you're on the unemployment line," Fordham sneered as he took the picture. "Lots of changes are coming to those who backed the wrong horse." The union boss stuffed the photo in his jacket.

Ray started to walk with Cat, keeping his eyes focused on Fordham's hoodlums. Dunn joined them at the front of the stage.

Terrified screams erupted from the bow of the *Stanley Rose*. Almost immediately, a massive fireball exploded, rocking the entire ship and sending people to the deck. Chaos swept through the crowd as the blast knocked over displays and tables. Panic filled the air as the costumed crowd pushed toward the stern. Then another fireball shook the gambling ship, sending fires into the night sky like rockets. Flames shot out of the open vents across the bridge, quickly catching the hanging paper and canvas displays on fire. The wind sent thick smoke and debris over the milling crowd as they reacted like cattle in a stampede.

Irish slammed his fist into a man standing in his way as he desperately pushed to get to the edge of the ship. He heard agonized shrieks from above and caught a glimpse of two people in costume suddenly jumped in desperation from the balcony area. After they struck the metal deck nearby with a sickening thud, their broken bodies continued to burn. Ray pushed forward, trying to guide his companions away from the floating dock where many people rushed toward.

As they fought through the crowd, Cat desperately held onto Ray's robe while using her shoulder to push through those standing in her way. She witnessed more horrific scenes as the wind sent flaming streamers raining down on a massed group near a stairway. Flimsy costumes quickly caught fire, giving the place an appearance of Hell. The flame-covered bodies spasmodically danced and twisted in fear and agony while she watched, then turned away.

Near the ship's railing, the photographer saw a woman dressed like Pocahontas trying to climb over the stairway rails. However, a beefy man grabbed the lady, pulling her away to take her place. The costumed woman tumbled down the stairs to the deck, where frenzied people stomped her in their panicked escape. Cat glimpsed the unmoving body, and she noticed the woman's one open eye blankly staring from a half-crushed skull.

J. Allan Dunn stayed right behind Cat, using his fists and feet to keep people from pushing him away from his daughter. His fearless need to keep his only child alive made him mean and ruthless. At the railing, a hysterical man and his wife tried to push past Dunn, screaming about their children at home. J. Allan used his elbow to smack down the terrified woman who pulled on his robe from behind. Dunn lashed out with his foot, striking the husband in the groin. The couple fell in the wave of crushing bodies as the trio finally reached the edge of the ship.

Pulling Cat next to him at the guardrail, Irish used his strength to hold off others grappling with him. He straddled the rail. Cat looked down, and fear filled her eyes.

"The water's too cold; we'll die." Cat's trembling yell suddenly turned into a scream as the *Stanley Rose* unexpectedly tilted forward when the ship's bow dropped.

Irish grabbed Cat and dragged her over the rail with him, letting their bodies fall into the water below. When they struck the cold water, the shock nearly caused him to inhale the liquid. Almost out of breath, somehow Ray got to the surface, coughing and spitting out the water that tried to drown him. The freezing, dark water held screaming and struggling victims around him. Still, Irish heard Cat's voice calling out to him. He got her attention with a yell.

Several yards away, he caught sight of Dunn landing in the water while the shamus struggled to remove his costume. His Seabee training snapped on as the man flipped the end of the robe up in the air and used one end to create an enormous bubble under the wet fabric. He tied the ends of the makeshift life vest off and yelled for Cat to join him. Irish reached out and drew her close to him. Soon Dunn joined them, and Irish had him create a similar temporary life vest. After J. Allan finished, Ray brought them together.

While the ship's flames illuminated the night sky, the shivering trio called out for one of the few water taxis circling the area. However, *Stanley Rose*'s stern finally lifted high into the air. The screeching of the twisting metal combined with the screams of those still aboard remained etched into the survivors' minds. Within a few minutes, the gambling ship went to the bottom of the bay.

The morning came, and most of those who survived the *Stanley Rose*'s sinking finally left. The survivors spent the night wrapped in wool blankets while sitting in hastily erected tents. Police officers interviewed many passengers, then released them to be accosted by reporters. The newshawks listened to the sad tales of loss and persistence while families came to the dock to retrieve the survivors.

Sunshine revealed the few passengers who remained. Huddled next to open fires burning inside large barrels on the pier, they watched the small vessels milling about the harbor. Many waited for news of loved ones. However, the boats that pulled next to the dock only offloaded the bodies found floating in the bay.

Irish stood next to the open fire in damp clothes, still quivering from the cold. Dunn and Cat had already left, taking advantage of the general disorder to avoid conversations with the police and reporters. Cat told Ray about her experience aboard the ship over the past two days during their brief time together. Fordham's men kept her locked up in a room for the time. He noticed the way Cat acted around J. Allan, so Ray assumed the woman heard Dunn and her mother's truth. He decided what the father and daughter would do from that point on was none of his business.

The shamus could have left earlier, but Irish hung around the dock out of curiosity. He listened in on the conversations and responses to the reporter's questions. When one newsman from *Beacon* came by, he recognized Ray.

"Say, aren't you a friend of Cat? I'm Stevens." The young man appeared just out of his school, but he already had the sagged, weary look of a reporter. "You came with the other passengers. What can you tell me?"

"Not much to tell; a fire broke out on the stern and bow, forcing everyone to take to the water," Irish shrugged his shoulders. "If it were two years ago, I would have said a torpedo struck the ship twice. You got a count on the dead yet?"

"No, they're still finding them in ones and twos, taking the bodies for the coroner. He'll be a busy man for the next few days," Stevens told him, thumbing toward a warehouse across the street. "Can you confirm the fires started at the same time?"

"The bow went up in flames first, followed by the stern," Ray explained. "The wind sent the flames into the decorations, which made it worse. Pretty damn suspicious, if you ask me."

"Yeah, I hear that as well," Stevens agreed, his attention suddenly on another small boat coming to the dock. The voice coming from the vessel was excitedly yelling that they found Fordham's body.

"I gotta go," the reporter said, then quickly left.

"Well, that answers my question," Ray said to himself as the troubleshooter started walking to the road. With luck, he hoped he might find a taxi.

~~~

Three weeks later, on a Friday, it was a quiet mid-morning as Irish sat in his office. His feet were back at their usual place plopped on the windowsill while he gazed at the building across the street. Over the last few days, he'd been
~~~

making phone calls to insurance businesses that might have an interest in a detective working for them when the need arose. Nothing turned up from his inquiries, but he sarcastically consoled himself that at least the receptionists he spoke with now knew his name.

He glanced over at a morning copy of the *Beacon* that he had just finished reading. The election came and went with no big surprise. Mayor Hopley and his gang of thieves kept power over Oyster City. A few days before the election, state investigators came down to hold an inquiry that lasted all of two days. When they left, their official tally of the sinking reported over a hundred dead and missing. He read that the sinking also injured another fifty people. The group of politicians agreed that the fire looked suspicious. However, the board found no evidence showing who or what had started the flames. In the end, they sold a lot of papers, while endless radio reports tried to whet the public fascination about the incident. All it did was make a load of money for those papers and stations. The case closed quietly, while the public found other terrible events to satisfy their morbid curiosity.

Lost in thought, Ray did not hear the footsteps coming up to his office or the door quietly open.

"Hello, Ray." Greye La Spina's silky voice immediately got his attention.

"Hello, Mrs. La Spina." He glanced over. "What are you doing here?"

Her long red dress whispered as she swept into the room. Greye closed the office door and locked it. She came around the desk and placed her hands on his shoulders.

"No need to be so formal, Ray. I'm here in peace. I brought you a gift."

He remained quiet, keeping his attention on the window while watching her reflection as she slowly massaged his shoulders. He could feel her energy behind him.

"All right, Greye, talk to me."

She let her hands slip away, pulling a small bottle of Irish whiskey from her purse. She sat the bottle down on the desk. "I came by to tell you I'm going away. Henry and I are taking a cruise to the Mediterranean."

"So, you've settled down and are a good wife now?" Ray could not leave the sarcasm out of his voice.

"Don't treat me that way," Greye told him as she picked the bottle back up and opened it. She took a healthy slug and gave him the bottle as she slid onto the desktop next to him.

"I might deserve it, but please don't do it, not today. We have all morning to spend together."

Irish took the bottle and looked at it.

"It's a little early in the day." He took a quick drink, thinking back to his last mickey from her.

"You and I can celebrate my departure. My husband and I are leaving for Europe, so I wanted to see you before I left." She reached down and took the bottle from his hand, taking another swig. He could tell she was trying hard not to say something. Then he noticed a red welt going around her neck, partially covered by the necklace she wore.

Greye slid off the desktop, bending over to kiss him softly on the earlobe.

"I have a case for you, shamus. Something to keep your logical mind occupied while I'm gone." She pulled a wad of bills from her bra and tossed them on the desk.

"There are five hundred dollars in that roll. It's all I have left in the world. I want to hire you to find someone." Greye walked back to the bedroom door.

"Who do you want me to find?" Ray grew increasingly intrigued by Greye's actions.

The bishop's wife turned and wagged a finger at him.

"No, we can't talk about it right now. Remember, pleasure before business, Ray Irish." She strolled into the room, where she started unzipping the back of her dress. He watched her slowly undressing in the next room, and the shamus rose from his chair.

"Well, you're making this damn difficult," Ray grumbled as he began removing his tie.

~~~

Late the same day, Irish came out of his bedroom to answer the constant knocking at his office door. He unlocked the door to find Lieutenant Arizona Campbell standing there. Ray opened the door and went to his desk.

"Saturday is quiet around here," the shamus told him as he sat behind the bureau. He uncorked the half-filled bottle of Irish whiskey left by Greye, filling a glass he pulled from his lower desk drawer.

"Yeah, well, it's my day off, and I was driving by," the policeman replied.

Ray laughed at the blatant lie, pulling out another glass.

"Then you can have a drink with me."

Arizona smiled and took a chair.

"Well, maybe just one. How's the business going?"

"Swell. I just got a case this morning. Now, what brings a policeman over on his day off?" Ray leaned across the desk, giving him a tumbler filled with whiskey.

"Something is bothering me," the detective told him candidly as he took a drink. Arizona remained quiet for a while. Irish just sipped on the whiskey.

"I still have several unsolved murders sitting in the files," he finally said. "They're driving me nuts. Somehow, there's a link, but I can't figure it out."

Ray nodded. He understood what his friend was saying.
~~~

"You said that Quincannon and Pendexter knocked each other off."

"Yeah, I know what I said. That was the people at the top telling me the official story." Arizona leaned forward, lowering his voice. "Now add in Plug Howard and Guy Young. Despite what the papers say, Fordham's people did not kill Howard, and Young damn well didn't hang himself. But that's not coming from me."

Irish sat up, his eyes alight. "What happened?"

"Both of them had their throats cut." The cop looked around the office as if someone might overhear him. "No witnesses, even in the jail, and someone drained the bodies of blood."

Ray leaned back in his chair, giving a little whistle.

"My God, what the hell is going on?"

The inspector leaned back in his chair. "Exactly my question." He downed the drink in one gulp.

<p style="text-align:center">~~~</p>

Two days later, in the early morning warmth of a rising sun, Ray stood by Pappy's newsstand, chatting about the events of the day. The newsy did most of the talking as Irish scanned the headlines, his mind in a trance, unable to interject much into the conversation. His thoughts kept coming back to Greye La Spina. Leaving that evening, she would soon be on a train away from Oyster City. However, her haunting eyes filled his mind, and he couldn't get her last conversation out of his head.

After spending most of their morning enjoying themselves in unbridled passion and lust, Irish held Greye in his arms on top of his small bed. He asked her about the line of abrasion going around her neck.

"That's a present from my husband," she sighed, laying her head on his broad, hairy chest.

"A couple of nights after we escaped from Guy Young, Henry came to my bedroom to tell me about all the stories he heard about me. At first, I thought he would kill me. Instead, my husband punished me. Put a dog leash around my neck, telling me he'd use that from now on to make sure his bitch stays home."

Ray remembered how her warm tears felt as Greye told about the mistreatment she received from her husband. He told her she needed to leave Oyster City, but she remained quiet. Finally, Greye raised her head and looked at him.

"You don't think I deserve it after how I've humiliated him along with everything else? I did worse to you." She laid her head on his chest again, looking at the recent knife scar on his chest.

"I know you'll never be able to trust me, but I'm sorry for what I did to you."

He was quiet for a moment.

"Yeah, you did me wrong. At times, you're a no-good tramp," Irish told her simply, while he stroked her hair. "You told me there was something between us. I'm not sure about anything like that, but the truth is that I can't hate you for everything that happened."

Ray let out a deep breath.

"But I'm all over the place. It's just I can't hate like so many do. I can't trust you because you were willing to let me die. You helped me when I needed it, and you also took a bullet to keep Cat alive. I consider that a fair trade between us. Not that I want to do that again."

She lightly ran her finger across his injury, then stopped.

"You're damn right I'm a no-good tramp. My first instinct is to grab the loot and run. It's all I know. We both realize that I only helped get Young because you forced me into it." Greye glanced up at him.

"Still, I had a dream that maybe you can teach me to be better. Do you think I could be like that little photographer you want?"

Ray softly ran his hand over her shoulder.

"Listen, you're more like her than you realize," he mumbled. "This damn world is full of hurt, and I think we've all seen too much death and cruelty. But I'm not the guy to teach anything to anyone. I'm just a drifter trying to forget things, whether that means staying busy or using the bottle. Hell, I'm not even sure what I'm doing here."

"I'd leave Henry if you asked me to," Greye told him. "Maybe I could learn not to care about money?"

Ray suddenly stopped moving his hand.

"I know," he replied. "You just need to leave this place and find a new start somewhere else. That would be the best idea."

"That could happen," she turned to him, giving him a brave smile. "Henry hinted I should just stay in Europe, leaving him to return alone. I could send you a telegram if that happens."

The sudden silence from Pappy brought Irish out of his thoughts. He gave his friend a quick smile.

"Sorry, lots of things are on my mind right now."

Pappy looked at him.

"I just said my wife asked me to see when you can come back over for dinner? She was pretty impressed with how much you ate. Emma keeps telling me I don't eat enough."

"Tell your wife thanks," Ray nodded. "I'll take her up on that offer real soon. By the way, do you have any books on the prior history of Oyster City?"

"Sure I do," the newsy said. "I got an entire stack from the library when they were getting rid of their old books. Some fool wanted to give them to a paper drive for the war effort. When you come over, I can bring them out."

"Swell, I'll swing by your place. I have a couple of things to finish up first." Ray waved as he left his friend to his work.

Later that evening, the shamus took a taxi to his new home. He was sitting on his bed, thinking about going to sleep, when he heard the distinctive sound of high heels coming up the wooden stairs. Since he was the only one living on the floor, Ray was pretty sure she would knock at his door. Curious, Irish slid off his bed and started to the front door. He reached for the handle after the third tap.

It was Cat, looking quite attractive in a polka dot, white and green dress. He smiled at the silly, green hat which completed the ensemble.

"Are you lost?" he asked.

She walked in with a smirk.

"Still, Mr. Hilarious, I see. Maybe you're in the wrong business. You need to tell jokes for a living," she told him. "I spoke with Pappy today, and he told me you had dinner with him and his wife a while back. How did it go?"

"Great food and friendly conversation," Irish replied as he closed the door. "He's a good man. Now, why are you hanging around here?"

She went to his desk, picking up the open bottle of whiskey sitting there.

"I have a piece of advice for you, shamus. People in this town won't be looking for help from a guy getting drunk at his desk. The same goes for getting clients when you have a crazy black man as a best friend." Cat's tone was critical.

"You forget I met Mrs. Purvey, so you find your friends and leave me to mine." Irish scowled at her.

"Aren't you going to offer me a drink?" she asked, her face turning bright.

Ray went behind and opened the bottom drawer, giving her a tumbler he pulled out.

"All right, enough of the dance, Cat. You don't drop in without reason."

The photographer put the bottle back on the desk and took a deep breath; her face turned to a frown.

"You're a damn ass when you want to be."

"And you can be damn hard to understand. So we're even. Now tell me why you're here, kid. I don't read minds."

"I'm not a kid, you know." Cat took a seat, looking out his office window. "You should have told me about Dunn. He explained everything about him and my mom. It was quite a shock, even though one of Fordham's goons spilled the beans when they kidnapped me."

"Well, it was none of my business, and I only suspected it." He sat on the edge of his desk, looking down at her. "How are you holding up?"

"I'll be all right, but I can't work for him anymore," Cat whispered. "It wouldn't be right."

Ray watched her, feeling an urge to reach down and lift her from the chair, holding her close. Instead, he offered advice.

"Listen, I'm hardly the guy to tell you what to do, but he's trying. Sometimes that's all a person can do. Give him that much."

"I suppose you're right. We'll see what happens." Cat glanced up at him. "You're usually not so sympathetic about him. I figured you hated him for all of what's happened."

Ray paused, thinking about her comment.

"No, I don't hate him. I don't hate anyone; life's too short for that. J. Allan Dunn is not my enemy, but I don't trust him. He's a product of the city." Irish stood, placing a hand on her shoulder. Cat put her hand on top of his.

"You know I could help you with your business. I have contacts," Cat told him, her grin returning. "After all, I helped you set this whole thing up."

Ray's eyes locked on her.

"As I recall, you practically forced me into it. But why all this interest in what I do? Why act like my right-hand man? I don't get it."

He saw the petrified look suddenly cross her face. Cat removed her hand from his, then looked away.

"Don't take what I say the wrong way," she told him. "You're a good guy, someone who'll fight for people, even when they're wrong. This place needs that, and I'm willing to help you get your detective work going. But that's it. What I do otherwise is none of your concern."

Irish walked around the desk, taking a seat in the wooden chair. He contemplated her words and actions.

"You won't make anything personal in this partnership; that's the bottom line, isn't it?"

She nodded sternly, her lovely eyes now steely.

"All right, you've made it plain. I'll do the same," Ray said. "I'm willing to accept help if it doesn't cost me too much. What do you have in mind? I'm not sure I trust you much more than your father in business."

Ray leaned back in his chair.

"I'll feed you information that I find, which could become a case for you," she told him. "If you land something, then I get a finder's fee. By the way, Max Brand is going to let me write for the *Beacon*. If you get information that I can use in the article, I'll let you keep the cut. It'll be nice and straightforward that way." She leaned over to pour a drink.

"Grab a glass, and we'll drink to it."

A couple of short glasses later, Ray told his new partner about some of his conversations and thoughts. Oddly to him, she believed the city would soon revive, informing him of a rumor about a new business coming to Oyster City. She even mentioned hearing about the bishop and his wife taking a long cruise together.

"No doubt, Bishop La Spina is trying to get that woman turned into something she'll never be," Cat said sarcastically.

Her comment reminded Irish about the late train the La Spina's would take that evening, and he mentioned it to Cat.

"Well, as long as that woman stays away from Oyster City, the better for everyone." It was clear the animosity remained for the photographer. Ray looked at the glass in his hand.

"Are you so sure the presence of Mrs. Greye La Spina matters in a place like this?" he saw the look she gave him. "Yeah, she's no good, but the entire chain of events since I've been here has got me thinking."

Cat, looking very comfortable as she leaned back in the chair, suddenly gave him an edgy look.

"I'm drinking, trying to forget some of it."

"Well, I can't," Irish confided in her. "Mark Fordham, the probable next mayor, dies on the gambling ship the city doesn't want around. We were lucky to escape with our lives; you know that. Those flames were all over the place, yet the state police and various boards can't say if the fire was deliberate or not. That ship was out there for over a year, but suddenly sinks when the next potential mayor is on it."

Ray suddenly paused as he mulled over the words.

"You said it. We were lucky. Probably just a firetrap that was waiting to happen, and run by a bunch of chuckleheads," Cat offered.

"Maybe, but now the foundation has its money back from the con job created by a few grifters who drifted into the city," Ray told her. "The bishop, who is from one of the original founding families, escapes with no hint of scandal. Hell, he's going on a cruise. Young tries to kill us for those bloody bonds, and he has powerful friends in the capital city upstate. Yet we're supposed to believe he committed suicide in jail. Word I have is that didn't happen."

He glanced at her, and the girl's expression remained stoic.

"How can a place be lucky to only a select few?" Ray asked. "Something in my gut tells me there's something rotten at the top."

She shook her head.

"It's like my mom always told me, fortune smiles on good people."

Irish turned his head to look at her; his scowl deepened. "You told me once there wasn't much of a difference between the gangsters and the people running Oyster City. Who are the good people?"

Cat remained quiet, but she frowned at the question.

"Worse, I have the rotten feeling that no matter who I helped, it was the wrong people." Ray downed the last of his drink.

~~~
~~~

The thick, foggy darkness of late evening covered Oyster City when Greye and Henry La Spina got out of the taxi at the train station. Taking the last train to Boston, the couple already had their overnight room ticketed and their trunk aboard. Greye stepped from the cab wearing a green dress and black-veiled cap, briefly watching the cabbie pulling the few remaining bags from the car's trunk. Her husband waved over a porter who took the bags.

"We're on the Boston train; we have a roomette." Henry showed his tickets to the robust porter, and the couple led their helper into the station, where the elevated platforms led to their train. Soon, they were standing outside of a Pullman car.

"My dear, why don't you go to our room? I have to make a quick phone call. It's something that I forgot to tell the Smyths the other night. I won't be too long."

Greye sighed, then followed the porter onto the train. They walked along the passage to her roomette. After the porter opened the door, he halted.

"I'm sorry, ma'am. It looks like somebody done messed up."

She looked past him and saw the enormous steamer trunk. The open lid showed it was still half-filled with clothing. Some of her clothes were lying on the bed.

"Just give me a few minutes to get the clothes out," Visibly irritated, she told the porter to place the baggage he was carrying on the couch in the room. "You can get someone to come back and take it to the baggage car."

After the porter left, Greye took off her hat and began moving the clothes from the trunk to the closet, muttering under her breath. There was a knock at the door, and she slid past the open chest. Just as she turned the handle, a hard push against the wood panel forced her back. Two masked people wearing black robes burst into the room. Before the lady could react, one of the masked figures punched her savagely in the abdomen. Greye crumpled over, unable to breathe, and the intruder shoved a thick wad of cloth in front of her mouth. Pushing her upright against the wall, the intruder pressed a dagger blade against her throat.

"Don't make a sound," a male voice growled as the other intruder quickly locked the door.

Greye's eyes widened when she realized the mask showed Death's caricature. The second masked figure started giggling at the sight, then came next to Greye. They forced her face down on the bed, where they bound her wrists behind her. After ensuring the gag in the wife's mouth remained tight using a towel hanging on the wall.

The figure with the Empress mask pulled a porcelain water bowl from under the small sink in the lavatory. She placed the bowl inside the steamer trunk while Death pulled the bishop's wife from the couch and bent her over the edge of the chest.

Greye heard the two intruders chant and saw the dagger next to her face. It looked similar to those on her husband's wall. Terror took over as she lashed out with her legs in a desperate attempt to free herself, trying to rise from her kneeling position. Death rammed the handle of the dagger into the back of her head, stunning Mrs. La Spina. But the bishop's wife continued her frantic struggle. The Empress grabbed at Greye's legs. Muffled sounds of grunting and groaning filled the room as the two robed figures finally subdued the woman again. They forced her back over the trunk, placing her over the bowl.

The whispers of ancient chants began again. This time, Death moved quickly, using the dagger to cut deeply into Greye's thin neck. As the dying woman's body shuddered, bucking in a futile attempt to remain alive, the bowl underneath turned red, filling with precious blood. The Empress enjoyed Greye's body trembling in her arms, giggling as the victim's struggles slowly subsided. The foul creature behind the mask suddenly quivered with orgasmic ecstasy while her prisoner bled to death.

When the blood finally quit spurting from the victim's neck, the masked intruders removed the bowl. Together, they unceremoniously stuffed Greye's corpse into the box. The Empress went inside the lavatory to pour the blood into an empty wine bottle, already waiting for the sacrificial liquid. Death began removing the clothes from the bed and closet, laying them on top of the body.

Three taps followed by another quick three taps coming from the door caused the killers to stop their work. Quickly closing the lid, Death eased past the trunk and turned the door handle. Bishop La Spina stood outside. He looked both ways down the aisle before he entered his roomette.

The Empress came out of the lavatory carrying the bottle of blood while Death pulled an empty suitcase from the dead woman's nearly empty closet. Pulling off his mask and robe, Death placed his costume inside the open bag. His thin, hawk-like face held piercing, gray eyes that matched his gray hair. Death wore a finely tailored blue suit, adjusting his tie while the Empress pulled off her mask and robe. The woman with the giggle smiled broadly at the bishop, then wrapped her costume and put it into the small suitcase. The brunette wore a nearly identical copy of the green dress that Greye wore to the train station.

"We have the sacrificial blood for tonight. It's a shame you can't be there," the woman's husband stated as he bent over to kiss his short woman on her cheek.

She smiled and lightly patted him on the shoulder.

"Carry it carefully for the master."

With a nod, the tall man placed the bottle into the suitcase and closed it, tightening the two leather straps which encircled the leather case. He quickly left the roomette, taking the bag with him.

Henry La Spina came around the trunk and sat in the chair. He watched the killer use a towel to clean the sink and the water bowl before placing the porcelain water bowl under the sink. After one last glance around, the brunette opened the trunk again, pulling back the clothes to view the corpse. The bishop leaned forward to look as well, picking up the ornamental dagger from the box. His face remained blank as he lifted the corpse's left hand. The crackling snap of bones and tissue filled the room when he cut the ring finger away. The man took the ring and finger, wiping the blood away with the small towel, before pocketing both in his dark suit pocket.

The lady's blue eyes were still alight at the murder as she watched the bishop clean the dagger. "It was so satisfying to watch the little bitch's blood fill the pan as she struggled. It was nearly as good as sex." Her voice was breathless. "That smug little tramp deserved much more for the mistreatment of your family name. She was really beneath you." She gave a wicked little laugh.

"True, but a man can make mistakes in a moment of weakness. I'm glad the Shadows could look past this error," Henry told her gratefully. "It's fitting that our master will have her soul for his enjoyment."

There was a knock at the door, and the Empress quickly threw the bloody towel on top of the body. After she closed the lid, she put on the black hat that the dead woman was wearing.

The bishop placed his feet on top of the trunk as he slid the dagger into the elaborate scabbard, putting the rare antique on the couch beside him.

"Come in!" he ordered.

"I'm sorry to bother you, sir. I'm here to get your trunk out of the way. We'll try to get it back to the cargo car, but the train is just about to leave. I can't imagine why my men left this in your room." A conductor looked into the cabin, while two unhappy porters stood outside.

"No need to fret, my good man." Henry removed his feet and locked the case before standing up, moving closer to the veiled lady, who looked out of the train window. "My wife and I had a last-minute change of plans. Just have this taken back down to the station. I've already called a man to pick it up on the dock tonight. We won't need that trunk anyway, just extra baggage." Henry watched the porters enter and get the steamer. Nothing showed the men caught on to the fact that the box was heavier than when it came into the room.

After they left, the bishop handed the conductor a five-dollar bill. "Please have a man bring us back a bottle of your best Rothschild when you can." The conductor tipped his cap and quickly left.

The bishop smiled at his guest.

"Well, Mrs. Smyth, my family's sacrifice should ensure our city's good fortune for a while."

"I agree with you, Mr. La Spina," she replied, but her eyes grew hard. "We'll make sure no such mistake happens again. There are suitable women among the elder bloodlines for your next wife. That will keep you from such difficulty in the future. I've learned it's far better to lose a distant relation than someone you decide to care about. The master does not forgive, as you well know."

There was a knock at the door, and the porter entered with the wine. He opened the bottle, filling glasses for his train passengers before leaving.

"When you get back from your cruise, along with the news about the unfortunate disappearance of your wife, the Shadows will find you a more suitable partner." Mrs. Smyth held up her glass in a toast, and Henry La Spina smiled, raising his glass as well.

~~~

Ray Irish stood in a mortuary, looking at the unidentified corpse of a woman. Blistered from the sun, the body's greenish -black skin covered the disfigured upper body. Most of the face's soft tissue was missing, eaten by crabs and small fish. The revolting sight wasn't new to Ray; he saw many cadavers in the same condition during the war. Drinking and drifting were his attempts to force such images from his memories. The coroner pulled back the sheet on the left side of the corpse. Only four bloated fingers remained, the ring finger severed.

"The body was in the water for about a month, no fingerprints or identifying marks. The killer removed the ring," the examiner stated, his voice monotone and sterile.

He observed Irish's reaction, then continued.

"It appears a four to six-inch blade is the weapon used to cut the woman's throat, but it's difficult to determine anything more with the damage to the corpse. Do you know her?"

"No, I didn't know her." Irish shook his head. His face remained a mask, withdrawn and emotionless.

Cat had left when the coroner pulled back the sheet. She was waiting outside, unsteady after puking up her guts from the sight and smell of the corpse.

"I'll drive," he told her.

On the way back to Oyster City, the car remained quiet except for the humming engine noise and tire's droning sound.

"What do you think?" Cat finally broke the silence.

"That was Greye La Spina," Ray replied in a monotone. "I've got a new case."

She paused, then glanced over at him. "I understand you want to believe that. Since I mentioned the state police found a woman's corpse the other day, you've changed. Ray, you can't be sure that's her. The *Beacon* reported Greye fell from the ship outside of Marseilles. The wire stated there were witnesses, and her husband was drinking with other passengers at the time."

He glanced at her, and his jaw tightened.

"Yeah, I checked. The ship barely left the harbor. They didn't find a body, and only one witness claims she fell overboard. You never heard of a bribe?" He shook his head. "No, she died before they left the city. That corpse we just saw
~~~

matches that timeline, and the wedding ring is missing. The body was in the water too long, so no fingerprints either."

"Why are you so sure of this?" Cat asked.

"Not long before she left, Greye came by my office and gave me five hundred dollars," he said. "She was getting pretty tipsy, but I asked her what she wanted." His thoughts went back to that day.

"Yeah, I can guess," she said smugly.

"No, you can't," Ray replied. "She wanted to hire me to solve a case."

"What case?" Cat's blue eyes examined him.

"Greye hired me to find her murderer," Irish said as he stared ahead.

The partners fell silent, each lost in unnerving thoughts. Road noise filled the cabin as the car returned to the dark metropolis known as Oyster City.

Die If You Want Praise

Ray Irish Occult Suspense Mystery Book 2

Chapter 1: A Ring and a Painting

The gun pointing at him encouraged his agreement.

"Any chance I get an explanation?" Ray asked.

The gunman slid the automatic back in his pocket and grinned.

"No need to worry yourself, gumshoe," he assured Ray as he backed out of the door. "I'm glad you have some sense. Just don't forget what I told you. No hard feelings, understand? This is just a business deal."

An instant later, the stairs squeaked as the visitor walked down to the street exit. Ray went to the office window and looked out, catching the green coat intruder getting into a black DeSoto passenger side. The car drove away, making a left turn on Cherry Street as the detective considered what the message meant beyond the obvious. He went back to his desk. Ray glanced back to the window, then shook his head as he sat in the chair. He leaned back in the squeaking chair while he rested his feet on the windowsill so he could look over the building next door. The *Morning Beacon* newspaper scrolled its flashing headlines to pedestrians above the street. The electronic news strip scrolling the latest news about a nationwide walkout of coal miners along with the dire threats of a worldwide heating crisis before the coming winter.

It's a damn crazy world.

After glancing at the office door again, Ray went back to reading his newspaper.

~~~

Detective Arizona Charlie Campbell sat at his desk, chomping on his unlit cigar. He looked at the autopsy report of the latest murder victim in Oyster City. His floppy face turned into a scowl at the description. Sydney Green's death read like a copy of the murder a month before. They found the corpse hanging by one leg. A young man from an excellent family found with his throat slit and the body drained of blood. He knew the kid had a few minor infractions, a bit of a troublemaker.

Nobody deserved to die like that.

"Are you planning on living in your office now?" The female voice came from the open office door.

"Hiya, Cat. What brings you here?" Arizona asked.

The freckle-faced girl slid into the chair across from him. She wore a green dress, and an outrageous black feathered hat topped her strawberry-blond hair.
~~~

"Looking for news," she told him casually while she beamed a smile. "You know, I've got to keep the pictures flowing to the paper."

"No, you only get photos when you hang out with the sergeant's desk and grab shots when we bring the crooks in," he reminded her. "Either come clean or leave. I'm busy."

Her smile turned into a slight pout when Arizona went back to the report.

"Alright, you've got me. I want to know more about those two missing teenagers," she confessed. "The police have been keeping a tight lid on this one."

"You're a photographer," Campbell reminded her. "Besides, there's nothing to tell. Two kids fall in love, and they leave town."

Cat leaned forward.

"You can't lie worth a damn," she said. "Jack Romano is the star quarterback on the football team, and he might get to college that way. Maggie Weber is one of the most popular girls in high school. They found their car out on Oldman Pointe, a known make-out spot for high school kids. Are you telling me they walked away from Oyster City, then hitched a ride to nowhere?"

He stared at her for a moment.

"Alright, I can't lie," he confessed with a sigh. "I don't know what happened out there. But you're barking up the wrong tree by coming here. It's a missing person's case, and they found the car outside our jurisdiction. Go bother the state police."

"Does that mean you're not working on this case?" Her question appeared framed as an accusation.

"Get off the reporter act with me," he told her. "I'm only telling you this because we're friends. Between you and me, I'm not sure what happened. But their parents came here, and I got the police chief to put a call into the state about it. They say they are making it a top priority. Even the district attorney is involved, ok?"

"Alright, Arizona," she said with a tinge of guilt. "I didn't mean to press so much. I met with Maggie's mother, and I promised I would ask."

Campbell took a drink of his cold coffee, and his face screwed up at the taste.

"Listen, I understand, but you can't come at me whenever something bad happens in this city," he said thoughtfully. "I've got several unsolved murder cases on my desk. I have enough trouble with those."

"Speaking of that, do you have anything on those murders?" She asked smoothly enough that the cop wondered why she wasn't a politician.

"I heard a rumor there's a link between the La Spina's chauffeur and that murder the other night," she lowered her voice. "Somebody cut their throat, isn't that correct?"

He scowled at her question.

"You're assuming your rumors are correct. I'm warning you right now; don't go looking for more trouble. Friendship only goes so far with me," Arizona told her firmly. His tone forced her to nod in agreement.

"Alright, I'll drop it," she told him. "How about getting a cup of hot coffee? It'll be my treat."

Detective Campbell grinned at her, his yellow teeth showing.

"I can't afford to be seen with you today. Everyone in the building saw you come in, which means everyone will know you're trying to press for information. I'll take a raincheck."

The woman stood, adjusting her hat.

"Well, it's your loss. I'll see you soon," she cheerfully stated as the woman walked to the door. "Maybe the desk sergeant will be nicer to me."

Campbell shook his head, but he kept his gaze on her nicely compact figure while she walked down the hall, the sound of the high heels tapping on the wooden floor. He told himself he would stop by her apartment soon with a bottle of rye whiskey. While he wasn't one of the high-class guys she liked to play with, he hoped a few drinks might warm her up. Besides, it gave him an excuse to see her and warn her again. Catherine was not the type to drop something. His gut feeling about the sinister similarity of the murders kept him up at night. Arizona did not need reporters discovering that someone drained the bodies of blood. He liked her well enough, but he did not trust her.

Catherine Bennett was the type of woman who would steal your wallet while making you feel good about it.

~~~

The sunshine shot through the dusty, open blinds, forcing Ray to turn his back against the annoying rays of the summer evening sun. Inside the Canton Noodle Parlor, Ray finished his shredded pork in hot garlic sauce with a fork. He never got the hang of using chopsticks. That afternoon, he was in no mood for a lesson. Sitting by his plate were the remains of a nearly empty tumbler of whiskey and water. Usually, Ray enjoyed the food and atmosphere. However, his day started rotten and went downhill since his strange encounter in the morning.

Gladys Peer, his crazy landlady, came by his office about a half-hour after the young punk with a gun left. She was looking for the rent, which the shamus did not have. He had already blown through his dough from the last couple of cases. He tried to appease Gladys with some half-truths, but Ray figured he would have only a few days before she returned. Later in the day, he tried calling Catherine Bennett, his occasional partner, who wasn't returning his calls. The last two dollars in his pocket told Ray that he had plenty of reasons to scowl at his food.
~~~

The small restaurant held a few people, and the nearby kitchen sounds seemed extra loud. Ray took several more bites, his jaw chewing like a machine, as he thought about the La Spina case. It grated on him that the murder case remained cold. The dead woman paid him to find her killer before she left Oyster City. While the bizarre request seemed nutty at the time, he changed his tune when he learned of the suspicious circumstances of her supposed death overseas.

Ray knew why!

He saw the body. Greye La Spina lay buried near the state capital. He was sure that her decomposed and mangled body was there with the rest of the unidentified bodies. All the corpses found by the state authorities along the Chesapeake Bay shores lay in the same potter's graveyard.

The problem was that Ray could not prove it. Hell, he couldn't even let the police in on his suspicions. But he knew Greye La Spina never left the United States, and he had used up most of her payment trying to prove it. His search for witnesses and records came up empty. Everything he found showed Greye leaving Oyster City on a train, boarding a ship to Europe, before drowning off Italy's coast. The police never recovered the body. Ray sighed and finished his drink.

As Ray slid out of the booth, a feminine figure suddenly blocked his path. He looked up to see a black-haired cutie standing in his way. She gave him a nervous smile and motioned for him to slide back. He retreated to his corner with a puzzled look filling his face. The girl slid in next to him. Her clothes were the latest fashion, but Ray noticed her brown eyes. He could have stared into the eyes for a while.

"Are you Mr. Irish?" Her voice had the lilt of a slight French accent.

"Yes. What can I do for you?"

He replied with a broad smile while his eyes gave her a quick look over. It was an exotic look he liked.

Huang, the owner of the restaurant, arrived at the table for his new customer. The lady glanced at Huang, and then she shook her head when the owner offered her a menu.

After the disappointed owner left, the woman placed a small, sealed package in front of Ray.

"I understand you once helped Margie Harris with a similar problem. Will you please open this, Mr. Irish? It is essential."

"Sure," he told her, picking up the box to inspect it before he broke the sealing-wax.

He remembered Margie. A down-and-out writer who witnessed a murder committed in a parked car along her street. The police couldn't find the vehicle or body, so they wrote her off as an attention-seeking nut job. It took Ray a couple of weeks to prove her story was accurate when discovering the body before finding the murderer.

I should have wrapped the case with a bow for the cops.

The man fumbled with the package as he remembered the case. Instead of giving him a medal, the district attorney threatened obstruction of justice charges against him. Only the reporter's articles about the police nearly blowing the case got the DA to back off. As for Margie, she had only a couple of nickels to her name, so he didn't get any money from solving the case. She promised she would pay him the extra hundred when she sold her story to the newspapers. Of course, the last Ray Irish heard from Margie came from a column in the *Morning Beacon*. She left for New York with a signed contract on the day she promised him the money. They were turning her story about finding the corpse into a Broadway play.

It was funny that Margie forgot to send him a check.

The painful jolt from bumping the still sensitive nub of his missing pinky made Ray drop the package on the table. Startled at the noise, she stopped scanning the room. He gave her a sheepish smile; then he focused on the box again. Irish missed her eyes suddenly widen when she glanced out of the window behind him.

"How do you know Margie?" he asked as he opened the bright red package.

"I met her at a reception on the night Margie's play opened," the woman said. "I mentioned the need to come here, and she spoke highly of your work. There's even a small part of your work in her play."

"Yeah, I'm sure," he replied sourly.

"Although, the actor who plays you in the scene is a much smaller individual," she observed as she scanned him intently before she glanced behind him again. "I was expecting to find someone more polished."

Ray let the comment go as he opened a white plush jeweler's box. After thumbing the catch, the lid opened. Stuck into the slotted purple satin lining of the box was a woman's finger-ring. It was a strange-looking hoop of gold wrapped around like the body of a snake, set with five diamonds on the back of the snake with the symbol of a pentagon. The large stones sparkled inside their platinum prongs like slivers of congealed fire. A unique design and expensive as hell, he guessed.

"What's this all about?" Ray looked at her.

"I need you to keep this ring and guard it with your life, Mr. Irish." She hurriedly told him. "My name is Orella Dela Cruz. I'll pay you a thousand dollars when I return for the package. People are after me, and they want it desperately."

Ray looked down at the ring in his hand.

"Well, you have to give me more than that to work with, sister. This thing looks like it's worth a lot more than a grand. What's your game?"

She attempted another smile, sliding out of the booth.

"I'm sorry for the mystery, but we cannot speak here. I promise that I'll come by your office tomorrow and give you a full explanation." She told him as she glanced at the window behind him.

"Please consider this valuable ring to be a retainer for your service." The woman pointed at the package. "Take a look at the wrapping, and you will discover more details."

Ray reached down into his lap and picked up the red wrapping, laying it on the table to smooth out the crumpled paper. He turned it over to inspect the inside. The document was blank. When he looked back at Orella, she was gone.

Ray hurriedly slid out of the booth after her, sending his drink to the floor. As he reached the door, he only caught a glimpse of Dela Cruz, who was already in a taxi, telling the driver to hurry away. Ray attempted to run to the street, but Huang caught him and grabbed him by his coat. The small man was swearing in a combination of Chinese and English, accusing Ray of trying to stiff him for the meal.

He glared at Huang, cursing him sharply before he reminded the restaurant owner that he came to the place several times each month. Ray watched the taxi speed away and returned to the building while Huang held open the door. The detective shoved the ring box into his pocket as he walked inside.

Moments later, the mystified man walked back to his office with the crumpled wrapping paper along with the broken wax seal in his pocket, along with the ring. He kept thinking of the girl's anxiety, and he replayed the warning from the green-coated gunman in his office that morning. Ray pondered the problem that just came into his life. When he reached the corner at Cherry Street, he decided to take a detour to see a friend.

<p style="text-align:center">~~~</p>

Footsteps echoed along the sidewalk in the early morning mist that blanketed Oyster City the next morning. Some might consider the early morning darkness and chilly haze bracing. Ray just grumbled to himself that he was a fool as he walked up to the Hopely Arts Center's front entrance. He saw Catherine Bennett waiting for him at the top of the steps. The strawberry-blond woman wore a light blue dress with a fox stole hung over her shoulders. As he closed the distance to her, the detective noticed her shiver, and the woman crossed her arms tightly around the fur. The man gave her a sly grin when he reached the top step.

"I hope you weren't waiting too long?" His intentional sarcasm caught her attention. Ray's dreams about the pretty stranger and her ring vanished at the insistent ringing of his telephone. He didn't appreciate Cat dragging him out of his bed.

"Oh, you're a riot!"

She cast an evil glance in their routine that was fast becoming their typical banter while the man grunted. He followed her through the lobby.

Cat worked for the *Morning Beacon* as a part-time photographer. Otherwise, her gold digger portfolio came from the rich boyfriends she kept happy. The attractive woman remained his sometime business partner, occasionally finding a case to throw over to Ray. It remained a way to keep him in business and to keep opportunities open for herself.

"It's your fault when you get me up at such a god-awful hour," Ray grunted. "Now, what is going on?" Her slightly freckled face kept the frown as she led him along, and he felt her apprehension.

"Reginald and his friends need your help. You're the troubleshooter for these kinds of things."

He looked around the place with a nod. Ray guessed Reginald would be the new man she mentioned the other day. She dated a wealthy guy so often; the names came and went for him.

Any gigantic building seems creepy enough in the dead of night, but hearing the faint echoes of half-muted personal conversations somewhere deep inside the building gave him the willies. The slap of his shoe leather, along with the tapping of women's high heels, on the white stone floor echoed in the musty-smelling air. The private detective came out of his early morning fuzz to wonder at several items that were amiss, including the fact no security guard greeted them.

"So, why the mystery?" he asked when he noticed her slow pace in the pale light. "Normally, I can't shut you up when you have something to talk about."

Cat shook her head like she wanted to forget something, her complexion pale, which fit the vast lobby's eerie atmosphere.

"You have to see this to believe it!"

Ray felt the tension and knew something unpleasant was waiting for him. He occasionally tugged at the rim of his Fedora out of habit. The man shuffled along with his unusual gait and slumped over posture, both permanent reminders of a Japanese artillery shell landing too close. However, his long legs allowed him to keep up with his silent partner. They passed the human-sized marble sculptures of Greek and Roman figures interspersed along the walls. Out of habit, he tried to scrutinize each ghostly white face in the alcoves, determining if he'd seen the sculpture in a book he'd read. However, the marble statues appeared out of place as he rounded a strange cubic thing that sat in the middle of the floor. At first glance, it looked like some alien spacecraft he saw in the pulp magazines linking Pappy's newsstand. Whatever the so-called art was, it cast strange shadows.

The whole place cast the same strange gloom as the rest of the damn city.

While they walked in the dim light, he fumbled to unbutton his long, dark gray wool coat. As they turned the corner into a large room, they saw a group of four waiting. The detective's stoop and shuffling walk caused the four men to mistake Irish for an old man at first. A slight man with slicked-back black hair and dark brown eyes advanced to them. Surprise crossed his face when he saw Ray's youthful but rugged look. He hesitated before he extended his hand.

"Mr. Irish? My apologies, I…well, I'm happy you came," he said with a slight Spanish accent. "I'm Harold Garza, curator for the Hopely Arts Center. We have a terrible situation and need your help. I know it's a dreadfully early hour, but Mr. Carter told me once of your help in a delicate business matter. Miss Bennett suggested we engage you immediately."

Garza's hand felt like ice to Ray, and he followed the director over to the three men waiting nearby. Ray nodded at Frances Carter the Third, who returned the nod. Dressed in a black tuxedo, the investment banker kept the same expression. His broad face wore a tight-lipped mask while deep blue eyes looked over Ray carefully. The prominent Oyster City businessman, who was also the Hopely Museum's chairman of the board, introduced Ray to the others standing next to him.

A few months before, Ray put an end to a blackmail scheme that involved sex-filled photos and letters involving Carter's young wife. Initially engaged to pay off the blackmailers, the detective decided on a different path. He discovered the hideout of a former husband who held incriminating evidence of Carter's wife. With the help of a smoke diversion started by Catherine Bennett, the shamus retrieved the blackmail evidence. He handed it over to Frances Carter, and the rich man's gratitude provided compensation enough to keep Ray's new detective business afloat at the time. It also gave him a developing reputation, which Ray welcomed as a newcomer to the city. His other benefit was Carter's pretty daughter, Samantha. Unfortunately, Frances Carter's gratitude did not extend to his daughter. Ray and Samantha had to meet on the sly for a blistering two-week romance before she called it quits. He couldn't forget that day since he felt like a fool for letting her get under his skin.

Standing next to Carter, a slender man with a V-shaped face and carefully clipped Van Dyke beard regarded the troubleshooter with an air of conceit. The attitude, along with a hawk-like nose, caught the detective's attention. As Ray learned, the art critic and a national journalist carried the improbable name of Marc Kiilu. He liked to dress like his artist brethren. Wearing dungaree pants and a green broadcloth shirt, he appeared out of place among those wearing tuxedos around him. While Ray never heard of the guy, those in the small group regarded Kiilu as a near equal to their social positions. In this manner, the art critic heartily agreed with the group's assessment, the superior air of his presence immediately grating on Ray. Killu's narrow, intense blue eyes steadily observed the detective in the gray coat as Ray turned to Cat.

Catherine stood next to a thin, brown hair young man named Reginald Kincaid, who brought her to the Center. He gave Ray the impression of a milksop, standing like an undertaker with his gray pallor, dark eyes, and black tuxedo.

Kincaid provided him with a weak, cold handshake that gave Ray the willies. The expression he gave Cat caused her to scowl while her lips pursed tightly.

You're fooling yourself, lady.

"Cat didn't give me a description of the problem over the phone, Mr. Garza," Ray turned back to his host, noting the back-and-forth glances among his new clients.

"What's happened and what you want from me?"

The curator nodded and, without another word, started toward the other end of the exhibition hall. His reluctant walk told the detective that they were heading into trouble. Carter and Kiilu followed behind the shamus, but deliberately, as if they would have preferred not to be there. The undertaker and Cat remained behind.

Walking through the darkened hall, they passed various exhibits hidden in shadows. Each person remained quiet while the noise of their footsteps filled the air. The sound mixed eerily above them as the echoes rained down from the high ceiling. Ray could make out two massive white pillars, one in each corner of the room. They gave the place a strange Greek look.

Garza came to a stop a few paces away from the column. Ray noticed the spotlight beam came from behind the massive pole, displaying a thick wooden plank nailed across horizontally. The display formed a crude-looking cross. In the harsh back light which temporarily blinded him, Ray moved aside, finally seeing the reason for his visit. A body hung from the wooden plank; the forearms nailed into the wood. The gray face and open mouth of the crucified man appearing like an eternal scream of torment.

Ray witnessed a lot of horrible death during his three years of hell in the Pacific; however, the scene made him pause.

The white marble floor had a pool of blood at the base of the improvised cross. The troubleshooter gingerly stepped around the pool, stopping to crouch as he gave a careful look at the long spear lying in the dark liquid. He noticed the spotlight deliberately placed behind the pillar and body to provide a morbid theater effect.

He drew closer to the blue-uniformed body hanging several feet above him and noted how the screams of the dying man would have carried throughout the place. Either the killer didn't care, or the victim was unconscious. There was no ladder in sight, but Ray knew the victim, along with the plank, required a platform to put the body where the feet dangled above the floor. It told him more than one person had to be involved.

Scrutinizing the body, Ray followed the large bloodstain that ran down the clothes from the stab wound on the man's side, no doubt from the lance on the floor. The trail of blood dripped across one of the dead man's black leather shoes.

The shamus noticed the railroad spikes driven through the victim's wrists into the support beam.

It was a coldly calculated, horrific way to die.

Recalling his Bible stories, Ray knew the victim must have spent a considerable amount of time suffering before he died. However, the lance made quick work of it. The whole thing appeared staged, yet somehow, he felt the scene carried a spontaneity. Irish could not get a handle on the reason for his feeling.

You don't kill an old night watchman just because he's in the building. He saw something.

"I take it you discovered the corpse. What time did you find the body?" Ray finally asked Garza when he turned back to the pale-faced director.

"We arrived about an hour ago. The doors to the center are closed to the public at five-thirty each day; however, I was in my office until about eight o'clock," Garza said. "Townsend was sitting on the stool by the front door when I left the building, just like he always does." Ray stepped over the hideous pool, which looked black in the light as he walked back to the group.

"Obviously, your night watchman ran into a killer who knows your schedules. From the amount of blood, I guess an artery got pierced by the lance." Ray paused as he tried to think through the killing. "I assume he is the only guard at night?" Garza nodded his confirmation.

"It's lunacy, sheer madness." Garza appeared to be speaking to himself while he stared up at the wall directly in front of the pillar.

"It's like some hideous joke."

"Yeah, some joke. They're supposed to be funny," Ray reminded him grimly.

"This isn't."

His gaze followed in the direction of Graza's eyes. When he saw the painting, Ray understood what Harold Garza meant.

As the spotlight beam passed from behind the corpse, the white light exposed a large, bright depiction of a crucifixion which hung on a wall across from the tortured man. It would have been the last thing the victim saw in his dying torment.

The painting dazzled with garish colors, and it looked like someone used a straw brush to brush the oils. The scene inside the picture showed Christ's crucifixion's classical image, except a vaguely uniformed man hung in the place of Jesus. Against a gray sky background and a cross of black, the pain-contorted, bleeding body in the picture stared back at the dead man on the pillar. Ray didn't bother to guess the artist's intent, but the image was nearly a dead ringer for the gruesome killing. Then, he noticed the spectators in the background along the bottom of the painting. Naked bodies wearing white, devil-like masks danced around the body. One disguise in the picture caused him to do a double take. The mask eerily reminded him of a chance encounter with a similar disguise several months before.

Ray immediately dismissed any idea of a connection. He arrived in Oyster City a few months before. The dark alley where he saw a similar mask had nothing to do with the painting. It had to be a coincidence.

"What the hell is this all about?" He finally asked, trying to understand the bloody scene.

"We don't know anything about it," Carter spoke up from behind. "When we arrived, I was leading the party through here into another room and found the body."

Ray glanced back. "Any ideas on why anybody wanted to kill this man? Better yet, psychopaths, you know of running around here?"

Garza shook his head, his voice a whisper.

"I mean to murder someone so fiendishly. Townsend is a night watchman."

"You're telling me he wasn't important enough," Ray sarcastically stated as he moved closer to the golden framed image.

Garza's face blanched at the comment.

"No, it's just Townsend was a nice guy who kept to himself," he said. "Our guard was a quiet person who got along with everyone."

Ray nodded, but his face remained skeptical.

"Was he married?" He asked as he glanced over. Francis Carter and Marc Kiilu remained like statues, keeping their distance from the display. Carter kept looking away from the sight in their strained silence.

Garza shook his head when he answered,

"No, he was single and retired. Townsend told me he was a detective with the Pinkerton Agency before they forced him into retirement."

"To live out his years in peace and quiet," the shamus commented aloud as he frowned at the irony. "Is the nut job who painted that damn picture still alive?"

He asked, trying to pull his eyes away. The scene on canvas made the horror of the reality that much worse. Harold Garza remained quiet, and his face went a couple of shades paler.

"What the hell does that have to do with this murder?" Carter suddenly snapped.

"It's showing us a copy of the crime, and someone deliberately placed the painting across from the murder victim. It doesn't take a genius to figure out why I would ask. Now, is the painter alive or not?" Ray held his ex-clients' gaze for a moment.

"Listen, we have nothing to hide," Garza hastily interceded. "I don't think any of us noticed this painting hanging there until now. You see, after we found the body, we didn't stay around for very long. Townsend was dead, and we had to determine our next steps. It's been a shock for all of us to see such a terrible death,"

"Yeah, killings can do that, I guess." Ray knew people reacted to murder differently, but he did not like the answers so far.

"Let's get back to who the painter was?"

"Gabriel Reece painted the picture, but that's not relevant to this killing," Carter said emphatically. "It just can't be connected to him."

"And why not?" Ray asked skeptically. "You've already said Reece is here."

"He's not the type," Carter told him.

"I can tell you that somebody has moved the painting," Garza insisted. "When I left the museum earlier, Reece's work hung on the wall over there." Ray looked over into a dark area across the room where the curator pointed. He couldn't see the other wall, but he assumed the man told him the truth. It would be easy to verify.

"Does Reece have any connection with your security guard?" Ray looked over the array of suspects.

"Gabriel is one of our talented local artists," Garza said. "I'm sure he must have met our night watchman at times when he came over in the evenings. We've displayed several of his paintings here. But they were never friends that I know about. You see, we use this area to show those local artists who are moving the art world forward."

"Where is Reece?" The detective asked.

Carter stepped closer, giving him a self-satisfied smile.

"I had Gabriel take Samantha out of here. They are in the Print Room. They arrived just a few minutes after we did, so he's not a suspect. He comes from a well-respected family within Oyster City."

Ray kept his temper at the dig. Carter could be a real ass when he wanted.

"How many more people came with you in the middle of the night?" he grumbled with a glare.

"Only Mrs. Rose Smyth joined us. She's in another room as well. As you know, Rose is one of the major sponsors of the artist community in Oyster City," Carter reminded him.

"It's understandable how shaken we were after seeing—that." Harold Garza interjected, and he looked visibly ill.

Ray frowned.

"Alright, let's go for the obvious question," he said. "What in the hell are all of you people doing here at four in the morning?"

Carter took the ball, outlining the night.

"It was around three fifteen when we arrived, Mr. Irish. We came over directly from my house. Earlier in the evening, I hosted a party for several prominent families," he explained. "We had a great night talking about the center and its future. Before I realized it, it was just after two o'clock. I believe Mr.

Kiilu suggested we come over to view the recent Raphael acquisition. He reminded us that the Madonna of Bogota just waited for us. Everyone left came over when I suggested a private screening, so to say. Nobody could refuse the offer, especially when a noted art critic came to town to see this painting."

"And you all came over?" Ray asked. He didn't try to hide his disbelief.

"None of you could wait until daylight?"

"You don't know much about the art world or its habits," Marc Kiilu's reply came with a tight-lipped, condescending smile.

"No, you're correct about that," Ray replied sharply, "But I've learned a lot about murders since I've come to Oyster City. There's never been one without reason. I'm trying to find a motive that might come into play here. Now, assuming a psychopath didn't kill your watchman, then maybe he walked in on another crime like a robbery?"

"But that's absurd," the curator's head jerked up at the thought.

"Why?" Ray insisted. "I read in the *Beacon* that your new Raphael picture is worth a fortune. I'm sure some of the other pieces in this building are worth a lot of cash to the right people. This crazy killing could be a great distraction from the main event."

"What could a thief possibly do with such a priceless artifact?" Kiilu asked, then shook his head at the detective's apparent lack of intelligence. "Every gallery and collector in the world would know someone stole it."

Ray stared at the arrogant intellectual for a moment. He debated how the man would handle a punch in the jaw.

"I suppose none of your society friends would purchase something under the table," he replied after a deep breath. "Has anyone doubled-checked the displays here to see if anything is missing?"

Garza's eyes widened at the idea, and he hastily shook his head.

"No, this is a large building; I haven't looked at our collection," he confessed. "Once we found the body, we were rather busy trying to determine our next steps."

Ray interrupted him impatiently.

"Listen, I'm a private detective," he reminded Garza. "All of you realize that this murder is police business. Why are they not here yet?"

Garza looked at Carter, and the chairman cleared his throat.

"You must understand, Mr. Irish, that we are in an unfortunate position. We have devoted much time and a lot of money to make this center a success," he explained. "If this brutal killing becomes public, it will cause great difficulty for the center. Not to mention the rest of us, of course."

"Perhaps, or it might become a moneymaker for you," Ray suggested. "I can see folks lining up at the door to gawk at the place where somebody bumped your guard off. At ten cents a head, you'll have this place rolling in dough."

He gave him a knowing look. Francis Carter's face went red at the thought.

"We couldn't possibly do that. Such an action would lower the prestige of this institution to nothing more than a sideshow carnival. We must find some way to keep out of any hint of scandal," he insisted.

Ray suddenly noticed Catherine and her undertaker date walk into the pale light at the exhibition hall door. He wasn't surprised at her curiosity, but he remained curious why she stayed away from the hideous display. Cat liked photos for the readers, the more gruesome, the better for her pocketbook.

"Are you asking me to get rid of the body and then eliminate any trace of the murder?" Ray's intentionally caustic response caused a stir among the small group.

"Oh, by God, we have no intention of such a thing!" Garza exclaimed. "Miss Bennett told us of your ingenuity, Mr. Irish. We're hoping you could advise us how to handle this matter with the least amount of publicity when we engage the police."

Ray had already decided on the course of action.

"Listen, Cat is a good egg. But publicity or not, the Oyster City police get very upset about someone interfering with a homicide," Ray warned them. "The cops would jail me in a heartbeat if they thought I was trying to cover up this mess. You can expect they'll run each of you through the wringer just for this delay. I'll play the intermediary if you need me to, but the police will come in the next few minutes. Now, where's your phone?"

The group stared at him like a deer in the headlights before Garza pointed out the direction of his office. Ray decided someone misinformed them about how the police would react, or they wanted to cover up this killing to save their hides. He decided he didn't have the patience to find out.

Ray passed by Carter, telling the banker he wanted a retainer check if the Hopely Art Center wanted him to hang around after the cops arrived. The stubborn look told Ray that he would not be getting any money for his early morning trip. He shrugged his shoulders and walked toward the phone.

Ray entered a room displaying etchings and block prints. He immediately noticed Samantha. A young woman in a white dress sat on a plush-covered bench near the entrance. She sat next to a young man, about her age, dressed in dungaree pants and a loud yellow shirt. A middle-aged woman sat on the other end of the bench, her gold dress too tight for her expanding figure. Ray's shadow crossed them in the dim light as he walked across the carpet. The girl emitted a frantic, surprised gasp, nearly jumping to her feet.

"Calm down, Samantha. I'm one of the good guys," Ray told her with a grin.

"Ray, why are you here?" She sank back with a deep sigh.

"That's the question I had. How are you doing?"

It had been a couple of weeks since he last spoke to the petite girl. He noticed she had changed her hairstyle. The stylish shortcut brown hair complimented her attractive round face. Despite her unnatural pallor and tear-stained cheeks, she looked great.

"That's a funny question. I'm not doing too well," Samantha replied sarcastically before going silent.

"Don't you have enough sense not to sneak up on people at a time like this?" The older woman's sharp voice interrupted the conversation.

"Next time, I'll wear bells, lady." He answered with a stiff smile.

"Are you the detective?" the young man with a porcelain face asked while he eyed Ray cautiously. He had long dark hair and imperious green eyes.

"Looking for Garza's office," Ray told him. "You must be Gabriel Reece."

Nodding, Reece waved a hand toward another door.

"In there," he told the shamus.

A few moments later, Ray called his friend, Arizona Campbell. He thought a direct call could help bypass any reporters hanging out at the police dispatch center. After only getting a couple of sentences out about the murder and Art Center, Ray moved the receiver away from his ear as Arizona loudly cursed the gumshoe.

"What the hell are you doing there? You know the procedures. Why haven't you called the police desk?" The lieutenant breathed fire through the line.

Ray took a deep breath.

"They wanted this thing kept quiet, so they called a shamus in for the job," he told him. "You know I'd look around, ask a few questions, and then tell them who the killer is. They must realize how well I can fix problems around here."

"Yeah! Well, you don't want my opinion of your reputation." The man on the other end of the phone loudly puffed while struggling to get out of his bed.

"Listen, they are trying to keep the reporters out of this for a while," Ray told him. "All the evidence remains just like when I arrived. Plus, you have all the suspects in one place."

"Well, damn it; keep your keister there unless you want me to slap you into a holding cell. I'll send someone over," Arizona told him, then he hung up with a loud click.

Samantha Carter remained on the plush bench when Ray entered the room again. The woman looked vulnerably appealing to the man. She sat leaning forward with her hands in her lap. Ray wondered why her father wasn't there, comforting the girl. He came closer to the bench, noticing Mrs. Smyth scowling at him. The old lady didn't like smart retorts from people of his lower social status.

"I take it you saw the mess out there?" Ray stepped next to Samantha, looking down at her. He didn't like how he asked the question. She simply nodded, and Ray expressed his condolences.

"Samantha, did you see the painting across from the body when you arrived?" He wanted to confirm her father's account of the events. She gave him a blank look, then shook her head.

"No, I didn't see that much. We came in late, and we found Dad and everyone standing in the hall. He tried to get me out of there, but I saw enough to make me sick." She told him her attention remained focused on the floor.

"Yeah, that stuff will do that to you. Where did Gabriel go?" He asked.

Vulnerable blue eyes glanced up at him and then retreated to stare at her hands again.

"He went to get a drink of water," she told him.

Her utterly flat voice gave Ray a gut feeling that something more than the shock of walking in on a hideous homicide affected the woman. He gazed at her for a moment, strongly tempted to reach out and place a comforting hand on her shoulder.

Instead, the gumshoe walked out of the room, meeting Cat at the lobby area entrance. Now alone, his photographer partner gave him a leer. She enjoyed watching his conversation with Carter's daughter.

"She's not your type, shamus," Cat told him in a breezy whisper. "After she dumped you, she went back after artists, people with talent."

"Yeah, that's hilarious," he replied in a biting tone. "Unlike you, Samantha Carter has class and scruples."

Cat glowered at him, but she held her tongue for the moment.

"Did you figure out anything?" she asked.

"Yeah, you're all involved." Ray shook his head with a tired scowl. "It's a damn puzzle right now. Anyway, you better hang around and have your alibi ready since the cops are coming. You know they'll be putting you and your new undertaker boyfriend through the wringer. I'm going out front to wait until they get here."

He brushed by her, going into the lobby. He stopped, turning back.

"I forgot to ask you something. Why haven't you got your news pals down here already? You're not the type to give up on some exclusive news and pictures."

"You don't know me as well as you think, Irish. Reginald asked me to keep this quiet." Cat explained.

"I get it; your boyfriend didn't want the publicity. You never cease to surprise me."

He walked away. The shamus didn't bother to look back, since he knew she was throwing daggers at him with her stare.

Ray and Cat had a strange partnership, and he still wasn't sure where he stood with her on any day. Despite her heart of larceny, he liked her in more ways than he wanted to admit. And Ray knew her attraction to him. Well, at least, he believed it in the way that she stuck with him. Always in control, Cat would not allow him to get too close. She reserved her attention for males able to afford her social climbing.

Halfway down the large hall, Ray stopped dead in his tracks, suddenly listening to the silence. The voices that once echoed in the other rooms' background suddenly vanished in the extensive building. He found the dark silence so intense that it carried a physical presence. Something inside Ray told him someone waited and watched. Then he heard the sound. Instead of a typical tapping noise of leather soles across a stone floor, the sound he heard barely whispered something different. Someone was deliberately tiptoeing across the cold marble.

The idea that someone snuck around a building that held a dead body forced Ray to pull his .45 automatic from an underarm holster. Sliding behind a large display of ancient Chinese porcelain, he peered around the lobby toward the sound. Almost immediately, he noticed a slight movement at the front entrance, near the exhibits of ancient statues he passed earlier. There were just a couple of dim lights casting a soft glow across the vast lobby, but he caught a glimpse. A shadow stealthily moved along to a place near a sculpture. Ray leaned against the display in front of him, peering into the shadows. For a long moment, nothing moved.

"Might as well come out," Ray spoke out as he took a different tack. "I've got you covered."

The response came in the form of a bullet sent his way. It went too high, striking a large pot on the shelf above him. Pieces of ancient pottery showered the detective, and he quickly backed behind the case. The shamus caught sight of the figure moving away before quickly exiting into another room through an arched doorway. He raced down the lobby to the entrance as he heard Cat's voice calling out in the dark hall. In another part of the center, a male voice yelled out something unintelligible.

When Ray reached the door through which the gunman had disappeared, he found the exhibition room filled with darkness. He quickly slid past the room's entrance, going behind a strange-looking sculpture. He expected the sound of gunfire. Instead, silence covered the area except for the sound of his winded breath. Nothing stirred in the shadowed room.

After a moment, his eyes adjusted to the blackness, and he determined his location inside a room. Filled with unusual displays which cast weird looking shadows, the shamus worked his way through the room, keeping close to the wall.

Despite feeling like a blind man searching for a needle in the sizeable area, he discovered as much as possible in the next few minutes. As he meticulously moved and slipped behind various displays, Ray determined the Center's layout. It held four or five exhibition rooms, each connected to the main lobby. Like a deadly maze, the place had multiple doors into other small spaces, most of which joined the main hall. Anyone could have popped off a shot and quickly ducked behind the numerous exhibits and floor displays. When Ray finally got back to the center of the main lobby, the suspects stood under the pale light of a single overhead lamp. The group, gathered in a circle, looked like they were waiting for someone to tell them what to do next. Only Cat was missing. The group gawked at the troubleshooter's gun, still in his hand.

"What in the hell were you shooting at?" Carter demanded as he stared at the man's hand.

"I didn't take a shot. But someone took out one of your vases by aiming at my head." Ray stated.

Garza went pale at the announcement. His expression confirmed the man was more concerned about losing an ancient artifact than the death of a certain private detective.

"I noticed someone sneaking across the lobby," Ray said as he looked over the group. "When I warned them to stop, they sent a bullet my way."

"The murderer?" Reece gasped. "Is he still here?"

"Maybe," Ray told them as he holstered his gun.

"Whoever took the pot shot at me might have gone out through the front door, but I probably would have seen that. Or they might have slipped out through a window or other exits I'm not aware of."

"But every window and door has an alarm," Garza told him.

Ray scratched his head at the news. Neither scenario seemed likely. He carefully observed those standing around him.

"Then, the person who took the shot is in this lobby right now," he said.

Garza looked apprehensively at the surrounding shadows, but Kiilu instantly realized what Ray suggested. He gave another one of his smiles, which made Ray want to smack the man's face.

"Are you accusing one of us?" he hummed.

"No accusations, just following the logic," Ray told him with a scowl. "Now, where were all of you when you heard the gunshot?"

Their answers didn't clarify anything. Reginald stated he was talking with Mrs. Smyth, who confirmed the man's story. Reece explained he was in the bathroom before he hurried back into the room. Kiilu claimed to have been studying the Raphael painting he had come so far to see.

Ray turned to Carter. With an air of superiority, he stated he called the police chief from a smaller office in the rear of the building. From the look on Frances Carter's face, he didn't get very far with the head of the police about keeping the murder quiet.

Samantha Carter told Ray that she and her father had been sitting on the bench when the shot rang out. Before he could question her further, the sound of sirens coming from outside the building signaled the police had arrived.

Chapter 2: Suspects Everywhere

As events unfolded at the Hopley Art Center, eight figures in white robes walked in the darkness on the other side of the city. The masked line followed a familiar footpath from the large chateau at the top of the hill. They followed the light of a single lantern, which guided them down from Andres Hill toward a massive catacomb. The white stone structure sat amid thick rows of ancient oaks and scattered headstones near the chateau. Hidden from the seldom-used street by the unmaintained brush which encircled the estate, the catacomb remained silent. One masked person struggled to pull open the iron gate. The screeching of rusting metal across the marble caused an owl to flap away in the night.

A ringing of fumbling keys cut through the air, followed by the scraping of a wooden door opening. The person carrying the lantern entered first. The figure walked past a polished coffin, going to the back, where two naked captives waited. Chained to the wall, the prisoners, one young male and a young female, immediately pulled at their bindings with the sound of footsteps coming toward them. Burlap sacks covering their faces twisted back and forth.

The eight masked figures looked over their captives as another lantern came to life, filling the gloomy room with a yellow light. The garishly painted masks thoroughly covered the face of each of the participants. Each disguise captured the image of the wearer's position within the cult. Large openings for mouths looked like a smile or a grimace, barely exposing the wearer's lips.

Death and Judgment stepped forward to release the male, each taking an arm to force the captive over a long stone bench. Their prisoner tried to resist, his gagged mouth giving a muffled yell. Death viciously struck his captive in the lower back several times, and the young man went to his knees. The two robed men dragged him to the bench, forcing the man over the cold stone slab on his belly. The prisoner's covered head faced an ancient crypt of stone with the name of Henry Andras.

As they tied his wrists and ankles under the bench, the masked figure of the High Priestess untied the young woman from the wall. With the help of the Empress, they forced the captive across the short slab. The young woman groaned in pain when her abusers tied her wrists and ankles together under the stone bench. The Empress looked down on her prisoner and fondled the captive's breasts.

"You like that bridge position in gymnastics," she laughed when the girl's body twisted from the pain and humiliation while she mumbled under her gag.

The capturers stopped tormenting their prisoners at the familiar squeaking noise of a wheelchair. A tall man in black, his pale face impassive, carefully guided the chair carrying a frail woman. The woman wore the mask of a demon. He helped her rise from the chair and gave her a silver-handled cane. They walked between the naked prisoners, but the shriveled figure under the red robe paid little attention to the captives. Instead, the old woman pulled a deck of cards and placed them on the stone. Shakily, she kneeled, using her cane for support.

"It is another new moon to make offerings to our master," the demon said to the group. The female voice was both ancient and controlling. "Mr. Wolfe, please pass around the wine."

The tall man wearing a stovetop hat nodded and quietly pulled a wine bottle from his coat's side pocket. He gave the bottle to the man with the Emperor's mask.

"Drink the sacramental wine to consecrate this new moon," the demon told him. "It comes to replenish the month just as we seed the innocent. The master welcomes Eisheth, Agrat Bat Mahlat, and Naamah on nights such as this."

The Emperor took a deep drink before passing the bottle. As each member consumed the blood-tainted wine, the woman in the demon mask shuffled her tarot cards on the bench. When she finished, the demon leaned back in the chair.

"My friends, it's time to enjoy ourselves with those meant to serve us. It is like the demon commands," she told them. She leaned back to watch the man in the mask of Death open his robe to reveal his erect penis. He positioned himself behind the male prisoner while the Emperor reached down and struck the captive across the back with a belt. The prisoner yelled a desperate muffled howl.

As the torture continued, the clammy atmosphere drank in the despair and violence that quickly filled the gloomy room. The robes fell away as the masked group split up to join in the young couple's forced debauchery. The captives resisted at first. Their screams and shrieks echoed when they felt the lash of leather across their bodies.

The woman behind the Demon mask heard the giggle coming from the other side of the bench. She frowned, glancing to see the High Priestess pull off the burlap sack from the female captive. The young girl had long brown hair and pretty eyes. The High Priestess removed the gag.

"What do you want?" A petrified voice struggled out of the young girl.

The High Priestess slapped her hard across the face several times.

"You'll remain quiet while you please your betters. We have plenty of night left, and I am going to enjoy every minute," she told her victim. She pulled back her white robe to reveal her lean body and sagging breasts.

On the other side of the bench, the woman wearing the Empress mask raked her long nails raked down inside of the girl's thighs. The action brought a pitiful cry along with trickles of blood from scratches. The girl relented at the abuse, letting her body go limp.

"Don't stop fighting, my little bitch. I like it when they fight," the icy voice of the Empress cackled as she dug her nails deeply into the thighs again. The anguished cry made the woman smile under her mask.

Amid the grunts and sobbing, mixed with the rhythmic slap of flesh, the Demon calmly sat on a pillow brought by her pale-faced attendant. As her servant lit candles next to her, she went back to her tarot cards. The old woman chanted homages to their master while she slowly turned over nine cards. Each card lay in a precise spot to reveal the past, present, and future of the Shadows. A sudden groan of pleasure, followed by the sound of slaps, occurred next to her when she turned over the Knight of Swords' card. The sight gave her pause, and she frowned again inside the demon mask. A gallant stranger kept reappearing in her deck as she lay out the pattern.

It was a bad sign!

There was an anguished cry from the male prisoner next to her, quickly followed by vicious punches from a man in the Judgement mask. The captive began crying as he accepted his next rape.

Finished for the moment, the person wearing the mask of Death leaned his back against the tomb. While he enjoyed the surrounding depravity, he placed a lit cigarette into the lip of the cover he wore. His eyes followed the tall naked figure of the woman wearing the Empress mask. She pulled up a small whip and began beating the female with it. After each lash, the victim's muffled screams only enticed the abuser to continue as the welts started to bleed.

On the other side of the bench, a whistled tune came from the High Priest's mask when he stood over the young man. The old woman wearing the demon guise nodded in time with the melody. It reminded her of when she was young and able to take part in her cult's merciless orgies. She turned over the last card and smiled when she placed the Devil card face up on the bench.

"My flock, our fortune continues. The tarot cards tell us this night is successful. As you remember, the rare blue blood super-moon will occur later this month. The master will come forth and give no quarter to those we battle," she told the group triumphantly. "The same knight appears before us, but the master will break him. Mental anguish and confusion await the dreams of our enemies while prosperity and wealth continue to rain upon us during the next month."

One of the masked figures gave a joyful cheer at the news as he passed along the bottle of wine to the Demon, who closed her eyes. The brutality would continue, then a blood sacrifice to Andras. As she listened to the sounds of the rapes, she slid her hand between her legs after taking a drink.

"Mr. Wolfe, you may entertain yourself with our male prisoner once the Shadows enjoy their pleasures," she told the stoic man behind her. "Then you may release him to our friends. Tonight, the girl will give us blood."

Mr. Wolfe remained quiet. His dark eyes took in the candle-lit scene. The new moon always meant one would live, and one would die within the tomb. The Chesapeake Bay would dispose of the girl's body. He knew well the verse from a book of their ancient creed.

Come to each new moon, deflower the children.
Suckled blood and wine brought forth dead kindred.
Andras, the winged angel sowing discord
Nightmares and death are poured

~~~

Lieutenant Montgomery Sirk sailed into the Hopely Center lobby with several policemen and Catherine in tow. The detective's perpetually grumpy face looked over the stylishly dressed crew of suspects. Then, he issued orders to his men to secure the building before turning to Ray.

"I got a call from Lieutenant Campbell about murder here," Sirk told Ray. "I'm not happy about this shamus. First, you bypass police procedures; then, I get hauled out of bed. Cat just told me she called you, but it don't make it right."

Sirk pulled a handkerchief from his coat pocket to wipe his bulbous nose.

"Sorry, a damn cold is coming on," he said. "Anyway, show me what you got."

When they reached the corpse, the cop turned a pale shade of green.

"Damn bad killing, alright. What have you got so far?" Sirk turned to Ray after he let Catherine retreat to find her date.

The policeman clasped his hands behind his back, listening to the shamus detail his version of the events. Sirk's potbelly extended from his gray suit coat as he paced. Ray told the policemen what he knew, including his escape from a bullet that took out an ancient vase. He also explained his theory about Raphael's painting, which raised Sirk's eyebrow. The policemen pulled a pocket notebook to enter his notes. The lieutenant kept up his annoying habit of clicking his tongue after Ray completed each sentence. After he finished his story, the cop put the notebook away.

"I see the hideous art up on the wall, but what about this Raphael painting you brought up?" He asked. "Did you check on it?"

Before Ray could open his mouth, Garza interjected.

"We tried to assure the private detective that the masterpiece had nothing to do with this murder. I did a quick walkthrough of the center, and nothing seems to be out of order. However, if it eases your concerns, please come with me."

The director led them across the large room, where a sign directed them to the Master's Gallery. As they passed the open entrance, the painting in question hung in the middle of an otherwise empty wall. Garcia found a switch that immediately sent a soft beam of light down from the ceiling, showing the painting
~~~

remained untouched. While the small group moved into the room, Ray recalled the paper's recent article about the item.

The Hopely Arts Center, initially established as an extension of the main museum, became an artistic attraction. To display the homegrown talent, Paul Smyth, a wealthy outcast of one of the city's founders, left Raphael's masterpiece to the art center.

When the display opened several weeks ago, the price tag on the painting, along with plenty of positive press coverage, sent the town into a publicity frenzy. Those who couldn't tell a Titian from a Rube Goldberg became instant experts on the past masters of the art world.

As he looked at the Raphael painting, Ray noticed the small sized masterpiece couldn't have been more than a couple of feet wide. Madonna and Child, painted in subdued blue, brown, and gold colors, appeared nearly new under the light. If pressed, the detective would have guessed the artist painted the canvas yesterday.

Sirk pulled a handkerchief from his pocket and blew his nose, cursing under his breath.

"Well, at least you have your painting. I suppose it looks pretty good, although one hundred and twenty-five thousand dollars is a lot of cabbage for that thing." The policeman remained unimpressed.

"You're amazed because the painting is so small. Yet, you're surprised the value of such artwork remains so high?" Kiilu asked with a patronizing smile. "You are missing the point. Jan Van Eyck's Madonna is only six inches by nine and recently valued at over a quarter of a million dollars in New York. You should not value something only by size. Raphael created this piece over six hundred years ago, yet his work remains fresh and vibrant. Note the perfection of the lines and the form, the clean…"

"Yeah, I get it," the policeman said dismissively. "It's a fancy piece of work worth a hell of a lot of dough. Now, I want statements from all of you witnesses."

Sirk told one of his uniformed officers to find a room for the interviews, and Garza suggested his office. Nodding, the police lieutenant ordered the group of suspects to the office. Mrs. Smyth and Francis Carter objected.

"Since it's nearly daylight, I believe we should meet at your office sometime later today to give you these statements," the banker told Sirk. "I mean, it's obvious that none of us had anything to do with the unfortunate guard."

"Mister Carter, it's too bad you feel that way," Sirk said with a bemused scowl. "However, if it makes you happier, I'm pleased to inform you that everyone in the building is a suspect until I say otherwise. That means you get to watch the sunrise with the rest of us."

As everyone began walking to Garza's office, Sirk took Ray aside.

"I want you to hang around after you sign your statement," he told him. "The police commissioner has already called me after Carter spoke to him. I might you're your collaboration with the statements coming out of this crew. Call it a gut feeling, but I doubt I'll get the full truth from some of them." Ray nodded, then followed the policeman to the office.

Several hours after dawn, Lieutenant Sirk finally released the last of his suspects from the smoke-filled office. He told those waiting in the lobby they could leave as well. Ray observed the scene while looking over a colorful abstract painting that looked like splotches of paint thrown at the canvas.

Striding towards the entrance as he sipped on another cup of lousy coffee he scrounged up, Ray noticed Garza and Kiilu heading out of the front door together. Their animated conversation probably centered on the famous painting inside. Fortunately for them, the police commissioner must have kept things quiet for the moment since no newshawks waited out front. Rose Smyth frantically puffed on a cigarette as she quickly hurried out, her thin pencil legs rapidly pacing across the marble floor.

As Ray neared the director's office, he got sight of Samantha Carter walking between her father and her boyfriend. By the large entrance doors, she glanced back and noticed him staring at her. Her lips parted slightly, like the woman remembered something. For a moment, Ray wondered if she might pull away from her escorts. However, Samantha Carter only hesitated for a brief second before the group pushed through the doors and into the sunlight.

He was about to leave his cup perched on top of a display case and follow the woman. Something in Samantha's eyes appeared to ask for assistance. But Lieutenant Sirk called out for him.

"Irish, come on in here."

The cop leaned back in an uncomfortable-looking art déco chair that sat behind a chrome-plated desk. He nodded for Ray to take a seat inside the stuffy room.

"Do you think Cat Bennett called you to protect that character she's with?"

Sirk had fingers locked together across his belly. He was looking through the large office window at Catherine, who had her arm hooked with Reginald Kincaid's. They headed toward an extensive black limousine waiting for them.

Ray shook his head as he sat.

"Hard to figure out women," he confessed. "Cat is the one that helped me with a couple of cases. Who is the guy she's running around with?"

The policeman's eyes bulged at the question.

"You don't know the Kincaid's? That's the family who got rich in that old ammo factory out by the base during the war," he explained. "Now, his daddy is a politician up at the statehouse. His kid is one that all the ladies want to take to the altar. I didn't figure Cat was that way. That's why I wondered if she got you in here to help protect Reginald."

Ray took a sip of the bitter coffee, raising an eyebrow at the thought. He sat the cup down on the desk and pushed it away.

"Need some whiskey in it," he said as he turned his attention to Sirk. "Since I've hit this city, the one thing I've learned so far about Cat Bennett is she's a complex piece of work. But I'll lay money that she's got no motive to bump off a night watchman or help her date to do it."

"Yeah, I don't think she's the type," Sirk agreed. "However, I need to tie off some things bothering me." The man thumped his belly.

"What do you think about this murder?"

Ray looked at him carefully. The detective was one of the few honest cops around, but he remained set in his ways about private detectives. The guy didn't have a lot of imagination. But at least, Sirk didn't treat him like he was a leper.

"From where I'm standing, Garza is the last to leave Townsend alive at eight; at least he says he did. Of course, this could mean the curator might have done the job before leaving. You'll figure that out during the autopsy. I guess Garza would be the most likely suspect since he's the last to see the victim alive. But we don't have a motive."

"Boy, you're a barrel of the obvious," Sirk told him sourly. "You know he couldn't haul that watchman up by himself. There's more than one involved in this killing, that's for sure. My guys think they figured out that the beam that the body was hanging on came from one of the storage lockers downstairs. A heavy mallet down there had blood on it, so they'll send it out for testing. The killer pulled a couple of those spikes from that weird art display on the floor."

Ray nodded.

"Yeah, after you sent me away, I hung around watching your men. It confirms the killer had to know this building pretty well, and they had to know the materials were available."

"The whole thing stinks just as bad as some of the alibis I heard." The cop rubbed his temples. "You heard Carter claim he was alone all afternoon and then at the banquet, which started at nine o'clock. He's off the list unless he somehow left early to kill the guy in the thirty minutes from the time Garza left."

"Yeah, that would be hard, but not impossible," Ray replied thoughtfully.

Sirk nodded at the observation.

"Then, there's that art critic Kiilu, a self-absorbed jerk. But I guess I can't arrest him for that. There's no motive. He's probably out unless I can find out something different," the policemen sniffed.

"Claims that he's only been in town a couple of weeks. He's staying at the Hotel Alexander. Unfortunately, he's got a good alibi as well. Kiilu was at Carter's party for a good chunk of the time with plenty of witnesses."

"Why has he been waiting around the city for so long?" Ray asked with a yawn. "I thought he came to see that darn painting everyone is so enthralled with?"

The lieutenant shook his head.

"He told my sergeant that he's doing some background for a column about the Hopely Art Center. According to Garza, Kiilu spent his time with many local artists in the city," he told Ray.

"I thought it was strange that Kiilu didn't bother to come to the Art Center until after Carter's party. Then again, everyone says he's a weird bird. They say he can pick out the next Rembrandt for the art world. Plus, his articles go out nationally, so I can't see where he has any motive to knock off some security guard."

Ray agreed with a nod before asking about Reginald Kincaid. The policeman gave him a grin.

"Yeah, you stepped out when I spoke with him. Mr. Kincaid has a pretty solid alibi," Sirk told him. "Miss Bennett, along with all the servants at the Kincaid mansion, can vouch for him. They were having dinner until late at the estate before going to Carter's party. I guess money could make people be your defense, but I don't see any motive there."

Ray gave another faint nod, remembering Cat's preference for cash.

"What about the Smyth woman? Carter mentioned she didn't like how Townsend treated her when she showed up early," he said. "Does she have an alibi?"

Sirk laughed at the question. "Mrs. Rose Smyth is an eccentric daughter of the man who donated the Raphael painting. You read about him in the paper enough times," he said. "But you're fishing in the wrong hole. You saw her; do you think she'll be dragging a guy up on that lumber for an execution? Anyway, I'm wasting time considering those involved with the Hopely Center. They don't seem to have any motive."

Ray leaned back.

"I don't know about that. Garza told me they were afraid of the publicity," the shamus observed. "You know the headlines blast out articles about this art center for a while now. Not that I believe it, but publicity might be a motive for everyone to be in on this."

Sirk thumped his belly with a laugh.

"Boy, that's an idea as crazy as the murder. That group of socialites is running scared at the thought of reporters shaming their proper names," he said. "The Smyths and Carters have been in this city forever. Why do you think Carter called the police commissioner? Your idea is just too weak as a motive. The only one left is Gabriel Reece."

"And Samantha Carter," Ray reminded him.

Sirk raised his eyebrow.

"She's a small woman, not much bigger than Rose Smyth," he said. "Yeah, I know Reece is pretty small as well. He couldn't lift Townsend alone."

Ray shot him a surprised expression.

"You're telling me a woman can't be the murderer? You can bet that someone had to know their way around here as well," he reminded Sirk. "The killer didn't just find a piece of wood and tools by luck. You just said it took two people, at least."

"That's right, I did," Sirk said as he drummed his fingers on the desk. "You know that Miss Carter was too willing to help cover for her boyfriend. She kept jumping to his defense every time my sergeant tried to get explanations about some of his vague answers. Neither of them has much of an alibi, either. You heard him tell us he was alone in his apartment painting until it was nearly time to leave for Carter's party." Sirk leaned across the desk.

"But I've got something interesting on Reece, which plays into my hands."

"You've got some reasoning behind this crazy murder?" Ray glanced over.

"There always is," Sirk declared with smug satisfaction. "You were going up the wrong tree with your ideas. Reece is the only one that benefits from this murder."

"How so?" Ray asked the cop as he suppressed another yawn.

"While my man was taking down their statements, Cat gave me the name of Jude Davis, who writes that art column for the *Beacon*," Sirk replied. "I called Davis, and he told me this Gabriel Reece was just another amateur until a year ago, annoying people in his attempts to get noticed. The top dog at the time was this guy named Felix Roman. I guess they considered him to be the next Michelangelo, but Felix disappeared after he'd got back from the war. Roman was so much ahead of the others that Reece could only move himself up in the pecking order when the other guy disappeared. Still, while Reece might be the best artist around here, but nobody would know. This city ain't New York or LA."

"Let me guess where you're going," Ray told him as he tipped back his hat. "Reece used his painting of the Crucifixion as the model for Townsend's killing. Once the newspapers get ahold of this, his name and his artwork will spread around the country. Hundreds of newspapers and magazines play up the connection with the murder, and suddenly, Reece will be famous. Is that it?"

Sirk leaned back in the chair with a smile.

"Got any other motive that's possible?"

"No, I can't think of anything beyond what I said earlier. It's a hell of a way to get people's attention if you ask me," Ray said. "I don't buy the idea that Samantha is involved. I know her, and she's not the type."

"Yeah, she mentioned she knew you from your work with her dad. But don't be getting any ideas about covering for her," Sirk warned him.

"If I wanted to do something like that, I would have done it before you showed up," Ray replied as his eyes narrowed. "She would have never been here, and alibis would have covered for her."

He paused while Sirk leaned back at the thought.

"I'm just telling you, she's just a kid, not even close to a person who kills someone. Besides, you saw how nervous she was," Ray reminded the cop. "You can bet that she was sticking up for her friend. It happens all the time."

Sirk's scowl deepened as he went quiet for a moment.

"Alright, I hear you, shamus. But I'm warning you to keep all of what I told you under your hat, Irish," he told him. "I can't pinch Reece just because I've got a beautiful start to a theory. If you're wrong about that little Samantha helping him, I need to have hard evidence to go along with the facts. The Carter family carries weight around this city."

"Yeah, Sirk, I understand," Ray said.

"You're new to Oyster City," Sirk reminded him. "Old families mean a lot around here."

Ray raised an eyebrow at the comment.

"Yeah, I've already run into that," he replied. "I don't need those folks throwing rocks my way. Anyway, I'm going home. Just another wasted night for me, from what I can see." He gave another enormous yawn before he got up from the chair.

~~~

It took two trips around the block for Ray to find a parking spot along 4th Street near his office. The *Beacon* building shaded the street below from the early morning sun. Most of the morning pedestrians were already inside their workplaces. Ray walked toward his office building, looking forward to sleep. His office's backroom provided him with an apartment of sorts, and he looked forward to the hard bed. The sound of his footsteps echoed in the narrow hall that led him upstairs. When he reached the top of the stairs, he stopped. The door to his office stood open. Automatically pulling his gun, the shamus crouched and slid next to the door. Slowly, he peeked inside. He noticed a pair of shapely legs first and followed them up to the woman sitting in a chair by his desk. Then, Ray observed the woman's companion, a small balding man with wide eyes carefully watching the gun. Ray kept the weapon pointed at them.

"I won't apologize about the gun," he entered his office cautiously. "I locked the door when I left."
~~~

The male visitor was short, round-faced, and plump. He held a small bag of peanuts in his hand like a little boy at a circus. His black suit and tie gave him the look of an accountant.

On the other hand, the female carried a shapely body, but her angular face coldly analyzed him with piercing blue eyes. Her blue dress shouted designer fashion, but Ray was no expert. He did notice the woman was a stunner. However, she also carried the air of supremacy, which immediately made him dislike her.

"We're sorry for the intrusion, Mr. Irish, but we must talk with you tonight." The husky female voice took charge as she slid one hand through her long blonde hair, pulling it over her shoulder. Ray decided it was a nervous habit.

"We would like to engage your services," she said.

"First, explain who picked the lock?" He asked, after glancing at the undamaged door.

"We simply had a friend of ours swing by and open the door for us," she replied airily. "It's so much better than waiting out on those dirty stairs for you."

"Yeah, I'll get my maid to sweep up next time," He grunted out sarcastically. "Listen, I'm tired and not in the mood for games. Who are you, and what do you want?"

She gave him a pleasant smile, but her eyes weren't friendly. "I'm Maria Andras. I'm sure you've heard the family name before. This is my cousin, Johann Weyer. As we stated earlier, we would like to hire you to find a misplaced object."

Ray slid his gun into his holster while closing the door. Going behind his desk, he took a seat, observing them.

"Misplaced would tell me it's lost. What did you lose, and why do you need a shamus?"

Ray knew the Andras name well enough. The family founded Oyster City, and members of the family still ran around like they owned it.

Maria pulled a long cigarette holder from her purse and held it between her fingers while her cousin quickly lit a match for her. Ray noticed one of her long manicured fingernails contained a broken nail. She inhaled deeply and blew smoke across his desk.

"It's a ring, Mr. Irish, a valuable and unique ring we would like you to find. If you can acquire the item, we'll pay a substantial amount for your time," she told him.

Ray hoped his poker face remained when he heard the story. "You have my attention, Mrs. Andras," he said. "But I'm still not sure why you need a private detective. I think you can get your maid to go through the trash."

Weyer interjected while Maria glared at Ray for his sarcasm.

"Perhaps we should explain further. A guest of the Andras house stole the ring," he told Ray. "We need to retrieve this ring as quietly as possible. It's a sensitive and very private matter between Maria and her guest; therefore, we don't wish to engage the local authorities."

Ray nodded as he leaned back in the squeaky chair.

"I see your problem," he said. "You mentioned a substantial sum to find this ring. How much do you think this piece of jewelry is worth to find?" He pushed back his fedora. He already suspected that his guests would feed him a story that might have some element of truth.

"Two thousand dollars when you return the item to me. I'll add five hundred if you can persuade the thief to return it to me personally," Maria told him, her eyes cold.

"I don't accept personal insults easily."

"Two grand is a lot of cabbage," Ray told her as he leaned forward at the mention of the price. "Tell me about this missing jewelry."

Maria blew out another poof of smoke from thin red lips, looking bored with his question. Then, she nodded to her cousin.

"It's a ring in the shape of a serpent and contains five diamonds," Weyer explained. "A quite exquisite piece of jewelry, custom made for Malcolm Andras, Maria's father. We must retrieve this heirloom."

"Who do you suspect?" He asked.

"We believe Miss Orella Dela Cruz took it," Weyer said as he squeezed on his paper bag. "She was a guest on the estate at the time, and after she left, the ring was gone."

"I take it you haven't contacted this lady," Ray asked.

Weyer blinked several times, glancing at Maria before he spoke. "No, she left early one morning with her luggage," he told him. "I went to the train station to check, but she hasn't left the city from there."

"Well, if it's stolen, why not go to the police?" Ray asked. "They are pretty good at sorting out these things. The detectives are known to keep the case on the hush for some of the wealthy families here."

Weyer twisted on the brown bag again, and Ray hoped the contents wouldn't explode across his dusty office floor.

"Miss Dela Cruz's father is the Spanish consul to the Philippines. He's currently in New York helping with the United Nations. Her mother is from an important family in Manila. It would not be helpful if a scandal started over this. That is why we're here."

"Yet, you're sure she took it," the shamus mentally worked through their story. "You don't suspect anyone else?"

"No, she made several comments about the ring before it went missing. I sent a wire to a detective in the state capital. He determined that she never arrived in New York, so she must still be in Oyster City." Weyer explained. "She's new to the country, so there's no place she can go otherwise."

"If I find her and she doesn't want to return the ring, what then?" Ray asked.

Maria chuckled before answering. "Don't worry, Mr. Irish. Orella's not a fool. She's quite headstrong, but I don't think she'll want the shame of incarceration upon her," she coolly replied. "If the girl remains stubborn…well, I've heard of your methods when dealing with gangsters. She's not much better. Bluntly, I don't care how you get the ring from her. Whatever you do, it must not reflect on our family. She is a foreigner, after all."

"Yeah, I'm pretty sure I get your drift. Well, let me see if I can track this woman down. We can go from there," he told his new clients. "I'll let you know what I find. Where should I contact you?" He fought the urge to yawn and stood.

Ray walked to the door. His visitors appeared surprised when he opened the door, dismissing them. Their expressions brought a brief grin to his face. Maria pulled the cigarette from her holder and pressed it into an ashtray on his desk.

"You can reach me at the Smyth residence on Andras Lane. The operator will know the number," Maria told him as she stood. Weyer waited for his cousin and followed her to the door. Ray noticed the sack of peanuts remained unopened as they walked into the hallway.

"I forgot to ask you something," he blurted out. "Are there any others looking for this ring? You wouldn't know a guy wearing a green coat and a tan hat?"

His question caused Maria to halt at the top of the stairs. Weyer nearly ran into her.

"No, I'm sure I don't know anyone like that," Mrs. Andras told Ray stiffly. The woman didn't bother to look back as she went down the stairs with her regal attitude.

~~~

Ray woke to the sound of knocking on his office door. The repeated blows on the door brought him out of an eerie nightmare involving stacks of cash surrounded by a black snake. The snake's head changed into a hideous, but familiar, skeletal face asking him for justice. It wasn't the first time the image came to him in dreams.

He stumbled out of bed, his face and chest covered in sweat. The mid-afternoon light coming through the half-opened curtain blinded him. Growling under his breath at the continued pounding on his office door, Ray walked from the back room where he made his apartment. Stuffing the tails of his wrinkled shirt into his pants, the shamus yelled out he was coming. Walking by his desk, he put his phone receiver back on the hook.

I guess the business day just started again.
~~~

Unlocking the door, Ray found Samantha Carter walking back down the stairs.

"Ray, you look terrible," she said after she turned back. "Are you alright?"

"I'm fine," he said with a grumble. He moved away from the door for Samantha to enter.

"It's a just lack of sleep. What brings you here? Your father will have a conniption."

"Listen, I'm of an age to do as I want. Aren't you happy to see me?" She asked, her eyes revealing hurt at his comment.

"Of course, I am," Ray told her with a sigh as he closed the door. "But you made it clear you needed time and space away from me, remember? I think I wasn't quite right for your friends."

He walked to his desk and sat in his chair, which squeaked like usual.

"It wasn't that way," she replied while taking a seat next to the desk. Samantha looked down at her hands. "Everything was moving too quickly. After all, we only went on a couple of dates. I told you that."

He gave her a frown, remembering their time differently.

"Yeah, your papa and his social circles had nothing to do with it," he told her. "Anyway, you didn't come here to retread old ground, did you?"

"No, that's not why I'm here," she admitted. "To be honest, I wasn't planning on coming here. But you were pretty clever when you helped my father. I need to talk with you."

"Well, that's something, I guess. I could tell that you wanted to say something to me as you left the art center," he said. "What is it?"

Samantha rose from the chair and walked to the single window in his office. She looked absently at the street below.

"I'm sure the police believe Reece Gabriel is a suspect in the murder of Mr. Townsend," Samantha told him. "Lieutenant Sirk came by our house earlier. I overheard him talking with my father about Reece. He had a lot of questions about Reece and his paintings."

Ray watched her profile, feeling a wave of sympathy wash over him. She'd never seen death before, let alone such a gruesome killing. But she needed to know the stakes.

"You're a suspect as well," he told her.

Samantha turned from the window. There was a hint of fear on her face.

"What…How can that be? Reece and I didn't arrive until after it happened." Samantha grew agitated.

"Exactly," Ray told her. "You're too close to the chief suspect. On top of that, you have a weak alibi, and you tried to defend Reece during the questioning.

If Sirk finds out you are covering something, you'll be up to your neck in trouble." Her eyes studied him as her face went pale at the thought.

"You don't believe that do you?" She asked.

"Do I think you committed murder? Not a chance," he said. "But you are the type of girl who would help a no-good rat try to get out of a trap."

"Reece is not a rat," she told him defensively. "He's an artist trying to express himself. His works communicate ideas that defy simple explanations. He's…"

"Save the speech for the socialites," Ray cut her off. "I wasn't talking about him. But since you bring it up, let's just say I can't discount that he's a suspect. Unless his alibi gets better, Sirk will keep him at the top of his list. That means you will be up there as well."

Samantha frowned at him as she came back to the desk.

"I don't know why I came to you. You're as bad as the police," the woman told him with growing fury.

"Listen, I'm giving it to you straight. You said you wanted my advice; that's why you came here," Ray reminded her.

"I'm not happy that you're in the middle of a murder investigation. You suddenly pop into my world again. Then you get mad when I give you the truth. I'm your friend, so I'll help you all I can."

He watched her anger slowly drain away as they went quiet for a moment.

"Is there anything I can do?" She asked as she slid into the chair next to his desk.

Ray shook his head.

"No, for now, you just need to keep away from Reece," he said. "Sirk isn't after you. But he's got a weird murder and more than a few suspects. As long as you are honest with Sirk, he'll be fair to you."

The room grew quiet again. Finally, Samantha rose to leave, and Ray went to the door, opening it for her. He placed his hand softly on her shoulder.

"Remember, I'll help you," he reminded her. She nodded and left. Ray shut the door and listened to the sound of her footsteps drift away.

~~~

By late afternoon, Ray looked forward to nursing his favorite drink, straight Irish whiskey. He had an untapped flask lying in a desk drawer, but he talked with Pappy first. His friend knew all the essential tidbits that were going on around Oyster City. Ray walked down Broadway until he reached the wooden newsstand that stood on a street corner a few blocks from the Hotel Alexander.

"Thanks for stowing that little box for me. It appears I have a few folks who want that thing," Ray quietly told his friend as he pulled a pulp magazine from the stand. He glanced around.
~~~

"I think I should take it out of your hands now. I want you to get in the middle of this. One side told me it's stolen."

Pappy grinned as he replied.

"Ain't that always the case, but don't you worry. I left it with Emma. Besides, there's nothing in the newspapers about such a fancy ring missing. That tells me the one that finds it, keeps it."

"Well, according to Maria Andras, her father owns it. They want it back." Ray said. Pappy whistled at the news.

"That woman is a real piece of work. They say she loves to cause problems for everyone else to clean up." He handed a paper to a customer who paid him. "From what I hear, I'm not sure you should trust her," the newsy said after his customer left.

"Yeah, I got that feeling as well. A guy named Weyer came with her. Maria mentioned her father was an Andras, but I don't know much about them. What's their background?" Ray asked.

"Malcolm Andras was a direct decedent of the founder of the city. He had three children, two boys, along with Maria. She married Phillip Smyth. In case you didn't realize it, Phillip is the brother of the Oyster City District Attorney." Pappy explained. "There are plenty of stories about Maria and her parties. She still lives on Phillip's estate, even though they got divorced several years ago."

"What is it with the rich and crazy in this city?" Ray wondered aloud as he scanned the latest stories in the magazine he held. "She claimed Weyer was her cousin. You know anything about him?"

"No, first I've heard of the name," Pappy shook his head. "But that's not surprising since I don't get invited out to the Smyth's estate or the Andras's estate for that matter."

The black man smiled grimly at his joke, and his friend nodded.

"Trust me; I don't think either of us will get invites to hang around those upper-class twits."

Ray went back to the stand and swapped out the magazine for the evening paper.

"Yeah, probably so," Pappy said with a grin. "By the way, I found out about that freckled face kid with the gun. He's a gumshoe like you. He goes by the name of Wilber Matthew."

The news caused Ray to look up from the headlines.

"Wait a minute, I know I haven't been around here long, but I've never heard the name."

"Yeah, that's because Wilber's from upstate," The newsy chuckled.

"A reporter told me about him. Somehow, he's hung around the state capital and kept his private investigator license. I guess a lot of shady stuff comes his way from the Jacobi gang."

"Like what?" Ray asked.

"Oh, like stealing, kidnapping, and even murder," Pappy told him. "I heard the guy would do anything for a dollar."

Ray went quiet for a moment, remembering Maria's reaction to his description.

"So, he stops by and says hello to me before I even know the score. I'll lay you odds that Maria Andras and her little fat boy partner went to him first. Weyer mentioned contacting a detective in the capital. Damn rats!" He grumbled before he changed the subject to the article he was scanning.

"I see one of the *Beacon's* reporters had an interview with Rose Smyth about the murder the other night," Ray commented after scanning the article.

"What's her story?"

"Yeah, she's a strange one. I'm surprised Rose came back to Oyster City after cutting ties with the rest of the Smyth family," his friend told him. "She's been rubbing their noses the wrong way by hanging around the art community. They are a prominent family and don't like associating with the riff-raff, even if they get some money out of the associations."

"Andras, Smyth, and some other prominent names appear to run the society pages," Ray commented.

"Folks who break with the families of the town founders have a nasty way of dying. Remember what happened to the bishop's wife."

Pappy reminded him as he handed a paper to a passing customer who dropped a dime into Pappy's hand. His comment struck Ray hard.

"Yeah, let's not bring that up." He said while he leaned back against the building.

"Anyway, I'm not buying this stuff with the outsiders. Every place has strange things happening, like those missing kids I just read about on page two. Probably just run off to the big city."

Pappy smiled at Ray.

"I don't want to burst your bubble, but you didn't read the entire article," he said. "They are missing, just like the others."

"Wait, what others?" Ray asked.

"Oh, off and on, we get teenagers who end up missing for a while," his friend said casually. "No rhyme or reason to it. Some of them come back, or they turn up in New York or LA."

"See, just as I thought," the shamus said smugly.

Pappy shook his head and glanced around with a frown.

"You don't understand about those that come back. Something changes them. The way I heard it, those wind up in institutions," Pappy emphasized under his breath. "And nobody knows what happened to the others since those that return aren't telling."

"Are you saying something's wrong with them in the head?" Ray asked. "Why isn't that all over the newspaper?"

"What good would it do?" Pappy shrugged. "Besides, most folks don't want anyone to know they have a crazy person in their family. I keep telling you that Oyster City has secrets that nobody is supposed to bring up. It's like that with these missing people. It just happens, and the people go on with their lives."

"Now, that's damn crazy," Ray told him.

"Maybe so, but you know I don't write the news; I just deliver it," he replied.

"Just remember the last time you got involved with those folks who play in the rarefied air of our city elders."

"I'll keep that in mind." Ray felt a chill go through him.

He suddenly thought of Samantha and wondered about her past. Irish never asked if she grew up in Oyster City or she was an outsider like him.

"By the way, what have you heard about Felix Roman?"

Pappy gave him a blank look at the question.

"Wait, I know that name," he snapped his fingers several times. "That's the artist who disappeared, right?"

"Yeah, I heard he came back from the war a while back," Ray replied. "I went down to the library today and looked through the newspapers during the war. They had an article about his return. His Sherman tank got hit by a German 88, and he ended up in the army hospital for a while."

"I can't tell you that much about him," Pappy confessed. "He was in the artist circles around here. As I recall, there was something that happened before he left—let me think." He handed over another paper to a woman who looked at Ray's nearby presence doubtfully. Ray guessed his crumpled suit made him appear a little too much like one of the low life thugs hanging around the docks. He watched the woman hurry away as Pappy came back to the conversation.

"I remember now," he said. "One of my regulars, a policeman, told me a little about his disappearance. I guess Roman's girlfriend called the police when he went missing. The way he explained it, Roman got it pretty bad when he was overseas. The cop told me he came out of the hospital and kind of went nuts. He attacked some art dealer at a reception, but it was hushed up."

Ray grew interested.

"You know why he attacked the dealer?"

Pappy shrugged.

"Never heard, but it didn't matter since he disappeared. But there's almost always a reason for attacking someone."

"Like what?"

Pappy laughed.

"When I was young, you went after someone because they had your money or your girl."

"Or both," Ray said while nodding in agreement.

~~~

Cat Bennett walked into her apartment, then laid her car keys on the table, looking forward to a quiet evening. She was tired and relieved. The woman hoped for some sleep and not nightmares. The *Morning Beacon* had her pictures, and she had a byline as well. Max Brand, her boss, only gave her the story credit reluctantly, but Cat expected that from the hard-bitten editor. She removed one of her high-heeled shoes when the phone rang. A scowl crossing her face, she limped across the room, walking on her tiptoes with the shoeless foot. She picked up the receiver.

"Is this Catherine Bennett?" A self-important female voice asked.

"Yes, who's this?" Cat leaned over and pulled off her other shoe.

"I'm trying to locate Mr. Irish, but he's not been at his office all day. Do you know where I might locate him? It's essential." The woman's voice was smooth and husky.

Holding her sarcasm, Cat replied. "Listen, I'm not his secretary. You…"

The voice interrupted.

"My dear Miss Bennett, I've heard all about your associations around Oyster City with this private detective. My name is Maria Andras. So why don't you be a good little girl and find him for me? You let him know I need to talk to him about his progress in my case. Have him come up to the estate tomorrow evening between six and seven, and there'll be fifty dollars in this for you. You can remind him there's an extra five hundred when he brings me Dela Cruz, but I won't wait much longer for some action."

The phone line went dead before Cat could say anything. Slowly putting the receiver back, she deliberated. She resented the woman's arrogance, but it was the cash she was offering. Plus, there might be something for her if she showed up at the Smyth Estate to collect. The reference to his case brought back Cat's earlier conversation with her partner. Ray didn't tell her about the details, but his brief description showed there was money involved if Maria hired him. Cat retook a seat and put her shoes back on.

~~~

Ray saw Cat Bennett waiting for him on the sidewalk by the door leading up to his office. He followed her up the stairs, trying not to think about her enticing curves.

When they reached the top of the stairs, Cat stepped aside and let Ray unlock the door.

"What have you got?" Ray asked as he stepped inside. He noticed a blue note slid under his door as she passed him. He placed his foot on it while he took off his coat.

"Why are you asking? I might come by to see you." She said with a sly grin. As she walked to the desk, Ray quickly picked up the note.

"You don't come here to chat," the shamus prompted her. "You're only here when you have cash in mind."

"Ok, then I want part of this deal with Maria Andras."

Cat told him while she pulled out his flask bottle of whiskey from the drawer. He hung up his coat.

"What a minute, that's not the arrangement," he said. "There's no story in this for you."

Ray took his flask from her.

"I got a call from Miss Andras, who's all hot and bothered to talk with you this evening. She told me about an extra five hundred, which I now get fifty percent." Cat told him as she reached out for the bottle. "Come on; I can help you. Remember, I can get the information from my friends."

Ray's face went sour.

"You can go shakedown your rich boyfriends, lady, and leave me out of it." He growled at her push. "I ain't one of your stooges."

She looked offended, but her blue eyes twinkled with amusement.

"How can you say such a thing?" she said, then paused. "Listen, I'm not your messenger, so you owe me for this."

Ray stepped around the desk, saying nothing. Then he pulled the cork from the flask.

"I'll give you a news flash," he told her. "Maybe I'm tired of this partnership. So far this week, I've got nothing but headaches from your help."

"Come on, quit the sourpuss routine," Cat said. "I'm the one that got you into that murder case the other night, remember?"

Ray took a swig from the flask, looking down at the brown-colored glass bottle in his hands.

"Yeah, the job that doesn't pay," he reminded her.

"That's not my fault. You need money, and I can help you investigate," Cat insisted. "The Andras family is loaded."

Cat slid onto the top of the desk. Ray didn't offer her the bottle, so she reached over and took it.

"Listen, I came up with a brilliant plan. I can sell exclusive pictures around the Smyth House to Max," she continued. "Phillip Smyth is the original hermit, and there are all sorts of rumors about what goes on in the house. You see, I'm not changing our deal at all."

She held up the flask in a toast and took a drink.

"We can still be friends," Cat's satisfied expression filled her face.

"Yeah, we're friends, alright," Ray replied with a stone look. "Go on with your idea."

"You can pick me up about six-thirty, and I'll tag along to get my fifty bucks from her. You can bet she'll never bother to send me a check. The rich never do," she explained. "While you keep her busy talking about the case, I can wander around and get some pictures."

"You plan on bilking me for a couple of hundred and have me introduce you to Maria," he said with a glare. "Then you run around for more pics to pull in even more money. Are you planning on extortion or just selling them to the *Beacon*?"

"Oh, quit making me out to be some grifter. The paper will pay me, and you make it sound so bad. Maria is a spoiled rich bitch, and everyone knows it," she said breezily.

"And you think nobody will notice you running around with that Watson camera of yours?" He scoffed while noticing that Cat did not offer him a cut of the money.

"Oh, you of little faith," she replied as she stuck her hand in her pocket. Cat pulled out a green box about the size of a cigarette package.

"It's a Whittaker Micro 16," she told him. "One of my friends got it for me. I slide this into a cigarette wrapper, and I've got my pictures. No one will ever know."

"Yeah, until you publish them. Have you met her?" Ray asked. "She might drop by the *Beacon* and put a bullet into you. Maria reminds me of a type to pull wings off angels just because she was bored."

"I'll be fine," she told him.

He stared at her for a moment.

"Alright, let's meet at your apartment," he said. "I'll drive you over."

Nodding, Cat slid off the desk and started for the door. "I'll be waiting, partner."

Ray watched her leave and pulled the note from his pocket. It was thick blue paper, folded over. Orella wrote in a hard to read cursive script, asking him to meet her at the diner next to his office at six. The shamus smiled as he stood—the chance to get back at his swindling partner for playing him as a sucker.

~~~

Ray was drinking coffee inside Frank's Diner a few minutes after Cat left. He knew the place well. The white walls needed a fresh coat of paint, and the white Formica counters were missing some edge pieces. But the coffee was good.
~~~

A couple of newspaper legmen sat in one booth. They were jawing with a thin waitress named Mildred, who had a Brooklyn accent to go with her squeaky voice, which filled the room.

From his seat at a table facing the large plate-glass window, Ray saw Orella Dela Cruz walk inside the diner. She glanced around like a dove in hunting season before recognizing him. Her dress was green, low cut, and fashionable. She wore an expensive fur coat, perfect for the chilly evening. She walked straight to the table, taking a seat with a smile.

"Mr. Irish, thank you for speaking with me," she said. "I know this must be quite confusing."

"No, I'm always getting pretty women coming to me with stolen rings," he told her with a bemused grin.

"I didn't steal the ring." Her brown eyes turned dark. "I took it back. It belongs to my family as much as your Washington Monument belongs to your country."

Her choice of words struck him.

"Well, Maria Andras and Johann Weyer say different, and they're willing to pay a lot for it. It was more than you offered."

"You haven't given it to them?" Her face went pale.

He shook his head.

"No, they promised me a bonus if you go back and apologize."

"Never," Orella replied angrily.

"Yeah, I figured it that way." Ray gave her a broad smile. "But that's how things stand right now. You have one side of this. Maria Andras has the other, and I have the ring, which puts me right in the middle."

Ray leaned forward, putting his elbows on the table.

"So, what's your story?"

Orella glared at him for a moment.

"You Americans always want gold. But if you are looking for blood money, I cannot hope to match what Andras will give you for the ring."

He frowned and pushed back his hat.

"Lady, get off your soapbox," Ray told her. "I was giving you the lay of the land. Unlike a lot of folks, I'm not trying to shake you down. Give me the truth, and I'll do the same. Now, why are you stealing this weird-looking ring?"

"I told you I didn't steal it; it belongs to my family," she insisted.

"Alright, it belongs to your family," he replied calmly. "Look, Maria Andras doesn't appear to want the cops involved, so I have my suspicions. Let's start with why it was on the Phillip Smyth estate?"

Ray stopped when he saw the waitress swiftly came to the table. He hated her timing, but he asked for a cup of coffee for his guest and a refill. Orella waited until Mildred left, then leaned forward.

"I guess I can see your point, Mr. Irish. Perhaps I can persuade you with the truth," she glanced around the room. "The ring is called Singsing of Multo. It is an ancient artifact given to my family by Rajah Gambang, King of Tondo, in the year 1405. A servant stole the ring from our house right before the Japanese invaded my country. You can see why it must return to my family."

He searched her face for clues on whether she was truthful. He got nowhere.

"I passed through your country, so I know a lot of stuff got looted during the war," Ray said. "But how did it get on Smyth's estate?"

Orella gave him a brief smile.

"I didn't realize you were in my country. My family lived in Manila, where my father worked for the Spanish consulate. A man named Abella took the Singsing, but the authorities couldn't get any information from the thief. Then, the war broke out, and things changed. My mother and father ended up in Australia. After the war, my father had a detective track down the servant, but he found Abella died in a Japanese prisoner camp. However, the detective discovered Calvin Villaflor, an antique dealer, purchased the ring. He escaped to the US."

She paused when the waitress returned. Then, she had a drink of coffee.

"We knew nothing more until my father arrived in New York to work for this new United Nations," she continued her story. "One day, my mother and I were shopping in Greenwich Village when we walked into an antique shop. We discovered Calvin Villaflor from Manila owned the store. You can imagine our joy at finding him."

"Yeah, I bet," Ray agreed. "I take it this dealer sold it?"

She nodded.

"Unfortunately, but he remembered the ring," Orella said. "It took a bit of persuasion, but he finally told us that Malcolm Andras purchased the Singsing when Mr. Villaflor opened his shop in New York."

She paused for a moment; a puzzled expression crossed her face.

"Is something wrong?" Ray asked.

"Nothing, it's just something I remember Mr. Villaflor telling us at the time. When we asked about the ring, he mentioned it was the first thing he sold in America," she told him. "He said Mr. Andras was waiting at his door when his shop opened on the first day. I thought that was strange since no one knew about the Singsing being in the store before that day."

"Well, that doesn't surprise me," he replied. "From what I've seen, collectors can be a strange lot, tracking down leads for their collection. I take it you found that Malcolm Andras was from Oyster City. What happened?"

"I discovered Mr. Andras died, and he left the Singsing to his daughter, Maria," Orella told him. "My mother had a private investigator get us more information about the Andras family. The man contacted Maria. He explained my interest in seeing the ring. We even made an offer to purchase it from her. Maria sent me a telegram inviting me to the estate. So, I came here last week."

The woman went quiet as she looked at her coffee cup.

Ray could tell by the change in Orella's expression that her encounter at the estate went poorly.

"Aren't you a little young to come here alone?" he asked.

"I'm eighteen," she said with a defiant pout. Then she paused.

"My mother and father didn't know I came to Oyster City alone. They believe I'm staying with friends. I believed I could do this by myself."

He gave her an admiring grin at the comment.

"Then your conversation about the ring didn't go well. What happened?"

Orella said nothing; she kept staring at her coffee.

"Did they not accept your offer?" he pressed, trying to get the story.

Orella looked at him; her face was dark.

"Maria is a kiki," she said venomously.

"What do you mean?" he asked, confused at the idea that Maria was homosexual.

"When I arrived, Maria was so very nice and pleasant," the woman continued. "During my stay, I joined their parties, but soon I grew uneasy. At first, Phillip and Maria appeared interested in my offer for the Singsing. Then, after one of their parties, Maria took me to an upstairs room with a servant of hers. We had a few drinks, and things suddenly became bizarre. I saw Maria put something into my drink, so I acted as though I drank it. She kept inhaling Benzedrine on the sly."

Orella lowered her voice and glanced around.

"She didn't think I understood such things. Then she told the servant to strip. Can you imagine?"

A look of disgust crossed her face.

"Of course, this shocked me and tried to leave, but she stopped me. Maria said she could make the poor girl do anything for us. That's when I discovered she likes woman lovers."

"My God, what a place," Ray replied. He took another drink of coffee.

"I'm sure that was difficult. What happened?"

"I left the room. I'm not like such people. Later, Phillip Smyth came to my room. He told me he didn't like me. That's when I discovered they invited to the house for…"

Orella looked at her cup for a moment, and then she looked at Ray; her brown eyes showed her resentment.

"I was to be their entertainment for the weekend if I wanted the ring. I grew angry; then I left the room. Maria caught me in the hall, and she slapped me. She laughed at me, telling me they would use me like a servant. As she came closer, I hit her. Phillip grabbed me and threw me back into the room. He began beating me. At first, I thought he might kill me, but finally, he left my room."

Ray kept quiet for a moment, thinking about her story.

"I don't blame you for smacking her," he agreed. "She probably needed a few more. But why didn't you go to the police?"

"I did just that," she told him. "But when I reached the phone, one servant warned me that Phillip's brother carried significant influence. I hung up and went back to my room. In my home country, it's dangerous to make such an accusation about powerful people."

"Yeah, well, we're not better here sometimes," Irish conceded. "You took the ring, then?"

"I stayed up all night thinking about it. It came to me I should go back home and have my father contact people he knows. I didn't have any other options. When I went down for breakfast the next morning, I told her and Phillip that I was leaving. He told me they never intended to sell the Singsing. They like to bring in outsiders like me for their fun. He called me nothing but a plaything, a toy. Then, that bastard called me a half-breed foreigner. I could not think of anything to do but leave."

Ray's eyebrow went up at the comment.

"Yeah, somebody needs to put a knuckle sandwich into his mouth," he said. "I take it you grabbed the ring on your way out?"

Orella nodded, tears welling up in her eyes.

"They displayed the Singsing in the library at the house," she said. "It came to me that I had to get the Singsing away from here. I walked by the display case as I left that morning. I stopped and found the case unlocked. I hoped they wouldn't miss it for a while. I've never done anything like that before."

Tears trickled down her cheek as she fumbled for a handkerchief from her purse.

"It's alright, sister," Ray said, reaching over to pat her hand. "For my money, they deserve a little payback."

Orella dabbed her eyes.

"I'm still not sure why you came to me at the restaurant?" Ray asked. "All you had to do was return to New York and give that ring to your dad. I thought diplomats remain protected from arrest. The police here won't be doing anything about it. Why didn't you just leave town?"

"That was my idea," Orella gave him a tired smile. "I tried to leave that morning, but they discovered the Singsing was missing before I could get to the train. The fat little man, Johann, was waiting for me at the station. I knew I needed to get a car or a bus. I didn't know what to do."

The growing worry filled her face.

"I tried calling, but my mother was not at home. I finally went to the Western Union building to send a wire to my father since I'm sure he would be at his office. While I was waiting, I met a helpful woman. She saw my bags, so I lied and told her I was waiting for my father to come to Oyster City. When she found out my father worked for the Spanish government and was in New York, she invited me to stay with her and her husband. That's where Pearl told me about you."

"Who are you staying with?" Ray looked at her strangely.

"Mr. and Mrs. Morris," she told him. "He's the president of Morris Bank."

"Yeah, I know Pearl, alright," he said with a forced smile.

"She's been very nice to me," Orella said. "I thought about borrowing their car, but I didn't know how I could ask them to drive me home. They would realize I lied to them. I had only a few dollars on me. I couldn't afford to risk it. When I mentioned I needed some help with a private matter, she suggested finding you. She even showed me your office building."

She took a drink of coffee. Her face turned sour, and she scooped sugar into the cup. Ray smiled at her actions.

"Why didn't you come up?" he asked.

"I did, but when I got out of the cab, I noticed a man dressed in a green coat staring at me," she replied. "When I walked by, he started following me."

"Wait, was he wearing a tan hat? Looked like he was just out of high school?" He asked, and Orella nodded.

"Do you know him?" she asked.

There was a flash of concern in her eyes.

"I know of him," he replied carefully. "He's a bum, so don't trust him."

"I thought I got away from him by going inside the drugstore on the corner," she said. "Then I watched for you and followed you to that Canton restaurant. Unfortunately, I didn't lose that man in the green coat. I saw him watching us from a car outside. That's why I ran out. My taxi driver was excellent. He lost him before I went back to Mrs. Morris's house."

"Smart girl," he told her approvingly.

As he watched Orella, he noticed her delicate features along with the soulful eyes which held him for a moment.

"My father has not returned my calls. The secretary keeps telling me he is out of town and unavailable," she said. "I believe my mother is out of town with him, but I don't have the number, so I can't get a message to her."

The woman paused. Her expression reminded him of a lost puppy.

"Mr. Irish, will you help me get it back to New York with the ring?"

"Only if you call me Ray," he said with a smile. "I don't trust my jalopy to make it to New York, so you'll take the train when it leaves in the morning. A personal escort for you, so there'll be no trouble. I want you to go back to Pearl's house and pack your bags. I'll pick you up at dawn tomorrow morning."

Chapter 3: A Snatch and Murder

Cat sat on her bed with the lights on in her bedroom. Her peach nightgown remained drenched in sweat. She pulled the covers around her, still shivering. A terrifying nightmare persisted in her memory. She had a few nightmares after a thug broke into her room a few months before. Her attack happened when she first got involved with Irish. But those dreams went away after the death of the hoodlum. But now, the nightmare that woke her remained fresh in her mind. She recognized her friends, but they were hanging upside down, blood pouring from their open mouths.

When she ran away, the people behind leering masks kept ripping at her clothes as she ran through a black forest. In a panic, Cat knew if she stopped, they would do terrible things to her. The dread she felt welled up as she ran, threatening to overwhelm her. Finally, when she pulled away from the shadowy figures, the scene changed, and Cat was climbing familiar stairs. But the stairs kept going upward into the far reaches of the sky. She climbed until she finally reached the door to her partner's office. When she entered the room, Ray was sitting in his chair. He had his feet propped up on the windowsill like normal as he stared out of the window. In his hand was a tumbler, but, to her horror, she recognized the liquid was blood. He gave her a familiar half-grin and handed her the glass.

Have a taste of nectar, child, and become the damned that rise with me.

The thought flashed through her brain when she looked back at the chair. It held a naked human body with a raven's head. As she tried to move away, the masked creatures were around her again. They grabbed Cat, forcing her to her knees as the raven-head creature stood and walked closer. The beak opened, and a sinister laugh filled her ear while the beast compelled the woman to drink the blood. Her gagging reflex forced her out of the nightmare.

Catherine's hands shook as she attempted to light a cigarette. She inhaled deeply, trying to get the nicotine to calm her. It took several minutes after going through the nightmare to realize she must have tasted the sweat on her lip. She still noticed the flavor of blood in her mouth. Cat threw back the covers and went into the living room, where she shakily poured a drink. Cat downed the whiskey in a gulp. The alcohol burned going down, but she was glad the foul taste was gone.

It's a damn lousy way to start the day.

~~~

The train station parking lot was little more than a gravel-covered spot situated around the main terminal corner. Ray nearly missed the entrance to the lot. The twilight haze and thick fog made the turn challenging to find. Passing the few vehicles already parked in the lot, he glanced over at Orella. Her focus
~~~

remained on the nearby line of train cars. His call earlier to the station informed them that the first train would leave in a few minutes.

They were behind schedule. It took longer than expected for Irish to extract his client from Pearl's house. The banker's wife was overly curious about his motives. Ray sympathetically smiled as he gave her a concocted story about working for Orella's father. In reality, the shamus hocked his watch and took a loan from Pappy to get enough money for Orella to leave by train.

Ray decided to walk into the station just in case Maria Andras still had someone hanging around. They planned to hurry through the lobby just as the train was about to leave. Orella would pay for her tickets after she got on the train. But they needed to move fast.

A single-story brick building with a chateau-like roof was their destination. When they got out of the car as another automobile slowed, then passed them. Ray went to the back of his Nash. He grabbed Orella's suitcases. She barely spoke as they hurried around several loaded carts near the freight side of the terminal.

Ray did not see the hulking man standing in the misty shadows. Instead, he caught the briefest movement next to him before his head exploded in pain. The shamus fell forward, unable to stop his face from striking the floor. The bags he carried scattered across the wooden platform. Irish took another slap from a leather sap across the back of his head that dazed him. He barely heard Orella's suddenly stifled scream.

The shamus forced himself to roll over and found two ugly mugs looking down at him. The young punk with the green hat held one hand over Orella's mouth. His other hand kept a gun pushed against her side. A large black man stood next to Wilber with a grin on his face. He kicked Ray, and his boot glanced off Ray's forehead. The injured man heard a loud curse from Wilber and the sound of footsteps running away. Ray could only watch in a stupor as Orella ran until Wilber caught her by the edge of the dock. The gunman whipped his pistol against the woman's head, and she fell from the platform. Ray pulled himself to his knees, but his mind could barely control his arms and legs.

"Get the car," Wilber ordered his partner, who leaped down from the dock.

Wilber jumped down next to the stunned woman. The big man ran to the end of the building, where he got into a gray car. The vehicle rapidly backed up while Wilber pulled Orella off the ground.

Ray tried to stand, but his unsteady legs gave way. He saw Wilber forced the woman into the backseat of the gray Frazer. They sped off while Ray committed all the details about the vehicle to memory. Nearly covered with dust, the license still revealed the seven numbers.

By the time the shamus walked into the train station, he could stumble forward in a reasonably straight line. He went to a string of phone booths, ignoring the stares coming from two uniformed porters standing by the main entrance. A dime later, Ray was speaking with Arizona Campbell. The voice on the other end wasn't friendly.

"Irish, what the hell are you calling me at home for? This is twice now," he told him.

"Listen, I've got a kidnapping for you. Are you still a cop?" Ray snapped.

He quickly explained what had happened outside of the train station.

"I didn't need a bunch of foot soldiers down here to make me repeat the story and waste time," he continued. "I've got the tag number and one of the thug's names. It's a shamus named Wilber Matthew from the capital. You call it in. If it's coming from you, the word gets out to your patrol cars immediately."

"Alright, I'll see what I can do," Arizona told him. "I take it that nobody saw what happened?"

"Yeah, they caught me coming from the parking lot. It was still dark."

"Alright, get your butt back to your office and wait for a call. Don't be a one-man show like last time. My guys will pick them up."

"Yeah, and I'll get old waiting for it," Ray sighed.

He gave him the license number, vehicle make, and color. When the shamus gave his verbal description of Orella, the cop whistled.

"She sure sounds like a lady I'd like to meet," he remarked. "What the hell are you into? Do you know why they kidnapped her?"

"No, I'm not sure," Ray lied. "I'll be at my place as soon as I can."

~~~

When Ray arrived back at his office, he noticed the lights were on. Inside, he found Cat waiting for him. She looked tired, yet her eyes were alight with anger directed his way. She had her brown camera satchel slung over her shoulder. He noticed she wore a pair of brown slacks and a green blouse with her hair pulled back into a ponytail. Her expression changed to concern when she saw his scraped and bloody face.

"Damn Ray, what happened to you?" She asked while she went through into his bedroom.

"Sit down while I get the iodine." The woman called out as she began rummaging through the cabinet hanging on the wall.

He went to his chair and pulled out his flask from the drawer, downing a shot before he sat down. Cat came back into the room, carrying cotton balls and iodine. While she worked on his injuries, Ray explained his injuries.

"Now you know why I didn't go with you last night. Things have changed," he said.

"You bastard, you should have called me. I was waiting for you and lost a chance at getting those pictures. I can't believe you were letting her leave with the ring." She told him while she pushed the cotton on a deep scratch. Ray winced, sucking in a breath.
~~~

"You're a damn fool!" Cat insisted. "Some foreign girl comes in with a big story, and you get your head kicked in. She could have made the whole thing up."

"Like hell, Orella didn't make up the story if I nearly got my head bashed in," he pointed out. "Maria Andres hired a two-bit gunman to recover the Singsing before I even got involved. Now that bastard just kidnapped her. Wilber must have followed me from Pearl's house. It means I screwed up. I should have been using my brain to get her out of town."

"You should have just given that ring back to Maria and pocketed the money. Why did you take this girl's side?" Cat asked.

Ray pulled away from her with disgust as he stood.

"Damn it, I'm not out trying to get the easy buck," he nearly shouted in his frustration. "The girl was scared and alone. You might not give a damn about that, but I do. Now, why are you here? Are you just going to chew on my ear about you losing some damn cash?"

He watched her glare at him for a moment.

"The police found Rose Smyth dead not too long ago." She went to his desk, where he leaned back in his chair. She pulled a cigarette from a brass cigarette holder, quickly lighting it.

"I just got the news from one of our legmen at the paper, saying they found Rose murdered inside her apartment," she explained. "I'm going over to the Richley Apartments to get some pictures for the *Beacon*. Do you want to come along, partner?"

Ray ran his hand through his hair. He could feel the knot on the back of his skull, and he heard the growl from his belly.

"The Art Center murder is a police case, remember? I don't know why I'm needed," he replied. "Carter made it clear I'm not getting paid to keep my nose in it."

"Well, considering Rose Smyth was at that murder scene, I thought you might be interested. But have it your way."

The woman shrugged nonchalantly. Ray realized she knew him too well.

"Yeah, maybe I am interested," he admitted. "But Orella needs my help now. The other stuff can wait."

Cat gave him a knowing smirk.

"Maybe so, but you'll want to stay involved in that murder case because you're as stubborn as a mule," she reminded him.

"You always have to figure things out. Did you forget about Samantha? That little damsel in distress that you're all clobbered over is a suspect, if my sources are correct."

She flicked the ash from her cigarette, and Ray glanced at her.

"Don't give me that look; I saw how you acted around her. Make her happy, and her daddy's got money," she reminded him.

Ray's face turned to stone at the suggestion. His head had cannons going off inside. Her smug attitude sent him into a rage.

"Who the hell are you to give me advice? You run around like a dog in heat when some wealthy guy looks your way," he countered. "Then you jump in the middle of my problems while you scam me like a damn grifter."

He turned away to the window overlooking the street, rubbing his head.

"You think all you have to do is bat your pretty blue eyes, and I'll roll over like a dog. Lady, I'm damn tired of you playing me for your sucker. Unlike you, I still have some scruples left."

He did not see the sorrow flash across her face at his comments. Cat bowed her head and deliberately placed the iodine bottle down on the desk. The woman stepped to the coat rack where she got her coat. The phone suddenly rang on the desk.

"Well, I'll leave you to your case, shamus," she told him coolly as Ray picked up his phone.

"Wait," he told her, but she didn't look back, closing the door with a bang. Ray held the receiver in his hand for a moment while a booming voice asked for him.

"Irish, this is Desk Sergeant Morley," the man's voice came through the line. "Detective Campbell told me to call you. We're looking for this car you called in. You need to stay put, and we'll let you know what we find out."

"Like hell, I'll stay put," Ray growled back at him. "Morley, you can tell Arizona that he needs to put out an arrest warrant on Wilber Matthew."

"Shamus, don't be getting yourself in a jam," Morley replied. "The lieutenant already figured you'd be howling something like that. The captain ain't putting out a pinch on someone just because you order it. You got that!"

"Yeah, I got it," he replied bitterly, then Ray hung up the phone and cursed at the empty room.

~~~

The gray four-door Frazer pulled up to a large barn with a single light still shining above its two doors. Dawn tried to break through the cloudy sky above the building. The remains of several cars and trucks, most missing their doors and body parts, dotted the nearby area. A few grazing cattle stood by the vehicles. As the driver opened one of the barn doors, Wilber ordered their prisoner up from the backseat floorboard. He led Orella inside the building with his gun pointed at her. The driver closed the door, and they forced her to the back, walking past several cars in various stages of repainting. Near the back wall, an old cot sat next to a small table and an old steel chair missing the padded seat cover. An iron stove stood between the table and the chair.

"Ulysses, get some rope," Wilber ordered his partner, then pushed her into the chair. The big man quickly returned with rope.
~~~

"Alright, sister, you're going to answer some questions about that ring you stole." He explained while Ulysses tied her hands behind her, wrapping the line through the metal chair back.

Orella shook her head.

"You can't make me talk. The police will be after you now for kidnapping…" Before the woman could say more, Wilber struck her with a backhand.

"Shut it, bitch." He spat out. "That damn shamus isn't going to do a thing for a little whore like you. He's still trying to figure out what truck hit him."

Wilber smirked when he heard his partner's grunted agreement.

"Tie her legs to the chair," he ordered Ulysses.

While his partner worked, the thug put away his gun, sliding it into a holster inside his jacket. Wilber pulled off his coat before he leaned close to the captive.

"Missy, you're going to tell me what I want to know. The only question is how much of a beating you take first."

Orella didn't have time to react. The punch to her abdomen forced the air from her lungs. Wilber grabbed her by the hair and jerked back her head.

"Don't worry, I won't mess up that pretty face just yet," he told her with a cruel smile. Ulysses laughed at the comment.

"Ya let me know when you're tired so that I can work her over some," he said to Wilber.

"You just get a fire going in that stove," Wilber glanced over.

"Now, where's the ring?" the shamus asked, waiting for a moment.

The hoodlum recognized the defiance in her eyes, and he struck her in the ribcage. After she let out a pathetic groan, he grabbed her by the hair and lifted her head.

"Babe, I can do this all night," he warned.

Orella shook her head, and her tormentor backhanded her. Blood trickled from her lip.

While Ulysses filled the stove with wood, he listened to the beating. The wicked punches forced grunts and groans from Orella. Wilber focused on the woman's abdomen, using her as a punching bag. When Ulysses got the fire burning, he turned back to see the woman's head hanging down. The woman gasped for air. He frowned, expecting their prisoner to fold quickly.

She's a cute dish; I hope he don't kill her too soon.

Fifteen minutes later, Orella's chair fell over on its back. She groaned in pain when her head struck the ground. The damage extended to her swollen face. Bluish bruising covered parts of the woman's upper body. The woman refused to give any information to her tormentors, who took turns beating her.

Ulysses stood over her, huffing. He took a swig from a small bottle of moonshine in his hand. He offered the hooch to Wilber, who knocked the man's hand away in disgust.

"That bitch ain't folding with this beating," Wilber coldly stated as he stared down at the woman.

Ulysses shrugged.

"She's tougher than most I've seen," he admitted. "Can't beat her much more without the dish dying."

Orella coughed, spitting out blood along with a tooth. Every breath hurt.

"We should have gone with the iron," Wilber glanced back at the stove after he kneeled by the woman.

"You made the wrong people mad. They want the ring and tell me I could pretty much do anything I want to you. I'm gonna make sure you spill the beans right now!"

Wilber went over to the stove and placed a long piece of an iron rod into the flames. As he watched the metal turning red, Orella struggled in her bindings.

"You know, there's a small town outside the capital where the Jacobi gang takes a few of their special prisoners." Wilber explained while he turned the rod amid the flames.

"There's a guy there named Max—Butcher Max, they call him. He's an expert at torturing. They say he came over from Spain after the Fascists won the civil war. He knows how to get information out of people. You see, it's more of an art than science in some ways. You have to keep the people alive while you make sure they know the pain will never quit until they tell you everything."

Orella's eyes fixed on the metal rod in his hand.

"Sit up her chair," he told his partner. Ulysses happily ripped off the woman's blood-stained top.

Orella desperately pleaded for release.

"Good Ol' Max showed me a thing or to," Wilber continued as he ignored her. He pulled out the red-hot piece of iron, then walked back to the bound woman. Ulysses stripped off her pale satin bra.

"No, please don't!" She mumbled out her words from her swollen and bloody lips. "I'll tell you everything,"

Orella frantically kicked out her feet as tears streamed down her cheeks.

"Yes, you will tell me all you know about the ring," the thug replied with a grim smile. "This will make sure of that."

Outside the building, the scream of agony caused the cattle to awaken and gallop away. They slowed, going back into a huddle. The screams and shrieks steadily weakened. Slowly, the animals slumbered again as silence fell over the area.

"Whatcha gonna do now?" Ulysses asked. He looked down at the unconscious girl. The smell of burned flesh made him fan the air. "Ya should've checked that shamus after I hit him. You want me to wake her with smelling salts?"

"Just stow it. She's told us enough. I'm going to make a call. I want to know if it's time to bury her." Wilber said as he picked up his coat. "Until I get back, you make sure she doesn't go anywhere!"

As Wilber walked away, Ulysses smiled as he looked down at their prisoner. Along her belly were several long burn marks. She held out until the third time her partner ran the smoking rod across her skin. Just before Orella passed out, she told them everything.

Ulysses took another drink as the barn door closed, and he bent down, untying Orella's hands and legs. He scooped up the unconscious woman and carried her over to a cot. The brute carefully laid her on the dirty cloth top as the effects of the booze and brutality flowed through him. He unhooked his overalls, letting them drop to the floor. Ulysses examined the woman for a long moment. Then he ripped off Orella's skirt before he crawled on top of her.

~~~

During the drive, Ray tried to keep his mind focused on the Dela Cruz woman and the ring. He didn't have the contacts to hunt for her through the underbelly of Oyster City. Worse, the kidnapper's ties to the Jacobi gang meant Irish needed to play it cautious. Stumbling around in the dark might get Orella and him killed. Still, the urge to do something gnawed at him. He blew it by letting Wilber get the drop on him. Until they found the car that drove away with his client, the shamus couldn't do much more at the moment. Still, he felt a growing urge to confront the bitch, Maria Smyth.

As he pulled in front of the Richley Apartments on 12th Street, the image of Greye La Spina crept into his mind. It was a reminder that he still had other unfinished business. He looked up at the five-story building which overlooked the road, making a vow to check up on Bishop La Spina soon.

The white and gray stone facade tried to combine three types of architecture and failed miserably. In his humble opinion, the luxury apartments held those with more money than taste. Sliding out of his car, Ray crossed the sidewalk and entered the building. It wasn't hard to figure out where the murder happened. A hulking policeman at the elevator pointed to the stairway door. He followed two reporters who were complaining about taking the stairs as they puffed on their cigarettes.

When he reached the top floor, Ray used his bulk to push past a couple of reporters who were trying to jawbone a young plainclothes detective. Next to the men, he saw Cat, who stood in front of a uniformed policeman. Ray recognized Stevens, one of the cops who worked that side of the city.
~~~

"I've told you a dozen times, no photographs, Cat," Stevens stated. "It's Sirk's orders. Now, why not be a good girl and stay out of the way?" He had his arms crossed, and Ray noticed how the woman pouted at his words. It was her usual tactic to work her will.

"Come on! You know my boss will throw me out," she pleaded.

Ray leaned against the wall, listening to her attempts to get past Stevens, when he noticed Detective Sirk at the far end of the hall. Taking advantage of the full exchange going on next to him, he slid along the wall when Stevens looked away.

The shamus got to Sirk before anyone noticed. He could tell the detective hadn't slept much since they last spoke; there were dark rings under his beady eyes.

"This doesn't concern you, shamus. Take a hike." Sirk grumbled.

"That's alright with me; I just got interested in the coincidental murder. It seems kind of funny how your victim was recently a prime witness at your other crime scene." Ray replied as he glanced past the policemen. The police photographer recorded the gruesome sight. He took his last shot before he started to put away the camera equipment. Sirk noticed Ray staring into the room.

"You've got a sick sense of humor if you think that's funny," Sirk growled. "This investigation is police business; you don't have a stake here."

"I understand," Ray replied while he took in the crime scene.

He saw the murder victim tied standing to a column. Someone slit the old lady's throat, causing her blood to pump out across her bathrobe. It reminded him of the dead guard back at the art center. He turned around to the cop when an idea came.

"Tell me, do you have a painting with the murder in there as well?" he asked.

The policeman's reaction told Ray that his guess hit the mark.

"Alright, how in the hell did you figure that out?" Sirk let out a long breath.

"It was a hunch. I saw the body positioned like a display, so I understand why you wouldn't let Cat in for pictures. You don't want it public, and this thing appears too coincidental, even to a guy like me."

The police detective looked at Ray for a long moment.

"You ain't wrong there. I guess you might as well look this over. Who knows, maybe you'll spot something useful for once. But remember, anything that you find comes to me. And nothing to the Cat about this."

Sirk warned him as the lieutenant led him inside.

"Of course," Ray said with a grin as he noticed she was still working on getting past Stevens.

More substantial than a small house, the apartment held a living room filled with white columns on a dark tile floor. The corpse of Rose Smyth stood because of the rope wound around her and a column near the fireplace. Gagged and her head held upright using a dressing robe belt around her forehead, the woman's thin throat presented a raw, open wound. Dried blood trailed down across the dead woman's covered chest. Rose's open eyes stared at a painting above the fireplace.

Ray stopped with a double take at the picture he saw on the mantle. It wasn't an exact duplicate, but it was close enough. The canvas showed a young female bound to a column. She had arrows sticking out of her body, and blood flowed down across the white clothes. The painting sat haphazardly on the mantle, leaning against a canvas of flowers that hung on the wall.

"The killer must have placed this piece on the mantle for this murder. But whoever did this slipped up. They forgot to bring along a bow and arrows." Ray said aloud as he stepped closer to the fireplace to look at the signature on the painting.

"Yeah, I noticed that," the cop grunted out. "I also recognized that Mrs. Smyth's robe is green, unlike the picture. Now get this, Reece signed that painting as well," he said. "I've already sent a man over to get my suspect. Just so you know, the dead woman collected his works, trying to promote him."

"I can't say I would put those pictures in my office. They're almost as bad as the real thing. Did you find the weapon?" Ray asked.

"No, the murderer took it with him. The best guess is a serrated knife by the look of the wound, but the coroner will have to confirm. Of course, no one heard anything, and nobody suspicious came in," Sirk told him bitterly.

Ray looked at the body for a moment and noticed the murder wrapped her to the column with rope. Then he moved out of the medical examiner's path when he and the ambulance driver finally pushed their way into the apartment. He observed the doctor do a quick inspection of the body before telling the driver to cut down the body.

"How did the murderer get Smyth to stand there while he wrapped that rope around her?" Ray asked aloud. He noticed Sirk watched the medical men place the body on the cart before covering it with a sheet.

"He probably just threatened her. She must have thought it was just a robbery, I guess. Too bad she didn't put up a fight," he told him. "Someone might have heard it. The maid found her, but nothing appears stolen from the apartment."

Ray did not buy the explanation, but he kept quiet. The evidence pointed to at least two people. The shamus slowly went through the rest of the apartment while Sirk finally allowed Cat to come inside the room for a picture.

Cat noticed Ray was already there, and she glared at him. The photographer tried to get a picture of Reece's oil painting. However, Sirk refused. She sighed dramatically, then took photos of the bloody rope and floor. She grumbled aloud that it was not enough for the paper's ghoulish readers.

Ray looked around, but there was no other place where the gruesome painting could have been hanging inside the apartment. Ray concluded the deranged artwork entered with the killer or killers. He mentioned it to Sirk. However, the lieutenant did not thank him. Instead, he rolled his eyes in disgust. It was another puzzle in his growing pile of dead bodies.

Ray started to leave, then paused in a corner of the room when a police escort came into the apartment with Gabriel Reece in tow. Francis Carter followed the group into the room as well. Intrigued by the scene, Ray listened to the police lieutenant question the men. He focused on their alibis while watching Cat, who stepped away several paces to get shots of Carter and Reece. He took it from her self-satisfied look that she was getting an exclusive array of images for her employer.

According to the police escort, they found Carter at Reece's apartment. The banker insisted upon coming along. Sirk's questions turned up nothing to Irish.

Reece claimed he was at the art center since it opened that morning. The director spoke briefly with Harold Garza about the Raphael painting. Carter insisted he was at his office all morning, meeting with clients before going to see Reece. They were about to leave for lunch when the police arrived.

When Sirk asked about the painting, Reece confirmed he painted it but sold it to an art dealer.

"Last I knew about the painting, it was hanging on a wall somewhere in New Hampshire," he told the policeman.

Then, the artist grew quiet as he went over to the picture and looked at his creation carefully. The way Reece looked at his picture surprised Ray. It was as though the painter was trying to remember something important. It reminded him of the times when a thought dangled in front of you, so close you could almost reach out and grasp it.

Reece caught Ray watching him, but the artist gave him a pointless grin. Eventually, Sirk let Carter and Reece go, warning both to remain in the city.

As Ray walked to his car, he kept thinking back to the look on the young artist's face. It seemed important, but he couldn't figure out any reason behind it. He could only guess that Reece spotted something in his art. Catherine's car drove by, but she paid no attention to him. As the shamus slid into his car, he wondered how long before she came back with her pretty smile, trying to convince him she was looking out for his best interests.

~~~

Arizona found Ray talking with Sergeant Morley about thirty minutes after the shamus arrived at the police station. The police detective had news for him.

"I've got a name for you on that car that you say snatched that Dela Cruz woman," he said. "I'm heading over to talk with him. You want to tag along?"
~~~

Ray gave his friend an annoyed look, then followed him down the hall. Taking Arizona's police cruiser, they drove along Broadway toward the docks. The street grew emptier as they got closer to First Street. It was a city section where most people stayed away unless they looked for sex, drugs, or gambling.

"It's taken you most of the morning to find out," Ray complained.

"Things like this take time. An ex-con named Ulysses Davis owns the car," Arizona replied evenly. "We've picked him up a few times. He's been in and out of jail for petty crime and assaults. His last heist with stolen cars got him a couple of years. According to Morley, there's a rumor that Davis does odd jobs for the Jacobi gang."

"Well, that matches what I heard about Wilber working for the Jacobi gang," Ray replied. "I don't see a connection, but who knows what Maria Andras is involved in?"

"What the hell are you saying?" Arizona asked as he glared at Ray. "Damn it, are you trying to tell me Miss Andras kidnapped this Dela Cruz woman?"

"No doubt in my mind about it," Ray nodded with a frown. "Wilber showed up at my office before Ms. Dela Cruz even got to me. He knew her name, warning me against taking the case. Somebody must have paid him to track her down. It can only lead back to Maria Andras."

"Yeah, you just put your hand into a hornet's nest with that accusation. I'm warning you that you better have your facts straight before accusing any member of the Andras family in this city. The woman has her ex-husband's looking out for her," Arizona told him. "You'll end up on the wrong end of the steer if you tangle with them."

Irish watched the houses pass by for a moment.

"I heard plenty of rumors about her," he mumbled. "I've met her, and she's slimy as a snake. But I get the feeling nothing seems to stick. Is that because of Phillip Smyth?"

Arizona remained quiet, which confirmed Ray's suspicion.

"I heard from Sirk that you've been hanging around his murder cases," the police detective finally replied, as he changed the conversation. "Now you have a client getting kidnapped. It seems like bad luck is following you around, Irish."

"Yeah, don't you know it," he said glumly. The men remained quiet for the rest of the drive.

The car pulled to a stop in front of a ramshackle Victorian home. A sign on the front welcomed new tenants, but Ray doubted anyone beyond drifters and prostitutes would stay there. Broken windows and dingy, flaking paint covered the front of the house. Rotten wood felt like it would give way with each step as they climbed onto the porch. Arizona knocked several times since the pull to the doorbell was missing. After a few minutes, an elderly man opened the door. He smelled like cheap hooch and fish. Arizona flashed his badge.

"What room is Ulysses Davis in?" His question was an order.

The man at the door blinked several times, and Arizona pushed past him. "I said, what room?" He growled. The man's shaky hand pointed up the wooden stairs.

"First door on your right," he said. "But he ain't in there. I haven't seen him."

"Fine, then we'll go up and look around." Arizona moved up the stairs quickly. Ray noticed the policeman pulled his revolver.

When they reached the door, Arizona pointed him to the other side, then knocked.

"Whad'ya want?" a slurred female voice asked.

The cop carefully opened the door. Inside the apartment, a chubby woman with dark brown hair sat on a worn couch. She had a thin, dirty robe over her worn out slip. In her lap was a half-finished bottle of gin.

Arizona walked in, looking over the room cautiously.

"Where's Davis?"

"Oh, it's you flatfoots," the woman leaned toward them. "I don't know where he is, now go away. Can't you see I'm busy?"

Arizona walked to the bathroom and glanced through the open door. Ray closed the door, stepping next to a beat-up console radio softly playing music. Ray recognized the Benny Goodman song as he watched the cop move in front of the couch.

"Goldie, I know you are still hanging out with Davis. Where is he?" he asked as he put away his gun.

He stood over the woman.

"I told you I don't know," she said, flashing her smile, showing the gold tooth, which gave her the nickname.

The smile was bitter, filled with spite.

Unexpectedly, Arizona reached down and slapped her hard across the face. Ray went rigid as sudden tension filled the room.

"Goldie, you remember me. I don't like people lying to me," Arizona said. "Now, be a good slush and tell me where he is."

The woman laughed at him and leaned back defiantly.

"Copper, all my men like to beat me. That's all you damn men are good fer. Say, who's your new partner?"

She winked at Irish.

"Ray, this is Goldie, a pro skirt who walks the docks and hangs out at Anthony's for her drinks," Arizona told him.

His eyes remained on the woman.

"Go to hell, cop," she spat out as she adjusted her robe, the springs groaning at her movement.

"Listen, you keep this up, and I'll haul you in. If you don't know where your boyfriend is, then tell us where he normally hangs out."

"I don't like you, copper, so you get no deal," she sullenly lashed out. "You can't touch me since I ain't turning tricks tonight."

The cop leaned over her.

"Yeah, but I might claim you're a common-law wife now," he replied with an evil smile. "You want me to get dirty and throw the anti-miscegenation law on you? You're living with a black guy, and that will make it easy for me."

Deciding the two stubborn people in front of him would do this dance for hours, Ray pulled his wallet from his jacket. He stepped next to Arizona with a green Lincoln bill he held tantalizing close.

"Listen, Goldie, I've got enough cabbage for you to fill the weekend with booze," he said. "But only if you give me the location of your boyfriend's normal hangouts. We'll leave, and nobody has to play dirty. Your guy gets some more time in the cooler, and you get plenty of booze. Is it a deal?"

Goldie looked at Ray suspiciously, but her eyes kept glancing back at the money he held. Finally, she took ten dollars from his hand.

"Alright, cutie, I'll make a deal with you," she said, placing the money inside her bra. "The bum's either hanging out at Ernie's garage on Muddle Street, or he's at the old horse barn."

"Old horse barn?" Arizona asked. "Where's that at?"

"That's gonna cost your friend five more, copper." Goldie gave him a drunken grin.

A few moments later, the men left the house, heading to Muddle Street. The police knew all about Ernie's, which held all-night card games. He told Ray the vice squad broke up games there several times a year. That was aside from the occasional murder, which was usually the result of some gambler trying to cheat another.

"Were you planning on running her into the station?" Ray asked.

"Nah, too much paperwork for her just to walk out in a few hours," he explained. "I was hoping she would break open with the threat, but she's damn stubborn. We have a history. I've picked her up a few times down on the docks. The woman's good at lifting wallets when she's not turning tricks. She's good at getting sailors into alleys for a quickie. The drunks forget to check their dropped pants when they're finished. Ulysses plays her pimp sometimes when he's not fixing up stolen cars. They're a real pair."

"That explains the reception, alright. You think she's on the level?" Ray wondered aloud.

"Well, we'll know soon enough. I'm a lowly cop. I can't afford to pay my informants," Arizona grinned as they turned up a quiet street.

After he parked the car, they remained in sight of the garage about half a block away. The place looked empty.

"We'll take the alley," the policemen told him as he nodded to the back alley.

When they reached the building, they heard voices coming from inside. Arizona pulled his service revolver when they reached the back door. There was a feeble light coming from the bulb above. Ray noticed a small rectangle about shoulder high on the door. He gave a couple of quick knocks. The voices inside the room went silent, and footsteps on concrete came toward the door. The peephole on the door opened.

"Whadya want?" A growling voice asked as a man's rugged face appeared behind the hole.

Arizona placed the barrel of his gun in the man's face.

"It's the police, Ernie. Open up, or you lose your head," Arizona told him.

With a click, the door slowly opened. Arizona pushed his body against the door, and it swung open wide. The large man barring the way fell backward, and the two men entered the room. Inside, they found a handful of people crowded around a card table.

"Lieutenant, do you want me to deal you in?" The cocky voice of a uniformed policeman asked as he looked over his shoulder at the intruders. Arizona scowled and pocketed his gun.

"Damn it, O'Brien, what the hell are you doing here?" the detective growled at the uniformed cop. "I ought to run all of your butts in and let you deal with the DA."

O'Brien laughed, but his eyes were dark. He took a drink from his silver flask.

"Hell, Campbell, stop flapping your jaw," he said. "This is my side of town, and I'm running ahead today. You can go kiss the chief's ass on your time."

O'Brien turned back to his game.

"Yeah, right after you get off your knees for him, you damn Paddy," Arizona shot back. The uniformed policeman got up from his chair. His face was livid, but he hesitated as Arizona stepped closer.

"Try it, O'Brien, and I'll finish it," Arizona warned him. "Your pension won't pay enough to fix your broken face."

As the men appeared ready to fight, the rest of the gambling crew around the table backed away. Ray looked at the men around the room, but none of them seemed familiar. After a moment, Arizona noticed O'Brien glance away, and he knew he won the round.

"Come on, he's not here," Arizona told Ray, and they left the building.

When they reached the car, Ray could tell his friend was about to explode. Ray slid inside while the policeman paced outside for a moment as he lit his cigar.

When Arizona got into the car, his face was still in a scowl. The vehicle remained quiet when he drove along the quiet street before turning toward Canal Street.

"Damn corrupt cops," Arizona finally spoke, hunched over the steering wheel and chewing on his cigar.

"Yeah, it's too bad you can't run them out," Ray observed. "There were always corrupt people anyplace you look hard enough."

"Christ, you don't have to look hard here," his friend grunted out through clenched teeth. "O'Brien's got payoffs from gamblers all along that street. That's why he wins, and there's not a damn thing I can do about it."

"You know anything about this old horse barn that Goldie spoke about?" Ray asked him to change the subject.

"Naw, but my guess it's a place for them to strip out parts from stolen cars or repaint them to resale out of state. Most crooks stay close to what got them cuffed in the first place," Arizona told him. "I still don't get the connection to kidnapping. It's out of this guy's league. Plus, Maria Andras's involvement with this guy makes no sense. I think you need to come clean with me."

"Sorry, but Orella is my client. You know I can't spill anything beyond her abduction." Ray chose his words carefully when he saw his friend debating the wisdom of keeping Ray with him.

"I'll tell you this much. Orella was at the Smyth Estate for a few days. They brought her in as some damn screwy entertainment that would give that whore Goldie a run for her money. Her father's some diplomat, and all I was doing was taking her home."

Arizona nodded.

"Alright, so you're helping her leave town, and these two mugs got her," the cop said. "That still leaves us hanging out here. I've only got your word on this."

"No, you have a tag number that gave you a lead. When we find Orella, you'll have everything you want," Ray promised. "And you'll have a full book of charges you can use to take down Maria Andras."

They parked next to a stripped car and waited for a moment. Nothing stirred around the large barn with it's wide-open doors. The gray four-door car sat near the door.

"Well, that looks like the car I saw," Ray told his friend. "I can't make out the plate yet."

"We'll soon see," the lieutenant quietly opened the car door. "You can come along, but don't get trigger-happy."

They took a quick walk over to the car. Arizona confirmed the license plate number. He pointed to the barn, and they followed a cow path through the grass to the edge of the structure. It remained quiet inside as Arizona led them to the entrance. He peeked around the corner, then pulled his service revolver. As he started around the corner, he waved Ray to follow. They took several paces before they stopped just inside the entrance.

Slowly twisting in the middle of the room was the body of Ulysses Davis. Hung up by one leg like some side of beef, the large man was naked but for his undershirt. The corpse had the other leg bent back, and the ankle tied behind his back at his wrists. A dark puddle of blood covered the concrete from the jagged wound along the man's throat. The lack of blood on the ground surprised Ray.

"Damn, not again." Arizona's disgusted expression filled his face as he crouched down to get a closer look at the dead man. "That's Davis, alright. What the hell is going on?"

Ray remained quiet as he walked around the building. Arizona followed along as they looked for Orella. Ray found the overturned chair and a cot in the back, along with her torn clothes. He also noticed the iron rod in the remains of the fire. The air still held the sickening odor. He remembered the stench vividly from his time in the Pacific.

"I think they tortured the girl for information. Wilber's going to pay before the cops get him," Ray vowed as he handed the blouse to Arizona.

The cop looked at the torn fabric and sniffed it.

"But why?" Arizona grimaced at the smell. He remembered the same burned flesh odor in Italy.

"Wilber wanted a ring that Orella gave to me. I was supposed to keep it safe," Ray admitted. "I didn't think she was in something this deep."

"You're not making any sense. First, you have a kidnapping, so where's this Dela Cruz woman? You can't expect me to believe that Wilber took off with the girl after he knocked off his partner and hung him up like a trophy," Arizona told him emphatically.

Ray shook his head as he dropped the cloth to the floor.

"I don't know what the hell's going on," he admitted. Ray turned his attention to the body.

"Maybe we got a lynching, and the Klan is involved? She's from the Philippines. They hate foreigners nearly as much as the blacks and the Catholics."

"No, this is just like another couple of murders I've got," Arizona growled out. "Besides, I would have heard about those racist bastards running around here. While there are plenty of people who hate the black folk in Oyster City, the Klan would have left a warning to everyone that they were back."

"You know this killing looks like someone staged it," Ray told him. "It kind of reminds me of those murders that Sirk is working on."

"What, those killings involving those artists and paintings?" The policeman commented as he walked around the body. "No, I'm not buying that. This murder is too much like the ones I've been working on," Arizona said, then went quiet.

"What are you talking about?" Ray asked.

"Never mind!" The policeman shook his head. "What we have is murder. This woman, Orella Dela Cruz, isn't here and Wilber is not around. Now I have to find them and figure out who the hell killed this guy?"

~~~

Maria Andras relaxed on her bed; her lithe naked body still held the sheen of sweat. Satisfied and content from her conquest, she watched Abby while her young maid slid on her black uniform dress. A sniffle came from the brunette as she hurried to dress.

"You're turning into a decent lover," Maria told the maid, sliding her hand along the inside crook of Abby's arm where several needle marks showed. "So much more experienced than when you arrived."

The maid froze at the touch, and Maria gave a wicked laugh before she rolled over closer to the white nightstand. She picked up her Benzedrine inhaler, enjoying the view of the maid's small breasts while Abby put her arms through the dress top. Maria inhaled deep breaths of the stimulant before she rose from the bed.

"Have my golden dress ready for me for this evening," Maria ordered when she stood next to the maid. "I have a special party going on tonight."

She grabbed the girl by her dark brown hair, forcing her head back. Maria gave her servant a long, probing kiss before she walked to the closet.

"Don't worry, my sweet, I have some pills to get you happy," she told Abby. "I can't have you all strung out on heroin. You'll need your strength. My friends expect you to keep them happy all evening. Maybe I should probably start charging them."

Walking into the large closet, Maria put on a peach nightgown. It was silk with a low V-neck and lace trim. When she came out of the closet, Maria went to her dressing table, where Abby stared into the mirror while she arranged her pleated headband. The maid had already thrown on her white apron, which remained untied.

Tomorrow, I've arranged for a new guy to work on the estate's gardens," Maria told her with a pat on the butt when she stepped behind her. "According to my sources, he needs the money. There's always a desperate nature to a junkie looking to get their fix," Maria told her as her evil grin broadened. She stared into the mirror at her victim while she tied the apron for the maid.

"I'll have you join us," her wicked tone nearly cackled in delight. "After all, you need to earn your money before I give you what you crave."

"You made me this way," Abby told her, with tears streaming down her cheeks.

Maria grabbed her maid by the shoulders and swung her around.

"You know I don't like tears," she slapped her with a hard backhand across the face.
~~~

The servant cried out, holding her reddening cheek.

"You backtalk me anymore, and I'll forget our deal. Do you want that?" Maria's callous tone dripped with venom.

"My last girl got so desperate for a kick that I heard she was turning tricks down at the docks with anyone who paid. Later, she jumped from the roof of a warehouse. It didn't kill her, so they put her in the nuthouse. Just remember that, my dear."

She pushed the maid aside, walking toward her bed. She smiled at the thought of a long, hot bath when she noticed a note in a red envelope on top of her dresser. With a glance at Abby, she picked it up.

"Did you bring this?" She accused the girl, who immediately looked around. Maria hurried over to confront her maid, shoving the envelope in her face.

"No, ma'am! I never saw that before," Abby told her fearfully, as she threw up her hands to ward off the expected beating. "You grabbed me as soon as I walked into the room."

Maria scowled, then ordered her maid to leave. After she left, Maria hurriedly ripped open the paper. Her face went pale, and she rushed out of her room.

They can't have her here!

Fifteen minutes later, Maria stood in a dirty room in the cavernous basement of the mansion. Next to her was Weyer, who hurried over next to the woman after he nervously closed the thick wooden door behind them. They looked down at the naked girl lying on a dusty antique sofa. A chain ran from the iron shackle around Orella's ankle to a bolt driven into the limestone wall. The drugged woman shivered involuntarily in the damp air.

"She gave the Singsing to Irish. He's the damn detective you suggested we hire." Maria's scathing tone focused on Weyer.

"Cousin, if you hadn't treated Miss Dela Cruz like one of your servants, losing the ring would never have happened."

He looked longingly at Orella, leaning over her to brush her hair from her face. Weyer frowned at the caustic looking burn marks running across her belly.

"It's a shame they tortured her for the information," he remarked. "Wilber did that to her?"

"Yes, he called me asking about what to do with her," she explained. "He got the little bitch to confess she gave that ring to that shamus, Irish, and they were trying to leave town. Somehow, the moron left Irish alive. I expected her to go away. Now she's down here, and that son of a bitch has the police involved."

"My, that Wilber is a brutish thug with no brains," he commented. "Still, you have her now. I'm sure she'll be happy to stay with you."

Weyer's sarcasm went unnoticed as he looked at his cousin. Clear to him, she was trying not to tell him something.

"Of course, you realize that having her in your home is risky. Servants are nosy, no matter how compliant you make them," Weyer reminded her.

Her glance revealed her tension, but Maria hid it well.

"I didn't have a choice," she told Weyer. "They left her here. My ex-husband left me a message this morning. She'll be here until the next full moon."

Weyer shook his head, letting out a whistle.

"You didn't tell me that the Shadows brought her here. They don't like mistakes. Do they know about the ring and Wilber?"

"I'm not sure," she confessed. "But I suspect Peter found out something from the police. She told Peter about her noble blood and their link to the ring. You know how close Phillip and Peter are."

"You have a problem if they suspect you've completely lost the Singsing," he reminded her.

"I'm not worried about that," Maria lied to him.

Weyer saw through the statement, but he let it go.

"Wilber came to the house this morning. He wants his money now after claiming he found his partner sacrificed," she continued to ramble on while she started pacing. "Unfortunately, he wasn't there when the Shadows grabbed this girl. Now I have to figure out what to do about him as well."

"Well, I'm glad I'm not in your shoes," he said. "He can't go to the police, but he could bring in the Jacobi gang into the picture. Phillip and Peter would not like that. They will not like the idea of more people becoming involved."

Maria's face turned pale.

"What do you mean? Surely, you don't think I'm afraid of gangsters," she replied. "Besides, I'm not the one that stole the Singsing. We have her now, so I need to pay off Wilber. That little man will go away with some cash."

"I'm not talking about Jacobi. While you are an Andras, I don't believe that pardons you from the wrath of the Shadows. Another mistake…well, I don't think you want them to return for you," he pointed out. "Even your ex-husband's connections won't help. You should remember the La Spina problem they took care of."

"I was born in Oyster City," she replied defiantly. "I'm too well known and heir to Andra's house, along with everything else, once that old lady finally cashes it in."

Weyer gave her an odd look before he returned his stare to the prisoner. He was enjoying the idea of his cousin's plight.

"Nevertheless, I'm glad I'm not in your place," he told her. "What do you plan on doing?"

"Obviously, she stays here," Maria said quietly, and she went silent. "I need to get the ring from that detective. Once I have that, the other things are just incidentals."

Weyer shook his head as he laughed.

"My dear Maria, you are always the same. Swat the hornet's nest, then hope someone else gets stung." He brushed his hand across Orella's forehead, then smugly smiled at Maria.

"I see several risks to your future, but I'm sure you have it all figured out," he told her sarcastically.

Maria's face wrinkled as she thought about her position.

"Alright, Johann, I know how you think," she told him. "Since we were kids, you've done the same thing when I run into a problem. Now, what risks do you see?"

She hated the way the grin on his face grew while she asked.

"I guess you won't mind coming down here daily to keep her quiet. Plus, you'll have extra time to keep the servants from noticing you coming down here," he told her off-handedly. "And surely, you have a plan for that detective named Irish and the cops. How do you plan on stopping people from asking too many questions? After all, you invited Orella over to the estate. Irish has spoken with her, so you don't know how much he knows. I'm glad you have this all figured out, and I'm sure you'll have no problems."

Weyer opened the door.

"What do you want?" Maria asked as her cousin started to walk out.

"Do you want my help?" He inquired as he paused.

"Oh, quit being impossible," she told him. "I know how your evil mind works. It's not the first time we've played this game. You know where my bedroom is, and I can bring some of my servants in for you. Just name your terms."

He smiled, turning back with his hand on the doorknob.

"Well, you are going to be disappointed, cousin. Your problem is too large for such a simple solution. While an orgy is an interesting offer, it's become rather cliché with you," he told her. "You've waded into a much deeper pool, and I've grown wiser over the years. We'll start with that Vashetu Emerald that you have locked away. I have someone interested in purchasing it."

"Never!" Maria's face filled with fury as she stepped toward him. "That was a present from my father. My mother would never approve."

Weyer smiled; his face looked like a troll in the shadows.

"I'm not bargaining with you," he said firmly. "I can fix your problems, but there's a very steep price for me putting myself in danger with the Shadows or the police."

"You're a bastard," she told him, then went silent.

Weyer stepped close, placing his hand on her cheek. His fingers were like ice.

"I'm not greedy," he said. "Since you're a dear friend, I'm willing to give you twenty-five percent of the cut. We're both taking a risk in this. Look at it this way; it's just sitting there in the safe getting dusty, and the money you get can keep you from relying on your monthly stipends. You wouldn't mind more independence from your ex-husband and your mother."

"I won't do it," Maria insisted.

Weyer shrugged his shoulders and returned to the stairs. He got about halfway up when he heard her voice as he expected.

"Alright, you fat little man," she told him scathingly, standing by the open door with fury filling her face. "You can sell the damn stone, but I get fifty percent of it."

Weyer glanced back, enjoying his new power over her. Her arrogant demeanor always grated on him. Weyer knew more of her secrets than she imagined. Besides, he did not like her. His knowledge gave him an advantage over her birthright if he played his cards right.

"Forty percent," he replied. "I'm going for breakfast. You can start by calling your dope peddler. You'll need to keep Miss Dela Cruz quiet until it's time for her to leave. Then you can call that detective to come over with the ring. Use your sexy routine and tell him you have the money; he'll go for it. I saw him eyeballing your legs."

Weyer started whistling as he continued up the stairs. Maria glanced back into the room before she closed the door. She locked it, making sure she kept the key while she grumbled about her treatment at the hands of the short, fat man.

Chapter 4: Reflections Will Kill You

After only a few hours of sleep, Ray forced himself out of bed. It was at the insistence of the continuous ringing phone sitting on his desk in the other room. On the other end of the line was Samantha Carter.

"Ray, would you mind coming right over to see me? I need your help," she said.

"Has something happened?" He asked, suppressing a curse when he stubbed his toe on the corner of the desk. Groggy from lack of sleep and worry, Ray had almost forgotten about the murders involving the gruesome paintings. There was a brief pause before she spoke.

"No, but I really must talk to you about a call I got from Reece. He was at the art center. Can you make it this morning?"

"Is your father there? If I show up, we'll have to explain," he reminded her.

"It's alright," she replied with a laugh. "My dad doesn't carry a gun, and he's at work."

"Alright, you can expect me in fifteen minutes," Ray told her as he was already looking back into the bedroom for his pants.

While he didn't believe in intuition, Ray pushed the gas pedal down harder than usual on his old Nash LaFayette 400. Something about the call bothered him. He could tell by the tone of Samantha's voice that she had something for him. He pressed his luck, running a couple of stop signs without killing himself. After a near-miss in his speeding frenzy, Ray grew sore with himself.

Sure, the woman looked great, and her kisses were hot and passionate. But he wasn't getting paid to keep his nose in this mixed-up mess of murders. Besides, it might be nothing. Probably just some left-over anxiety Samantha had from not telling the cops about something trivial.

Hell, she'll tell me about an overdue library book from when she was a kid.

His stomach growled, reminding him he should have stopped off to do some damage to a couple of eggs and a minute steak. He had plenty of time. However, the gnawing feeling coming from his stomach wasn't just the hunger, and Ray continued pushing his vehicle to keep up the pace.

The two-story stately white home on Clipper Avenue rested on one of those large, deep lawns that appeared to go back for acres. In this part of the city, that could be possible since the Carter family had plenty of money. Parking at the curb, he started walking to the house along with a long gravel walkway. About halfway up the immaculate green lawn, the shamus noticed the blue front door stood partly open.

Any other day, he might have decided it probably meant nothing and walked to the door. But Ray remembered the destroyed Chinese porcelain back at the Art Center that came from a bullet aimed at his head. He decided to take a long sweep around to the side of the house, where the long driveway went to a large garage.

A row of thick green hedges lined the path. He made it to the first window, which appeared partially opened. Carefully stepping through the Azalea bushes to peek inside, the shamus heard a gasp on the other side of the neatly trimmed shrubs behind him.

A middle-aged woman stared at him from the other side of a hedge. Her fat face held a mixture of shock and outrage as she had a watering pitcher in her hand.

"Hey there, mister, just what do you think you're doing?" the woman yelled, her gravelly voice startling Ray.

The guilty look on his face didn't calm the situation.

"I'm calling the police," she barked at him before she started toward her yellow house.

The nosy neighbor's round form shook like jelly as she hurried across the lawn. Then he heard a door slam from inside the back of the Carter house. The heavy sound of footsteps running across the wood floors came through the window.

Ray rushed around to the end of the house. As he ran up the back steps, he nearly collided with a masked person running out of the house. A flash of silver caught his eye, and his experience from the war kicked in. Ray grabbed the intruder's arm while using his attacker's momentum to twist away. Both of them tumbled into the grass. Ray landed awkwardly on his back, unable to grab the bandit, who quickly rolled to his feet. During their brief struggle, the knife went flying into the bushes.

Ray pulled his weapon, but the intruder was already running past the garage. When he reached the back of the structure, all he found was dense foliage and the sound of someone frantically scurrying through the underbrush. The thick brush heading down the hill to the back street could have hidden a tank. Ray followed the vague direction of the sounds before they disappeared. He continued down the sloping ground until he heard a car start up and hurry away with the sound of screeching tires. Cursing under his breath, he put his gun away and retreated to the Carter house.

Rummaging through the bushes, Ray eventually found the knife and went inside the house through the open back door. Passing through a tidy kitchen, he went to the door leading to the dining room. As he placed his ear on the door, he heard a sound like muffled half cries.

When Ray burst into the room, the first thing he found was a large dining room table forcing him to go around. He looked into the next room, where he discovered a gagged Samantha Carter sitting tied to a chair. The woman frantically struggled to turn her head in his direction as a blindfold covered her eyes. Muffled yells trickled through her gag. He dashed to her chair, which faced a large fireplace. He stepped behind to remove the cloth covering her eyes. She suddenly reacted at his touch, frantically trying to twist away from the shamus, no doubt expecting impending death.

"It's alright now; you'll be okay. It's Ray Irish," he told her softly, and Samantha fell back in the chair as he untied the blindfold and gag.

"My God, he nearly killed me." She blinked several times, shaking her head.

Samantha stared up at a big oil painting on the wall across from her while Ray worked on her bound wrists.

"Christ, save me!" she exclaimed.

Ray looked up from behind her and joined the woman to stare at another gruesome canvas. In the gold-framed painting hanging above the fireplace, two corpses sat inside a traditional living room. A woman in white, blindfolded and gagged, had blood covering her front from a severed throat. Next to the woman sat a man with terror covering his face. A knife was sticking out of his chest while a straight-edge razor rested in the man's hand. The detective noticed the shadow of a masked man in the background, the white face of the mask smiling at the scene. He instantly guessed the canvas came from the same crazy painter, Reece.

"Damn!" Ray cursed as he let the implications sink in. "It looks like the bastard tried to make another copycat murder. Too bad I couldn't catch the SOB."

Samantha's face carried a mixture of ongoing fear and immediate relief as she finished removing the gag around her neck.

"I was going to die the same way as that woman in the painting," she shivered. "It's the same picture that Lieutenant Sirk spoke to my dad about the other day."

Ray used the knife to cut through the rope wrapped around her arms and legs. That was when he suddenly appreciated the neighbor's loud warning about the cops, which scared the killer into flight. Otherwise, Ray might have witnessed Samantha's murder from the side window.

"It was Reece who did this to you, wasn't it?" He asked as he held out a hand for Samantha, who took it as she stood. The woman shook her head, unsteady on her feet, while she gingerly touched the side of her head.

"No, I didn't see him. He had a ski mask on. But whoever attacked me was taller and stronger than Gabriel. You said you saw him," she told him.

"Yeah, he and I collided at the back door. You're right; he's bigger than Reece," Ray agreed. "How did he get in?"

"I'm not sure, but the back door's usually unlocked. I thought I heard my father in the kitchen. When I walked into the living room, someone hit me from behind. I fell, and before I could do anything, he was on top of me." She paused, trying to catch her composure.

"He didn't say anything, just gagged me and wrapped me up with rope. After he put me in this chair, he moved the painting so I could see it better. Then forced me to face that painting while he placed the knife on my cheek," Samantha told him in a whisper.

"Then, he cackled with a laugh like a crazy man as he put the blindfold on me. The bastard wanted me to know that he was going to cut my throat just like that picture."

"I heard my neighbor yelling at someone about calling the police," she continued. "Then I heard him curse and take off into the next room."

"Yeah, that was me. Can you give me any more details about the guy?" Ray asked.

Her face went blank, and she shook her head.

"I'm sorry, no. He just had on a black shirt and dungarees. I've never had this happen before."

"It's alright, I'm just searching for how you can identify the guy," he gave her a reassuring grin.

"Is that painting by Reece?" He asked, nodding with a frown at the framed canvas on the mantel.

She paused long enough for him to look at her.

"No, that's a picture by Felix Roman," she finally conceded.

"Really!" The surprising answer forced him to review the canvas again.

"I heard something about him the other day. They say he was good." Ray looked back at the canvas. "But it's pretty gruesome."

He decided against saying anything more when he noticed the woman's eyes light up at the mention of the guy's name.

"You shouldn't judge the image against the past," she chastised him lightly. "Although I have to admit that I never liked that picture. Everyone believed Felix's work to be the best in a generation. He liked to say all of his passion was a rebellion against the standard. He gave me that painting, and my dad insisted on putting it there. It just gave me the creeps."

She paused, lost in memories.

"Yeah, I'll agree with you there," he told her.

"When Felix came back from the war, his injury left him disfigured. Felix only allowed me to see him in the hospital one time. That was only while the bandages still covered his face. He couldn't even talk to me, so he wrote notes. When he got out, he wouldn't let anyone see him," she explained with pain crossing her eyes. "Then, an art dealer in the capital convinced him to show several of his pieces in an exposition. I didn't even know about the show, but I heard people kept looking at him and not his art. The whole thing just drove him away. I don't think he could endure people pitying him. All I know is that his personality changed. He became resentful with those of us who tried to help. One day he vanished, just left me a note. Nobody has heard from him since that day."

Ray turned his attention to the painting, hating it but trying to find clues in the canvas.

"From your tone, I would say you still care deeply for him." He told her. "It's funny how you never mentioned him to me before."

"I don't see why that should concern you," she replied with a flash of fire when Ray turned to her. "Listen, we had a few good times, but you don't own me."

"Maybe not, but it explains things to me now. Let me give you my rule number one for those who want my help." Ray said to her. "If they tell me the truth, I find it a lot easier to help. It also keeps me from walking away."

A long pause turned the room silent, and she finally took a deep breath.

"I'm sorry I spoke like that. You did save my life." She tried to smile. "Felix and I were to be married before he joined the army and left to go overseas."

"Yeah, I get it," he told her.

He didn't want to keep plowing the same ground about her old boyfriend.

"Now, why did you call me this afternoon? Did you know your life would be in danger?"

Samantha gnawed on her lip before she spoke.

"Gabriel Reece phoned me just before I called you. He discovered something about a painting at the Art Center. I've never heard him so excited. He said he had to talk to me before he would go to the police." She looked at the delicate watch on her wrist, then smoothed her dress. "He should have been here by now. I wanted you to be here to listen to his story." Ray walked across the room as he listened to her. He frowned at the thought, but tested his theory.

"Do you think he's going to accuse Felix Roman of Townsend's murder?" He asked her. "I remember how you reacted when I walked into the exhibition room when you were with Reece. There was more bothering you than just that body. You noticed something about the painting hanging above the night watchman, didn't you? What was it?"

Her eyes widened, and Samantha's face reddened.

"I should have told you what I noticed at the time," she said. "I remembered that the same painting was in Roman's old studio at one point. When we were waiting for the police, Reece told me he copied that painting before Felix left town. He told me to keep it to myself since the Art Center didn't know, and they paid him good money for it. When he called me this morning, Reece told me he saw Felix's picture down at a thrift store. The owner of the shop said that Felix is still around town. Reece told me he could prove it."

"Then you got nervous that Reece would point the finger at Roman. That means your ex-boyfriend would be under the gun," he finished his thought. "Is that why you wanted me to stop by?"

Samantha frowned, but she didn't dispute what he said.

"Last year, I met with Felix's doctor before he got out of the hospital. The wound permanently scarred him," she explained. "Felix left me a note saying he saw too much in North Africa. The bitterness made him leave. I just can't believe he committed the murder. Only a lunatic could have done those horrible things to that poor man in the art center."

"And Mrs. Smyth," Ray reminded her.

She nodded, looking at her hands.

"Well, you might be right," Ray conceded as he touched her shoulder gently. "However, you need to remember that right now, everyone who was in that art center is a suspect to the cops. If what Reece says about Felix Roman is true, we can't rule him out as a suspect. They know it took more than one person to lift Townsend's body upon that makeshift cross after the murderer or murderers nailed him down to the beam."

Ray lifted her head, forcing the woman to look at him.

"It means that whoever killed the night watchman must have had help. I'm pretty sure you're smart enough to recognize that," he told her. "The fact you wanted me to come over tells me you can't convince yourself that Roman isn't involved somehow. Whoever just tried to kill you had to know something about this painting being here. Someone knows a lot about you and your dad. There are no coincidences here. Somehow, there's a plan behind all of this."

Her eyes searched his, trying to work through questions in her mind.

"No, I won't believe Felix has anything to do with that," she declared adamantly. "Other people know about his paintings. Lieutenant Sirk came by the house yesterday. He was asking us about all the paintings that my dad collected," she told him. "I overheard the policemen tell my dad about the painting in Rose's apartment when she died. That's what got me to thinking about copies. You know how artists like to improve their techniques by copying other painter's works."

"No, I didn't know that," Ray said.

"Well, they do, but Felix and Reece were rivals. Felix didn't like Reece, not one bit," she replied. "And he didn't like him copying his paintings. Right before Felix joined the army, they argued about it. It's obvious that the police believe Gabriel's involved in this."

Her blue eyes avoided his.

"Are you telling me that Felix Roman might have set up Reece to be the fall guy?" Ray asked.

"No! If you knew Felix, you would know that's impossible," she said firmly. "I believe someone else is trying to put this on both of them. Someone is trying to confuse the police with all of this stuff about paintings. Look how Lieutenant Sirk keeps his focus on those who painted those pictures. They're artists; it doesn't mean that Reece or Felix Roman murdered anyone. I thought you might see my point. It makes no sense for either of them to kill a guard and Rose, does it? I needed someone to believe me."

Ray stared at the woman for a long moment. It was hard to tell, but he believed she was trying to protect her friends from Sirk.

"Well, you're making sense to me. Alright, I'll try to keep an open mind," Irish promised.

She gave him a sad smile.

"Thanks," Samantha said. "It makes me miserable to know that someone might use those paintings in murder."

Ray cocked his head at the thought.

"People are people, no matter what clothes you put on them," he replied. "I've seen some people that look like choir boys turned into deranged killers because Uncle Sam trained them. Others might kill just for kicks, or maybe their roommate snored too loud."

"Not everyone in the world is like that," she said with a frown at his cynical observation. "I know, without a doubt, Felix wouldn't kill me. We were in love."

"Maybe Roman is jealous because Reece took his place in your affections," Ray explained as he glanced down at the knife in his hand.

"But that's not true," she protested. "Gabriel and I are just good friends. I've known him for many years. He's not like that at all."

"You might feel that way, but I'm willing to bet that your two boyfriends don't. Jealousy can do strange, terrible things to people," Ray told her as he gave a thin smile.

"Listen, Samantha. I'm not saying anyone is a murderer at this point," he continued. "It's a pretty mixed-up case so far. Townsend's murder would only enhance Gabriel Reece's fame, if not his reputation. What little I've learned about artists, if Felix Roman is involved in the killings, he wouldn't want to put Reece out there as the top dog."

He took another glance at the painting on the wall, his face displaying a gnawing concern.

"You know, there's still something bothering me about this picture," he said. "I feel something is staring us in the face, and we just can't see it."

Samantha started for the phone, telling him.

"I need to call my dad about what happened. I'll be right back. Shouldn't we call the police about this?"

"Wait a minute," Ray exclaimed as something clicked inside his mind. She stopped in her tracks.

"The killer is following a pattern about the deaths shown in the paintings. On this canvas, two dead people seem to be lovers. Was he waiting for Reece to show up after your death? I don't see another chair that would work in this room, although he could haul in a chair from the kitchen, I suppose."

Samantha came back to the fireplace, and her strength impressed him. Some people he knew would have fallen apart after her experience. Instead, the woman peered closely at the painting.

"Maybe they overheard my phone call," she suggested.

Suddenly, Samantha turned to him, her eyes wide.

"You said there might be two killers. Could they have split up, deciding to commit separate murders?"

Ray reacted immediately to her thought, dashing toward the phone on a small table by the window.

"Or worse, you said Reece was already supposed to be here. What's his address?" he called out as he tapped on the receiver handle, trying to get an operator.

A minute later, Ray had Lieutenant Sirk on the telephone line, telling him to meet at Reece's place. He demanded that Sirk get a squad car over to the apartment. When Sirk asked for details, Ray quickly barked back that there was no time. The shamus hung up. He realized the lieutenant would want his scalp for his action, but he was willing to risk it. Samantha stood by the door after grabbing her purse.

"I'm going with you," she stated, making it clear she was not asking.

"Of course, you're not getting out of my sight until we get the answers sorted out," he gave her a forced grin.

As the car careened through the streets to Reece's home, Ray kept trying to get to the apartment while not accidentally killing the woman sitting next to him. When they arrived a few minutes later, there were no police cars yet. The building was several blocks away from Carter's home, which made Ray suddenly wary. His attempts to get Samantha to remain behind went nowhere. With a deep breath, Ray slid out of the car and entered the building. He took the stairs two steps at a time to the third floor, with Samantha hurrying as fast as her heels would allow. Reaching the closed door of Room 4A, he put his ear to the wood and heard somebody moving around inside.

Ray pulled out his .45 Auto and quickly pushed through the door. He nearly tripped over an artist's easel by the door. In the middle of the room, the body of Gabriel Reece sat in a chair. His position looked precisely like the man in the oil painting back at Carter's house. Blood soaked his shirt, coming out of a hole in the man's chest. However, there was no weapon. He glanced over at Samantha. She had her clutched hands pressed to her mouth, trying to keep a desperate scream from erupting. The anguish and disbelief filled her face at the horror in front of her.

He was about to reach for her when Ray heard movement coming from the bathroom. He made his way to the closed door and listening carefully. Inside the room was the faint sound of a grunt and movement. On the floor, he noticed tell-tell spots of blood leading to the door. He slowly turned the handle, but the door handle would not move. Inside, an inhuman wail erupted, and Ray immediately kicked in the door.

Sitting on the tile floor with his back propped against the white bathtub, Francis Carter the Third stared at his blood-covered hands. In one hand, he still held a bloody knife.

"Don't try anything stupid," Ray told him while keeping his gun leveled at the man.

The suspect blinked several times, trying to come out of a trance.

"You don't think I could have murdered him?"

"Nah, I always see people covered with blood and carrying a knife," Ray replied.

Carter looked past the gun pointed at him.

"Gabriel asked me to visit. We were to discuss a painting of his which he was trying to persuade the Arts Center to purchase."

He looked down, shaking his head as he spoke.

"I found him like that."

Disbelief covered Carter's face while Irish inched closer.

"And you decided to take the knife to the bathroom as a souvenir. Yeah, that happens all the time," Ray replied.

Carter's voice cracked as he explained.

"I pulled out the knife and tried to cover his wound with my hands. It was a natural reaction to his chest wound, something I remembered from Civil Defense training. I was trying to save him."

He dropped his head.

"I was too late. There was no pulse."

Carter looked at him, hope fading from his face.

"I got sick, so I had to come in here. I don't know why I just picked up the knife again."

Ray listened to the desperation in the man's voice while he glanced over to see the remains of lunch inside the toilet bowl.

"Well, you drop that thing, and I'll let you explain it to the cops," Ray told him mildly.

Francis Carter glanced up again before a bitter laugh leaped out of the distraught man. Finally, he gave a deep sigh and dropped the weapon to the floor as Carter's daughter stepped next to Ray. She slipped past him and joined her father in tears. As they embraced, Carter cried with her.

Just a few minutes later, the noise overwhelmed the main living area of the small apartment. Lieutenant Sirk paced back and forth in front of Carter. The policemen held off the reporters who struggled to get inside the apartment while a plainclothes detective covered the body with a sheet. The suspect sat on the couch next to Samantha, her dress stained in dry blood. Lost in their grief, the father and daughter barely exchanged a word.

Over the next hour, semi-organized chaos filled the studio apartment of the dead man. The medical examiner, a slight man who looked like he might blow away in a storm, arrived to give a quick inspection of the body. He officially declared Reece dead. While flashlight bulbs flared from the police photographer getting morbid pictures of the scene, a fingerprint man calmly continued doing his work. Everything centered around the framed copy of Felix Roman's painting of the two corpses. Seeing a duplicate of the same picture at Carter's house gnawed at the shamus like a mouse on cheese.

Sirk's sour expression changed as he listened to Ray give his statement to the sergeant. The policeman had a smug smile when the shamus got to the story of how he found Carter in the bathroom. Sirk had a murder suspect caught holding the knife. In his eyes, the capture of Francis Carter tied up his cases nice and tight.

For his money, Ray did not like it. He watched the usually confident Carter, who sat slumped on the couch with his now clean fingers pressed against his temples. The suspect looked close to shattered; his eyes keenly followed the corpse when the medical examiner and a policeman removed the body from the chair. He had a gut feeling that Reece meant more to the businessman than the price of a painting. A wealthy and busy person made transactions by phone, not going to the guy's apartment.

Lieutenant Sirk started questioning Carter, who began repeating his story. After listening for a moment, the cop grew angry.

"That's a lie!" the tired cop thundered. "You and Roman committed Townsend's murder to increase the value of those paintings that you own. Then you decided to take out Reece to cover your tracks. While you took care of Reece today, you sent Roman to kill your daughter. The only thing that saved her was Irish getting there in time. We just figured it out faster than you could hide all of this using the idea a lunatic is responsible."

"No, you're crazy. I haven't seen Roman since he disappeared," Carter told him in a tired, dejected voice.

His confident frame transformed into a crushed old man. His eyes pleaded with the small group, who observed his movements.

"Your wrong about my father," Samantha interjected. "Like I told Ray, the person who attacked me wasn't Felix Roman. And it wasn't my dad. The person was thinner and shorter."

"I swear to God that I would never hurt my daughter or Gabriel," Carter insisted as he looked up.

Tears welled up in the man's eyes.

"I couldn't do such a thing. You're just looking for a scapegoat."

"Like hell, we've got you, and you're behind the eight ball. The victim's blood covers you, and you have no alibis that stand up." Sirk told the man gruffly, before he turned away.

He walked over to Ray with a broad grin.

"Well, that closes the case. Hell, we will even make the evening newspapers," the cop told the shamus triumphantly.

Ray continued watching Carter. The man appeared lost in another world.

"I don't know about that," Ray replied. "This setup smells like a dead fish. The guy I ran into wasn't Carter, and Samantha swears it wasn't Roman. Now give me a motive on why Felix Roman and Francis Carter kill Townsend in the first place?"

Lieutenant Sirk kept his grin.

"I wondered when you would ask that. The guard got in the way, and the plan fell apart. Guess who owns most of the paintings made by Gabriel Reece, and quite a few of Roman's as well?"

He nodded at Carter before continuing.

"And who do you think will make a mint on the art when the press spins this up? We got a dead artist along with links to the murder." The policeman asked Ray rhetorically.

"I don't know about that," Ray replied. "Samantha just told you she only knew about that one painting made by Felix Roman. Why have two exact copies of the same oil painting unless you're trying to kill two people in two different locations? Reece and Roman are the only ones we know about who could make the copies. This doesn't add up."

"Hotshot, you need to remember that witnesses are usually wrong on height and weight anyway," Sirk told him. "Anyway, it doesn't matter about copies of paintings. Maybe this Felix character got an idea to sucker two people at the same time. Listen, we caught Carter with his hands covered in blood. He had to kill Reece. I don't need any more evidence. That alone will get a conviction. With Samantha Carter's statement, I can put out a warrant for Felix Roman. Once I get him in jail, I can sort out the rest of the details."

The detective glared at Ray.

"Besides, why should I argue this out with you? You're nothing more than a witness at this point," he said crossly. "You better remember that."

Ray wasn't paying attention since his focus remained on Samantha Carter. She looked dreadful, her pale face overwhelmed by the pain at the loss of a close friend along with the murder accusation against her father. Her dress was bloodstained from holding her father.

"Well, I'm going to take Miss Carter back home?" He told Sirk in a hushed voice. "She's going through a lot right now."

"No, I want you to hang around to finish your statement with my sergeant," Sirk ordered him, still upset at the questions coming from Ray. He didn't like the shamus undermining his arrest. When Sirk looked over at Samantha, he relented.

"I see what you mean," he told Ray with a grumble. "I'll have one of my men take her home."

Samantha overheard the conversation and gave Ray a weak smile. While she insisted on staying with her father, Sirk forced the woman to leave. A policeman who looked too young to be out of the academy escorted her. Before leaving, she bent over and kissed her father on the forehead. Ray stared at the door after they left, then he finished his statement with a nearby sergeant.

~~~

It was early afternoon when Ray drove to his office, lost in thought. He strongly doubted Carter had killed anyone. The whole murder scene was surreal. The cold and calculating killing involved a painting like the one in Carter's house. Sirk believed Carter tripped up, staying just long enough to be captured. While it was easier for Sirk to wrap up the killings, Ray just couldn't buy it. The underlying motive for the murders made no sense. Even a first-year lawyer would point out that Francis Carter was wealthy. A few extra thousand from a mad scheme to raise the value of a few paintings remained far-fetched. Something else drove the murders around the pictures.

The only glimmer of hope came when Ray convinced Sirk to monitor the rest of the suspects found in the art center after the murder. He pointed out that he didn't have Roman yet, leaving a possibility that others knew his whereabouts.

He pulled his Nash into an open spot in front of Frank's Diner. It was a place where the newspaper reporters from the Beacon hung out. As he got out of his car, Ray noticed Cat inside the diner. She was chatting with a few of her reporter friends. She recognized him, then turned her back to him as he walked by the window.

So much for reconciliation.

Ray went up the stairs to his office. When he walked inside, he looked around, half-expecting to see someone waiting for him. Disappointed, he went behind his desk and took a seat. Ray looked out the window at the building across the street. He was tired, but he could see Orella's face as he stared out at the afternoon traffic. Ray turned the chair around and picked up the phone. After ringing the front desk of the police station, he finally reached his friend.

"What's the news?" he asked.

"Sorry, Irish, but I don't have much for you," Arizona told him. "I've checked the police in the capital, and they haven't seen Wilber. He's been a thorn in their side for a while now, so they're willing to help. I gave them a description of his car and license. If Wilber's still around, we'll find him. I also contacted the state police as well."

"What about his partner?" Ray asked. "You have any clue why someone killed him?"

He went quiet for a moment.
~~~

"Nothing I'll say over the phone. I stopped by to talk with Goldie, and she's skipped town," Arizona said. "Nothing is coming from her about what happened. Don't worry; we'll find this Dela Cruz girl."

"I have an idea that she's in a place you won't be looking for her," Ray grumbled.

"And where's that?" Arizona asked.

"That's something I can't say to a cop." The shamus told him before saying goodbye.

~~~

Ray found Pappy at home that evening. His newsy friend lived in an apartment several blocks from where Ray made his home and office.

"I need the ring," Ray told Pappy as he walked into the living room. "That damn Andras bitch double-crossed me. I'm pretty sure that she kidnapped my client as well."

Pappy whistled at the news, directing his friend toward the dining room.

"Emma hid it for me," he told Ray. Pappy disappeared into the bedroom, and Ray sat at the dining table. As he waited, Ray looked around the immaculate apartment. He almost felt the presence of Emma in the room.

Emma died several years ago. Her husband believed her ghost remained in the apartment. While the whole idea threw him at first, Ray had grown to accept his friend's reality. He'd seen enough death during the war to take the view that some people go a little crazy. If it helped him to get through the day, then Emma was still living there.

Pappy was a friend.

Ray lived by the motto that you don't abandon friends. Twice a month, he came over to have dinner with Pappy and his wife. As they ate, he could almost see the dead woman sitting in the chair next to him.

"Well, here's the ring," the newsy said as he came into the room. He handed Ray the Singsing of Multo. "You know, I almost don't want to give it up to you. My Emma tells me she can feel the power of that thing."

"It's just another high-priced piece of jewelry that people are fighting over," Ray replied sarcastically.

"You're wrong there, my friend," Pappy said as he walked into the kitchen. "Emma felt its power, and I went down to the library to find out more about it."

He raised his voice from the other room.

"That Singsing has an ability to bring ghosts of relatives into the presence of the living. One book even had a legend about the rulers using the Singsing to look into the future." Pappy walked back into the room, carrying a pot of coffee and two cups.

Ray looked at the black serpent coil. He felt the hairs on the back of his neck rise. The five diamonds gleamed nearly black in the light. He shook his head.
~~~

"It's old," Ray gave his friend a dubious glance. "My apologies to Emma, but legends don't mean it's a fact."

Pappy grinned as he poured the coffee.

"Emma told me you'd be skeptical. She said you look tired," he said.

"Why don't you stay for dinner?"

"I appreciate the offer, but I'm not hungry right now," Ray replied.

"Besides, I've got to swing by the Morris house and find out more about Orella's time with them. But if you don't mind, I'll tell you how you can help me. Can you check up on Orella's Dela Cruz's father? Maybe check with your reporter friends at the paper tomorrow."

"Sure, I'll check on this, but what about Cat?" Pappy asked. "She's your inside person at the *Beacon*."

"Yeah, she's not talking with me at the moment," he told him. "It seems I was too nice to the girl who got kidnapped. I called her out for it."

"You made her mad again," the newsy protested. "I told you that you need to take her out to dinner more often. You get more using honey than you get by using vinegar."

"Sorry, Pappy, but Cat brought this on herself. You know she's double-dealing all the time," Ray said. "I'm supposed to apologize for telling her the truth. I don't see that happening."

He sighed and shrugged his shoulders.

"Right now, I have bigger problems," he told him. "I have to find this girl. She's got no one here but me. I need to know who Orella's father is and what he does. She told me he works for the UN. She hasn't received any messages from him for some reason. I smell a rat somewhere."

"Alright, I'll check up on this," Pappy promised. "Are you sure we can't whip up some food? No matter what you say, my wife tells me you look hungry."

"No, thanks," Ray shook his head. "I have to go see Pearl Morris. It's still early in the evening, so hopefully, she won't be three sheets to the wind tonight."

~~~

"Ray Irish, is that really you?" Pearl asked when she entered the foyer of her home. "You left in such a hurry the other morning that you didn't get to meet my husband. Come into the study; we just finished dinner." She excitedly hooked her arm with his and directed him through the dark double doors. The butler followed them and closed the doors behind them. Inside, the large room held a blue tufted couch in the middle of the room with a coffee table and two side chairs. Light oak shelves lined one wall near a fireplace.

He found her husband, James Morris, standing by a small, mirrored bar. The top of the cabinet was open, and he had a drink in his hand. While he saw Pearl's husband on board the *Stanley Rose* before, this was the first time Ray talked with him.
~~~

"Nice to finally meet you!" The man's tone was professionally tolerant as he gave a firm shake of the hand. "I recognize you from that night on the gambling boat. What brings you to our house?"

"I'm sorry to bother you this evening, but I wanted to ask you about your recent guest, Miss Dela Cruz. She's a client of mine. Orella told me she was staying with you for several days," he explained. "I'm afraid someone kidnapped her. We're trying to find her."

"Oh, how dreadful," Pearl spoke up. "Why would anyone do such a thing?" She pulled away from Ray and went to the cabinet.

"What will you have, Mr. Irish?"

"Oh, a shot of whiskey would be great," he replied. "Did Orella call or meet with anyone while she stayed with you? She mentioned she had a difficult time trying to get a message to her father."

Pearl carried over a partially filled tumbler to Ray. She led him to the couch while James took the seat across from them.

"I'm not sure, she said. "You see, I found her at the Western Union station. She looked so out of her element that I offered to help. She stayed with us until you arrived to pick her up. I know she tried calling her father from here several times."

James Morris took a sip of his drink, observing the scene.

"Yes, my wife has a bad habit of picking up strays," he said before taking over the conversation.

"Mr. Irish, are the police involved?"

"Yes, they are," Ray assured him. "Since she was a client, I'm giving them a hand. One kidnapper is Wilber Matthew. He's a thin guy who likes to wear a newsboy cap and a green coat. Did you happen to see him hanging around?"

"No, I can't say that I have," Morris told him.

"But I saw him," Pearl interjected excitedly. She went on to tell Ray about the encounter with Orella.

"But you didn't see him around when I drove by to pick up Orella, did you?" The shamus glanced over at Morris, who observed his wife.

"No, I didn't," she said with a frown. She swirled her drink, nearly spilling it.

"Mr. Irish, the girl was rather quiet during her brief stay. And…well, she wasn't one of our friends," Morris spoke up. "I remember she told us she was staying at the Phillip Smyth estate for a few days. I'm fairly sure something must have happened there. My wife invited her to stay with us only because of the Smyth name."

Ray caught the glare between the husband and wife.

"Now, James, we've been over this," Pearl said with a forced smile.

"Miss Dela Cruz needed help, and she has sufficient means to employ Mr. Irish. Her father is an important diplomat."

Her husband grunted his disbelief.

"Did Orella mention her stay at the Smyth Estate?" Ray asked.

"No, not really," Pearl said. "As you suspect, she was rather upset when we met. Orella remarked on her distaste for Maria, but she was upset with Phillip Smyth as well. You know he's the ex-husband of Maria."

The woman lowered her voice.

"I hear he's quite difficult with people, especially those who aren't from this country. Since he's a leader in the community, I'm sure he has his reasons." The woman went back to looking at the glass in her hand.

She appeared entranced by the melting ice as she continued talking.

"My husband and I were at a charity event for the hospital. Mr. Smyth stopped by to mention his work with the asylum. He knows James, of course. Smyth's on several boards in town, including one of my husband's rival banks."

Ray noticed James get up, returning to the liquor cabinet.

"As you can see, Mr. Irish, my wife likes to keep tabs on all the social events." He poured another drink. "Phillip is not a charming fellow, that's for sure. He's known for his rather violent outbursts. I suspect Miss Dela Cruz did not meet his peculiar standards."

"How so, Mr. Morris?" Ray asked.

The answer he got wasn't a surprise.

"She's a foreigner, of course. Dark skin and all," Morris told him. "And she's a Catholic. Not a good combination, I'm afraid."

"Despite my husband's reservations, she was quite charming to be around," Pearl hastily injected with a forced smile.

"I hope you find her soon."

Ray quickly finished his drink and stood to leave.

"Yeah, so do I. Listen, if she happens to call you, please let me know," the shamus put on his fedora. "I'll let myself out."

~~~

When Ray reached his office, he had a messenger waiting for him. He recognized the young boy was sitting on the steps leading up to his office. It was the newspaper boy who worked the corner near his office each morning.

"Tommy, what are you hanging around here for?" Ray asked.

"A man paid me a dollar to give this envelope to you," the boy explained as he handed over the paper. "It's important, the man told me."

"Thanks," the shamus told him as he handed his young messenger a quarter. Ray walked up the flight of stairs while he ripped open the fine grade paper. Inside was a note from Maria. His face grew hard, and he shook his head at the delicate written lines in the letter, which gave off the same arrogant attitude. But he held the trump card in his coat pocket.
~~~

It took several minutes for Ray to get Maria Andras on the phone. Her voice was smooth with a touch of rattlesnake venom.

"You've been difficult to reach, Mr. Irish. I believe you have the ring we want."

"And how would you know that?" he growled.

"It's quite simple," Maria told him. "Orella stopped by to let me know before she left town."

"Yeah, and I'm telling you that you're a liar. She never volunteered to see you," Ray roared into the phone while he stood up. "Lady, you are making me angry. Now, where's the girl? You want the ring, then you better come up with Orella."

"I'm just quaking that you might be upset, Mr. Irish. My only interest is that Singsing ring," Maria replied firmly. "You want that foreign bitch so bad, then you hand me that ring."

"It's not a game, you bitch," he replied. "Keep stalling, and I'm bringing the cops into this."

There was a long pause before Maria's bitter voice came across the line.

"If you decide to bring the police into this, you will lose," she said in a voice filled with scorn. "Do you believe the district attorney and the police will listen to a second-rate detective? I'll have you thrown in jail for stealing the ring, along with your little foreign girl. You show up at Oldman Pointe in the next 30 minutes with that ring, or you can deal with the consequences. This is the only chance you have to make things right."

The click in his ear came before Ray could respond. With a curse, he placed the receiver back on the phone carrier. A few minutes later, he was driving down First Street, heading out of the city.

So much for the idea that I hold the cards!

Ray recognized Maria Andras wasn't about to let him bluff her on who had the stronger hand in Oyster City. Her last name and family associations left him in a bind. Getting on the wrong side of the DA meant problems for him. On top of that, he couldn't expect any help from his friend, Arizona. Cops were unlikely to risk their careers trying to buck those running the corrupt system. He would have to use the ring as bait. Show them the prize and make them come to his terms. Maybe he could force Maria into a bargain, since they would be out of the city.

Damn it, you can still fix this. Just get Orella away from the bitch.

He briefly considered the .45 auto in his pocket. He could see putting a bullet into Maria and enjoying the idea. Then he shook his head.

Get a hold of yourself; you're tired, you dumb shamus.

In the darkness, he nearly missed the turnoff from the main road. He followed the gravel single lane path to the well-known make-out spot for teen lovers that overlooked Oyster City. Trees lined the way as he drove along. He slowed just before the parking area.

For a moment, he thought he saw a light reflection coming from next to the path. The shamus slowed the car, but he didn't see it again, so he drove into the secluded parking area. His neck hairs rose when his headlights revealed a large yellow Packard parked near the bluff edge. Maria and Weyer stood by the long, expensive car. He pulled to a stop a few paces away and slid out of his car.

"Alright, Mr. Irish, where's my ring?" Maria asked him when he stepped in front of them. "I don't have all night. Guests are waiting for me."

"Yeah, I can't say I care about your problems," he told her as he looked past her. He tried to see inside their car. "Where's Miss Dela Cruz? I told you she is part of the deal."

"And I told you she isn't here. She's on her way back to New York," Maria said with a fake smile. "Johann took her to the station this afternoon."

His eyes narrowed.

"You're too cute," Ray said. "Orella called you a kiki, but I've got better names for your type. Now, quit playing games, you worthless broad. Where is she?"

"Honestly, she's not with us. But we can complete this transaction, and it will pay you well."

Weyer hastily interceded before his cousin could say anything. Maria's stern expression reminded Ray of a mean weasel. He looked at the tubby man.

"I'm sure you can use the money, Mr. Irish. Let us focus on your selling us Singsing right now," Weyer explained.

"I'm telling you to hell with the ring. I still don't believe Orella left town," he replied. "She is in this deal, or I just walk away. I'll stay away from Oyster City and watch you sweat."

"Mr. Irish, I can show you her train ticket stub if you don't believe me. It's right here in my pocket." Weyer opened his jacket to reveal an envelope.

He pulled it out to show Ray.

"I have no reason to lie about this. The girl told us you had the ring before getting to your office to engage your services. She wanted your help, and you failed to protect her," Weyer explained.

"Think about it! You're the reason she had to leave. You have been less than honest with us. She knows that you've lied to her after I told her you kept the ring. She went back to her father. You could have finished this transaction and split the money with her. Yet, you continued to hold on to the ring."

Irish looked at the man. He recognized the lie, but the shamus had no choice. Ray still needed to go along with the charade to learn about Orella's location. He hoped for some luck as well.

"Yeah, I was keeping my cards close to my chest after my run-in with your hired man," Ray explained.

"Your guy Wilber was already looking for the Singsing. A lot of lies have been floating around."

As he spoke to Weyer, Ray failed to see Maria's glance behind him.

"Well, it appears we might have been less than truthful," Maria suddenly agreed. Her manner was unexpectedly smooth again. She slowly began stepping toward Ray, and he didn't like it.

"Do you have the ring or not?" She asked.

"Yes, I have it," Ray said as he tapped his chest pocket. "Now, we were discussing Orella's whereabouts. Prove to me she's on that train!"

"You have got to be kidding," Maria spat out. "Let's get this over with."

She walked to the car and pulled out a small suitcase. She stepped toward Ray and flipped open the case. He saw a stash of greenbacks under the harsh glare of headlights. It was hard to keep a poker face when he saw the money.

"Hell, you're just like the rest of this city," she told them with an evil smile just as Ray heard the sound of a footstep behind him. Before he could turn around, he felt something striking him in the back of his head.

Irish went down like a falling tree, landing face-first in the dirt as the ink of unconsciousness washed over him. Wilber stood over the shamus. He slid his gun into the shoulder holster with a self-satisfied grin.

"Quit standing there like a baboon. Get the ring," Maria ordered Wilber.

He scowled at the woman, but he crouched down and riffled through Ray's coat.

"He's got a couple of things I can use," he told Maria matter-of-factly.

Wilber picked up Ray's .45 auto pistol, and then he held up the Singsing, which sparkled black in the headlights.

"He's not too smart of a cookie," Wilber chuckled.

He turned to his partners.

"And now we talk about my money. That little suitcase you're holding is your down payment."

The thug smiled at the rage on the woman's face.

"You slimy hoodlum," she replied with venomous spite. "Don't you think you're keeping that ring?"

Wilber's boyish face kept his grin, but his eyes were dark.

"Lady, right now, I could plug you both with his gun and walk away with everything," he explained. "Is that what you want me to do? Or do you want to talk some sense?"

He turned Ray's gun toward Weyer, who was slowly backing away.

"Don't move, fat boy,"

The man halted, and Wilber turned his attention back to Maria.

"You tried to keep me out of the picture tonight. I had to follow your car up here to find out the truth. You planned to forget about my cut in this deal. I don't like rats like you two!"

Wilber's icy stare remained on Maria.

"Irish has it right about you. You're a double-crossing dike bitch. And it's going to cost you. My partner got killed, and I know you had something to do with it."

He waited for a response, but Maria remained quiet.

"It's not smart to clam up with my heater pointed at you," he explained. "If I let you and fat boy live, it wouldn't take much for you to leave me hanging out to dry. An anonymous call to the coppers and I'm swinging from a rope for my partner's death. So, I'm going to protect myself."

Wilber's grin turned deadly.

"You're going to come up with more, or I'm killing you here!"

Maria continued glaring at him, but it was Weyer who spoke up.

"What are your terms?" He asked.

"If you want this ring, then it'll cost you another suitcase of cash, two thousand." Wilber placed the ring in his pocket.

He stepped in front of Maria and reached for the suitcase. When she tried to pull back, he shoved the barrel of the gun in her face.

"You hophead little bitch, hand me that now or I'll kill you."

Reluctantly, she gave him the suitcase. Wilber stepped back with a triumphant smile.

"As I said, it's your down payment," he told them. "When you come up with the rest of the cash, you get the ring."

"You can't do this," Maria growled out furiously. Her thin face twisted in rage. "I swear I'll have people who'll track you down and kill you. Now give me that ring."

Wilber pulled back the trigger on the .45 auto.

"Lady, you must really want a bullet. You need to get off the bennies."

"Alright, alright, we'll agree to what you ask," Weyer hurriedly interceded as he stepped next to Maria.

"That ring is more important than anything else. You have a deal."

The man's words caused Wilber to pause.

"But as part of this deal, you get rid of this detective. Make him disappear. That saves all of us any more problems. Maria will get the money for the ring. Is it a deal?"

The thin shamus looked at Weyer, then back at Maria. Finally, he nodded.

"Alright, but don't get cowardly on me. You tie the guy up, and I'll get my car," he told them.

Wilber slowly backed away. Weyer hurried to open the Packard's trunk and pulled out a length of cord. He tied the unconscious man's hands behind his back.

When Weyer finished, Wilber arrived in his car. He pointed his gun at Maria as he slid out of the seat.

"You can help the fat guy load my rival into the trunk," he said. "A little dirty work might do you some good."

Maria caught herself as she was about to reply. Instead, she glared before going to help Weyer lug Ray into the trunk. When they closed the trunk lid, Wilber got into the car.

"I'll expect your payment for the ring tomorrow evening," he told them through the open window.

"You'll get my call with the place and time. Be there, or I'll keep this damn thing and turn it over to friends of mine."

"What will you do with Irish?" Weyer asked. "Nothing can come back to us."

"Don't worry, pop. I'll cover everything up nice and tight. For this kind of money, I'll make sure the shamus dies on a country road. But I can always have the Jacobi gang to come after you if you suddenly get stupid. After our trade, I don't want anything to do with you."

The cousins remained quiet as they went to the Packard. Maria got behind the wheel before she turned on Weyer.

"So much for your damn ideas," she told him viciously. "You've bungled this so you can come up with the money."

"Just shut your mouth! Without my idea, your body would be in the back of Wilber's car and your soul in Hell. Now, let's go home," he said. "We'll need to come up with the cash and talk with your ex-husband."

Maria started the car, then paused.

"What the hell are you talking about?" she wheeled their car around the old Nash in the way. "I won't have Phillip involved in this. He'll kill me."

"For the ring, Phillip will help you," her cousin said. "You can't keep him out of it any longer."

"No, I can't," she replied.

The hairs on her skin stood up when she thought about the idea.

"We have an arrangement since the divorce. If I go to Phillip, he'll want me to repay him for the trouble. I can't do it. He's too brutal. You don't know him and what he expects."

"He's the only one who can take care of Wilber for us," Weyer insisted. "You and I both know that."

He tried to keep the smirk off of his face. Maria was afraid of Phillip, and he enjoyed the sight. While the man didn't know what caused their divorce, he saw the deep welts and bruises on her back before. He could make an educated guess.

"You know this Wilber might just come back for more money," Weyer reminded her. "He knows how much we need the ring. You're the only one who can get Phillip to use his influence on the district attorney. I can't do it since I'm not one of the family. We will pay the money to get the ring back," he explained.

"When the brothers are through with Wilber, he cannot pin anything on us, and we'll have the money back."

"What do you mean?" she asked.

"Don't you understand? Wilber is a killer. He murdered his partner," Weyer said with a thin smile. "Phillip can instruct the police to shoot him down as the killer. With Irish out of the way, that will shut up our only potential leak. No matter what Phillip wants, getting rid of Wilber should make you smile."

~~~

In the basement of the Smyth Estate, Orella struggled to wake from the fog that flowed through her mind. She shivered violently and tried to curl up in a fetal position. Her stomach protested in agony, but the woman was so cold. The sound of a chain rattled when she moved. Her ankle stopped, suddenly grabbed by something. Sluggishly, she slid her hand down her leg, and she found the metal bracelet attached to the chain. Her delicate fingers tried to pull the bracelet off her ankle, and then she grasped the chain. Orella yanked again and again. Her stomach hurt enough that tears came to her eyes at the effort. The chain would not budge. Desperately, she looked around in the darkness, but her fog-filled eyes found nothing but indistinct shadows. She tried to lift herself off the sofa, but fell back as her head spun. Ominous shapes filled the surrounding shadows, and she realized she was naked. Slowly, Orella pulled herself into a ball, trying to keep warm despite the pain of her injuries.

I'm trapped in hell. A cold hell!

Then, her mind drifted back to the barn where they tortured her. The black man who helped kidnap her stood naked from the waist down. His lecherous grin came to Orella when she remembered the man getting on top of her. But she could barely move, and her belly hurt so much from the burns. Orella drifted away again. It was so much like a terrible nightmare. Disjointed and unreal, she did nothing as the man raped her.

Then, the lights inside the barn went out. Still drifting in and out of conscious thought, Orella heard the grunted scuffling noise while the pain of weight lifted from her body. When the lights came back on, the man who hurt her hung upside down from the ceiling.

Around him, black-robed figures wearing masks stood chanting. Then she watched as one person in a death mask cut the screaming victim's throat. Orella remembered trying to look away, but she could not move her head from the sight. As the dying man wiggled on the rope, she felt a weird mix of thankful horror. The chanting increased as one of the robed figures put a bowl under the dying man, gathering the blood. Slowly, the people stepped toward Orella. She recalled
~~~

the urgent panic filling her. She screamed, but the sound came out in a hoarse whisper. Her throat still burned raw from the brutal treatment earlier.

Falling from the cot, she tried to crawl away, her mind filled with agony at the movement. Orella stopped at a pair of polished black shoes as one of the masked figures stepped in front of her. She rolled over on her side and saw the person wearing the emperor's mask cocked his head.

"A little thing like this will do quite nicely for the full moon," the deathly voice said. "Peter says she's noble blood. That's perfect. Too bad we missed the other shamus."

A robed person wearing a mask of a priestess stepped close and savagely kicked Orella in the head. The prisoner drifted into unconsciousness again as giggling laughter came to her.

She'll be fun to play with.

Orella could not be sure if the statement came out as a voice. Time and the fog in her head became one as the woman drifted again into her cold hell. The effects of the drugs they put into her kept coming in waves.

Eventually, the fog slowly receded again, and Orella finally pushed up from the couch. She cried out from the stinging pain of her belly. The woman accidentally slid off the couch and landed on the cold cement. She heard the chain rattle near her foot again. Painfully reaching out, she found the links and followed them with her fingers to the wall. Then, Orella began to twist and pull on the chain.

Chapter 5: Double Cross

Inside the large home, people in black robes sat around a five-sided table. Above them, the night sky sent in a trickle of light through the glass cupola ceiling. Tarot card masks covered their faces while watching their leader, the Demon's masked figure, who held the five-sided gold cup. In the middle of the table, there was a silver bowl with incense burning. Behind her, two people wearing the faces of Death and Judgment stood by the door.

"As normal, I'll start our meeting with a tribute to our master," the Demon picked up a bottle next to her and poured the red liquid into the cup, then into the silver bowl. She waved the incense over the container. The woman drank the blood of Ulysses Davis, then passed the vessel to the Magician next to her. The Demon began chanting homage to Andras as the blood went to the Magician while the others waited for their turn. Soon, the room filled with the voices in tribute to the Grand Marquis of Hell. When they finished, the Demon lifted her hands, palms up.

"Master of the infernal legions, we seek your sharp and bright sword," she commanded. "Come forth in your winged form to complete our mastery over the city. Sow discord among your enemies and blind them from the truth."

The group watched the Demon staring into the bowl. A low growl erupted after a few moments from behind the mask when the robed figure suddenly went stiff. The incense smoke grew intense, clouding the room while a foul smell filled the air.

"Servants of Andras, I arise at the full moon," the growling voice boomed. "Through blood, you will commune."

The Magician retched at the overpowering smell of Sulphur next to him. As the room temperature dropped, the masked figures noticed frost forming from their breath when they exhaled.

"A body taken among the believers, a servant of my needs. At the terminus of the next full moon, finish your deeds," the voice's ominous tone carried across the room. "A powerful body will cross the vale into the world of the living. Curse those who doubt; the legions come forth unforgiving."

Suddenly, the threatening voice coming from the figure of the Demon went quiet. The body in the chair relaxed as the masked head lulled. Death stepped forward and looked at the incoherent form.

"You have heard from the master," he told the group as he scanned the seated members. The man in the Judgment mask stepped next to the table.

"A great honor comes to us. One of us will give their body to the master, and their soul will become his servant," he told them happily. "When the Singsing of Multo returns, the power of Andras will be invincible."

Judgment turned his attention to the Empress.

"You have two days to get the ring back to its resting place in the library. If you fail, you will give your blood for Andras to cross over into our world. The decision is final!"

"Wait, I'm a Shadow and family; you cannot do that. There are plenty of sacrifices available. You have one of ancient blood."

Her voice rose in pitch when the woman abruptly stood. The chair slammed into the wall.

"The group agreed to the decision before you arrived," Death told her. "This is not the first warning, and the moon returns soon. All things come back to the non-believers."

"I'll get the ring back, I promise. But you know this is not my fault. Someone should keep that ring locked away," the woman tried to explain.

"Yes," Judgement agreed. "That is why you have two days."

~~~

Wilber turned off State Route 67. He decided to take the gravel road back to the capital. State cops might have a speed trap on the highway. Getting stopped with a kidnapped person in the trunk was something he didn't need at the moment. Once he found a secluded spot, he'd pump a couple of bullets into the head of his rival and leave the body along the road. It meant less competition and a bonus for him in the end.

Not a bad night's work, he thought.

Wilber slowed because of the heavily rutted road while placing his hand in his pocket to touch the ring again. He grinned and turned on the car radio. It took a few minutes for the tubes to warm up. Soon the orchestra sounds of a classical piece came through the speaker. He frowned at the slow number, and he hit the brakes as the road got worse. Wilber felt like he was riding a tractor with the ruts on the gravel.

In the trunk, Ray felt the bouncing as a tire iron glanced off his skull. Fully awake and in pain, he initially panicked before he figured out his location. While he bounced around among the few tools, he worked on his bound wrists. Relief flooded over Irish. Whoever tied him was an amateur. It didn't take long for him to free his arms, then his legs. In the darkness, he felt around until he found the tire iron. The shamus tried to pry open the trunk lid. However, no light and lack of leverage points caused Ray to lose the tool when they hit a large bump.

Wilber heard the noise coming from his car trunk and decided his passenger needed a permanent rest. No vehicles passed him in the last couple of miles, and no lights showed in his rearview mirror. He slowed the car and pulled halfway into a driveway entrance. The deep ruts in the path bounced his vehicle, and he hit the brakes. He heard his captive sliding into the backseat with a thud.

Wilber grinned.

That hogtied shamus is in for a surprise when he gets it with his own rod.
~~~

The man turned off the motor and the lights before he slid out of the car. He looked around carefully, pleased with the isolated area. The entrance path led into a dark field, and trees overhung both sides of the gravel road. As he walked around to the rear of the car, his leather soles crunched on the gravel. Wilber pulled the gun he retrieved from Irish.

After glancing around, the thug grinned while put his key into the trunk. Just as he turned the handle, the heavy lid flew up. The edge glanced off the gunman's chin, sending him backward. Before Wilber could recover, Ray sprang from the car and landed on top of Wilber. The men rolled around in the dirt until Wilber cuffed Irish in the head with the gun. However, the thin man wasn't fast enough to point the weapon at Ray.

Irish pushed them into the main road, and they wrestled for control of the firearm. Only the sound of their grunts broke the stillness. Wilber attempted to gouge at Ray's eyes while the shamus held on to the man's wrist. Then, Irish elbowed Wilber in the belly. He followed with a nasty headbutt. Blood trickled down both men's forehead.

Pow!

The gun went off. The bullet struck the ground. Ray felt the hot, spent cartridge pop from the receiver and hit him in the cheek. He slammed his knuckles into Wilber's ribs quickly several times and wrested the gun away from the smaller man. The thug went down to his knees, winded by the rib shots. Rolling to his feet, Ray held the .45 auto on the man.

"Alright, get on your feet. Where the hell is Orella?" he demanded.

"I don't know," Wilber told him as he caught his breath.

"Like hell! You're going to spill it now. A couple of bullets in your knees should refresh your memory," Ray growled out.

"You think they won't put you on the gallows for the murder of your partner?"

He aimed the pistol at the man's leg.

"Alright, alright," Wilber told him, apparently relenting. He paused when lights from a truck came over the hill.

As the lights came toward them along the narrow road, Ray waved his gun. He forced his prisoner to stand behind the car trunk as the oncoming vehicle lights grew brighter. The truck pulled an extended trailer behind it. They heard the vehicle picking up speed coming down the hill.

"Just stay out of sight. We'll finish our conversation after this trailer passes," Irish slammed the trunk lid down.

As the truck passed, Ray saw the outline of the driver inside the cab, who paid no attention to them. Ray lifted his gun hand to shield his eyes from the expected dust. In an instant, he saw movement from Wilber as his hand reached into his jacket.

Irish charged him before Wilber pulled his weapon free. Ray glanced off the thug before he slid into the narrow ditch. Desperately trying to keep upright, Wilber kept backing into the road. With a scream, he fell under the back wheels of the trailer. A sickening crunching noise reached Irish over the engine of the vehicle. The driver never slowed.

It took Ray a moment to recover while the dust settled. He stepped next to the body. In the starlight, he crouched down and checked for a pulse on one arm. In the darkness, he could only see the dead man's vague gray clothes and Wilber's deformed head. He grabbed the ankles of the body and dragged it to the front of Wilber's car.

Ray turned on the car headlights, and the corpse was in worse shape than he thought. His face looked horrendous, with an elongated and mashed tire mark engraved into the skin. He quickly went through Wilber's clothes and found the ring, which he promptly pocketed. When he pulled the dead man's wallet, Ray found several twenties, which he kept.

That's payment for trying to bump me off.

He walked back to the vehicle and turned off the headlights while he debated his next moves. The road remained quiet as Ray slid into the car. Calling the state police about the accident would give him nothing but a headache. They might not believe his story. Certainly, Maria and Weyer would not give him any cover. He wiped his prints from the wallet with his handkerchief and placed the leather item in the glove box with a sigh. After starting the car, the shamus backed away from the body before turning the car to follow the truck's path. While he didn't know where he was, the heavy vehicle would lead him to the main highway. During the drive, Ray tried to piece together the missing pieces. Maria must have made a deal for Wilber to get rid of him. There was no other explanation for waking inside the trunk. The smarter move would have been to kill him at Oldman Pointe and leave the body there. Wilber must have wanted a nice, quiet place where the corpse remained hidden for a while. Ray decided Wilber must have held on to the ring for safekeeping after finding out he couldn't trust his clients. Probably to make sure he got paid.

I can't say that I blame him, but what about the suitcase of money?

It was still a couple of hours before sunlight when Ray finally reached Oyster City in his trusty old Nash. He parked along the street in front of his office and felt the energy leave him. He was exhausted, and his head pounded like a drum with each movement. When he carefully touched his injury, he guessed his skull must look like a cracked egg if they did an x-ray.

His brain couldn't turn off the drive back. On his way back to the city, he finally found the highway. He made it back to Oldman Pointe, where he found his car. While he quickly wiped his fingerprints off every spot he could think of inside Wilber's car; Ray stumbled upon the small suitcase on the floor behind the driver's seat. The money was a welcome surprise, and he took the case with him as he slid out of the car.

As he drove away, Ray decided the cash in his possession gave the whole evening a nice, ironic twist. When he reached the city limits, the tired man decided not to alert the police about Wilber's car and corpse. There were too many loose ends, which he could not tie up if he reported anything to the police.

It's better to let the whole incident slide until I find Orella.

Ray was running on empty. The clock showed just after 4 AM, and the diner next door opened at 6. Ray took a seat in the chair behind the desk and leaned back. His eyes immediately closed.

After two hours of restless sleep, he jerked awake when the grotesque images of Greye La Spina's corpse ran through his memory. When she jumped off the mortuary table and tried to attack him, Ray nearly fell out of his chair. Scrambling to avoid the ghost coming at him, the man finally woke. He sat there, his wide eyes slowly recognizing the blazing billboard on the building across the street.

"These damn nightmares are going to kill me! What the hell do they mean?" His voice boomed inside the quiet room. Only the silence answered the shamus.

Shaken by the experience, he staggered from his seat and went into the bedroom. After a quick bath, he went next door as Mildred turned on the neon light, declaring the diner was open. He wobbled to a booth. Mildred came next to the table.

"Ray, you look like death warmed over. You need some coffee?"

"Steak and eggs as well," he agreed with a nod.

"Alright, honey," the woman purred. "Everyone's been having trouble sleeping." She turned, then glanced back.

"Just let me know if I can help, sweety."

He watched her strut away. The man recognized the danger in her idea because Mildred was on the hunt.

After she returned with his food, Ray picked at his plate, lost in thought. Nothing on Wilber's body showed Orella's location. But something kept gnawing at him about the kidnapped woman. The brief exchange with Wilber convinced him that the thug did not know where she was. But the dead man carried the Singsing ring. Ray could only guess at the reasons. The only thing he knew for sure was that Maria and Weyer were still in a bind about getting it back.

Suddenly, Samantha slid into the seat across from him.

"I saw you as I was going to your office. My God, you look worse each time I see you. What's wrong?"

He looked at her pretty, delicate features. Irish gave her a tired smile.

She's too sweet to be hanging around a guy like me.

"Nothing now that you're here. It's a better question for you," Ray replied. "How are you holding up?"

She frowned.

"I'm alright. I saw my father yesterday. He's got an excellent lawyer, but he's changed," Samantha told him. "It's almost like he gave up. I've never seen him this way."

Mildred came to the table. Samantha ordered a coffee. After the waitress left, Ray took a sip from his cup.

"Listen, you and your father have nothing to worry about. Sirk has more holes in his case than Swiss cheese," he said in a reassuring tone. "You just need to keep your chin up."

"It's tough. Dad's wife won't even see him," Samantha said. "While she and I never got along, my hatred for her has grown. She believes what the papers are saying about my dad. I think she went back to our vacation home in Rhode Island."

"Don't let it throw you," he told her. "I remember her letters when I worked on that case. Your dad should have thrown her out with the other trash when he got the letters back."

She smiled at the comment, and there was a moment of silence after the waitress returned with her coffee. Ray finished his buttered toast.

"I hate seeing my father sitting in jail for something he didn't do. Can't you help him?" Samantha asked.

Ray sighed as he motioned Mildred for a refill on the coffee.

"I'm sorry, but there's not much I can do," he said. "We're down to just a few suspects left, and they seem to have pretty good alibis. Unless you've got something that has some teeth, Sirk's not going to listen."

"I don't have anything like that," she admitted. Her eyes gave Ray a haunted look. "I know you'll think I'm crazy, but I get a sense that someone's following me. I had the same feeling when I drove to your office this morning."

Her words caused Ray to glance out of the front window of the diner. The traffic grew busy as the daylight broke through the early morning clouds.

"Let's finish our coffee and take a drive," he told her.

He wanted to test her theory about being followed.

A few moments later, they were heading along Peach Street in Samantha's yellow Studebaker. As she drove, she told him about her last few days.

"All I've been doing is running around or working on the Azalea bushes in our yard," she said. "I need something to keep me from worrying too much. I tried meeting with Reece's parents, but they're a wreck right now. All I could do is to give them my condolences. I felt so inadequate."

"Yeah, I know what you mean," Ray absently replied as he scanned for cars following them.

He didn't see anything suspicious. Irish noticed the strain from her loss of a friend and her father's incarceration. He told her he was sorry for her pain.

"I'm alright. Really, I am. But you look terrible. I almost didn't recognize you this morning," Samantha confessed. "What's going on? Have you got another case?"

He nodded and remained quiet, briefly thinking about Orella.

"There's a client who got kidnapped, and the guys who did it are dead," he explained. "It's one reason I'm not getting a lot of sleep. In fairness, you look pretty tired as well. You have to rest. Getting sick won't help your dad."

"I'll try." Samantha turned on Main Street, heading to the docks. "The tension makes it tough. I've never had such bad dreams until this whole thing started."

Her words caught Ray's attention.

"Really! That's strange," Ray said, trying to stop the mental picture of Greye La Spina's decaying body, which flickered in front of him.

"The same thing happened to me about a day or so before the Townsend murder. You're probably right about the stress."

"Well, as my instructor liked to say, *In Somnis Veritas*," she told him grimly.

"What does that mean?" He asked after trying to remember the little bit of Latin he knew. "I'm not the college type."

"In dreams, there is truth," she replied with a smile. "It appears St. Martin's College for Women gives me a way to baffle private detectives. It's funny, but when we were dating before, we didn't talk about our past."

"Yeah, we didn't talk about much at all. Not that I'm complaining, since it's kind of hard to bring up those things when you're in the back seat," Ray said with a grin.

She glared at him, and he noticed her face turn red. Then she laughed. Her air was light, almost like her usual self.

"Alright, you have me there," she confessed. "I think that's what scared me about where things were going. It was a whirlwind around you. To be frank, I felt like I was too far over my head with you. Believe it or not, but I thought you were trying to dominate everything. You don't know me as you think."

Samantha glanced over at him.

"I'm sorry if I hurt you."

Taken aback by her comment, Ray remained quiet. She was correct. He got hurt more than he wanted to admit, and he told her that.

"Well, I have a knack for screwing up things. It's kind of hard for a guy to admit he's vulnerable at times," he explained. "It's not the way my daddy raised me. Anyway, if you're willing, we can restart once we get your dad out of this."

"I would like that," she said. "But only if we can discuss our past."

Samantha looked over at him with a smile.

"What type of a guy are you, Ray Irish?"

He paused at the question, trying to give an answer.

"Alright, I'll give it to you with both barrels. I'm the type who leaves the second year of college to join the Seabees during the war," he said with an air of resignation.

"When I got back to the states, I tried to find the bottom of several thousand bottles of whiskey. I came into Oyster City on the top of railroad cars. I helped a guy from taking a beating by hoodlums is the reason that I'm a shamus. Not good enough to make a living at it, but not planning on doing anything different."

He went quiet as he looked over the harbor, mostly empty of any watercraft. Ray reflected on the statement and decided it was accurate.

"My type is a lot less than you deserve."

He noticed her expression changed from thoughtful to stubborn. To his surprise, she pulled into an empty parking lot. After she went to the back of the lot behind a few open iron ore cars, she stopped the vehicle. Samantha turned off the engine and slid over next to him.

"You need to let me decide what I deserve, Ray. I'm not daddy's little girl," she told him.

Samantha leaned over, putting her face close to his.

"You might be better than you realize. Now kiss me."

~~~

About thirty minutes later, Samantha Carter drove back downtown. While Ray suggested they find a hotel and stay together for the rest of the day, she resisted the idea. Instead, they agreed to meet that weekend. As she turned the corner at Broadway, Samantha mentioned seeing Kiilu outside the police station the day before.

"He mentioned that he just left after trying to see my father," she said. "Kiilu offered me his sympathy, and then he told me that Lieutenant Sirk forced him to remain in Oyster City until the grand jury finished their work."

"That seems strange to me," Ray told her. "Sirk never mentioned it."

"Well, the jailer mentioned Kiilu walked by him, but he never asked to see my dad," she replied. "I asked what the guy did, and the cop told me that Kiilu stared at the bulletin board that holds the wanted posters. He spent several minutes there."

"He's a flake; maybe he enjoys looking at the criminals," he suggested. "All I know is he's a jerk."

Samantha smiled.

"I agree with you. You should have seen him at my dad's party that night before we went to the museum." She slowed for a turn. "He was playing the belle of the ball, carrying on with everyone. He kept the spotlight on himself all night. Is this the spot?"
~~~

Ray nodded, and she stopped her car in front of Pappy's newsstand.

"I've got some things I have to follow up on, but I'll come by later and make sure you're alright," Ray grinned.

"Just remember, you have to leave when I say," she said with a smile. "My neighbors can be nosey about men coming to the house, especially if a man doesn't leave at an appropriate hour."

"Well, I better come by early," he quipped.

Irish got out of the car, wiping her lipstick from his mouth with his hand. The woman laughed and threw him a handkerchief. Ray wiped the red away from his hand, then stuffed the perfumed cloth into his pocket. Pappy smiled when Ray came to his stand and took a paper.

"She's a pretty one," the newsy stated with a smile as he took the dime.

"Yeah, that's for sure," Ray agreed. "I used to think she was smart until she took a liking to me."

Pappy laughed at the comment.

"My Emma was the same way," he told him while handing a paper out to a customer. When he turned back to Ray, Pappy's expression turned severe. "I have to tell you that you look like hell. What happened?"

"Everyone notices my good looks this morning. But I have backstabbing clients, and more questions," Ray grumbled. He bypassed the events that gave him a swollen face.

"Listen, I'm in a hurry. But something that Samantha just told me got me to thinking. Do you know anything about Harold Garza, the curator of the Hopely Arts Center?"

Pappy gave him a long look before he said anything.

"He's been there for quite a while. Came in from the West coast but can't tell you much more than that," he told Ray.

"According to the papers, he had a lot to do with Rose Smyth and her Raphael painting coming to Oyster City. I would think the mayor would give him a medal for all the publicity."

"I wonder if Garza somehow benefits from Rose Smyth's death. It's strange, but every time I've seen him, he's been hanging with Kiilu," Ray replied thoughtfully. "I think I'm going to check with Sirk."

He opened his paper and checked the columns. He frowned after reading through the section about lifestyle and arts.

"I noticed Kiilu didn't have his column in the paper for the last week," he explained. "But here's the explanation saying he's on an assignment. Well, I guess his alibi about being in Oyster City pans out then. But I still think something's wrong with the guy. I just can't put my finger on it."

"Well, I got some news for you," the newsy interrupted him. "Cat found out that Orella's father has returned to New York. He and his wife went to

Washington for a couple of weeks. His name is Victor Dela Cruz, and he works for the Spanish Ambassador's Cultural Office. According to Cat, he's been calling around, trying to track down Orella when Cat called him. I guess he's coming to Oyster City." He smiled as he handed out another paper. He glanced at his friend, who kept reading an article.

"You know, Cat came by to tell me. That means she wanted it to get back to you." Pappy shook his head. "She was all full of herself since she got Arizona to issue a missing person alert on this Dela Cruz girl. The national newspaper wires picked up the story, so she's getting some attention. I still say that you need to make up with her. Cat's still pretty sore with you, but she is your partner."

"Yeah, I'm not the kiss and let's make up type. Not when I'm in the right," Ray explained before he yawned.

His action caused Pappy to yawn as well.

"The nights have been quick. Too many dreams," the newsy complained.

"Yeah, same here," Ray confessed, then looked at his friend oddly. "You're the third person to mention dreams to me. There must be something in the air."

"It could be. My regular customers seem moody. I should start selling them coffee out here," Pappy said with a beaming smile. "I've been a regular therapist for some of them. They keep telling me about being chased."

Ray grunted, still half focused on his paper. His friend offered a morning newspaper to an older lady walking past his stand.

"As long as they don't start talking about shadows in their dreams," he commented, then turned the paper over. He didn't see Pappy's distraught expression.

"What did you say?" his friend asked anxiously. Ray looked up.

"What? All I said was shadows in the dreams," he replied. "Why do you ask?"

"That's the same expression some of my customers told me." His friend replied.

Pappy walked back and forth in front of his stand, pulling his hat and scratching his head. Ray watched him with growing interest.

"Now that I think about it, there's something that I read once. In the past, people were having trouble sleeping," Pappy told him. "It was pretty creepy stuff, if I remember right."

"You sure you weren't reading some of those pulp magazines you have on your stand?

Ray's joke didn't get a smile from Pappy. His friend tapped his temple while he tried to remember the story.

"No, something at home…hmm, it'll come to me. I usually remember such." He stopped in mid-sentence and snapped his fingers.

"I got it. It was about Oyster City. Some strange things were happening last century. A few people got hung over it. It was like those old witch trials in Salem. It was over a hundred years ago, I'm sure. The story is in one of those large journals that I've collected."

Ray yawned again as he folded up the paper and slid it under his arm.

"Well, you have fun with your research," he said. "I think I need to drop by a hotel and chat with someone before I go visit with Arizona."

Ray hustled over to the Hotel Alexander, where he noticed Leroy James, the hotel peeper, standing by the row of phone booths. He immediately walked over to the retired cop. Leroy always grimaced like he had a toothache whenever Ray came near him.

"How's life treating you?" he asked the hotel cop.

"Better when you're not around," Leroy replied as he shifted his weight. "My feet hurt, and I have enough going on with the state Legion convention in the city. Damn call girls are running in and out of the rooms. I don't understand why these men can't bring their wives and keep things respectable."

"Well, guys will be guys," Ray's flippant response caused the ex-cop to frown.

"Say, did you hear that one of the big shots from the Spanish embassy is coming to the city tonight?"

"Hell, you're just a barrel of good news, shamus. You say, this evening?" Leroy asked as he pulled out a notepad to write the information. Ray nodded as he smiled at the man's habit.

"Since I've done a favor for you, let me ask a question," he said. "Have you seen much of the famous art critic Kiilu? I figured he would be another thorn in your side. You know those artistic types."

"Oh, I've noticed him alright, dressing like some circus freak," Leroy told him, then paused and shook his head. "No, I can't say I've heard anything. He's been really quiet. To be honest, I don't remember seeing him outside of his room that often. Why do you ask?"

"Well, he's a strange bird, and he was around with the rest of those art lovers who got caught up in those murders you've been reading about," Ray said. "I'm not sure he's on the up and up. Can you do a guy a favor and check out his room? He's a writer. Let's see if he has any tidbits about the Townsend and Smyth murders. I'll throw a Lincoln your way for the trouble."

"Yeah, seeing I have to monitor the rest of the hotel, I won't make any promises," Leroy told him skeptically.

Ray nodded as he left. He knew Leroy was not about to miss out on an easy ten spot.

~~~
~~~

Later that day, Ray found himself inside the office of Lieutenant Arizona Campbell. He stopped by to ask about progress in finding his missing client.

"Like I told you on the phone, if I get a lead, I'll let you know. In the meantime, you just have to wait," Arizona told him irritably.

"Well, I've been doing some thinking about this, and I'll let you in on a surprise that you're not going to like. I believe Orella is still alive. I also think I know where she might be," Ray replied. He saw Arizona let out a sigh.

"That doesn't sound good," the cop said. "When you come up with ideas, it means something bad for me. Remember your idea to catch that racketeer, Guy Young? That didn't go so well."

Ray's sly grin caused the cop to scowl.

"Yeah, and I've got the missing finger to prove it. You're going to really love this one," the shamus sat in a chair. He paused briefly, debating the wisdom of his next move.

"I think Orella Dela Cruz is at the Smyth Estate," he said.

Ray would have loved to have a picture of Arizona after his comment. The cop almost bit through his unlit cigar.

"Damn it, you're off your rocker," Arizona told him after spitting out the hunk of tobacco still in his mouth.

"How in the hell did you come up with this idea? As I understand it, that place is crawling with servants," he dismissed the idea. "Nobody in their right mind puts a kidnap victim in a house that has parties going on there nearly every night, not to mention all the guests running around. On top of that, the brother of the district attorney and his ex-wife are well-respected citizens of the city. It's more likely they took her out of the county. It's more likely that Wilber and his partner killed her. Then, Wilber or Jacobi's gang took out Ulysses."

Ray leaned forward.

"You don't believe that. We both know that Smyth and Andras are low-life vermin with money," Ray replied. "Listen, you told me that none of your snitches are giving you anything. Normally, that means the person is dead. But I'm confident she's not. We only know that someone beat and tortured her for information. I'll tell you why. Maria wants an expensive ring that Orella had. She hired Wilber, and he's missing. She can't afford to kill her."

"Are you not telling me something?" The detective put the cigar back in his mouth.

"If you can't find Orella or Wilber, then it stands to reason that nobody would think to check out a place that's off-limits," Ray avoided a direct answer. "A big estate has plenty of places that servants don't normally go. That tells me that since the snitches are quiet, then Maria and Weyer had no option but to take her back to the estate."

Arizona leaned back in his chair, and his broad face wrinkled up like he smelled a foul odor coming from Ray.

"You're reaching here," the cop replied.

"Yeah, I agree it's a stretch, but look at this from my side," Ray insisted. "I've got an expensive item with questionable ownership that I believe my client owns. Then, her parents haven't heard from her, so she's still around here. It's an indisputable fact that I've got a couple of rich monkeys who brought in a shamus to kidnap Orella.

"Except you can't prove it at this point," the cop interjected.

Ray frowned.

"Alright, I can't prove it to you cops yet," he paused, debating how much he would divulge to the detective.

"Just between the two of us, I'll add to the mix something you don't know about. Wilber tried to knock me off for the damn ring after doing a deal with Maria Andras and Johann Weyer," he said. "Wilber told me he didn't know where Orella was. Now you know why I think the girl is out on the Smyth Estate. Where else could she be?"

The policeman stared at him for a moment.

"He could have been lying," Arizona said, then went quiet after he pulled the cigar from his mouth.

"You're playing with fire; you know that." He leaned over to retrieve a bottle of Bromo-Seltzer antacid from his desk while he belched. The detective added the tablets to a glass of water.

"You do this to me every time."

"Listen, I have no probable cause beyond your word to get a search warrant on that place. On top of that, you know there is no way in heaven and hell that the district attorney will sign off on such a warrant to raid his brother's house. It would be all over the papers in the morning."

"Yeah, I figured as much," Ray agreed with a bemused smile. He waited until his friend drank down the medicine. "It only means that someone needs to get over there and find her."

"Are you crazy? You get caught out there, and it'll be your PI license and 30 days in jail just for trespassing," Arizona told him. "Just for kicks, the DA will probably slap on enough charges for you to get a few years in prison."

"Then, I guess it's a lousy idea, and only an idiot would try something like that. I'm glad that I'm not like that." Ray stood and put his hat on.

Arizona saw the look of determination on Ray's face, and he shook his head.

"Make sure that Smyth and his ex-wife aren't around and find some way to distract the servants, you lunatic. Just don't be mentioning my name if they nail you," he warned.

Irish opened the door, then turned back.

"Tell me something, do your vice cops know of a place where the hop-heads hang out?"

"Yeah, I'm sure they have some ideas," Arizona told him. "Why the sudden interest in dope?"

"Just something that Orella told me about Maria," Ray replied. "I take it she's a dope fiend. Someone supplies her. It also would be a way to keep your prisoner nice and quiet. It might be a way to find that distraction you were speaking about."

"Christ, you're making my stomach acid start up again," Arizona said. "Go talk with Stoddard down at vice. He can give you the list of lowlife hangouts. But remember to let me know if you find something. There's a murder involved in this case as well."

~~~

Ray patiently waited in the dark confines of Musso's, a bar at the corner of Regal Avenue. It was a dive and didn't pretend to be anything different. He was getting used to the foul stench of stale beer, rotgut whiskey. It almost overpowered the flowery fragrance from giggle-smoke and tobacco.

In their sequin costumes, a group of musicians hung around two large booths in the back, and their smoke drifted to the front. Surrounded by their instrument cases, most band members spoke in a slang that Ray could not comprehend at times. However, he got enough to understand they were preparing for their gig at a nearby dance club. Pappy's tip about the place was right on the mark. When he walked in, Ray saw the musicians taking deep drags of their homemade marijuana cigarettes to go along with bottles of beer.

A broken jukebox sat in another corner. There were two women in simple dresses, a red-head, and a brunette at a table next to the silent equipment. Ray kept his attention on them when they entered the place. The women barely spoke to each other and dressed better than the rest of the patrons. They were out of sorts and nervous. Ray noticed they did not order drinks.

"Get me another glass of Kentucky Tavern from an unopened bottle on the shelf," Ray told the bartender with a growl. The tall, thin man frowned and turned his attention away from the girls. He pulled the bottle from the shelf.

"Most people don't complain," the bartender told him.

"Well, most people coming in here already loaded," he replied foully. "They don't care if you water down your drinks."

Ray glared at him.

"I do care!"

After the bartender grumbled under his breath, he filled the tumbler on the counter. Ray paid him and took his first drink while a dark-haired man entered the bar from the back door. He passed Ray on the way to the girl's table.
~~~

The policeman's description of him back at the station was accurate. Sporting a thin mustache, the man had a dapper hat on, and he wore a white and black herringbone coat. A sometime musician and full-time pusher supplied the wealthy clients through their servants. According to Stoddard, the man's name was Porkpie.

Ray took his glass and went over to a nearby table, making sure to sit with his back to the trio. He could see their suspicious glances at him from the mirror behind the bar. But Ray dropped his chin and kicked up his feet on a nearby chair, and the pusher reconsidered his misgivings. Almost immediately, one girl began working on Porkpie for drugs. While he didn't understand a lot of the jargon, Ray figured out the red-head woman was Eva. The transaction between them went quickly, but Ray noticed the woman's voice quivered as they conversed. Either Reece's servant must have been new to the game, or she needed a fix.

"What about you, Abby?" Porkpie asked, turning to the brunette. "Are ya layin' down the hustle today?"

"I need a tin of Mickey Finns, and she wants poppy tears," she told him. "She wants them today."

Ray perked up at the conversation. He understood enough to realize they were discussing knock-out drops and opium. He glanced in the mirror behind the bar to watch the girl. She had an innocent look with a slim body. Her eyes carried a haunting sadness.

"What no beenies today? What gives? You know I don't carry around much of the other stuff," the man told her.

"I don't know," she replied. "She just needs it."

It'll cost you more lettuce, lady. You got it on you?" Porkpie inquired suspiciously.

"Yes, I have enough. She paid me before I left," Abby told him as she laid several greenbacks on the table. The dope pusher laughed at her.

"Yeah, ya don't skim any for yourself," he told her scathingly as he pulled two thin cigar tins from his jacket. "This is all I got. If you need more, I'll be here tomorrow." He took the money and handed the tins to her. The women at the table froze when a tall musician walked by Ray and sat at their table.

"I glom'd on to you two choice bit of calicos," he told the women confidently. "How about coming over with us cats? We've got some good Indian hop."

Abby tried to turn him down, but Eva appeared interested in staying. Ray finished his drink and walked out of the bar to his Nash. When the girl emerged from the bar, he watched her walking along the street while he started his car. She went to the bus stop and waited. When the bus finally arrived, and she got on, Ray began following the bus.

<div align="center">~~~</div>

Abby walked up the dingy steps inside the Cooper Building, heading back to the apartment of her friend Eva. Even though it was her day off, Maria Andras insisted Abby fill her time getting drugs.

The pills and tablets were for elegant parties, which turned into cesspools of depravity when a select group of wealthy addicts gathered. Maria and her ex-husband ran the show and used her as a personal present for their friends. Trapped by her heroin addiction and working for the sadist who got her addicted, she still believed she was better off. While Abby could no longer control anything in her life, she wasn't working the streets. Her only source of happiness was the ethereal high of dope.

Quickly shutting the door after entering her apartment, Abby went to the table covered in dirty dishes. The stench struck her, but she only thought about the syringe in her purse. Then, the woman jumped at a heavy knocking at the door. She tried to ignore the sound. However, a few seconds later, the knocking grew insistent.

"Damn," Abby said aloud as she stomped to the entrance. She hoped the landlord was not looking for money again. Instead, a large man pushed inside. Abby let out a startled yell.

"Can it, lady," Irish told her. "I'm only here to ask a couple of questions. I don't care what you're doing otherwise."

"Get out of here," she insisted.

"Don't get stupid. You're carrying too much dope in that purse to argue with me. Oyster City vice won't walk away from that," he explained.

Ray closed the door when he recognized the fearful despair on her face. He had seen the same look during his time recovering in the naval hospital when too many guys came out of their injuries addicted to morphine.

"Are you a cop?" she asked.

"No, I'm a shamus. I followed you from the bar where you got your drugs from Porkpie. You work for Maria Andras. What's your name?"

"Abby…Abby Brown. What do you want?" She slowly backed away.

"You're buying drugs for Maria Andras." Ray stepped toward her.

The woman glanced around in a desperate attempt to think of a way out.

"Don't bother lying to me."

"Yeah, they're for her," Abby hung her head. "She's hooked on bennies and always needs the stuff for her parties."

"But that's not what you got for her. I overheard what your pusher told you. Something's changed about your purchase this time," the shamus insisted.

"No," she admitted. "For some reason, Miss Andras wanted this stuff. She didn't tell me why."

"That's a nice employer you have. If the cops catch on, then you're going to jail, not her."

He noticed her avoiding eye contact with him.

"Have you seen Orella Dela Cruz inside the house in the last couple of days?"

Her surprised expression made him step uncomfortably close.

"You remember her! Your boss invited her to stay at the house. Thugs working for your boss kidnapped her," Ray pressed the woman back into the wall. "If I find out you know something, drugs will be the least of your problems. There's murder involved in this thing. Think about that and what you'll need to do for those butches in prison when you get there. Now, you got one shot to tell me the truth. Have you seen her?"

"I swear, mister, I've not seen the lady since she took off that morning." Abby insisted as tears welled up in her eyes. "She was nice to me. When I carried her bag to the taxi, I could see that she was upset."

"I'll bet you know why she took off, don't you? He asked.

She nodded, the woman's face showing her distress.

"You don't understand. We have to do these things for Andras."

"Yeah, I get that you're addicted. A guy can spot that a mile away. But you can be a dope head without Andras," he told her. "What's she got on you?"

The girl shook her head.

"I can't tell you. Just leave me alone."

Her pathetic voice disgusted Irish.

"I'm tired of asking. What does that bitch have on you?" Ray grabbed her and forced her to look into a mirror hanging on the wall.

"Take a good look at yourself, lady. You're about to come apart, and Andras will throw you out with the rest of the trash," he growled.

"Come clean with me. I swear that I'll help you."

"You can't do anything," the girl moaned while pulling away. She looked out of the dusty window for a moment. Then she placed her forehead on the glass.

"Try me," Ray insisted. "Look at it this way. You either work with me, or I call my friends at the police station about you. It's your choice, but I've got a woman in trouble. How long do you think you'll last long inside a jail cell? Cops are good at breaking people. Maria's not going to be touched unless you tell me what she has on you?"

The woman continued looking out the window. He noticed her hand kept clutching and releasing her purse. Finally, she pulled away from the window and went to the worn Sheraton chair. Abby slid into the chair.

"Alright," she wearily pulled out a cigarette. "I got busted a couple of years ago and I'm still on probation. I can't afford another arrest, or they add it to my charges and throw away the key."

Ray took a seat on the arm of the small couch nearby. It was an ugly green and looked battered like the rest of the furniture.

"What happened?" He asked.

"I drove the getaway car for my boyfriend after he robbed a store. I didn't know about the robbery, and they gave me probation. Phillip Smyth hired me as part of my rehabilitation program," she scoffed and lit the cigarette. "When I went to work for them, I was clean, I swear to God."

"Yeah, until you ended up around Maria," Ray replied.

"Not just her, her damn husband, as well. At first, they treated me nicely enough. Then, they started coming to my room at all hours, insisting I have a drink or snort this," she recalled as the bitterness came out. "Then…" She paused.

"Well, one morning, I woke up, and there's a cop standing over me. The son of a bitch forced me out of my bed, claiming that I stole Maria's jewelry. He was holding my purse. It had some of her items. He threatened to take me to the station."

Ray remained quiet, noticing the long pause. She was avoiding the full story.

"What happened next?" He asked, already guessing he knew.

"The policeman told me it was a felony robbery. He knew all about my past." She paused and looked away. "I made a deal to keep me from going to jail. He hauled me back to the Smyth House. The cop talked with Maria, and then he left." She stopped.

"It sounds like someone slipped you a Mickey and put jewelry in your purse. Did Maria pay off the cop?" Ray asked.

Abby nodded, taking another deep drag on her cancer stick.

"I do what they tell me. Either way, I lose. It's my word against the cops and Maria. You need to go away and leave me alone."

"Not until we finish this," Ray reminded her.

He removed his fedora and scratched his head. He wanted to help. While she was in a nasty bind, the shamus had enough on his plate at the moment.

"The state line isn't that far away. Why haven't you left?" he asked.

Abby gave him a skeptical look as her green eyes widened.

"Where would I go?" She asked, stamping out the butt of her cigarette. "I don't have any money. My family's disowned me. Phillip Smyth carries a lot of clout in this town. They put out a warrant for my arrest, and I'm in prison. I avoid that when the son of bitch O'Brien comes by once a week to see me."

"O'Brien, you mean the big, uniformed cop with a thick accent? Why does he come here?"

The woman's hurt turned bitter. For a moment, she remained silent.

"He's the cop that holds the stolen jewelry case over my head. Maria pays me sometimes, but it's not enough. O'Brien comes by here once a week. When he gets done, he pays me in dope," her eyes teared up when she looked at Ray.

"Do I need to give you all the details, mister?"

"Alright, I get it. You're in a tough place. And I've got a missing client." The shamus glanced out the window, then he stood and began pacing.

After a moment, he looked back at her.

"Listen, the way I see this, you got only one option. If you stay a slave to that bitch, Andras, you'll still end up in jail when she finally tires of you. You know that, don't you? That cop will find him another girl."

He waited for a response, but the woman stared at the charred cigarette butt in the ashtray.

"It's time for you to quit playing the sap," he told her. "I've got an idea, but it means you have to take a risk and get yourself straight."

Her eyes looked up, and he could see the hurt behind them. She blinked the tears away.

"I'm not sure I can do it," she whimpered. "You don't know what it's like for me. All I can think of is getting another shot." Abby lowered her head. "I don't want to feel anything."

"Listen, I've had friends in the same boat. They got out of it. You can do it as well. You're strong enough," he stiffly crouched by the chair.

"I promise that you're not alone anymore. You work with me, and we'll nail the bitch and get you out of this mess. You can help save someone from ending up like you. It'll be tough, but tell me everything that's happened?"

Thirty minutes later, Ray heard enough about Abby's recent past to make him livid. Abby told him through tears and several cigarettes about her experiences. Maria began injecting her with heroin while she was unconscious from the spiked drinks. Before long, Abby became a slave on the Smyth estate. After she told Ray some things that Maria Andras required of her for her money and drugs, he held up his hand.

"Stop, I've heard enough," he said. "That bitch needs to take a hard fall. And I think I can fix this for you. But we need leverage. Now, I have good reason to believe that Orella Dela Cruz is inside the house," Ray told her. "Is there any place where servants aren't allowed?"

"No, not really," Abby shook her head. "Well, the only places that I've never been to are the basement and the attic. Nobody goes into them much. The staff isn't allowed to go into an area of the basement where they store the wine," she said to him. "They tell us that servants stole from there in the past."

"Yeah, well, I'm not buying that. It's a good place to start. I'll need a diversion so I can get into the house and look through the place," he said. "You'll need to help get me in there and keep the staff from getting nosy."

He recognized the trepidation crossing her face, and she kept looking at her purse.

"The longer you take to decide, the longer it will be before you get your fix," he told her softly.

After another moment, Abby finally relented.

"I'll help, but if they catch you, you can't say anything about me," Abby insisted.

"Don't sweat it. Nobody will worry about you. It's my head in the noose when I step inside the house. The good news is that if Orella is there, there's no way the district attorney can protect his brother from kidnapping charges," Ray assured her.

"Nobody is that big in town. We need to find a night when Maria and Phillip are not at the estate. That way, you aren't exposed. I'll walk in and check around."

"And if the missing woman isn't there?" She searched his eyes.

"Then I leave nice and quiet. Nobody is the wiser. I'll still get you the hell away from them. Do you have any ideas when I can get inside?"

The maid clutched her hands again, and then her face lit up.

"They're not going to be home until late on Friday night," she said nervously. "There's a big event at the Hopley house with the mayor. It's rare, but Phillip will go as well. That means most of the servants will be gone for a few hours. I'll bet only the butler and a few others will stay around the house."

"Then I'll plan on showing up after they leave," he told her as he pulled out his business card. He gave it to Abby.

"Don't let anyone find this card on you. Hide it if you have no other choice. You can call me if anything changes, or you run into a problem."

"You can't tell anyone I'm talking with you," she said, her voice dropping to a snivel. "I can't handle jail."

"Just hang on for a couple of days. We'll get you through this," Ray told her as he handed the woman a twenty. "This money is a start for you. I'll find someplace to help you get out of this habit; I promise."

He walked to the front door, placing his hand on the doorknob. He glanced back at the woman.

"One more thing, Abby. From now on, you're with me, or I give you to the cops. Should you betray me for that needle, I've got enough on you that you'll be an old lady before you leave prison."

Ray walked out.

~~~

"Have you heard from Wilber?" Weyer asked Maria as they stood on the portico overlooking the front lawn. The sun was falling, casting red light across the area.

"No, something is wrong," she replied as she held out a hand for the railing, nearly spilling the glass of wine in her hand. "I tried calling his office. Nobody ever picks up."

"This is getting dangerous. We don't have a ring," he reminded her.
~~~

"You don't need to tell me." She spat back caustically before taking another drink.

"I think Wilber skipped town. You better talk with Phillip again. You're in real trouble," he said as he watched her.

He noticed the woman shivered, and it wasn't from the temperature.

"Wilber's greedy, and he'll be back," she assured him. "And I'm not going back to see Phillip again. He's going to get his brother looking for Wilber. That's enough. My wrists still hurt from being tied up, the rotten bastard."

"Well, you married the sadistic brute," Weyer replied casually. "I seem to recall you liked that about him."

"Not now," she spat back angrily. Her words sloshed. "Fun is fun, but Phillip likes to hurt."

She paused, shivering again.

"You know that my mother arranged the marriage," the woman lowered her voice like she was telling him something confidential.

Weyer tried to keep the disgust from expression. He understood the reason for the arrangement. Maria and Phillip were both bisexual sadists and needed a marriage that looked suitable for the upper crust in Oyster City.

"Keeping the families together, my mom told me. She knew my girlfriends were nicer to me." Maria turned back to the house and held up her glass.

"To my mother, for keeping it in the family," she yelled her toast.

"You need to get back to reality, you damn fool," Weyer told her. "Put the bottle down for a minute. They'll expect that ring soon, and we need to find Wilber. I'll check with a police officer I know. In the meantime, you play whatever game Phillip wants."

"The Shadows better get her out of there soon," Maria said aloud, not paying attention. "I'm tired of dealing with the little bitch. I'm not a nursemaid for a rat that they're just going to kill."

"Keep it down," Weyer told her as he glanced around. "You better not let the servants find out, or all hell will break loose. The way that room smells, you're not doing much beyond doping her. You're lucky those burns haven't gotten infected. Otherwise…," he said, then stopped with a sigh.

The man knew she was beyond listening. He gave her a thin smile.

It shouldn't be this easy.

"I don't care if she lives or dies," the woman retorted before she took another drink.

"You're too drunk to deal with," he observed. Weyer took her by the arm and turned Maria to face him.

"Unless we find Wilber, the Shadows will use you for the next sacrifice," he declared. "You don't seem to realize that your neck is on the line, not mine."

She shot him a scared glare before going back to her drink. Weyer turned away, leaving Maria looking out over the lawn. The man walked to the double doors leading inside. While he headed down the grand staircase of the house, Weyer beamed at his cousin's actions. He noticed the goosebumps on Maria's skin when he mentioned the Shadows. His cousin was rightfully afraid. The thought pleased him.

So much the better for his plans.

Maria failed to ask Weyer about the Vashetu Emerald he sold. The stone gave him a nice sum in his bank account, and he wasn't about to remind Maria about the money.

Marion Underhill, from a prominent family in the city, purchased the jewel. During his conversation with Underhill, Weyer discovered Marion knew about the missing ring. It was only a passing comment. However, it confirmed that the Underhill's had connections to the Shadows. Over the years, Weyer found it paid well to keep his mouth shut while looking for opportunities. Now, the pieces were in places for him to make his next move. He would play the innocent victim to Maria's ideas. If his suspicions were correct, Weyer would receive a gratifying reward for his efforts.

Chapter 6: Death Hurts

A reddish haze came through the curtains when Ray scrambled out of his bed. He had his gun out, and his wide eyes kept darting back and forth. He searched for the hideous demon that woke him. The shamus stumbled around the bed to the closet, pointing his gun at the dark shadows inside. Convinced it was not a nightmare, he kept scanning the room, for the masked figure burned into his memory. It took several moments for him to convince himself there was nothing in the quiet bedroom.

Trying to shake off his fear, Ray went back to the bed and slid the gun into the holster, which hung from the headboard. He sat down and shook his head. His nightmares came from the war. The men he knew and the tragic events he witnessed still seared through his subconscious. Yet, for the last few weeks, every one of the terrible dreams involved the robed figures with masks. They swirled around him like ghosts while he walked in pools of blood. It was enough to make a guy wonder about his mental state. Slowly, he rose and scratched his head as he went into the bathroom.

Maybe a hot shower and coffee might snap me out of it.

After Ray got dressed, he walked out into the office. He just sat behind his desk when the familiar knock of Gladys Peer came from his office door. His landlady always tapped SOS in Morse code on the glass window covering the top half of the door. When he unlocked the door, she came inside. Her expression revealed she expected someone else to be with him.

Gladys had a vivid yellow dress with green polka dots that made her look like a strange librarian. Her dainty glasses always remained perched at the end of her bulbous nose. The woman's fat face reminded him of Mrs. Santa Claus with her twinkling green eyes.

But Gladys was not jolly, as she placed herself by his desk. Before she had a chance to say anything, Ray had already pulled out his wallet. He handed her the rent for the next two months. His crazy landlady gulped down her surprise as she took the money, quickly folding it into her purse.

"Since you've taken care of your responsibilities, I'll forget your impatience with me the other day." She took a seat in front of his desk. "Mrs. Purvey doesn't like to be treated like a doddering old maid."

Ray kept his smile semi-pleasant. Gladys wrote under the pen name Mrs. Purvey, and she took on the persona when she worked. The woman enjoyed referring to herself in the third person when she spoke to mere mortals.

"So why is Mrs. Purvey talking to a shamus? You handle the society types, and I'm just another deadbeat guy," he went to his chair.

He remained standing, leaning over the chair back.

"Mr. Irish, rumors have you in the company of Samantha Carter recently. You know she's one of the most eligible ladies in Oyster City," she replied while pulling a notepad from her purse. "Her father is a suspect in a foul murder. My readers want to know how you could entice such a creature." She paused and cleared her throat.

"I mean, you're not from one of the…let us say, established families in the city."

"Let's just say Samantha is a fan of democracy. She's not living in a world of aristocratic types around here," he replied in a mocking tone.

The woman missed it. She smiled and leaned forward.

"That's what I thought," she said in a conspiratorial undertone. "Modern women are so that way. It's changing the world."

"That I believe," he replied.

Ray took a seat and leaned back with a yawn.

"Listen, there's not much to tell here. I don't think I appreciate a column about Samantha. Her father's problems have her attention. Not some nutty column about society types. Those are people with more money than brains."

He saw her face blanch at the comment.

"Sorry, that's not exactly what I meant," Ray told her in a hasty retreat. "The lack of sleep is getting to me. It's just Samantha is a good friend of mine. Your readers don't want that. They want to know that she's actively involved in proving her father's innocence. That's the truth."

Gladys stared at him for a moment, and her face gathered its regular pasty coloring.

"Yes, Mr. Irish, I like your angle on it. I think I can do something with that. Don't worry," she said sympathetically. "The nightmares are getting to everyone. I was telling Cat just yesterday about staying away from coffee before bedtime. That'll stop the restlessness."

"Is she having nightmares too?" He glanced over at the woman.

His concern caused a grin to form on her thin lips.

"Yes, like many people," Gladys said. "She was telling me how these dark figures were chasing her, like people with creepy masks covering their faces. It reminds me of the old stories that our grandparents used to scare the children about the shadow people of the past."

"That's strange; I've had something similar in my dreams. Never heard of those old stories or people having the same dreams before."

Ray rubbed the stubble on his chin.

"Isn't that interesting? I told Cat it was probably the stress," Gladys said. "You know that she's been looking into those missing kids?"

The shamus shook his head, still thinking about the woman's comments.

"No, I didn't. Why the interest?"

"A mother of one of those missing teenagers came to her. Cat believes she might have tracked them down." Gladys put away her notepad and pulled out her compact.

As she looked into her compact mirror, she suddenly paused, then looked past it to Ray.

"I don't know what happened between you two, but she's been a grouchy bear all week," she complained.

She touched up her lipstick. Ray noticed she was waiting for him to respond.

"Well, she's a big girl. She'll come out of it," he said.

"I think she would welcome your help. You know she cares for you, even though she'll never admit it."

Gladys briefly feigned a smile as she put away the compact. He noticed that her front teeth still had red lipstick on them.

"Well, she's got a heck of a way of showing it," he growled, then went quiet for a moment. "I'll tell you what. The next time I see her, I'll see how she's doing."

He leaned back in the chair, which squeaked loudly. He inadvertently sighed, and the woman beamed as she stood.

"Well, Mrs. Purvey has to finish up her column," she told him. "I'll be sure that my observations about Samantha Carter remain sympathetic. I like the girl, although I have to admit that I'm worried about her choice of men."

She walked to the door, quickly letting herself out.

"You and me both," he softly replied as he turned to stare out the window.

After a long moment, he looked back at his messy desk. He was tired, but he couldn't go back to sleep. His brain remained foggy, like the dense clouds that came off the bay occasionally. His hands reached for several unopened letters, which he slowly opened. The first one was from his bank. He threw it on the pile with the others. It reminded him to drop by and put cash into his depleted account.

However, the second letter immediately caught his interest. The return address had the handwritten name of Jefferson Tweed from New York. Ray tore open the envelope and tried to decipher the scribbled note in the letter. When he finished, Ray leaned back in his seat and let loose with a long whistle. The image of Greye La Spina flashed through his mind. He recalled the day that his lover predicted her death, and he accepted payment from her to find her murderer. Now, he might have the proof to get the dominos to fall. Unfortunately, he wasn't going to New York until he could wrap up his current work.

A police siren brought Ray out of his thoughts. He leaned over to look down at the street and saw the black and white car moving fast along Peach Street. Soon, the car was out of sight, and the siren a distant memory. Out of habit, he rolled his chair back to the wall and turned on the radio. As he waited for the tubes to warm up, he adjusted the dial to the police band. The shamus picked up the habit from the reporters across the street. They listened in on the conversations from dispatchers to the police cruisers for their next news scoop. He rolled back to his desk and opened the rest of his mail.

As Ray threw away the envelopes, the radio blared out dispatches to the police cruisers throughout Oyster City. Most of the radio traffic was in coded messages, which he was gradually learning after buying the radio a couple of months back. When he heard a familiar address, he turned his head towards the sound. He waited as a chill filled him. The voice repeated the same address.

Samantha!

Ray pulled up to Carter's house as Lieutenant Sirk stepped down from the porch. The front lawn swarmed with police. When Ray reached the house, a sergeant stopped him.

"It's alright, let him through. He needs to see this," Sirk told his man.

"What happened? I heard the call about a policeman getting shot," he asked the lieutenant.

"That's what we're trying to figure out," Sirk said. "Come with me."

Ray followed him to the entrance. Just inside the door, a uniformed cop lay face down on the floor, his body sprawled across the wool rug. A blood pool gathered around the head. There were powder burns around a small bullet hole in the back of his head. He looked at the wall and saw a spattering of brain and blood across the wallpaper.

"The neighbor called us about seeing an intruder sneaking around the house," the policeman told Ray. "Our guy walks in and gets it in the back of the head. The neighbor told my sergeant that she heard the gunshot and saw Samantha's car drive away." Ray scowled at the news.

"You're not telling me that Samantha Carter did this," he insisted.

"No, she drove away in her car, but a man was sitting in the front seat next to her," Sirk said as he clamped down on his cigar. "Unfortunately, the neighbor didn't get a good look at the passenger. I've already got an all-points bulletin out, along with a description of the girl."

"Damn it," Ray cursed.

"You can say that again," Sirk replied as he glanced at his policemen, who searched the lawn and driveway for evidence.

Ray moved to the side of the front entrance, his eyes following the path of the bullet. The killer must have waited for the policemen to enter the front door and then shot him from behind. While he listened to the exchanges between the detective and his men, Ray noticed Roman's macabre painting above the fireplace was missing.

"This kidnapping blows up your theory about Francis Carter." There was no satisfaction in his statement as Ray stepped next to Sirk.

"I already told you there were two people involved here. This kidnapping confirms my notion that Carter has an accomplice," the cop replied irritably. The thought of a kidnapped woman got under his skin. "Carter must have tipped off his partner, so he had her snatched to keep her quiet."

"Come on, let it go. First, it's a pair of killers who decide to knock the woman off, along with Reece," Ray replied cynically. "Then, after one murderer gets caught, the other culprit kidnaps Samantha. What the hell for? And why take that painting?"

"Damn it, I didn't say I had this thing figured out." The policeman's bulging eyes flashed. "Not yet anyway. I'll get the truth out of Carter. It has to be Felix Roman, and I'll get him even if I have to use a rubber hose on Carter, by God."

Sirk turned to his uniformed sergeant, who stood nearby.

"I want all the suspects that were in the art center hauled down to the police station," he ordered. "If they get to squawking, then bust them as a material witness. We'll get straight answers about where they were when this Carter woman got snatched, or I'll throw them in the cooler."

~~~

During his drive to the police station, Ray kept thinking about the paintings. While waiting for a traffic light to change, he noticed the many telephone lines suspended above the street. Each line carried the signals back to the central office, where an operator would control the next phone call's path and direction. It reminded him of the case.

It's a web of hidden messages that lead to one place.

Harold Garza charged into Sirk's office with a policeman in tow. The director was indignant about being hauled away in a police car. Sirk refused to offer sympathy. Instead, he told Garza to shut up before he told him about the kidnapping of Samantha. Garza fell back in a chair by Sirk's desk like a giant hand pushed him.

"Why would someone take her?" His dark eyes searched the Sirk for an answer the policeman didn't have. "This is so unbelievable. I still can't believe Carter killed Reece, and now this."

He looked between Ray and the cop.

"You don't have any idea who kidnapped her?"

Before anyone could reply, Kiilu entered the room.

"This is an outrage," he fumed. "Why am I here?"

"Enough with the beefing," Sirk growled at him. "Sit down unless you want a jail cell. Someone kidnapped Samantha Carter. Where have you been?"

"I was going to the hotel when your detective arrived," Kiilu said. The detective on Sirk's team nodded agreement.

"Then where were you before that?" Ray's voice came from behind the open door. Kiilu paused, glaring at the shamus who stepped into view.
~~~

"I was coming back from several places, if you must know. I've been trying to track down an artist by the name of John Adams," he told them. "He was a lead given to me by Mr. Carter."

"You can bet we'll check on that," Sirk told him. He turned back to Garza.

"As for you, my guy had to wait for you to return to the art center. Where were you?" He pulled a handkerchief to wipe his nose.

"I…I was coming back from lunch," Garza replied. He looked like a little boy caught with his fingers in the cookie jar.

"Can you prove that?" Sirk countered.

"Yes…well, I would prefer to talk with you alone, detective. It's a delicate matter with a married woman," Garza said as his eyes darted around the room.

Sirk scowled at him, then left the room with Garza. A few moments later, they returned.

"I have someone checking up on your stories," Sirk told Garza. "Until we get this sorted out, you will keep yourself available. I still have to talk with Cat Bennett and Reginald Kincaid."

"Detective, why aren't you searching for Carter's daughter?" Kiilu asked. "I think hauling us down here is a waste of time. I agree with Harold that Mr. Carter is unlikely to be the murderer of that night watchman. Yet, according to the papers, you caught him in the act of killing Reece. While I don't know why he would do such a thing, have you considered maybe his daughter is involved?"

Ray watched the art critic as he leaned against the wall. His dislike of the man intensified.

"Yeah, the lady shot a cop in the back of the head with the same gun that someone tried to kill me with at the art center," the shamus replied with venom. "Then she took off with a duplicate painting that was setting in Reece's apartment. Oh, and a stranger helped her as they drove away. There's a witness."

Garza stared at Ray.

"I don't understand," he said. "What are you saying about the two paintings?

"The painting at Reece's apartment is the same as the one that hung above this fireplace," Sirk spoke up. "Didn't you know there are two of those paintings?"

"That's impossible," Graza insisted. "I saw the painting that Felix Roman gave to Ms. Carter just before he left for the army. I tried to have him display it in the center, but he refused. Roman told me it was a gift to his one true love. I can't accept that he made a copy."

"The kidnapper had some reason to grab it." Ray joined the conversation again as he considered the puzzle. "So, who made the copy, and how did Reece get it? Felix Roman was his rival, and they didn't get along, according to Samantha."

He glanced at Harold Garza, who leaned forward in the chair.

"Well, some painters will make copies of other paintings to improve their technique and brushwork." The director continued with Ray's thoughts. "At times, it's difficult to tell one picture from the other. This type of thing has been going on for ages."

"You're on to something there," Ray looked at Garza. "The duplicates and paintings of Roman and Reece are involved at least one murder and attempted murder. They also tie back to the killing of the night watchman. We're still missing the link."

"This is not getting us any closer to finding Miss Carter," Kiilu suddenly reminded them. "Are we to listen to this when a woman is missing?"

"Slow down and hear me out," Ray looked at Sirk. "You have the word out about her kidnapping. Everyone is looking for Samantha now. We've covered that angle."

"However, when you think about the actions of our killer, I don't think whoever kidnapped her is still on the road. He went someplace with the woman and the painting. We have someone who just shot a cop, yet he still wants to grab a painting and kidnap the woman. That means she's important to this case. The same thing goes for the picture. We have two copies of the same image used as the model for one murder and nearly another."

"Alright, I'll agree it doesn't make sense," Sirk replied. "But you're flipping back and forth like a bookie with a tip sheet."

"I'm just following the trail, which keeps coming back to the paintings. I keep asking why they are necessary. Then, Mr. Garza told us that artists make copies of other works. Samantha said the same thing," Ray explained.

"Yeah, so what?" the cop asked.

"It begs the question of the original motive for killing Townsend. A crazy man didn't kill him," he told the group firmly. "What Garza said about copies finally clicked with me."

The shamus scanned the room.

"How does someone steal something valuable and then hide the fact?"

Nobody took the bait. Blank stares came back from those around him.

"How hard would it be for a talented artist to make a copy of an original masterpiece, like maybe a recent Raphael acquisition called the Madonna of Bogota? That's why the murderer had to get the duplicate painting out of the Carter house," Ray said.

"What the hell are you talking about?" Sirk growled. "We're talking about Samantha Carter, remember? I think you have that Madonna picture on the brain. It's a big step from there to your damn idea about that Raphael painting, which, I'll repeat, was never stolen."

The cop put his hands behind his back, his belly extended as he thought.

"The picture that was hanging there in Samantha Carter's house was no Madonna," the cop reminded Ray. "And we already know Reece painted the original one he gave Miss Carter. I think you're just grasping at straws."

Ray shook his head.

"No, I'm threading all the strings of this nasty web together," he told him. "Samantha is part of this because she knows something. You agree that string number one is the link to paintings. Remember that all the murder scenes had something to do with art. And the killings have matched the paintings, but not exactly."

He looked at Sirk, whose expression revealed suspicion about Ray's mental state.

"Listen, I know what I'm saying appears far-fetched at first glance. But think about what I'm telling you. When I arrived, the first thing that happened to me was the potshot aimed at me back at the art center. We assume it was the murderer. Ok, but why? Why try to bump me off? It tells me that the killer didn't plan on my arrival at the center before the police. Cat threw a monkey wrench into someone's idea when she called me. It also says that some of this scheme is very deliberate, and some of it relies on improvising as things occur."

The lieutenant shook his head.

"I don't understand," he said. "You act like this is all one big production."

"That's the link that came to me. Almost everything we saw comes down to staging and diversion. This whole damn scheme is full of it. You have to go through the details to sort it out," the shamus told them as the excitement he felt became palpable.

"The night someone killed the watchman, we find his body staged, and the painting moved near the corpse. A scene planned out."

"But why kill Townsend at all?" Garza asked.

"That's right," Sirk agreed. "The night watchman was old and unlikely to stop anyone if they were stealing something. There's no motive to knock him off."

"Exactly! I think Townsend walked in on something. He probably wasn't that hard to overcome, but the killers wanted to throw the police off track," Ray said. "But I couldn't figure that angle out. Why try to fool the cops with a murder?"

"And you have an answer," Sirk asked after lighting his cigar.

"Because they needed time. What better way than to stage a crazy-looking murder? Same with the second murder, but this time, the killers brought a different picture before they cut Rose Smyth's throat despite what the canvas showed. That suggests improvised like the death of the policeman. But it's still connected. It's the only reason that can account for her death. We know no one robbed her. She also had only one line of the web leading back to the museum, the Raphael painting."

"That's too weak. We know that the paintings of Reece will increase in value now. That's why Carter planned it," Sirk reminded him, then scratched his head.

"No, that doesn't make sense if Roman is involved. Why would he help Reece get rich and famous? He hated Reece."

"I wondered about that as well. You could almost think that his rival knocked off Reece."

Ray leaned against the wall.

"But I think Reece noticed something inside the art center. Samantha called me that morning. She wanted me to meet with her and Reece. On the phone, Samantha claimed Reece found something and needed to discuss it. Then, suddenly, someone kills Reece, and now she's missing. They stumbled into the truth."

"I think I'm seeing what you're getting at. Alright, I'll agree, pretty obvious. The killer was there to get Ms. Carter and the painting. Still, the killers didn't need to take the painting, even the copy. And there's nothing solid to tie this murder into the other murders. It's just speculation."

"You didn't find any shell cases at the crime scene," Ray said. "I'll lay you odds that the killer carries a revolver and the bullets in your dead cop match the one that destroyed that vase in the Center. That tells us the same person probably just kidnapped Samantha. That's the tie-in."

The stunned silence told Irish that he had got their attention.

"I'll bite on that if we find the killer," Sirk agreed with a slow nod. "It fits in with the idea that the killers improvised some of this. But I just remembered a flaw in your idea. What about Carter? You caught him with the knife."

Ray nodded.

"Yeah, I agree. He's the prime suspect at first glance. But let's assume for a moment that Carter's telling us the truth," he replied. "He comes in on a dying person with a chest wound. In the Seabees, we learned you try to cover the wound immediately. Assuming he had similar training when he found Reece with a blade in him like that, Carter might have just instinctively pulled the knife out. Lieutenant, you told me that the knife used to kill Mrs. Smyth had a serration. But I noticed the steak knife in Carter's hand had a regular sharp blade. It means the killer improvised again and grabbed the knife from the kitchen. Are you still with me?"

Sirk stopped his pacing at the question.

"Then, Carter gets sick when he realizes Reece is dead. But that could have happened when he just realized he just killed a guy," the cop replied half-heartedly.

"So, there's reason to doubt your theory, Lieutenant. You've been on the force for quite a while. A person could react either way, correct?" Ray asked.

"I don't know," Sirk's face dropped as he thought about it. "I suppose it can happen. But it's still pretty thin."

"Well, let's add one more thing," Ray told him. "I'm willing to bet that Francis Carter has something more than a business relationship with Reece. When I watched him, I saw a shattered man. I've only seen that type of reaction when it's someone close who dies. Someone who carries powerful feelings and affections for another person."

Garza leaned forward in his chair.

"You may be correct, Mr. Irish. I jokingly asked Miss Carter when she and Reece might wed. She told me Gabriel would never marry her," he said. "At the time, I thought she meant Reece didn't have the same social status as the Carter. But your idea just reminded me of something Rose Smyth said. She mentioned Carter went over to Reece's apartment nearly every day."

Garza glanced around the room.

"I don't want to speak ill of the dead, but Mrs. Smyth implied something was going on between those two men."

"Christ," the policeman shook his head at the news. "Just when you think you know people."

Sirk walked over to the window and looked outside.

"If that's true, it could have been a lover's quarrel, and he killed Reece."

"Alright, let's accept that logic," Ray told him. "Then explain who kidnapped Carter's daughter?"

As he kept working through the details, Ray noticed Sirk started to make the clicking noises with his tongue again. It was an irritating sound but seemed to help the policeman think.

"Maybe there are more than just two people involved? It could be an inside job with outside people," the detective thought aloud.

They could see by his expression that Sirk didn't' believe his idea.

"It can't be a coincidence about what happened with Reece and now Samantha. Somehow, the killers figured they knew something, so they came after them. I tell you that whoever is doing this is using the paintings to throw us. It's a diversion from the primary goal, which always points back at the art center."

Sirk frowned at him for a long moment, then began pacing the floor again.

"You're still grasping," the cop said. "Where's the solid proof?"

"Sirk, do you really believe anyone would risk a hangman's noose unless the goal brings a fortune? None of Reece's or Roman's canvases would bring enough cabbage for me to risk my neck," Ray said. "Carter has plenty of money, so even when the news spreads about the links with the murders, maybe they get a few grand. I can't buy that's the motive."

"Alright, give me a motive beyond a lover's quarrel," Sirk challenged him. Ray gave him a sly grin.

"You're not going to like hearing it. There is one item in that art center building, which might be worth the risk. The painting by Raphael would be something that people might kill over," he said. "I think a lot of folks might try to steal that. That's why the art center is alarmed and has a night watchman."

Kiilu let loose with his patronizing laugh.

"Mr. Irish, are you sure you haven't been out in the sun too long?" he told him sarcastically. "The painting's still there."

"You're correct," Ray replied with a glare, then he spoke to Kiilu as he would a child.

"Inside the museum, there is a painting that people say is a masterwork by Raphael. But remember, all the murders show diversion and distraction. I'll try to make it clear. Can anyone here guarantee the real McCoy is hanging in the gallery at that museum? Not one of you can guarantee that, can you?"

Garza suddenly snapped to attention at the idea while the lieutenant stared dumbfounded at the shamus. Kiilu let loose with a condescending whistle during the silence. Ray glanced over while he considered how good it would feel to slam his fist into the guy's face.

"Are you saying that the Madonna painting in the Hopley Art Center is a forgery now, and these killings are just a way to cover up the switch?" Sirk paused while he allowed the idea to marinate in his mind. Doubts showed across the inspector's face as he considered it.

"That sure would change the focus on suspects," he conceded. "Maybe someone not even at the art center."

"Whoever is running this show is a devious son of a bitch. Remember, the people who killed Townsend had plenty of time to stage the whole thing. The group of important people showed up to see the famous painting, so they're convinced when they see it. Now, with everyone's attention on the murder, who's going to worry about a Raphael painting? I think that's why the killer took a shot at me when I mentioned the painting."

Ray looked around the room.

"I mean, there's no other reason for someone to take a shot at the guy just showing up at the scene of a murder."

"Then explain the murder of Mrs. Smyth and the killing of Reece today." Kiilu pointed out as he stroked his hatchet-face. "They both had paintings involved, according to what you said."

Ray remained quiet for a moment while he looked at the art critic.

"Alright, here's my guess. I said the bastards that did this need time. They need the diversion continuing until the police arrest someone. Case closed; they leave town. Since they can't hang twice, another murder maintains the facade.

My best guess is one murderer joined the group of people who came with Carter to the Art Center. Therefore, that person has to be involved with the others. If we prove that Madonna painting is a fake and the noose will almost be around the killer's necks."

"I'm not convinced about your idea, Mr. Irish. However, if it will settle this, I suggest we have the painting examined." Garza rose from his chair. "Fortunately, we have Mr. Kiilu still here. He can help us with this. After all, he is one of the foremost experts in the United States."

The art critic looked uncomfortable when the eyes focused his way.

"Gentlemen, I will stake my reputation on the fact that no such forgery exists except in the mind of this private detective who has only this wild theory. However, if it will ease the lieutenant's concerns, we can do a simple test. By employing the use of chemicals, which I can administer, we can quickly date the work."

"No, we cannot do such a thing," the curator spoke up, looking like he might have a stroke. "Using chemicals on such a masterpiece would be too dangerous; it's reckless. Besides, there are other methods we can employ."

The director gazed at the art critic, who shrugged his shoulders.

"Enough of this," Sirk interjected. "I can't have any potential suspects looking over the painting. While I still say Ray has a fixation on that damn painting, I'll bring in the folks from the state historical museum. Those eggheads can decide the best way to figure out whether or not the painting is a fake."

The policeman gave a slow exhale, scowling at Ray.

"Until that happens, we still have to find Samantha Carter," Sirk told them. "I'm going to see our other suspects. Because this murder case remains open, each of you will have a uniformed cop outside of your front door."

"Wait, why are you doing this?" Kiilu asked. "I have to return home. My editor is already screaming about my column."

"It's for your protection," the lieutenant told him with a grunt. "Maybe we still have a homicidal maniac on our hands. I'm assuming Irish's crazy theory is full of holes, but I'm going to make sure that none of you gets killed."

"Or that they try to leave town," Ray smirked as he opened the door for those in the office.

~~~

Ray pushed through the small group of reporters, who kept peppering him with questions. He went to his car, put his hand on the key to start the engine, then stopped. Instead, he waited, watching the remaining suspects leave the police station while he smiled to himself.

Sirk's ham-fisted approach, while unintentional, might be a stroke of genius. The action might force the killer or killers into a risky move. Ray looked down as Kiilu and Garza left the building. He covertly observed their harried
~~~

conversations with the reporters. When they got in Garza's brown Hudson, he started his car.

Ray followed the men downtown, where he saw Kiilu get out of the vehicle after pulling in front of the Hotel Alexander. He pulled his car to a stop next to the curb and waited until Kiilu walked inside. After a moment, he slid out of his Nash and entered the lobby of the hotel. The shamus glanced around for Kiilu, but the art critic was already entering the elevator.

Ray went to the front desk and asked the clerk for Leroy James. A phone call later, Leroy emerged from his office at the back of the building.

"What's up?" he asked.

"Kiilu's room," Ray told him. "What did you find out?"

"Not much," Leroy said as he pushed back his hat. "You said he was a writer. I didn't see any typewriter or paper in the room. He must send in his articles on the phone."

Ray nodded, pulling out a ten-dollar bill for the hotel detective's trouble.

"Well, I doubt that. It appears someone is pulling a con," he replied. "It's time for me to check up on the guy."

"Are you going to Sirk on this? I heard he's the one running the show," Leroy advised.

"Yeah, I probably should," Ray agreed. "But I haven't got anything but a strong suspicion at this point. You know Sirk likes proof. Just keep an eye on this fake Kiilu to see if he leaves without the policeman stationed in front of his room. I'll keep a watch out of the back of the hotel."

Ray yawned as he waited inside his car. Night shadows fell across the street, and the streetlights turned on. Finally, someone opened the back door of the hotel, near the garbage cans. Instantly, he recognized his suspect as the man walked out of the hotel. Glancing around, Kiilu headed down the alleyway and went around the corner.

Ray started his car and slowly drove through the alley until he reached the street. He saw Kiilu sliding inside a yellow and red taxi parked along the sidewalk. Ray waited a moment; then, the detective carefully followed the cab as it drove away. He backed off the gas pedal, making sure not to lose his prey. Fortunately, the taxi driver kept to the main streets as the cab meandered through the city. Ray wondered if Kiilu had his driver on a sightseeing tour. Eventually, the taxi reached the town's edge, coming to a slum section of abandoned warehouses. Large two-story buildings lined either side of the street. Now abandoned, the buildings were various shops used for the ammunition plant operations. When the war ended, the contracts stopped, and the plant closed. Any visitor to Oyster City would not be hanging around this part of the town, let alone a prominent art critic.

The taxi came to a stop in front of a dark building with large roll-up doors and a cargo ramp. Ray slowly brought his coupe to a halt about half a block away, turning off his headlights. The only light on the street came from a single streetlamp above the cab where Kiilu paid his driver. As Ray watched, the driver tried to get his passenger to reconsider leaving the taxi. Kiilu left the car. He took a glance around the area before he walked to the corner of the building. He swiftly disappeared down a side alley.

Sliding out of his car, Ray grabbed a flashlight out of his glove box and took off after his target. As he crossed the street, he pulled out his gun. Dark alleys were not his friends when following a murder suspect. When the shamus reached the corner of the building, he couldn't see much, but he heard footsteps going up iron stairs, followed by the creak of a door opening. Ray worked his way down the dark alley, almost missing the ladder which led up to the fire escape for the building. As quiet as he could manage, Ray climbed the ladder, although every step seemed to ring out on the creaking steel contraption. Finally, the shamus reached a door, nearly hidden in the shadows. When Ray slowly pushed the door open, he could see no light.

The man paused, listening, but there was silence inside. Crouching low, the man pushed through and found himself in a dark room. Keeping his gun pointed into the darkness, he flicked on his flashlight. It was an empty room with a wooden door in front of him. The area was silent as a grave, and he heard footsteps on the other side of the door. The old boards under his feet creaked as Ray moved to the door. After a moment, he slowly opened the door, breathing a sigh of relief that the hinges remained quiet. Stepping into a narrow hallway, the shamus pressed his flashlight against his coat. He let just a small sliver of light reveal the doors on either side of the hall. Old posters from the war effort hung on the wall.

Ray slowly crept along, listening for any sound in the eerie quiet. Finally, he heard voices ahead of him at the last door on the left. The man groped forward until he reached the doorknob. A soft light escaped from under the door. He heard Kiilu's voice.

"Listen, it's elementary. That private dick followed me, and he'll be here any second. I told you that every plan requires adjustments." When Ray heard movement inside the room, he turned off his flashlight, pocketing it. Slowly, he pushed through the door with his gun in hand. He pointed at a smiling Kiilu who leaned back against a messy desk filled with containers. A glance around revealed they were the only ones in the room. Gun centered on the suspect; Ray stepped forward.

"Don't move, Kiilu, or whatever your name is. We need to settle this now."

"Oh, by all means. I've been waiting, Mr. Irish. Now you can meet Felix," the bearded man replied with a sneer.

Ray expected the other man, but not a fist swinging from behind him. The detective spun around, only to get smacked in the jaw with a knuckle that struck like concrete. Immediately after the blow, the attacker pushed a shoulder into him with a tackle into the wall. A jolt to Ray's wrist sent his .45 Auto to the floor. The clatter of the gun caught Kiilu's attention, and he sprang forward to retrieve the weapon.

Ray had other problems at the moment. His attacker hooked a muscular arm around the detective's neck, sending them both to the floor on their knees in the struggle. Ray clawed at the arm around his neck, and then he tried to grab his attacker's hair. The pressure tightened around his throat, and Ray pushed back hard, trying to press his attacker into a wall. However, the man held on to Ray, who struggled to breathe. Kiilu let out the same condescending laugh that the shamus hated.

"Felix, you can stop now. I'll take care of this problem," he said. The man held the auto in his right hand and a snub-nosed .38 revolver in his left, each one pointing at Ray. An evil grin now replaced the man's arrogant smile.

Felix Roman let go of Ray and backed away. The shamus got to his feet with a strained effort, looking at Felix. The stout man had long, thick black hair and bright green eyes, but a person wouldn't have noticed that at first. Instead, Ray stared at the hideous hole in the middle of the man's face. Ray saw plenty of nasty injuries inside the military hospital while recovering from his wounds. Still, his shocked expression showed at the sight. It is hard to tell where his missing nose ended, and the mouth started with the middle section of his opponent's face caved in.

Above them, two floodlights hung from the ceiling, run by batteries that sat perched on a dusty shelf next to the artist. Ray noticed the artist wore a worn and paint covered shirt and dungarees. An easel covered with splotches of paint sat next to the old desk where Kiilu leaned. Haphazardly laid across the top of a nearby table were cans of colorful paint, along with a candle and a long-bladed serrated knife. In one corner of the room, an army cot was the bed used by Roman.

"You got a little too nosey, shamus. You should have just let that dull copper run the show. It would keep you alive longer." Kiilu observed his target, glancing around.

"Well, it took me a while to figure out that you're no art critic," Ray replied. He decided to play on Kiilu's ego.

"It bothered me you were supposed to be in the city all week and only wanted to see Raphael's painting after Carter's party. There were only two suspects left after Carter got thrown in the slammer. I knew for sure when you didn't even have a typewriter in your room. You were sloppy. By the way, just who are you anyway?"

"I guess it won't matter to let you know the truth," the man holding two guns shrugged. "Morton Anderson at your service, and, of course, you know Felix Roman, one of the greatest artists of this generation."

He flicked the barrel of the revolver toward his partner in crime. Ray nodded at the artist, then turned back to Anderson.

"Then, I take it the real Marc Kiilu is no longer putting out his articles?"

"Absolutely not," Anderson explained. "I couldn't afford to have him accidentally show up in the newspapers somewhere. He was just another piece of the puzzle needing to be solved. When you start in on a big haul like this, you can't stop at anything. I couldn't afford to make the mistakes that Otto Wacker did when he sold all those fake Van Gogh's back in the 20s. A person must learn from the mistakes of others."

"You've been doing your homework," Ray replied, trying to keep the man talking while he searched for a way out of his jam.

"You don't spend three years in the big house without something to dream about," Anderson replied. His eyes lit up as he laid out his achievement. "I knew the key to any successful heist like this would be a diversion. The stroke of luck was finding my partner. I read about his return to Oyster City, the famous local artist who everyone pitied. I had to track him down in New Hampshire, but Fate laid the cards on my table. Swap the famous painting with a forgery, and I would turn up as the influential art critic to maintain the work's provenance. I had to set up the whole thing for enough time to get away; the entire scheme was simply brilliant in form and function."

"Yeah, brilliant until something went wrong," the sarcasm dripped from Ray. "You botched the job and had to kill people to cover up the crime."

Anderson gave him a thin smile, glancing at his partner, who studied both men.

"One always expects hitches with any big haul," the killer replied. "I snuck into the Art Center multiple times over the week to understand everything about the building and the people working there. Still, that imbecile night watchman woke up from his nap early. Unfortunately, my partner struck him too hard, leaving us with the problem of a body. But, as you figured out, I had a backup plan. Mr. Roman already told me about Reece's feeble attempts to copy his rather morbid works. Born of inspiration that night, I simply took advantage of the opportunity. Felix knew all about the workshop in the basement of the Center."

"Yeah, just like taking the pot shot at me. You figured if I got knocked off, cops would think the killer nailed me during the escape. But you missed something that Reece figured out about your scheme." Ray said, then Anderson nodded his agreement.

"Well, I couldn't take a chance. He could have gummed up the works. I noticed him gawking at that Raphael painting the next morning. When we spoke, he seemed rattled, and I knew he must have bought into your idea about a forgery. I found out from Garza that Reece called Carter's house from the museum; I couldn't take the chance that some punk with a brush figured it out. That's when I moved quickly to fix the problem."

"Yeah, I bet it was the same with the Smyth woman," Sirk replied. "A loose end to tie up, and you were afraid she might recognize the Raphael picture switch as well. You and Felix must have scared the hell out of her to tie her to that column so easily. But your mistake came in using that painting. The murder had nothing to do with arrows."

"You're cleverer than I realized. Yes, we had to improvise quickly. Felix created that copy from memory. He saw it in some shop while he was out of state. It came in handy when we needed it. Once Mrs. Smyth opened the door, and she barely recognized Felix standing in front of her. But her horror of his facial injuries forced her into a compliant old lady. It appeared she could not understand the events even as I bound her to the column while my friend placed that painting for her to see."

The man smiled in memory of his work.

"While I doubt that the woman would figure out about the forgery, her death made it easier to throw sand in the eyes of the police with my little charade. Once they arrested Carter, the whole scheme worked out nicely for me to slip away. Reece became the counterfeiter, and Carter killed him. In the end, it doesn't matter as long as the coppers remain clueless."

Ray glanced at Felix, recognizing the growing distrust in the man's eyes at the calloused way Anderson spoke about the murders. The scarred artist appeared upset at the revelations coming out during the conversation.

"I know you made the forgeries for him," Ray spoke to Felix. "I don't think you're a killer. Your girlfriend told me you saw too much death overseas. Tell me, why are you willing to be hung with him? You know they'll be looking for you."

Roman had difficulty getting out the words. But the anger was clear.

"And why not? Why shouldn't I get some of the gravy after what happened? Look at me! I'm a sight no one could stand to look at, like an ugly piece of human art," he said. "The rich people wanted my paintings to shock them, but not when I came around their estates. Dealers told me to stay home. Once my works meant rebellion to them, then they only wanted to pity me."

"I guess Anderson pitched the idea to get back at those who hurt you," Ray interrupted as he kept his focus on the artist. "Pull a con on the rich and run away. He told you the entire plan would be a piece of cake, didn't he? But it went south on you."

Felix nodded with regret showing in his eyes.

"I'm not a murderer. I didn't want to hurt Townsend; he was a good guy. He tried to run away, and I hit him," he told Ray. "Anyway, it's too late now. Like Anderson told me, I get the chair for one murder or ten. Once we have the money, I can get away and have anything I want."

"So, you're in this because people gave you some dirty looks. Hell, I've seen guys in worse shape than you in the Camp Lockett Convalescent Hospital. They were in the same boat as you. The only difference was they came back from the war and restarted their lives with the gals who couldn't recognize them anymore." Ray turned to the man with disgust in his expression.

"Damn it, you just ran away and hid like a little boy. Look around; you're still hiding. People around here told me you were some great artist. I don't buy it. I think you're too afraid to stand up and show everyone what pain and suffering mean," the shamus continued.

"I'm warning you, shamus, to keep your mouth shut," Anderson interjected, but Ray recognized the effect of his words on the artist.

"And here's a news flash for you, Felix. You didn't kill Townsend when you struck him." Irish glanced at the man holding the guns. "You screwed up when you followed Anderson's lead and nailed him to that column. A dead man couldn't pump out blood like that from the chest. He'd probably lived if someone hadn't stabbed him to finish him. Did your partner tell you about another of his mistakes?"

Anderson yelled at Ray to shut up as he stepped closer. Felix turned his stare to his partner, partially standing in front of Ray.

"You swore he was dead," he told Anderson. "You're the one who speared him with that lance. I trusted you. You said it would make the scene fit perfectly for the cops."

"You've been relying on your partner's smarts for too much." Ray interrupted again. "If Gabriel Reece recognized that Raphael painting as a phony, then how long is it before others figure it out? I'm going to give you another news flash. The cops already have a warrant out for you, Felix. They believe you did these murders on your own. They think you're a lunatic. I'll bet your partner didn't tell you that either."

Ray inched his way behind the artist, keeping his eyes glued on the guns held by Anderson. The gunman focused his attention on Roman now, his eyes narrowing as the truth came out.

"You know that means nothing," the ex-con tried to explain. "I've said all along that the whole idea expects they'll figure out the forgery eventually. Once we get away from Oyster City, the original painting will turn up somewhere in Europe in a few months."

The man stepped from the desk.

"Listen, Felix, haven't I been straight with you since I've let you in on this whole setup? I told you I'm getting a good fence to handle this. A hundred and twenty-five thousand, and there'll be no trace back to us. Everyone will believe that Mrs. Smyth was the dupe who had the forgery all along. Now, get out of the way so we can finish this shamus and get the money."

"Felix, that still leaves you hanging out by yourself." Ray reminded him. "Ask your partner about Samantha Carter getting kidnapped. Did he tell you about that? I bet she's tied up downstairs. She's the sacrifice in that painting of yours. You remember the one piece of art you left in her house? Did Anderson tell you he took it with her? Your painting contained a man and a woman. Wake up! He kidnapped Samantha to die. You and she have to die for your partner to pull off his scam without sharing a dime with you."

Felix Roman's mutilated face immediately turned red with rage as he looked back at Ray. With the hideous, disfiguring hole in the man's face, he seemed genuinely evil.

"Wait, you never told me you had a thing for her." Anderson slowly turned a gun toward his partner. Felix took a step toward the gunman.

"I told you I saw Reece hanging around the girl and figured he had told her everything. I had to do it. We couldn't take the chance. Besides, she'll never love you; just look at yourself."

Ray kept up the heat.

"Anderson's already set you up. Remember, the cops are searching for you, Felix. The police don't know about your partner. With one of those damn paintings hanging above your body, they'll say you went nuts from your war injuries. Case closed by the cops. Anderson will have no witnesses and all the money, laughing at you while he takes a ship to Europe."

Anderson gave a panicked half-laugh as he backed into the desk. The entire room seemed to stop for a couple of tense seconds while Anderson decided who to shoot first. Ray helped the choice along by diving behind the wooden easel next to him. A slug from the .38 struck him in the thigh, causing him to let out a howl. But the diversion allowed Felix to rush his partner.

Ray's .45 auto spit out two bullets when Anderson turned on his partner. Felix's body shuddered from the impact of lead striking him. Yet his fury carried him forward. The artist ran into Anderson, sending them across the top of the desk.

Despite the pain from his wounded leg, Ray scrambled over to join in the melee. A gun fell out during the fighting, and Ray grabbed his .45 back. Before he could point the weapon, Ray caught a wild kick from Anderson in the head. The blow sent the shamus back, tumbling over paint cans. He remained on his feet. However, his gun fell to the floor.

Felix clamped one powerful hand on Anderson's gun and the other around his partner's windpipe. Turning purple, Anderson's face showed his panic. Anderson kept striking his fist on Roman's powerful forearm during the melee, but the locked grip remained around his grip. His increasingly frantic struggles caused him to kick out. Ray jumped into the fight again, trying to pull the enraged Roman away. The artist refused to release his partner's throat. During the struggle, Ray took a kick in his wounded leg. He fell back into the office door in pain, sliding to the floor.

Ray painfully struggled back to his feet as Felix visibly weakened from his wounds. With vengeful desperation, the maimed man grabbed the knife from the table. Before Ray could react, Roman slammed the blade into his onetime partner's chest. Almost immediately, death ended the struggles for both men.

When Ray got to the desk, Anderson's body slid to the floor like a broken doll. Felix Roman's audible death-gasp echoed slightly, and he fell across Anderson's body. The artist's fingers remained clamped around the wooden handle of the knife, still stuck in the corpse. Morton Anderson, his eyes staring up in stony surprise, seemed unable to grasp how quickly his plans fell apart.

Scanning his wound, Ray discovered the bullet went through the meaty part outside his thigh. It hurt like hell, but he would live. The shamus was happy that the lead missed his rebuilt thigh bone. After recovering his gun, he made a quick search of the office. He found the small and rare stolen Raphael painting. It looked like the other to his inexperienced eyes, but Ray decided that he now had the original masterpiece. He tucked the rolled canvas under his arm after failing to find a working phone.

A hell of a lot of people died over the damn thing.

Working his way to the main floor below, Ray opened the many doors while yelling out for Samantha Carter. When he entered a large open dock area, his flashlight beam revealed someone sitting between two abandoned pieces of machinery. As Irish approached, the dim light showed the woman was sitting perfectly still in the same white and green dress. He held the flashlight beam on the woman who had her back to him. Ropes wrapped around the woman, holding her to a high back rocking chair. Smiling, he limped across the cracked, damp cement floor. Ray paid only slight attention to the framed picture near her as he got closer. Soon, he recognized the painting. The same one taken from Carter's house. It leaned against one of the massive steel instrument panels next to the piece of machinery.

Irish ignored the pain of his injury as he limped along toward the still woman. The surrounding air carried the stench of wetness and decay. Several candles near the picture gave a faint yellow light to the area. He glanced at the gruesome colors on the canvas, which were highlighted by candlelight.

"It's alright, Samantha. It's Ray!" he told her softly. The shamus came around to her side, and he stopped.

Her head slightly bowed forward. At first, it seemed like Samantha was saying her prayers. The beam of his flashlight revealed a dark, glistening stain across the front of her dress — a dumbfounded man locked on the color he recognized. Ray stood there, staring at her corpse while his mind went over the last of the case.

Anderson killed Samantha just before he arrived, forcing her to look at the painting just a few feet away. The devious bastard expected to finish Felix once they killed Irish. A suicide by a crazy artist after two more murders. Then, the son of a bitch Anderson expected to walk away. Samantha's death was the last senseless act of a brutal killer.

I'm so sorry!

Carefully, Ray Irish reached out softly and touched her brown hair. While knowing she would never move again, the man suddenly made a childish wish.

Come back to me!

He imaged her looking up at him in relief at his touch. Her smile of thanks filled her mind. Instead, Ray felt his finger brush the cold skin of her body. That was when he let his brain finally grasp the fact he failed. Unlike the heroes of his childhood books, the shamus arrived too late to save the damsel in distress. Ray Irish was to blame for her murder.

He let his gaze drift down to the candle by Samantha's feet. It looked like a votive candle from a church. For the first time since the war, he asked himself the same useless question.

Why do good people die when there are so many bad ones who really should?

He remembered the last time he asked the question. Hunkered down in a stinking foxhole on Tulagi, the frightened Seabee asked God the question while he endured an ungodly Japanese artillery barrage. Tonight, the same answer came back to the detective, just as cold and lifeless as a body.

Nobody knew!

The pain from his observation ran through him as Ray scowled at the painting. It grew fouler. The man sat down his flashlight before he calmly picked up the canvas frame with both hands.

Suddenly, he lifted the piece high over his head before he slammed the artwork across the instrument panel. Again and again, he savagely battered the wood frame into chunks. It took several moments of beating, tearing, and shredding to destroy the hideous artwork. In his rage, Irish did not hear his howls of desperate fury echoing throughout the building while he ripped apart the canvas into long pieces of shredded confetti. When he finished, Ray gasped for air, and he could only feel a numbness envelop him except where his injured leg ached from his effort. After a moment, he glanced at Samantha's corpse before he slowly hobbled away.

Eventually, Ray exited the building, gently taking the steps down after opening the warehouse's side door. He looked out at the flickering lights of his corrupt city. Usually, such a scene might give him a sense of comfort. Instead, the view weighed on him like the chilly air that descended around him. Making his way to his car, Ray knew it would take more than a couple of whiskey shots to ease his pain. After he called the cops, he would relive the night again for the official police record. The man would need to repeat every turn of events and explain every terrible mistake that the shamus made. Worse, it would take time for Ray Irish to forget about the dead girl in the basement.

Chapter 7: Brown Bottle Flu

Arizona arrived at Cat's apartment late in the evening. He came along with a bottle of decent wine that he picked up along the way. The salesclerk told him it was a sophisticated brand that his wealthy clients preferred. The big man grew nervous as he turned the manual doorbell.

This feels worse than hitting the beach at Anzio.

"Yeah, yeah, I'm coming," her irritated voice grew louder after he turned the ringer the second time.

Cat opened the door dressed in a blue sleeveless nightgown and a hastily thrown on a pale blue robe. She gave him a surprised smile as her hair fell across her face. The sexy look struck him dumbfounded for a second.

"Sorry…I know it's late, but I thought I would drop by with a gift," he groped for the words. "I mean, it's about time to return the favor for all the coffee you buy me." He held up the bottle of wine with a grin.

"The guy says only the best people drink this stuff," Arizona told her. Cat laughed and opened the door wider.

"I guess I can trust your word for that," she grinned. "Come on in, copper. I take it this is not an official visit?"

"No, I'm off duty," he replied, following her into the small kitchen. He stood there while Cat pulled down two glasses from the cabinet.

"Sit down and take a load off," she told him when she noticed him standing like a statue. After the big man sat on the couch, Cat slid in next to him. She handed him a corkscrew, then watched him fumble around while trying to open the bottle.

"Is something wrong?" Her tone was mischievous.

"No, not at all," he glanced over. "I'm not usually drinking this stuff." He finally removed the cork and poured the wine into the goblets she held.

Arizona leaned back and took a sip. While not something he would buy again, he thought he did an excellent job of hiding his distaste. Then Cat laughed at his expression.

"I take it you're more of a scotch man," she told him.

Arizona chuckled with a nod.

Cat rose and went to the small liquor cabinet near the radio. She turned on the radio and came back with a tumbler full of scotch whiskey.

"Alright, you can quit making faces," she handed him the glass.

She sat next to Arizona again and leaned back on the comfortable couch. Her face lit up in playful delight when she noticed his eyes glance at her cleavage, highlighted by the low V-shape cut on her nightgown. The woman was used to the ogling, taking it in stride as her way to control men. Arizona was not a great-looking guy, and he dressed like a banker back in the 20s. However, Arizona carried a quiet and honest demeanor. He always treated her like a lady. It was a character trait she found rare in Oyster City.

"Why did you come over?" She decided he needed to quit smoking cigars. They stained his teeth.

"Now, don't give me this nonsense about buying your coffee. I only did that once." Cat smiled when his face grew slightly red.

"Well, to be honest, I wanted to see you. You've always been nice to me. I like your company." Arizona confessed.

"I see," she said casually.

Cat took another sip of wine. They had the same expensive swill in the estate homes that she occasionally went for parties. Cat learned about upper society's tastes and refined character for the last couple of years. It was a crock, and she knew it. However, the dividend from finding rich guys meant you never had to worry about your next meal.

"I wondered how you might react to me coming over," Arizona's voice interrupted her thoughts.

"How do you mean?" She wondered.

"Well, I'm kind of dopey — not one of the pretty guys I've seen you with. Plus, I realize you and Irish are pretty close," he said.

"He and I are just partners," Cat replied quickly, then sighed when he glanced at her.

"Look, nothing is going on between us. Besides, I never thought of you as dopey."

Her words made him grin.

"Well, I would like to take you out sometime if you're willing," he told her. "Maybe go to a Cagney movie?"

"That might be fun," she said, then glanced over. "I'm curious; why don't you just come out and ask me?"

"I don't come from the upper crust, and a cop isn't going to rack in the cabbage," he replied.

"I'm not a gold digger!" Cat sat up rigidly. "You aren't going to get girls to go out with you when you insult them."

"I didn't say you were a gold digger," he calmly replied as he watched her. "But you must know about the rumors if you react like that. Listen, I don't have a beef about those you go out with."

He sipped on the drink as the room went quiet but for the music coming from the radio. After a long moment, Cat turned to him after staring at her wineglass.

"I hate people like you and Irish," she told him, but there was no malice in her tone. "You always have to observe everything, don't you? You think you know someone just because you deal with lies and deceit all the time. But you never bother to ask them about their past."

"Some people don't like to bring up their past. Irish is that way," the cop reminded her. "On the other hand, many people lie about everything, so they don't know the truth anymore. Why bother asking them?"

He sighed.

"But either way, cops and private dicks are bound to pick up bad habits, I guess. We hardly believe anything unless we see it. Even then, we're not sure."

"Did you grow up poor, Arizona?" Cat finally spoke after another long moment of silence.

"Poor as church mice," he replied affably. "My folks had a few acres along with a darn mean mule that was lazy as sin. Somehow, my folks raised two brothers and myself. Even though we couldn't scrap two plug nickels together, I still got an education. It wasn't fun, but I learned one thing."

"What was that?" she asked.

"My pop taught me you never look over the fence, wishing you had the neighbor's prized bull. Envy was always one of the seven deadly sins," he told her as he adjusted his gigantic frame on her couch. He laid his arm across the back behind her. "When I think back, I believe it's easier to figure out your genuine friends when you got nothing."

"How so?" her eyes observed his expression.

"When a guy goes into a bar on payday, he'll have a thousand friends," Arizona told her. "Check out how many friends you have in the same bar when they find out you're suddenly unemployed."

After a moment, Cat nodded to herself and leaned back against his arm. His words were gentler than what Irish told her. However, they told her the same thing. Chasing the wealthy men gave her an intoxicating dream. It also gave her the same low-class stench she so desperately wanted to escape.

"I wouldn't tell you to lay off if you decide to ask me out some time," she told him. "For now, let's enjoy the music for the evening." He nodded, and she felt him relax next to her.

They remained quiet, sipping on their drinks. The two people remained lost in thoughts of their respective pasts and future. She frowned when the phone suddenly rang.

~~~

Irish did not know his location other than it was a somewhat familiar-looking room. Time left his world, and it could be night or day. Ray did not give a damn. Time meant nothing but returning to everything that he wanted to forget. As he lay on the comfortable bed, he was willing himself not to think of anything. Ray wanted to feel a comfortable numbness spread over him like a warm blanket.
~~~

However, there was a dizzy feeling as the room spun. He realized his stomach churned with unsteady nausea as well.

I'm too drunk to get to the bathroom.

The shamus took another drink of Old Rock Rye. He still claimed he disliked the taste, but he was far past caring. The brown flask was the only thing decent they had in the liquor store. It helped him block out thinking about Samantha; just considering her name opened a deep wound.

He took another drink. It was harsh and burned his throat, but it warmed. The drunk smiled to himself after an involuntary shiver.

"Trying to hide again, Ray?" the coldly familiar woman's voice whispered the question in his ear.

"Are you going to forget about me as well? You took me to bed, then took my five hundred. Now, you hide inside of the bottle. It seems like that's your solution most of the time."

Ray refused to look over at the direction of the voice. He knew Greye La Spina sat in an ugly plaid chair near him.

"Greye, you're not real. Take a powder and go back to the grave," he told her.

"Why don't you look over? We used to be so close," the ghost whispered. "Now you want to run out on me. Look at me, lover! Don't you remember?" He felt the tug of war inside. Finally, Ray turned his head toward the chair.

The ghost of Greye La Spina reached down and took an empty flask of whiskey from the floor. It wasn't the woman as he remembered. Instead, she appeared to him as the corpse he saw in the morgue. The body of his lover lying on the table after the autopsy.

The spirit tossed her head back, trying to drink the last drops of whiskey using lips that were eaten away by the creatures of the bay. Her bloated body was unrecognizable with a sallow skin of blue-green. Greye looked him over with her empty eye sockets.

"I've buried worse-looking corpses," he told her bluntly. "Why are you coming to me this way?"

"You damn crumb, you want to whine about your problems. Look at me. I'm never to rest. You haven't found my murder yet, so how else can I get your attention?"

"Just go away and leave me alone," Ray looked away. "I'm done with this stuff. I'm no detective."

"Then give me back my money. Then, I'll go away, hotshot." Greye mocked him.

The ghost rose and came closer. Irish smelled the rotting flesh, the same sickly odor on those nasty islands where he spent the war.

"Oh, wait, you can't return my money, you crud. All talk and no action, just like a guy."

She leaned down.

"Kiss me, Ray."

"Get away from me," he screamed.

After throwing his bottle at the image, he rolled away. His body slid off the bed and slammed into the dresser with a heavy thud. Ray saw a pair of shoes in front of his face, and he glanced up.

"Time to go to sleep, shamus," the ghost of Hugh Pendexter said as he looked down at Ray.

Greye's assassin brother carried the sliced neck wound of his death. The blood looked fresh on his suit.

"I always hated that damn mustache," Ray growled at the ghost.

Then, he finally passed out.

The pounding on the door felt like someone was beating his head with a hammer, but he refused to move. One eye opened, and he saw a blurry bottle on the nightstand. Ray was back in his bed. The brown bottle was on its side and empty. Next to his head was a shattered alarm clock on its side. The few remaining shattered glass shards slowly came in and out of focus.

The pounding started again as one opened eye stared at the bottle. He licked his dry lips. Outside the room, there was the rattle of keys. It sounded close, yet muffled. A moment later, people entered the room. He rolled over, expecting more ghosts to complain about him. He saw an upside-down man coming to the bed. Ray did not realize that his head hung over the edge of the mattress.

"Alright, mister, your time here is up. Out you go," the voice demanded. "We don't need no drunks hanging in my rooms."

"Get out, you upside down troll," Irish groused. "I've paid you for the damn room!"

"Your three nights are up," the voice said. "I want you out of my hotel in ten minutes. Don't make me call the state police." The figure stomped away, passing by two people standing in the doorway.

Ray rolled over and suddenly found himself on the floor with a thud. He groaned as the fire in his leg turned blazing hot. The shamus picked up the bottle, verifying it was still empty. Then, someone grabbed the bottle from his hand.

"Out of bed, Irish." Cat threw the bottle into a trash can.

"Get the hell out of here," he spat out. Before he realized what had happened, a pair of hands lifted him off the floor.

"You smell like piss and booze," Arizona fumed as he shook his friend. "You ain't getting into my car like that. Into the shower, shamus," he forced Ray into the bathroom.

Cat followed. Together, they quickly stripped him down to his underwear. The water was icy when it struck him, and Ray let out a stream of curses. Still, he took the soap and began rubbing it over his tee-shirt. His sodden brain could barely decipher whether his head would explode or he would puke.

"Alright, why the hell are you here?"

He coughed out after Arizona forced his head under the stream of water for a second time.

"Pappy sent us to find you," Cat told him. "Arizona discovered your car nearly wrapped around a tree. For a moment, I thought you might have died."

"You're damn lucky to be alive. I had your Nash towed to a garage," the policeman told him.

"Yeah, I have all the luck of the Irish," he replied bitterly. "Tell it to Samantha Carter."

"Is that what this drunken escape is about? You damn fool, stop beating yourself up," Arizona gave a deep sigh, and he shook his head.

"Listen, I spoke with Sirk. He told me all about that ex-con who slit her throat. The son of a bitch is rotting in hell. You solved the case. Hell, the art center director thinks you're a damn hero for getting their precious painting back. You even made the newspapers. People will come to get your damn autograph. You figured out a mystery that got good people killed."

"Samantha was one of them. I blew it, and I got her killed. I should have let Sirk know about my suspicions. He could have picked Anderson up," Ray countered as he turned off the shower. Cat handed him a towel.

"Hell, they could have beat the information out of him in jail if I had any smarts," he continued.

"You've got another missing girl who needs your help. Or don't you remember that case, you damn fool!" Cat snapped. "You can't read minds or look into a crystal ball. Now, buck up and snap out of it."

Livid, she stomped out of the room.

Drying his face and hair, Irish got out of the shower, suddenly realizing he still had on his underwear. The bloody bandage covering his leg wound remained unchanged since the doctor put in a couple of stitches.

"Great, now I have to dry off in wet clothes," he said sullenly. "Hand me one of another towel so I can check this leg."

Arizona gave him the towel, getting a look at the man's scarred legs for the first time. He decided Ray must carry around an angel on his shoulder.

"Those Navy docs did a hell of a job on you," he told Ray. "Next time, don't lead with your feet."

The shamus glared at him, still holding the bloody bandage in his hand. Then he realized the cop was joking.

"Yeah, they decided to use me as another Frankenstein experiment," he grumbled. He looked around the bathroom.

"Where the hell am I? I don't even know."

"It wasn't hard; we just had to follow the bottles," Arizona smirked. "State police sent out a wire about the wreck, and your name was on the registration. We came to the closest motel. Get dressed; we have a long drive."

He left, closing the door behind him.

After a few minutes, Irish came into the room. He was drier, and his bandage was in the trash. The wound was healing. He took his pants back from Cat, who sat on the bed. She glanced at his scars, then looked away while Ray sat next to her to put his pants on. As dizzy as he felt, Ray would have fallen on his face otherwise. When he finished, he remembered that wet boxers under wool pants were damn uncomfortable.

"What day is it?" he finally asked.

"It's Friday," she told him. "The owner told us you came in and that you haven't left the room. Do you remember that?" Ray slowly buttoned his shirt, shaking his head.

"No, I barely remember walking into this place," he said.

Suddenly, he stopped when the familiarity of the décor struck him. He groaned from his head, pounding at him as he bent over. Ray pulled back the edge of the large wool rug that covered most of the wood floor. The red bloodstain was still there. He glanced at Cat, who suddenly stood up, her face going pale.

"This is the same room," she said. "I can't believe it."

"What are you two talking about?" Arizona asked as he kneeled to look at the stain. "Do you know something you should talk to police about?"

"No, but we recognized the room," he told him bitterly as he recalled his time there. Irish let the rug drop from his hand. "This is the same room that Pendexter got his throat cut."

"You mean that guy who tried to knock off Guy Young a few months back? The state police and the papers claimed it was his partner that killed him."

He looked at them suspiciously.

"What the hell do you know?"

"Nothing," Cat said too quickly. "We saw the room when we came here looking for Greye La Spina. Pendexter was her brother."

The policeman stood. He glanced at Cat, then at Ray.

"Well, I guess that'll have to do," he told them. "Doesn't matter anymore, I suppose. The racketeer and his cronies are six feet under. Did you come to this room deliberately?"

"Hell, I don't remember," Ray lied as he sat down on the bed again.

He could still see Greye's ghost and remembered what she told him. His face was pale, and he had trouble keeping his focus as he stared at the chair. The room seemed to wobble. Finally, he put on his shoes.

"All I remember is the booze and nightmares," he said aloud.

"The hotel owner told Cat you were talking to people in here. You scared the hell out of him. It appears you're meeting with the ghosts now," Arizona said with a grim smile. He noticed the shamus staring at the chair, lost in thoughts.

"Come on, let's get moving," the cop told him. "You can dry off in the car. We're running behind."

After Ray finished tying his shoes, Cat handed him his coat, along with his gun and holster.

"Your wallet's in the coat," she told him coolly while she walked to the door. "I've got your hat."

Ray limped down the stairs, going into the sunlight, and he paused, grabbing the door for a moment to keep his nausea down. When he finally got to the car, the man immediately threw up behind the trunk. After his violent retching finally receded, he climbed into the back seat. Arizona drove away. Uncomfortable bouts of silence fill the car as they took the highway to the state capital.

"Where're we going?" Ray finally asked.

"Arizona and I are meeting the parents of Jack Romano. He's the kid who went missing. I finally tracked him down," Cat said. She turned around from the passenger side to look back at him. "You can stay in the car and sober up while we're there. We don't have time to take you to your office."

Ray scowled at her, but leaned back for the ride.

"Don't get me wrong, but why did you come for me?" He asked after a couple of miles passed.

"Christ, you're pathetic at times. Pappy called me and said you were missing. He got worried when you failed to get your paper that morning."

The image of his friend handing out papers near his stand crossed Ray's mind as he looked away from her glare.

"Have you forgotten about that kidnapped girl, Orella Dela Cruz? You've got a case to finish, mister, so you better get yourself together. Her father is in Oyster City, and I've already met him. Believe it or not, he's hiring you to find her. I told him you're already on the case and that you were checking out leads. He doesn't need to know you're checking out the bottom of whiskey bottles."

Ray remained quiet at her cutting remark. He tried to focus his thoughts, which swirled around like the ghosts in his room. Samantha's death gave him an excuse to pickle his brain in self-pity, just like coming back from the war. He felt like a damn fool. Worse, he forgot about Orella. The woman needed his help, and he ran away for three days. He swore to himself that it would never happen again.

"Yeah, I'm glad you didn't mention it," he grumbled. "I've got a knack for drinking at the wrong time."

"Yeah, that's pretty obvious," she replied bitterly as the fire flashed in her eyes. "Maybe you need to quit feeling sorry for yourself, so Orella doesn't end up like Samantha Carter?"

"Alright, enough!" Ray snapped. "Maybe she's already dead. You can beat me up or get me up to speed. Has our police detective turned anything up on Orella's kidnapping?"

"Still nothing," Arizona spoke up. "There's not much to go on. Her family hasn't heard from her. None of my snitches know anything about it. It's like she's vanished. One thing that you should know. They found Wilber along the road outside of the state capital. The state police don't understand how he got out there when they found his car just outside of Oyster City."

The policeman looked back at Ray through the rearview mirror.

"All we have is your half-baked idea," he told Irish.

"Listen, Arizona told me about your idea. I think it's nuts, but he agrees Orella might inside the Smyth estate," Cat glanced at the cop when he interrupted.

"No, I said we didn't have any other leads."

"Anyway, we can't just send her dad to their house and accuse them," the woman continued. "Her father wants answers."

"The last time we talked, you told me I was a fool," Ray reminded her. "Now, why are you so interested in my case?"

Before she could respond, Arizona took over.

"Cat's making sense, Ray. As a cop, I'm stuck about where to go with this investigation," he explained. "You know I need evidence or a body, especially with the Smyths and their connections. We know murder is involved somehow with this kidnapping. But I got nothing to show for it."

Trying to pull his mind back into the case, Ray barely nodded.

"I have one of their servants who told me that the house could hide Orella. It has areas off-limits to the servants. And I have the ring that Maria wants back, or at least I did." he started going through his coat to find it.

When the man held the ring out for Cat to see, she surprised him with her apparent disinterest in the expensive item.

"I've also found out that Maria's a junkie and has her servants doing the dirty work, getting her drugs, and fueling her sex parties. You won't believe what she's doing to them for her kicks," Ray told them. "Anyway, Maria hired Wilber to knock me off. He didn't get it done, and I've got the ring."

"Anything I need to know about Wilber?" Arizona asked in a tone that remained even. However, Ray knew he was fishing. He came clean about what had happened.

"Not much to tell. After he slapped me with a sap, I woke in the trunk of his car. He stopped on a lonely road to finish me. Then, the bastard let a truck run him over."

Arizona glanced back in the mirror with a deadpan look.

"And Wilber's car ended up miles away."

"Yeah, that's how it went down. Still, Wilber left me high and dry about Orella. I'm still sure he didn't knock her off since he still had the ring," he continued. "When I think about it, my only guess is that shady shamus wanted to milk more money out of Andres and her cousin."

Ray caught himself before he mentioned the cash he found with Wilber.

"Where does that leave you?" Cat glanced back.

"The only option left is going into Maria's house," Ray replied. "If I find her, Arizona has evidence, and that bitch gets taken down. Unless something's changed, I have to be there tonight since they're out to Mayor Hopley's party. The place will be nice and quiet."

"What if she's not there?" she asked.

"Then it's back to square one," he said with a shrug. "If she's alive, the girl has to be on the Smyth estate. Someone murdered the partner of Wilber for a reason. It must tie into why she's missing. If Orella's dead, then where's her body? Why not leave it at the barn when Ulysses got killed? They would have just paid Wilber to go away if he did the job."

"I haven't heard what you just told me about breaking and entering," the policeman said as he glanced in the rearview mirror.

"Actually, a servant will let me in, so I'm not breaking the law," Ray's sarcasm caused Arizona to grunt.

As they got closer to their destination, Ray asked Cat about her discovery of the missing teenager. She frowned.

"I got a tip from a reporter with the *Morning Capital*," she said. "He told me that some of the missing kids turn up at the lunatic asylum. So, I started making some phone calls and came up with some leads. I drove up and spoke with a nurse who used to work there. She told me that before she quit, a kid matching Jack's description arrived. The nurse also told me about the treatment of the patients they get."

She shivered involuntarily.

"It's barbaric. Anyway, I drove with Jack's parents when they went to the place to check out if he was there. I was planning on getting some pictures, but they can't get in to see their boy. At first, the staff wouldn't admit he was there. Then, they claimed Jack was under a state arrest for his mental illness. I had Arizona check on that."

She looked over at the large man wearing the bowler hat.

"Yeah, I checked. Nobody with the state or the city has any record of picking the kid up," Arizona explained. "Somehow, he's in this asylum, and nobody appears to know how he got there. That's the reason I'm coming along. Those parents need to see their kid, and I need to find out what happened to the missing girl."

"Out of your jurisdiction," Ray reminded him. "Kind of like my invite tonight."

"Yeah, but I have an open investigation into the disappearance of those kids," Arizona replied. "It doesn't matter since I'm there to keep the peace."

"What do you mean?" Ray asked.

"Jack's dad threatened to kill the doctor the first time he was there," he said. "He claimed the doctors are abusing his kid after a nurse explained his treatment. The boy's become withdrawn, unable to communicate."

"The family wants to take him home, but the doctor insists Jack has to stay for more treatments," Cat told him. "I swear that someone is trying to use the state bureaucracy to keep the kid in there."

"It'll be interesting to see what this is about," Ray leaned back in the seat.

Forty minutes later, they saw the gray stones of walls which surrounded the asylum. It looked like a massive medieval fort. The gray turrets on either end of the building overlooked the grounds, towering over their car as they pulled into the courtyard.

After coming to a stop, Ray put on his coat. His shirt remained damp.

"You don't need to come inside," Cat told him. "You look like hell."

"What you and Arizona said about the kid bothers me. Someone had to bring him here. Otherwise, the police would have this boy in jail. And you can bet that the reporters had their headlines lined up. Cops don't take a suspect to the looney bin first."

He slid out of the car, slamming the door behind him. Cat turned to Arizona.

"That's the only way you can get him away from his problems," she smirked. "Give him something that doesn't make sense, and he'll stay on it like a dog with a bone."

"Yeah, I know," the cop replied with a smile. Arizona wiped his brow before putting his bowler hat back on.

"At times, he reminds me of you."

They found Mr. and Mrs. Romano arguing with a fat woman in a white uniform inside the building. The parents were having difficulty getting past the duty nurse. She insisted the doctor in charge left instructions telling her that the boy was off-limits to the parents. Arizona went to the desk and showed the nurse his badge.

"Lady, this boy is part of a police investigation. Now, you're going to let me see Jack Romano, or I can have the state police come here," he told her. "If the parents need to get a writ of habeas corpus, that means the lawyers and reporters will soon camp out on your doorstep as well. Do you want your boss talking with the whole circus that will cause?"

Uncertainty filled the woman's face before calling a male nurse, who led them to Jack Romano's room. What they saw inside caused everyone but the nurse to hesitate. Inside a padded room, they found a young man sitting on the floor, leaning against the wall. The star quarterback of the Oyster City High School wore soiled white pajamas. His handsome face, drained and pale, matched his thin body, which carried the look of a traumatized addict. The kid didn't recognize his mother when she rushed to his side. Ray watched the slow response from the patient as his father and mother crowded around him. The boy attempted to shutter out answers to his frantic parent's questions. None of his words explain how he got there.

"He looks like a damn POW," Ray growled aloud to the male nurse, who just shrugged his shoulders.

"That happens with some patients," he casually explained. "They start violent and end up mild as anything once doc gets through."

Jack's father rose to confront the nurse.

"What's happened here? My boy's got marks on the side of his head," he said.

"Yeah, the doc prescribed electroshock therapy and a lobotomy. That's why he's no longer complaining," the nurse told them. "The treatment makes them snap out of their delusions."

"You son of a bitch, he can barely talk," the father yelled an instant before he struck the bigger man in the white coat.

His punch nailed the nurse in the jaw. Arizona and Ray jumped in, separating the two men. While he held the boy's father, Ray noticed Jack was staring at him. Tears streamed down the boy's face. His mother clung to her son; her face covered in her tears.

Arizona pushed the male nurse into the hall while Cat and Jack's father followed them. Ray went to Jack and crouched next to him. Something in the young man's look reminded him of a corporal he once knew.

A Marine who might have been seventeen if not younger struggled with a brain injury after an enemy shell exploded close to his foxhole. Irish spent the better part of ten weeks watching the kid while Ray healed from his surgeries.

"We're going to get you out of here," Ray assured the boy in his mother's arms. There was a flicker of gratitude in the patient's eyes while the bitter arguing going on outside the room drifted away.

"Can you tell me what happened? I promise we're going to get whoever did this to you," Ray explained.

Over the next few minutes, the shamus learned a few things from Jack. The young man slowly let loose with coherent streams between his meandering answers that described beatings in a graveyard.

When Ray asked about the people who did it, Jack's answer sent chills through Irish. He determined that masked people in robes kidnapped him and his girl. Tears flowed while he told of Maggie Weber's repeated rapes.

"They hung her…l.like a pig," he shuttered out. "Cut her…throat. Drunk…bl.bl.lood…laugh..ter."

Jack's statement brought back images of nightmares and recent murders to the shamus. Ray's foul mood turned black when he realized Jack held something back, and he suspected the reason. Maggie wasn't the only one raped.

"I swear to God that we'll get them for you," Irish replied with his fury barely held in check.

"We'll figure this out. You just get better."

Irish placed a hand on his shoulder, and then he left the room. Ray glanced back as he went through the door. The boy's mother continued to weep as she held on to her boy. When he found Arizona and Cat at the end of the hall, a doctor had joined the male nurse. Their pathetic attempts to explain only caused Jack's father to grow angrier. The doctor kept trying to say Jack was a violent person when he arrived.

"I'm using proven procedures for helping your son," the doctor briskly explained. "We will continue our treatment. He's suffering from hysteria and manic episodes that are coming from the lies he is telling. He's made up all sorts of wild stories to cover up for what happened to the missing girl. We have to assume he must have hurt her. The tales are his way of shutting out what happened."

"What are you talking about?" Arizona interjected. "What tales?"

"The boy is having delusions. He claims masked creatures kidnapped them. He talked about being taken to a graveyard where strange rituals occurred," the doctor said. "That never happened. It goes with his need to shift blame away from him, of course."

His condescending tone infuriated Ray.

"You piece of garbage. That kid is telling the truth. He wasn't making up a story about these people in costumes," the shamus confronted the doctor. "You bastards went into his brain. Your damn treatment is as bad on him as those who assaulted him."

"You son of a bitch!"

Jack's father pushed the doctor into the wall. He had his fingers gripped tightly on the man's white coat. While Arizona cut off the male nurse who tried to intervene, Ray stepped next to the struggling doctor.

"You touch that boy again, and I'll help this man kill you. We'll make it look legal, you son of a bitch," he swore in an ominous growl. "Now, you've got five minutes to discharge him to his parents, or you deal with me next."

"Why aren't you stopping this?" The doctor coughed out to Arizona;

The cop paid no attention to the male nurse, who ran back to the nurse's station.

"It's out of my power, bud. Besides, I might join them in beating some sense into you if you don't get that kid out of here," Arizona warned him. "I have to make a call to the parents of the girl. Do you want me to have them come to see you as well?"

"What's happening here?" A small, balding man in a black suit exclaimed when he drew closer to the group.

He stepped next to the doctor, pulling him away from Ray and Jack's dad.

"I'm Doctor Wolfe, and I'm in charge of the facility," he declared. "You have assaulted Doctor Williams."

"Nonsense. We're just explaining the situation to him. You're breaking the law by holding on to a minor," Arizona confronted him. "Aside from hurting your patient, your staff is impeding an investigation."

"You have no jurisdiction here," the man stiffly replied as he confronted the policeman. "Now you will leave immediately."

"Don't push me, you pencil-necked bureaucrat. I've got a good mind to let the press know all about your staff impeding a kidnapping investigation," Arizona told him. "And I have a reporter with me. The lady here can tell everyone in the state. The people in the governor's office will be down here, looking into what you're doing."

"Not only that, but I'm also close friends with Reginald Kincaid," Cat interrupted. "You should know of him, since his father is a state senator. You might remember he's the one making a name by going after corruption in the agencies. Do I need to draw you a picture?"

"Now, young lady, let's not get so hasty. I'm sure we can come to an agreement and avoid such wild talk," Wolfe assured them.

His strutting rooster manner grew edgy as he looked between Arizona and Cat.

"Fine, you have Jack discharged to his parents, and we'll walk out peacefully," Arizona told him.

"I can't do that. The patient is a ward of the state at the moment," Wolfe said. "You have no right to hamper our treatment."

"The police chief of Oyster City knows exactly where I am and what I'm doing," the policeman said as he clamped down on his unlit cigar. "By the way, I checked around. No policemen brought this kid here. Now, that means someone's lying about what happened. Do you want to press me on this? Hell, I would like to see how much heat the governor will take before you earn a jail cell."

Immediately, the facility administrator gave orders to his staff, and they hurried away. After his orders, Wolfe went to the nursing station at the end of the hall. Ray watched as he made an urgent phone call. The bureaucrat was yelling at his staff when Jack's father came up to thank Arizona for the help.

"We'll take Jack home. We'll get the best doctors we can find. He'll be back like he used to be," the father told them. His tone was one of hope, not confidence.

"Sure, time with family will make a world of difference," Ray chimed in optimistically. "That's the great thing about young kids is their resilience. I've seen it before."

"Yeah, I'm sure he's right," Arizona agreed.

Thirty minutes later, the trio was speeding along the highway back to Oyster City. Only the road noise filled the inside of the car as the occupants remained locked in their thoughts. Each person struggled with the scene inside the asylum after they finally left with Jack and his parents. Wolfe escorted them from the building, still promising retribution for Arizona for overstepping his authority. His demeanor had changed from anxiety to smug assurance. Ray noticed the difference in the man when he returned from his phone conversation.

"I thought that doctor was going to pee himself when you threatened him," Arizona interrupted the silence.

"It took a lot for me not to beat the son of a bitch," Ray confessed.

Cat glanced over, the suffering she felt for the boy showing on her face.

"It's vicious what they did to that kid," she said bitterly. "Fifty years ago, you could have shot him and walked away."

"Too bad we can't bring back the golden days. The bastards juice their brains with drugs and electricity, then tell the parents that the kid has a mental problem," Arizona said. "I had a buddy who had battle fatigue. He looked a lot like that kid after they got through with him. I swear to God that those damn doctors got that crap from the Nazis."

"Well, the Nazis didn't wear robes and masks," Ray commented. "Someone kidnapped and abused him and his girlfriend for a reason. It was tough to understand, but the kid talked like they put her upside down and bled her."

"Are you sure that's what he described?" The policeman asked sharply. His face went slightly pale, and Ray noticed.

"Yeah, I'm pretty sure of it," the shamus confirmed. "Jack described her hanging like we found Ulysses in that damn barn. Have you got other murders like what he described?"

"I need to figure out who dropped Jack off there," Arizona told him, disregarding the question.

"You can get the state police to investigate," Cat said. "You warned Doctor Wolfe about that."

"Right, what I told them was a load of malarkey," the policeman confessed. "The police chief would have my head on a platter if he realized I was using his name like that. Hell, it still might get back to him. The doctor was pretty upset. Unless you've got some connections, no state patrolman will look into that place. Hell, the damn staff is probably a bunch of relatives of the governor for all we know."

"It still makes me angry," Ray replied. "Someone put Jack in there. Worse, I think it might have a link to other cases. Pappy tipped me off about other missing kids. Put your victims into an insane asylum, and who's going to believe their stories?"

He caught Arizona's involuntary nod at the suggestion.

"Well, that's something I can check on," he told them. "When I get back, I'll see how many people from Oyster City missing person's reports are ending up out there."

"I swear I've had nightmares about those figures that Jack's describing." Ray looked out the window of the car.

"You know that doesn't make any sense? Everyone has nightmares," Cat remembered a recent one of her own.

"The way the kid described the people, and the robes remind me of something I saw one time in an alley back when I helped your father escape some hoodlums. Also, I've seen some of them in my dreams recently," he explained.

"Figures were dancing around in black robes," Arizona told them. "The masks look like some strange Mardi Gras masks."

"Wait, you've seen these things?" Cat's voice broke as she stared at him.

Slowly, the cop nodded.

"And I tell you it's stress," Arizona said firmly. "I thought about it since I overheard one sergeant complaining about dreams. These cases are affecting us. We're probably remembering some of last year's Halloween costumes the kids were running around with."

"Yeah, Gladys mentioned stress to me as well," Ray interrupted him. "But it doesn't explain why we're having the same nightmares about the same type of figures. That's the strange part."

Both Arizona and Cat grow quiet at the observation. As Cat noticed the outline of Oyster City in the distance, she glanced back at Ray. He appeared lost in thought, his face sour and intense.

"Ray, I want to tell you I'm sorry about Samantha's death," she said. "I didn't know that you and she were so close. I wouldn't have made the remarks I did had I known."

Ray did not appear to notice her apology. His eyes remained fixed on the side window as the scenery passed by them.

"Yeah, well, skip it," Ray finally said in a near growl. "She's gone. That's it."

Cat peeked over at Arizona, and he shook his head. His expression told her to leave Ray's latest wound alone.

~~~

A proper shower, along with a shave, gave Ray the feeling that he might survive after he got back to his office. He went next door to Frank's for a bite to eat. His leg still hurt, but he could cope with the pain.

After he finished, he called Cat, and they met at her car across the street from his office. She had changed into a tight red dress that accentuated her figure. It was a view he usually enjoyed, but he hardly paid attention as she walked around the front of the car. They didn't speak much on the quiet drive over to the Hotel Alexander.

It was nearly dark when they stepped out of the vehicle. The couple met Victor Dela Cruz in the lobby. A medium-sized man with closely cropped black hair and a long mustache, Orella's dapper father wore a black double-breasted suit. He carried an air of sophistication and manners when he bowed and kissed the back of Cat's hand before the introductions. Cat's face turned red, but Ray noticed she enjoyed the attention.

"Have you any news?" he asked them with a slight accent.

"We're working on something this evening to see if we can smoke her out," Ray told him.

"I'm sorry, what do you mean?" the diplomat asked as his face filled with confusion and concern.

"What he means is we might have a lead to her whereabouts," Cat hastily interjected. She beamed a smile at Victor, who suddenly came to her side.

"You must excuse me for I don't know, how do you say…slang," he took the woman by her arm and led her to an open table. Ray scowled, but followed along.

"It appears you have made progress. This is good," the man observed.

"Yes, we should know more tonight," Cat replied confidently.

Dela Cruz's attention remained on Cat, and she was eating it up. After Victor ordered drinks, Ray sipped on a club soda while sitting across from them. He hated the taste of the drink, finally sitting the glass down. He silently watched as Cat gave a brief update to Victor. Most of what she told the man was a series of lies. When she asked Dela Cruz about the Singsing of Multo, Victor regaled her with their illustrious family history. It was the same as Ray heard before from Orella. When Victor asked for more details about the ring's location, the shamus interrupted.
~~~

"By the way, where's your wife?" Ray asked Victor during a brief pause. "I'm sure she's upset about Orella."

He watched the man pause briefly, then smoothly accept the changed direction of the conversation.

"Mrs. Dela Cruz has been so upset by the developments, the doctors advised she remain in New York," he explained while Ray leaned back in his chair, studying the man.

"Yeah, that's too bad. I'm sorry that she's in poor health," the man told Dela Cruz. "Hopefully, we'll get some news for her soon. I'm sure you'll want to send word to her when we know more."

"But, of course," Dela Cruz agreed. "Now, about the ring, I was hoping…"

"If we're going to find your daughter, Cat and I need to get moving since we're running behind," Ray quickly rose from the chair. "We might not be back until late, so don't wait up. We'll let you know what we find out."

Ray was already in the hotel lobby when Cat finally caught up.

"I thought you were going to give him their ring. Why didn't you?"

"A couple of reasons," he replied. "First, he's not what I'll call a doting father and husband. He's eyeing you more than worrying about his daughter. He didn't even bother asking to join us. I'm not sure how much I trust him."

Ray paused at the lobby door with a thought.

"Besides, it's possible that I'm wrong, and we might need that ring if Orella's not there. The backup plan is to set up a swap with Maria Andras for Orella."

"How can you give it back to her?" Cat stopped in mid-stride, stunned at the idea.

"Who said I would? I said we would set up a trade," he said with a tired grin. "After all of I've been through, Maria can hang before she gets the ring now."

"Still, you were abrupt with Victor," she scolded him as he held the door open for her. "I got him to pay your going rate for the last couple of days, plus a finder's fee for the ring. Not bad work, if I say so." Ray glanced at her self-satisfied smirk.

"How much is your take?" he asked sarcastically. "Or does that come later, after I'm not around?"

Cat's face went dark at his comment, and she remained silent until they got into her car. She put the key in the ignition, then pulled her hand away.

"Why do we have to act this way? I can't understand why you can't be nice to me when I help you. You needle me with nasty comments. So, what if I have a few dates with guys who find me attractive? We have a good time, and they pay for all the nice things. You never know what might come out of it," she breathed.

Her stare remained on the large steering wheel in front of her.

Ray glanced over, somewhat surprised at the question. At first, he wanted to tell her he'd seen enough in life to know that her act wasn't any better than the whores he met in the past. In his mind, at least there's some honesty there. They require cash up front.

No, I can't do it! She's saved my ass too many times.

"I don't know," he finally sighed. "I like to think you're my friend, even though I realize we've been digging at each other for a while." The silence filled the cab of the vehicle for a long moment. Cat started the car and drove away from the hotel. Three blocks later, Ray finally spoke again.

"I like you, and I told you that. It's just…sometimes the things you do just grate on me," the shamus confessed. "Just like in the bar with you and Victor where you're going along with it. Hell, I wondered if I was holding you up. He's a married man with a sick wife. The situation didn't even throw you a curve."

He stared out the window, barely noticing they followed the road up Andres Hill. The large, park-like area covered a large section in the middle of Oyster City. It held many of the great estates where the wealthy namesakes of the city founders lived. He glanced over at Cat and saw her dark expression.

"I told you at the start that we had a business partnership, nothing more," she reminded him. "I don't need your approval for how I act with men. You act as you own me."

Her tone was accusing, but Ray decided not to take the bait.

"No, that's not it," he told her. "You've saved my butt a couple of times, so I owe you. That's why I'm going to give you some free advice. I've watched you with your game for too long. You play hot with every guy that has a name or fancy suit, married or not. And I'm telling you, they're not in your league."

"Meaning I'm not classy enough." Her face turned livid when she spat the words out.

"Damn it, that's not what I said," Ray told her. "I'm saying those frauds aren't good enough for you. They're using you until some damn socialite comes along, and they dump you. It makes me mad you don't want to see it. Seeing you do this…well, it sticks in my craw, alright?"

"You're not my dad," her voice rose. "And you don't know everything. Some of those guys would have married me if I was interested. But I'm not. I told you once that I don't want people running my life. It's never happened, and you're not going to change me. Just go back to your bottle."

"Yeah, I'm too drunk to see you for what you are," his mocking grunt escaped. "You're too much like your dad and the rest of this damn greedy city. I guess I need to forget that image of a young girl with innocent blue eyes. I'll shut my mouth and watch you happily degrade yourself. Is that fair enough?"

He waited for Cat to blow her top. Instead, she went quiet. Her face remained screwed up in a raging turmoil, and her eyes blinked rapidly. Then she pulled her car to the curb.

"Get out," she told him, her eyes focused straight ahead. Ray nodded and slid out of the car. He looked back in the open window as he shut the door.

"Well, I tried. I'm not sure you know what you want. But wise up, lady. Otherwise, I'm sure Victor will be happy to show you his room."

Irish immediately regretted his words as he walked away. He was wrong to hurt her.

He glanced at her gray Olds coupe, which sped past him, taking a corner with the tires squealing at the hard turn. Ray continued on the sidewalk, heading to the Smyth estate. Half a block later, he let it sink in that he had no vehicle. Getting out of the estate fast no longer remained an option for him. He shook his head and cursed.

Damn Irish, you're such a dumb ass.

~~~

Peter Smyth's piercing gray eyes scanned the court briefs lying on the desk. They absorbed his concentration as he focused on an upcoming court case. As the county's district attorney, he prided himself on his ability to memorize essential details. Such things proved useful in beating his adversaries.

Hunched over the desk, Smyth carried a posture similar to a bird of prey. A single desk lamp illuminated his thin, hawk-like face while dark shadows filled the rest of the room. He heard the light knocking at his office door and looked up with a scowl. It was long past closing time for his office. He saw the shadow of a man outlined in the opaque glass in the upper half of his door. The rapping came again, and he took a deep breath.

"Come in," he said impatiently. He watched the door open, and a familiar man entered.

"I'm busy, Weyer. Come back tomorrow," Smyth told him as he went back to his briefs.

"Mr. Smyth, this won't take long, and it's vitally important. It concerns your brother and his ex-wife," Weyer said as he entered the room and closed the door behind him.

Smyth didn't look up from his papers.

"That can wait," the district attorney replied, his tone irritable.

"No, it cannot. I'm afraid it involves a ring known as the Singsing of Multo," Weyer continued. "It's missing, and Maria is having difficulty getting it back."

Smyth glanced at him.

"What does that have to do with me? Are the police involved?"

"No, but two private detectives are. But it's clear you're not interested, so I'll take my leave," Weyer said.
~~~

He turned and went to the door.

"Why are you telling me this? I'm curious about your interest in this affair," Smyth told him.

"I've spent enough time on the Smyth estate to hear and see things over the years," Weyer replied.

He turned from the door.

"I think it's time you know that one of your favorites is so high on bennies and her parties that she's making poor choices. It might come back to those who, shall we say…use the shadows of the night."

He started fidgeting with his hat, and Peter Smyth raised an eyebrow at the comment. He turned his full attention to his visitor.

"That's an interesting observation," he told him. "I know Maria has always been headstrong. My brother looks past that, unfortunately. As a distant relative, you've always remained involved with Maria, but you stay out of our affairs. Why this sudden change to discuss family matters? I thought you only handled antiques and special purchases for the relatives."

"Let us say that I've tried to keep her from making poor decisions. However, she's made it a mess of this," Weyer explained. "A simple exchange for cash has turned into a missing girl with her father sending telegrams. There's a rumor the girl's father is coming to Oyster City. Plus, the shamus who had the ring is missing now after taking the money from Maria. I can't track the man down, and as far as we know, he still has the Singsing."

Smyth held his temper. However, Weyer saw the anger sweep through the man's expression before it quickly faded. He recognized the man prided himself in control.

"I should look into this with Phillip. He still influences her," Smyth told him. "Tell me the full story."

Weyer spent the next several minutes giving his version of the events to Smyth.

"And what of this shamus named Wilber? You say Maria hired him?" He asked Weyer.

"Yes, against my judgment. Maria heard of him through one of her drug contacts. Wilber's tied into a gangster name Jacobi. I warned her we needed someone we could control. Like I said earlier, Wilber took the ring and quite a bit of money."

"And this local guy, Irish, is involved as well. That might become a problem. I've heard about him. He's making a name for himself, according to the papers. Not brilliant, but tenacious," Smyth said. "You recommended him to Maria. Can you control him?"

"That's doubtful now. The problem is that Irish knows Maria betrayed him. He worked with the missing girl, trying to get her out of town. There's a possibility that he already knows too much about the ring. As far as I can tell, he's not been around for several days. Maria paid Wilber to remove Irish. That hasn't happened. My guess is Wilber took off with the ring and money. I need help to track him down."

Weyer avoided mentioning his role in failing to get rid of the private detective.

"What's Maria's plan to find the ring?" Smyth asked.

"I'm not sure," Weyer admitted. "She's showing little incentive, I'm afraid. She told me that her mom would support her no matter what may occur. I believe that leads to carelessness, such as the disappearance of the Singsing. If that item gets to New York, it will be difficult to retrieve."

"That ring is precious," Smyth said firmly. "Do you think Irish is still looking for the missing woman?"

"Yes, he made it clear with his actions that he will come after Maria about the kidnapping," Wilber replied. "I don't want to be around if that missing girl should suddenly turn up. Rumors would come out immediately, even if you could keep a lid on it. Phillip might rely too much on his ex-wife. You can see why I came to you. I believe you can handle problems like this. Sometimes, it's necessary to move people out of the way if they become a burden to a group."

"You believe Maria is a burden?" Smyth asked.

Weyer nodded firmly.

During a long pause, Peter Smyth looked over at the man, who remained visibly nervous. Finally, Smyth nodded.

"It appears we have a similar outlook, and I believe we need to address your concerns. You and I should discuss this matter over sherry at my place," he said to Weyer.

"Why don't you come by after we return from the mayor's party?"

~~~

The sun fell behind the horizon as Ray stood in the shadows across the road from Phillip Smyth's estate. The whine of a motor and the creaking sound of the gates opening caught his notice. He watched the long black limousine pulled through the entrance. The lights from the vehicle flashed across his position. Ray remained as still as a statue. The pale driver sitting in the front seat's open cab did not see the shamus standing there as the car turned in front of him. Ray caught a glance at Maria and a thin man sitting in the backseat. After the car drove away, he cautiously walked across the street. However, the gate closed before Ray got to the entrance. Scanning the quiet street, he began walking next to the wrought-iron fence that encircled the estate. The large house of stone sat across a vast front yard; its windows were mostly dark. White Grecian columns leading up to the portico reminded Ray of a government building.

No doubt, they consider themselves to be the ruling class of Oyster City.
~~~

When he came to the corner, he found an opening between the stone corner post and the next section of iron bars. Squeezing through, Ray worked his way across the lawn. Hesitating at the slightest sound, he finally reached the corner of the house. In the shadowy darkness on one side, he walked on the stone footpath until the trail led him around the back.

A nearby door opened, causing Ray to slide up against the ivy-covered wall. Ray watched a servant step into the darkness, heading away from the houses. Moving around to the door, the shamus looked into the door window. Inside, he saw a woman dressed in a light blue dress with an apron. She was smoking a cigarette and chatting with a man in a black butler's uniform. As he watched, Ray did not hear someone coming up behind him.

"Come on," Abby whispered to him. Ray whirled around, his fist ready to punch the woman before he recognized her.

"Damn, you're quiet. Where'd you come from?"

He softly asked as he tried to gather his wits. He saw her nervous grin in the pale cast of light coming from the door.

"I thought you detectives weren't afraid of anything?" She asked sarcastically. Her tone revealed her worry.

"Only in the movies," he whispered. "Now, what's your plan to get me inside?"

"There's another door to the servant's entrance," she said. "I'll go in first, and you follow me when I give you the signal. There aren't many people here right now."

Instantly she took off along the paving stones leading to the other side of the house.

They silently passed the back of the house until Abby stopped at the servant's entrance. She went inside while Ray came next to the door. Looking through the cracked slit of the partially opened door, he waited until Abby waved him inside. Without a sound, she led him through a narrow hall until they reached a door. Quietly, the servant pulled a key and opened it. She hurried him inside, and he went down a couple of steps on the dark stairs. She closed the door and pulled down on the light cord hanging from the ceiling. When they reached the cellar floor, Ray saw a small alcove filled with wine racks. The rest of the cavernous area was dark. He turned to her after she turned on another hanging light. It showed a path through dusty crates and trunks to doors in the distance.

"Some wine cellar! Abby, this place is enormous. Do you have any idea where to start?"

He asked quietly. She shook her head.

"I've never been down here before," her hushed voice slightly stuttered. "I stole the key from Maria's table."

"Alright, I want you to look around those rooms." he pointed into the dusky shadows on one side of the basement. "I'll take these behind me. We should have plenty of time, but we need to be quiet. Let me know if you find anything."

Abby nodded and walked away slowly. The first door she opened was into the room stacked with rows of wine bottles.

"See, I told you they had wine down here," she whispered excitedly.

"Good for you," he told her. "Now, let's find this girl."

As Ray left, he didn't see the pout on the maid's face at his comment. He wandered away, moving among the piles of discarded furniture, dusty trunks, and crates. Around him, he heard nothing but the sound of his footsteps and the occasional creak of the massive beams above his head. Thick stone walls cut across the basement to support the beams. Walls connecting the rooms made a hallway that looked like a drunk designed it. He entered some of the dark areas through doors, while others just had open entrances.

As he walked deeper into the maze along the backside of the house, Ray had to search for lights that hung down between the beams. Everywhere he looked, piles of boxes, trunks, and crates got in the way. It appeared like the complete history of the Smyth family sat around him. Layers of dust covered most of the items.

He reached the far end of the basement where the boilers sat, grimy and dark. Ray jumped when one of the boiler's burners suddenly kicked off. The flames gave the area an evil look as the yellow light filled the space. With a deep breath, he began working his way back to the stairs.

Halfway back, the area opened up along the wall. Ray noticed Abby's shadowed figure at the far end. She was poking around and disappeared from his sight after making a turn.

Ray came to a stop while his face filled with worry. Maybe he misjudged Maria and Weyer. They might have hired a couple of thugs to do their dirty work and remove Orella permanently.

There are plenty of abandoned buildings in Oyster City to hold a person or bury a body.

The thought got under his skin, and Ray shook his head impatiently at the idea.

No, Orella was still alive. She had to be.

He was about to go to the next room when he heard Abby jiggling a doorknob around the corner from him. In the basement's stillness, he grinned when she cursed aloud. Finally, she called out in a hushed whisper to Ray. His expectations grew as he hurried around the corner. Abby had her ear next to the door as she waved him over.

"It's locked," she whispered. "I thought I heard something moving inside, but I can't find a key."

"To hell with a key," he told her.

Ray stepped back, looking at the door, and decided it would break. He threw his body at the wood. The loud snap from the frame filled the air when he slammed into it. The strike plate gave way and opened. He fell into the room, landing on his knees.

Then Ray felt something strike him in the head. He went down on his side in a painful daze as he grabbed his head. There was a stifled scream in the air, and it took a few moments before he saw two people looking down at him.

Orella crouched down next to him, trying to lift the shamus, while Abby watched both of them in silent bewilderment. When he got to his knees, Ray realized the prisoner was naked, her breasts in front of his face. Then the stink of her body odor hit him. He moved to a standing position while the girl held on to him.

"I'm sorry I hit you," Orella slurred out as she leaned against him.

"Never mind that. We need to get you out of here," he told her.

As he moved toward the broken door, the woman stumbled. He grabbed at her as Orella slid to her knees. She trembled while Ray pulled her up. He noticed the long, pus-filled wounds which ran along her stomach.

"Here, this will keep you warmer," he whispered as he quickly pulled off his coat and wrapped it around her.

Abby hurried out of the room ahead of them as he led Orella toward the stairs. A broken chain dragged behind the prisoner as they made their way through the basement.

The effects of the drugs in her body caused Orella to collapse again after taking several steps. Ray lifted her, then held her up by throwing the girl's arm over his shoulder. He ordered Abby to lead them out of the house.

"I got loose from the wall, just kept working the chain back and forth," Orella rambled as she tried to keep moving her legs. "I couldn't get the door open. They keep coming and giving me drugs."

The prisoner started repeating her story.

"Shhh! You can tell us later. Let's get out of here first," Ray whispered as they ascended the stairs.

When the trio reached the door at the top of the stairs, they heard voices coming from inside the house. Ray pushed through the door and retraced his steps outside.

"Get her out of here," Abby whispered hurriedly. "I've got to get the key back to Maria's bedroom."

Ray nodded and hurried his client along. Half dragging her with him, the shamus went to the exit and entered the backyard.

When they reached the patio edge, Orella stumbled again, nearly sending them both to the ground. Frustrated by the slow progress and the noises coming from inside the house, Ray picked the girl up in his arms and started carrying her. As the pair came round the corner of the house, they nearly ran over a man smoking a cigarette in the shadows.

"Hey, what are you doing?" The dark figure yelled out as Ray pushed past him.

Then, the sound of footsteps followed him along with yells for him to stop. A nearby window lit up as they hurried by, and he noticed a maid's face looking out. The glare from the lights behind him allowed him to follow the stone steps to the lawn. When he stepped on the grass near the front of the house, he met a small group of servants who stopped him. Ray noticed Abby standing with them.

"Hold it, mister. You're not going anywhere." A thin, balding man stated firmly.

Ray let Orella's legs drop to the grass. She wobbly stood next to him. The shamus pulled his gun and pointed it at the man in the black butler suit.

"You need to back off and go away," Ray told them firmly. "This girl is not going back to that house."

The small group moved back, and he returned to guiding Orella across the lawn. He heard servants running into the house. Ray glanced back to see the few remaining staff staring at him.

With his arm around Orella, he finally reached the corner of the fenced yard where he entered the estate. The distant wail of sirens came through the air. At first, he welcomed the sound. Then he remembered Maria Andras already had at least one corrupt cop on her payroll. He cursed himself for not thinking about the possibility of a policeman stopping him. The way his luck ran lately, the shamus expected the DA to show up with them.

Ray's brain began working overtime as he tried to figure out his next steps. Orella remained mildly incoherent, hardly able to stand. He had to get in touch with either Sirk or Arizona, but Irish had no options left.

Neighbors won't have a problem noticing that I have an injured, naked woman in my arms.

With a resigned sigh, Ray continued to help Orella along the sidewalk. While they were moving away from the Smyth estate, he knew someone would see them before too long. It would be only a matter of time. With rising panic shrugging through him, Ray kept looking for a parked vehicle.

Damn these rich bastards and their parked cars with chauffeurs.

Ray felt the girl weaken next to him, forcing him to stop. Orella began mumbling next to him, and he tried to keep her quiet. As he started to pick her up, a familiar voice yelled out as a car drove up next to them.

"You damn fool, get her in the car," Cat scolded.

Moments later, Cat's gray coupe turned down a side street. Ray was in the back seat, and Orella rested her head on his lap. He ran his hand across the unconscious woman's forehead, which was clammy and sweaty. Orella constantly shivered under his coat.

"We need a doctor fast," he told Cat quietly.

She turned up another street to get back on 9th street. It was the quickest way to the hospital.

"She's got a heck of a fever going on." He pulled back the coat again. The burns on her abdomen were leaking pus with a terrible odor that struck his nose.

"There are several terrible burn wounds on her belly where they tortured her. By God, I want those bastards to pay for this," he swore bitterly.

"I'm heading to General Hospital," Cat told him. "The emergency room will take care of her. We can call Arizona from there."

"Thanks for returning," he told her. "For a moment, I thought about taking her back to the cops. But Maria might have one or more on the payroll."

Cat remained quiet, but she nodded as she looked at him in her rearview mirror.

"When we get there, you call Arizona. If he's not around, then call Sirk. He's honest," Ray told her while looked down at Orella. "They'll fix those bastards. Phillip Smyth can't cover for Maria now."

After Cat parked in the hospital's driveway, Ray carried Orella into the building. He placed her on a gurney located by the doors, while Catherine rushed to the phone booth. A nurse immediately hurried toward the gurney, attempting to intervene when the shamus pushed into the dark hallway. The admitting nurse started asking him questions about Orella, which Ray hastily answered. Most of the time, the shamus told the nurse that he did not know. He noticed the nurse eyed the exposed links of a chain and ankle cuff still wrapped around Orella's leg.

Halfway down the corridor, a male attendant joined them and quickly took control of the gurney. As they wheeled Orella away, Ray explained more of the story to the nurse. He stopped when he saw the nurse's eyes look past him. He heard footsteps come up from behind.

"Hands in the air," a voice told him. Ray tried to glance back and got whacked on the side of his head with a pistol butt. He went to a knee while a uniformed policeman quickly cuffed Ray's wrists behind his back.

"What the hell are you doing?" Cat yelled out as she rushed into the room.

"You're that photographer from the paper," the policeman said. "Lassie, you're under arrest as well. Hanging around with scum like him. Now you're getting a cell as well."

There was an ominous grin on his face.

"Turn around, or I'll give you a bump on the noggin as well."

"O'Brien, you can't arrest us," she insisted.

The giant cop smirked as he clamped his handcuffs around Cat's wrists while she faced him. His partner pulled Ray from the floor.

"O'Brien, we just got an injured girl in the emergency room," Cat tried to reason with the cop. "What the hell are you doing?"

"Damn it. We found Orella Dela Cruz, the kidnapped girl. They held her prisoner out at the Smyth estate," Ray joined in while he shook his head.

"Blaming Phillip Smyth, now ain't that a laugh," O'Brien said with a chuckle as he pulled the .45 auto from Ray's holster.

"We heard all about your trespassing on Mr. Smyth's property. We'll add in plenty of other charges beyond breaking into his estate. You also threatened witnesses. You better be getting a lawyer, shamus. The DA put out an all points on you."

He turned to Cat.

"Now we have the little photographer girl as your accomplice. Didn't your folks teach you that robbing the rich folks gets you thrown in jail?"

O'Brien spat out his sarcasm, along with a bit of drool.

"Yeah, but they didn't say anything about what happens to dirty cops on the take," Cat replied.

The cop sneered before he struck her with a backhand. Ray rushed O'Brien, putting a shoulder into him. His charge pushed the policeman into the wall. The other policeman pulled Ray off of O'Brien, who slowly got up. O'Brien's eyes were dark with anger. He looked around and noticed the nurse and a doctor were watching the scene.

"Shamus, we'll play it your way," he grabbed Ray. He pushed the shamus to the door and outside. The other cop took Cat's arm and led her to the police car.

O'Brien directed Ray behind the car. He stopped the shamus, turning him around before he punched the handcuffed man in the stomach. Ray doubled over, trying to get his wind when the cop grabbed Ray by his hair. Then, the cop slammed his prisoner headfirst into the trunk. Irish dropped to the pavement, blood streaming from his face. He heard Cat screaming for the policeman to stop. The pavement went around in circles as the shamus lay there in a half-stupor.

"Lassie, he needs to quit resisting arrest." O'Brien stepped closer to Cat with a gleam in his eye.

His partner laughed at the joke as he pulled Ray up from the ground.

"There's talk going around that Irish is involved with the rats who killed Detective Howard a few months back." O'Brien stated. "I'm going to help the boys when they use the rubber hoses on you."

He punched Ray several more times in the belly. The handcuffed man dropped to the ground again. O'Brien ordered his partner to help him drag their prisoner to the police cruiser. They pushed him into the back seat. Ray groaned as he flopped over on his side. Then, the policeman turned to Cat.

"You don't open your mouth against my report about Irish resisting arrest. Otherwise, I'm going to make sure the butches in the cell block get you alone in a quiet cell for the rest of the night, girlie. Do you get my meaning?"

O'Brien shoved the woman to the car.

"Now, get back there with your boyfriend," the dirty cop nodded to his partner, who opened the door.

Catherine remained quiet as she slid into the seat next to Ray. She gently lifted his head with her cuffed hands and placed it in her lap. As the police car drove away, she felt the warmth of his blood on her thigh.

~~~

It was long after midnight when Arizona arrived at Ray's jail cell. His broad face held a grimace as he chomped on the thoroughly chewed cigar between his teeth.

"I heard O'Brien arrested you," he said. "Resisting him is not a good idea."

"Yeah, I tried to resist with my hands handcuffed behind my back," Ray mocked the event. He moved carefully since his ribs still ached.

"At least, I don't see double anymore. That son of a bitch roughed up Cat just for kicks, as well." He noticed Arizona scowl at the news. R
ay asked about Cat.

"She's mad as a hornet and pacing like a caged tiger," the cop told him. "Cat called me as you were getting arrested. She's yelling for…"

"What about Orella?" Ray interrupted. "How's she doing? You can't let anybody get to her."

"The doc says she is stable, but she's unconscious. They pumped her full of sulfa drugs for the infections," the cop explained. "I got there and put one of my guys outside her door. She'll be alright."

Arizona paused and glanced around.

"You have bigger problems right now. The district attorney has you over a barrel on this one," he told him quietly.

"What are you talking about? Didn't you arrest Maria and Weber? They kidnapped Orella," Ray blurted out. "The bastards had her chained down in that stinking basement."

"Cat told me everything. Right now, Orella is unconscious, and she can't back your story. Cat only saw you by the street with the missing girl," Arizona told him. "Maria Andras and Phillip Smyth claim Orella was never there. They have servants making claims you broke in to steal something. They even told the DA that you pulled a gun on them when they tried to stop you."
~~~

"Yeah, the servants tried to stop me. Even when they saw me carrying Orella out of there," he explained. "Listen, not all of them are going to back Smyth. Maria's maid, Abby, helped me find her."

"I believe you, but you're up against it now. Sirk got a search warrant. They found the Singsing ring in your office. According to Phillip Smyth, the ring was there on his estate yesterday," Arizona said. "Do I need to draw you a picture?"

"Christ, you saw that damn ring, so you know that's a lie. They're pulling out the long knives." Ray said as he began to pace inside the small cell.

"That damn DA is a rotten son of a bitch. Why don't you put some heat on the servants? Check on Abby. She's the maid and addict on top of it. She'll back my story if you get her away from the house."

"I can't touch them. After I made sure Miss Dela Cruz was safe, I went over to the Smyth house," Arizona told him. "The chief of police and the district attorney told me I couldn't work on the case. They took it over."

The police detective paused and looked around.

"I listened in on some stories coming from Maria and her ex-husband. They don't make convincing liars. However, their story sounds better than yours does for the moment. Worse, there's a rumor that you're a suspect in the murders of Detective Howard and Quincannon, La Spina's driver."

"The district attorney is investigating a petty robbery. It's a damn good thing I had nothing to do with those murders." Ray tried the irony to convince himself. But he knew from the detective's odd look he was on a one-way track to somewhere he did not want to go.

"You better be worried. Planted evidence can suddenly show up along with a witness if Smyth puts you in the hangman's noose," he warned him. "Now, keep your mouth shut, no matter how much they squeeze you. You still have charges against you, and there's no way they'll let you out on bail. The DA will argue you're a flight risk. And there'll be some cops showing up to interrogate you. You know, they might get rough."

"I don't have a choice but to wait and hope, is that it?" he asked.

"Yes, that's how things look," Arizona confessed, glancing around again. The jailer remained at the other end of the passageway.

"I'll get back to the hospital. Once the girl comes around, I'll have her tell me everything. Also, I'll check on the maid if I can swing it," he told the prisoner.

"Just remember to get somebody there with you," Ray suggested. "With your boss and Smyth involved, be careful who you trust."

Arizona nodded in agreement.

"When I get the evidence, it should be enough to back off some of those after your scalp," he replied. "Smyth can't afford a scandal with his brother and Maria Andras in the middle of it. Just keep your head down and your mouth shut."

"Alright, you have the lead," Ray told him.

Arizona turned to leave, then halted.

"Just don't get the idea that any justice will come from all of this," the policeman warned him. "People leave town, charges get dropped, and documents end up missing. It's Oyster City."

~~~

Following a barely palatable lunch two days later, Ray retreaded the same path to an interrogation room on the police station's third floor. He'd been there before. The prisoner walked gingerly as possible, trying to avoid moving around too much. Long before sunrise, a couple of cops coming off duty stopped by his cell. It was the second time they took him to the out-of-way room.

Instead of asking questions, the two men used fists and rubber hoses on Ray until he could not rise from the floor. After they finished, they picked him up and plopped him in a chair. The men asked about the murdered detective and Ray's involvement with Detective Howard at the Hotel Alexander. Ray kept his lips sealed and got another round of punishment before the policemen hauled him to the basement. They forced him into a bitter cold shower to clean up the blood and sweat.

His clothes were still damp as he walked along with another jailer who led him. Coldly efficient, much like the robots in the comics sitting on Pappy's newsstand shelves, the guard remained silent. Reaching the end of the hallway, he opened the door and forced Ray into the room. Inside, the shamus found a gray-haired man sitting at the table.

"Have a seat, Mr. Irish," the man told him, and the jailer forced Ray into a chair across the table. Ray let out an involuntary groan.

"That'll be all. Wait outside," the man told the guard, who silently left.

After the door closed, the man stared at Ray for a moment. His hawk-like face held piercing blue eyes. Ray remembered seeing the same scowl in the paper several times. He stared back at Peter Smyth, the distinguished district attorney of the county.

"I looked into your background. Since you've come to Oyster City, you've been in the middle of many nasty murders," Smyth told him. "I don't think that's a coincidence.

"Yeah, I had to figure those cases out for your guys," Ray replied. "I walked into town and found out how damn foul and corrupt this place is. It does seem strange that the district attorney isn't interested in all the sleaze that goes on here."

"You know who I am," the district attorney replied.

"Sure, I've seen you in the papers. It's not hard to hear about you since Oyster City has more murders than Chicago," Ray said. "Plenty of other crimes as well, even a batch of cases involving missing children. It seems some of them
~~~

end up in the lunatic asylum. Yet somehow, our famed DA finds time to focus his efforts concerning some petty robbery involving his brother."

"I see you've done some homework about my city," Smyth replied. "But it doesn't matter, really. You're a guy on the way out."

Ray leaned forward.

"Let's cut to the chase. Why did you bring me here? Your underlings get paid to do this banter with a prisoner. You don't bring in a guy for a chat unless you don't want something on the record. If you've got something private to say, then I'm all ears."

Smyth gave him a thin smile. The man's intense blue eyes were ice cold.

"You still think you're a hotshot, eh? Listen, mister, I've dealt with your type before. Don't make me angry, or I'll let the cops start on you two times a day," he warned. "Everyone breaks if you put enough on them."

"You're getting me nervous," Ray growled back. "Your boys are good, but I've seen plenty of people at their worst. Hell, I helped kill a few of the bastards, so quit trying to frighten me. Let's get down to business," Ray tried to control the situation.

He glanced back at the door, wondering if Smyth might set him up for a fall. A lot of terrible thoughts ran through his mind.

"We both know I had nothing to do with stealing anything at your brother's house," he told Smyth. "Something's not sticking; otherwise, I'd have seen a judge this morning and would have probably bonded out."

"I could hold you for something bigger," the DA told him with a deadly glare. "Maybe I want to fit you for a noose. Those unsolved murders might have your name on them."

"Only I wasn't in this city when they started. It's too risky for your position. I don't think you want to try that route," Ray kept a brave face as he worked through the details. "Plus, we still have the girl I took out of the basement, despite what some paid-off witnesses might say. She'll testify to that, and you don't want that in court."

Ray's confidence suddenly took a nosedive when he saw Smyth give him a smug smile.

"Well, about this girl you are so certain about," Smyth drummed his fingers on the table as he spoke.

"We need to have you examined for mental issues. Maybe a trip to the lunatic asylum would change your mind. You had nothing to do with Ms. Dela Cruz's rescue. Two members of our fine police force found her by the side of the road. Someone mysteriously drugged her before they took her to the hospital. That's what the official police reports showed me this morning. The nurse at the hospital even claims you came into the hospital with Miss Bennett after the Oyster City police arrived with the injured Dela Cruz woman."

The blue eyes of Mr. Smyth held his prisoners for a moment. It felt too much like a snake looking at a mouse for Ray's comfort.

"As for your supposed witness, I should tell you that Victor Dela Cruz took his daughter back to New York City this morning," Peter Smyth said. "Her father was eager to get her to a specialist near their home. I went to the station to wish them the best. I'm afraid you have no witnesses to support your position."

Ray tried to keep on his poker face at the news. However, he felt the sweat start in his palms.

"Now that you realize your terrible position, I'll give you more to worry about," the DA continued. "Rumors came to me you're involved in the killing of a policeman. It's only fair to warn you we will look deeply at your role in that unfortunate affair."

"That would be the noose you spoke about," the shamus observed.

The district attorney nodded. Ray shifted in his seat, trying to think of something to break out of the chill that filled him.

"If you brought me here to smirk at me, don't waste your time? I know too much about Maria and Weyer. They kidnapped and tortured Orella over that cursed ring. Running the girl off to New York won't stop that. I'll make sure reporters will eat it up what I say about the Smyths. I'll make damn sure that everyone hears the truth. You keep pushing me, and I'll make your brother's life hell on earth," he promised Smyth.

The man replied with a hollow laugh, and it turned into s mirk.

"Hell on earth! How amusing. Perhaps I would enjoy seeing that." the DA leaned back in his chair.

"Mr. Irish, I'm not here to listen to your empty threats. I'm here to guide you. As you've figured out, I could throw you in front of a judge and grand jury," he continued. "If you know anything about me, I can get a prisoner to trial fast and quiet. The newspaper wouldn't care a bit about you. In the end, you will go away to prison for quite a while. That supposes that you survive our jail."

He paused for a moment to let the idea sink in. The man tapped on the edge of the table with the gold wedding band on his finger.

"Now that I think of it, I believe you had something to do with the capture of the notorious gangster Guy Young. It's unfortunate, but sometimes our prisoners feel the need to commit suicide, just like Mr. Young did. You might consider that possibility if you don't heed my advice."

The statement confirmed Ray's belief. The gangster that Irish helped bring to justice never committed suicide.

"Yeah, I get it. You're the dealer, dealing yourself a hand." Ray's tone dripped with spite.

Why is he telling me this?

His mind scrambled for a way out of the box he felt closing around him.

"Quite right, Mr. Irish," Smyth agreed. "You can put things together. You're fortunate that my brother is a more forgiving person than I am. He enjoys his solitude. Any trial would tax him and his ex-wife," Smyth explained. He stood up from the chair, leaning forward with his fists on the table.

"By the way, I should tell you that your partner, Catherine Bennett, has already seen the light," the DA told him. "The official police report states she picked you up, and only you, in front of the Smyth estate. Now that Miss Bennett's realized the error of her ways, I'm afraid it's only your word against Ms. Andras and my brother. It's highly doubtful any reporter will run a story now."

Ray leaned back in his chair, and his eyes narrowed.

"Alright, you've let the other shoe drop," he said. "What do you want?"

"Shamus, you will pack up and leave town. Your private investigating days are over once I revoke that license. As long as you keep your mouth shut and walk away, you'll have no problems with me or the police after you leave," he stated. "I'll make sure the police escort you to the city limits."

Ray watched Smyth's face as the man spoke. It looked confident, almost cocky. He wanted to smack the grin off his face. Then he remembered the fact that the man across from him was a lawyer. A damn good lawyer with a trained skill at telling lies with a straight face stood across from him. He offered to let him walk away. He suddenly wondered why the deal. If Smyth had him all boxed in, there was no need to be lenient.

Arizona must have gotten something from Orella.

Somebody didn't want publicity. Or someone was afraid Victor Dela Cruz might make trouble. He was a diplomat with friends in Washington, no doubt. While the Smyth's were big fish in Oyster City, they were only small minnows outside the city. Ray pushed his luck.

"I'm not sure I like your idea," Ray finally replied. "This place might be corrupt, but it grows on you, if you know what I mean. Your men might beat me every night. Yet, eventually, I will get a lawyer. Hope springs eternal to a guy like me. I might risk bringing back my star witness, who went to New York. That is, if you can't persuade your brother to drop the charges."

Smyth's smile disappeared, and his voice went icy.

"Don't test my patience, shamus. The only way you'll leave this jail alive is to sign the statement downstairs. However, I'll make everything crystal clear for you. You're no longer welcome in Oyster City," he said.

Smyth stepped around the table, then paused behind Ray. He looked down at the prisoner, who remained facing forward.

"You know that it's the time of year where the fog comes out at night. You will sign the paper to walk free this time. I suspect that the next time you're in the newspapers, it will occur after you go into an alley and get your throat slit."

The DA opened the door.

"That'll be a damn appropriate death for a guy like you."

Smyth walked out of the room while Ray stared at the closing door. He felt a frigid chill go through him when he remembered the last time he wandered into an alley. There was a masked figure who watched him from a window.

Chapter 8: Change of Plans

An hour later, Ray Irish finally left the police station. He signed the paperwork, and no charges hung over him…at least for the moment. The shamus walked down the steps, putting his wallet into his pocket. He made it about half a block when Cat's gray coupe drove up next to him.

"Get in!" she yelled out through the open window. Ray slid into the car next to her.

"A friend told me they released," he said. "Are you alright?"

"Yeah, I'm fine. Some leech working for Smyth took me into a room and told me to sign a statement. It was a made-up lie about the hospital. It didn't have anything at all about Orella. I didn't want to sign, but he told me if I didn't, then I'd go to prison with you," she quickly explained. "I'm so sorry, but I had to sign it."

"Forget it," he replied. "I know you had to do it. They forced me to do the same thing. Did they hurt you?"

"No, but it was my first time in jail. I guess there's a first time for everything," Cat said with a forced smile, then turned serious.

"Listen, Orella and her father left town. I got to the hospital when they were loading her into an ambulance. Victor told me they were going back to New York. I'll bet you can't guess who was there."

"Peter Smyth," Ray replied grimly.

"How did you know that?" she asked, nearly forgetting to stop at the stop sign.

"I met our illustrious district attorney a couple of hours ago. He offered me a deal. It involves me leaving Oyster City," he told her.

"Did Arizona talk with Orella?"

Cat nodded, and Ray carefully leaned back in the seat, trying to keep from breathing too deeply.

"Well, that explains why they released me. Arizona must have gotten something," he stated.

"That must be it," Cat agreed. "I spoke with him only for a moment, and he told me he got Orella to sign a statement which confirmed everything you said about her kidnapping. Arizona didn't say much, but I could see something was going on when the DA showed up with Victor and Orella. After the train left, I drove to the police station to let you know. The desk sergeant hardly spoke to me, and he wouldn't let me see you."

She paused when they came to a red light.

"Ray, the sergeant claims you're a cop killer, and I wasn't getting any help from the police anymore. I had to go to the *Beacon* to get a legman to ask around about you. That's how I found out you were getting released this afternoon."

She noticed Ray wince when he tried to change his position in the seat. His face remained puffy and bruised around the nose.

"You're hurt, Ray. That's not from the other night, is it?"

"No, as I said, they're gunning for me. Arizona warned me to keep my mouth shut, and he was right. The DA had some of his corrupt cops pound on me for fun each morning. Today, he hauled me into a room for a private chat. I'm pretty sure that Smyth is pushing the idea that I killed Detective Howard, along with Greye La Spina's boyfriend and driver. It's got the police force up against me. Smyth gave me two options, and one of them is a grave. He's not a subtle guy."

"They can't do that," she said, then stopped. "Damn, maybe the bastard can. He'll put every crooked cop against you. If you even sneeze wrong, they'll haul you to jail."

"Yeah, and I bet I end up like that gangster, Guy Young. Smyth reminded me that Young died by suicide," he told her.

Cat frowned as she turned a corner.

"I remember you told me it wasn't a suicide," she said with a glance at him.

She saw his familiar grimace when Irish focused on coming up with a solution.

"What are you going to do?"

"The bastard ain't running me out of town," he replied bitterly. "I don't run off easily. Besides, I've made some promises that I mean to keep."

"That's good," she told him and then went quiet. "I want to see Arizona, but I'm not sure I should. We're both toxic, like radiation, with the police right now."

"You're probably right," he agreed. "Let's try a phone call from my place."

He looked out of the window of the car as she turned toward his office.

"Tell me about Victor taking his daughter back to New York. Did you get any idea why?

"He said that he wanted to get a specialist for Orella," Cat explained, her expression turned bitter.

"I think Victor got paid off to leave. For a guy with his daughter in such awful shape, he seemed a little too upbeat, if you know what I mean. The rotten bastard was still making eyes at me when they carried his daughter on the train on a gurney,"

She refused to glance over at Ray, believing he might give her one of his darn smug grins.

"That girl is still pretty sick. I overheard her nurse saying that she's going through withdrawals. They must have had her on narcotics the whole time."

"Is she going to be alright?" Ray glanced over.

"I guess so. Victor had a nurse with her for the trip." Cat turned in front of his office.

"Are you going to be alright, or do we need to get a doc?"

"I'm fine," he told her. "At least my ribs hurting takes away the pain in my legs from that bullet wound. I need to find a chair, and then I can try to sort out my next steps."

Cat went quiet as she pulled in front of the building.

"I could use a drink," she confessed as she slowly led the way to his office.

Ray limped up the stairs, where he opened the door. He went to his desk and pulled out a half-empty bottle as she came next to him.

"Pour it yourself," he picked up the phone receiver. "I'll try to call Arizona."

Ray waited as the phone rang for a while. Finally, he hung up.

"No answer. I'll try again later," he told her.

She handed him the bottle. An uncomfortable stiffness fell over the room.

"I need to know why you showed up after I got Orella?" he finally questioned her. "We didn't part on good terms."

She frowned and took her glass to the nearby chair. Ray's eyes followed her, wondering at her struggle.

"I won't lie; I was so mad at you. But I only got a few blocks, and I had to stop," Cat told him. She focused her stare on the glass in her hand.

"It took a while for me to calm down. That brutal thing you said to me about Victor Dela Cruz kept swirling around in my head," she explained. "It was tough, but I finally had to be honest with myself."

Cat's blue eyes turned to him for a moment.

"For all of your flaws, you've always told me the truth whether or not I like it. I need that right now," the woman whispered.

"Do you really think I'm a whore?"

The pain in her voice at her self-indictment struck Ray.

"No," he immediately shook his head. "Look, I'm not the one to say you're wrong. But it's just you always think money and status will solve everything. I don't know how to keep my trap shut when I should."

Cat nodded as she looked down at her glass.

"You know, someone else told me something similar the other night. I guess there's something in what you say," she said so softly that Ray nearly missed it. Cat was silent for a moment before lifting her head; her eyes were moist.

"As I sat in the car thinking about it, I remembered that I still owe you for saving my life." Then, she took a drink. "I always say I don't like people owning me."

The woman went quiet.

"Anyway, I came back and waited. I figured you would probably need a ride."

Ray took a slug straight from the bottle.

"Yeah, I picked a hell of a time to start an argument," Ray admitted. "I was playing it too high and mighty with you. Then I realized I needed you. To be honest, I half expected to be wrong about Orella's location. I had to do something. I was lucky that an arrogant fool took a kidnapped girl to their house."

"Well, you called one right," she said.

"This time," he replied. "And, by the way, you don't owe me anything." He held up his hand when she tried to argue.

"No, no, hear me out. I've had my butt hauled out of the fire a couple of times by you. Hell, you came looking for me while I was playing a drunk again. We're square," he said firmly.

"It's none of my damn business how you run your life. Like you said, I'm not your pappy."

A brief smile came to her lips at his statement.

"Ray, you take things a lot more personal than you want to admit. When I heard Samantha was dead, I came by to talk to you. You know, see how you were," Cat cautiously said as she looked at the drink in her hand.

"However, you were already gone. I knew you were trying to forget, and that's something I can understand. The thing is, I did not know where you went, so I could only hang around. I hate feeling that way."

She went quiet for a moment.

"For all of your faults, you've tried to be my friend."

Ray watched as his friend kept glancing at him.

"Yeah, as you pointed out, I've got a bad habit of feeling sorry for myself."

"I'm sorry, I shouldn't have said that," she replied.

"Forget it!"

The silence hung the air.

"I'm going to let you in on something. I've done things you won't believe. Hell, I had a mother who left me alone when her guys came by." She stared ahead as she spoke. "I could see she was lonely, and I soon figured out that some of her boyfriends were no good. But she never let her guard down while she remained with me. I don't know what my father told you about her. But I sometimes wonder if I'm turning into her."

It was one of the few times Cat mentioned her mother to Ray. His chair squeaked as he leaned his elbows on the desk.

"J. Allan Dunn may talk a lot, but he's not the type to tell me about your past," Ray replied. "The way he explained it, he was the primary cause of some of the bad things that happened as you grew up."

"Well, that's not true," she said. "Dunn wasn't around, but my mother had a bad habit of finding the wrong guys." She took another drink.

"When I got older, those same jerks turned their attention to me."

Cat sat down her glass and shivered involuntarily.

"But that's not important." Her tone was sympathetic. "What is important is that you've been a friend, even when you act like a jerk. I'm sorry for treating you like you are the problem."

"Well, at least I'm good for something," Ray joked. "But I'm hardly the one to give out advice. Maybe I'll get a brain and keep my nose out of other people's business."

He leaned back in his chair when she grinned.

"You'll never do that. You're too much of a busybody." The woman stood and came around the desk. Standing behind him, Cat placed her hand on his shoulder.

"Maybe we can start again?"

"Cat, you never have to ask," he said as he patted her hand. "I'll stand with you." She nodded happily.

"Thanks, I promise that I'll remember that from now on," she said as she squeezed his shoulder. He winced, and she quickly pulled her hand away.

"Sorry!"

"Don't mind my groans; it's just finding a place that doesn't hurt. Thanks for coming back to me. I did not know what I was going to do with a naked girl in my arms."

He turned the chair and beamed a smile at her. Cat shook her head, suppressing a laugh.

"Alright, you'll never change," she told him. "Now, let's stay serious; what are you going to do about Smyth?"

"Well, I don't think there's much I can do to get him off my back," he confessed. "I need to find out what Arizona has. Maybe Smyth might turn his fire toward Arizona."

He stared absently out of the window for a while. Cat watched him. Despite several nights in jail, he was holding up well. The woman liked his relaxed appearance when he became thoughtful.

"You know what? I might have an idea. I think a trip to New York is in order," Ray suddenly told her.

"Why would you do that?" she asked.

"I can think of several reasons," he told her. "But the key to the idea is making sure Peter Smyth knows I'm heading out of town. That ought to make him think he's scared me. Besides, it'll give me an alibi for something that will soon happen. I'm going to check out that ocean liner that took Greye La Spina and her husband to Italy. I need you to keep things from going crazy while I'm gone."

Confusion filled Cat's face.

"Why Greye La Spina? She's gone, and nobody is going to find out whether or not your theory is true."

"For better or worse, I'm still on Greye's case," he replied. "I had a letter come in the other day from a detective who I asked to look into her death. He says he found a witness who states she never made it to Italy."

Ray placed her hand back on his shoulder.

"You can pat me on the back now. I know I'm right about what happened to her. I think my New York detective might have the proof."

"What about this alibi? I didn't know you had a crystal ball," she told him.

He shook his head, and his confident smile faded.

"It's better that you remain unaware," Irish explained as he patted her hand. "A grand jury can put friends on the witness stand if my crazy idea goes wrong."

~~~

Ray arrived at Pappy's newsstand as he was closing up. The two men worked to secure the stand, and Ray walked with his friend to Pappy's apartment. The sound of their footsteps echoed as they followed the sidewalk past the dark storefronts. With the evening crowd light, a few patrons entered the two restaurants across the street. However, their neon lights reflecting colorfully on the windows the men walked by.

"Are you sure about this idea?" Pappy asked Ray after he laid out his plans. "It seems to me this girl might not go along with the idea."

"It's a risk," he agreed. "But I got a feeling that she'll come through. When I saw her at Musso's this afternoon, she agreed to the idea. I think a bit of revenge appeals to her, along with a fast train out of town."

"Not to mention some cash from you," Pappy reminded him.

"Well, that comes from Andras," Ray grinned at the irony. "I'll let you know when I get back."

The two men turned the corner, and Ray noticed his friend appeared unusually quiet. He asked Pappy about it.

"You're as bad as my wife," the newsy told him. "I was thinking about those dreams everyone is having. You know, I said I might have something about those shadows in the dreams. Well, I found it in that old newspaper journal. It was worse than I thought."

"What happened?" The shamus grew curious.

"In July of 1792, a mob gathered in the town square, just a few blocks from here. They lynched several prominent citizens of Oyster City," Pappy told him. "The newspaper stated the mob dragged several men and women from their homes before they took the prisoners to a large tree where they hung them."

"Hell, that's not unusual," Ray replied. "A hundred years later, we still have lynching because some damn bigots don't like the color of your skin. You know that as well as anyone."

"You don't understand," Pappy told him patiently. "This is the white folk getting lynched by their own kind. The citizens formed a posse to stop these people from something they feared. The whole episode overwhelmed the town. Do you want to know what scared the people the most?"

He stopped Ray.

"One article mentioned strange dreams and the rise of a demon."

"Are you telling me the whole city had nightmares?"

Pappy nodded, and they started toward Pappy's apartment again.

"It sounds a bit like the Salem Witch Trials," Ray observed.
~~~

"Well, other similar events have occurred in all parts of the world," his friend agreed. "However, this instance brought down the state militia. The county sheriff rode to the state capital on his horse in a panic. He claimed a mob killed a cult that worshipped a demon. Despite the soldiers taking over the city, I can find nothing, stating that anyone got arrested for what happened."

"Well, it's a great story, but I'm not buying everything written by one person claiming to be a reporter," he told Pappy. "It's like some of those supernatural movies we saw when we were younger. I think they call it mass hysteria."

His friend laughed when they arrived at the building, which housed Pappy's apartment.

"My Emma told me you would say something like that.," he said. "You want to come up and see those papers I found?"

Ray looked at his watch and shook his head.

"Sorry, I'll have to take a raincheck on that. I need to get over to Cat's place first and then to the train station. However, you can do me a favor while I'm gone."

"Sure, what do you need?" Pappy smiled.

"After I leave, I need you to spread it around among your police customers that I'm in New York City. Don't be too obvious; mention it casually," he told him. "I need the information to get back to the district attorney."

"You got me curious, Irish," Pappy glanced over at his friend.

"Remember what happened to the cat that got too curious," Ray reminded his friend. "Just keep it low key, and you don't know much beyond my trip out tonight on the train. Keep it that way. I'm meeting with Cat and Arizona for dinner. I'll see you as soon as I get back."

<center>~~~</center>

Ray spent the rest of the evening with Cat and Arizona at her apartment. The large policeman sat on the couch, his bowler hat tipped back, and he had a drink in his hand. He chewed on his stogie between drinks.

"I wondered why you hadn't stopped by to see me," he told Arizona.

"Yeah, I've been pretty busy," he replied. "The chief's got me on a short leash right now. It appears I'm not doing enough on the murders of Detective Howard and La Spina's driver. He suggested you would be the logical suspect."

"Hell, I'm getting damn popular," Ray said.

"Don't believe that," the policeman scoffed. "I only came over since Cat told me you're heading out of town. I can't afford to stop by your office. But you never told me Cat cooked so well."

He grinned at the woman who came out of the kitchen.

"It's rare that I get to do it," Cat confessed. "Most of the time, I'm eating at a restaurant. But I'm changing some of my bad habits."

She gave Ray a wink as she handed him a drink. He smiled.

"I know Peter Smyth is gunning for you," Arizona said. "Where are you heading to?"

353

"New York City," Ray told him. "I'm following up on Greye La Spina's death. A detective sent me a letter saying he's found something strange about the cruise."

"You'll have to tell us about it when you get back," she told him. "Shouldn't we be heading out?"

"Yeah, we need to get going if I'm to make that last train," he agreed. "You coming along?"

"Sure, why not?" Arizona replied. He finished his drink, then followed them to the door.

"How long are you planning on staying?"

Ray opened the door.

"I'm not sure. A few days, I guess. But Smyth hasn't seen the last of me," he promised.

<div align="center">~~~</div>

Leaning back in his seat, Ray looked out of the cabin window as he grew anxious. The train would leave in five minutes, and his expected passenger had not arrived. Despite the assurances and money handed off, he could have misjudged.

"I'll bet you're glad to see me," Abby told him as she slid into the seat next to him. It took a minute for her to catch her breath. The servant looked different in the brown tweed coat and dress. New confidence exuded from her, and he liked her look.

"Well, I was getting a bit nervous," he confessed. "Do you have it?"

She nodded, then pulled her green hat off.

The Singsing of Multo looked like an ornament. She retrieved the familiar ring from among the feathers.

"It went better than I expected," she glanced around with a nervous grin. "Nobody was around the library, and I grabbed it on the way out of the back door. I even showed off my hat to some of the other servants. Nobody figured it out."

"Aren't you a clever one? Any problems getting here?"

The girl shook her head.

"No, I followed your plan. Miss Andras has a party going on, so the servants are pretty busy with dinner and drinks," she told him, then paused. "She'll be in for a rude surprise when she comes looking for me."

Her tone was bitter and triumphant.

"I told you that revenge would be sweet," he agreed with a sympathetic laugh. Suddenly, the train began moving, and the cabin jerked forward.

"We're on our way," her excited smile broadened.

For a moment, the woman reminded him of an innocent child. Then Abby started to drum her fingertips on the armrest. She remained addicted to narcotics. He pulled out his wallet. Then, the shamus looked around the car before giving her two hundred for the ring. The passengers in the train car remained locked in their worlds, either reading or talking.

"You'll have your choice coming pretty quick," he told her quietly. "From what you told me, in a few hours, you're going to be needing a syringe. I can't have you getting crazy on me, but it's still a few hours after that before we get to Philadelphia. Can you do this without shooting that stuff in you?"

Abby nodded firmly.

"I know I'll have the shakes, but I won't let that bitch keep me this way," she said. "I've tried to cut back on the stuff." She paused and leaned closer.

"It's just I'm not sure that I can do this alone."

"Listen, if it gets too bad for you, we'll hang out in the club car and fill up on coffee and cigarettes. I'll be with you until we get there," he told her. "You can do this; just let me know if you need help."

"Are you always this nice to a dope fiend?"

Ray noticed the shade of suspicion in her question.

"You're cute, but as I told you before, you don't need to worry about my motives," he reassured her.

"I've seen some of these problems when I healed in the hospital. Good men who just got hooked because of their injuries. I see the same in you."

Her uncertain appearance lightened as one passenger walked by them.

"It's been ages since I've been on a train." She paused for a moment, then turned to him and patted his arm.

"I'll be alright," she promised.

The next morning, Ray walked off the *Marylander* alone in New York City. He arrived from Philadelphia. Weary from lack of sleep, he moved with the busy hustle of passengers as they pushed into the elegant Grand Central Terminal. His first time in New York City caused the shamus to act like a wide-eyed visitor. He stared at the massive celestial ceiling as he crossed the stone floors. Across the road, there was a grand staircase that caught his eye. He could almost see dignitaries coming down from above. Then, he looked at the four-faced brass clock at the top of the information booth in the terminal center. It was just after seven in the morning. When he exited the building, he joined the mass of humanity trying to get a taxi.

On the long drive out to Queens, Ray smiled to himself when he pictured Abby waving to him as he left the Pennsylvania Hospital. True to her word, she held up well during the train trip to Philadelphia.

By the time they reached the central terminal, she was full of coffee and a few sniffs of benzidine. Ray escorted her to the hospital that he looked up at the Oyster City library. When they finally got there, she clutched at her bag, which he guessed still held a syringe. However, she walked confidently into the dark and quiet room with Ray. It took a bit of convincing for them to get the night nurse to admit her. However, with a few dollars he put out to the doctor in charge, Ray was confident Abby could change things with her life. Even better, she was away from Maria.

Despite the Andras and Smyth family connections in Oyster City, he was confident that Abby remained out of reach as long as she stayed out of state. A private detective might track her down. However, it would not be too easy. Leaving Oyster City, Ray had Abby take a taxi to the bus station first and buy a ticket to New Orleans. Next, Abby went to the train station in another cab. She already had the train ticket Ray bought a few days before. He doubted anyone would stop in Philadelphia to look for her since their tickets went to New York City.

It's even less likely they might look for Abby at one of the leading institutes for recovering addicts using money from Maria Andras.

When his driver interrupted his thoughts with a sudden stop and colorful curses at the offending vehicle, Irish came back to his destination. He planned to stop by Orella's home. Ray grinned at his driver's thick accent while he looked out at the drab scenery.

Cat got Victor Dela Cruz's address for Ray before he left town. They lived in a house somewhere in a place called Kew Gardens. When Ray mentioned the area, the cabbie rambled on about the United Nations using the Queens Museum and all the changes coming to New York. According to his driver, the foreigners coming in since the war overwhelmed the area. He claimed they were cheap tippers as well.

When they finally arrived at the house, Ray found himself mildly surprised. He didn't expect the Dela Curz family to live in a small suburban Tudor-style house from the '20s. Ray expected diplomatic staff would adopt a newer and more expensive home.

The shamus gave the taxi driver a healthy tip as he slid out of the car. At the door, he met Victor. The man's face revealed his disbelief and suspicion. Ray wondered what Peter Smyth told Orella's father.

"Mr. Irish, what brings you here?" he asked, as his eyes narrowed.

"I wanted to see how Orella is doing," Ray said pleasantly. "I'm spending a couple of days in the big city, so I decided to check on how she's recovering from her ordeal."

"Thank you for inquiring. Really, you should have just phoned. My daughter is doing much better," Victor told him. "Unfortunately, she's still unable to see visitors. Doctor's orders, I'm afraid."

Ray saw through the lie, and he noticed the man remained in the doorway.

"That's too bad," he replied. "Since you took off so soon, I was concerned if you still cared about recovering the Singsing of Multo."

Victor's eyes widened at the comment.

"Well, the health of my daughter is more important. We just haven't thought much about it," he replied.

"Well, I would be interested in it, father." Orella's voice piped up from inside the house. Soon she stood by her father.

"Mr. Irish, please come in," she told Ray. "We're happy to see you."

"I was just explaining that you're not yet well," Victor hastily interceded. "He can come back at another time."

"No, he'll come in now," she told her father firmly as she opened the door wider. Victor stood aside as Orella took Ray by the arm as he came in. He removed his fedora as they went to the couch.

"It's great to see you, Ray. As you can see, I'm feeling much better," Orella told him.

Her eyes were bright. Orella wore a pale-yellow dress. Ray took a seat, and he noticed the woman stiffly moved when she sat.

"Father, don't you need to get to work?" Orella asked. Victor hesitated before he nodded.

"Yes, I'll see myself out," he said. "Your mother will be in the kitchen if you need anything."

Victor left the room, his face red.

"You look great," Ray told Orella. "I'm glad to see the doctors have got you fixed up."

She smiled and leaned closer to him.

"Confidentially, I still feel pretty lousy at times, but I heard your voice at the door," she breathed. "I'm glad you came over since my father…well, he should go to work."

"As long as you can see me," he told her. "I don't want to cause you problems."

Orella beamed at him.

"No, you can't cause me problems. I needed to thank you for saving me," Orella said. "The doctor tells me I still need to rest, but I'm about to go crazy staying in my room. I don't like confined places now."

Ray frowned.

"I can see why. Listen, I have a present that might cheer you up," the shamus told her. "Now, close your eyes and hold out your hand."

Orella looked at him suspiciously, but she did as told. Ray placed the ring in her open palm. He grinned broadly at the shocked expression on her face. Immediately, she hugged him. That's when he noticed a pretty woman in a white dress watching them from the hallway. She stepped into the light of the room, and Ray tried to pull away from Orella. The woman smiled at his clumsy attempt.

"Mr. Irish, I've heard so much about you. I'm Yana, Orella's mother," she stated.

Orella turned to her mother and showed her the ring. Yana sat next to her daughter, and Ray noticed the strong resemblance between the two. In many ways, Yana looked like a slightly older copy of her daughter.

"You've done our family a great service," Yana said as emotions flooded her face when she looked up from the ring. "How can we ever repay you for this?" The big shamus grinned.

"Well, I'm a newcomer to this city. We might have dinner this evening," he said. "I'm sure you know of a good place to eat."

"That's a great idea, mother. See if you can get my father to come with us," Orella told her. There was a flicker of misgiving in Yana's eyes, but she smiled.

"I'll see what I can do," she promised. Orella gave her mother the Singsing.

"I'll make sure we lock it in a safe place. In the meantime, I'll get us coffee. I won't take no for an answer, Mr. Irish. Come into the kitchen when you finish catching up."

She rose and walked into the next room.

As they sat on the couch, Orella kept glancing at Ray while he played with his hat. Neither could find the words to restart the conversation. Finally, Ray opened up.

"It's hard for me to tell you this, but I don't think any justice will come from your ordeal. Peter Smyth protects Maria and her cousin," he told her. She nodded, patting his arm.

"I expected as much," she told him. "My father took me out of the city because the district attorney warned him. He probably took some money as well. It happens in many of the countries I've lived in."

"Well, it's not supposed to happen that way here," Ray grumbled.

"You can't blame yourself. I'm amazed you found the ring. How did you get it?"

"Let's just say that I had some help," he told her with a sly smile. "It just kind of ended up in my pocket on the way here. I don't think anyone will come looking for it here, but I can't guarantee it."

"Then you've nearly answered my prayers for revenge against Maria," she said brightly. "My father will pay you what I promised for the recovery."

"That's unnecessary," he said, looking down at the delicate hand on his wrist.

"But I insist," Orella said. "I'm not the type to forget a promise."

Ray grinned.

"Whatever you decide, but so that you know, there's a delicious irony in this case. Andras and Weyer already paid me for the ring," he said. "Sometime, I'll have to tell you the total story when this thing calms down. Now, let's go get that coffee if you're up for it?"

Orella nodded and carefully rose from the couch. She hooked her arm with his, and they went into the kitchen.

~~~

That afternoon, Ray arrived at a dingy building on East 126th Street in Harlem. He checked the directory before heading up the flight of stairs to the second floor. He found the office of Jefferson Tweed. It was Pappy who put Ray in touch with Harlem's toughest shamus. He knocked on the door and heard a gruff voice tell him to enter. Inside, he found Tweed sitting behind a battered desk. He
~~~

was a large black man with a boxer's face, scarred from several years in the ring. His nose carried a crooked bend, but his eyes brightened when he saw his client.

"Irish, it's about time you showed up. You owe me some cash," Tweed said.

"Maybe so," he agreed. "But let's see what you have first."

Tweed opened his drawer and placed a document on his desktop. Ray stepped closer and inspected the paper.

"Talk to me," he said as he read it.

"You have a signed affidavit from the ship's porter, who was a crewmember on the MS Vulcania last year," Tweed told him confidently. "He swears that Greye La Spina did not come aboard the ship in Genoa. In fact, he saw Bishop La Spina in Genoa frequently with a blonde woman who did not match the description of his wife."

Ray glanced up, surprised at the news. It was the break he had been waiting for.

"You're sure about this witness? How much did you pay him to open his mouth?"

Tweed smiled; there was a gap in the upper row where one tooth was missing.

"Not a lot. I noticed his name on the ship's manifest when the *Vulcania* docked last year. The porter handled the upper-class cabins where your Bishop La Spina stayed. The porter's been with the Italia Line since the end of the war," he told him. "I went to the ship to meet with him when it docked a couple of weeks ago. The captain confirms he's reliable."

"According to this porter, what happened the day they left Genoa? You say Greye wasn't on board. That could mean she stayed in Italy," Ray replied as he took a seat, still reading through the document.

"I thought of that already. The porter came aboard when the ship was returning to the United States," he told Ray.

"According to the ship's log, Greye La Spina went onboard in New York and left for Italy with the ship. Yet, according to the Italian police, they have no record of her arriving in Genoa. Even better, somehow, there's a record of Bishop La Spina and Greye arriving in Naples."

He gave Irish a knowing smile.

"I'll bet you think a bribe is in this somewhere," Ray replied.

"Only thing that makes sense," Tweed insisted. "I think that Bishop La Spina must have brought someone aboard the ship in New York, and that same person disappeared before the ship left the harbor. Then he bribed the correct people when the Vulcania arrived in Naples. The porter told me most of the officials in the ports would accept payment to change the records."

"Did this crewman see Greye on the trip?" Ray asked.

"No, but the porter only got on with the *Vulcania* when it was heading back to the states," Tweed said. "The company was moving around some of their crew to other ships. They replaced the porter who served the bishop and his wife when they crossed the Atlantic."

"What happened to him?" Ray wondered.

"He left the company, and I haven't been able to track him down," Tweed told him. "I have my suspicions he might be hard to find now. He was a fascist sympathizer of Mussolini during the war. I think that might be why the company moved around their crew. The communist party is powerful in Italy now. Maybe he's wanted for war crimes?"

"Damn, that's too bad. But it looks like I have something to go on," Ray admitted.

"Did anything else come up in your conversation with this crewman?"

"Yeah, he told me that the bishop sure didn't act like a holy man," Tweed said with a nod. "The porter described him as a nice guy with an eye for the ladies. La Spina almost always came back from his travels among the villages with various expensive trinkets. On the day they left Genoa, the porter told me it shocked him when the captain stopped the ship and sent out a lifeboat to find Greye La Spina. The porter went to the bridge and saw the captain talking with the bishop and a couple of other passengers who insisted Mrs. La Spina fell overboard. The porter told me he had to keep his mouth shut. He didn't like the odds of keeping his job if he argued with passengers."

"Anything else?" Ray asked after he pulled out his wallet and laid the money he owed on the desk.

"Not really," Tweed said. "The porter only mentioned that the bishop liked his knives. He came back with several rare daggers that they had to store in the ship's safe."

"Why am I not surprised?" Ray replied, as he pocketed the document. "Thanks for the help with this."

He left Tweed counting his money as he went to find a hotel room.

~~~

That evening, Ray sat at a table in the *21 Club* in midtown Manhattan. Across from him were Orella and Yana. As they left the house, Orella's mother informed them that Victor would be working late with his duties at the U.N.

Ray didn't believe the excuse, but it wasn't any of his business, he decided. Both women looked stunning in their pale blue dresses. They could have been sisters. Ray noticed leering glances from a row of men sitting at the bar when they entered the club. He expected a few wolves to come over when the women finished dinner, if not sooner.

"I'm the envy of every red-blooded guy in the club tonight," he told them with a broad smile after the waiter went for their drinks.

Orella blushed slightly at the comment. Yana returned the smile, her hazel eyes dancing with delight.
~~~

"I can see why my daughter came to you," she said. "You have a gift for making women feel comfortable, Mr. Irish."

"Please, call me Ray. I consider it a gift," he boasted. "By the way, I'm warning you. I brought you ladies into a dangerous area tonight. I've seen the wolves at the bar. They'll keep your dance card full."

Orella glanced back, then leaned over to whisper to her mother, who nodded as she laughed.

"We'll heed your warning, Ray. But Orella and I have been through the lion's den before," Yana said confidently as a waiter brought their drinks.

It was nearly three hours later when the trio left the club. Ray spent the bulk of his time with Orella, who wouldn't leave his side. She rejected two of the wolves who came by the table. However, the young woman grew visibly tired after dancing with Ray a couple of times. Yana had her share of men stopping by, but she remained quietly aloof to them. She took Ray to dance while Orella rested. Ray inadvertently brought her into his arms. She teased him lightly about it, but she did not move away.

During the drive home, Irish enjoyed his quiet conversation with Yana. He glanced over at Orella, who had her head nestled on Yana's shoulder. He learned that the woman was a direct decedent of Hara Humamay, Queen Juana of Cebu, an early ruler of the Philippines. Yana married Victor while she was very young. They lived primarily in Australia and Spain during the war. Orella, like her mother before her, went to France at a young age to study. It was the reason both women had slight French accents.

When they reached the Dela Cruz residence, Victor had not yet returned. After they got out of the cab, Ray was about to leave, but Yana insisted he come inside for a moment. The shamus pulled a Lincoln from his wallet and told the cab driver to wait. When he entered the living room, Orella gave him a tired smile.

"Doctor's instructions, off to bed," her mother ordered her.

"You get some sleep," Ray agreed. "I'll drop by tomorrow."

Orella nodded and told him goodnight as she walked into her room. Her mother followed her.

A few moments later, Yana returned. She led Ray out into the darkness of the front entryway and closed the door. Yana stood close to him, and he could see her eyes searching his in the dusky light. He glanced over at the taxi, which remained at the curb. The driver's cigarette glowed in the dark of his cab.

"What did you want to tell me?" He asked, growing uncomfortable by her proximity and silence.

"Orella's young and inexperienced," she whispered. "She's a lot like I was when I married."

"Yeah, I can see what you mean," he agreed. "Are you concerned about me?"

"Yes, that's it exactly," she replied. "You saved her life. She told me everything that happened, including what those rotten bastards did to her. Do you realize that one of them raped her after they tortured her?"

"My god, I had no idea," he said. "I just saw her infected wounds. The only good thing I can tell you is both of them are dead. That I know for a fact."

"Did you kill them?" She asked, and she noticed he hesitated.

"I saw one fall under a truck," he said carefully. "He was trying to knock me off. The other one got his throat cut, probably by the thugs he hung around."

"I see," Yana said quietly. "Then, Orella can go on with her life. There's no need to seek justice against them."

She softly cursed in French, but Ray didn't understand the words.

"I still have a beef with the people who set this up," the man reminded her. Then he stopped.

"No, you're right; Orella doesn't need to go after Maria. Let me handle that."

He saw Yana smile at him as his eyes became accustomed to the dark, shadowed area.

"You must know that Orella will follow you to the ends of the earth. All you have to do is ask her," she told him.

Ray scratched his head at the thought; then he remembered Samantha.

"You're worried that I'll ask her?"

Yana nodded in agreement.

"Well, I like her," Irish admitted. "But right now, I wouldn't ask anyone to join me. She's in New York, and my town is a corrupt place called Oyster City. It wouldn't be fair."

The woman smiled at his answer.

"That's good," she told him. "I don't know much about you, Ray Irish, but you've got the look of someone who's seen evil. I would guess some of it."

"Yeah, you're right about that," he confessed.

"Perhaps she needs someone with a past. Maybe she doesn't. Either way, she's enamored with you. I just wanted you to know that I can see why. Like I told you earlier, you have a way that women feel comfortable around you. Go back to your hotel and sleep well. We'll see you tomorrow."

Yana reached up, placing her hands on his shoulders, and forced him to lean down. She kissed him on the lips before she quickly turned and went inside the house. As Ray walked to the taxi, he ran his hands through his hair before putting on his hat. As he slid into the cab, he looked back at the house, thoroughly confused about Yana Dela Cruz.

~~~

Many miles away, inside the circular room, four black-robed figures sat at a five-sided table. The pale light of a partial moon flowed from the glass cupola ceiling. Multiple candles on the table revealed the unmasked people who waited for their leader. Their masks lay on the top of the table in front of them. A small
~~~

old woman entered the room carrying her demon-like disguise. A flowing red robe covered her frail body, and she wore a golden headscarf.

"Why are we summoned?" Betty Andras asked as she took the last seat. "We already know that the Singsing of Multo is missing yet again. Can Phillip not secure this ring?"

Her tone was deathly.

"I've just come from the police. They have determined a servant who has left the state stole it," Peter Smyth told her, his blue eyes glaring at Betty. "We might try to track her down, but it will be difficult. She's probably sold it to a pawnshop."

"This is unacceptable," Mrs. Julie Smyth spoke up. "We've prepared everything. A person of royal blood and a gem of power gathered for our needs. Now, we have nothing."

"Only because of incompetence within one house," Betty told them, staring at the man sitting by the Judgement mask. "Phillip, I question your commitment to our cause. Can you stand in front of the master after this?"

"It was not a Smyth who lost the ring and allowed outsiders to get too close to the Shadows," Julie spoke up.

"Quiet!" Betty raised her hand. "Phillip can defend himself."

She went silent, waiting for his response.

"If you're asking me to cut my own throat, you'll have a long wait, Betty. Our houses share the blame," Phillip told her. His voice carried no hint of turmoil or angst. A heavily weathered face held the same piercing blue eyes as his brother. He also had large ears, which he tried to hide with his long shoulder-length hair. His tall formed hunched over as he leaned forward.

"You wear the mask of the demon Andras, our master. Tell me, Betty, have the cards changed since our meeting in the crypt?"

"Fortunately, the master remains with us. And we've seen a growing number of people affected by the nightmares," she said. "The coming cycle remains powerful, even without the Singsing ring. Fates that guide us insist we continue our journey."

"Then, we must proceed." Henry La Spina rose from his chair.

He pulled a golden dagger from beneath his robe. When he tossed the weapon on the table, Julie jumped, then nervously giggled. She smiled sheepishly at those who glanced at her.

"I've gone through our forefather's scriptures again," Henry told them. "It's been 152 years since the last blue blood moon cycle, and our master became one with the living. Unlike the last time, there is no one to stop us now. I've ensured no church in Oyster City carries a genuine believer as their leader."

He paused, looking at his comrades.

"To safeguard our success, I suggest we find a new sacrifice for tomorrow night. And we all know there is only one person suitable as a substitute."

He pointed to the mask without a person at the table.

"We did not invite The Empress for a reason," he said. "I say that she must atone and become a sacrifice. It appeases our master for her mistakes by allowing the ring to leave. This entire affair is a farce unless we do this."

"I agree," Phillip cut in quickly. "She carries a line of noble blood, which few of us have."

"But she's one of us. Outsiders and derelicts are easier to dispose of. No one cares what happens to them," Julie spoke up. "We got rid of the mistake that Henry made."

She smirked at the bishop, who returned an icy stare.

"They don't carry the power needed. But you also carry noble blood in your veins," Harry pointed out.

"It's the Empress or the High Priestess who are the most suitable since the ring is missing. Perhaps you wish to hang in her place? Do we risk the wrath of our master?"

Julie glanced around the table at the faces watching her. She turned to Betty Andras, who remained unusually quiet.

During the conversation, the woman pulled her deck of tarot cards and slowly turned them over. Above the room, a cloud covered the moon above, creating a hauntingly dark atmosphere to descend into the room. The timing caused the small group to glance up at the darkness.

"She is a friend, but we must consider the demands of our master," Julie finally spoke to Betty. "You must say something."

After a moment of careful consideration, Betty nodded her head.

"Peter came to me with this idea already," Betty confessed as she scanned the familiar faces at the table.

She knew each of them since their birth and their mothers and fathers. Her daughter went to school with Julia.

"While I might have fought the idea a few years ago, I've changed my mind after hearing the details. Now, I've dealt the cards to guide me."

On the table, one card showed a man with swords stuck in his back. The other card revealed a tower under siege.

"I'm afraid the Empress will face the shock of her life." The lady's indifferent tone surprised many around the table.

~~~

The sunlight glared past an opening in the curtain, hitting his face and forcing Ray to roll over in his bed. As he came out of his deep slumber, he heard a faint rapping on wood. At first, he thought someone was knocking on another door down the hall. Then he heard the knocking again, and he realized it was at his door. Struggling out of bed, Ray grumbled to himself as he walked across the room. He decided against looking for a robe. He unlocked the door and partially opened the door before he stopped.
~~~

In front of him was Yana, who looked up. She wore a black and white polka dot dress. The woman smiled as Ray moved behind the door.

"Mrs. Dela Cruz, what brings you here? Is everything alright?" He asked while peaking around for Orella.

"It's just me, Ray. Orella is doing fine. She's still at home,"

Yana entered the room. After looking over the furnishings, the woman turned around.

"She's expecting you before you head back to Oyster City on the late afternoon train. I made sure she stayed home to rest since last night was quite tiring for her. She'll want to take you to the train station."

"I'm sorry about that," he told her, still holding his hand on the knob with the door partially open. "I probably should have waited a few days before I showed up. Wait a minute, how did you know I was leaving this afternoon?"

"You're not very observant for a shamus," she teased him, glancing at the scars on his legs.

"Aren't you going to shut the door, or will you just let strangers pass on our conversation?" The shamus closed the door and went to a chair by the bathroom. He took his pants off the back of the chair and sat down.

"You had your return ticket in your coat pocket yesterday when we first met," Yana explained as she went to his bed. She picked up his shirt, and then she threw it back on the cover. "I noticed it when I was sitting next to you."

"You'd make a good detective," he stated, visibly impressed.

"So, what brings you over here?"

"I was thinking about you last night," she said as she stepped closer. "You know, I didn't sleep well after you left. How did you sleep?"

"Best rest that I've had in a month," he told her as he stood. "Getting away from Oyster City helped stop the bad dreams."

"Yes, I remember you mentioned that at the club," Yana drew close to him. "I'm glad you're well rested for the coming day."

"Yeah, I suppose," he grudgingly agreed. Ray tilted his head, his face filled with curiosity. "But I'm trying to figure out where this conversation is going."

"You're a detective," she teased him again as she took off her hat, which matched her outfit.

"Let us look at the facts. Number One, you realize my husband did not join us last night. He stated he must work late, like so many times before. However, I know he spends his spare time in an apartment across the street from his office. The office secretary lives there."

He frowned at the news, thinking of Cat's conversation with Victor.

"I see you have your thoughts about Victor as well," she coolly observed. "And it leads to Item Number Two. I'm a lonely woman who is only a few years older than you. You find me attractive. I've seen it in your eyes. Let your shamus mind chew on those facts for a moment."

"And you are here for revenge against your husband?" he surmised.

"No, revenge is the first time a lonely wife has an affair," she told him. "I'm here because I like you, Ray. We see things in a similar light." Yana reached up and put her arms around his neck. Ray put his hands on her waist, debating whether to push her away.

"Can you deduce my reasons for being in your room?" she asked him. Her voice was husky, and her eyes bright with desire.

"I've got a pretty good idea," he admitted as he wrapped his arms around her. "Not that I'm complaining, but how does your daughter fit into this situation?"

"I thought about this after you left. You and I have experienced the world," Yana told Ray. "We understand that it's filled with rotten people. Some of them walk among us with their nice clothes and fancy titles. Others, like you, are good at heart. Yet, they must do things that nobody else will do. It makes life difficult, but honorable."

"You think I'm honorable?"

His incredulous tone made her laugh.

"Of course you are. You proved it when you returned the Singsing. Once you leave, I will guide Orella to more suitable men. Her attention must go to others who are less experienced with life and all of its problems."

"I see. You want to protect Orella from the pain I could give her," he sighed.

He went silent as the smell of her perfume tantalized his nose. The man looked into her eyes.

"You're a smart cookie, Yana. But that only fixes Orella's problem. I don't see myself returning to this city anytime soon."

"I'm not looking for a commitment, just your company for the next few hours. Lock the door and let's enjoy the morning."

Yana lifted on her tiptoes and planted a passionate kiss on his lips. Ray pulled her close and twisted the skeleton key in the lock.

~~~

It was past midnight, and Ray was back in Oyster City. He stood in a phone booth inside a grease joint while he let the phone keep ringing. Arizona's gruff voice finally came across the wire.

"I'm back in town at *Vinnies* near the docks, and the coffee is lousy. You should know the place. No one will notice that you're having coffee with a marked man," Ray told him.

"Yeah, I know the place. Go away; I'm in bed," the cop replied.

"I have interesting news from New York that you better listen to," he said. "Nothing that's for the phone."

There was a grumble. Then Ray heard a click in his ear as Arizona hung up.

While he's waiting at the counter, Ray sipped on the bitter coffee and picked at his greasy ham and eggs. His thoughts kept slipping back to Yana and Orella.
~~~

After Yana left his hotel, Ray took a taxi to see some sights, but he hardly got out of the car at each stop. The driver tried witty observations at each stop off. However, Ray hardly noticed. His driver grew silent after his questions were unanswered. Finally, he had the sullen driver take him to the Dela Cruz home.

Inside, he had a pleasant lunch with the whole family. Victor remained distant but polite, like Yana. However, Orella was excited to see him. She eventually dragged Ray away from the house to talk alone. They walked around the block several times as she kept asking questions about his past. Ray kept his answers light and boring. Eventually, the girl told him she was coming back to see him in Oyster City soon. Ray forced a smile. Then, he reminded her she should wait a while since Maria and Phillip might still cause problems. Her cheerful expression turned dark at the thought.

"Then you will come back here to see me. I'll take you to the best spots," the girl suddenly insisted.

Ray promised he would return, and she smiled at the idea.

"I think everyone will like that," she held his arm tight.

The family drove Ray to Grand Central Terminal. Both women hugged him while Victor watched him, apparently relieved that the shamus was leaving.

Inside the coach, Ray pulled off his jacket, and he found an envelope inside his pocket. He ripped it open and found a letter along with a check for a thousand dollars. The elegant cursive script was from Yana, informing him that Orella told her about the ring's recovery fee. At the end of the brief note, Yana thanked him for being there.

I'll be just a fleeting memory. Orella will recover and find a good man.

"Is the coffee that bad here?" Arizona asked as he took a seat next to Ray.

"Yeah, and the food is just as bad," Ray responded drily. He ignored the glare coming from the cook, standing a few feet away. The fat man with the stained clothes walked back into the kitchen.

"How's Miss Dela Cruz?" The policeman asked after the waitress brought him a cup of coffee.

"She's darn tough," Ray replied. "She was out at dinner and dancing a couple of nights ago. Says she's coming back, but I warned her that Andras and Weyer would remain untouched by the law."

"Damn, you're an ass," Arizona declared. "No, you're right; keep her away for the moment. By the way, did you hear about the robbery on the Smyth estate?"

The shamus shook his head.

"That damn ring everyone wants is gone. Stolen again, and I heard that the district attorney had a conniption."

"It's a wonder he didn't come looking for me," Ray commented as he observed Arizona glance over.

"What makes you think he didn't? A couple of uniformed cops went by your place and tracked down Cat as well," he said. "It's lucky for you we took you to the station that night."

"Yeah, like I always say, luck of the Irish," the shamus replied casually. "Anyway, I can picture a couple of upset people. It breaks my heart."

"Yeah, I'm sure it does," Arizona drolly agreed before he grimaced at the bitter sip he just took. "They claimed a servant by the name of Abby stole the ring. There's been no trace of the girl. The chief even assigned a couple of men to check out all train and bus stations between here and the capital. They came up empty. Best guess is the maid hauled the ring out of the state, either by bus or train."

He turned to Irish, leaning his elbow on the counter.

"By now, she pawned off somewhere, and the girl isn't coming back. Andras claims the maid had an addiction to drugs. Funny, but I remember you telling me about Abby helping you find the Dela Cruz girl. Conveniently, you left that night."

Irish gave him a cryptic grin.

"A pure coincidence, I'm sure. But that's not why we're here. I can officially add another murder to your collection of mysterious killings." Ray changed the subject.

"What the hell are you talking about?" Arizona asked as Irish pulled a piece of paper from his pocket.

"You're looking at the evidence against a certain Bishop La Spina that we know. It's one reason I went to New York City."

He showed the detective the affidavit from the porter on MS Vulcania.

"We now know for sure that Greye La Spina wasn't on the ocean liner when it left Genoa. Her supposed drowning occurred a few hours after the ship left. I have a signed document from the crewman who knew the woman was not on board the ship. The man thinks the bishop must have bribed people."

Arizona's scowled at the news.

"Still, it's mighty thin," his friend finally stated. "You've got no corpse and a respected citizen who's loved by most of the city."

"Oh, I know where her body is," Irish stated. "Her body is in a pauper's grave out by the state capital. Greye never left Oyster City alive. Her body washed up after being dumped in the bay."

Arizona grimaced again after taking another sip of coffee. He put the cup down on the counter in disgust.

"You're right about the coffee. Now you're giving me heartburn," Arizona told him. "You think I'm crazy enough to charge Bishop La Spina with the murder of his wife on this flimsy evidence?"

"No, I'm just telling you what I've found so far. This paper is part of it," Irish explained. "I know where they buried Greye's body. The next stop is Boston for her dental records. By the way, I saw Greye's body at the state morgue. She had her throat cut, just like Quincannon and Ulysses. Also, the murderer cut off her ring finger on the left hand. Unless you can point to another missing wife from Oyster City, Greye La Spina fits the picture of the victim pretty damn well. And it gives the appearance of a pattern here, doesn't it?"

Arizona kept staring at the document as he tipped his bowler hat back on his head. Ray knew him long enough to recognize the man was seriously considering the idea.

"There's a bit more. Ever since Peter Smyth introduced himself to me that day at the jail, I've been thinking about his shielding of Maria and his brother," he went on.

"Henry La Spina runs with the same crowd. His driver and his wife nearly robbed him blind. Somehow, the bad guys got killed, and Henry came out on top. Add to the mix is Howard. He's a cop, but we both know that Howard came as crooked as a witch's hat. There may be a link between all of them, and the bishop is the logical suspect given his connections."

"You have nothing but circumstantial evidence," Arizona said reluctantly.

Then he gave the document back to Ray.

"You hang on to this. Official files can get lost in this town," he signed. "I guess I'll need to look into it. Tell me, are you ever going to hand me something that doesn't stink?"

"I might," Ray replied with a sly grin. "But I wouldn't count on it."

<center>~~~</center>

In the bright light of the blue blood moon, a small group of masked people stood around a dull gray stone crypt. The moonlight filtered through the tree canopy over them, giving them a view of the single rope hanging down from the massive limb above.

"Where is the sacrifice for tonight?" A voice asked from behind the mask of the Empress. "There are no candles and goblet."

"As you know well, the victim left town with her father. We've lost the noble blood because of your bungling," the woman in the demon mask said.

Her shaky hand pointed her cane at the woman.

"Maria, you knew tonight's sacrifice was important to our line. Yet, your self-indulgence has left the Shadows with little choice. Therefore, we have decided upon changes. Bring him forth!"

A thin man in Judgement's mask led another masked man to the crypt from behind the tree. The stranger held a wine cup; his Bacchus mask covered his broad face. Underneath, Weyer smiled like the drunken god whose mask he wore. His short stature and enormous belly stood out under the ill-fitting robe he wore. He toasted his comrades.

"Bacchus joins the circle to help bring forth the Master," Judgement declared. "Tonight, we will install our brother, who brings us the sacrifice. Our priest will give the rites for the Master to join us." He looked over to the High Priest, who came next to the Empress.

369

"The master will need a vessel to enter our world, and the blood of a noblewoman will nourish him while he rises." Henry La Spina told them from behind his mask of the Priest.

"Noble blood runs inside the Empress. Prepare her!"

"What a minute? What is going on here?" Maria Andras threw off her Empress mask. Her pale face showing the rising fear, she retreated from the crypt. However, she backed into Mr. Wolfe, who silently walked up behind her.

"No!" she screamed out.

A brutal punch delivered by Wolfe sent the woman to the ground. Bacchus and Judgement picked up the woman by each arm while the High Priest gagged her with a thick strip of white cloth. As Maria came out of her stupor, the High Priestess stripped the robe from the woman's body, leaving only her silk bra and panties. The man in the mask of Death guided the old woman in front of Maria.

"Are you sure of this, Betty?" Phillip asked. "Even when we were married, I've never liked her that much, but she's your child."

She glanced at Maria, then she nodded. Her daughter desperately tried to wriggle out of her bindings.

"There is no better way to bring forth Andras," Betty announced triumphantly over the muffled sound of Maria's pleas.

"The death of an Andras, who remains barren, makes no difference to the family. Other members of the Andras family exist to support the Master. Prepare my daughter for the full moon."

The Demon stepped back to the tomb while the remaining Shadows ripped the undergarments from Maria's shivering body. They dragged her along the ground to the grave. Her mother ordered Mr. Wolfe to bring out the case with their votive candles and the golden goblet. As Betty prepared the top of the crypt for the coming sacrifice, she paid no attention to the sounds behind them. The muffled cries from Maria turned into a desperate rage while she fought the Shadows. When they attempted to tie the woman's leg, Maria kicked out, landing a blow into Henry La Spina's crouch. He went to a knee, catching his breath while Weyer grabbed Maria by the hair and punched her in the face. The action stunned her, and Peter finished tying her ankle.

"It's unfortunate for my daughter, but we must address the Singsing's loss for all to witness and take heed," the Demon patiently explained to Wolfe.

"The rule of the Shadows is merciless yet fair. The Master's attendants must always put his interest above those of the family. You show wisdom in your nature," Wolfe agreed in a hollow voice seldom heard by others. He pulled a pocket watch from his waistcoat. "We don't have much time left before the full moon."

"It is hard to lose a daughter," Betty confessed. The woman didn't look back at the muffled screams. A giggle came from the High Priestess as she raked Maria's breasts with long fingernails while the men pulled her aloft.

"Remember how much you like doing this to our victims," Julia smirked. "The master's servants will enjoy you the same way."

"The dreams tell me he will rise from the grave and walk among his servants," Betty continued. "Maria's blood will give us the power necessary to complete the ceremony."

"Everything is ready," she told Mr. Wolfe with satisfaction.

Her eyes filled with tears, Maria still struggled while dangling by one leg above the tomb. Her head was only inches above the stone top of the crypt as the moonlight coming through the tree flickered across her lean, white body. Maria's smooth skin, so carefully pampered before she arrived, now showed the scratches and bruises from her abuse. With her arms tied behind her back, her struggles reminded Weyer of an image he had once had.

In a dream, he saw a white worm writhing on a hook. He laughed to himself as he joined the Shadows reformed in a circle around the tomb. Each member began lighting the candles.

"Bacchus must pass the initiation of the blood," Judgment declared as he held out the golden goblet. The people behind the masks watched Bacchus confidently between Judgement and Death. The man behind the Bacchus mask reached out and pulled Maria by the hair.

"Dear cousin, you've belittled me once too often," he whispered into her ear. "Think of it. I've taken your place, and now I get to kill you. Try to enjoy yourself when Andras gives you to the infernal legions for their pleasure."

With grim satisfaction, Weyer used the ornate dagger of the Shadows to cut his cousin's throat. Judgment hurriedly placed the goblet under the dying woman's head. As the blood flowed into the cup, the woman's death throes caused her body to jerk and spasm.

Mr. Wolfe came to Bacchus. He retrieved the dagger as chants of the group broke the silence of the night. The tall man stood next to the new member of the Shadows, as they called out their master.

Bacchus picked up the goblet, now nearly filled. He held the cup up to the group's approval before he brought the drink to the large opening of his mask. For all of his bravado, the man almost spat out the warm liquid. Knowing such a move would mean his death, Weyer forced the blood down his throat as the night went silent. He hurriedly handed the cup to the Priestess. While the dark ceremony continued, Betty Andras chanted the ritual to summon their master.

When the last member of the cult took a drink from the cup, the ground beneath them suddenly quaked. Terrified screams shot from the masks of the Priestess and the Priest while everyone staggered from the shaking soil beneath their feet. A loud crackling snap filled the air as the top of the crypt split open while the Shadows hurriedly retreated.

Barely able to hold her position, Betty used her cane to steady her body while she watched in fascination as the rotting corpse of her ancestor came to light. The corpse of Maria Andras fell on top of the ancient remains when the rope gave way. A sudden gale whirled around the graveyard, and the wind lashed at the Shadows.

On his knees and silently praying for deliverance, Henry La Spina saw the massive old tree topple. He rolled away, barely avoiding a thick limb landing on him. The branch fell across the back of the man in the Judgement mask, sending him into the stone. The group scattered in the howling tempest while the violent shaking sent nearly everyone to the ground. Then, as suddenly as it started, the earth stopped moving, and the wind went still.

Julie Smyth, her High Priestess mask hanging around her neck, looked up to see her husband slowly standing. His smashed Judgment cover lay on the ground next to the broken crypt. The tree branches scattered around the man fell away as he rose. He picked up the mask, cocking his head as he looked at the large amount of his blood showing inside.

Smyth stepped away with no sign of injury on his face. His face looked paler as he gazed over the area. The man's blue eyes held a paralyzing glance.

When Peter stared at his wife, she shivered at the change in his eyes. They blazed with an evil intensity that made him look mad. But the man gave no hint of recognition to his wife. As the Shadows slowly gathered themselves, they came back to the crypt. Most had lost their masks during the turmoil. Only Death still had on his cover as he pushed through the broken branches. He stood next to the figure of his brother. He still held the goblet with a small amount of blood.

"Your master arises!"

An ominous voice filled the air as Peter took the goblet from his brother. He drank the remaining blood and then tossed the cup. Bacchus fumbled with the golden goblet as he tried to catch it.

Andras, a Noble of Hell, stood in front of his followers in the form of Peter Smyth. He stepped through an open spot among the branches as Phillip followed him. Mr. Wolfe came before him. He immediately kneeled, handing his new master the golden dagger.

"We go to my house where each of my earthbound servants will submit to me," Andras told them.

"Andras, the Shadows brought you forth," the masked demon woman told him as she hobbled before him and bowed. "The greatest of hell's demons and master of tells of all things past and future, we follow your wisdom and guidance."

Peter looked her over, then grabbed the older woman by her throat. After lifting her in the air, the demon smiled while observing Betty's desperate struggles for breath. Then there was a loud snap that filled the air as his hand crushed her neck.

"Your old, frail body gives me no pleasure, but your soul might," the ominous voice growled as he glared at his followers. "I lead the legions from hell! I don't follow the luck of tarot cards."

He let the lifeless body of Betty Andras fall to the ground a few feet from the tomb. Then, Andras began walking toward the house the bore his name while the human attendants obediently followed him.

Drink with the Devil at Midnight

Ray Irish Occult Suspense Mystery Book 3

Chapter 1: Nightmares among the Living

On the night of the second full moon for the month, Johnny Jacobi entered a pillared white marble building in Oyster City. He felt the blast of cold air that reminded him of a morgue when his henchmen opened the large doors that led into Peter Smyth's office. The tall, thin gangster glanced around the room, and his eyes immediately fell on the regal-looking man sitting behind a large walnut desk.

Peter Smyth leaned back in his padded leather chair as the group entered his office. His long fingers began tapped on the chair arms while his thin lips curled into an unpleasant smile.

Jacobi immediately halted when he noticed someone hidden in the shadows at one corner of the room. The man stepped into the light, and the gangster immediately thought he saw a walking corpse. A pallor face with the blank expression of a dead man nodded to the visitor.

"Mr. Wolfe is my assistant," the man behind the desk assured Jacobi. "He's unarmed. There are no police in the building."

The gangster nodded as the servant brought a silver tray with a piece of paper on it and placed the plate on the desk. Wolfe silently receded into the shadows. Jacobi turned his attention back to his host. Peter Smyth wore a finely tailored blue suit, conservative cut and expensive. His eyes carried the glint of amusement as he watched the gangster's uneasy movements.

"I don't like meeting with coppers in their office," Jacobi replied sorely. He unbelted his stylish gray trench coat and pulled off his gray fedora.

"You'll notice that I didn't bring any lawyers." He told Smyth as he directed his two thugs to stand on either side of the doorway. "Am I going to need legal eagles for this little chat?"

"You will benefit from your trip to Oyster City," Smyth told him, disregarding the question. "Consider it the start of a partnership."

"I don't make deals with coppers," Jacobi scoffed. "I make or break your type. Now your message said something about my business connections with Guy Young. He's dead, so don't think a DA can threaten me about his operations. Besides, I heard Young committed suicide in your jail. I brought along my muscle just in case you tried to get too smart. Now get to the point, or I'm leaving."

"Let me see if I can't persuade you to stay and listen to my offer," Smyth cautioned. The blue irises of his eyes suddenly turned black. They reminded the gangster of two endless tunnels. Instantly, the room grew bitter cold. The hairs on the back of Jacobi's neck weren't from the cold. The expression on the DA's face scared him.

Behind him, Jacobi heard his gunmen grunt out in pain. He glanced over to see his men's grizzled faces turn pale with a mixture of disbelief and fear. The men dragged their pistols out from the holsters under their arms. Jacobi's hoodlums physically struggled to control their movements. With wide eyes, they stepped closer to their boss. With trembling hands, they pointed their revolvers at Jacobi. When they pulled back the hammers on their weapons, the gangster jumped from the chair.

He yelled for them to stop as he backed into the desk. Trying to get out of their line of fire, he slid toward the side of the room, but the wall stopped him. His men shakily adjusted their aim. Expecting the worst, Jacobi screamed for them to stop as he crouched on his knees.

Then, the two thugs pointed their weapons toward each other. The nearly simultaneous blasts from the gunshots filled the room. Both men crumpled to the floor like marionettes on strings. The shaken gangster slowly rose from his crouch. His wide eyes frantically surveyed the scene as he carefully stepped between his dead men. Each corpse had a trickle of drying blood sliding from a bullet hole in their forehead.

"Obviously, they meant little to you." Smyth's unholy voice broke through the stillness. "Now, Mr. Jacobi, have a seat so we can discuss what you'll be doing for me."

Jacobi didn't move for a moment. He couldn't. As his brain tried to process what had happened, he slowly turned back to the man behind the desk.

"What the hell are you?" he finally gasped out.

"That's an interesting turn of the phrase," Smyth observed. "Let's just say that my dominion reeks of Sulphur and my assistants enjoy inflicting pain and suffering."

"Now, take a seat!" he ordered the gangster firmly as he pointed to the leather chair across from him. "I have plans for you."

He waited until the shaken man finally sat in the chair. The entire time, Jacobi's bulging eyes stared at Smyth.

"On top of the tray, I have a list of people who need to be—well, let's just say they will meet an untimely demise," Smyth told him. A grin crossed his face as he watched Jacobi gazing at the piece of paper like it was a snake.

"Go ahead, pick up the paper. It won't harm you. It will make you quite wealthy and even more powerful," Smyth assured him.

Carefully, Jacobi picked up the sheet and looked at the typewritten words. His eyes widened at the names on the list; then he glanced up at the Oyster City district attorney.

"Yes, that's correct. Each one of those individuals will die in the coming days," Smyth informed him. "Nearly all of them are important names in the state. Your responsibility is to remove those people from the world of the living."

"How?" The question came out of the gangster automatically.

"Well, that's up to you now. You control Baltimore and influence various parts of the state through your illegal enterprises. I know your organization has unsavory people who can take care of those persons who oppose you," the DA explained.

"Now, in return for your efforts, I'll give your criminal organization free rein inside of Oyster City. The police will not bother your gambling, racketeering, and any other illegal operations that you intend to set up."

The DA leaned forward with a bemused smile.

"Well, as long as I receive a slight cut of your profits, that is. Mr. Jacobi, you will find this city very accommodating for your work in the future."

Jacobi shifted his position in the chair and glanced over at the silent, solitary figure in the room's corner. He turned his focus back to Smyth.

"The Oyster City district attorney promises me his city for a cut of the profits. But why are you looking for me to do your dirty work?" the gangster finally asked.

Smyth gave an impatient sigh.

"I suggest you look at our meeting as an opportunity. The type of work I'm giving you is your natural calling," he told the gangster.

"Since many of the people on the list live in other parts of the state, you have the manpower to eliminate them. That is something I lack for the moment."

Jacobi slowly nodded in agreement; his thoughts still attempting to understand the creature before him. Then he shook his head.

"I don't get it. You've already got some strange power over people to do that to my boys. What's your game?"

He glanced down at the list again.

"That is nothing to concern yourself about," Smyth informed his new partner. "Let's just say you're helping me and I'm helping you."

"Well, I don't like it. From the names I'm seeing, you're having me take all the risk. I get bumped off; you get all the gravy. Free rein in one damn city doesn't seem like a fair trade. I'll have all the coppers in the state trying to knock me off," Jacobi insisted.

The demon behind the desk stopped his grinning. His deathlike expression made the gangster even more uncomfortable.

"That's a consideration, of course. Let me add a little sweetener to the pot for you," Smyth stated smoothly. "Aside from my office looking the other way at your enterprises, I'll ensure a few of your most trusted associates fill the openings because of those untimely deaths. Perhaps you might take on one of those roles. It means civility and dignity attached to your name. I believe you can understand how such arrangements will benefit you. The governor and others will accept your associates in those positions."

"I knock off your competition, and some of my boys get to replace the honest Joes, is that it?"

Smyth nodded at Jacobi's question. He recognized the gangster was in the bag.

"Those are the terms for you. There is only one condition," Smyth continued. "I expect your people to use the same method of killing whenever they murder someone on the list."

Jacobi crooked his neck at the demand, his eyes dropping to look over the list again.

"You want it to look like the same guy is killing them?" He paused as he thought about the idea.

"You might have something there," the gangster continued. "It'll be harder to trace back to my involvement in this scheme. It could appear that a crazy inmate escaped from the asylum. The papers will forget all about my organization for a while."

"That's one consideration, of course. You see, fear and insecurity are my specialties," Peter Smyth agreed.

~~~

Ray Irish lay on a bed, watching the moonlight streaming into the hotel room. The traffic sounds of New York City streamed through the half-opened window. A beam of light landed on his brown fedora, which hung on the top rail of the chair that sat near the foot of the bed. He sighed lightly and tried to turn off the thoughts swirling around his brain.

He couldn't sleep! And the reason lay right next to him in the bed.

Ray glanced over to see the sleeping form of the pretty woman. She was on her side; her black hair covered most of her face.

You're a damn fool! She can't get caught up with a guy like me.

Orella Dela Cruz came from a respectable family. Aside from her fantastic, exotic attractiveness, she was a beautiful person. Orella held all the naïve and trusting values that Ray once carried. She also made Ray out like he was a knight on a white horse since he rescued her from her kidnappers. Sure, the girl kept pestering him with phone calls, telegrams, and letters.

He remained charmed by her attention. Having a loving and kind person by your side felt good. It was something Ray needed after dealing with the foul, corrupt world of Oyster City. However, he knew she must remain in New York City. Ray wanted to stop their relationship.

Hell, that's a lie! I could have stopped the whole thing with a letter. Instead, I wanted to see her, to hold her again!

He rolled over to face the wall. It was tough admitting that he was such a heel. Ray should have told Orella to leave when she showed up at this door. Instead, he took the easy way and took her to bed. She could never understand how his life worked. Playing a shamus was the role entrenched in him now.

Worse, the world he lived in carried too many rotten parts for Orella. The daily interactions with crooked people made him just as bad as those he took the money from at times. His constant struggle to chase the next shamus job for rent money meant he was nothing like a white knight. Frustration and heartache sent
~~~

Ray back into a bottle too often. His life yelled out to the world that Orella didn't deserve the fate of staying with him.

Irish heard Orella mumble in her sleep and she rolled next to him. He felt her small breasts brush against his arm. The man felt the tingle of excitement, and Ray frowned. She needed someone better, and he just made it worse.

Carefully, Ray slid out of bed and quietly made his way to the bathroom. He closed the door and turned on the light. He recognized the stupid man standing mirror and looked out the open half window. The neon lights of the building across the street blinked out

Yana's face flashed into his mind. The two women looked like sisters. Only a few years older than Ray, Yana needed him occasionally as well. They committed adultery in the same hotel room the night before. It was bad enough that he really liked Orella, but he wasn't smart enough to stop screwing the girl's married mother.

Sometimes, you're such a damn fool!

~~~

As Orella Dela Cruz walked to the front of the old church, she felt the happiness which was missing from her life. She stopped at the front row of pews and smiled at those watching her as she showed her the white wedding dress she wore. It was her mother's. Yana beamed at her daughter. After her mother hugged her, Orella took her father's arm. Victor Dela Cruz, his head held high and proud, slowly stepped with her to the sound of the organ music.

When they got closer to the altar where a tall thin man in priest's clothing waited, Orella heard the music change. The sound became ethereal and eerie. She glanced over at the organist. Panic built inside of her when she saw the figure in black turn toward her, revealing a hideous mask. She recognized the same costume from the night of her kidnapping.

In a panic, she turned to her father. However, he was no longer at her side. Instead, a large black man dressed in blue denim coveralls stood next to her. Ulysses, the thug who tortured and raped her, stood next to her. He looked straight ahead. His throat showed the open gash from his murder. Orella backed away in horror. But with each step, her feet gradually refused to move.

The woman turned to the front pews of the church. She screamed out in horror. Dressed in the same black robes, the people in the seats put on similar, grotesque masks.

"Come, my child, stand with your husband," the deep voice echoed in the room.

Before she realized what happened, Orella felt Ulysses pull her to the altar and move away. With no will of her own, she watched a tall, thin man with white-gray hair leering at her from behind the platform. As he pointed to her left hand, Orella looked down. Instead of a wedding ring, she found a grotesque ring
~~~

that wrapped around her finger like the body of a snake. Five diamonds on the ring carried the symbol of a pentagon.

"Now hand me the ring," the man demanded.

Orella felt herself pulling the Singsing ring from her index finger and handing it to him. She stepped back to find a familiar presence move next to her. She knew it was Ray Irish from a glance out of the corner of her eye. Orella smiled at the thought of him with her.

"You may kiss the bride," the gray-haired man declared with a sinister laugh.

Orella turned to Ray. Instantly, she recognized his complexion was an off-color blue. Then she turned to him, and he looked back with dead eyes. There was a wicked gash across his throat. Irish pulled her into his arms, and Orella screamed herself awake.

It took a long moment before she realized she was lying on the floor, covered in sheets. Irish fumbled around with the bedside lamp before the blinding light made her look away. He slid next to her as Orella began crying.

~~~

The last remaining blood trickled down from the gaping neck wound on the corpse. Hanging upside down by one leg, the naked female body twisted slowly in the moonlit night.

Nearby, two naked people wearing hideously distorted masks of a High Priest and a Magician lifted themselves from the high grass. Finished with their rape of the semi-conscious victim, they casually redressed in their ceremonial robes.

"My turn," said a small, tubby man wearing the mask of Bacchus.

He passed a broken crypt where he paid no attention to the skeletal remains inside. The object of his desire, a naked young man with his arms bound tightly behind him, vainly struggled while mumbling through a gag. His pleading caused Bacchus to laugh as he shed the rest of his robe.

The remaining members of the cult paid only passing interest at the spectacle. Sated by their gang rape of their female victim before they sacrificed her, the small group smoked cigarettes and sipped on blood tainted wine. While they whispered among themselves, they paid no attention to the grunting noises coming from Bacchus and the pleas of his victim.

The only unmasked individual remained aloof to the spectacle. Long and lean, the gray-haired man stood by the body of the hanging female. There was no need for a mask. Andras, a demon brought forth from Hell, now lived inside Peter Smyth's body.

"Death and Andras are the same; there is no need to hide my face," he told his followers on the night of his return to the earthly realm.

Dressed in a scarlet robe, Smyth quietly surveyed the Andras cemetery where his followers held their sacrifices. The full moon of the caused his gray
~~~

hair to look nearly white in the moonlight that streamed through the leafless tree. His hawk-like face turned to his followers; coal dark eyes focused on the fat man wearing the Emperor's mask. Andras stepped toward the crypt as the Priest and Magician joined him.

"Since my return a month ago, my followers have pleased me with sacrifices and offerings. However, there is much work left for us to bring forth the other legions of my kind," the demon's told the group.

"On the night of my return, the most devout of my followers showed their fidelity to me. Except for two of you. Tonight, we will address this error."

He turned his attention to the man in the Emperor's mask.

"Hopely, you're one of my Shadows who were not present during my return. It appears that you were conveniently out of town," he stated.

The demon held up his hand when the mayor tried to interject.

"I don't want your excuse. I know the reason for the trip. Going to Washington, DC, was an attempt to feather your nest. Bluntly, it gives me doubts about your commitment to me," Smyth warned, as his voice took on an eerie echo.

Hopely felt the hairs on the back of his neck rise at the sound, which mimicked the echoes of the catacomb that the Shadows sometimes used for their rituals.

"Master, I swear it wasn't about me! Please let me explain," the fat man begged as he pulled off his mask.

He slid off the crypt and tried to step closer. He stopped when he saw his master's dark expression, and his plump face grew pale as he backed away.

"I met with our congressmen and one of the state's senators about adding our people to their staff," Hopely stammered out. "You understand your servants can help you in positions of power. The only time the people in Washington would see me was on the day of your return. The Shadows knew of my absence and agreed."

Smyth's piercing stare remained black.

"Tell me more," the demon said.

"I went to Betty Andras with this idea," Hopely insisted after licking his dry lips. "After my election problems a few months back, I came up with this plan. To control beyond Oyster City, I realized the Shadows must spread our influence. We would start with those leaders who need our votes in this city. You see, it benefits everyone. You will benefit most of all."

Peter Smyth stared at the mayor in the uncomfortable silence. A long groan from Bacchus with his orgasm broke the silence. Smyth glanced over, then turned back to the mayor. A foul smile spread across his lips.

"It's clear you must learn obedience. You could have come to me on your own before the night of the sacrifice. That your idea has merit is the only reason I'm not snapping your neck."

"Yes—yes, master…, I'm sure…" the mayor started.

"Shut up, Hopely! There's more. It's a new era when I came into the human world. Your unquestioned loyalty begins with following my orders," the demon continued.

"I've always worshipped you. I've cut the throats of the sacrifices and drunk the blood on full moon nights since I was a young man," Hopely insisted. "I give my prayers to the legions of Hell. What more can I do to convince you?"

"Bah! Such things mean little during the orgies among your friends in the darkness," Smyth replied.

He paused and motioned the half-naked form of his human wife to join them. Julie Smyth still wore her mask of the High Priestess. She glanced at the others before joining the mayor.

"On your knees, woman," Andras ordered.

Julie Smyth giggled nervously after removing her mask. Obediently, she opened her husband's robe.

"On the night of my return, my followers followed me to my home. Each of the Shadows pleased me as all servants should," the demon explained. "Now, you will join my wife. Get on your knees."

Hopely blanched and refused to move.

Peter Smyth ordered the Shadows to gather around him. They formed a circle around their leader. A man dressed as the Magician forced Hopely down next to Julie.

"Those who disobey the will of Andras will suffer before they die," he whispered into the mayor's ear. "You're not special. We've all done as he's asked. Our master doesn't accept free will."

"Wait, I'm one of you! We all know each other," he pleaded to his friends. "The rule is to force a Shadow to be a servant to the others. We take those that we want. We are not slaves!"

"I demand obedience at all times," the demon growled. His eyes turned black.

Hopely clutched at his neck; his mouth opened wide. The man's tongue stuck out as his throat compressed. Panic filled the mayor's face in the dim light as he slowly choked himself. He knew he would die soon unless Andras released him.

"Man of nothing. You're nothing but my plaything," Smyth told him. "I determine if you live or die in this world. For your defiance, the Shadows will use you as a whore until daylight."

Released from the demon's spell, Hopely nearly fell over. The man in the magician mask got him back to his knees. The mayor visibly shook while Julie put her arm around her partner. She giggled after she whispered to Hopely.

A satisfied grin crossed the demon's face as his followers started pulled off their robes again. Their unexpected entertainment meant for a long night, but they would not displease their master.

A few feet away, Johann Weyer pulled off his mask as he arrived with his rape victim. He forced the man to crawl on his hands and knees to the group.

"Master, is it time to bleed him?"

With a nod, Smyth held out a golden dagger, then turned his attention back to his wife and Hopely, who worked to please him. Weyer went to the master and took the weapon. He put his mask back on while he went toward the next sacrifice. Recognizing the peril, the bound man attempted to escape by rolling away. He only got a couple of feet before the headstone stopped him. Bacchus cackled in delight and walked over.

When he reached the young man, the killer kneeled and embedded the blade into his victim's throat. Blood spurted across the ground while the dying man thrashed in his binding. Bacchus walked over to join the rest of the Shadows as their animalistic groans and grunts filled the air. The moonlight faded behind the gathering clouds.

~~~

It was early morning when the moon receded from the night sky. A choking fit woke Catherine Bennett out of her terrible nightmare. She gasped for breath while holding her hands to her throat. She twisted around in the bed, trying to find the killer. It took several seconds for the woman to realize no one was trying to murder her. Still, she felt the burn of thin wire wrapped around her neck. A bright light blinked on in her face.

"Dear, what's wrong?" Marion Underhill asked as he rolled over from turning on the lamp. "Did you have a nightmare?"

"Yes, …something like that," she choked out as she still felt the cold wire on her neck. It felt so real that she searched around the bed briefly. Cat paused, then hurriedly got out of her bed. She didn't bother with a robe as she hurried over to a tall mirror mounted on the wall. However, there was no mark on her neck, only the slight red finger marks from grabbing at her throat. In the reflection, she saw Marion get out of the bed and walk toward her. He was half-dressed.

As she leaned forward, pressing her forehead on the mirror, he pulled her into his arms. They looked at each other through the reflection of the mirror.

"What happened?" he asked.

Cat sighed, smiling at the mix of sympathy and concern on his boyish face.

"I—I thought my necklace was strangling me," she lied. Marion smiled sympathetically.

"It's on the nightstand," he told her. Still embracing her, he led her to the side of the bed. Cat saw her present hanging from the unlit lamp. She leaned back against him, enjoying the embrace.
~~~

"I'm sorry I got home so late," he whispered in her ear. "Our ceremony took longer than expected. I didn't realize you were having a nightmare." He kissed her lightly on the cheek and reached around to caress her breast.

"No, dear, not right now," she panicked slightly and pulled away. Cat turned to see Marion's bewildered expression. She pulled her robe off the end of the bed, not catching the flash of anger in his eyes.

"I'm sorry, it's just the nightmare got to me. You go back to bed. I'll come to back after I get a drink of water."

"Are you sure you're alright?" His mechanical tone went unnoticed as she kept feeling the necklace.

"Yes, I'll be fine in a while. I need to shake off these heebie-jeebies," Cat replied while putting on the silk robe. It was a present from Marion as well. She stepped to him and gave him a quick kiss on the lips.

"Don't worry, I'll make you late for work when the sun rises," she promised him. Cat tried to sound seductive, but it felt phony. However, Marion accepted it with a grin, and then he yawned as he went to the other side of the bed. He finished undressing and pulled his pajamas off the end of the bed.

Catherine walked out of the bedroom, clutching the lapels of her pale blue bed jacket closed. Crossing the small living room, she went to the open liquor cabinet. The nightmare remained crystal clear in her mind. With a shiver, the woman poured herself a drink from the first bottle she found. The gin caused her to cough, but it warmed her after she got it down. Her hand shook as she filled another glass. The nightmares continued nearly every night. They were getting to her.

Going to the couch, Cat realized that her relationship with Marion slowly changed over the last several weeks. At first, he took her to the swankiest clubs and parties where she enjoyed pretending like she was just another distinguished guest. Then, he brought her expensive gifts, and soon they were lovers. Marion made her apartment his second home over the last month. She realized he was becoming too much like a husband. While Cat enjoyed the attention and the benefits, she felt a trap slowly encircling her.

As she sat there, sipping on the drink, she suddenly remembered something Ray Irish told her once.

"You run around like a dog in heat when some wealthy guy looks your way!" He said in a fit of anger.

Cat picked at the silk cloth of her robe, looking at her leg that lay exposed to the soft light of the room. She knew Ray and the other men enjoyed looking at her body. She used tight skirts and blouses to her advantage. Cat used to think that tempting men gave her the way out of her life along the docks. Now, she wasn't so sure.

There's a word people use for what I am.

Funny, Irish was a big, honest brute, but he never called her a whore. Even after taking advantage of him, Cat recognized that Ray never let her slights overshadow his loyalty. Also, when she fell into the pit of self-despair, the woman knew that she could rely on the shamus.

Still, it wasn't enough. Catherine Bennett had to rise above everyone, even if she crawled across the skeletons to get there. She sniffed lightly, refusing to let the tears fall, then took a long drink.

Being a tough bitch got Cat through the tough years of watching her tramp mother. She made it out of the waterfront tenements by playing men like a fiddle. While her life didn't meet the expectations of some people, she wasn't about to stop her search. Someday she'd laugh at those who insulted her.

Looking for something to take her mind away from the growing self-pity, she noticed her half-finished letter to Jack Romano's parents. Slowly, her eyes focused on the paper lying on the coffee table. For a long moment, she stared at it. Memories of her first encounter with a desperate young man flooded over her. Jack's parents came to her for help in finding their missing child, along with his girlfriend. With a little digging, she tracked the boy to the state insane asylum in the capital. Abused by his kidnappers and mistreated by the bastards that ran the center, Jack left the place as a stuttering shell. Jack's girlfriend was still missing and presumed dead.

With a sigh, she picked up the letter. After reading the words, Catherine shook her head and downed the rest of her drink. Tears tumbled down her cheeks. She crumpled the paper in her hand.

Why do I care about crawling to the top social circle of this damn city?

Chapter 2: A Dame on a Bridge

Two weeks following the Shadow's murders, the newspapers were on to other tantalizing news. The sacrificial victims were missing, according to the paper Peter Smyth held in his hands. Missing people never keep the interest of the public for very long. Looking up, he noticed their arrival next to the Andras mansion. He waited as Mr. Wolfe stepped out of the chauffeur's seat of the black Packard limousine.

"The fog is coming in heavy tonight. As instructed, I've had the old lady's furniture removed from the master bedroom and replaced with your items from the Smyth house." Wolfe said as he opened the back door of the car.

Smyth stepped out and looked at the fog as it shrouded the estate.

"Very good," the demon told his servant. "It's too bad that we'll have no moonlight for tonight. Make sure you have lanterns for our walk to the cemetery. And ensure that our guests in the basement have food and water. I don't want them to die prematurely."

"Of course, master," Wolfe said impassively. "By the way, I've instructed your new manservant to have your mail and messages waiting at your desk."

"Can I trust this one? I cannot have a mistake coming from human frailty," Smyth growled.

"Jarvis is from my brother's family and loyal to me and therefore, to you. He is also mute. He'll remain quiet at all times," Wolfe said.

"Would you like dinner this late? The blue moon rises during the witching hour."

"Yes, yes, that is a good idea," Peter agreed. "In the meantime, have that pretty little servant girl in the basement bathed and brought to me."

"Is she to be your sacrifice tonight? The second moon of the month is not strong," the servant advised.

"No, the bitch is only for my pleasure tonight. Tell my wife of this world to join us," the demon explained. "You know how much Mrs. Smyth likes to abuse our captive guests. Julie believes she is entertaining me while she enjoys her shallow desires."

The servant nodded and helped Smyth remove his coat.

"Humans amuse me. It makes me wonder when I'll sacrifice Julie. Perhaps on the next coming eclipse, which will bring forth more of my kind," he mused.

He let out a mocking laugh as he walked to the library. Smyth stopped at the door, then glanced back.

"Tonight, we'll use the butler from the Smyth estate for our sacrifice," the district attorney instructed his servant. "Since he's already ill, we don't want him spreading his virus to the others. It's always better to remove the weak."

"Very good, my master," Wolfe agreed as he bowed. "I'll prepare everything for you."

The man walked toward the basement door as Andras entered the library.

~~~

A thick fog rolled in from the Chesapeake Bay and the houses along Clover Street were lit up as the families inside finished their dinners. A gray Hudson slowly passed a small cottage style house, nearly coming to a stop. The car's driver looked out the driver's side window at a man and his boy watching TV. The vehicle sped up to turn left at the nearby corner. Halfway around the block, the car turned into the alley and parked behind the empty garage. Pausing for a moment, the driver carefully slid out of the vehicle. Then, he partially closed the door, making sure not to make any noise. The stranger pulled down his brown fedora low across his forehead and hiked up the collar of his gray trench coat as he walked down the alley. Only the sound of his shoes crunching on the gravel path reached him as he glanced around the houses on either side of the lane. When he reached his destination, the man crouched between the bushes that separated the backyard from the narrow road. In the growing darkness, he remained hidden from a neighbor's window.

From his vantage point, the man again scanned the area before focusing his attention on Mr. and Mrs. Romano's house. A yellow light coming through the kitchen window revealed Mrs. Romano standing in front of the kitchen window. She was looking down, apparently washing the dishes. After she turned from the window, the stranger in the trench coat pushed through the bushes and into the yard. He went to the darkest shadows along the back wall of the house and waited. Several days of observing the house installed the family's routine in his mind.

The stranger pulled a length of flexible wire from his coat. The piano line had two wooden handles attached on either end as he heard Mrs. Romano called out for Jack to take out the garbage. Soon, the young man exited the house carrying a large paper bag. He headed to the area behind a small one-car garage where two battered trash cans sat. After going behind the building, Jack Romano noisily pulled the top from the metal container and tossed the paper bag inside. Just as he placed the lid back on the trash can, he felt something slide by his face. An instant later, the wire tightened around his neck. The young man grabbed at the piano wire, but his hands couldn't stop the intense pressure. The man in the trench coat pulled Jack away from the cans while his victim struggled to remain upright. He turned and kicked. However, the experienced killer used his weight advantage to force the boy to his knees, then to his belly. He kept the garrote around Jack's neck, grimacing as the boy's struggles slowly subsided. Seconds later, Jack Romano died face down in the gravel of his backyard. As the killer stood above the body, he heard the voice of the boy's mother came across the yard.
~~~

"Jack, don't forget to put the lids on tight. We don't want the animals to get into the trash," she called out. Metal pans clanged as the mother continued her work. She didn't see the killer quickly leave back along the alley.

On the outskirts of Oyster City, the gray Hudson pulled over to a nearly deserted diner. The killer in the gray trench coat went to the back of the room where the phone booth stood. He closed the door and dialed a local number after putting in a nickel. The ringing stopped when someone picked up the handset. The killer heard breathing.

"Another job finished," he mumbled.

There was a click as the line went dead. The man looked at the phone and shook his head. After he left the booth, the killer sat down at the counter. He ordered a cup of coffee. As he lit a cigarette, the killer thought back to his phone call. He swore that heard an uncanny hollow laugh reach him just before his receiver went silent.

~~~

Officer Larry Lee yawned as he turned his police cruiser onto the old coast road leading to the abandoned wharves and the Chesapeake Bay. New to the force, he was still trying to get used to the graveyard shift. Driving past the deserted gas station at the corner of Andras Lane, the policeman noticed the large Packard parked at an odd angle by the edge of the dark building. The policeman overlooked the sight at first. He stopped at the intersection, then glanced over at the car again.

An expensive car next to a closed business didn't make sense!

He drove on, then decided to investigate. By the time he turned his large vehicle around on the narrow highway; he had noticed the lights on the rear of the Packard come on. When the police cruiser reached the small, gravel parking lot of the garage, the suspicious vehicle suddenly sped away. The car turned on to Andras Lane. Whipping his police cruiser around, the policeman started after the Packard.

As he passed came close to the building, a dark figure stumbled out into the headlights in front of him. Unable to stop in time, the police car struck the person. Lee heard the sickening thud, and he glimpsed the dark figure flip over his hood as he slammed on the brakes.

Jumping out of his car, Lee found the body outlined in the beam of his headlights. While the dead man lay on his side, the policeman noticed the open eyes staring at him. Lee walked over to the body, purposely avoiding looking at the eyes. When he crouched to verify what he already knew, Lee cursed under his breath.

How in the hell am I going to explain this?

The dead man had on a black uniform. When the cop reached into the man's jacket, he grimaced from the smell. His touch caused the body to roll over on its belly. The gleaming golden handle of a dagger embedded in the man's back came into sight.
~~~

"What in the hell…" the cop rose from his crouch. Immediately, Lee ran back to the car to call police dispatch.

Lieutenant Montgomery Sirk arrived at the murder scene about thirty minutes later. The ambulance had already arrived. Men in their white uniforms were leaning against their vehicle, smoking cigarettes while they chatted with Officer Lee. The cop quickly moved away to join the detective as he slid out of his car.

"Alright, what the hell is going on?" Sirk asked as he walked over to the body, now covered by a white sheet from the ambulance. The police cruiser lights continued to light up the area.

Lee explained what had happened while trying to downplay his role. Instead, he pointed out the dagger in the dead man's back. Sirk bent over and pulled back the sheet to look over the body. His perpetually grumpy face remained somber, but he wrinkled his bulbous nose at the smell coming from the corpse. The dagger remained in the body.

"Hand me your handkerchief," Sirk ordered Lee. He took the cloth the officer handed him and covered his hand before he pulled out the murder weapon. A whistle escaped from one of the ambulance attendants, who looked on.

"You got that right," the detective agreed as he looked over the jewel-encrusted handle.

"Alright Lee, run me through this again slowly," Sirk told him as he held on to the weapon.

"As I drove through the lot, I didn't see him until he came running from that side of the building," Lee pointed toward the side of the garage.

"Hmmm," the detective murmured as he waved Lee to follow him.

For the next few minutes, the two men scanned the area for additional clues using Lee's flashlight. All they found were a few barely visible footprints and a tire track which might have come from the Packard.

"Well, it looks like this tramp got it right when you showed up," the detective concluded. "Probably scared the murderer off when you turned around." Sirk pushed back his fedora and scratched his head thoughtfully.

"I don't get why someone killed this beggar with such a fancy knife. Hell, damn thing's worth more than the car you saw," he told Lee.

"Maybe the dead man stole it, and the killer wanted it back?" The patrolman offered.

"Yeah, that's a possibility, I guess. Alright, I've got a special assignment for you. You keep the murder weapon wrapped up while you go back to headquarters," Sirk ordered. "I want that evidence locked up in the evidence room. Don't go showing it around and make sure the lab guys to go over it for prints."

Officer Lee dubiously nodded as he accepted the bloody rag.

"What about my handkerchief? It cost my wife 45 cents!"

"You're taking one for the team," Sirk told him with a grin. "Welcome to the big leagues."

When he arrived back at the police headquarters, Lee was still trying to determine how to approach his wife about the loss of his handkerchief. His wife was small, but she had a temper. Mrs. Lee was also frugal and not happy with his choice of professions since Lee returned from his stint in the Navy during the war.

No, I'll hear about the loss of the damn handkerchief for a while.

Lee sighed as he walked in the quiet hallway to the evidence room. Near the door, he saw Detective Arizona Charlie Campbell coming down the hall toward him. The patrolman instantly recognized the big man with his bowler hat perched on his head.

"I heard you found a corpse," Arizona said. "What'd you and Sirk come up with?"

"It was pretty strange," the policeman replied as he gave him a quick recap. He unwrapped the weapon for the detective to inspect.

"Found this fancy knife stuck in the victim's back. The guy came out of the shadows when I was trying to catch up with this Packard that I noticed by the garage," he explained. "Sirk thinks the victim must have been a hobo. He told me to have this thing checked for fingerprints."

Arizona held the weapon using the blood-stained cloth and examined it.

"Yeah, those might be genuine diamonds and rubies in that handle."

He gave an admiring whistle as he handed the weapon back.

"Make sure it doesn't get lost in the evidence room. Expensive stuff can walk away. You say the corpse was a hobo?"

"I guess so. The man wasn't carrying any ID," the patrolman told Arizona with a shrug.

"I don't remember anything about a missing guy that fits his description. He had a scraggly beard, and he stunk to high heaven. It was funny since the clothes he wore were in good shape. I haven't smelled anything that bad since going into those rotten POW camps in the Philippines."

The detective was walking away, but stopped.

"What do you mean about the clothes?"

"Well, the tramp had on a butler uniform that looked in good shape. Well, most of it anyway. He ripped up his coat pretty bad. I guess he ran through thorn bushes, trying to get away from the murderer."

Lee paused.

"You think that he could have swiped the clothes from one of those rich estates up along Andras Lane?"

"You mean you found him at the gas station there?" Arizona's voice perked up as he asked.

"Yeah, that's the place," Lee agreed. "I noticed a Packard stopped at that garage, so I figured they had a breakdown. When I finally got turned around, the car was hurrying away. I couldn't make out who was in the vehicle."

Arizona scowled.

"You sure it was a Packard?

"Yeah, I'm pretty sure. It was one of those big fancy jobs with the wraparound grille. I couldn't figure out the color or get the license number," the patrolman told him as he unlocked the evidence room door.

"Tramps don't go around in expensive cars or get murdered with jewel-encrusted daggers," Arizona grumbled to himself. He watched Lee take the weapon to the open box on the counter. The policeman closed the lid and locked the box.

"Let me have the key," the detective ordered Lee. "I'll make sure the lab boys check it for prints first thing in the morning."

The policeman looked at the key as he handed over.

"Are you taking charge of this case now?" Lee asked as he noticed the detective's troubled expression as the lieutenant put the key in his coat pocket. Arizona didn't reply. He pulled off his bowler hat and wiped his forehead as he hurried along the hallway toward the stairway.

~~~

A Packard came to a stop at the drive leading through the gates of the Andras estate. The driver, his face covered by the mask of the High Priest, shakily pulled the hand brake before he killed the engine. He looked over at his companion.

"What are we going to tell them?"

"He's dead," the man behind the mask of Judgment replied. "That's the truth. You're the one who left the dagger in him."

"Yes, but you let him escape in the first place," the driver replied. "What you think Andras will do?"

Phillip Smyth shrugged.

"Whatever he feels like doing. It's Andras in the body of my brother. I can't influence him."

Henry La Spina remained quiet for a moment.

"That could mean both of us will suffer. Phillip, you and I have known each other for years."

He paused as the air between them hung heavy.

"The Shadows aren't the same anymore," the bishop finally stated. "We've debased ourselves to where all we do is amuse Andras. We're no longer human, just animals who must follow their master. Whatever idea comes to mind, we must accept it like his lapdogs. My wife…" He went quiet.

"Your wife isn't any different from the rest of us," Phillip's voice hardened. "You had us kill your first wife for Andras."

"It was revenge," La Spina stated flatly. "She was not worthy of standing with us."

"We all know that. I used my ex-wife as a sacrifice so she could no longer endanger the Shadows."
~~~

The bishop glanced over.

"It was revenge as well," he insisted while he removed his mask. "Greye and Maria were so much alike that we used the Shadows to get rid of them from our lives."

Silence filled the car.

After a deep breath, Phillip nodded.

"You're right. You and I think the same. We know that a blood sacrifice helps to eliminate the undesirables in our midst. Andras enjoys only blood and pain."

"And commanding that we abuse and rape each other for his entertainment. We're nothing more than servants. He used Hopely to make sure we stayed in our place. It won't be long before we end up like that damn butler," La Spina complained.

"Careful about what you say," his friend warned. "Andras will do more than rape you next time."

"Tell me the truth. Do you like how he runs the group?"

Phillip glanced over and took off his mask.

"No, you and I both know the new members are not worthy of joining the Shadows." He sighed. "I've seen Andras. He knows every weakness we have."

Silence filled the Packard as each man looked at the mansion.

"I think we purge our mind of the lost dagger," Phillip suggested. "We killed the butler when a policeman showed up, which is the truth. You and I can recover the dagger without our master's knowledge."

"It's risky," Henry reminded him.

"Do you want Andras to use us to please him like a whore again? Just stick to the truth and forget the dagger. He won't ask about it," Phillip insisted as he opened the car door.

"We brought forth a demon from Hell, and now we must live with the consequences!"

The bishop opened his door.

"This is not the deal that our ancestors gave Andras."

~~~

Ray Irish walked into the dive bar where his ex-boss, J. Allan Dunn, insisted they meet. Only a couple hours before, the shamus arrived at his office, where the ringing phone greeted him. After spending several weeks in New York, he briefly considered letting the phone ring. However, his lack of funds forced the private detective to pick up the handset.

Dunn's squeaky voice insisted that he had some information that Irish needed to know. Despite his reservations, Irish went to the bar before he could unpack from his trip. He guessed he owed the guy a conversation. After all, it was Dunn who put Irish into the whole shamus racket. J. Allan Dunn was part of
~~~

the stinking, corrupt organization running the city, but Ray got along with the guy.

After several drinks and a couple of hours, J. Allan failed to convince Ray about his half-baked ideas regarding the changes going on at City Hall. As Director of Public Works, he worked for Mayor Horace Hopely and took care of all construction and sanitation projects. But that didn't stop J. Allan from adding fees and kickbacks to pad his bank account. Of course, that was after Dunn sent some of the graft into Mayor Hopely's bank account first.

Married to Hopely's cousin, J. Allan held a minor position within the family structure which he tried to use whenever it suited him. Dunn also firmly believed the mayor was in danger, which it kept repeating to Irish. Inside forces threatened to knock everyone off their gravy cart of corruption. While the idea might carry some water at first, Dunn's clue jumped into fantasyland when he explained his reasons.

"I'm telling you, there's a major power play going on from Peter Smyth. He's taking over the mayor's office," Dunn told him as he glanced around nervously. The thin man was a walking jitterbug.

"Are you telling me that our district attorney controls the mayor? Come on, unless he's got something over Hopely, there's no way that blowhard mayor is letting Smyth run the show," Irish told him.

"I know it sounds crazy. But you've been out of town according to what Cat tells me. You wouldn't know about it," the director replied.

"I was in New York for a few weeks," Ray said. "Nothing around this city changes that much."

"You don't know what Horace is doing. It's never in the papers, and none of it is good," Dunn complained. "I mean, Hopely put Phillip Smyth in charge of a new department that we all report to now. You know he's the DA's brother," he gave an exasperated sigh.

"That means Phillip and Peter know about everything going on."

"Let me guess? You're worried that the district attorney will now start hauling grafters off to jail. I don't think you need to worry that they're coming after you. Peter Smyth strikes me as a ruthless SOB who's just as dirty as everyone else in this city. Could be that Phillip wants to play in the game now. It sounds like the mayor just set things up for him. You told me all the old families in this place stay tight as fleas."

The thin man slammed down his drink, spilling part of his whiskey on the counter. Then he glanced around sheepishly.

"Irish, I tell you something is wrong. Maybe I can't put it into words, but I know it. Feel it in my bones," he assured him. "There's one more thing!"

He stopped and cast his gaze around the room. The few customers were busy wallowing in their drinks, paying no attention to the two men conversing at the bar.

"No one has seen Maria Smyth and her mom, Betty, for over a month." He leaned forward to whisper. "I'll bet you didn't know that Betty Andras ran this town. She was a strange bird that dressed like a gypsy, but she had her hands on everything involved with politics. Mrs. Andras ran the whole thing from her house. I saw her order Mayor Hopely around like he was her butler. Now, no one's seen her. I checked, and her servants aren't around either." He grew quiet, glancing around.

"I saw Peter Smyth driving to the Andras House. I think he's moved in there."

Ray grunted at the news.

"I don't know about this old lady, but Maria and Phillip Smyth deserve a lot worse after what they did to Orella," he told Dunn. "I think your imagination is running wild. That bitch Maria hightailed it out of town when she lost that Singsing ring. I bet Phillip kicked her ass out the door after cops started showing up at the estate. He couldn't afford the publicity," Ray assured him.

"She probably convinced her mother to go with her. Hell, they're rich. They took the servants along with them."

"No, my wife would have heard about Maria's trip. She told me that nobody knows where she's might be. Maria Andras would not leave town without a lot of fanfare," Dunn insisted.

"I swear that something is wrong up at the Andras House."

Irish frowned at the thought. Dunn had a point. Maria liked the attention. She thrived on it. He tipped back the last of his drink.

"Dunn, you need to get another hobby. Even if something is going on, what do you want me to do about it? Peter Smyth still dreams about putting me behind bars. I'm not running up to say hello to the Andras or any of those families. You're stuck with whatever Hopely is doing."

The thin man frowned and downed his whiskey.

"I suppose you're right. But it doesn't make it any better." He agreed while sliding the glass tumbler between his hands.

"By the way, how's Catherine doing? She's not been returning my phone calls." He glanced over at Irish. "She's my daughter, and I would like us to go back to something we used to have. I don't guess I blame her."

"She's fine," Ray replied. "I guess that she's still learning to handle all the change since you explained you're her father. It's going to take some time, I suspect."

Dunn looked down at his tumbler.

"Thanks for the encouragement, even if it's a lie. I'll see you later."

The man rose from his chair.

Not long after Dunn left him, Irish stepped out into the night. A fog quickly enveloped him as it rolled through Oyster City. It was a fall of fog and mist. The shamus took Fleet Street on his walk back to his combined office and home. The waves of mist saturated his trench coat and fedora, leaving Irish to wish that he'd driven to the bar. But he had the car in the shop again. It was just another problem, which went along with the random thoughts that swirled around his head along with too many glasses of whiskey.

Taking a deep breath, he tried to clear his head as he took the narrow footpath to the bridge. He kept thinking about what Dunn told him. Something in the back of his mind tugged at him. It was like an old memory from childhood, something so familiar yet lost over the winds of time and distance. Then, a fleeting image of a pretty woman came to him again. The presence of Greye La Spina returned. He always felt her ghost when he got a few too many drinks in him. Her spirit continued to remind him he still had not solved her murder. Greye was never subtle when she lived and, most certainly, not as a ghost in his head.

The menacing stone entrance to the pedestrian bridge came up faster than he expected. The stone assembly looked like a gun turret from an old fort. But the look was deceiving, since the complete structure was only a few years old. The city built the bridge during the war to help the defense workers reach the manufacturing plants on the outskirts. However, the war economy had turned bust for Oyster City, leaving Ray on a lonely path.

He scanned the thick fog around him. A firm belief swept over him that someone was following him. He felt it in his bones, but when he slowed, no sounds of footsteps came to him. Continued glances over his shoulder revealed nothing, either. He glanced back again just before he took the metal stairs to the bridge.

Hell, anyone could follow me in this pea soup!

Irish had reason to remain on his toes. Returning from a trip to New York, he had just heard about a string of random murders occurring throughout the state. Ray knew a crazy cult remained hidden in the shadows of the city. He'd seen their strange masks and costumes in the shadows of alleys and windows. Irish suspected something sinister remained behind the obscure figures. However, they remained nothing more than people hiding behind their costumes. Still, when he saw them in his dreams, Irish started to believe their menace had something to do with the strange killings in Oyster City. While he joked about the figures as ghosts, Pappy remained convinced they were an omen. His friend believed the masked figures carried on a tradition from a dark chapter in the city's history.

Pappy also says his dead wife's ghost still lives with him.

Stepping across the bridge, Irish couldn't see the Murphy River and the railroad tracks below. It was well past eleven o'clock and the thick fog wrapped through the open structure with a swirling gray mist. Familiar landmarks were nowhere in sight. Only the sound of his footsteps carried with him as he crossed. As he tugged down on his fedora, the shamus tried to avoid focusing on the shadows near the edge of the bridge.

Damn fool, your imagination is playing tricks on you!

He focused on the underlying sense of peace in the stillness. It was about the only time he felt alone in downtown Oyster City. Everything around him looked muted and gray. There were no bright neon lights and no constant rumbling noise of trains below. Only a string of dim lights coming from above showed him the way. The city seemed to have gone to bed in this swirling cloud. Only the sound of his leather soles on the wood created the slight echo as he started across. It was a peacefulness that couldn't last.

Nearly halfway across the bridge, he saw movement in front of him. At first, it looked like shadows moving through the mist. A pale face of a woman in white momentarily came into focus and then disappeared amid the swirling haze. Irish thought he heard heavy footsteps, but the sound stopped. He slowed his pace, concerned about who might wait for him. Ray swore he heard persistent whispers coming through the fog. He took a few more steps, trying to figure out what was ahead.

Refusing to move as the whispers ceased, he waited. Finally, Irish forced himself forward. He didn't see anything at first. Movement caught his eye. Ahead and above him, the flutter of a gray pant leg moved. A woman perched on the parapet came into view before the outline disappeared again. Immediately, Irish began running toward the woman.

People didn't climb upon bridge parapets to get a better view, especially not on a night like this.

Irish heard a distant sound, like footsteps moving away. With a knot filling his stomach, he quickly covered the remaining distance. However, his focus remained on the figure that looking down into the nothingness below.

She screamed when he grabbed her pant leg. The woman tumbled forward, her arms flailing to grab at the empty sky. The woman caught hold of a steel beam next to her as Irish grabbed her leg. He tugged back with all his weight, and she lost her wet grip on the steel. The woman landed on top of him, sending them both to the wooden deck of the bridge.

Ray cursed loudly, using most of his learned profanities when she rolled across his leg.

"What the hell are you doing?" Irish barked after he automatically pushed her away. He retrieved his fedora next to him and stuffed it on top of his head.

Gingerly, he rose while trying to ignore the pain in his leg. The woman sat up, holding her elbow. She whimpered softly, talking to herself.

Ray watched her for a moment.

"Are you hurt?" he asked.

The woman still whispered, appearing not to hear his question.

"Lady, I asked if you alright?" Irish got louder.

Great, a drunk.

Finally, he reached down and took her by the arm.

"Come on, let's go," he growled as he pulled her to her feet.

She was taller than he expected. Her waxen face had a red splotch high on one cheek. Dull eyes searched his face, trying to comprehend who stood before her.

"They couldn't make me do it," she told him.

Her reaction convinced him she was drunk.

"Hey, you two, what's going on?" A voice came out of the fog. "What are you doing on that beam?"

A patrolman came into view out of the mist. He had a tight grip on his nightstick.

Irish turned to him.

"It's my—my girl," he sputtered out. "She was looking over the edge and got dizzy."

"Easy now," the cop said. "My gray hairs don't mean that my eyes couldn't see that the girl was up on that parapet. She was going to jump, wasn't she?"

"No, she was just trying to get a better view, and she got nervous," Ray lied. "Isn't that right?"

He put his arm around the woman, who remained in a trance. Slowly, she nodded in agreement.

"Listen, it's late. Can you give us a break?" Irish asked. "You don't want to haul us in for a bunch of paperwork."

"Let's see some identification," the cop ordered, and Irish dug out his wallet.

"Maybe I understand. I got a nervous wife too," the policeman said, then pointed the flashlight beam on Ray's shamus card and his concealed weapons permit.

"Well," he said, "if it isn't the famous Ray Irish. Since when does a shamus ask for a cop for a break, unless he's in the middle of something that smells like trouble?"

The policeman flashed the beam of light in her face again. She held up her hand.

"What's your name?" He asked.

"Florence Smith," she mumbled out, then glanced over at Irish. "I'm—I'm here on vacation," the woman added hastily. "I don't have my purse with me."

"Yeah, I'm sure. Everyone comes to Oyster City for vacation," the cop replied as he stared at her.

His broad face slowly dropped the suspicion.

"Are you drunk?" he asked.

The woman shook her head, refusing to look him in the eye. The cop's expression changed as he glanced at Irish.

"Alright, take your girlfriend home and no more bars. Maybe I didn't see anything with the fog and all. But I don't want to see either of you around here again."

"We're leaving right now," Irish agreed. "Thanks!"

Irish steered Florence toward the end of the bridge. The woman stumbled after a couple of steps. She held on to his arm for support. He noticed how she moved carefully, almost rigidly. He thought she was expecting something to jump out of the fog.

They remained quiet. Irish kept glancing at her, thinking about her suicide attempt. He had little patience for such thinking.

I saw too damn many good kids screaming to live!

They came to the end of the bridge, which led down to the sidewalk. The woman paused, then gingerly went down the metal steps. As they started down along the trail, Ray noticed that a car's engine had started. He glanced into the fog, but he couldn't see the vehicle in the distance. The policeman's whistling and heavy footsteps slowly faded away when he took the other path after leaving the bridge.

Florence pushed away from Irish after she tripped while stepping down off the curb.

"You drunken fool. Suicide is for cowards," Ray said gruffly.

"I'm not drunk!" she insisted. "They didn't get me off the bridge. Just leave me alone. You don't need to worry about me."

"You heard the cop. I'll find you a cab. You go home and sleep it off."

The shamus took her by the elbow. Florence stopped and pulled away from him.

"You son of a bitch, you don't know anything," she lashed out. "I suppose you didn't see the three people right there? They were telling me to jump or they would push me off the bridge?"

She turned away. Ray hesitated while he watched her hurrying toward the road. Despite the internal warnings going off in his head, Irish caught up with her and grabbed her arm. She grimaced when he stopped her.

"Hold up, sister, and calm down. I might have heard footsteps in the fog, but I didn't see anyone. The policeman came from the same direction as I did. He didn't see anything; otherwise, he'd have said something. It still doesn't explain why you were trying to take a nosedive into the river."

Florence tried to break free, but his grip was firm. Pain filled her face, and she quit resisting. She looked away and then dropped her head.

"Just leave me alone," her voice trembled with resignation. "They'll find me and kill me anyway."

Irish stood there in quiet confusion after he released her. He couldn't figure out her game. Maybe she was drunk and nuts. But he recognized the look of despair on her face. He also recalled the footsteps near them on the bridge. Ray took a deep breath.

"Listen, I'm hungry. Let's find a diner. Some food will sober you up."

"Damn it, I told you I'm not drunk," she lashed out again. "They gave me a pill."

"Alright, they gave you a pill," he agreed hastily. "But you and I need to leave. That cop will come back this way to make sure we're not hanging around."

Ray gently took her by the arm.

"Come on, let's talk."

Halfheartedly, she followed his lead. After a few steps, she glanced at him.

"Are you really a private detective?"

There was a tinge of desperation in the woman's question.

"You heard the man. I don't go around lying to cops for the most part." The shamus gave her a forced grin. "Now, let's find a taxi."

Thirty minutes later, they were sitting inside *Frank's,* the diner next door to his office building. Irish had difficulty trying to decide about the woman. After their coffee arrived, Irish spent the first few minutes trying to get her sober enough to make sense while they waited on their food.

He recognized she was a troubled married woman. Her clothes told him she had money. She wore gray suit pants and a yellow silk blouse. He'd seen clothes like that in a store window on Broadway Street. The store was too rich for his pay. However, her case might be a winning combination for a private detective with few clients.

Then again, maybe she's crazy enough to put a slug into me.

In the fluorescent light, Ray watched her manner. He liked what he saw across from him at the table. While not a stunner, the woman in front of him wore her brown hair short and her blue eyes had an earnest quality. Her round face showed the strain of her worry. Florence sported a diamond ring on her left-hand ring finger. The clothes were expensive and smart looking, but you couldn't tell from how crumpled and wrinkled they were. He suspected she had worn them for several days.

However, Ray also noticed a bruise on her right temple above the red mark he saw earlier. The injury appeared recent. He guessed someone struck her with a fist.

"Drink the coffee; it'll help. What brings you to Oyster City? The cop knew you were lying. Most people don't show up for a vacation," he said. "This place is not on the way to anywhere."

"Yes, it was a lie," she agreed, then hesitated.

"Mr. Irish, I swear I didn't have any drinks. People took me to that bridge. They are hunting for me, and I'm desperate."

"Well, let's start with the basics. Call me Ray. Now, I've already noticed that you're married. However, you haven't mentioned your husband."

Her eyes dropped at the statement.

"Yes, well—my husband is a marketing executive, so he spends a lot of time on the road," she explained.

"Alright, I'll let it go for now. Let's start with your real name."

Irish waited until the waitress placed their meals on the table. After she left, Florence remained quiet. Her eyes kept glancing at the windows looking out over the quiet street. He picked at his food while she silently debated.

"I'm not hungry," she finally told him. "Whatever they gave me is wearing off."

"Then, let's get to the truth. Remember, I'm a shamus. I can't help you unless you let me. Why don't you consider yourself as my client? That means that I must keep my trap shut if you're worried about the wrong things coming out."

She stared at him for a long moment.

"Mr. Irish, I don't have much money," the woman sighed. "What I mean by that is my husband gives me an allowance to run the house. I won't be able to pay you much."

"You tell me you're desperate. I believe you. You said you're alone despite having a husband," he told her.

"I see a mark on your face, which tells me someone struck you recently. We can talk, and if I can help, we'll go from there. Is that fair enough?"

Her eyes widened, and the woman placed her hand on her face, rubbing the bruised area. After a brief pause, she finally nodded.

"My name is Florence Rice. What I'm going to say will sound crazy," she warned him. "But I swear to God that it's the truth." Florence paused again.

"There were three people who took me to that bridge. They wanted me to kill myself or make it look like a suicide."

"Hold on here," Irish interjected. "Start with giving me some background here."

Hurt and pain filled her eyes, and he thought she might break down. Instead, the woman took a deep breath.

"It starts with the leader of those hyenas who drove me to the bridge. Dr. Elmer Horne is a psychologist who runs the Horne Clinic," she said as her voice trembled.

"You mean that place just outside of town?" He interrupted. She nodded. He heard that the exclusive clinic held the loonies from wealthy families.

"You see, I got away from him. But his associates found me before I could get to the phone. I was going to call my husband, my friends..." She stopped and stared at her clasped hands.

There were tears in her eyes when she looked at him again.

"You have to understand. A few months back, Horne pressured me to sign the papers," Florence stated.

"What a minute. You're all over the place with your story. Slow down. What papers?"

There was frustration in Ray's question.

"Commitment papers," the woman stopped and composed herself after taking a deep breath.

"Dr. Horne made me commit my mother to his clinic." She stopped again.

"Well, that's not exactly the truth. Jim, that's my husband, pressured me to sign the papers as well."

"Let me try to explain. When my mother went into the clinic several months ago, I thought I was helping her. But it was the start of this whole nightmare. Two weeks ago, the doctors called me to tell me that my mother injured herself from a fall. They asked me to come to the clinic. My husband and I rushed down to Oyster City to see her."

Florence stopped suddenly. He waited while she pushed back her plate.

"When I went inside, the nurse wouldn't let me see her. They took Jim into another room, and the staff wouldn't let me leave. I waited in a room for a while, then Horne came inside and claimed I was a threat to the community. He had his staff lock me inside a room. That is why I had to escape today."

Irish nearly spit out his eggs at the information. The woman across from him escaped from a mental institution.

She must be stark, raving mad!

He briefly glanced at an empty phone booth at the back of the diner. Florence didn't say anything, but she recognized his sudden change when she looked up.

While Ray took a drink of coffee to get down his food, he slowly dropped his concern. There was something in her desperate and frightened demeanor, along with the pained expressions in her eyes, that told him she wasn't a nut job. He'd seen mental cases from the ravages of war. She didn't match up to his experiences. Plus, Ray certainly remembered the sound of other people on the bridge. He looked around.

"Alright, this place is too public for our conversation. We'll go to my office next door so that we can talk in private." He pulled out his wallet and laid the money on the table. "Besides, we'll have a drink if you're interested."

Florence smiled a little, as if she wasn't used to it. She slid out of the booth and went toward the door. She didn't seem to notice that the diner had no other customers. A minute later, they climbed the stairs to his office.

"You don't believe what I'm telling you," Florence told him while he held the door open for her. He flipped on the light switch and pointed her to a chair by his desk.

"You could have called the police from the diner," she said as she sat in the chair.

"I believe you," Ray lied with his best poker face.

"You're not a good liar." Then the woman took a deep breath. Her body slumped in the chair.

"It doesn't matter, I guess. I'm out of ideas, Mr. Irish. I just need someone to listen to me. Then you can send for the police."

"The police aren't always the best option," he told her. "You said you escaped. Where's your husband?"

"I don't know. Still waiting at home, I guess. He never returned to the clinic as far as I know."

She kept fiddling with her wedding ring as she spoke.

"Horne told me that Jim signed the commitment papers. I called him a liar. I wouldn't believe it."

She paused, looking at her ring.

"I still don't," she mumbled.

Ray opened the desk drawer and pulled out a bottle of Irish whiskey and two tumblers.

"Alright, let's start this again. Why don't you just lay your whole story out for me from the beginning?"

Irish filled the glasses halfway and slid over one to the woman. She picked it up and took a small sip.

"Start with your mother," he told her with a smile. "What's going on with her?"

The woman choked on the drink.

"I don't drink much," she apologized. After a moment, she opened up.

"About six months ago, my mother's neighbors complained about some of my mother's antics, which were getting worse. She lives in Annapolis alone, you see."

"What antics?" he asked after downing the glass. He poured another one. Irish figured he needed a couple more of them tonight.

"After my dad passed away several years ago, mother grew erratic," she told him. "Nothing dangerous, mind you, just forgetful. She'd forget simple things like her address or her way home. One time, she got on a bus and ended up in front of the capital. The neighbors kept an eye on her, but I should have been there."

There was bitterness in her tone. Irish guessed the husband had something to do with it.

"What happened?"

"Well, everything got quiet for a while. I would call mom's house, and she wasn't home, or she was too busy to talk. Then, out of the blue, I got a wire telling me she was seeing a doctor named Elmer Horne. I have no idea how that happened. I thought he was just a family physician. Then I learned he was treating her as a therapist of some sort. Anyway, Horne suggested that my mother meet someone named Dr. Wolfe. I guess he runs the asylum near where my mother lives."

Dr. Wolfe was a name Ray recognized, and he sat up in his chair.

"I know the guy. What happened next?"

"My husband and I went to visit her at her house several weeks after meeting with Horne. I almost didn't recognize her," Florence said after placing the tumbler down on the desk.

"Mom was a different person, mumbling to herself and afraid of everything. She did not know who I was, and she attacked me. You must understand, her behavior worried me, Mr. Irish. After that happened, Dr. Horne convinced us to put my mother into his private clinic. I only found out later that Horne has a partnership with Dr. Wolfe. I was trying to make sure that my mother wouldn't hurt herself. You have to believe me."

"What about your husband? Why didn't he help you straighten this out?" Irish asked.

"Jim seemed supportive. As my mother got worse, he started to side with the doctors," she explained. "I told him we should take her to our home, and I would look after her. Well, we had a large fight about the idea. Eventually, I signed the forms to have her committed."

"There's something I don't get. Why are you so involved? Doesn't your mother have a lawyer?" he wondered aloud.

She paused as the question struck her.

"She has a lawyer, of course. However, I have power of attorney over her estate. She set that up after my father died." The woman said.

"Mom wasn't able to handle the investments and such. My family owns quite a bit of real estate in Baltimore. You know buildings and such."

"Your husband pressured you to get your mother into the clinic rather than having her stay with you. I take it you know why?"

Irish hoped she wasn't too naïve about her husband.

"Jim is always home late because of his clients. He told me I couldn't take care of my mother and our household if she moved in with us. But I don't think that was the only reason," she admitted.

"Not that he'd admit to it, but I think her decline scared him. He never liked coming around my mother. At times, he didn't enjoy being around me, either."

The shamus remained quiet at the comment. Florence lowered her eyes to stare at the glass in her hands.

"Take me through how you ended up in Horne's clinic," Irish suggested.

"As I said, we came to the clinic to check on my mother. We stopped by the Duchy Motel. Joe decided we should stay for a few days. The first day, the nurse told me that my mother could not see me since she was on painkillers. That evening, after dinner, I remember feeling drowsy after Joe drove back to the hotel." She told him, then took another sip of whiskey. "When I woke the next morning, I discovered heavy stratches on my arms. My husband told me the hotel staff found me behind the building, near the trash bins. I was sleepwalking. I have to admit, it scared me."

"That's understandable. You are under a lot of stress." Irish smiled.

"Well, you don't understand. I suddenly had the same symptoms as my mother," she finally told him. "Joe mentioned he was afraid of me. He suggested we return home."

The shamus leaned forward in his chair.

"I see," he replied. "You understand your husband took you out to the clinic, and they wouldn't let you leave. It seems clear to me."

Florence thought about his observation, but she shook her head.

"No, I know it looks terrible for Jim, but I talked with Dr. Wolfe. He said that my problems came from my mother's troubles. The doctor told me that all I needed was some rest. He told me it would only be a few days. Then I saw the bars on the windows." Her reply came with a tone of detached disbelief.

"To be honest, I like your husband less and less," Irish confided.

The look in the woman's eyes told him she agreed, although she wouldn't admit it aloud. Florence noticed the detective's face turn to a scowl when she mentioned the asylum.

"Did you see your mother while you were in the clinic?" Irish asked.

"No! The staff kept telling me she was too ill. Then Horne insisted that my recovery required isolation. But they did nothing like treatment. I just sat in my room most of the day," she said before finishing the drink.

"You can't trust anyone," he pointed out. "That's why you gave the cop a false name. You suspect the police are looking for you."

"I wanted to go to the police, but they won't believe me any more than you do," she said. "The police would just ship me back to the clinic."

"There's one big difference," he replied. "I heard someone else on that bridge. That means there's truth in your story. Otherwise, it's a strange coincidence which I don't believe. Your answers to my next questions will convince me."

Florence's eyes showed hope for the first time.

"I'll answer anything you ask me," she declared.

"Alright, let's start with your escape," he told her. "How did you get out of there?"

"I didn't have a plan, really," Florence replied. "It just kind of happened. Every morning, they would give me a pill that made me barely able to function. In the evening, they locked me in my room. I don't remember much during the days, just a vague routine where they would take me to a courtyard with other patients. I noticed they only had a few nurses. It didn't matter since I think all of us were on drugs."

"One morning, I spit out my pill when the nurse turned away before escorting me. I just acted like I was on the drug. Most of the patients just stumbled around or sat in a chair and talked to themselves," she explained.

"At one point, I decided to find my mom. I snuck inside, but I never could find her room. I guess she might be on the next floor, which was locked. However, I discovered lockers where they stored the patient's clothes. That's where I found what I'm wearing. I rolled them up in a bag that had my last name on it."

"Smart girl," Ray told her with approval.

Her initial smile turned to a frown.

"Well, not really. They still caught me today," she confessed. "Anyway, I rolled up those clothes in a towel and hid them in my room. This morning, I decided to escape. It wasn't tough to get out of the buildings. The attendants were not watching me during the lunch period. I took the towel from my room and snuck out of the building. After I got away through a hole in the fence, I changed clothes and got to the road. I hitched a ride from a farmer. I was almost inside the motel when they found me. They caught me walking across the parking lot. I didn't even get to a phone to call anyone to help me."

"They probably guessed you would return to the only place you knew in Oyster City," Ray told her.

Florence looked down in embarrassment.

"It's alright. I would have done the same thing. You say there are three of them. Give me their names."

"It was Horne and his nurse, Velma Ohr. Also, that creep Sam was with us," she spat out. "I don't know his last name. He's a big brute who likes to hurt people. The creep kept coming into my room after the lights were out. He would come close to my bed and tell me nasty things he planned to do to me."

"Yeah, I get it; he's a son of a bitch," the shamus agreed. "Forget about him and tell me about how you got to the bridge."

"Horne was furious that I escaped," she explained. "It was already dark, and the fog was coming in when they drove me back. Sam insisted they should kill me when they got back to the clinic. Then Horne suddenly pulled off to a side road. They pulled me out of the car, and Horne ordered the nurse to hold me."

She paused, glancing away.

"That's when Sam beat me. I couldn't breathe. He kept punching me in my stomach until I begged them to stop."

Florence paused. After another sip, she took a deep breath. The drink helped as she retold her tale.

"They pushed me back in the car. He had the nurse try to shove a pill into my mouth, but I bit her finger. That's when Sam slapped me a few times. That must be how I got the bruise on my face."

Florence stopped, her head drooped, and Ray waited patiently.

"This time, the nurse forced the pill down my throat. I don't remember how long it took, but we got to that bridge. Sam helped me out onto the bridge and the whole thing felt like a dream. Horne kept whispering in my ear about how the pain would soon go away. I felt them pushing me along, and I could hear their voices urging me up on the railing."

Florence stopped, looking down at her glass.

"I don't know if I climbed, or they helped me. All I remember is Dr. Horne telling me I would no longer feel any pain. He kept telling me to step forward. That's why I was sure you saw them."

Ray stared at her for a long moment at the statement. Despite his initial suspicions, he found himself believing her. If she was lying, the woman was damn convincing.

"I told you that you wouldn't believe me," Florence stated with a resigned frown. She finished the rest of her drink and sat the tumbler on his desk. Then she stood and staggered. Florence caught herself by grabbing the desk's edge.

"I'm tipsy now," she confessed. "I'll be leaving now, Mr. Irish."

Ray rose from his chair and cut her off as she started for the office door.

"No, you've got no place to go. Instead, you're going to bed and sleep this nightmare off. You forget that you're my client," he insisted.

He directed her to his bedroom in the back room of his office.

"But you don't believe me. Why are you helping me?" Her suspicion was obvious, but she used his arm for support.

"Let's just say that I'm starting to believe you," he admitted.

He guided Florence to his unmade bed and turned on the lamp.

"One last thing. I want you to pull up your blouse," he ordered.

Florence's eyes widened in shock, and her face turned red. She took a deep breath and hesitated. Then Florence started to take off her blouse.

Ray shook his head.

"No, it's not like that. I just want you to lift your shirt so we can see your belly."

With a suspicious glance at him, the woman did as he told her. Ray moved her closer to the light. Florence looked down and noticed with surprise at the dark blue splotches covering her abdomen from the beating she took.

"I thought you moved around like you were in constant pain. Those bruises confirm your story. Don't you worry now; we're going to fix the bastards who did that to you. They deserve a world of hurt," he explained.

He carefully sat her on the edge of the bed. Florence looked up at him.

"Thank you!" She burst out, her shoulders shaking as she tried to hold back the tears.

Ray walked to the door. Holding his hand on the doorknob, he decided her husband was a fool or dirty bastard. He glanced back at his client.

"Don't thank me yet. You've never slept in that uncomfortable bed," Irish replied with a grin. "There's aspirin in the bathroom. Take a couple to help with the pain. I'll see you in the morning."

He closed the door and went back to his desk.

Gordon Brewer

Chapter 3: The Bishop's Wedding

Catherine Bennett showed up at Irish's office just after sunrise. As usual, she didn't bother to knock. Cat just opened the door and entered like she owned the place. In a way, she did since Cat set up his accommodations when Ray got started as a shamus. His on-and-off partner silently walked around the desk, coming up behind Ray's chair. Ray's head nodded as he leaned back, his feet propped upon on the windowsill. It was his normal position so he could look across the street at the *Beacon's* scrolling news banner.

Cat put her hands on his shoulders, and Ray jerked awake, nearly tipping out of his chair. He glared at the good-looking girl, who returned a bemused grin.

"Did you hear about the Boston Braves winning the championship?"

Ray smelled her perfume as she leaned over him to look out of the window at the scrolling ticker. He glanced over at her cleavage partially exposed through the blue blouse. His mental flash of her without the clothes came to mind, but he dismissed the idea. Cat continued to make it clear they were partners in business, not in bed.

"Yeah, it's easy to keep up with the news from here," he told her sourly as he pulled his sock-covered feet from the windowsill.

The chair loudly squeaked as he turned to face her.

"Since when do you follow baseball?"

Cat laughed and slid into the chair next to his desk. She placed her purse in her lap.

"Alright, smart ass, then answer this," she said. "Did you get my message about Henry La Spina?"

"Yeah, Pappy told me yesterday when I picked up the morning paper," he replied. "I take it you're going to show up at the wedding?"

"You bet," she told him as she took off her latest fashionable hat. Cat used her fingers to comb through her strawberry-blond hair. As usual, her blue eyes twinkled with excitement at the possibility of money.

"I've got a new Universal Mercury camera to try out. It's small enough that I won't look too obvious," Cat declared. "I figured you'd be interested in coming along."

"Yeah, a great way to waste my day. I'm betting neither of us is on anyone's invite lists for this party," Ray responded with a sigh.

"Come on, Cat. When you leave a message with Pappy, then show up like this. You want me to help with your scheme."

"Now, how can you think such a thing?" she told him airily with a broad smile.

Despite his gruffness, she knew he would help her.

"I figured if you came along, you could figure out how to get us inside. It's against my better judgment having you along, but you have a knack for getting into places. Plus, we can get some exclusive wedding photos."

"I get it," he replied. "You get paid, and I help provide you the way in."

Cat frowned.

"No, you're getting fifty percent. I told you I'm changing my ways," the woman insisted.

"I thought you believed me."

"Sorry, but it's been a long night. I remember the last time we went through this."

He bent down and picked up a shoe. He put it on as he continued.

"I don't want to be stuck holding the bag again."

"Don't be like that. I wasn't my fault that the guy had no money. You know that!" Cat reminded him. "You're just stubborn."

"He found enough cash to take you out on the town for a couple of weeks. You forget I hear things on the street as well," he replied with a glare.

Cat's smile turned into a surprised expression, which made him feel better.

I'm a detective, remember!

"Anyway, I've been true blue after I stopped dating Reginald," she quickly insisted.

Ray gave her a knowing smile, but he let it go. The shamus knew that Cat still considered every guy with a thick wallet to be her next conquest.

"Alright, I'll join you on this wedding," he said, to change the subject. "I want to see the show. I'm interested in Henry La Spina's actions. His bride must realize what happened to his last wife," Ray said bitterly.

He thought longingly about a cup of coffee as he tried to shake the sleep out of his head.

"Well, that's doubtful, since only you have this murder theory about Greye La Spina. The rest of the world knows that the bishop's wife died by accidental drowning," she told him after glancing at the closed bedroom door. Typically, Ray didn't keep it closed.

"Besides, she's marrying Henry, whose family carries a history of status and decorum for Oyster City." She used an upper-crust accent which sounded overly dramatic.

"I believe the new bride is some distant relation to the Andras family. She'll be the toast of the city, of course."

Yeah, exactly where you see yourself, Ray thought.

"It sounds like the bishop kept it close to his family friends this time," Ray observed coldly.

Cat nodded as she watched his jaw tightened. She wasn't going to convince him that Henry La Spina didn't kill Greye. Cat glanced again at the closed door. She was sure someone was in the other room.

Ray's bedroom opened slightly, and Florence stuck her head out of the door. She was wearing Ray's robe.

"I heard voices, and I got curious," Florence admitted.

Then, she saw Cat's glare, and she apologized while trying to retreat into the bedroom.

"Florence, it's ok. Come on in," Ray spoke up. He noticed Cat's scowl, and he had trouble suppressing his grin.

"This is Catherine. She's a photographer for the *Morning Beacon*. You might have seen their building across the street."

"Cat, meet my new client. Mrs. Rice has a problem that I'm trying to solve."

Ray quickly finished tying his other shoe and stood. He stepped around the desk next to Cat.

"Since I'm helping you, then I need a favor," he told her. "Florence has some people after her. Do you know of a place where she can hide out until we can get her problems worked out? It's just for a few days."

"What's going on?" Cat asked in a clipped tone.

"It's probably best not to know too much right now. Let's say the cops might have a wire out on Florence and she's in hiding. I need to talk with Arizona about the whole thing. Also, I'll need to get a lawyer involved pretty soon as well."

"That bad, huh?" she asked.

Cat looked over at Florence, who felt like the woman was appraising her value.

"Alright Ray, I've got a place in mind. You know Betty. She's out of town for a few days," she told him.

Cat recognized from Ray's blank look that he did not know who she was talking about.

"You know, Betty, the artist," she insisted. "You met her at Reginald's party? I'm watching her pet kitty, so your client can stay there."

"Yeah, I remember now. That thin gal who liked to blow smoke in a guy's face," he said with a frown.

He turned to Florence.

"Go get dressed, and Cat can drive you over," he told her.

"I didn't say I was her damn driver," Cat complained.

"You want my help with the wedding; then you'll do me this favor," he growled. "We still have some time before the wedding starts. I need to talk with Arizona. Then, you can complain to everyone for the next week about how much I'll owe you again."

"You're damned right I will," Cat fumed.

Florence glanced at the bickering partners before she walked back into the bedroom to dress.

Catherine drew close to Ray.

He waited for the comment.

"I guess you're back to married women," she observed coolly. "That didn't work out too well the last time."

"Stow it," he snapped. "Florence has been through hell and back. I discovered her last night on top of the pedestrian river bridge. Florence escaped from a damn head doctor and his cronies who beat the hell out of her. They nearly had her trying to jump from the bridge."

He gave her a quick recap of his case. Cat's eyes widened.

"Are you saying she escaped from an asylum? What the hell is wrong with you?"

She blurted out.

"Listen, I thought the same thing at first, but she's not crazy," he told her. "They put her and her mom into Horne's clinic out on the edge of town. My guess is they're interested in the old lady's estate. Here's what makes me even more suspicious about this place. It's partially owned by a shrink we both know and hate."

"Who?" Cat asked.

"Remember Dr. Wolfe? It seems he and Dr. Horne are partners," he explained. "Something is wrong there, and her husband might be involved somehow. That's what I'm going to figure it out."

"You believe this Dr. Horne and her husband might be involved with Wolfe? Wow, if she's not crazy, there might be a great story in this," she told him with growing excitement.

"I get the exclusive on this."

"Your generosity is showing again."

"Hey, it's a great idea. Joey at the *Beacon* is getting tons of notice since he started working on those murders that the crazy man is committing with a garrote," she told him. "His stories are picked up by AP and INS now with his name on the byline. That's big stuff for a reporter."

Despite the excitement in her manner, she suddenly went quiet, and she walked to the window. Ray missed the sorrow that crossed her face, but her change surprised him. He waited for a moment.

"Alright, I get what you're thinking," he agreed. "But you have to be nice to Florence."

Cat continued staring out of the window.

"What about her husband?" She finally asked quietly. "Why isn't this woman going back to him?"

"I told you that something wrong is there," Ray admitted. "When we talked last night, she tried to support him. Still, I don't think she trusts him anymore."

He went quiet as Florence came out of the bedroom in her disheveled clothes. She wore no makeup, but the woman carried herself with renewed confidence. Ray escorted her to the door.

"While Cat's driving you to this place, I'm going to talk with some friends and get the lowdown on those doctors," he told her. "I want you to keep inside that apartment and don't answer the door for anyone except Cat and myself. Here's a Lincoln to get you by until I get some news."

Ray slid the ten dollars into her hand.

"I'm the client, remember?"

Florence insisted as she tried to give the money back.

"You don't have your purse or any money. We'll settle up later," he stated firmly.

Outside the building, Cat led Florence to her gray Oldsmobile coupe parked at the curb. During part of the quiet drive, the photographer appeared lost in thought. Then she started glancing over at Florence.

"He's a good man," Florence spoke up.

"You mean Ray? Yeah, well, he's a sucker for a woman with a sob story," Cat replied.

"Yes, he admitted as much," Florence agreed and paused for a moment.

"He didn't tell me about you. I'm sorry, but I admit that I overheard some of your conversation in the other room. Do you work for him?"

"No, we're partners!" Cat snapped over the noise of the wind coming through her open window.

"Listen, there's no reason to stare daggers at me," Florence replied. "I just met Mr. Irish a few hours ago. He's the only person who believes me, let alone trying to help me."

"That's what your husband should do," Cat reminded her.

"Yes, you might think so. You can tell me about it the next time your husband lets you sit inside an insane asylum," Florence countered.

Cat went silent at the comment while her passenger looked out the side window. Florence pressed her fist to her lips, refusing to let the tears start. The stony silence filled the car until Cat turned her vehicle into a parking spot in front of the St. Mark building.

"Alright, you're in a tough spot, and you've convinced Ray to help you," Cat finally conceded. "Now, I'm helping him. That doesn't mean I'm sure about you."

"I'm not a lunatic," Florence stated flatly.

"Well, if you're involved with Wolfe, I'm not so sure," Cat told her as the car stopped. "But we'll find out soon enough."

Catherine got out of the car while her passenger slid out on the other side. They stepped to the sidewalk, and Cat stopped.

"Are you sure you don't want someone to contact your husband?" She asked Florence.

The woman shook her head and continued past Cat to enter the building. After following her, Cat took the lead toward the wide stairs. The building carried the Art déco style of ten years earlier.

"Betty will be back come Monday, so you'll need to be gone by then," Cat stated.

After a climb to the third floor, they stopped at the front of the door marked 3B. Cat fiddled with the door lock for a while until she finally unlocked the door.

"Seeing you didn't bring any luggage along, there's a dry cleaner across the street for your clothes and a store around the block for anything else. Irish is in the phone book, if you need to call him." Catherine said as she put the apartment key on the kitchen counter. She watched Florence as she looked over the room.

"While you're here, you can take care of Betty's cat."

Florence let the comment go as she followed her to the door.

"Thank you for your help."

"Yeah, you can thank Irish," Cat dismissed the gratitude. Instead, she glanced back at the woman. "For your sake, I hope you're not lying to him about your story. He can't take on a deadbeat client. He's had too many of them already."

"You know, a few weeks ago, your attitude might have intimidated me," Florence told her with a sigh. "But now, I think it's pathetic. I'm stronger than you."

Cat suddenly turned around at the comment. However, Florence continued.

"Listen, you might act like you're protecting Mr. Irish from me. But we both know that's not the truth. I overheard enough at his office to figure your game out, Missy. I know a woman who plays a similar game. You like to control and manipulate. You get away with it right now because you're young and pretty. But Ray's got you figured out. That bothers you."

"How dare you say that?" Cat blurted out.

"Listen, you do not know about my past. In my opinion, Irish doesn't deserve to put up with your guff," Florence told the woman with a thin smile as she shut the door.

She left a bewildered Cat standing in the hallway.

~~~

Irish called Lieutenant Arizona Charlie Campbell of the Oyster City Police Department as soon as Cat left with Florence. His friend was not pleased to hear from him.
~~~

"Damn it, do you want me to get fired? They can't see me on the same street as you right now," Arizona grunted out. "The district attorney made it clear to the police chief that he wants your head on a platter."

"Listen, I'm just offering to buy you breakfast," Ray told him. "Besides, if you play your cards right by me, I'll start sending Cat to bother you more."

There was a gruff laugh on the other end of the line.

"Alright, I'll take you up on that. I'll be at Vinnies since nobody can stand their coffee," Arizona replied, then hung up.

Ray arrived at the old greasy spoon by the docks about twenty minutes later. The big detective was already there. He sat in the back of a corner booth where he could watch people as they entered the building. Arizona had an unlit cigar clamped between his teeth, and his bowler hat sat perched at the end of the table. He unconsciously ran his hand through his sandy hair while his icy blue eyes followed the shamus to the table. When a fat waitress waddled over to get Ray's order, Arizona smiled and told her his breakfast was on his visitor. Then he ordered more toast.

"I see you didn't waste time," the shamus spoke after the waitress left. The cop's plate was nearly empty.

"Alright, Irish, what do you have up your sleeve? You don't buy me breakfast unless you want a favor," the cop reminded him.

"It's a favor for both of us," Ray assured him. "You remember Dr. Wolfe back at the asylum?"

"Yeah, I remember him alright. Damn shrink tried to get me fired," he replied. "I didn't tell you he called my boss about us at the asylum. He wasn't happy about my work to get the Romano kid out of his loony bin."

"Then here's some payback for you. Your favorite shrink has a tie in with another head shrink named Elmer Horne." Ray leaned back.

"Horne's the guy that runs the clinic on the outskirts of town. You might have seen a police report coming out about an escaped patient."

Arizona paused, waiting until the waitress finished refilling his coffee. He waited until she went behind the counter.

"Dispatch put out something early this morning about an escaped looney," the cop replied. "The wire said a real nut job they were transferring from Horne's clinic to the state asylum escaped."

"A woman escapes from a private clinic for the wealthy," Ray replied. His grin turned to a smirk. "Is she like another Ma Barker?"

"No, just a delusional wife who could hurt herself or others," Arizona explained, then stopped. "Alright, where is she?"

"I have no idea," the shamus replied. "But what if I told you that Horne tried to force her to commit suicide before they ran away when a flatfoot patrol came along?"

"Then, I would say you're as nuts as this woman," the cop replied. "I heard nothing like that. What the hell are you involved with now?"

"I'm not sure," Ray confessed. "I don't know much, but I'm clear on a couple of things. First, somebody beat the woman. Second, the woman was nearly at the breaking point when I met her. At first glance, I might have written her off like the report you saw. Then I found out her husband's not quite the supportive soul she married. Plus, let's add the fact that her husband got the old lady put in the same place before his wife. Would you be interested now?"

"No! You're connecting dots again. Probably means nothing, but you need to get paid," Arizona fired back.

"Hell, I always need to find money," Ray frowned. "But have you finished connecting the dots with that Dr. Wolfe and the Romano kid showing up at the state asylum? There's a devious rat somewhere in the mix. I'm sure this supposed crazy woman and her mom have money, and that's the reason for the whole thing, but I need to check things out. I'm going with that gut instinct you talk about."

"Right now, it feels like indigestion. It always happens when I'm hanging around you. Look, your suspicions won't mean anything if you don't turn this woman over to the police."

He paused, rubbing his chin.

"Maybe you're way off track here. Listen, I don't like Dr. Wolfe, but it's a long shot that he's involved in some scheme. From what I know, he's got too many political connections. Besides, he and Horne got the law on their side. If the woman's committed, it's up to the court to hammer it out about releasing her."

"That doesn't sound like the detective I know," Ray pointed out.

He grimaced after he sipped the bitter coffee.

"Yeah, that's because I'm on a short leash. The press might have forgotten about Detective Howard's murder, but the police chief hasn't. I'm about this far away from walking a beat again," he said as he held out his thumb and index finger, which were an inch apart.

"It's too bad," Ray replied. "He was a dirty cop involved in something. They shouldn't be hammering you about that."

"Well, it goes with the territory," the cop grumbled. "I'll give you a word of advice about this woman. If the Peter Smyth catches wind that you are involved with some crazy that's on the run; he'll jail you and get them to throw away the key."

"Alright, I hear the warning," Ray conceded. "I'll be a good boy. But I've got something even better for your stomach. Cat's got me pinched to help her get into Bishop La Spina's wedding."

"I won't be within ten blocks of you. I'm still partial to the idea of a pension," Arizona replied gruffly.

He sighed.

"Ray, you need to quit helping her schemes. It just gets you both in trouble. One of these days, she'll step into something that's going to get her hurt. Cat deserves better."

Irish went quiet for a moment.

He's worried about Cat hanging around me. That's a new one!

"Well, she's a stubborn girl, and you've seen how Cat ropes people into working for her," Ray finally replied. "I'll see what I can do."

He stared at his friend for a moment. He didn't see how the cop and Cat fit together.

Well, stranger things have happened.

"You do that. Just remember what I told you about Smyth," Arizona warned Irish.

An hour later, the shamus stood, leaning against Pappy's newsstand. He watched his friend, who greeted the morning rush of patrons. The newspaper was selling well, and his friend beamed a smile as his daily customers handed him a dime. A regular fixture at the corner of Main and Broadway, the thin black man with gray hair, overheard most of the news and rumors going on within Oyster City. He was also one of the few real friends that Ray counted on.

"Pappy, you're too cheerful this morning," he complained when the line of customers thinned out. "You must be sleeping better."

"No, I'm still getting those damn nightmares. But the money is nice. The murders and bank robberies will always bring in more business," Pappy replied. "With this serial killer running through the state, the *Beacon* and I are raking in the dough."

"Making money on death seems to be the going thing here in Oyster City," Ray agreed. "I stopped by because I needed information. Mariam Wolfe, he's the doctor who runs the state asylum up at the capital. You know who might have the dope about him?"

"Best check with a guy named Oscar Hewlett. He's the reporter who works for the *Sentinel* in Annapolis," his friend told him. "I remember Hewlett did a couple of articles about the asylum before Dr. Wolfe became head of the place. I guess it was quite a mess and Wolfe got appointed by the governor to clean the place up."

"He's a reformer?" Ray asked. "I would have never guessed that. He seemed more like a typical bureaucrat."

"Well, that was the idea. But with our governor, it's all about who you know," Pappy stated with a rueful grin.

"I'll bet you don't know that Dr. Wolfe has ties to the Andras family. He married a cousin, I think. Anyway, Hall is your man about the juicy things going around the capital."

"What do you mean?"

"It's politics. There's always something beginning covered up," his friend explained with a grin. "The tailored suits and perfume don't change human nature about power and money."

"Yeah, I see what you mean," Ray agreed as he placed a quarter on his friend's newsstand and took the latest issue of *Planet Stories*. The cover showed a pretty, curvaceous redhead firing at a strange mist with a futuristic ray gun.

"You owe me a nickel," he rolled up the magazine.

"Trying to expand your mind now?" Pappy ribbed him.

"I just like looking at the pretty damsels in distress on the covers," Ray joked as he left.

On his trip back to his office, the shamus stopped by the garage where his Nash Lafayette 400 was waiting. He gave another twenty to his mechanic, who warned him that his junker would soon need brakes. The thought grated at him as he slid into the car.

Someday I'll get a well-paying case to trade the old jalopy in for a newer one.

As he drove to his office, Ray debated his new client's problems. When he got to his desk, he placed a call to the *Sentinel*. According to the switchboard operator, Oscar Hewlett wasn't in the office yet. Ray left his number for the reporter to return his call. Leaning back in his chair, he put his feet up on the windowsill and looked absently out the window. Then he reached over and called a familiar number. His lawyer picked up on the second ring.

"I can't wait until someone develops a way that I know who's calling me so I can ignore your phone calls," Robert Bingham complained.

"Come on, you're my legal eagle, and I need your advice. I've got a well-dressed client who's got some problems with a husband and doctors," he replied. "He's some marketing executive, so I'm sure there's money there. I believe there's a large estate with a living mother as well. That should be right up your alley."

Irish could almost hear the man licking his lips at the thought of money. The lawyer instantly became friendly.

"Is she looking for a divorce?" he asked.

Ray gave a thin smile at the comment. He quickly explained Florence's problems and Dr. Horne's involvement.

"I'm guessing a divorce will end our sad tale. The husband's name is Jim Rice. According to the wife, Mr. Rice, had her committed to Horne's clinic. He also worked out a way to get his wife's mother put there as well," he explained.

"Now, are you interested?" His smile broadened when he heard the lawyer fumble with the phone.

He's already tallying up his bill.

"Yes, I might be interested," Bingham replied. "Now, give me more detail."

Ray recapped much of what Florence told him, and the lawyer stopped him as he finished.

"Are you sure she's not nuts?" The lawyer's skepticism remained.

"She didn't beat her belly to get black and blue marks," Ray growled. "One of the doc's assistants did it to her. I think Horne has a scam going on with his patients. I don't think it's a coincidence that her mother is sitting in the place as well. Isn't there something you can do to keep them away? I guess there is some legal mumble jumbo magic you can do to keep the doctors and cops away while I investigate this thing?"

Bingham whistled at the news.

"Well, I can file a civil action against the doctors to start the process. If her husband went to a judge about her, then we're limited in some of our options," he explained.

"I can get in front of a judge here in Oyster City. It would muddy the waters and cause problems for the other side. We can claim all sorts of things. I'll need to find sympathetic docs for our side. Remember, another judge could throw her back in Horne's clinic. Or they might commit her to the state asylum for evaluations. There are no guarantees here."

"Right, I understand," Ray replied. "You start your paperwork. In the meantime, I'm going to follow up on a few leads. If I get hard evidence, it'll make your job easier. Just don't forget that she's my client."

"Tell me where she's staying, and I'll drop by to speak with her. If she agrees with me helping her, you will have to follow my lead," the lawyer warned Irish. "You're a loose cannon. I can't save you from hanging yourself, but I can keep you from killing the golden goose here."

The shamus scowled at the comment. He took a deep breath and gave Bingham the address of where Florence was staying. He wanted to believe that a lawyer would fix her problems. However, he wasn't confident.

People playing for large stakes aren't likely to fold their cards at the first sign of legal trouble.

"Right now, she's pretty jumpy," Ray told him. "I've got the day pretty full since I promised I would go to LaSpina's wedding. Let's meet with her this evening. Between the two of us, we can lay everything on the table for Florence."

~~~

Inside the cathedral, Catherine was happily taking pictures with her new camera. She remained oblivious to the stares and whispered comments coming
~~~

from the people in the nearby pews. Ray wasn't paying attention. Instead, his mind was on the recent events with the woman at his side.

Before the ceremony started, he and Cat snuck into the Saint Sergius Cathedral early and waited in one vestry. The door let enough light in for them to stand in the quiet confines. The smell of her perfume and their closeness during the wait filled the room with an unsurprising tension. Ray whispered a few lewd jokes, and Cat's face reddened. She laughed and returned a dirty limerick of her own. Irish gave her a surprised laugh and drew closer. To his surprise, she went to her tiptoes and kissed him on the cheek. Ray smiled and put his arms around her. For the first time, she didn't resist as he kissed her.

Unfortunately, a surprised parishioner opened the door. The spell broken; they glanced over at the embarrassed woman before they quickly left. They joined the bride's wedding party. Cat immediately pulled her camera and appeared to forget the moment.

On the other hand, Ray kept wondering about the spark he felt for her. She drove him nuts at times, but Cat could make him feel good. He also remembered Arizona's warning, and he wondered if the woman could ever settle down with one man for long.

At first, good manners and social etiquette ruled the day. However, Cat's unexpected comment to him about the glances they were receiving drew him out of his thoughts. Irish overheard a nearby whisper from two busybody old maids about their intrusion. Ray looked over at their place next to the aisle. He gave them a fake smile, then asked them to switch seats. However, they politely refused. Ray leaned close to the woman.

"You might want to reconsider. The lady next to me is a lunger, and you never know when the coughing will start," he whispered.

Immediately, the old maids got up and hurried away.

"What did you tell them?" Cat asked when she took her seat next to the aisle.

"Unfortunately, you have a severe case of TB," Ray smiled.

He glanced over for her approval. Cat had already started taking several pictures as the organ started playing.

The spring wedding was majestic as intended, despite a fit of coughing by the priest during the ceremony. His display left an uncomfortable pause just before the couple exchanged vows.

A skinny, platinum blonde with a hook nose and green eyes, Myrna Valentine, came from a prestigious family in town. Her refined and grand style of dress radiated money and class. The bride's dress was to die for, according to Cat. To Ray's eyes, she wasn't a looker, but he noticed how happy she appeared when the priest finally declared the couple man and wife.

Henry La Spina carried his substantial bulk with a sphinxlike humbleness. While he stood taller than Ray, there was a softness to the man from the years of quiet living. As bishop, he ran several institutions along with a foundation. And Ray believed without a doubt that La Spina killed his first wife.

Before her death, Greye La Spina hired the shamus to find her killer if she never returned from the cruise she and Henry were taking. It was a debt Ray still owed his former lover.

Ray kept watching the front rows where the cream of Oyster City society sat. Peter Smyth sat next to his wife, Julie. Phillip Smyth, Peter's brother, sat with Mayor Hopely on the other side of the aisle. Also, in the row were several other people that Irish didn't recognize. He guessed they were the wife's relatives.

As he looked over the rows, he noticed Maria Smyth failed to attend the wedding. Maria's missing this event seemed out of character. His eyes came back to the animated conversation going on between Phillip and Hopely. From the agitation written all over the mayor, the scene appeared to confirm J. Allan Dunn's concerns.

They left the ceremony just after the couple finished their vows. Cat prodded Ray to hurry along, trying to get a good vantage point. Irish trailed after her, stopping at the back of the church to watch those in the front pews. They left by a side entrance after a quick conversation with the newlyweds. Settling into a nook by the front doors, Ray and Cat watched the crowd leaving the building. Several of the onlookers opened a pathway on the front steps, waiting for the wedding party to leave the building. The sunshine warmed through his suit coat, and he felt the start of sweat trickling down his back. Ray Irish observed the genial groom and smiling bride descend the front steps of the Saint Sergius Cathedral.

When the bishop and his wife exited the building, the milling people crowded around the couple as they passed by Cat, who got several more photographs. When the couple reached the sidewalk, the rice flew at the couple, followed by the toss of the bride's bouquet back into a small gaggle of women.

"That's one lucky girl," Catherine piped up as she stood overlooking the scene. "She looks very much in love. Even Henry appears happy."

Ray's focus was on the freckle-faced woman leading him. She looked lovely, with her strawberry-blonde hair pinned up under her beret. Cat's white and yellow dress flowed nicely over her curved body. He drank in the picture, noticing the woman wasn't sarcastic like usual. Instead, Cat looked wishfully at the scene. It was a side to her that was unexpected. Still, he disagreed with her observations.

"That woman does not know what she has gotten into," he said with a growl. He glanced over at the bishop, who looked like a politician trying to get votes.

"Well, his bride is not a grafter like Greye," she replied. "I swear I've never seen the bishop act that way around a woman. He's a man in love."

"Don't expect it to last. That woman just married a murderer," Ray shot back. "Let's see how long she lasts."

Cat turned back to watch La Spina's new bride, Myrna Valentine. The bride spoke with an older woman who was crying while Henry beamed a smile at her. She took his arm, and they posed for several pictures from a rival newspaper photographer who was waiting by the car.

Reluctantly, Ray had to admit the couple looked like they were quite smitten with each other. Henry nodded for the driver to hold open the door of the black limousine. As Myrna began waving and calling over her maid of honor, Irish suddenly grabbed Cat and pulled her in front of him.

"Quick, get a picture of her before they leave!" he ordered. Ray pushed through the onlookers. "Cat, I need you to get pictures of the bride's hands."

"Come on, out of the way, the press is coming through," he said as he pushed through the crowd. When they got only a few steps away, the newlyweds turned for their car. However, the harried movement of two people coming toward him caught the bishop's attention. Ray noticed the nearly imperceptible change in La Spina's expression when he saw them rushing toward him. Cat began snapping away on her small camera. As the groom and bride entered the car, Ray leaned over to Cat and nearly shouted into her ear.

"Remember the hands of the bride!"

Henry La Spina's voice rose above the din coming from the well-wishers as he hurried the driver to leave. A moment later, the large vehicle was turning the corner a half a block away.

"What the hell was that all about?" Cat finally asked as Irish led her away from the multitude of people.

"When you get those pictures developed, I want to see them," Ray told her after she broke from his hold.

"What did you see?"

She watched him shake his head.

"Not here, let's go," he insisted.

Ray hurried her along. He waited until they were in his Nash before explaining.

"I don't know if you can do it, but we need to blow up any pictures of the bride's ring," he finally told her.

"Why? What's so important about that?"

"Because that ring she's wearing is the same damn ring Greye wore," Ray declared. "I'm sure of it!"

"You're crazy! You can't possibly know that," she replied.

Irish glanced over.

"I saw it more than enough times. Let's go to your darkroom at the *Beacon*. You can try to prove me wrong," he declared.

An hour later, Cat stood over several flat tubs while she completed the final wash on her photos. After developing the negatives, she enlarged the images; confident her partner was on the wrong path.

But why am I so sure Ray is wrong?

She sighed as she considered her partner's fixation on Greye La Spina's death. A few weeks after the woman's disappearance, Ray persuaded Cat to drive them to the morgue in the capital. She shivered when she recalled the horrible sight of an unidentified corpse laid out on the porcelain table. Aside from seeing that the body was a woman, Cat knew there was little to positively identify the corpse.

The fish and crabs ate away most of the fleshy parts of the face, hands, and feet, along with the soft tissue of the breasts. However, the coroner told Ray that the victim had a deep slash across her throat. The fact that someone cut off the left ring finger Ray about the identity of the corpse. Cat had photographed dead people before, but the condition of the body and the smell of the room got to her. She left the room in a hurry before the coroner finished his conversation. On their drive back to Oyster City, Ray tried to convince Cat that she saw the remains of Greye La Spina.

Cat refused to believe. To believe such a thought shattered her beliefs in Bishop Henry La Spina. He couldn't be a cold-blooded killer. Over the years, the man went out of his way to support Cat and her mother. Brought up on the docks, Catherine met La Spina when he ran the mission. She always assumed the bishop helped them because of his compassion for her mother's plight. It was something she couldn't forget. Cat would not let her image of Henry become sullied by Ray's need to solve a puzzle.

While he waited, Irish was on the phone, trying to get through to Florence at the apartment. However, the busy signal kept buzzing in his ear. He hung up while scowling at the black phone. Ray hoped his client wasn't naïve enough to call her husband. He could almost imagine how that phone call would go. Cat came into the room, interrupting his thoughts.

"I wonder who she's called," he said aloud.

"Are you talking about your new girlfriend?" She asked.

"Yeah, the line is still busy. I don't like the idea of my client being on the phone," Ray glared at her. "Did you get anything?"

Cat shook her head as she swung two sheets of photographic paper in the air to shake off the remaining water drops.

"Well, between the crowd and our moving around, I don't think you have any evidence. I blew up the best ones from the negatives, but they're pretty blurry," she replied. "Look for yourself."

Irish took the photos from her. His inspection confirmed Mrs. La Spina's finger had a ring, but the details were impossible to identify. As he walked around the room, his scowl deepened.

"He's not a killer. There are a thousand things that might explain the similarities of the ring. I'll bet Henry just used the same design for her."

Cat's eyes danced in triumph when she saw his reaction.

He handed her the photos, as his frown remained. Cat placed them on the top of the desk next to her.

"Yeah, the bride had no choice in the matter," he reminded her testily. "I'm betting he told her it was a family heirloom, given to him by his dear, sweet mother. You still can't disregard the fact that I have a witness that says Greye La Spina wasn't on that ship going to Europe."

"I can't, but there are other possibilities, aren't there? With all the publicity, Greye might have taken off after a payoff from the bishop's friends," Cat pointed out. "She was a grifter, after all."

Ray shook his head.

"No, she had her flaws, but Greye would have let me know. Hell, at least she would want her money back from me. I recognized how much she feared her husband. You didn't see her expression when she told me to solve her death if she never came back from her trip."

He saw her expression, ready to argue with him.

"No, don't give me that look," he interjected as he held up his hand. "Greye knew something was wrong. I think she might have seen too much or known too much about La Spina. That explains the motive and why she never got out of Oyster City alive."

"But you never got a dental match on that corpse you made me take you to see," she reminded him.

"Only because I haven't tracked down her dentist in Boston," he explained.

Ray stepped closer.

"Cat, I know you are sympathetic to this guy. I understand he helped your family. But you must admit, I've got some strong circumstantial evidence. Instead of beating me up with your ideas, why don't you help me prove to myself that I'm on the wrong track?"

He watched a smug smile spread on her lips.

"Alright, shamus. I've got an idea for you about that ring. Have you considered that you're going about this the wrong way?" Cat offered.

She lit a cigarette and began puffing.

"What do you mean?"

"Well, the ring on Henry's new bride had to come from a jeweler. I'm betting it's a copy from a local jeweler. Find out who made it and maybe that'll stop this nonsense," she said as she exhaled a ring of smoke.

"You were waiting to spring that little idea on me at the right moment," he guessed.

Cat nodded as he hovered close to her. Her bright blue eyes looked into his eyes.

"You know, if you weren't smoking those damn cancer sticks, I'd give you a big kiss right now," he told her.

"What makes you think I'd let you?

"Because we both know that I'm better than those boys you like to hitch up with," Ray insisted as he placed his hand on her hip. He leaned in, and Cat waited, feeling nervous anticipation. He caught himself and slowly brushed by her.

"You'll figure it out sometime," he teased as he walked to the door.

Cat leaned against the desk and took a deep puff of her cigarette. She noticed her hand shaking as she exhaled.

"Damn you," she said under her breath.

~~~

Henry La Spina carried his new bride into their house, slightly irritated that his butler failed to open the front door. He quickly forgot his annoyance when his wife kissed him on the cheek.

"The house is just amazing," Myrna told him. "I promise I won't make too many changes."

He laughed as he slowly lowered her to the floor.

"Mrs. La Spina, you can make all the changes you wish. It's about time for me to think of the future," Henry declared as he looked around the quiet house. "I don't understand why the servants aren't here to greet you."

Myrna wrapped her arms around the big man and brought him close, giving him a long kiss.

"So much the better," she breathed. "Why don't you show me the bedroom? We have time before the reception this afternoon."

"Yes, we have an hour or so," he agreed as he looked at his watch. He took his wife's hand and led her past the foyer and up the long-curved staircase.

"After the reception, we'll go to the train station. By this time tomorrow, you'll be in Niagara Falls," Henry told her as he swept her up into his arms. As he carried his new wife into the bedroom, his laughter suddenly stopped. Myrna looked over to see a line of people in robes standing by the bed wearing masks.
~~~

She only recognized Peter Smyth. His eyes looked her over, and she suddenly felt fear welling inside of her.

"We're welcoming your bride to the Shadows," Peter stepped forward as the bishop let his wife slid from his arms.

"What the hell are you doing?" he demanded.

"Henry, your wife is lovely," the demon Andras observed. "Since you've been spending so much time with Myrna, your friends feel neglected."

Peter turned back to Henry and placed his hand on the bishop's shoulder. Henry felt a painful sting in his arm, and he winced.

"I had not forgotten your incompetence last month. You let the man escape. Now, you've forgotten your master," the demon said ominously. "We'll fix that problem today."

Henry's eyes widened as Myrna's hand dug into his arm.

"Honey, what is going on?" She asked her husband, the tone of her voice rising in fear. Henry ignored her.

"We must give her time to come into our circle," he implored Andras. "She's not like us. Myrna's never seen our world. You cannot force her into such things."

"Nonsense. Time is too short for such things. My brothers are waiting for their return. I've given your servants the day off, compliments of you. The Shadows will welcome the bride to our fold." The demon's eyes went black at the statement. "I have the bloody signed oath from your family inscribed upon the gates of my world. She must accept her fate on this wedding day."

Myrna pulled away from her husband, slowly backing to the door. However, several robed people cut off her escape route.

"Henry, this joke isn't funny," she sputtered out as her husband stepped next to her. Her fear-filled eyes kept glancing at the people around the room.

"I'm sorry, Myrna. I'd hoped I could bring you into the Shadows gradually," he told her. "We have no choice. Come with me."

As Henry stepped closer, his bride screamed in panic as she pushed by him. Two of the masked figures grabbed her arms before she reached the door. She screamed. The men quickly covered her mouth with a gag.

"Take her to the basement," Andras told his followers.

Chapter 4: A Dark Apartment

Ray Irish spent the afternoon interviewing multiple jewelers about the wedding ring of Myrna La Spina. While he found most of the shop owners happy to discuss the design, no one received business from the bishop. After entering the fifth shop, he decided their reluctance to steer him to the correct source came from their competitive business nature. The man in the shop explained it best to the shamus.

"Yes, Goldberg's across the street carries many types of wedding rings," the owner stated. Then, he lowered his voice and leaned closer to Ray. "But he is not a real designer, you know. He has a brother in New York, and he has copies brought in."

Irish nodded in agreement, then mentioned Bishop La Spina was the customer. The man gave him a thin smile.

"No, his family won't do business with Jews. You might try Underhill's down the street. He thinks a lot of himself. I've heard that the Andras and Hopely family send work to his shop."

A few minutes later, Ray   walked along Broadway, where he noticed a small neon sign flashing *Underhill* through a large shop window across the street. He suddenly remembered Cat telling him she was dating a gem dealer with that name. Avoiding the light afternoon traffic, he swiftly crossed the lined brick pavement. Inside the long, narrow shop, chrome cabinets lined the walls on one side. Crystal vases and delicate figurines accented the expensive décor. Ray ignored the urge to wipe the soles of his scuffed shoes before stepping on the elegant red carpet.

A young woman gasped lightly when Ray entered. He saw a couple standing at the end of the counter. He wanted to laugh at the woman's flustered face, which turned red. The man behind the counter hurried toward Irish. He pulled a handkerchief he pulled from his tailored blue suit coat pocket to wipe remnants of lipstick from his lips.

"May I help you?" the man slowed his pace as his eyes scanned Ray's clothes suspiciously.

The shamus said nothing as he stepped to the jewelry display case, looking over the rings inside. He glanced up when the shop owner made his way along the counter. Underhill had a pencil-thin mustache and piercing eyes. Ray decided women would go for the guy's delicate, angular face. A touch of gray hair around the temples of his brown hair gave the owner a look of wisdom.

"I said, may I help you?" the owner asked again. He carefully placed the handkerchief in the pocket. It was clear the shamus was not meeting up to the standards of the shop.

"Yeah, I'm looking for a ring," Irish replied as he kept scanning the examples inside the case.

"Obviously," his frosty reply made the shamus glance at him. "Might I suggest something in another cabinet? What you're looking at are custom designs."

Ray reminded himself that a punch to the guy's nose would not help him get information.

"I'm looking for a certain design," he said. "Are you Marion Underhill?"

"Yes, I am. Did someone recommend my store?"

"Yeah, you could say that," Ray told him as he took a different tack. "Cat Bennett spoke highly of it. I'm a friend of hers."

Underhill did not warm to the recommendation.

"I see. Well, I must warn you that our client list is quite exclusive," he sniffed.

"Maybe you can help me out. I've got a girl who's pushing me about marriage," he lied. "My girl noticed a ring on some lady, and she just went wacky about it. I'm trying to find something similar. Cat told me you are the expert on such things; the best in the state, according to her."

"She's correct about that," Underhill said proudly. He pointed into the case. "You see that ring? It is just a model, of course, but it reflects my signature style. I used a similar design for a ring that Nancy Cunard purchased. She met me in New York to pick it up."

"Amazing work," Ray agreed, although he did not know who Nancy Cunard was and didn't care. "I see I came to the right place. So, every ring is unique to the owner."

"Of course," the shop owner replied. "My clientele can afford such individual styling."

"Do you make these items yourself?"

"No, I'm the designer and owner of the store. I employ several expert jewelers who work in the back," Underhill explained.

Ray nodded and leaned over the case.

"The one I saw is quite similar to the one in the next row down." He pointed in the case and described the La Spina ring. "The way my gal swooned over that one, I guess you've made a few of them?"

"No, that reserved for only a few families," Underhill stated. "I think you might be mistaken."

Ray shook his head.

"No, I'm sure that's the design alright," he said. "Bishop La Spina's bride wore it. You know, I have a pretty excellent memory of such things."

"Yes, that came from my shop." Underhill's face brightened as he spoke. "It's a delicate thing, refined and tasteful. I remember…"

Ray saw the man's eyes suddenly narrow.

"Where did you see this ring?" He asked. Ray grinned in triumph.

"This morning at Bishop La Spina's wedding. But something about it told me I'd seen that same ring before on another lady."

"Well, I believe you must be mistaken. I highly doubt what you saw was a ring of mine," Underhill cautioned. His eyes were rapidly blinking as he spoke.

"Now, please don't waste my time. I suggest you try another shop."

Underhill quickly dismissed the shamus before he walked back to the woman by the counter. Ray felt the man's eyes following him out of the building.

As Irish walked several blocks over to Pappy's newsstand, he whistled a Benny Goodman tune. He enjoyed the reaction of Underhill and all it implied. He did not doubt that La Spina got the ring from the jeweler and there was only one wedding ring in existence.

Cat will choke on this news.

He already believed it, but the shop owner unwittingly confirmed his suspicions. Underhill had ties to other renowned people in Oyster City. Whether those connections were strictly business deals, he wasn't sure. Ray hoped that a conversation with his friend might clear it up for him.

Pappy was leaning back against the wooden wall of his newsstand when his friend walked up. Ray pulled up next to the dozing man and pulled off a magazine from the shelf. The noise woke Pappy.

"Trying to catch a nap before the evening rush?" Ray asked.

Pappy laughed and stood up from his stool

"You might say that. Two editions a day are wearing me out with this serial killer on the loose," he replied between yawns. "What brings you by?" The man crouched down to organize some of his comic books along the bottom shelf.

"A guy named Marion Underhill got my attention today when I stopped by his shop. Cat told me she's been dating the guy. What do you know about him?"

Pappy stopped, then glanced up.

"Are you getting nervous about Cat and him?" He asked with a mischievous grin. Irish glared back at him.

"Not likely, given how the guy was playing a kissing game with his help when I walked in. Marion's just another pretty boy with cash." Ray declared.

"Well, you're probably right," Pappy smiled. "His grandfather built the business, but he took over when his dad died in an accident. He was too young, most people thought. I hear the ladies flock to him."

"Yeah, I figured that out. He carries an attitude of sophistication and has loads of expensive jewelry," Ray stated as he flipped through his magazine.

"I'll tell you this much. Greye La Spina's murder led right through his shop. The wedding ring I saw on the bishop's wife today was the same one Greye wore. Underhill supplied the ring and boasted about it to me. Then, he got nervous when I mentioned the same ring was on two different women. It strikes me he knows something about La Spina."

"Underhill comes from one of the founding families of Oyster City," Pappy pointed out. "I don't need to remind you it's a small group and they don't like strangers. I warned you about this since the day you arrived."

He paused.

"Did I hear you right? The second missus has the same ring as the first?"

Ray nodded quietly as the newsy worked on another shelf, which held the western pulp magazines.

"What are you thinking?" Pappy asked after a glance around.

"That Underhill, La Spina and some of the rest of these founders were involved in getting rid of Greye. I can't figure out why. I mean, she would have left if someone paid her to go away. Then, something about this city keeps coming back to me. When I was in New York, I slept like a dead man. As soon as I get back to this damn place, the nightmares with Greye start up again. I keep getting an odd feeling there's something connected here."

Ray shook his head and glanced over with a sheepish grin.

"You see, I've been reading too many of your damn magazines!"

Pappy said nothing.

"When I first arrived in town, you told me strange things happened to those who went against the founder families. Also, you pointed out that bizarre killings occur in Oyster City. I'm believing this town carries a jinx."

Ray continued as he noticed his friend avoided looking at him. Pappy avoided eye contact with his friend, and the shamus watched him for a moment.

"Alright, spill it! You displayed your magazines just fine."

The newsy stood and walked around to the other side of his stand. He fiddled with the newspapers from the morning. Ray put his magazine back on the shelf and leaned against the wood.

"It's Emma," Pappy finally blurted out.

He looked around the stand, but the street was quiet. The policemen who lazily leaned against the streetlamp down the block was out of range.

"She tells me darkness is falling over the city," Pappy said. "Emma believes a demon rose on Andras Hill recently. It's worse than last time."

"Pappy hold up here. I remember that story you told about a lynch mob killing the town elders because they worshipped the devil or something," Ray replied. He had trouble keeping his disbelief out of his tone.

"But you expect me to believe that's happening now. Come on; it's 1948."

"Emma said the demon rose on the last full moon. She recognized the signs from dogs howling in the night. I remember it as well because the sounds woke me that night," the newsy insisted. "She knows these things. The demon gets his strength from the blood and the moon."

Ray listened in amazed silence as he examined his friend. Pappy refused to look up. He continued to move small stacks of his morning paper around.

"Ray, I know you think that I'm off my rocker," Pappy said with a sigh. "I swear on a stack of bibles, everything I tell you is true."

"Listen, I trust everything you say," Irish replied. The shamus held up his hand when his friend tried to interrupt.

"Now hear me out," Ray continued. "I never told you I knew a guy who saw ghosts before. His dead father warned him to get out of a foxhole just before a shell landed on it. So, if you say Emma is with you, I believe you. But you admit that a demon coming around Oyster City is hard to swallow. It's not like this place needs the help of evil."

Pappy nodded.

"I understand. It's difficult for me to tell you everything. However, you need to know something that Emma wanted me to tell you when you first came over to dinner. I refused to say anything about it at the time."

He glanced over at Ray.

"Alright, I'm a big boy. What didn't you want to tell me?"

"That night, you arrived for dinner; you made such a good impression on my Emma. She expected you would walk away after I set a place for her," Ray's friend explained. "When we were cleaning up after dinner, Emma insisted I say something about Greye La Spina. She wants to protect you."

Pappy paused.

"I'm sorry, but I refused to tell you that Mrs. La Spina would die. I guess I didn't want you to think I was off my rocker. But you need to listen to me. Emma tells me they will hurt and kill more of your friends. She knows bad things are coming to the city."

Ray didn't know how to respond at first. He realized the man earnestly believed what he told him. Irish also knew the ghost of Greye invaded his dreams.

"What does she know about Greye La Spina?"

"The demon's clan does terrible things to people to please their master. Greye gave them the blood for their ceremony," Pappy explained.

"Greye La Spina was a thorn in the bishop's side," Ray admitted. "But to sacrifice her for a demon? I'm not sure what I can say."

"Emma says that you know the truth. You have an aura around you and that you've seen the sacrifices to Andras. Each person sacrificed like a lamb in the Old Testament."

Ray's face drained at Pappy's description. He recalled in vivid detail the dead people with their throats cut in sacrifice. He never considered the idea that Greye's chauffer and the thug hanging from the barn were sacrifices. His drunken conversation with Greye's ghost told him to search for her killers. Her dead brother's spirit was with her in the hotel room with the same horrible wound. He shook his head, trying not to accept what Pappy told him. He'd known Pappy for a while and never considered him crazy.

Yeah, he's eccentric, but not nuts.

"Listen, Ray; there's a reason Andras rose from the hill bearing his name. People think they named the cemetery after their ancestors. I've read the old newspapers, and the demon's name came up one time. One newspaper article claimed that Henry Andras swore he was the demon just before they hung him and his family over the town square."

Pappy went quiet as a woman pushing a baby carriage passed the stand.

"His followers never stopped trying to bring him into the world. He is one of the legions who follows Lucifer. His followers will come after you because you know too much about them."

"What do you mean? I don't know anything about this," Ray insisted.

"It's the people in masks," his friend stated as he fumbled with the stack of newspapers.

"Emma warns you to stay away from the people with masks."

Irish felt goosebumps rise on his arms. He witnessed a robed figure with a mask a few times in the dark recesses of alleys. Ray even felt like they might be following him. He never told Pappy about the mask figures, only the shadows he saw in his nightmares.

"The spirits are restless, and they speak to my Emma about the ring you took from Smyth. What's happening scares the spirits. That means you've got problems," Pappy declared.

"Alright, for the sake of argument, these followers might be after me. But why? I'm just a dumbass shamus. Besides, that ring is far away from here, never to return," Ray reassured his friend.

"You are a threat, and you know where that ring is at," Pappy glanced up. "Emma says those in masks need the ring. To give more strength to Andras, they kill, but the Singsing means something special to them. You're in danger because of it."

Irish began a slow pace back and forth on the sidewalk.

"How am I supposed to investigate people in masks or stop these dreams?"

Pappy avoided eye contact as he focused on his shelf.

"Emma can't see everything, but she tells me that there are still people who follow their ancestors," he sighed. "They're the ones who brought this thing from hell."

"That could be anyone," Ray grumbled, then stopped.

"There might be something in something that Dunn told me about the old Andras woman. He said she and her daughter are missing. Then there's the bishop who has blood on his hands."

He looked over.

"I wouldn't rule out any founding families. They carried the creature into this world." Pappy said, then he stopped working.

"My wife told me you should find a tarot reader. It might help. But be careful. A demon can enter your mind."

Irish smiled when he heard the worry in Pappy's tone.

"You tell Emma not to worry; I'm always lucky."

~~~

The darkness slowly filled the master bedroom of Henry La Spina. On the blood-stained bed, the bishop lay on his belly next to his new wife. Myrna remained curled up in a fetal position, wrapped in a bedsheet. Her pale face expressionless, her mind continued to deny what she had experienced on her honeymoon.

"I promise, it will get better," Henry reached out to comfort his wife. She recoiled from his touch like a snake slithered next to her.

Henry didn't blame her. He recognized her tortured agony and betrayal. She experienced something that he witnessed at a young age. Henry grew accustomed to seeing sacrifices over the years. At twelve, he bled his first victim. Henry La Spina remembered the old woman's terrified reaction when he sliced open her throat.

Myrna witnessed the sacrifice of a naked man hanging upside down in the basement. The victim was a bum kidnapped from a dark alley the night before. While she screamed through the gag, Henry tried to help her by explaining the importance of the Shadows. His words had no effect. Attempting to escape from the horror of the basement, Myrna soon felt the wrath of Andras. He ordered the Shadows to ensure Myrna drank a blood tainted glass of wine. She had no choice with a still dripping dagger pointed at her throat by the man in the Bacchus mask. Myrna promptly threw up. For her insubordination, the Shadows tied her to the wall and whipped her. Ultimately, she drank several glasses to stop the beating.

Peter Smyth turned her around to watch the naked men grouped around the woman with a priestess mask. When she removed her disguise, Myrna recognized Julia. A ritualistic orgy played out before her while the alcohol and drugs slowly had its intended effect on their recruit. Myrna looked upon her husband while he enjoyed the pleasure of another woman and then another man.

After Andras released Myrna from the wall, he led her upstairs to the master bedroom. On her bed, the demon brutally raped her. His ominous voice declared her to be the mother of his children. His eyes went as dark as night. Her willpower draining away, Myrna wanted to cry and scream out at the same time. Then, a numbing nothingness overwhelmed. Andras became her sole purpose. To please the master became the only thought in her mind.

Before long, the Shadows slowly gathered around the bed. Julie Smyth chanted the words given to the founders of the cult by Étienne of France.

Andras, Great Marquis of Hell, commander of a demon legion, I invoke you to accept our sacrifice. Embed your servant into our woman, so we may rule all through corruption and vice.
~~~

When the beast finished with Myrna, he ordered the Shadows to hold Henry down on the bed. It was a reminder of who ruled over the Shadows. Andras whipped Henry using a leather belt. The demon gave Myrna the bloody belt to continue the brutality. After Henry declared his undying allegiance, Andras finally let Myrna stop. She collapsed next to him as the Shadows exited the room.

As Henry looked at his wife next to him, he knew his words were shallow and worthless. He never expected to feel such powerful emotions about her when he asked her to marry him. After all, the La Spina family always married for position and power.

While his first wife was a mistake caused by Henry's weakness for beauty, he took care of the error. Greye La Spina repeatedly betrayed him, then rubbed his nose in the mess she created by her graft. He felt no regret in his role in having Greye die as a sacrifice to the demon. At the time, Henry felt pride in bringing Andras into the world through his revenge.

The woman next to him was a delicate creature he grew to care about. Henry never expected to find something like love to enter his world. Sexual gratification came from domination. Control and power made the world, and he followed the same nihilistic belief of his forefathers. Service to Andras always remained the staple of family ties within the old families of Oyster City. His carefully built facade of being a pious priest within the Christian community fooled everyone in Oyster City. He held only contempt for followers of a weak god. Henry maintained his allegiance to Andras.

"You know that I never wanted this for you," he told her quietly. "We've grown up with our rituals. It works to keep our families on top of the rabble we must rule. You will learn this is for the best."

He wasn't sure that she heard him.

As he lay there, the bishop's back burned from his injury. He didn't want to move. He felt a fury filling him. No one questioned his loyalty, because Henry always remained a staunch believer.

Yet Andras humiliated him. Beating him was an intentional act designed to show the demon accepted nothing but complete submission from his human followers. As a product of wealth and status, Henry never felt helplessness and betrayal. Henry was part of corrupt and ruthless families who used other people for their gain. However, he believed he understood the emotions Myrna carried. She would survive by joining their ways. Henry would ensure that. But the future looked bleak for his family.

Andras just shattered any belief that Henry might have about his role in the future world. The demon devastated his dream of having a son to continue the family. Instead, Andras would use his wife to bear children. All the legions of hell might follow his son when they rose from the depths, but Henry La Spina's name did not matter. The rise of Andras was a hollow victory for the Shadows.

Curse my blinded ancestors!

Raised on the stories of his family and the allegiance to Andras, Henry knew the history of how they settled in the village that became Oyster City. The La Spina family maintained their power and influence by their worship of Andras. All the sacrifices, including the mob lynching of his great grandfather, were necessary to achieve the ultimate goal. He and the Shadows finally brought Andras into their world. Their satisfaction in the accomplishment soon changed after he killed Betty Andras, the leader of the Shadows.

Henry believed he understood the demon's plan. Spreading his influence across the state, Andras intended to unleash his brothers from below. That left the human followers with a choice. They would keep their power and control over the city in name only. The Shadows were no longer in control of their world. Since Andras took over the body of Peter Smyth, the demon made it clear that he didn't need the Shadows. Henry La Spina recognized the mistake of his forefathers. However, he also knew he had no choice. The bleak future for the La Spina family required a break from the past.

~~~

The night sky descended upon Oyster City as Ray pulled his Nash into a parking slot at the front of the St. Mark building. Just before he left his office, he tried calling Florence. No one answered. Turning off his car, he glanced up at the apartment where Florence was staying. A sliver of light showed between the curtains.

As he slid out of the front seat, Irish continued to mull over his client's husband. Earlier in the afternoon, he called Jim Rice about his wife. Ray claimed he was a reporter with the *Beacon* who was working the story about Florence's escape. Jim Rice appeared genuinely upset about his wife, anxiously asking for the latest news. When Ray pushed into questions about the mother-in-law and the estate, Rice's tone immediately changed. Before long, Jim threatened to call the paper's editor about his treatment. Then he abruptly hung up.

When Irish arrived at the apartment door, he knocked, but there was no answer. He glanced around, trying to decide if Florence left to get dinner. However, in the dimly lit hall, Ray noticed the light shining from under the door. The shamus tested the doorknob and found it wasn't locked. A warning bell went off in his head, but Ray ignored it as he called out. Silence returned his greeting; then, he saw two green eyes in the shadows along the floor. A cat came out from behind the chair and slid around his ankles. The shamus smiled at the animal.

"Hello there, kitty. Where's everyone at?" He stepped into the room.

That was when Ray noticed the leather soles on a pair of shoes sticking out from behind the couch. He eased over to get a better view. Irish discovered the body of a man lying face down on the carpet. As he stepped closer, a movement along with the rustle of cloth caused Ray to look over.

"Hey, mister!" A loud, gruff voice announced.
~~~

Immediately, Ray's cheekbone caught the butt end of a revolver. By the time his falling body hit the floor, he was unconscious.

"Alright, bring her out," the large thug growled back into the dark bedroom. While his partner forced Florence into the room, he picked up the fireplace poker lying next to the corpse. Her mouth gagged, and her arms bound behind her, the woman could only let out a muffled cry. The brute holding the poker smirked at the woman, his boxer's face twisted in delight at her fear.

"Don't worry sister, you're gonna live," he told her. "But you can watch me finish your hero. I'll leave his brains all over the carpet."

"Don't Slim," the other thug told his partner. "Boss wants this quiet. Coppers are dumb. Put that poker in his hand and let the shamus take the rap."

At first, the man resisted the suggestion, and he lifted his arm. Then, an evil grin came over the man holding the poker.

"Parker, I think I like that idea," Slim crowed before he placed the weapon in Ray's hand.

"Now the cops can wake him up to haul 'em off to the gallows." He boasted, like the idea was his own. "Come on, lady. You got people waiting for you."

Slim carefully surveyed the hall as he led the way. The men took Florence out of the building by the back alley. Halfway toward the next building, they came to a black limousine. The rear door opened and a small, balding man in a blue, three-piece suit stepped out. His dark eyes focused on the woman as he directed them to put her inside the car.

"Any problems?" Dr. Wolfe asked.

"Yeah, just a bit. When we got to the floor where the apartment was, we saw the woman let a little guy into the place. I went up to the door and listened. He's a lawyer named Bingham," Slim explained. "I pulled my gat and went inside. Dumb broad didn't even lock the door." He smiled while he glanced at his partner, who pushed the barely resisting woman into the car.

"The little guy got really talkative when I pointed the gun barrel at his head. He told us about the shamus who got her the apartment, and he's checking on you and your partners. He told me this Irish has your clinic figured out."

"What happened?" The impatience in the doctor's tone caused the thug to grin.

"Don't get all huffy. I was trying to tell you. The lawyer tried to get to the phone when your crazy lady tried to escape. Parker took care of the lawyer with a poker. I slapped the girl around some to get her attention. We were about to leave when that shamus showed up. I gave him a nasty headache," the thug boasted.

"You left him alive? I can't have that," Wolfe swore.

"It's alright," the man assured him. "He'll take the wrap. The lawyer and the shamus got into a fight. His fingerprints are all over the poker. The coppers will enjoy beating a confession out of him. Nobody will believe his story, anyway.

Don't worry; we got it covered. We'll call the cops after you leave. They'll arrest the shamus. Anything he says ain't going to keep him from the hangman."

Wolfe shifted his glance back to the vehicle.

"I guess that will have to work," he gave a resigned sigh. "You make sure that you make that call when we leave. Then, let your boss know I appreciate his service."

"Sure thing doc, but where's the money?" The brute insisted.

The small man pulled out an envelope and handed it over. Slim smiled.

"Jacobi says he'll have some more crazy suckers for you to treat pretty soon."

Dr. Wolfe nodded before he slid back into the car. He directed the driver to pull away, watching as the two criminals walked down the alley toward the sidewalk. He turned back to look at Florence as she struggled to free herself from her bindings. In the facing seat across from her were three additional passengers. Her eyes darted back and forth at the familiar faces.

"I don't like using those people," Dr. Horne complained. "I have people who could have taken her back."

"You let her escape," Wolfe replied as he glared at the older man. "Worse, you've killed her mother. To compound all of this, you nearly screwed up the whole thing by your inept attempt to have Mrs. Rice commit suicide."

He paused as Florence's muffled wail filled the car at the news of her mother's death. The two doctors looked at her for a moment before returning to their conversation.

"Damn it, Horne, you didn't clear any of this with me. Only a fool wouldn't consider the legal problems."

Horne returned to a sullen silence while crossing his arms. With a head full of wavy, disheveled gray hair along with his horned rim glasses, Horne carried the look of a mad scientist. His white lab coat didn't cover his thin arms, which rested on his flabby, middle-aged belly. Despite his frustration, he recognized Wolfe was the only one who could extract them from their difficulty. His political and social connections meant too much to the partnership.

"You can play the psychologist at the clinic, but don't forget who runs things. My arrangement with Jacobi got those men to fix our problem," Wolfe continued.

"Please remember that it was my idea." Horne lowered his head to look over the top of his glasses. "Rich suckers with estates need my treatment; therefore, you need me. Don't forget that!"

"And you don't want to tangle with me, Horne. I have only so much patience with failure." Wolfe turned to their prisoner, who desperately fought with her bindings. The look of rage on her face caused Wolfe to smirk.

"Mrs. Rice, I assure you that your mother died peacefully. Her death was far better than the slow descent into a wasting disease of the brain."

He turned to Horne again.

"By killing the old lady before Florence's husband put everything into place, you've delayed our progress. Once the judge receives formal notification of the mother's death, her estate will go to Florence. Now we must…"

Their prison interrupted Horne again with her violent struggles.

"Sam, please sit next to our patient and ensure she keeps quiet. You may do as you need. Make sure you don't leave any visible injuries on her," Wolfe told the big man in a white coat sitting next to Horne.

Sam's thick lips curled up into a wicked smile at the prospect. He moved next to Florence, who flinched as he took a seat by her.

"Unfortunately, your escape and your mother's demise have left us with a predicament. As you might have guessed, your husband called his friend, Dr. Horne. He gave us your location," Wolfe explained to her.

"You really shouldn't have mentioned divorce to him. It's now obvious that your situation poses a danger to everyone. The engagement of a detective and a lawyer means we must adjust our planning."

Wolfe paused as he pulled out a cigarette case. He took a cigarette from the line inside and lit it. Dr. Horne rolled down the window slightly with an annoyed grimace. Then, he rolled down the window separating the passengers from the driver.

"Find us an isolated place," Horne told the driver, who nodded.

Florence suddenly tried to escape by frantically going toward the car door. A grinning Sam pulled her back into the seat. Her muffled yells forced the doctors to glance over briefly. They returned to their conversation after Sam slammed his fist into Florence's belly. She doubled up in agony, struggling to breathe.

"I say it's time to reconsider our options. I agree that our facility here in Oyster City is not suitable for Mrs. Rice," Wolfe told Horne. "Her death might bring unnecessary attention to the clinic. The old lady's estate is too large for us to make any more mistakes."

Horne went quiet, and only the noise of the car came into the cabin while the two doctors looked out of the window. They remained silent until the limousine pulled off the road. They turned into a dark, deserted gravel lot near the abandoned army base. Florence visibly shook from fear as the car stopped. The driver turned off the lights. Only the burning end of Wolfe's cigarette showed inside the dark interior of the vehicle.

"Let's get rid of her," Horne insisted. "We can dig a hole in those woods right by the car. Nobody will find her."

"Your incompetence continues to bother me. I just told you we must play for time while Mr. Rice has the court make him the administrator of the estate. If she's dead, there will be an investigation and potentially months of delay. What happens if the police, or the judge, want to interview her? We can turn her into a compliant imbecile with drugs and electroshock, but we need to have her alive. If she's missing, there will be questions from other family members and delay."

Wolfe turned on the light in the cabin. He looked over at their prisoner, who remained in a fetal position.

"Then what's the solution? Her husband will want to know what we're doing," Horne pointed out.

"It doesn't matter. I still don't trust your friend," Wolfe replied after Horne closed the window. Horne frowned at the implication.

He glanced over at Florence.

"This conversation can wait. She doesn't need to know."

"That doesn't matter now. We won't let Mrs. Rice out of our control again," Wolfe dismissed the warning. "We will do this my way from now on. Once we have control over the estate, we'll take care of our patient."

"What have you got in mind?" Horne reluctantly asked. "A reporter called her husband with questions this afternoon. I think Jim's getting nervous."

"First, we need to keep the police out of this. Next, we need control over Jim Rice." Wolfe ran through his options calmly as he inhaled the smoke.

"It's too risky to keep her in the clinic, and we can't kill her right now."

The red of the burning tobacco grew intense, then subsided.

"We have our medical records of her mental state," Horne interjected. "We can back up anything that Jim tells the court.'

"Obviously," Wolfe said as his lips pursed with a thin smile. "But we need complete control over her husband, and I believe your screw up might inadvertently give us the leverage we need."

"What are you saying?"

"The old lady's death! We'll tell Jim Rice that her death means the electric chair for him unless he follows our plan to the letter. I'll let him know when I get back to the capital."

Horne's face paled as he slowly nodded agreement.

"Alright, but what about his wife?" he asked his partner.

"I'm getting to that! You know, I finished a book by Alexandre Dumas just the other night. His story just gave me an idea concerning our patient," Wolfe stated as looked out into the dark woods. "Mrs. Rice can't live, and she can't die for the moment. I believe we'll need to put her into purgatory instead."

"What are you talking about now?" Horne's voice cracked slightly.

"Mrs. Rice will become lost," he said half to himself. "Like an anonymous face in the crowd—yes, that works." Nodding to himself, he turned to Horne.

"Tonight, you'll inform the police that your people found her and returned her to the clinic. If they need to see her close out their concerns, you'll make sure she's drugged, as I mentioned before. But I don't think it will be necessary after I contact the district attorney." Wolfe stated as he leaned back in the seat. He exhaled a puff of smoke.

"After that, it's only a matter of filling out the proper paperwork. Your friend, Mr. Rice, can use her escape to help his legal takeover of the estate."

"It's pretty risky," Horne insisted. "You're assuming the police will not want more information."

"Then, I want her at the state asylum as soon as I'm ready." Wolfe paid no attention to his partner. "We'll have her processed in as a Jane Doe. You understand how paperwork can lose her. She has no one to protect her, and nobody could find her. Florence Rice becomes lost to the world. After that, we can dispose of her at any time."

Florence shuddered at the news. Desperate rage filled her. She tried to lash out with her feet at the doctors, who presented her upcoming life of torment and death with clinical detachment. Sam quickly struck her hard several times until she stopped. The two doctors only glanced over before returning to their planning.

"She's not to leave her room until my people come to get her. Do you understand? Nobody else but the police can know that she's in your clinic," Wolfe stated.

"To the rest of your staff, let them know she's already transferred to the asylum."

"I don't like this. Losing a patient in the state system is no solution. She can still talk." Horne leaned forward as he pointed to Florence. His partner gave a massive sigh.

"Don't argue with me. As long as Florence Rice remains my guest, and no one knows where she is, her husband will remain under our power. We'll have control of everything. Once I inform Jim Rice about her location, he'll dance to any tune we want. He's behind the preverbal eight ball. While she lives, we control him and the money. Now, do you understand?"

Horne recognized the implications. They were double-crossing his friend.

"Damn, I thought you were too calm about this. You make it sound so simple," Horne complained.

"Of course, it's simple to you after I've explained everything. However, I'm not asking for your permission. We'll stick to this plan. I won't accept another mistake," Wolfe paused, stuffing out his cigarette in the small ashtray on the arm seat. "You saw the people who will come for you, Dr. Horne. I don't take prisoners."

Horne's briefly glanced at the dim outlines of the others in the car, and he let out a sigh.

"Doctor Wolfe, I believe that you'd betray your mother. Alright, but I think we should drive to the asylum tonight. You can put her away."

"No, not all my doctors are as corrupt as you. I must arrange things. I'll let you know when I have everything in place. In the meantime, you will release the body of the old lady to an undertaker. You can fill out the appropriate death certificate to ensure she died of old age. Remember that Mrs. Rice doesn't talk with any of your staff," Wolfe growled. "I want you and Sam to be the only ones to handle our valuable patient. You keep her filled with tranquilizers during her stay. That will ensure she can't talk with anyone."

"Alright, I'll take care of everything. Sam, you heard the order," Horne told him. "When we get to the facility, you are the only one who will watch over her. If she gets away, it's your hide on the line."

"Sure thing, boss," Sam replied happily as he lightly stroked the woman's hair.

Florence tried to pull away. Wolfe opened the glass partition and ordered the driver to take them to the clinic.

Chapter 5: The Setup

"Alright, wake up," a gruff voice finally pierced through the dark fog. The beam of light shining in his face finally woke Ray. He tried to reach for the painful bump on his cheek. However, the steel grip of someone's hand immediately twisted his arm behind his back. Before he could react, Irish was in handcuffs. Two men lifted him from the floor.

"Well, well, if it isn't the clever shamus," a familiar voice caught his attention. Ray looked over at Lieutenant Sirk, who was frowning at him.

"Why did you kill him?"

The prisoner shook his head weakly.

"What?" Gradually, he recognized the body, and the memories returned.

"Come on, Sirk. You find me on the floor with my head nearly pounded in. You know damn well I didn't kill him."

"Says you," the cop replied sternly. "I've already got the victim's name of Robert Bingham. My men already rousted his secretary out of her house. She tells us he's your lawyer, and you were meeting him here tonight. The apartment only has you two in here, and you had the murder weapon in your hand."

"Use your brain. I'm not likely to kill a guy and hang around for the cops," Ray replied.

"You can tell it to the judge. The lady in the apartment below says she saw you coming up the stairs. Then she heard a man yell. Here's what went down from my view. You and your lawyer go to this apartment and get into a fight. You kill him and then you knocked yourself silly, thinking you'll have an alibi." Sirk insisted. "But it won't work."

"Take him to the station," he told a uniformed policeman standing behind Irish. Sirk stepped away when he noticed the coroner walking down the hallway to the apartment.

"Come on!" the cop told Ray as he pushed him forward.

It was about an hour later when Sirk finally showed up at the interrogation room where Ray sat. He still felt woozy, and the side of his face swollen, which partially closed his left eye. He didn't get any sympathy from the detective as he sat across from Ray.

"Are you ready to talk?"

Ray glared at him.

"What do you want to know? That I pounded my face after taking out my lawyer for no reason. Come on, give it a rest, and start using your brain."

The sarcasm dripped from the shamus as he adjusted his position in the hard, wooden chair. His hands were numb from the cuffs pinching into his wrists behind his back.

"Alright Irish, I'll admit it looks like a frame job," Sirk conceded. "But I've seen your work. You think that you're a bright boy. Maybe you struck Bingham too hard, and then you figured you needed an out. You might have continued to pound on the victim's face until it was unrecognizable."

"Yeah, but I didn't smack my face with the butt of a pistol to knock me out. You got a theory for how I did that?" Ray challenged him.

"I could be you ran your face into the mantle and say some hoodlum did that to your face. It's possible for you to cover up murder this way. Thing is, I might not believe you did it, but I've got to do my job with evidence. Evidence points to you right now. I've got your prints on the murder weapon. You are lying by the body when we arrive, and you got no witnesses. Now give me your story."

Ray gave a humph.

"If you're having a hard time with this case, just wait until you hear my story," he told him.

The shamus gave the cop a brief version of his client and her arranged meeting with Bingham. He pointed out his client was still missing, and the clinic was abusing the woman before she escaped and came to him for help.

Ray toyed with the idea of giving Sirk the full story, but he decided against explaining everything he knew. It wasn't going to do him any good and might make things worse at the moment. Sirk might determine that Florence and Irish were in on the murder together.

Sirk patiently listened as he filled his pipe and lit the tobacco. He blew aromatic smoke into the air.

"Listen, I admit putting Florence up in the apartment. Maybe you can become a real detective instead of taking the easy way out here."

"One thing about you," he said between puffs, trying to keep his pipe lit. "You always come up with interesting stories. Somebody hits you when you enter the apartment. You say you didn't get a look at them. You also tell me you have a client who is missing. The problem is she's an escaped patient from a clinic. You say that you do not know where this client is. I'm afraid you'll need to find a talented lawyer."

Sirk slid back in the chair and rose. Another man entered the room. His bulky frame filled a well-worn suit, and his blue eyes weren't friendly. With a broad face, flabby jowls, and a misshapen nose, the stranger carried a menacing air with him. Sirk walked by the man silently and left the room. The stranger came to a stop next to the prisoner.

"All right, shamus, I've been listening to your bullshit story. It's time you tell the truth," the stranger said gruffly.

"Who are you?" Ray asked suspiciously. "I thought I knew all of the detectives."

"The name is Devine, on loan from the Baltimore PD," he said. "The DA asked our chief for some help with the murder of Detective Howard. There's a rumor going around that you and Howard didn't get along."

"Yeah, I have a problem with cops getting their graft from racketeers," Ray replied.

He wasn't expecting the massive backhand from the cop.

"I didn't ask for your lip," Devine stood with his hands on his hips. "You'll answer my questions when I ask them. Now, Sirk's got you dead to rights on one murder. Why not come clean on killing Howard?"

"You go to hell!" Ray spat out.

However, the next strike caught him in the ribs. He painfully gasped for air like a fish out of water.

"We've got all night shamus," Devine warned him as he took off his coat. "I'm sure you're just another asshole that thinks you're too smart to get caught."

"You remind me of those damn shore patrol goons." Ray got out between aching breaths. "I don't break, you worthless bastard."

The goon with a badge gave Ray a cruel grin as he rolled up his sleeves.

"Yeah, the guilty suckers always tell me that!"

~~~

"Here you go, a nice clean bed for you," Sam pushed Florence to the edge of the railing. He forced her to bend over and untied her bound wrists. The attendant squeezed her nearly numb wrist hard enough for her to cry out in pain. With a cruel laugh, he wrapped a leather restraining strap around her wrist before he forced her on top of the sheets.

"Hand me your other wrist," he ordered. Florence complied, and the man grinned after strapping her legs to the bed. Sam stepped back; his ugly face turned worse from his thoughts as she struggled in the straps.

"I'll leave your clothes on for now," he told her. "When I come back, it'll be nice and quiet for me to strip off your fancy duds."

He stepped close and touched her cheek. Florence turned away. Sam savagely ripped off her gag. She let out a strangled yelp.

"Oh, you think you're too good for me?" he spat out as he gripped her jaw and forced her to look at him.

"I remember when you walked by me the first day — all prim and proper with your nose in the air. Too bad, I recognized your act. Now you heard the doc. I'll be working late the next few nights just for you, my special patient."

"Open your mouth," the thug in white ordered. His stubby fingers dug into her cheeks as he forced her mouth open. Sam shoved a pill into the back of her mouth. She choked before finally swallowing the dry, bitter tablet.

"There's a good girl. By the time I get back, you'll be in another world. Don't worry baby; it's not enough for you to forget. I'll make sure you remember me long after they haul you away," he declared triumphantly.

He leaned over and kissed her as she struggled to turn her head away to avoid his lips. Florence listened to his whistling as he closed the door. The tears
~~~

fell as she struggled with her bindings. After several minutes of fruitless effort, the woman finally stopped. Breathing heavily, she recited a prayer that her mother taught her.

~~~

In the circular room at the top of the Andras' house, Peter Smyth sat at a five-sided table as his followers entered the room in their black robes. The glass cupola ceiling reflected several candle lights placed around a silver bowl in the middle of the table. Deep in thought, the demon paid no attention to those watching him as the room remained quiet.

The last people in the room were Henry and Myrna La Spina. Henry's wife reluctantly took her seat at the spot where the Empress mask resided. Her husband sat across from her while Julie Smyth took the seat next to Myrna. Horace Hopely kept glancing at their master from his place next to Julie while fiddling with his Emperor's mask on the table.

Behind his brother stood Phillip Smyth in a red robe. He wore the Judgement mask. Next to him was Marion Underhill, who waited impatiently in a black gown. The mask in his sweaty hands was the grotesque image of a magician. He rocked back and forth on his heels; the creaking of the wood floor caused the others to glance at him. The jeweler remained an unfamiliar figure to most of their meetings, including their sacrifices.

"Your minds tell me of your concerns about this sudden meeting," Peter's voice filled the room. "One Shadow came to my brother and sought my guidance." The demon paused.

"Underhill, you have news for us. I can hear it in the palpitations of your heart."

"Yes, Peter. It concerns a man who came to my shop. He asked questions about La Spina and his wife. I believe he recognized the ring that Henry gave his new bride," Underhill blurted out. "He said it was the same one that Henry gave his first wife, Greye. She was..."

"What are you talking about?" Henry interrupted. "There's no one who could know."

His sudden pause caused everyone to look in his direction. He turned to Peter Smyth.

"Master, it has to be that shamus," the bishop hastily explained. "Irish was with Greye when Guy Young and his men tried to kill them."

"She was with him in more ways than you think." Andras gave him a deadly glare. "You're a bumbling fool. I have all the images and thoughts from this body that I inhabit. After Peter Smyth cut Greye La Spina's throat in your cabin on the train, her spirit never passed into my realm. It appears God left her in this realm. I know her ghost reaches out for him."

"But she was a sacrificed for your benefit," Henry insisted.
~~~

"The death of your cheating wife benefited you alone, priest. I can read your heart. Her death allowed you to have this one," he pointed to Myrna, who listened to the conversation with dread filling her features.

"I won't be tolerant of another mistake, La Spina," the demon warned.

He paused, rubbing his chin.

"The fact that this detective remains Oyster City means he must have allies. That makes him a threat to my plans," Smyth stated, mostly to himself.

"He is only one person," Phillip Smyth pointed out. "We can have a cop or gangster just kill him."

"No, while he has little power against us, we must find out what he knows and those who support him first," the demon declared. "As I recall, this Irish has a female who works with him."

He turned to Underhill.

"Do you know of this person?"

"Yes, that's Catherine Bennett. She has ambitions," the man replied. "In fact…"

"Yes, I can see her in your mind," Andras interrupted. His face twisted into a sly grin. "You are bedding her while using her ambition against her. A devious proposition which will prove useful to us."

"How?" Surprised and terrified, the jeweler could only get out one word.

"For the moment, you will make her your closest ally. Find out anything about Ray Irish. You will discover his allies." the demon leaned back in the chair.

He placed his hands together and gave a satisfied smile.

"After that, we will invite this detective and his allies to one of our parties. Her ambition will lead them to their deaths. I can envision a host of ways in which to deal with them."

The demon stared at Underhill.

"Do you understand?" He asked.

The jeweler nodded, licking his lips.

"Of course, I'll do as you command." He stammered out.

The door to the room opened, and the cadaver-like form of Mr. Wolfe peered inside. The demon nodded his head. Wolfe retreated, then forced a bound prisoner from the basement into the room. The gagged, white-haired woman could barely walk. Her ripped and dirty servant uniform hung on her thin shoulders. Wolfe pushed the woman to the edge of the table and forced her to bend over. The servant's wide eyes searched the room for help as Wolfe slid the bowl under her head.

"It is not a night of the moon; however, Myrna must complete a sacrifice," Andras told the bishop and his wife. "You will complete tonight's sacrifice. Your act will cement your bonds of blood between your soul and my realm. Come, mother of my child!"

Andras declared as he rose from the chair. He pulled a golden dagger from his robe and handed the weapon to Myrna. She visibly shook when she took the weapon. Then, she dropped the knife on the table. Tears fell down her face, and she appeared ready to faint. Henry grabbed her by the arm as he retrieved the dagger. He led her closer to the terrified servant.

"You will be the sacrifice if you disobey," he insisted while whispering in Myrna's ear.

"Come, I'll help you."

He placed the handle back in the hand of the shaking woman. Together, they extended the blade to the throat of the housekeeper that Henry knew since he was a child.

~~~

The ringing, sliding sound of steel woke Irish from a deep sleep. Standing at the entrance to his open cell door was a uniformed cop.

"Alright shamus, get your ass up, you've got a ticket out!" There was disappointment in the man's voice.

Bleary-eyed and frightfully sore, Ray carefully crawled out of bed.

"Who sprung me?"

"You'll find out when you go through processing," the cop told him. "Now get a move on before I close the door and let you rot."

A few minutes later, the shamus stood at a counter where a uniformed policewoman diligently spread his few possessions in front of him. He hardly noticed his wallet, twenty-one dollars, along with his gun and holster until the woman forced him to identify the object. The groggy fog filling his mind came from several hours on the hot seat along with a few rounds to his belly when Devine didn't like his smart attitude.

Ray's temper rose while he thought about the abuse he took. The shamus paid scant attention as the woman quickly typed out several forms. After Ray signed several pages, he watched the humorless woman finish her paperwork. He didn't hear his visitors arrive behind him.

"You're damn lucky the evidence came out on your side," Sirk's voice growled. "You didn't make any friends with Devine. I'd watch out for him."

The detective and Catherine waited for him.

"Yeah, I'll keep an eye out alright. That son of a bitch decided to beat out a confession. He'll be lucky that someone doesn't follow him into an alley some night."

Ray's bitter reply came while he gingerly put his holster over his shoulder. Then, he focused on putting on his suit coat.

"That might sound like a threat," Sirk said.
~~~

Irish glared at him.

"Take what you want out of it. Cops get a reputation for being thugs for a reason. You knew what was coming. Before your new girlfriend showed up, you knew I wasn't lying to you." He jammed his pistol into the holster.

"I always told people you play straight. I'll remember your crap the next time someone asks me to figure out a murder."

"Get the hell out of here," the cop spat out.

He pushed past Ray and continued toward the jail area.

Cat grabbed Ray before he could follow Sirk.

"Calm down before they haul you away," Cat pulled him toward the entrance.

"Arizona told me that rat Devine is working for the District Attorney as some special detective. He claims the guy's got a lot of pull. Also, Devine started still spreading around a rumor that you are still the number one suspect for Detective Howard's murder."

"I don't give a damn! Sirk proved he's just like the rest of these damn corrupt cops here," Ray lashed out.

He noticed a couple of uniformed policemen took notice of his outburst. The shamus gave them a dirty stare as Cat pushed him away. Halfway down the hallway, he broke free and outpaced her to the doors.

"Damn it, Ray, don't forget, I'm on your side!" she panted out as she grabbed the door handle.

He turned his battered face toward her. His fury remained.

"I tired of worthless flatfoots beating up suspects instead of using any brains they might have." Ray pushed through the door.

When he reached the steps leading to the sidewalk, he stopped. Cat stepped next to him and remained quiet for a moment.

"So, how did you spring me?" Ray finally asked.

"I didn't, not really," she confessed as she continued following him outside.

"When I heard they arrested you, I went to see Arizona. I found him with Sirk, and I overheard some of the conversations. Sirk got the evidence which got you off. The coroner says that Bingham's murder happened before you arrived," Cat explained.

"After they hauled you away, the coroner noticed dried blood from Bingham on the floor underneath you. Sirk confirmed you didn't have any bloodstains on your shirt, so you could not have done it."

"Yes, that damn Sirk still let Devine grill me for most of the night," he fumed as he moved quickly, despite his unusual gait. "You got anything else?"

"Yeah, I heard Sirk say that one tenant saw two men and a lady leaving the building through the alley. He agrees that somebody wanted you to take the fall after they took your client. Slow down," she insisted.

Grudgingly, he slowed.

"Did you tell them about Florence?"

"Yes, but only a little bit. Damn it, don't give me that look. The cops have decided that Florence was involved in the murder of Bingham. Arizona told me she's already back at the clinic and it'll be up to the DA about charges. He probably won't press charges against an insane person as long as she remains in the clinic."

"Sure, a terrified woman escapes from a nuthouse. Just for fun, she kills her lawyer." Ray's tone dripped with sarcasm.

"Then I walk in, and she tried to cave in my thick skull to frame me for the murder. Oh, and she walks away with two new friends from the clinic. Are you buying that crap?"

"Of course not. Sirk told me that the police chief would insist she did it. She's a ready-made patsy, and you just got in the way. Someone already got to the DA," she explained. "When Sirk talked with Dr. Horne, he told him that the district attorney already knew about Florence and her mental breakdown. It's clear that the whole thing was a setup."

"And the cops don't have to do their job. Damn, from the pan to the fire for her," he replied as he carefully touched his upper cheek. He winced.

"Do you have some aspirin?"

"No, I don't," Cat took him by the arm. She led him along the sidewalk. "You know you look like hell warmed over, hotshot. Since you won't go to a doctor, there's a drugstore around the corner."

As they took two seats at the counter of Gottschalk's, Ray ordered a couple of coffees along with jam and toast. While the soda jerk got their coffee, Cat went to the pharmacist's counter. She came back with a small tin box filled with aspirin.

"What's next?"

"Like I have a clue," he grumbled after downing a couple of tablets with some coffee. He ordered the soda jerk to refill his cup.

"By the way, I talked with one of the *Beacon's* photographers who took pictures at Bishop La Spina's first wedding," she told him. "He's checking to see if he can find the negatives for me. I'm still telling you it's a wild goose chase."

"Well, that's some news. It sounds like you are coming over to believe the bishop's not what he pretends to be." His smirk hurt his face.

"I still say you're wrong. Henry La Spina is too nice to hurt someone, even if she deserved it," she flashed at him.

"Maybe, but I don't think his wife deserved a slit throat just because she screwed around. Anyway, I still owe Greye," he told her.

He quickly downed the food, followed by the rest of the hot coffee. He ignored the scalding fluid burn the inside of his mouth.

"Drink your coffee. I've got work to do," he insisted.

"Greye is dead, and you still want to chase after her ghost." Her face turned sour.

"Now, you're going to get in the middle of this crazy woman's problems. It'll be just like the murder of Samantha Carter."

Cat paused.

"Remember what her murder did to you? I don't want to see you killing yourself with a bottle."

Ray didn't catch the sympathy in her voice.

"Don't bring her up!" he growled out. His bruised face turned into a mix of rage and pain.

"You know that's not how it works. Florence Rice came to me for help. I have some bastards try to frame me for murder. I can't just let her rot in that clinic."

Cat glanced around at the other patrons sitting at the counter. She gave a feeble smile at their growing interest.

"Keep it down," she warned him. Cat put her hand on his shoulder.

"Listen, I didn't believe her story at first. I was wrong. There's something there, and she needs help. I'm just worried about the cost to you. Her husband has the backing of the doctors and cops. You can't just charge in there and accuse them of the murder of Bingham. Nobody's giving you a confession and hanging themselves in the process. If you don't watch out, they'll throw you in the looney bin to keep her company."

"Well, I'm damn well going to do something," he insisted.

Cat nodded and went quiet. She finished her coffee with shaky hands. Ray glanced over to notice the absent expression on her pale face as he slid off the counter stool.

"Let's go to your office," she suggested. "Maybe we can put our heads together and come up with something that doesn't get you thrown back in jail."

The two of them barely spoke as they walked along Peach Street. After they walked into the office, Ray headed to his bedroom.

"Get us a couple of drinks," he told her. "I want to check out the damage on this once handsome face."

She surprised him by missing a change at a nasty reply.

When he stared into the mirror, Ray barely recognized his reflection. Half of his face remained swollen, with the white of one eye nearly completely bloodshot from a broken blood vessel. He lightly splashed lukewarm water from the faucet on his face and carefully dried his face. Ray re-entered the office after changing his clothes.

Cat had a half-filled glass of whiskey waiting for him on his desk. Ray noticed she had nearly finished her drink.

"What are you thinking?" she asked, leaning back in his chair, which barely squeaked.

"This case centers on Pete Rice and Florence's mother," the shamus grimaced. "Florence's husband might be a weak link. When I called him, asking questions like a reporter, he suddenly got nervous about publicity and hung up on me."

"What about the clinic? Maybe Arizona can check it out for you?"

"No, I can't do that to him. He's on thin ice with Detective Howard's murder. Arizona's got a dead cop with no suspects," he told her.

"My best bet is to track down Pete Rice in Baltimore. If he's worried about reporters calling him, I might get something out of him when I met him in person."

"But Florence is back in the clinic," she pointed out. "Maybe you need to get another lawyer after Horne and his staff."

"It'll take too long," Ray explained. "Besides, I don't know any lawyers who'll work for me around this town. You know the DA has a target on me. Bingham only worked with me because he took risky cases."

"And he charged you double for it," she reminded him.

He nodded as he paced in front of the window. Ray stopped and turned to her suddenly. He winced from his aching stomach muscles.

"Damn, that hurts. I swear that I'm gonna get that bastard cop for what he did," Irish swore.

After composing himself, he continued.

"What you said comes back to Dr. Horne. He must have sent two goons to your friend's apartment. One of them killed Robert Bingham because he was talking to Florence. That means the trail leads to the clinic again."

"You can't go out there," Cat cautioned, then took another drink.

"If Horne calls in the cops and they catch you there, what do you think the district attorney will do? Smyth will have you in prison for years," Irish noticed her hands still shook. He carefully sat on the edge of the desk.

"Alright Cat, what's going on with you? That's your second drink already," Ray observed.

"I don't know what you're talking about," she looked away. "Shouldn't you get tickets if you're heading to Baltimore?"

"When you start talking straight with me." Ray slowly sipped on his Irish whiskey.

After several minutes, the tense silence in the room finally overwhelmed her.

"You're right. Something bothers me about all of this," Cat finally admitted and downed the rest of her drink. Shivering, she placed the empty glass down.

"All of what? What are you trying to tell me?"

"Damn it, I'm not sure," she told him.

Her shoulders sagged. Cat stared out of the window. The latest news came across the wire headlines displayed on the building across the street.

"It's got something to do with that."

"What's the newspaper building got to do with it?" He glanced over to where she was looking.

"It's funny. You sat at this desk every day, reading the latest news coming across the wires on that display. But you've never caught on."

Cat went silent for a moment and held up her empty tumbler. Ray picked up the whiskey bottle and paused. She glanced over and pounded her glass on his desk. He scowled and poured more for her. From her rambling thoughts, he wondered if she'd started with morning with a bottle.

"It was the night that our newspaper reported on another of the garrote murders," Cat continued. "I saw our headlines going out in the *Morning Beacon*; then I saw the news coming in from New York, Boston, Baltimore, on and on. You know what? Not one of those big-city stories had anything about some crazy murder happening. Not one of them!"

"Come on, that means nothing. When I arrived here, you told me crazy things happen in Oyster City," he replied.

She shook her head.

"No, you don't understand! It's been that way since I can remember. Now, it's worse. Each of us has nightmares we agree don't make sense, yet they seem to be the same dream. Since we've met, think of all these insane things that have happened to us," Cat insisted.

"Cat, come…"

"No, listen to me. We're on a ship that explodes and sinks, nearly killing us. You got knifed by the same thug who broke into my apartment. And then, we're nearly killed by a bunch of gangsters because of Greye La Spina."

The woman looked at him, her lips trembling. Her blue eyes searched his face.

"I think this is a cursed place," Cat finally said.

"That's the whiskey talking." Ray glanced away, but she noticed the surprised expression on Ray's face.

"Oh, don't worry, I'm not as drunk as you think I am. But add this to your list, shamus." She gave him a condescending smile. "Think about those nightmares everyone has. I didn't tell you about one that keeps coming back to me."

"It's a nightmare. Comes from…"

"Have a taste of nectar child and become the damned that rise with me," she interrupted him.

His face paled.

"Where the hell did you hear that?" he demanded.

None of us can sleep a full night…" she turned away, trying to stop the tears that started rolling down her cheeks. The woman placed her empty tumbler on the desk.

"That's what you told me in my nightmare. I remember running away from people who were wearing these crazy masks."

Cat continued to stare at her lap.

Ray's dumbfounded expression remained. Shocked, he downed the rest of his drink without tasting it. She had just described a nightmare he remembered. In it, he gave her a glass filled with blood. He shook his head and sighed.

"What is it?" she asked when she glanced up.

"Wait, you saw this too. That's why you recognized the words."

"We all have strange dreams. I might have just overheard you say something at some point," Ray maintained. "I've mentioned those damn masks before. You can't take this too far."

"Don't do this to me!"

"Do what?"

"I'm just trying to explain my feelings. You're so damn bull-headed you don't even realize that I'm worried about you," Cat sniffed, then she reached over and grabbed the flask from him.

She took another swig and looked out of the window. Her tears caused her mascara to run down her cheek. Her vulnerability surprised him. Catherine always tried to keep her emotions in check around him. His mind went back to the description of her nightmare. Ray couldn't find a logical explanation for her remembering an exact line from his dream.

After she gathered herself, Cat pulled a silver compact from her purse and looked in the mirror.

"Damn it; now I look like a mess," she suddenly blurted out. The woman got up and stepped toward the bedroom.

"I hate this city. Nobody can seem to catch a break. This place kills good people; even poor Jack."

Cat entered the bathroom and began using the mirror to touch up her makeup.

"What are you talking about?"

His voice carried into the room as Ray got to his feet.

"Jack Romano, he'd dead. Didn't you know?" Cat called out, then she stopped and stepped back to the doorway of the bedroom.

"Oh, that's right. You were out of town. I guess you couldn't have heard about it when it happened. Jack was one of the first garrote murders. The son of a bitch murdered that poor kid in his backyard."

"That has to be a sick joke."

Disbelief and a growing fury filled his face. Cat told him about the boy's murder. When she finished, there was a look of death in his eyes. She only saw the expression once before. It scared her.

"Who's the lead reporter in these murders? I want some details," he demanded.

"It's Joey Reiser. I told you he's investigating these murders," she replied.

"Then I'm going to see him. You want to come along, or drink your day away?"

Ray was already at the coat rack getting his fedora. She rushed back into the bathroom; her face growing red with anger.

The shamus hurried down the stairs. Cat followed along while hanging on to the handrail. Irish was already across the street when she reached the sidewalk.

"Damn it, wait up," she yelled out.

Ray paid no attention and was inside the building when Cat finally got across the street. Taking the stairs two at a time, Ray saw Joey at the far end of a big and busy room. Desks filled the area, but the reporter sat alone in one corner. Joey typed away, oblivious to the heavy smoke coming from an array of cheap cigars and cigarettes. Ray pushed through a small gaggle of reporters concerned about the upcoming World Series.

"Hello, Joey. You know I could make a small fortune if I put a cigarette girl in this place," Irish said without a smile.

"Irish, I thought I saw you coming this way. I heard you got arrested," the reporter glanced up. "What the hell! Did the cops do that to you?"

"Never mind my face," he replied. "Tell me about Jack Romano, that kid who got it over on the southside of town."

"It's in my articles, and they cost 10 cents when you get the paper," Joey continued typing, his glasses perched precariously on his thin nose. "I've got work to do."

"Don't give me the business," Ray growled as Cat joined them. "I want to know about these murders."

"Come on, Joey," Cat agreed. "Ray knew the kid. You know he'll return the favor."

The reporter looked up at them, and his blue eyes glinted at the idea.

"Alright, but don't complain when I need a heavy to help get some information out of a source," he said with a cagy grin.

"Yeah, I get it. Now, what have you found out about Romano's murder?" Ray asked.

"To be honest, there's not much to go on," the reporter leaned back in his chair. "I guess you've heard most of it. It's the same guy using a wire to kill people all over the state. The kid was the only one in Oyster City so far."

"Any theories about the killer?" The shamus asked impatiently.

"No, just someone that's pretty strong and deliberate." Joey shrugged his shoulders.

Then he pulled a file from the desk. "Whoever's doing it doesn't seem to follow any pattern that I understand."

"How so?" Cat spoke up.

"Well, take Jack, for example. All the other victims are important people in their town. You know, civic leaders who are involved with something important around the state. Then, the guy knocks off some basket case." Joey suddenly stopped when he saw Cat's face.

"I'm sorry, Cat. I forgot you know the family."

"Do the cops have any leads that you've heard about?" Ray picked up the latest paper sitting on the desk and glanced through the most recent articles.

"There are no suspects that I'm aware of. The son of a bitch is cold, precise, and he doesn't make mistakes. Every time, he finds an isolated victim and the killings are quick," the reporter stated as he reviewed his files. "The killer always uses a length of wire, probably piano wire. It's a damn gruesome way to go. As I said, I can't figure out why the killer knocked off the kid."

"Because he was just a kid?" Ray glanced up from the paper.

"Well, that's one point, but remember, the rest are people of influence. They go to the same fancy places and pal around with the gangsters and politicians," he explained. "Also, the manic only got one woman so far. So, there doesn't appear to be a pattern. Mrs. Johnson got it a few days ago. She was an odd bird with money that the governor placed in charge of the anti-corruption group. Made headlines because she was a woman, but the committee wasn't going to investigate anything the governor wanted to keep hidden. That's why it doesn't make sense to me."

He paused, thinking aloud.

"These murders appear random but don't, if you know what I mean. Kind of like the nightmares I've had."

Ray glanced over at Cat at the comment. She tried to remain stoic, but her eyes told him she heard the comment.

"It sounds like a crazy person with a mission," the shamus commented.

"You could be right. There's something else. Nobody in Oyster City except the kid is dead. I mean, we have our share of rich and important people," Joey stated. "I can think of several who would make a good stiff for this killer."

The reporter shook his head as he put his file back on the desk.

"I guess the kid was just in the wrong place at the wrong time. Can't tell about these crazies, I guess."

"Yeah, maybe. But it doesn't make sense. Someone that precise and careful wouldn't make a mistake on the victim," Ray said, mostly to himself. He hurried away, and Cat caught him by his sleeve.

"Don't forget me! I've got a stake in this," she insisted. "What are you planning?"

"I'm not sure," he confessed. "It appears I need to be in two places at the same time."

Chapter 6: A Trip to Nowhere

Later that day, Ray was back in his office. After leaving the *Beacon*, he and Cat pulled into his usual booth at the diner next to Ray's office. As they were talking over coffee, Cat puffed on her cigarettes. It filled the air around them like a low hanging smog. Mildred came to the table and gave Ray an ice bag for his cheek. Irish thought he saw a hint of resentment in Cat's eyes at his special treatment. The idea caused him to grin before he went back to his problems.

While Ray promised her that he was heading to Baltimore, Irish didn't tell Cat the whole truth. He followed another path. On the way out of town, the shamus turned toward Dr. Horne's clinic. He owed it to Florence to help her escape. However, he didn't need Cat to be involved in something that might come back and bite them.

Once he got the prisoner away from the clinic, Ray planned on stopping by the *Sentinel* newspaper. While the reporter had never called him back, he intended to have Florence tell her entire story to the reporter. He needed political pressure. A sympathetic reporter would bring that to her cause.

For her part, Catherine promised she would have Dr. Horne's past investigated by a reporter from her paper. As they talked about the possibilities, Cat appeared more understanding of his client's plight. She even suggested that she could tip off a reporter for the possibility that other patients were in the same boat.

Light a fire to smoke the cockroaches out.

Ray reached the outskirts of town along Route 67 when he turned onto the narrow road leading to the Horne Clinic. He waited for nightfall to sneak into the clinic. Ray hoped Florence was still there. If not, he decided the medical records would tell him. One way or another, he would find his client and help her escape.

He saw the sign to the clinic and pulled his car off the road before reaching the gates of the facility. Ray slid out of the front seat and quietly stepped along the way to the entry. A drowsing guard listened to the radio from his perch inside the guard shack. Passing behind the hut, the shamus slipped into the compound through the open gate.

As he walked along the road, Ray followed the partially lit path into the main compound. He walked by a line of overgrown shrubbery, punctuated by several unlit light poles. When the shamus reached the center of the facility, he found three buildings laid out in a semi-circle. A two-story structure in the middle of the cluster had two lamp lights over the main door. The other buildings were dark.

Ray headed to the front of the main building when he noticed a small pointing to the small administration building on his left. The sign made him change direction, deciding to check out Dr. Horne's office first. As he approached the dark building, Ray kept glancing around for any guards. The shamus noticed light coming from a single window on the ground floor at the corner. Gliding up to the window, he peeked through to see two people inside on a couch. He did a double-take when he glimpsed a half-naked man thrusting into a bored-looking woman. The platinum blonde woman's fake cries of enjoyment barely came through the closed window. Swiftly passing around the corner, Ray found the side entrance.

Irish quietly entered and followed the hallway to the single light coming from under an office door. The sign on the door told him it was the office of Dr. Horne. With a grimace on his face, he pulled his .45 auto and carefully entered the room. The woman's half-closed eyes suddenly widened when she saw Irish standing over them.

"Shut your trap, lady." He growled. "Horne, you and I are going to talk."

The doctor froze, then he looked up at the barrel, which was pointing at his head. Horne's gray eyes were wide with fear; he slowly nodded.

"Get your ass moving! You're taking me to Mrs. Rice." Ray ordered. The doctor fell off his lover in a mad scramble to find his pants while the woman curled up in fear and embarrassment.

"Who are you?" Ray growled at her.

"Velma—Velma Ohr," she stuttered out.

"Yeah, you're in with the rest of these thieves. Alright, you whore, get your clothes on. You're coming along," Irish motioned to her with the barrel of his gun. Her fear quickly turned to anger. She glared at him while pulling on her bra.

"Horne, I know the entire story. You and Wolfe might think you can steal the estate with Pete Rice, but I got news for you. Now, you're about to go down hard. You got a murder pointing at you now," Ray told him smugly. Horne's face drained at the news as he put on his glasses.

"You get only one warning," he told them. "You two are taking me to Florence Rice. Get stupid, and you die."

"You'll never get away…"

Ray stopped the doctor in mid-sentence when he backhanded him with the barrel of his gat. Horne went to his knee, grabbing his cheek. The strike left a bleeding welt.

"Keep talking, and you'll look worse. You tried to pin a murder on me."

The shamus waited impatiently while his captives hurriedly dressed. He led them out of the office and down the hallway. Growling for them to move, he forced the two prisoners across the courtyard under the pale-yellow lights overhead. When they entered a large building with peeling white paint, Ray spotted someone at the end of the hall sitting at a small desk. He grabbed the doctor by the shoulder.

"Go straight to the desk," Ray ordered in a whisper. He pushed Horne in the back with his .45 auto. "Keep it calm and steady."

The group moved to the end of the hall.

"Good evening, doc," a male nurse in white said absently. He missed the wound on Horne's face as he focused on the stranger behind the doctor. Irish stepped to the side and leveled his gun at the slight man.

"On your feet," he ordered.

"Hold it, mister, don't shoot," the attendant automatically raised his hands. The large key ring hooked to his belt jingled from his shaking movements.

"Just get in front of the doc. Just take us to Florence Rice's room," Ray commanded.

The man hesitated as his confused face paled. He glanced back and forth between Ray's gun and Dr. Horne.

"But she's not here. She escaped a few days ago," the man insisted.

"Don't make me angry," the shamus growled back. "The police know Mrs. Rice returned here. Do I need to beat on the shrink?"

"He wouldn't know," Horne suddenly declared.

His confidence returned; the doctor tried to take charge.

"There's no need for violence. I'll take you to her room."

"Alright, everyone will go see her," Ray told him.

The doctor led them down the hallway and into another corridor, where they encountered a locked gate. Nurse Ohr glanced back at Ray. He noticed she watched him with an odd expression of fascination. The shamus slowed and told the male nurse to unlock the gate. Halfway down the hall, Horne pointed to a cell door.

"Open it," he ordered the man with the keys. The attendant hurriedly opened the door. Ray took the man's keys before he forced them to go inside the room.

Inside, they found Florence strapped down on a bed. Ray directed the men to a corner of the room. Then, he ordered Ohr to unstrap Florence.

"The whole gang's here," the woman on the table giggled groggily. She stopped when she recognized Horne.

"I'm going to kill you," Florence told him flatly before disappearing back into her drug-induced world. She turned over on her side, and the hospital gown slid away to expose dark splotches that covered her breasts, belly, and thighs.

"Then I'm going to kill everyone," she giggled. Her head rolled back and forth as she repeatedly sang, "dirty bastards, dirty bastards…"

Her condition infuriated Irish. He grabbed the nurse by her arm and pushed her across the room.

"Bitch, get over with the others!" Ohr fell into the wall as she kept watching the pistol in his hand.

Ray turned to Horne.

"What have you done to her?"

He stepped closer, pointing his weapon at Horne.

"She just on tranquilizers to keep her quiet; they'll wear off in a few hours."

The doctor's condescending tone wore on the shamus.

"And you beat the hell out of her again, you worthless piece of crap. I should give you a bullet for what you've done," he spat out.

Ray pointed the barrel of his weapon at the shrink's face. The nurse cried out in fear and backed away to the wall, where the male attendant joined her.

"I'm in no mood to ask twice. Those thugs that got Florence don't come cheap. Where'd you get them?"

"I don't know what you're talking about," Horne fear showed but held his ground.

However, Ray was in no mood to give him credit. He struck him across the side of his face with the barrel of the gun. The blow sent the doctor's glasses flying.

"Alright, we'll get tough," the shamus snarled. "I'll like hurting you."

Ray sent the doctor to his knees with a wicked punch to his mid-section. Horne looked like a fish out of the water while clutching his belly. Irish glanced at the doctor's fearful companions, who kept their eyes on his gun like they were following the movements of a cobra.

"You've got one more chance before I put a bullet into your knee," Ray warned the doctor.

He lowered the gun to point at the man's leg. "It's the last time I'll be nice about this."

Horne struggled to get the words out. "You're a dead…man—Jacobi will…find you!"

"Are you telling me that you have that damn gangster involved?"

The doctor nodded and finally caught his breath. There was a smug grimace on his face when he looked at Ray.

"You're a dead man," he said again. "Killing me won't matter now. Jacobi knows all about you and that dead lawyer. I'm surprised his guys haven't already rubbed you out after the police released you."

Ray paused, his mind trying to grasp the news. He went over to the bed. Horne's story changed everything. He had to get Florence out of their clutches and away from Oyster City.

"Come on, Florence. Let's get going." The shamus tried to wake the woman. She barely reacted until he lightly slapped her cheek several times.

"Irish, is that you?"

She tried to lift herself from the bed and failed. Ray helped her up when she nearly slid to the floor. He placed her arm over his shoulders and started toward the door.

"You'll never get away with this," Horne spoke up. "If the police don't get you, that gangster's men will. Just leave the woman, and you might get out of this alive."

Ray turned back with a sneer on his face as he pointed the weapon at the doctor.

"I don't think so. Jacobi might be your ace up your sleeve, but your game is up," he said with more confidence than he felt.

"Once Florence is out of the state, I'll have her talk to the reporters. How long do you think your clinic charade will last? A few newspaper headlines will have the state looking at you. I'm betting that Wolfe and Jacobi might decide they don't need you. I'll let you think about that while you're waiting for someone to release you."

Irish closed the door.

~~~

Marion Underhill was waiting outside Cat's apartment when she arrived. He had a broad grin and held a bouquet of roses.

"Come on, get dressed, we have a party we're late for," he held out the flowers. Cat smiled and sniffed the fragrant flowers. When she took the package, thorns pushed through the paper wrap and pricked her.

"Ow! That wasn't smart," she flinched and looked down. Cat turned back to her lover.

"That was so sweet of you. But I thought we were staying here tonight," she gave Marion a disappointed pout.

"Then, you better get changed fast," he told her. "This is a real shindig with the mayor and a lot of other big shots. I was dropping off a piece of jewelry for Mayor Hopely and his wife's anniversary. He suggested I bring you along at the last minute. Come on; you'll love it."

"Alright, I've got a black dress that's perfect." Cat grew excited as she fumbled for her keys.

"Here, let me take those," he offered. Underhill took back the bundle and followed her into the apartment.

"I'll hurry," she told him as she rushed to the bedroom.

"Alright, I'll put these in water," he agreed as he went to her kitchen. While he worked, Underhill glanced through the open door as she hurriedly changed. He enjoyed the voyeur view when she removed her dress.

I think others will approve of that body tonight.

As Marion drove Cat to the party, he kept glancing over at her. Finally, she asked him what was on his mind.

"Well, I saw your friend, the big detective with the funny limp, the other day. He came into the shop about a ring he saw. Did he tell you about it?"

"You mean Ray Irish? Yeah, he's got this idea in his head about a ring he saw. He's in Baltimore on a case," she replied.

"Why do you ask?"

"Oh, no reason. It just seemed odd at the time. You look beautiful tonight," Marion changed the subject. "I'm so glad you're coming with me."

Cat smiled at the compliment. She wondered if Marion was jealous of Irish. The thought amused her.
~~~

"I'm excited you asked me. While I went to a few of these events with Reginald at one point, but you seemed reluctant to invite me. I thought you were afraid I might embarrass you," she told him.

"Pfft, more like I didn't want you to be bored to death," he replied. "Don't worry; they'll eat you up. I heard the Peter Smyth took a liking to you."

"I don't think so." Cat pulled out her compact and checked her lipstick. "He's not a pleasant person."

"Well, you have to admit, getting arrested doesn't make the day of any district attorney," Marion said with a grin. She glared at him, then surprise filled her face.

"Yes, I heard about you and Irish involved with some diplomat's daughter," he said smugly. "Rumors spread around this town like wildfire."

"And you still want me to meet these people? Aren't you running a risk?" She wondered.

"What risk? I'll have the prettiest date at the party," he declared.

The cocktails were flowing freely when the couple arrived at the mayor's home. It was across the street from the La Spina house. When Marion pulled along the curb, Cat saw Henry La Spina and his new bride crossing the street. The bishop wore a black tuxedo while his wife's light green dress showed white in the headlights.

"I took some pictures at their wedding," Cat said as she watched them. "She was a lovely bride."

"Yeah, very nice," he agreed with a smirking grin. "I spent time with her after the wedding. She's got a lot to learn."

Marion realized Cat's expression questioned his statement when he opened his door. He turned back to her.

"What I mean is, she has a lot to learn about how to handle Oyster City society here." He slid out of the car seat before going around the car to open her door.

"Come, my lady, I want to show you off," he told her with a grin as he held out his hand.

They met an ancient servant at the door of the Hopely house. After the servant showed them inside, Cat cast him an amused glance.

"He looks like he just got out of the grave," she whispered to Marion, who laughed loudly.

Marion introduced Cat to the mayor and his wife. Jean Hopely struck Cat as an exceedingly happy, blue-haired woman. She wore a black dress that bulged in odd places, trying to keep the overweight woman's flesh confined.

"My dear, you've been the talk of the party already," Jean told her. She took Cat by the arm. "Come, there are so many people who've asked about you. Watch out for the wolves."

Before the new visitor could stop her, Jean whisked Cat into the multitude of people dressed in fashionable dresses and tuxedos. She glanced back to see Marion and Hopely, who watched her with bemused smiles.

Cat met a half-dozen people who appeared happy to meet her. It was hard to hear with a band in the background. But Cat enjoyed meeting those who ran the city. However, she kept feeling like someone was staring at her. When she scanned the crowd, Cat could no longer see her date. Still, piercing blue eyes were watching her. The hair on the back of her neck rose when she identified the person.

Peter Smyth!

The district attorney stood tall and dignified, appearing next to his brother, Phillip. Catherine had dealings with the DA before, and she decided that must be the reason for the stare.

Well, I'm just as good as the next girl in this society soiree!

For an instant, she thought Peter read her thoughts. Cat turned her attention back to her talkative host. She glanced back and noticed Peter and Phillip walking toward her. They ignored several extended hands from other partygoers. When they got to Cat, Jean interrupted her conversation. She gave them a broad smile and introduced herself to the brothers.

"Oh, I'm quite familiar with Catherine," Peter said in a tone that both fascinated and concerned her.

"But I'm pleased to meet you under better circumstances. I'm sure it was quite a nightmare while you spent time in jail."

His smile appeared more of a leer.

"Marion has spoken highly of your skills."

"I'm flattered," Cat replied. "I didn't know you knew about my photography."

"Of course, they know," Marion leaned over her shoulder as he joined them. "Good to see you, Peter."

The lawyer acknowledged Marion with a slight nod. Phillip tugged at his brother's sleeve.

"Yes, well, if you'll excuse me, I'm needed. I look forward to seeing you again," Peter told Catherine. "Perhaps before you know it."

As he walked away, Marion pulled Cat closer.

"You've made an impression," he whispered. He steered them to the bar. "Peter doesn't normally go out of his way to talk with people."

"I feel like I'm a turkey, and it's too close to Thanksgiving," she replied. Underhill suddenly burst out laughing at her quip. Cat smiled and chuckled as well.

When they got their drinks, Cat felt the stares again. This time she noticed Myrna La Spina looking at her. The newlywed could have been a wallflower as she quietly stood by the wall. She kept stabbing her untouched drink with her cocktail umbrella. Curious, Cat strolled over to meet the newlywed.

"Hello, I'm Catherine Bennett," she introduced herself. "I've known your husband for years. The mission that his church runs is a great service for the community. My mother used it when I was growing up."

Myrna gave her a faint smile at the news. However, her expression remained distracted.

"I'm glad to hear it," she replied. "I spend most of my days there."

Cat carried on a one-sided conversation for a short while. Her comments on Myrna's wedding finally caught the distracted woman's attention.

"Yes, I hope that day was happy for everyone," Myrna replied vaguely.

Cat noticed the woman appeared to be fighting back her tears. Myrna suddenly swallowed down her drink in one gulp and stopped a servant who carried a tray of more drinks. She took one of them after placing her empty glass on the plate. Myrna realized that Cat had stopped talking. The bishop's new bride gave her a quick grin.

"I'm afraid I'm not good company this evening. Please excuse me," she said.

As Myrna walked away, Cat turned to find Marion behind her.

"Did you have an interesting conversation?" His tone was unusually challenging.

He smiled as he handed her another drink.

"She appears a little upset," Cat replied. "I'm afraid I did most of the talking."

Marion turned to see Henry join his wife.

"I guess becoming a bishop's wife takes a lot to get used to," Marion said.

"Now, come with me. I'm going to show you off on the dance floor."

~~~

On the other side of town, Ray Irish was practically carrying Florence out of the building and across the compound. The woman tried to find her footing. However, the rocks and bushes caused her to stumble several times along the way. When they reached Ray's Nash, the interior light revealed her bloody feet as he helped her to the back seat. He pulled a blanket from the trunk, which he put around her.

"Keep down while we drive. We're getting out of town. I'll take you to someplace safe," Ray told her.

With a tired nod, Florence fell back onto the seat. She was fast asleep when Ray took Highway 50, which led to the ferry that went to Baltimore.

As the car reached the outskirts of Easton, Florence woke long enough to ask where they were.

"I'm driving to Matapeake to catch a ferry," he told her.

"I thought I heard you say something about driving me out of state. Was I dreaming?"
~~~

"It was a bluff," he admitted. "I thought about it for the last thirty miles. I don't like the odds. One phone call to the FBI would mean kidnapping charges against me. Your story has no solid evidence to support it. We can't take the risk."

He sighed.

"To be honest, I didn't have much of a plan other than getting you out of there. Nowhere in Oyster City is safe. The only idea that I've come up with is to get you to your friends to hide and see what shakes out. I'll stir up trouble in Baltimore when I investigate your husband."

"That's not much of a plan," she told him.

"Yeah, I'll try to do better," he replied.

The sarcasm was not intentional, but he was tired.

"Now, what about your friends? Are there any that can help? Who can you truly trust? Even better if you can think of someone who your husband won't know or suspect."

"There's Beatrice Bauer," she told him after a long pause. "She was a mentor for me before I met Jim. We were very close. She's a librarian at the Baltimore Public Library. Of all my friends, Bea is the only one that my husband doesn't know. I can't imagine that he would remember her."

He glanced back at her in the rear-view mirror.

"That should be perfect. Just keep the blanket on. Nobody can see you in that outfit. We're taking back roads but, for all I know, the ferry at Matapeake might not be running when we get there."

"I thought you were dead at first, and then they said you would get the blame for Max's murder," she said. "Dr. Wolfe and Horne decided they needed me alive…"

Tears were in her eyes; Florence dropped her head.

"They told me that my mother was dead. They killed her. I know it."

"You can tell me more when you get some sleep. Don't worry; you'll get justice. Just trust me and sleep for a while," Ray told her gently.

Florence agreed silently and pulled the blanket over her as she lay down.

She was asleep when Irish drove up to the dock where a lonely shack stood under a single streetlamp. A small parking area next to the building held a few vehicles. The ferry sat in the water, just past the gate. With its red running lights and green overhead lights, the vessel carried a holiday atmosphere.

However, the place looked deserted. Ray slid out of the car when he saw someone moving inside the shack. A stout man wearing a uniform stepped out under the light. As he drew closer, Ray noticed the guard's suspicious eyes looking over the shamus and his car.

"You still running across?" Ray asked.

He suddenly realized his black and blue face was attracting attention.

"Yes'm if you have three dollars," the man told him with a heavy accent. "Where ya heading?"

"Baltimore," Ray replied as he pulled three bills from his wallet.

"Then, I'll get the gate. Ya almost missed this one. Weren't going to be running until the morning after she leaves," the guard took the money and kept talking as he headed to a wooden barrier placed across the road.

He moved it as Ray got back into his Nash. The guard waved him forward and guided the car along the dock and across the ramp that led onto the ferry.

Ray glanced back to find Florence asleep under the blanket. He got out of the car to stretch his legs and knock the sleep away. The ferry was a flat bottom steamer that probably held a dozen cars in total. Only his Nash and a large truck were on the ship when he heard the whistles blast above him.

Several sailors suddenly appeared from below decks to cast off the lines that tied the boat to the dock. The only other passenger was the truck driver, who came running from the dock at the last minute. He came from the back of the ship, walking past Ray's car. Ray turned to watch the activity on the deck and didn't see the man glance inside his Nash.

The trip across to the south docks of Baltimore took several hours. Ray stayed near his car most of the time. The trucker stopped by near the end of the trip, and the two men spoke briefly. The trucker appeared a bit too curious, so Ray gave him a quick lie, which the man seemed to accept. Then, the sounds of the ferry's whistle broke up the conversation. Not long after, the ship turned into the bay to dock. A short time later, the shamus backed off the boat and turned the car toward Beatrice's place.

About thirty minutes later, Ray's Nash pulled in front of a tiny bungalow. It took several rounds of knocking before a tall woman finally opened the door. She looked them over from behind a pair of pince-nez glasses. The prim gray-haired lady reminded Ray of his high school teacher with a formidable gaze from her green eyes. She wore a flashy red Chinese robe. Then Ray noticed a younger woman standing near the entrance. Her pretty face went dark when she saw Florence as Ray put his coat over her shoulders.

"Florence, what happened?" Beatrice asked.

"I'm aright, but we need your help," she explained. "Can we come inside?"

"Of course," Beatrice stepped aside, allowing them to enter. They passed the other woman, who stepped next to the couch in the living room. She remained quiet while she listened with interest.

"Bea, I'm sorry for coming here," Florence told the older woman, who wrapped an arm over her shoulders.

She led Florence away from Ray.

"I have no place to go and nothing to wear. I can't trust my husband to help me."

"Lady, I'll cut to the chase," Irish interjected. "Your friend is in trouble and needs a place to hide for a while. Her husband is involved in something that stinks. He had her committed to a mental asylum. The police might be looking for us. If they catch her, they'll claim Florence is nuts and involved in a murder. That's what you're up against. Can you help her or not?"

"Murder!" Bea stared at Ray over her glasses. "And who are you?"

"I'm a shamus, and Florence is my client," he explained. "I can't fill you in on all the details, but she's been through hell."

"Of course, I'll help," she exclaimed as she tightened her hold on Florence.

"Come with me, dear."

She glanced back at Irish.

"You can go into the living room while I find Florence some clothing. Amy can get you some coffee."

Ray noticed the scowl from the other woman, but she remained quiet. Beatrice led her friend away with assurances of her safety. Ray followed them halfway down the narrow hallway. Bea led Florence into a second bedroom, where they sat at the edge of a tidy bed. Ray went back to the living room and passed by the master bedroom. There is a queen-sized bed inside with the cover, and the sheet pulled back on both sides.

When he entered the living room, Amy sat on the modern couch. It carried square lines and chrome. As he looked at the woman, he noticed she wasn't planning on offering him coffee. He also realized she might pass for Florence's thinner sister. However, Amy wore her brown hair shorter, and her blue eyes were paler and striking. The woman also had a dusting of freckles across her nose. It gave her the look of someone just out of college.

Amy avoided his momentary stare. Ray scanned the pale green room with uncomfortable looking squared-off furniture. Near the tiled fireplace, a desk held a typewriter and well-ordered stacks of papers. Modern paintings with vivid splotches of paint covered the walls in the room. Ray stood in front of one. He paid the canvas no attention. His tired brain considered his limited next steps.

"That's *Woman in a Red Armchair* by Picasso," Amy's voice intruded upon Ray's thoughts. "Do you like it? Bea is friends with the owner's wife."

"It's not to my taste," Ray grumbled absently. "Do you have a phone book around here?"

With a sour expression, Amy pointed to a small table with a black phone on it. Ray nodded before he went over to find the home address of Jim and Florence Rice. He wrote the address along with the phone number to Beatrice's house.

"Tell Florence that I'm going to see her husband," he told Amy. "She'll need to get a lawyer today. I'll be back as soon as I can. Just don't let her run around in public."

"Her husband won't be up yet," Beatrice told him as she stepped into the room. She handed Ray his coat back.

"Why don't you stay for coffee? I'd like to know more about what's happening. The sun won't come up for a couple of hours,"

Ray paused as he thought about the offer.

"Thanks, but I think I need the element of surprise here," he decided. "Either way, it's a Crapshoot. Besides, the less you know right now, the better for you if this all blows up. We have enemies."

Ray walked out the door and to the car. He glanced over to see the two women looking out the window as he pulled on to the street.

When Ray arrived at the dark house of Jim and Florence Rice, he drove past slowly before coming to a stop two houses away. As he walked back to the house, he glanced at the two parked cars across the street. They were empty.

Stepping onto the lawn, Ray looked over the sizeable colonial-style house. The other homes in the neighborhood, all with a similar design, were dark. He walked around the side of the house. The lights were out inside as he ambled up the back porch. He tested the locked back door.

The shamus paused as he debated his options. Coming back at daylight was too risky with neighbors seeing a stranger hanging around. The dark house implied either that the doc had not called Jim Rice yet or there was nobody inside.

Well, flip a coin; I might not get another opportunity to get this bastard.

Ray looked around in the darkness, then slowly pressed his elbow against the pane of glass in the door. While the cracking sound of the breaking glass barely made any noise, to Ray, it sounded like an explosion in the still night. Large pieces of glass fell inside as he carefully put his hand in to unlock the door. He entered slowly.

The crunch of his leather soles on bits of glass caused him to pause. Then, he moved forward while feeling his way across the kitchen. Ray guessed right about the location of the stairs near the front of the house. He could make out outlines of furniture from slivers of light coming into the house from the street. Ray heard the steady beat of a grandfather clock nearby as the shamus carefully went up the stairs. At the top, he felt along the railing until he saw double doors to a master bedroom.

Ray pulled his .45 auto from the holster under his arm as he entered the room. In the soft light coming from the street, he saw the large bed in the middle of the room. Drawing closer, the man noticed two mounds under the covers. He felt along the wall and found a switch. The light flicked on to reveal a man and woman in the bed.

"Are you Jim Rice?" the shamus asked when the startled man woke.

The blonde woman tried to roll out of bed.

"Don't move, lady," he growled out. "Nobody's going to get hurt. I'm here for some answers."

"Who are you?" The man pulled up the covers.

Irish nearly laughed at the futile gesture. Florence's husband had a narrow nose along with darting eyes. His accent was pure New York.

"You need to come clean, Rice. I already know the bimbo here isn't your wife," Ray stated.

"Plus, I've got the goods on you. You and Horne committed your mother-in-law and wife to the same clinic while you tried to steal the old lady's estate. Does that get your attention?"

"I don't know what you're talking about," Rice insisted. The husband glanced over at his girlfriend.

"Not a good time to play dumb. Didn't Horne tell you that your mother-in-law is dead? That means you've got a murder charge coming." Irish bluffed confidently.

"So that you understand, your wife has escaped from the clinic earlier this evening. She's in hiding, ready to talk. When daylight comes, you're going to have a lot of company with cops and reporters."

Rice's face turned gray at the news.

"You idiot, I told you this wouldn't work." The blonde stared at Jim as her fear poured out. "I'm not going to prison for you."

"Ellen, shut up," Rice spat out. "He doesn't have anything."

"Come on, we're going to see the cops about your little scheme," Ray waved them out of bed with his gun. "No need for your clothes."

"Listen, there's no need for the police," Rice countered. "I've got money. What will it take for you to forget you saw us?"

Ray paused, deciding to take advantage of the man's sudden generosity.

"How much? Horne offered me a lot to go away earlier," he lied. "I think Wolfe will do the same."

He saw Rice light up at the idea.

"Five grand tonight," the man offered. "Another fifteen, when I settle some things."

His beady eyes kept staring at the gun in Ray's hand.

"You mean wait until you settle the old lady's estate?" Irish suddenly grinned. "It's too bad for you that I'm an honest shamus. I've already got a client. Your wife came to me, and she wants you put away for a long stretch. All you did is just confirmed my suspicions. The cops are going to love you. Now, out of bed, before I get angry."

He forced the couple down the stairs after turning on the lights. The blonde was wearing a blue nightgown which barely covered an enticing body. Ray believed she used too much makeup trying to cover her a rather plain face. Rice wore blue pajamas. The man stood well over six-foot-tall, even with his stooped posture.

"Go out the front door and head down the street to my car," he told them.

"I can't go out in public like this," Ellen complained.

"Fine, get a coat from the closet," he replied as he opened the front door. Ray continued watching Ellen as he slowly went backed up to the entrance. The shamus felt the hard jab of a gun barrel poke him in his back.

"Don't move and give me the gun," a familiar voice ordered.

With a sigh, Ray lowered his weapon. The glare of a car's headlights passing by the house momentarily illuminated two large men standing in the doorway as he glanced back. Before he could react, a hand grabbed Ray's gun. Another pair of hands spun the shamus around. The rock-hard fist that struck the shamus in the nose sent Ray back into the living room. Blood spurted from his nose. As he tripped over the carpet, the detective saw his attacker coming at him. The thug pummeled Ray as he struggled to rise from the floor. Unable to stop the heavy blows, Irish endured the pounding for a moment, then he fell unconscious.

Irish woke in the backseat of a car, his arms and legs tightly bound. The thugs didn't bother to gag him. It meant they didn't care if he yelled. However, he wasn't in the mood to talk. He glanced around and saw the back of heads of two men in the front seat. They remained quiet.

After a series of long stretches of rough roads, the car finally stopped. The thugs pulled Ray off the floor and from the back of the black Plymouth. They hustled him towards a small ramshackle building. In the darkness, the structure looked like a barn. It had a distinctive lean to one side.

"Come on, you have a date with Max," Slim told Ray.

"You're the son of a bitch that blindsided me back in Oyster City," Ray growled.

"Yeah, but you got other worries right now, fella. Butcher Max wants to chat with you, and he knows how to get information out of people." Slim pushed the captive through the door, which had a single blacked-out window.

A short, balding man stood by a heavy wooden chair with straps. He wore dungaree pants along with a red flannel shirt. His massive biceps filled the sleeves of his shirt.

"Strap him to the chair," Max told them with an aristocratic Spanish accent. His face was chubby, but his eyes were cold and deadly as he surveyed his next victim.

"Come on, Parker, give me a hand," Slim grumbled as he forced Ray to the chair. The two thugs quickly strapped him into the chair. When they finished, Parker placed Ray's gun on the table next to the small telephone generator. Wires led from the table over to the chair.

"Mr. Irish, even here your name has made the papers," Max told him in apparent admiration.

"However, I should warn you that nothing can save you now. It will make things much easier for you if you answer my questions. Do so precisely and accurately, and you will find your death quick and painless. Like you, I have a reputation. I'm known for extracting information from reluctant people for my employer."

"I'll save you the trouble. Florence is out of the state, and soon the reporters will write all about that worthless husband of hers," Ray opened up. "Now I don't know what Jacobi has on her husband, but I'll bet your boss doesn't want the publicity."

The Spaniard began laughing, quickly joined by the other thugs.

"You're a funny man. You don't realize why you're here, do you? Rice is of no consequence to us," he said. "You spoke to the wrong people on your trip here."

The shamus instantly thought of the truck driver on the ferry.

"Let me guess? Horne got out and made some phone calls," Ray stated. "Somebody put the word out about me."

"Yes, they already knew your car, and the ferry operators always write down the vehicles and license numbers that cross on their ships," Max replied.

"And that means Jacobi has ties to the ferry company. I should have guessed." The prisoner grumbled.

"You don't strike me as a man of great intelligence. Anyway, you're here to provide information on an item you stole a few months back. Our client wants a ring back. You will provide me that information before you die," Max told him with a smile that sent a shiver down Ray's back.

"You're crazy. I don't have any damn ring," he growled out.

"Please don't insult my intelligence. You know the whereabouts of the Singsing of Multo, that most powerful ring from the Philippines. Since you are the last person to have it, and the Smyths are paying me handsomely to determine what you did with this ring. You can start talking with my partners while I prepare my instruments."

Slim suddenly slammed his fist into Irish's belly. The force knocked the wind from him; however, Ray could do nothing while several hard punches struck his abdomen. The grunts of pain escaped him while he tried to suck in the air. Max paid no attention as he slid iron pokers into the front opening of a nearby stove.

"Shamus, it's time to tell us about the ring," Slim told him. Ray's drooping head shook his refusal. Instantly, he received another punch from Slim. This time, the massive fist struck Ray in the face. His head whipped back, and blood immediately flowed from his nose again. The stream of red spilled down his chin and dribbled on his shirt.

"I'm not giving you anything."

Ray spit the blood from his mouth.

"That's what you think," Max said, then he clamped a wire around his arm. The torturer paused for a moment as he looked out of the door of the shack.

"The wind must be picking up outside," he told Parker.

Then, Max instructed the thug to crank the handle on an army surplus telephone generator. Electrical current surged through Irish, sending him into convolutions. Max ordered Parker to stop.

"A servant girl took the ring from the Andras estate," Max said. "Our sources believe you are involved and helped the woman to escape. Where is the ring?"

"Go to hell," Irish panted out.

"I'll let you think about that statement. We have all the time we need," the torturer replied calmly.

"Parker, please start again. I'll let you know when to stop."

This time, Max let the shamus experience several rounds of excruciating electrical torture. The man stood there impassively, watching as Ray's contortions soon covered him with sweat.

The last series of convulsions finally caused the chair to tip over sideways, with Ray striking his head on the packed dirt floor. As he lay there trying to recover, he barely realized the wetness of his pants came from his pee.

Ray barely recognized Slim come over and left the chair upright. Ray's head snapped back and forth with each backhand from the thug. He was beyond pain and unable to speak. His mind could only focus on the odd angles that he saw his torturers working. Ray slowly realized he would eventually break or die.

"He's nearly out of it," Ray heard Slim's voice.

"Our guest will wake up when I use these pokers," Max told the thug as he pulled an iron rod from the stove. The tip was nearly white in the dimly lit room.

"Open his shirt!"

Slim ripped open Ray's clothing as instructed, then stopped when he heard a growing roar coming from outside. Max stepped toward Irish with the poker.

"What the hell…" The words barely got out of the thug's lips before the front wall of the building exploded inward.

A massive black car slammed into the building, dragging Parker under the front bumper. Ray heard the thug's cutoff scream, but he could only watch the chaos surround him. The scattering debris struck Slim as he tried to run to the back of the shack. He went down under a collapsed section of the wall.

Some of the debris struck Ray, sending him and the chair over on his back. The car stopped only a few feet away. While coughing and shaking his head to keep the debris out of his face, the shamus heard the creaking of the driver's door as it opened. Through the dust, Ray saw a pair of high-heeled shoes.

"Get those straps off of him," he heard Florence Rice's voice.

Ray only saw the lower half of the woman's body and a revolver in her hand. Her green dress made her look overly dressed for his rescue. Max came into view with his hands in the air. However, his self-assured manner remained.

Florence forced the torturer to Irish, where he struggled to remove the straps from Ray's arms and legs from the straps. Irish groaned as he rolled away. Despite his pain, the shamus got to his feet and grabbed Max. He slammed him to the ground, then picked up a splintered board. Ray placed the pointed end against the torturer's throat.

"Alright, you foreign bastard, it's time for you to talk," he grimaced. "You have information that I want. What's the arrangement with Jacobi and Smyth? Talk now, or you died in this accident."

Fear filled Max's face from the first time he dealt with retribution from one of his victims.

"I don't know the details," he exclaimed. "I just know he wants the ring, and you have the information."

"That's not enough," Ray pressed down.

"All I heard was something about shadows needed the ring. That's it, I swear," the Spaniard insisted.

"Then, what's Jacobi's interest in Florence?" Ray asked.

"I told you already; he doesn't care about the woman. Wolfe has the arrangement with him," the man stated. "I don't know the details."

"Ray, look out," Florence screamed as her gun went off.

Her shot missed Slim, who pulled himself out of the debris. Irish viciously kicked Max in the head before he ran to Florence. They ducked behind the car while Slim pulled his gun. His bullet struck the vehicle's fender next to Ray's head. The dust momentarily blinded him. Florence rose up and took another shot at the thug. Slim fell back behind a pile of the broken wall with a nearly inaudible groan. Wiping the dust from his eyes, Ray saw Max working his way to the turned over table.

No, you don't, you son of a bitch!

The shamus took off after the torturer. He arrived at the table when Max reached for the .45 pistol on the ground. Ray crashed his body into the smaller man, sending them over the top of two overturned chairs. Ray felt the heat from the hot poker near his face as he almost landed on top of it. Max was quicker.

Wrapping one arm tried to wrap around Ray's neck, he swung around the gun. Ray twisted his head and bit down savagely on Max's arm. Blood flowed as the torturer screamed in pain. Ray rolled his body while he grabbed his opponent's wrist. His move pitched Max over. The shamus grabbed the pistol, and the two men wrestled over the weapon.

Just as Max forced the gun barrel toward Irish, Ray spotted the poker. He grabbed it and whipped the steel into Max's face. The torturer fell back, losing his grip on the weapon as he held his hand over his seared flesh. When Irish pulled the gun away, causing the firearm to go off. The bullet struck Max in the belly. While the man died screaming, Ray felt the tug on his clothes. It was from Florence.

"Come on, my car is outside," she yelled in his ear.

They left the shrieking man on the ground. The shamus followed her toward the open space that used to be a wall. Another shot rang out, and they saw Slim moving toward them. He stooped with one arm injured while pointing his heater toward Florence. She turned, then fired her revolver. Slim went down from a bullet in the chest. Ray caught up with Florence, and they rushed out of the building as flames peeked through the broken wood.

"It's over there," Florence said.

Ray noticed a dark DeSoto coupe in the light.

"You drive," he told Florence when they reached the car.

As they sped away, Ray watched the fire quickly spreading over the building.

"I don't know how you found me, but I'm damn glad you did," he told her.

"I overheard you tell Bea about going to see Jim," she explained. "It took me a while to talk her out of this car so that I could follow you."

"And the revolver?" He asked.

Florence went quiet. They turned on to a rough, paved road.

"I thought about killing Jim for what he did," she finally admitted. "But I drove up when those men were taking you away. I guess I didn't have any choice."

"Yeah, you had a choice." He glanced over at her, suddenly concerned about her motives.

"Still, I'm damn glad you followed me. You were good there. How did you learn to shoot like that?"

"My daddy taught me when I was younger. We had a small farm where we spent the summers. He might have been a businessman, but he wanted me to know how to protect myself," Florence explained.

Ray slid his .45 auto into his holster. He let out a slight groan as he moved.

"Are you alright?" She glanced over.

"Yeah, I'll survive. At least those bastards won't torture anyone again. It was a gutsy call to run their car into the building. However, you overdressed for my rescue," he joked.

"Thanks," a quick grin flashed across her face. "Maybe I should have told Bea that before I left. Anyway, I didn't know how many of those people were in there. I decided to bring in the tank. I saw it in a movie once. It sounded like they were forcing you to talk about some ring. What's that all about?"

Ray was taking stock of the damage to his face. He carefully probed around with his fingers. Her question reminded him of another problem in his life.

"It was another case, nothing for you to worry about," he lied. "At least they didn't do that much more damage to my face."

He inhaled when he pressed into a sore spot.

"I'm going to need a new suit and shirt. The sun will be up soon."

"What about Jim?" Her tone turned unpleasant.

"I suspect that he's gone into hiding now," Ray told her. "It'll take some time for me to track him down with his mistress. You have to get back to stay with Beatrice."

After catching the surprised look on his client's face, Ray suddenly realized that Florence didn't know. He apologized for springing the news on her.

"It doesn't matter, I should have known," Florence replied while her stunned expression quickly changed into a grimace. "He won't like what I'll tell him."

Ray lifted his head and looked her over. The dim dashboard light glowed, showing her determined and embittered face.

"Just remember, we'll get you out of this. Jim and his two doctors will spend a long time behind bars," he assured her. "Maybe even worse if they can prove your mother died because of them."

"Along with that bastard Sam," Florence took the next turn. "He needs to get it as well."

Ray nodded. They went quiet with their thoughts as the car passed a sign telling them they were in Baltimore again.

Chapter 7: Making It Right

Florence pulled into the narrow driveway at Beatrice's house as the sun rose. The spindly woman was at the door about to give Florence a lecture before she saw Ray.

"Get in here," she waved them inside while holding the door open.

The librarian immediately questioned Florence concerning her whereabouts. Florence recapped Ray's capture and escape from the thugs as Bea led her into the living home. They left Amy behind with Ray. She glanced uncomfortably at the injured shamus in ripped and bloody clothes.

"Come on; you can clean up in the bathroom," Amy told him. She led them to the back of the house.

"What happened?" She asked.

"Let's just say that Florence saved my bacon," he explained.

"Don't use the towels in there; I'll get old ones for you use." She ordered when she stopped at a small closet.

Ray went to the bathroom entrance.

"I have a stake in this if the police suddenly show up," Amy said as she came back. "Are you saying it's better that I don't know?"

"Yeah, that's one way of putting it," he agreed. "I'm sure your friend will let you know the details."

He slid past her into the bathroom.

"Not likely," Amy sniffed, then disappeared.

The shamus quickly stripped down to his undershirt. He carefully washed his face, trying to avoid the many bruised areas. As he got a good look at his reflection in the mirror, Ray decided he looked like a punch-drunk fighter who lost the last couple of fights at one time.

"You look like hell." Amy stood at the doorway after returning.

"Just another normal day." He ran his wet fingers through his scalp, trying to find more injured places.

Ray felt the woman's inspection of him, but he continued working on cleaning his wounds.

"Did you lose your finger in the war?" she finally asked.

"No, that was a present from a gangster in Oyster City," he glanced at his hand, and slowly made a fist.

Even his knuckles hurt.

"Florence will stay here until I get this sorted out," Irish changed the subject. "I'll get a hotel, so it's safer for everyone. Any place to get secondhand clothes near here?"

Amy shook her head.

"There's no need for you to leave. Bea already took off with Mrs. Rice to get you clothes. At least that's what they said."

"It's Monday," Irish pointed out. "I thought she worked at the library."

"Bea told me she's calling in sick today. Mrs. Rice will get her full attention." Amy bitterly replied.

She pulled away from the door to look into the living room as they heard the front door open and close.

It dawned on him how much he didn't know about his client or the other women in the house. Ray kept glancing at Amy through the reflection in the mirror while he dabbed the towel on his face and neck. She wore a nicely tailored pantsuit. Given her hostile attitude toward him, he guessed her experiences with men drove much of it.

"You got any iodine?"

She glanced back.

"It's in the cabinet!" Amy's replied curtly.

She walked into the living room as Ray used a piece of toilet paper to dab the stinging liquid on the worst of his cuts.

"What do you do around here? I assume you probably work somewhere." He raised his voice as he stepped to the bathroom entrance.

Amy acted like she didn't hear him at first. She was looking out the front window.

"I'm a writer," she finally told him as she came back to the bathroom.

"Any stories I might know? I'm partial to science fiction myself." Ray picked up his ripped and bloody shirt from the floor. He put it in the sink and turned on the water again.

"I doubt it. I write poetry and articles for literary magazines," Amy explained. "You don't get rich, but it's my passion. You might look under the name of Amy Salzer."

Puzzled, the woman crossed her arms as she watched him.

"Why the sudden questions about me?"

"Trying to understand things that I observe," he admitted. "For instance, the relationships between you three women are opening my eyes. Did you know Beatrice gave Florence a gun?"

Amy's eyes narrowed.

"Yes, I overheard Mrs. Rice tell Bea about the terrible things her husband did to her before she left Baltimore. I'm sure she told you about her husband beating her. She showed us the marks on her belly. He's just a pig, just like all men!"

The shamus suddenly stopped wringing the water out of the fabric when he halted. He glared at Amy.

"She lied to you. Her husband might be a louse, but those bruises came from those damn thugs at that clinic." Ray picked up his coat, deciding it would need dry cleaning or thrown away.

"Even though Florence saved my life, it was dumb for you and Beatrice to let her go. Those thugs could track find this place if they got the license plate number from the car."

He shifted his focus to the woman. She faced him with her hands defiantly placed on her hips.

"I get it," Ray pushed past her with clothes in hand. "You got a thing against guys. Funny, I never knew that Florence is a lavender like you. Now, you're upset because she's getting kindness from your girlfriend."

"How dare you!" She followed close on his heels.

Ray stopped and turned. Amy barely avoided running into him.

"Listen, it doesn't take a genius to see what's happening. Since you and Florence have a similar look, I guess Bea likes the appearance. She's probably the butch, and you get to play the wife."

"You're a son of a bitch," she spat out, her face red.

"That's probably true," he quipped. "But I'm not getting involved in some damn lovers' spat between you three women. My job is to keep Florence alive while putting some rats in jail."

"And you're not doing a good job of that, are you?" Amy crossed her arms in satisfaction.

"Listen, you need to get over yourself," he told her. "Otherwise, Jacobi's men will make sure we all end up dead."

The woman's face filled with fury, but she recognized the name.

"The gangster? Is he involved? You should have told us."

Ray nodded.

"You're probably right. Then again, you've kept showing me your damn low regard for men since I arrived. Maybe, kiki's like you can't think any differently. Next time, don't consider a guy your enemy until you know him."

He waited for her to explode, but instead, she turned and left the room. He gave a grim smile as she slammed the bedroom door.

Yeah, I've been around the block, lady.

About an hour later, Florence and Beatrice arrived back at the house. Florence handed Ray a used suit, along with a white shirt. He grumbled a thank you before telling Florence he was getting a hotel room before he went looking for her husband.

"I think you might want to get out of state," he offered.

He didn't expect her to take to the idea. He was correct.

"We've been discussing this mess and Bea wants me to stay here," Florence paused. She smiled at Beatrice. "That is, as long as I don't run off without her."

Amy entered the room, and the smile fell away from Florence. The tension caused Ray to speak up.

"Did you happen to get a morning paper? I want to see the news from Oyster City."

"It's on the front porch," Bea told him. "Go get your clothes on."

Ray went back to the bathroom. When he returned, Florence was waiting with the newspaper in her hand. The other women were quietly talking in the kitchen. He only heard the clinking sound of dishes along with running water.

"There's nothing about my escape," she said. "I'm surprised. It doesn't make sense."

"I don't like it," he agreed with a whisper. "With Jacobi involved, Horne and Wolfe probably don't want the cops involved. They will have gangster friends looking for you. That makes everything much more dangerous until we can expose them. After I get a room, I'm going to contact a newspaper contact I have."

"You think anyone knows that you and I killed those men of Jacobi's?"

Ray swore she had a bit of pride in her question. But her expression carried a worried puzzlement.

"No, I don't think so. I didn't see anyone following us. We only saw cars passing us as we met them. Still, we can't be sure. Max might have told Jacobi he found me. You need to be careful."

He paused.

"Make sure Amy doesn't start talking. She's not your friend," he warned her.

"Remember, I'm crazy," Florence replied with a smile. "I know Amy doesn't like me, but she will do anything Bea tells her. I didn't tell you that Bea and I always had a special relationship."

Florence paused at his smirk.

"Yeah, I've already figured out some of that. To be blunt, I don't care. I've got a gangster trying to kill me," he explained. "It's probably safer for you here. Just remain out of sight. No more following me. Got that?"

Before Florence agreed, the other women entered the room. The tension hung in the air, but Ray didn't care. He went to the phone and called the taxi company. Fifteen minutes later, Ray entered a cab and directed the driver to Florence Rice's address to get his car.

<div align="center">~~~</div>

Myrna Bennett arrived at the Salvation Mission House early. She spoke with Mr. Davis, the director, for a moment before she slipped back into the kitchen. Since her introduction into the Shadows, the mission was the only place where the woman could get away from her husband. She had lost all hope that Henry La Spina would take her away from the hideous world they lived.

Enduring the terror of her forced involvement in a cult of demon worshippers, Myrna found solace working with good people helping others. She also enjoyed cooking and found it took her mind off thinking about her problems. As she worked, Myrna didn't hear the person coming up behind her.

"I got your note, Mrs. La Spina. Is there something I can do for you?" Catherine Bennett stood by the door.

"Miss Bennett, I'm glad you could come over this morning. I know it was pretty early after all the festivities last night." Myrna went to the door and glanced out into the hallway before shutting the door. "I think we should have our conversation in a quieter place."

The woman motioned for Cat to follow her. The two women went into a room with racks of shelves partially filled with canned goods. Myrna shut the door behind them.

"I understand you are friends with Mr. Irish. There were a few articles about him in the newspaper. I know that the district attorney hates him. Can I trust your friend?" the bishop's wife asked.

"Yes, Ray is one of the few in Oyster City that you can say that about," Cat agreed. "That's part of the reason so many people don't like him."

"Then tell me why you trust my husband, Henry? You say you've known him for years."

Puzzled, Cat thought she misunderstood the woman's question.

"What I meant was I remember him when he was coming to this building. He was always so cheerful and supportive when my mom and I came here. It helped my mother at the time. He meant a lot to my family," she explained. Catherine felt uncomfortable as Mrs. La Spina's continued nervous glances at the door.

"Would you go to Henry and trust him with your life if he wasn't wearing the garments of a bishop?"

Catherine crooked her head at the question.

"I'm not sure I follow you."

"You have fond memories because he's a man of the cloth." The woman paused and lowered her voice.

"When I spoke to Marion Underwood about you, he mentioned your work for the newspaper and this detective. I overheard him talking about Mr. Irish coming to his shop the other day concerning a ring that Henry's first wife wore. Do you know anything about that?"

"Yes, Ray has a theory about your husband's first wife," Cat said, then she turned red.

"I'm sorry, but it's a crazy idea. I don't want to upset you. Let's drop it."

Myrna shook her head.

"It's too late for that. Did you know that Marion Underwood told Peter Smyth about Mr. Irish coming to his shop? Would you like to know Peter Smyth's response?"

Catherine hesitated and shook her head.

"Marion would have told me!"

The bishop's wife gave her a sympathetic smile.

"My dear, you're as naïve as I was until my wedding day. Mr. Underwood is no better than my husband."

Cat backed away as confusion filled her face.

"Why are you saying this? I don't understand."

"Because I don't want to end up like Henry's first wife, or worse!" Myrna paused as her pained expression caught Cat's attention. "I need to know everything. Henry told me that his wife fell overboard while they were on a cruise. I'm convinced that didn't happen. Now, what does your friend believe?"

"You have to remember that there's no proof and Ray was upset by her death." Cat tried to avoid telling her.

"Why was Mr. Irish upset? Miss Bennett, I realize I'm asking a lot from you. But I must know about what happened."

Cat took a deep breath.

"You see, Ray and Greye were having a relationship. Irish believes that your husband had something to do with Greye's death," she told Myrna. "Listen, the story is pretty morbid. Do you really want to know?"

She was surprised by Myrna's sudden laugh.

"Catherine, you can't possibly imagine what morbid is. Please go on."

Cat hesitated, then finally she nodded.

"You're not going like it, but Ray took me over to a morgue that handles the bodies that wash ashore. He found an unidentified woman who he claims is Greye."

Myrna's face paled slightly. "Why does he believe it?"

"The woman's left ring finger was missing," Cat replied.

"And someone cut her throat," Myrna stated.

She looked down at the ring on her finger. The woman pulled it off and held it up for Cat to see.

"Mr. Irish is correct. I'll never wear this again!"

Myrna went to the door. She pressed her ear to the door for a moment before coming back to Cat.

"I can't tell you more, but we're both in danger," Myrna insisted. "You do not know how bad it is. I want Mr. Irish to get me out of Oyster City. I'll pay him well for this help. There are others involved who might be watching you."

Cat couldn't reply. She remained dumbfounded by the comment. Myrna came closer and put her hand on Cat's shoulder.

"Catherine, I'm not crazy, but I'm terrified! You should be as well. You could be the next one they want. I saw how Peter and Phillip Smyth watched you last night. Didn't you feel everyone watching you? The Shadows like what they saw."

Cat remembered the same feeling from the party. However, the woman's words about shadows surprised her.

"I thought it was just my imagination. What do you mean by shadows?"

"It's what the group calls themselves. These are powerful people who have made a deal with the devil. Peter Smyth has plans for you. And nothing would surprise me concerning my husband," Myrna replied bitterly.

"Will you deliver this message to Mr. Irish for me? I have to leave town, and I need help."

"I suppose I can. But Ray's out of town, so I'm not sure how soon he'll get it. Maybe you should explain more to me. Talking about it might help," Cat offered.

Myrna glanced back at the door, then took Cat by her elbow. She guided them to the far side of the room.

"I'm taking a tremendous risk by talking with you. I'm living in a nightmare since marriage. Mr. Irish and you might be the only ones who can help me."

The bishop's wife hand's visibly shook as she spoke.

"I see that you're afraid. I'm Ray's partner in many of his cases, so give me more details. Are you afraid of your husband?"

Myrna nodded, but she remained quiet. Her internal struggle was clear; her eyes fixed on the floor.

"Henry's involved, but there are others," she slowly admitted. "I swear to God that they're insane. How did I know that the dead woman you saw had a slit throat? I've seen this group string up people to kill them in rituals. They made me…"

She stopped and looked up at Cat.

"Nobody can stop them. That's why I must run away. Someplace they'll never find me. But I can't just leave without protection to help me escape. I want to hire Mr. Irish for this."

"Who else is involved?" Cat asked. Her tone verged in disbelief, and Myrna glared at her.

"No, I'm risking my life and yours by telling you this much. But we're both dead if you say anything to anyone other than Mr. Irish. Whatever you do, don't trust Marion Underwood. He has connections everywhere."

"Why? What's that supposed to mean?"

"It means I've seen what my husband's capable of doing. He and Underworld fear Peter Smyth, and they will do anything for him." Myrna stopped when she recognized the mix of confusion and suspicion in Cat's face.

"Catherine, ask yourself why your boyfriend is suddenly so interested in you. Why were you invited to the party at the last minute? Peter Smyth told him to do that. You must keep quiet and remember you're in danger, just like me."

The bishop's wife started to leave.

"Alright, I'll go to Ray for you. I won't tell anyone about this conversation," Cat caught Myrna before she got to the door.

"How do we meet with you?"

Myrna looked at the door, then whispered to Cat.

"Don't come to me. I'll call Mr. Irish at his office. Remember what I told you about Marion. He and Henry are part of the same group of people who will destroy us if we don't get out of Oyster City."

~~~

Ray Irish found Oscar Hewlett sitting at a small desk. The *Sentinel* reporter had a pipe dangling from his mouth while he listened to a police broadcast coming through the receiver. Ray stood by, staring at the reporter until the man looked at him.

"Is there something I can help you with?" Hewlett turned down the volume. He focused on the battered face of his visitor.

"Yeah, I'm Ray Irish. I've been waiting for your call for a few days," he replied.

Hewlett remained confused.

"I'm not sure what you're talking about."

"Yeah, start checking your messages. There's a clinic down in Oyster City run by a corrupt doctor named Horne. I know he ties into a man you know pretty well," Ray told him.

"Who would that be?"

"Dr. Wolfe at the insane asylum," he replied. "You wrote articles about him. I went over to the library and looked them up. You know Wolfe is dirty. He and Dr. Horne are partners at that clinic. I also tie them to Jacobi's gang. Are you interested in a front-page story now?"

The reporter's mouth opened, and his pipe fell on his desk.

"Are you sure?"

"I wouldn't be here unless I was. Do you want this exclusive, or should I let you get back to chasing the next police case?"

His mocking tone caused Hewlett to chuckle.

"Alright, I'm an ass for not returning your call. Now, tell me what's going on." The reporter leaned back in his chair. "Did Jacobi's boys do that to your face?"

Irish grabbed a chair from another desk and sat down.

"Yeah, his boys did a number on me. First things first," he declared. "Are you willing to write a story about Jacobi? He's not going to like that."

"Well, as you know, Jacobi's a bad customer," Hewlett agreed. "And I'm not stupid enough to take him on directly..."

"Then you're no good to me," Ray interrupted.

"Calm down and let me think!" The reporter lifted his notebook.

"If you say Wolfe's involved, then I can focus on the story about him and his partner. But first, I have to know if your story is worth my time."

Irish quickly gave a recap of the last couple of days to Hewlett, who began taking notes. He explained their escape and his trip to Baltimore.
~~~

"Alright, I've got an angle. I'll keep the story about Florence and her mother getting railroaded by the husband, along with Wolfe and this Horne character." The reporter's eyes brightened as he already pictured the headlines.

"Well, Jim Rice will not like you anyway," Ray explained about his phone call, posing as a reporter.

"Are you trying to take my job?" Hewlett chuckled. "Damn, I wish I had photos of your escape. Alright, we've got a great story. I take it that Florence Rice is your client. Can I interview her? I'll need pictures as well."

"Alright, I'll arrange it," Ray told him. "I'll call and let you know where and when. One thing though, you keep this story from the cops."

Hewlett leaned forward.

"Yeah, you've got a reason to be suspicious. Where are you staying?"

"Not yet. I do not trust anyone at this point. I'll call you with the news," Ray told him. "And this time, check your damn messages."

"Alright, I'll make sure of it. You might already know this, but having Jacobi as your enemy makes your days limited here. He makes his money from the rackets and gambling. His boys also control the docks and have ties with the ferry operators."

"Yeah, I get it," Irish replied.

"A lot of people get paid to look the other way. Supposedly, he's been pushing his operations down to Oyster City since Guy Young killed himself," the reporter explained.

Oscar leaned back in his chair, trying to remember something. Then he did a double-take.

"What a minute, Irish! Now I recognize your name. You're the one involved in the capture of Guy Young. I read the wire about your gunfight with his gang."

There was a hint of admiration in Hewlett's voice. Irish nodded.

"Then you're damn lucky that Jacobi let you go."

"It wasn't luck, but we'll skip it," the shamus explained. "Do you know why Jacobi would work for Wolfe and Horne? There aren't any ties that you know about them. I think Wolfe has a tie to Peter Smyth, but I'm not sure."

The reporter shook his head as he lit his pipe. The fragrant aroma of the tobacco soon filled the air.

"Nothing I've heard. All I know for sure is that Wolfe and Smyth went to the same schools together. I believe Wolfe has an older brother who works for that rich old lady down there. What's her name?"

"You mean Andras?" Ray asked. "I'll have to look into that connection. In the meantime, I'm tracking down Florence's husband, Jim Rice. He's got some floozy who's probably still with him. I'll let you know where Jim might have landed when I call you."

"A bit of advice when you look for information around here. Anything that involves Jacobi will get back to him. Make sure you have your back covered and keep a low profile," Hewlett warned.

Fifteen minutes later, Ray went back to his room. It was inside a fleabag hotel with a good view of the street, along with a quick escape down the back stairs. After sitting on the bed, the shamus put in a call to Beatrice's house. She answered, and Ray told her that Oscar Hewlett would interview Florence about her experiences.

"Are you sure that's a good idea? She's still a wanted fugitive," Bea reminded him.

"Yeah, it's a risk, but this reporter has written about Dr. Wolfe. He's legit," he told her. "Plus, the heat might get people nervous. That's alright at this point."

At the end of the discussion, Bea agreed with his idea and told Ray she would take Florence to meet the reporter. Ray thanked the woman and told her he would call when he found Florence's husband. Then, he suggested they remained out of sight when the story broke.

"I won't be out there since I'm a target right now. I'm guessing it might take a few days, so sit tight and keep an eye on things."

As he put down the receiver, Ray let out a long breath before he picked up his hat.

Time to track down a rat!

~~~

Late the next morning, Florence sat on a bench in a quiet nook as she waited for the train. Bea sat next to her as they whispered. The two women drove straight to the station after Florence's interview with the reporter. The reporter or his continued assurances that the story would be front-page news impressed neither woman. Hewlett promised Florence that he would seek justice on her behalf against the corrupt doctors and her husband.

"I'm not sure about this," Florence told Bea. "I mean, Irish helped me. Maybe I should stay."

Bea shook her head.

"Florence, I'm so happy to have you back. But you've already forgotten what I've told you. You can't trust any of them. Hewlett can't force the police to throw those bastards in jail. Last night, you agreed these men are both just using you for their benefit. It wasn't any different than when you were in college. Men use you for their purposes. That detective is no different than your husband."

"I don't think Irish is like Jim," Florence argued.

"My dear, don't fool yourself. This detective knows your mother had money," Bea scoffed. "He also knows that we've had a relationship. Amy told me he called her a kiki. Can you trust someone who insults my friends?"

Florence's face grew dark at the news.
~~~

"Now I don't trust him, and you shouldn't either. Haven't I always guided you to do the right thing?"

Bea put her hand on the woman's shoulder.

"No, you're right. I must make things right. Amy's idea will put this to rest," Florence agreed.

"Plus, you will get justice. Honey, you agreed about everything last night. Even better, no one will ever know."

Bea carefully watched her lover. She frowned at her hesitation.

"Florence, if you don't think you can do this, well—it's really up to you. You know that I'll protect you."

Florence looked down at her lap. She saw the chrome barrel of the gun in her purse. As she considered her options, the woman felt a surge of anger well up inside of her. Then, the whistle of the train arriving broke through her thoughts.

"You're the only one that understands me."

"Of course I do. Now you don't worry about a thing. Amy will handle Mr. Irish and the reporter. We must do this. I'll be with you each step along the way."

Bea leaned over and kissed Florence on the lips. Florence wrapped her arms around the woman's neck and returned the kiss passionately. Bea pushed her back while she glanced around.

"No, dear, not in public. We have our roles to play in Baltimore," Bea reminded her. "Come, it's time."

The two women stood with their overnight bags in hand. Together, they went out the door to the train platform.

~~~

Two days later, Ray Irish finally tracked down Jim Rice. It took a few greenbacks to bribe the man's accountant to find what bank Florence's husband used. After that, Ray staked out the bank while sitting in his car or waiting at the diner across the street from the bank. He sat at a table looking out the front window on the second day. The shamus suddenly spotted Ellen entering the bank. The blonde's tight green dress and white hat made it clear she wasn't trying to hide her presence.

After throwing a tip on the table, Ray hurried across the street and got into his car. Rice's mistress came out of the bank several minutes later. She went across the street to a waiting car. Ray recognized Jim Rice inside the vehicle behind the wheel. The shamus immediately did a U-turn with his Nash. He slowed to a crawl, waiting for the couple to pull out of their parking space.

The shamus backed off and carefully trailed the car to the outskirts of Baltimore. Gnawing in the back of his mind, Ray could not shake off his concerns about Florence. When he called the house, Amy told him that Beatrice and Florence were out shopping. The woman snippily told him to call back later. After
~~~

he hung up, Ray tried to reassure himself about his client. As he followed his quarry, the shamus kept wondering if he should have kept Florence with him.

Jim Rice took his time, stopping off at a liquor store and a grocery store before his vehicle finally turned into a parking lot of the Lazy A Motel. The U-shaped building sat between the main road and the railroad tracks. The bright stucco walls, flat tile roof, and cast-iron railings stood out like a sore thumb. A vast, rusty steel train maintenance building sat across the road about fifty yards away.

Ray stopped along the road and watched as the couple turned into an open garage between the guest rooms. They quickly entered their accommodations at the end of the building.

Well, I located them, but now what?

As he sat in the car, Irish mentally laid out his choices. The police might be interested, but at this point, Ray had no proof against Rice except the word of his wife.

Florence was still a fugitive from a mental clinic.

On the other hand, the newspaper's headlines that morning carried Hewlett's story about Florence. The article was sympathetic to his client's plight. Plus, the photo of her did an excellent job of showing the distraught woman abandoned by a heartless husband. To Ray, it left only one option. He would get Hewlett over to the motel before Rice skipped town.

A half-mile down the road, Ray pulled into a café parking lot. He found the phone and called Hewlett. The operator told him that the reporter hadn't shown up at the office yet. Ray left the operator the number at the café, silently cursing under his breath as he hung up. He went to the counter where a fat man sat on a stool, looking bored. Ray ordered a coffee, and then he went back to the phone booth.

Bea answered on the second ring. He overheard her call out to Florence.

"Listen, I know I've been out of the loop, but I found your husband," he told his client. "Did you see the article about you?"

"Ah…yes and I appreciate your help. What are you going to do?"

"I'm waiting on a call back from Hewlett. I think he needs to confront your husband before the cops to help protect you. That article should get the police looking for Horne and Wolfe. However, I'm still worried about Jacobi's men out looking for you. You need to be cautious," Ray warned. "Where have you been? Amy has been the only one around."

"I can explain when you come to pick me up at Beatrice's house," she said. "Don't send Hewlett out there unless I go along with him. I want to see this. Where did you find Jim?"

Ray told her, then he tried to talk her out of coming along.

"Are you sure you want to be with Hewlett? It's likely to get pretty rough."

He didn't like the idea of her meeting up with her husband's mistress. There was already enough publicity about Florence. She didn't need more photos of her confronting Ellen.

"Of course, I'm going along. I'll explain what happened to me when we meet," the woman stated. "Why don't we set up everything when you get here?"

"Alright, I'll be over there in half an hour."

Ray hung up the phone and went to the counter. He slammed down the coffee and burned his tongue before heading out the door.

When the shamus arrived at Bea's house, he noticed her car was gone. He went to the door and knocked. Suspicion filled Ray's face when Bea opened the door. She had a smug look that bothered him.

"Where's Florence?" He asked.

Bea glanced back at Amy.

"We're not sure," she replied with exaggerated innocence. "I don't believe she told us where she was going."

Ray peered over at Amy, and he noticed she avoided his gaze.

"Alright, you two, what are you hiding?"

"I don't know what you're asking us. Florence asked for the keys to my car, and I let her borrow it," Bea told him. "You're the shamus; you figure it out!"

"Lady, what game are you playing? I only got Amy on the phone when I called to check-in."

"It's a shame, but I don't know what you're talking about. I'm sure Florence will let you know when she wants to talk with you."

The woman's tone of arrogance sounded like fingernails running down a chalkboard. He grew angry.

"I'm tired of your stalling," the detective stated. "Now, I want the truth. Otherwise, I'll call the cops about you and your girlfriend there. I'm sure they'll find interest in your breaking the sodomy laws. The publicity won't be good for you and your job. I'm not bluffing. Now where's Florence!"

Beatrice stared at him coldly and drew a deep breath after a glance at Amy.

"I knew you were a bastard the first time I saw you. Alright, mister, you want to know what happened. Florence told us what those men did to her in the clinic. I escorted her back to Oyster City. There's only one thing she could do. She decided to stop the evil Horne and Wolfe. Florence struck back. She's doing this for herself and for everyone who's different."

"You insane bitch! What have you done?"

"I'm fixing the problem," the woman said triumphantly. She stood tall with her arms crossed and her face screwed up in bitter fury.

"Dr. Wolfe's treatment to fix the problems of people like Florence, Amy, and myself. I saw what he's done to girls like us."

Bea stopped as a wave of emotion overcame her momentarily. Amy came to the woman and held her.

"Patty committed suicide because of that shrink. I've seen how you think. You're no different from Wolfe," Amy told him. "That bastard drilled into her brain. When they finally released Patty, she killed herself."

"Look." Irish tried to calm the women. "I'm not like Wolfe. I'm trying to help Florence. She's your friend, remember? Now, tell me what's happened."

"You're a rutting pig who only wanted the money," Bea countered.

"But there's nothing you can do now. I gave Florence my gun, and I went with her while she took care of them. Florence shot each of her tormentors down like dogs. Once Florence finishes with her husband, I'll help her leave the country. She'll be free."

"No, you just gave her to people like Dr. Wolfe, you wicked bitch. They'll judge her insane, and you know it. Otherwise, you'd be with her now."

Ray turned and hurried to the door.

~~~

When he arrived at the Lazy A Motel, Irish found Bea's car parked behind Jim Rice's vehicle. He sprinted to the open door. Inside he found an emotionless Florence sitting in a chair beside the door. Her husband lay face down on the floor. The spreading pool of blood gathered by at the woman's feet. Ellen, Jim Rice's mistress, lay sprawled across the bed. Her open, vacant eyes stared at the ceiling. The woman's blue blouse showed three rings of blood on her chest.

"It's finished," Florence whispered. "The bastard won't hurt anyone anymore."

Ray surveyed the scene quickly, and then he stared down at his client. He saw a woman who carried the same vacant expression of battle fatigue he saw in the Pacific.

That bitch Bea drove her into this!

His hand shook with furious rage when Ray carefully took the gun from Florence's hand. He sincerely hoped there was a special place in hell for Beatrice. Then, the shamus wiped the weapon with his handkerchief. After dropping the murder weapon on the floor, he took his client by the hand.

"Come on, Florence, let's go to Bea's car," he said. Ray led the woman outside. As they walked to the car, the shamus glanced around the quiet parking lot. Ray opened the driver's side door and told her to get inside. He kept the door open for a moment as he's scanned the parking lot and the nearby windows of the building. The traffic on the road in front of the hotel was light. Nobody looked out of the adjoining room windows. It appeared that no one heard the shots.

Or no one cared!

"I didn't have a choice," Florence's voice broke her silence. "The train was passing by, and I couldn't even hear my husband plead for his life."
~~~

"Drive straight to your house," he finally told her firmly. "I'll follow you in my car. We'll decide what to do."

The ride to Florence's home seemed to take forever. As Ray followed, he watched as Florence drive deliberately and her head never turned. Finally, she turned Beatrice's car into the drive at Rice's home. Ray parked behind her. Florence remained in the car until he opened the door. Then, the shamus led her inside through the unlocked front door.

"Take a seat," he said.

The woman sat on the edge of the sofa. After a moment, Florence glanced around the room as she came out of her trancelike state.

"Why bring me here? I could have waited for the police at the hotel."

Her eyes remained fixed on the wedding photo of her and Jim that rested on the shelf across the room.

"I don't owe the cops anything. However, I need to know something. Are you ready to die for killing your husband and his mistress?"

She blinked several times before the question finally got through. Florence looked over at Ray for a long moment.

"I'm sorry, but you don't know the entire story. I've killed four people in total," she confessed. "Everyone who had something to do with this scheme against me is dead."

"Yeah, Bea told me she went along to encourage the whole thing. Your so-called friend put a noose around your neck; you realize that, don't you?"

His growling voice didn't get through. Florence continued to recount her past two days.

"Bea and I took the train to Oyster City while Amy covered for us. I made sure that worthless bastard Sam was dead. Remember, I promised I would kill him when you helped me escape?"

Her distant smile told Ray the woman was reliving everything.

"Sam told me about how he liked to hang out at one bar after he finished his shift. He'd rape me, then he'd leave work to get a drink, just like it was part of the job. I waited for him to leave that bar."

Florence suddenly looked over at Ray.

"It was funny. Sam didn't believe I would shoot him in that alley. He laughed at me; then I put a bullet in the bastard's balls. It was so easy. I smiled at him as he begged me not to shoot again. He died knowing I pulled the trigger."

Florence chuckled softly.

"Dr. Horne made it easy as well. His name was in the phone book, and I just walked up to the door of his house. When he answered my knock, I saw panic and fright in his face. He got it in the belly."

Ray stared at his client. He silently grew angry for her. Many people drove Florence Rice into the broken, twisted person in front of him.

"On the train ride back, I finally realized I was almost free of everything. Horne and Sam would never hurt me again." Her monotone voice continued with the same detached expression.

"But when you told me where my husband was hiding, something inside me decided I must confront him. I wanted to see Jim's eyes when I told him what his sweet wife had killed two men in cold blood. I had to see the fear in his face for what he put me through."

She dropped her head.

"I guess I'm really crazy. Even though I should say I'm sorry to you, I didn't believe you. I knew you wouldn't get those bastards. Bea told me there was no chance. She was right; it was the only way."

Florence went quiet for a moment before turning back to the shamus.

"You want to know something funny? I thought I would feel satisfied with Jim dead, but I don't."

"What do you feel?" Irish asked.

"There's one of them left. Doctor Wolfe needs to pay now. My only regret is I won't get a chance at him, will I?"

"No, you're not going after him," he replied with a growl. "It ends here for you."

"I hope you get him. I know you're going to try. Maybe not for me, but for what he's done to others."

"You don't have to worry about that," Ray told her.

Florence nodded, then sighed.

"You know, I got married to a jackass because I couldn't be satisfied with hiding myself away like Amy. I wanted to pretend that I was like everyone."

She paused, looking over at the shamus.

"You know, the husband, the house, kids. I guess I got what I deserved."

She shrugged.

"Then I look at your beat-up face. It reminds me of how you tried to help me. Do you want to know something funny? I told your partner, Catherine, that you didn't deserve the guff she put you through."

Florence gave a weary chuckle.

"I guess I'm one big hypocrite."

"Listen, I do not know what you've gone through, but I know something about vengeance," Ray said. "I know how it tears at you."

He took a deep breath.

"Why couldn't you trust me?"

"I don't know," she stated, then slowly stood.

Florence walked over to the picture on the shelf. The black-and-white image showed her and Jim smiling together after their wedding. She pulled the photo out of the case and ripped it apart.

"You're right about one thing. You don't know what I've gone through." Florence's face turned to fury again. "I'll never forget what they did to my mother and me. They'll burn in Hell with me!"

Then, a thought came to her, and she walked into the other room. Ray observed the woman as she went to an interior wall where a painting hung. She pulled on the edge of the frame, and the picture opened like a door. Inside the wall behind it was a safe. She opened it and retrieved a bag.

"Here's some of the money Jim saved over the years. Last I knew, he had around ten thousand in here. My husband didn't believe in putting everything in a bank," she re-entered the room. "He probably used some of this cash to keep his whore happy." Florence tossed Ray the bag as she stepped by the bar. She poured a drink into a large tumbler.

"It's yours. I'd rather you have it than the vultures who will descend to rip my mother's estate apart. I don't believe you knew that she owned this house. It was a wedding gift. Here's to my mom," Florence held up her glass in a toast. The whiskey splashed from the glass.

"Now, call the cops. It's finished, and I intend to be quite drunk when the police arrive," the woman took a deep drink.

She coughed from the burning effect of the whiskey going down.

Ray opened the bag and pulled out a wad of greenbacks. He unrolled five c-notes and put them in his pocket. After placing the bundle of money back into the bag, he stepped next to the bar and set the sack on the countertop.

"You've paid me for my time and expenses. That was the agreement. Instead of getting drunk, I suggest you pack your bags and find the first boat out of the country," Ray said. "I don't think they can get you when you're in Cuba or maybe further south. Pretty soon, the cops here and in Oyster City will look for you."

He walked to the entrance.

"That's assuming that the state police don't have a warrant out on you as well. Somebody will eventually figure it out."

Florence sat her drink down.

"You mean you don't want the money?"

"It's blood money, lady! I took the case to help you, not just take your money. Despite my outward appearance, I still have a conscience," he replied.

"Wait, why are you doing this? I had the impression you were all about getting justice. Don't I deserve punishment?"

With his hand on the doorknob, Ray started to open the door, then he paused. He refused to look at her.

"Lady, you saved my life. I owe you a chance to survive. That makes us square. There's no justice to be served by the state executing you. Too many people helped you on your descent to hell. I have my ideas on justice when the paper comes out and the police start nosing around."

Ray opened the door.

"Don't go!" Florence implored him. "I'm not sure what to do."

She stepped around the bar and came toward him.

"Listen, you could come with me. Take a vacation away from here. I have enough cash to get by for a while, and you can help me get started again."

Irish shook his head.

"No, you need something else." Ray paused, looking down at the floor. "Besides, I'll still have to deal with Jacobi on my own."

He took a deep breath, thinking of his mistakes.

"I guess I should have driven you out of the state. Hopefully, the pain for you will go away. Maybe it was justified in your mind. But that need for vengeance has already torn your soul. You damn well have no reason to feel anything for Bea or Amy. They helped push you into this pit. Beatrice and Amy got you to fulfill their darkest fantasy. They're as evil as Wolfe and Horne. Amy hates with a passion, and my guess it has something to do with a man. Bea wanted you to strike out at all men because of her loss. Wolfe had something to do with that. I think that's why she helped the whole thing along. Beatrice sure didn't like you."

"No, that can't be right! Bea wouldn't do that to me." Florence's voice rose.

"Take off the blinders. Why didn't they come with you? Why did they help you murder, but they have no plans for your escape?"

He glanced over.

"You didn't see it because you had one thing on your mind. They took advantage of your deep hurt and a need for revenge."

He noticed her face pale from recognition.

"As I said, I owe you my life. So, I'll let you walk away this one time, but I'm not helping you anymore."

"But why not?" She asked. "I'm not crazy; I just want to get away from all of this."

He took a deep breath.

"Lady, this is one time that I'm not sure what I'm doing here is the best thing for anyone. But you're on your own, and you should leave before the police come here. As much as others have harmed you, I'm not sure what to do."

The shamus looked at the quiet street.

"The problem is, I really believe that you started to enjoy killing people."

Irish walked out, closing the door.

Chapter 8: A Wall of Daggers

After leaving Bea's house, Ray Irish stopped by a gas station where he called Hewlett. This time, the reporter answered. Hewlett immediately began the conversation by congratulating himself on his article. His good cheer came from all the attention it was getting.

"Before you can't get your enormous head out of the door, would you like a follow-up?" The shamus interjected.

"I've tracked down Jim Rice. He and his mistress are dead. Cops are heading there now."

"Crap, why didn't you call me first? Where is he?"

"Well, you get an exclusive," Ray stated. "You didn't hear this from me, but the killer left the murder weapon in the room. Beatrice Bauer supplied the murder weapon. You can confirm that with your buddies at the police station."

"Wait, wasn't that the tall gal who was with Mrs. Rice?"

"You got it. Oh, you'll love her explanation. I'd run over to her house and interview her about why she gave the gun to Mrs. Rice. I'll let you figure out the interesting relationships. You can start with Florence, who was the girlfriend of Miss Bauer before Amy."

"Christ, what a story and a twisted sex scandal to go with it. You've just made my day. The religious groups will have a field day with the opinion columns about this stuff," Hewlett stated after a long whistle.

"What about Florence Rice? Is she the killer? Did the cops arrest her?"

"I have no idea. All I know is that I'm off this case. You'll have to track down my ex-client on your own. You might try her house, but I doubt that she's there." Ray told him before hanging up.

Irish made an anonymous phone call to the police. He briefly told the desk sergeant, who answered about the bodies at the Lazy A Motel, then hung up. Ray walked away from the phone booth. He wondered whether the reporter or the cops would get to the motel first.

~~~

The next day, Irish was leaning back in his chair with his feet propped up on one of the open windows that overlooked the street. He yawned, still carrying the effects of his long drive back from Baltimore. He opened the morning paper, and the headline yelled out about the recent murder of Sam Conner. The police were officially looking for Florence Rice, who escaped from the clinic. The paper declared the woman insane and extremely dangerous.

As he read about the details and suspicions concerning the murder of Sam Conner and the shooting of Dr. Horne, Ray whistled. There was no mention of anyone helping the woman escape from the clinic. While he was happy that he wouldn't have to explain his role in assisting a murderer to escape, Ray wondered about the reason.
~~~

He suspected Wolfe might rely upon Smyth to take care of Irish. Later on in the article, he found out that Dr. Wolfe would temporarily take over the operations of the clinic. However, another article mentioned that the state patrol seized medical records from the clinic. Because of the questions about patient mistreatment brought out by reporters from the *Baltimore Sentinel,* the governor's office was taking heat. When he turned the page, he briefly wondered if Florence Rice took his advice to leave the country.

Well, I guess Florence and I both came up short.

Then Ray frowned when he saw the picture of Phillip Smyth on the second page. The image brought home the fact that Smyth sent Jacobi gunning for him. Soon, the word would get back to the DA that Irish was still alive and kicking.

Pappy was correct, that damn Singsing Ring is coming back to haunt me!

Irish worked with Abby, a servant girl, to retrieve the ring from Peter Smyth's estate a few months back. Ray gave back to the rightful owners in New York. Now, Jacobi was working for the Oyster City district attorney to retrieve the Singsing.

That part puzzled him. Phillip Smyth had the reputation as a strait-laced prosecutor who strived to keep gangsters out of the city. He knew Smyth hated him. But Ray never considered the idea that Peter Smyth would go to such great lengths to find the object that his brother held on their estate.

Recently, Orella told Ray that the traditions about the Singsing of Multo came from its extensive spiritual power. Even Pappy warned him about people coming after the ring's power. Of course, Ray dismissed the idea. It was just a ring. However, those thugs trying to find it weren't joking. Torturing the information out of him meant Smyth was playing for keeps.

Irish viewed Phillip Smyth like the rest of Oyster City, a rotten core under the quiet façade he displayed. All Ray knew was he had to keep a low profile while he figured out his next steps. He'd also need to warn Orella and her family to be careful. Someone might track down the servant girl who stole the Singsing. After all, Abby was an addict, and he never knew if she finished her treatments.

Ray heard footsteps coming up the stairs to his door. He reached under his jacket and placed his hand on the grip of his gun. Two knocks later, Arizona Campbell's enormous frame entered the room.

"You're going to get a poor reputation if anyone sees you come here," he told the cop as he quickly removed his hand from the gun. Ray noticed the man glanced back at the empty stairwell before he closed the door.

"Don't worry, I came up the back way," his friend took off the bowler hat he wore and used a handkerchief to wipe off the leather band. Irish realized the cop wasn't joking.

"You're face looks like a meat grinder got to it. What happened in Baltimore?"

There was a genuine concern in the detective's question.

"Well, I met up with some of Jacobi's thugs. But that's not the surprising part. Are you sure you want to hear what they told me? It points to a connection that's big enough to rip this town apart."

Ray studied his friend.

"Why do I come here just to get an upset stomach?" Arizona asked with a sigh. "Alright, what do you have?"

Irish briefly told the cop about Max's attempt to torture him for the information about the Singsing ring.

"I swear Max insisted Jacobi got his orders from Phillip Smyth. Now tell me, what the hell is a district attorney doing giving out instructions to a well-known gangster?"

"Son of a bitch!" the big cop exclaimed. "That's all I need to hear. We've had rumors that Jacobi wanted to move into this city for a while. It's hard to believe that those sitting high and mighty over Oyster City are bringing in a gangster."

Arizona shook his head at the idea, then crossed the room to inspect the office. The policeman examined the bedroom through the open door before he went to one window that looked down at the street.

"Still, the way this city operates, I guess I can't dismiss your idea," Arizona said while still looking at the street below.

The room went quiet, except for the light street noise outside.

"Alright, you're not here about my health. What's going on?" Ray finally asked. "You look like you're about to jump out of that window."

Arizona remained silent for a moment. Then he glanced back.

"It's as crazy as what you just told me. I've got a problem. It concerns someone in that elite circle at the top," he replied.

The cop glanced back at Ray.

"It's Henry La Spina and his collection of daggers."

Irish nearly fell out of his chair as he dropped his feet from the windowsill.

"You got something on him?"

"What I have is dicey and hot as hell," Arizona grumbled. "Nothing we say will leave this room, got it?

"Whatever you say. Irish leaned forward in the chair. The creaking noise filled the room while the policeman started pacing as he gathered his thoughts.

"Alright, I have a dead guy that we found at that old gas station by the state highway a few weeks back. We thought he was a hobo at first. However, the guy had on a tuxedo type of uniform."

The cop paused and looked over at Irish.

"You know what I mean, an outfit that a butler might wear. I have no missing person's report that matches, so I got to thinking that the dead person might be a servant for someone in Oyster City."

Before Irish could reply, Arizona outlined the murder and the large Packard leaving the scene.

"The cop who found the body brought in the murder weapon. They found it in the dead guy's back," he explained.

"You got fingerprints?" Ray asked, not trying to conceal his growing excitement.

"No, the lab guys found nothing on the weapon. I went and checked this morning to confirm what they had." Arizona paused and looked out the window.

"Alright, what else?" The shamus sensed something was wrong.

"They've lost the murder weapon. It's gone."

Ray dropped his head. Arizona glanced over.

"Yeah, I know it was a dumb move. I should have taken the damn thing to a safe deposit box," the cop admitted. "I might have known someone would grab it. The damn thing had rubies and diamonds in the handle. It was too much temptation for a bunch of low paid technicians."

"Yet, I can tell you don't believe that's what happened," Irish declared. Arizona went to the chair next to Ray's desk and sat down.

"No, I don't. In any other police station, I might. But not here in Oyster City," he agreed and then went quiet.

Ray opened his desk drawer and pulled out a bottle of Jameson whiskey. He poured two glasses and handed one to his friend.

"I'm still on duty, but I'll take it. The murder weapon reminded me of the dagger you told me about before. Then, I remembered something that Cat said to me about the dagger you saw in the room where Greye's brother got his throat cut. Well, I checked with the state police, and they claim there was no weapon found at the crime scene," Arizona explained.

"Let me guess; you think there are too many coincidences here," Irish observed.

He held up his glass.

"Welcome to my world."

"Yeah, damn it. Then, you had to tell me about Henry La Spina's dagger collection. Now I can't get it out of my mind."

The cop took a sip of his drink, then slugged back the rest of the glass.

"Still, it doesn't prove anything. Best I have is Bishop La Spina, who likes to collect old things."

"Maybe so, but a guy's dagger collection tells me differently," Ray said. "I don't think a lot of priests collect deadly weapons as a hobby. Now the question is, what's an honest cop to do? That's why you're here, isn't it?"

There was no satisfaction in his voice. Ray understood his friend's dilemma. He poured another drink, but Arizona left it untouched.

"Well, a young hot-shot detective would get a search warrant and check out La Spina's house."

Arizona went back to the window and stared at the building across the street.

"But here, in Oyster City, I'm going to get a flat no from the chief of police before I can even get in front of a judge. Hell, you know how it is. If I'm lucky, I'll probably get demoted to walk the beat around the docks."

"Ah, but you'll still have your pension," Irish replied, then frowned from the glare he got from Arizona.

"Yeah, poor joke."

He paused.

"Can you identify the dagger?" Ray asked.

"Sure, I remember it well enough." Arizona turned back from the window. "I should have a picture of it. One of the lab guys hadn't developed the negative yet, so I can get the camera. What's with the grin?"

"You get the negative developed. I believe that someone needs to look at that wall where the bishop displays his collection."

"That's called breaking and entering," the cop reminded him.

"Listen, it's not illegal for a servant to let in strangers. A guy could work himself inside to verify whether any of the dagger's match. It shouldn't be too hard."

Before Irish could reply, the men heard the footsteps hurrying up the stairs to Ray's office.

Cat entered the room. She hesitated when she saw Arizona. The big detective smiled while fumbling with his hat.

"I'm sorry," she told them. "Am I interrupting something?"

"No…nothing like that," Arizona glanced over to Irish. Ray just smiled. At times, his friend acted like a schoolboy around the woman.

"What do you have on your mind, Cat?" Irish asked.

Her face turned red.

"I need to speak with you alone," she told Irish. "It's important!"

"It's alright, I have to get back to work," the cop told her.

Arizona put on his bowler hat and stopped at the door.

"Ray, I'll get that picture and get back to you."

The cop smiled at Cat before he left the room.

"What's going on?" She asked.

Cat took a seat next to the desk and lit up a cigarette.

"Curiosity killed the cat," he warned. "You shouldn't run off Arizona. He's taken a liking to you."

She didn't return the smile.

"Like you always tell me, stow it. Damn it, I've been waiting for you to get back and this is serious."

"Alright, I'm all ears," he frowned.

Then Irish leaned back in his chair.

The woman inhaled deeply before starting. Cat told him about her encounter with Myrna La Spina. She outlined everything the new wife told her, including the warning about Underwood. Ray leaned forward as he listened to the story. Surprise and excitement filled his face.

"Then she believes me about Greye?"

"Yes, she pulled off her wedding ring after I told her about your theory."

Cat stepped to the window and went quiet for a moment.

"Listen, I had a hard time accepting this," the woman turned back to Ray. "But I've been thinking about all the connections. I'm sure that Mrs. La Spina is terrified. You need to talk to her. Maybe when she calls, you'll understand why I'm changing my mind."

Ray let a smirk hurt his face.

"I'm betting this idea sticks in your craw a bit."

"Yeah, but I still say you're nuts," Cat countered mildly. "I've told you before that this town has too many strange events. I can't forget that."

Cat slid on to the desk as Ray turned his attention out the window. He was looking at the scrolling news banner across the street again. It reminded her of a question she had.

"Speaking of crazy, the papers claim your client killed one person and shot another in the last few days. That can only mean Florence was here…"

"It's finished, let's leave it at that," he cut her off. "There was nothing but pain in that case. Florence Rice is gone. She's not coming back."

The woman slowly nodded, surprised at his abrupt answer.

"Alright—I'll let it go. I guess it explains why your face is carrying all those bruises. So, what are we going to do about Mrs. La Spina?"

"You mentioned she would call me. How do we get word to her I'm back in town?" Ray asked.

"I'm not sure. Myrna was afraid and told me she would call you. That's all I know."

The shamus carefully pulled a notepad from his desk drawer. He noticed the stiffness of his muscles remained as he wrote down the connections that Cat had pointed out earlier.

"I'm formulating an idea. Mrs. La Spina claims she's afraid of her husband. Arizona was just here telling me about a murder that might have a link to the bishop's wall of daggers. You have a boyfriend who's suddenly interested in me after I stopped by his shop about that wedding ring."

He circled each point as Cat leaned over to view the notepad. In the center of the paper, he drew a stick figure.

"Of course, the antique dagger they found at the scene of the latest murder is missing. Does that remind you of anything?"

Ray glanced up to see her expression at his question.

"You don't think it's the same dagger that we found in that hotel room where Greye's brother died?" Her eyes widened at the news.

"It's crazy."

"Why? They found no murder weapon. It's the only evidence that appears to tie these killings together. We know that most of the murders involved the killer cutting their victim's throats. We know someone drains the blood from the corpse most of the time. I've been thinking about that. A few hundred years ago, we would think vampires were around."

He leaned back in his chair, pushing up his hat.

"We just don't have a motive."

"Until now! You've just told me a story about Myrna La Spina claiming there are important people in this town who are killing people in a type of ceremony. Another clue is Mrs. La Spina saying that her husband is afraid of Peter Smyth. And we still have the nightmares we've talked about for six months. There has to be a connection between all of this."

"Maybe it comes together, or maybe you're just trying to make connections that aren't there. Ray, what you're saying is difficult to believe," Cat replied. "The woman is terrified. I guess we need to meet with her."

She went silent for a moment.

"But the nightmares make me want to believe. I've seen…well; they scare me."

Ray sprang from the chair.

"I'm afraid as well," he told her. "I'm not the smartest person around, but I can add up the events. They aren't good. I've told you that I saw people wearing robes and masks in the shadows of an alley. I was with Arizona when we found that thug who raped Orella. He was hanging upside down with his throat cut. La Spina's driver died similarly. Then, I've had my share of nightmares about those robed people. Hell, we even have Arizona saying he's had those nightmares as well. To top it off, Pappy claimed a demon is out there. He warned me about the history of this place. He even says Emma knows about that damn Singsing Ring."

"Come on; you know Pappy's kind is always afraid of spooks and goblins," she stated.

Ray glared at her. He'd almost forgotten about Cat's prejudice.

"Pappy's my friend," he growled back.

Her expression told him she wasn't changing her mind. After a pause, he finally continued.

"Even a skeptical guy must concede there's something strange going on in this city. Myrna's involved because she married into the La Spina's family."

Cat slowly nodded.

"This is just so unbelievable. Even if I say you're correct, what can we do?" she asked quietly.

"Hell, like I know the answer to that. I don't like feeling that we both have targets on us. It makes a guy think that I should get back on the train that brought me here."

Ray grumbled aloud.

"Listen, the damage to my face comes from Dr. Wolfe and his ties to Jacobi. Jacobi is working for Phillip Smyth. That means I've got two guys out to get me."

"No! Smyth is a self-righteous jerk, but he's not corrupted enough to bring in that gangster." Cat replied. "There's no reason for him to do that."

"Why?" Ray glanced at her. "You said it yourself. This city is rotten to the core. Smyth, La Spina, the mayor and a handful of others run things. Your father, J. Allan, tried to convince me that Smyth appeared to be taking over. Any of them or all of them could be involved with Smyth."

Cat went quiet for a moment. As she thought about the corruption inside Oyster City, it made some sense that gangsters and the district attorney worked together. The thought left her disgusted and worried when she looked at the shamus. Irish had that determined scowl on his face again as he looked at the building where she worked.

If I were as smart as I think I am, I would find some way to get you to join me, and we would drive away from this damn place.

She recognized that her idea would never happen once he got hooked on fixing a problem.

"I understand you'll want to figure it out. Even if it means somebody gets hurt," Cat stood, putting her purse over her shoulder.

"Alright, I'm going across the street to do some research. Maybe there's something in those murders that ties these things together." The woman started for the door.

"You never know what some reporters might know but haven't bothered to look into."

"Don't talk too much," Ray suddenly warned. "If Myrna La Spina is telling you the truth, then the information that gets back to this group is dangerous to you. It could come from people you might trust."

Cat stopped and looked back.

"Just stay away from Underwood."

Irish turned back to watch her. Cat gave him a sly grin. The shamus narrowed his eyes at the look.

"I don't need my partner getting herself killed by her new boyfriend," he declared.

"Sure, that's what you can tell yourself. Don't worry about me," the woman let out a chuckle as she left the office.

~~~

The next evening, Cat waited inside Ray's office. Amid a small cloud above his desk, she finished her second cigarette since Arizona and Irish left. Cat angrily stabbed the stub into the ashtray.

It wasn't right for them to leave her there!

She arrived just as the men were heading over to Henry La Spina's looking for the dagger. When she tried to join them, Arizona refused. Cat tried to argue with him, but the cop wouldn't budge. He even threatened to take her to the jail and book her on a trumped-up charge if she followed them.

As the policeman shoved down his bowler hat on his head, she realized Arizona would not give in. Worse, her business partner refused to back her. When Ray pointed out that Cat couldn't take any pictures, the woman cursed at him. Like usual, Irish gave her that same careless grin, which only increased her anger. The whole thing frustrated her.

Men are bastards! She once again decided.

She understood the danger involved. Cat followed them to Ray's car. After the two men got inside, the shamus looked out the open car window and reminded Cat she would have the inside scoop on everything when they retrieved the murder weapon.

"You can take a picture of the dagger when we get back. Your editor will love that," he told her as he drove away.

Still upset, Cat went back upstairs to the office and picked up the phone. She decided the reporter could unexpectedly show up at the bishop's house to keep an eye on Ray and Arizona. The woman started to dial the number to one of her reporter friends when she heard footsteps in the stairwell.

She placed the receiver back on the phone stand when two small knocks came from the door. She saw a petite woman's shadow outlined in the obscured glass of the door.

"Come on in, he's always open," Cat said sarcastically.

Slowly, the door opened, and Orella Dela Cruz entered the room. Her expression soured when she recognized Cat. Orella glanced around the office.

"Is Ray not here?"

"No, he's on a case," Cat sniffed when she saw Orella's suitcase. "Did you just roll into town?"
~~~

The visitor nodded. She stood by the open doorway, apparently unsure of her next move.

"You can come in and wait if you want," Cat finally offered.

After an uncomfortable pause, Orella closed the door and sat her suitcase by the empty hat rack. She trudged to the tall window, which overlooked the street. Cat's eyes narrowed while watching her visitor.

She didn't understand why Orella was there. Plus, it bothered Cat that the woman held such a clear passion for Irish. Orella was too young to see him for the hard-headed and stubborn person he was. She couldn't know about Ray's penchant for drunken rage when the world fell on him.

Besides, she's a foreigner!

"Do you know when Ray will return?" Orella asked while she glanced down at the street.

The few people walking on the sidewalk moved through the streetlight, disappearing into the night shadows.

"He'll be back soon," Cat replied as she dramatically opened her purse and pulled out a key from her bag. She held it up.

"I guess he never gave you a spare key. What brings you back to Oyster City? The last time you were here didn't work out very well for you."

Orella glared at Cat as she turned to face her.

"Ray told me about you. You act like his jealous wife."

Cat's face turned red, and she stood up.

"You don't know him. Did he tell you about Samantha Carter and how he fell apart after her murder? I was the one that helped him out of the gutter, not you."

Orella crossed her arms.

"Ray told me about her. He admitted how much her death hurt him. We spent a lot of time together in New York. He saved my life. I know more about him than you think."

"I'm just giving you some free advice, sister. Irish is a good guy, but he brings trouble when you get…"

Cat's face suddenly went pale when she recognized the ring on Orella's right hand. The strange-looking band looked like the body of a snake. Five diamonds embedded in the tips became a pentagon symbol near the head of the snake.

"I've seen that ring before!"

Orella looked down at her hand.

"This is the family ring that Ray got back for us," she explained. "It's been in my family for many generations."

"It was in my nightmares," Cat replied.

She stared at the band like it was a real snake.

"They were terrible dreams, filled with my friends and blood."

Orella's pretty face turned pale at the comment. There was a brief recognition in her eyes that Cat caught before Orella glanced down at the family heirloom again.

"No, it's not possible," she said. Orella appeared to be trying to convince herself. She went quiet for a moment.

"I've had nightmares as well, but that can't be from this ring," Orella finally said. "But my pleasant dreams always showed me carrying it. That's why I wore this treasure. Something wanted me to see Ray."

The room grew quiet again. Then the two women heard footsteps coming up the stairs.

"It must be Ray and Arizona," Cat said.

However, a massive man in a black suit entered. His pockmarked face showed no emotion as he surveyed the room. He quickly stepped into Ray's bedroom, looking around. A tall, thin man with a gray trench coat and gray fedora slowly walked into the office. He looked over at the women with hard and unforgiving blue eyes. Cat recognized the gangster from pictures in the papers. She quickly moved over next to Orella.

"Where's Irish?" Jacobi asked.

"We haven't seen him," Cat replied. "We just found the office was open and came inside." She took Orella by the arm and started leading her to the door.

Jacobi refused to move aside.

"You're a liar. I know you're that photographer who works over at the *Morning Beacon*," he replied.

Jacobi looked her over before turning his attention to Orella.

"This cutie could work in my whorehouses. I heard the shamus hung around slants and darkies."

One of the thugs cackled at the crack. Jacobi told him to shut up.

"Now, where's Irish?" Jacobi asked again.

"I'm not lying; he didn't tell me where he was going."

"Well, then you two are coming with us."

Cat continued toward the door, and the two large men cut her off. One grabbed her arm. There was a gun in his other hand.

"You'll do as I tell you or I let them hurt you," Jacobi told Cat. He took her by the arm and forced her to the desk.

"Now, get a pencil and paper from the desk and write what I tell you. Otherwise, Irish will have two bodies in this office when he gets back."

~~~

As Irish and Arizona sat in Ray's car two houses down from Bishop La Spina's home, the two men watched the quiet house. Earlier in the day, Catherine told them about a formal party which the La Spina's attended every year. Her
~~~

information led them to pick this time of the evening to sneak into the bishop's house. However, the La Spina's had not left for the evening.

Glancing at the massive white stone United Church building, Arizona chomped down on his unlit cigar. Sitting next to him, Ray hunched down in his seat with his fedora covering his eyes. When they arrived at the house which overlooked the large stone mansions of Park Street e a couple of hours before. At first, the two men chatted about various topics. However, the conversation dried up, and silence filled the car as the two men retreated into their thoughts.

Ray understood Arizona's concerns about losing his job, or worse, if their plan went wrong. He encouraged the policeman to let him go inside alone. However, Arizona rightly pointed out that Irish hadn't seen the dagger for several months.

Arizona wasn't worried about his job as much as he didn't want to believe several murders involved the bishop. Henry La Spina came from an old Oyster City family. Such ties meant a lot within the upper society circles in the city. Worse, he still remembered seeing the corpse of a local criminal hanging like a sacrificial lamb after having his throat cut.

When he added up all the murders in the last year inside Oyster City, the 'Chicago smile' made up the vast majority. If La Spina is the prime suspect, it could mean even more of the city's elites were involved.

Arizona pulled off his bowler hat and wiped the inside leather band. He could be putting his neck on the line. Arizona didn't want to end up like Detective Howard. Corrupt as he might have been, Howard didn't deserve to die like that.

"Here we go!" Ray's voice brought Arizona out of his thoughts.

The cop looked up to see the La Spina's car backing out of the drive. The driver carefully pulled into the street. Both men saw the bishop was in the rear seat.

"His wife's not with him," Arizona observed.

He let out a deep breath.

"Looks like a change of plans. Can you keep Mrs. La Spina busy for a while? Maybe get her to send the servants off for something upstairs? I'll come in from the garage entrance, just like we discussed before."

"Listen, Mrs. La Spina might help us. Catherine's conversation with her tells me she might come over to our side soon enough."

Ray slid out of the car.

"I hope you're right," the cop whispered. "Just keep the lady busy and away from that room."

The two men crossed the darkening street. They separated when Irish turned and took the steps to the front door of the bishop's home. The policeman continued walking until he reached the front walk that led to the church. He followed a path to the front doors of the church, where he stopped and waited among the towering columns of the building.

The servant who answered the La Spina's front door was unknown to Irish. The man stood nearly as tall as the shamus and broader through the chest. He reminded Ray of Greye La Spina's murdered driver.

"I'm here to see the lady of the house," Ray told him.

"She's ill, get lost," the man barked. As he tried to close the door, Ray shoved his foot in the door.

"Say, I told you to get lost," the servant told him.

Ray pushed the door in, sending the man back into the foyer. Mrs. La Spina was standing halfway up the circular stairs.

"I believe she'll want to see me," Ray stated. "It concerns her new husband."

"I'm gonna rip your head off," the servant started toward him.

"James, stop!" Myrna commanded.

The big man paid no attention to the order. Ray waited as the man came at him with his head low and arms outstretched. It was a wrestling move Ray had seen before. The shamus struck the servant squarely in the nose with a vicious jab. He slipped away from the man's arms, then hit him again in the back of the neck. James fell headfirst to the marble floor.

Ray looked up at the thin woman on the stairs. At first, he thought her look of bitterness focused on him. Instead, he realized her stare focused on the unconscious servant. She came down the steps.

"If you're Ray Irish, you've just made a mess of everything," Myrna said.

She looked down at her servant.

"James works for my husband. He tells him everything."

"I wasn't planning on him attacking me. Now, come with me." Ray glared. He motioned her to follow him.

"Any other servants we need to worry about?"

"No, the cook has left for the day. What are you doing?" She suspiciously asked as she joined him.

"We're letting a cop come in," he told her. "Where's the door to the side entrance?"

"It's the one on the right," Myrna hurriedly told him with fear in her voice. "You didn't tell the police about me?"

"No, the police don't know about your message. Don't worry, Arizona is the only cop who thinks your husband might not be an angel."

Ray slid open the paneled door.

Arizona stood on the outside porch, trying to get the door open. His face paled when the external light turned on. Then he saw Irish. The cop quickly slipped inside.

"What the hell are you doing?" He asked Ray.

"Improvising! Now come on and look over that display. Mrs. La Spina and I need to talk."

The trio went back through the foyer to the library, where Myrna quickly opened the door.

"He got a headache trying to kick me out," Ray explained when he noticed Arizona eyeing the servant. They went inside.

The study looked the same since Ray last visited. A large oak desk sat in front of the family coat of arms displayed on the wall. The subject of their search covered the area around the display. Rows of ancient ceremonial daggers carefully hung on small shelves. The shelves were full.

Arizona crossed to the display while Ray took Myrna aside. They stood by the massive stone fireplace. Ray carefully looked at the woman, trying to determine her motive as she glanced between Irish and the policeman.

"What's he doing?"

"There's a dagger stolen from the police investigation," Ray explained. "We think it might be on the wall."

She looked at the display.

"It's the second dagger down from the right," she told Arizona.

"I've got it!" Arizona declared after he gave her a surprised glance. He took out a handkerchief from his coat pocket and pulled one dagger from the wall. He stepped back to them while putting the weapon in his coat pocket.

"How did you know?" The detective confronted Myrna.

"Well, for one thing, there was an open space on the wall when I arrived at this house after the wedding. I noticed someone added the dagger to the display several days ago."

"Do you remember if your husband placed it there?" Arizona asked as he pulled out his little notebook.

The woman shook her head.

"No, it was just there one morning. I assumed my husband placed it there." Myrna admitted. "However, others have access to this library."

Her obvious sidestepping of the question caused the policeman to stare at her.

"Come on; you can ask her more in the car," Ray interjected.

Arizona nodded and led the way out the door. As they passed through the vestibule, Ray noticed the servant slowing moving as he regained consciousness. The trio went out the side door and hurried along the driveway to the quiet street.

When they got to the car, Arizona got in the back seat with Myrna. He began to ask her questions about the dagger. Ray pressed on the gas pedal and glanced over at the La Spina house when the car passed them. The front door remained closed as they continued toward Ray's office.

Irish listened in to Arizona's questions. Myrna kept her answers short. When Ray interjected some of what Cat told him, the woman finally opened up with her story. At first, both men had difficulty believing her wedding night ordeal. The events seemed too much like a dark horror story. The woman briefly told the policeman about those involved in the Shadows and their attempts to bring Andras into the world. She tried to detail the orgies and rapes committed along with the legend of the master and his return to lead chaos on earth.

"Look, I know what I'm telling you may appear irrational. But you must believe me. I'm not making up this story. This group of Shadows wanted a demon to arise. They insist its Peter Smyth. After you came over, I can't go back to that house or my husband," she insisted. "They'll make me one of their sacrifices."

"Mrs. La Spina, please understand. What you're telling me is difficult to believe," the policeman replied.

"Like hell," Ray spoke up from the front seat. "Myrna, tell Arizona about the people who died in these rituals."

When Myrna told Arizona about the servants who they sacrificed, she had to stop. Her anguish and grief were no act.

After gathering herself, she explained the rituals inside the round room and the cemetery on the Andras estate. It was the manner of the victim's death that shook Arizona. Either she knew something, or it was pure coincidence that she described the murder victims. Arizona didn't believe in coincidence. He reached over and softly patted her shoulder when the woman finished. Arizona looked up to see Ray watching them from the rear-view mirror.

"We've all had the same nightmares for the last few months. I know others in the city have these damn dreams as well." Ray reminded Arizona. "I know it's as strange as it gets, but her story matches the murder of that thug, Ulysses. We found him hanging upside down with his throat cut in a barn. Add in those other murders, and you have a motive behind them."

"Come on; you don't believe that the district attorney is a demon? They'll be throwing all of us in the looney bin." The policemen looked back at the woman.

"No disrespect, ma'am but if your husband comes looking for you; I can't put down what you told me into a report. They'll put you away and throw away the key."

She nodded.

"I understand," Myrna stated. "I'm not a lunatic."

She hesitated and looked down.

"I might have condemned my soul forever. However, I'm willing to swear on a bible in front of God that what I've told you is the truth."

Arizona leaned back in the seat and slowly exhaled.

"Mrs. La Spina, maybe you witnessed these things. But you have to admit that I'm in a real bind here. What I did back at your house with this damn shamus is illegal. We may or may not have a murder weapon someone stole from the police. Now, you're asking me to believe something that no court in the land would buy."

"Look, even if Smyth isn't a demon, you have to consider something else. Enough people believe in this whole legend to sacrifice humans with that dagger in your coat," the shamus reminded him.

"It means you have a responsibility to take down these Shadows. Isn't that part of a policeman's job?"

Arizona glared at him before silently getting out of the car. Ray slid out as well. As they went up to the office, Arizona told Ray that he took a nearly empty glass next to a bottle of scotch that the bishop had on his desk before he left.

"I swear to God that I'm going to stand there and watch the lab guys dust the dagger and this glass for fingerprints. If they match Bishop La Spina, then I'm arresting the bastard."

"It might destroy your career," Ray warned.

"Then so be it," Arizona told him. "It's time to get the roaches out into the light."

Ray opened the door and noticed Myrna carefully scanning the room as she entered. He frowned as he looked around for Cat.

"I was hoping Cat was still here. Come on in, it's not much but it's home," he joked, then paused when he noticed a suitcase by the coat rack.

Ray glanced back in his dark bedroom before turning to the woman.

"Mrs. La Spina, we'll find a place for you to lie low. Do you have any family you can go to?"

Myrna nodded, then gave him a look of fright.

"You don't think Peter Smyth will go after them, do you? I hadn't thought about that."

"I'm not sure, but it means your relatives are out," Ray told her as he walked into the bedroom.

He remained focused on who came to his office.

"We'll come up with something," he called out. Irish didn't see anything in his bedroom to show who arrived with a suitcase.

"Ray, come out here," Arizona voice demanded.

The shamus walked back into the office area to find the detective holding a sheet of paper in his hand. His grim expression told Irish something was wrong.

"This is in Cat's handwriting, and it's not good. Jacobi has her. He wants you to meet him in the warehouse district about the Singsing ring. He wants you there at midnight."

Ray hurried to the desk and read the note given to him. As he scanned the document, Myrna came closer.

"Cat's been kidnapped. What…"

"Damn it! That son of a bitch is getting bold. He's got Orella as well." He threw down the note.

"What are you talking about?" The cop asked.

"You see that line about my girlfriend is with her. That means Jacobi has Orella as well. Now I understand why the luggage is here. It's Orella's family that has the ring," he explained. "I hope like hell that she doesn't say anything by mistake."

"This is not good," Arizona agreed as he picked up the phone.

He tapped the receiver a couple of times to get the operator.

"What are you doing?"

"I'm getting my guys involved. We need to rescue Catherine. That's going to take some men and extra firepower," the policeman replied.

Ray placed his hand on the phone carriage, hanging up the line.

"No, that'll get both of them killed," the shamus growled. "You know there are too many cops on the take to keep this thing under wraps. Jacobi will know about whatever you're planning before it happens."

Arizona slammed down the phone, barely missing Ray's fingers. Myrna jumped at his action.

"Damn it; you're not running the show. I know the police force a hell of a lot better than you do. That means I can get men I trust. I'm not leaving Cat to that bastard!"

Ray drew closer.

"Arizona, we don't have time to coordinate this as a police raid. It's nearly eleven now. You know the warehouse district has locals with eyes who keep a lookout for cops. Damn it, let's say that you get a car full of cops. What makes you think you can get your guys in there without someone seeing your men?"

The shamus watched the policeman's jaw tighten.

"I'm not saying that we're not leaving Cat or Orella to those bastards. But I think it's only you and me on this. If Smyth is calling the shots and using Jacobi for this, then are you willing to risk their lives on it?"

His words caused Arizona to pull his hand off the telephone.

"Hell, Cat and I almost got killed the last time we took on a gangster. Guy Young somehow picked up on our plan. This time, you have to get inside there without being seen."

The cop turned away. Arizona glanced over at Mrs. La Spina, then stared out of the window for a moment.

"Alright, if it's just you and me, then it means we need a diversion," he finally replied. "You keep them busy while I sneak in from the back."

Arizona turned around with a determined scowl on his face.

"Yeah, me keeping a gangster busy seems to be my trademark around here," Ray snorted. He went to his desk and opened a drawer. He pulled out a spare .38 revolver, which he placed in his suit coat pocket.

"But I don't have any better idea."

He retrieved his .45 Auto from his shoulder holster, then pulled out the seven-round magazine. It was full. Ray rummaged around the drawer and found a handful of more cartridges, which he pocketed. He glanced over at Myrna after putting the gun back in the holster.

"We need to drop you off on the way," Ray told her. "Gladys Peer might be the best option for you at this point. She's eccentric, but a good person. She can get you out of town on the first train in the morning."

To Ray's surprise, Myrna shook her head.

"No, I'm staying with you."

"Ma'am, you can't come with us. We can't protect you," Arizona warned. "Take my advice; you get on a train. You get out of this city."

"And go where? You two are the only ones that I can trust at this point. I can't put your friends in danger because of me. Mr. Irish already said that I can't go back to my family. The decision happened when I left the house with you."

Myrna's eyes were moist, and her hands shook.

Ray placed his hand on her shoulder.

"I admire your gumption, but you really shouldn't do this," he told her softly. She tried to smile.

"Don't you think that you have enough to worry about right now? I've read the papers. This gangster is bad. But I've seen worse. Besides, Catherine needs help. I'm not brave, but I don't think I have any good choice here."

Ray sighed.

"Alright, we don't have time to argue about it. When we get there, stay in the car and keep your head down. If things go wrong, then drive out of town and don't look back." He turned to Arizona.

"You know that we do not know how many of Jacobi's men will be waiting for us."

"Then we stop by the police station. I've got an idea to help us level the playing field." Arizona headed for the door. "We'll take your car."

Chapter 9: The Warehouse

Ray walked along the empty street to 102 Dock Street, arriving at a dark warehouse which loomed over him. The fading paint on the brick front revealed the name of a once-proud company "Peace Livery."

Not likely, Irish thought.

Ray looked around the quiet street. Nothing moved, and the only sound came from a sign across the street which squeaked with each light breath of wind. He carefully made his way to the corner of the building; then he looked down the side of the warehouse. A side door stood partially open underneath a weak yellow lamplight.

They're making it easy for me to get killed!

After another glance around, Ray moved along the wall to the door, where he pulled out his .45 Auto. It was dark inside the building. Before he went inside, the shamus reached up to break the lightbulb with the barrel of his pistol. The glass exploded like a gunshot, louder than he expected. Ray pushed next to the door, waiting for the sound of movement. It remained quiet inside.

He quickly slid through the entrance and placed his body behind a wooden barrel. Glancing around the barrel, he made out the surrounding items. The strange outlines of old machinery, boxes, and even horse-drawn carriages which sat under dusty tarps filled the area.

Beyond the first row, a couple of lights showed the rest of the low-slung room where more equipment and vehicles sat. Ray's eye followed the massive beams that supported the exposed wood floor above him. Hearing footsteps coming from above, the shamus carefully and quietly worked his way to a dark spot between two dusty funeral carriages.

That's appropriate.

From his new vantage point, Irish spotted the two women on the edge of an open area. The gangster had Cat and Orella tied together with their backs against a massive support beam. He breathed a sigh of relief. They appeared anxious, but unharmed. He noticed they were whispering to each other.

The middle of the building carried light down from above and revealed several more pieces of machinery. As Ray looked around for Jacobi and his men, he eyed the chains and pulleys dangling from a massive iron beam in the center of the building. There was light coming from the second floor and the noise of the footsteps above him. Fortunately, the sound indicated a single person.

The steps slowed to a stop. He decided that one of Jacobi's henchmen stood on the second floor. The shamus guessed the man watched over the open area where the women were standing — probably holding a rifle on the women.

"Alright Irish, come on out into the light!" Jacobi's voice came from the shadows behind the women. "My men watched you as you entered the building."

Slowly, Ray rose from between the carriages.

"There's no reason to keep the women, just let them go," he yelled out.

Jacobi and two of his men came out from behind the women. They stepped into the light of the open area. Behind him, Ray heard movement. When he glanced back, he saw two more of Jacobi's thugs who between him and the entrance. The glint from the pistols in their hands caught his eye.

"Alright, you've got me surrounded, just like you planned. Now just let the women go!"

Ray kept glancing between Jacobi and the men behind him. Slowly, he stepped away from the carriages.

"Nobody followed him, boss!" A voice yelled out from the second floor.

"Hell, you must think I'm a really dangerous man," Irish smirked as he peered up at the thug standing on the second floor overlooking the main floor.

He turned back to Jacobi, who smiled grimly.

"No, not really! I'm just careful. A few of my men mysteriously died after they invited you to one of my special places to discuss that ring. I'm pretty sure you got lucky that time to knock them off. However, your luck has run out this time."

Ray casually put his hand in his coat.

"Oh, you mean Max. Do you want me to tell you how he begged for his life after he ratted you out? He told me all about your partner, Peter Smyth. I hope I didn't inconvenience you."

He gave an arrogant grin. Ray felt the cold sweat break out along his lower back. He hoped he wasn't visibly shaking.

The gangster didn't react as Irish expected. Instead of anger, Jacobi sneered.

"There are always more men like Max. Enough of the bull session, shamus! You're going to tell me where that Singsing ring is. That's your only option."

Ray noticed Orella react to the statement.

Fortunately, she remained quiet as Ray carefully moved next to an abandoned cart.

"The gun in your coat won't do you any good, shamus. You can drop it!" Jacobi ordered. "I've got enough men to make sure you can't do anything."

"Just let the women leave. They don't know where the ring's at," Ray tried to bargain. "Once they're out of here, I'll tell you where that damn ring is at."

"Let me have him, boss. I'll punch it out of him."

The thug behind Irish pounded his fist against the horse-drawn hearse door.

"Shut up!" Jacobi ordered.

The gangster leader stepped next to Catherine. He pulled out a pistol from his coat and pointed the barrel at Cat's stomach.

"The word on the street is that you're sweet on this one! Since I lost a couple of good men because of you, I'm going to give you once chance to spill your guts. Otherwise, this bitch gets it in the stomach. She'll die slow!"

The gangster's foul grin showed Ray that Jacobi wasn't bluffing. Ray glanced over at Cat, who stiffened.

"Alright, I'll talk. I don't have that damn thing. It's in New York somewhere." Ray moved to the right, trying to keep the men behind him at an angle.

"Where?" Jacobi shoved the gun barrel into Cat's gut. She grunted.

"You dumb bastard, Ray's telling you the truth! He sold it, and we split the money," the woman lied. "Hurting us doesn't get it back here."

Jacobi suddenly struck her across the cheek with the gun.

"Shut up! He's gonna tell me exactly where it is!"

Ray reacted by pulling out his gun, which he immediately pointed at the gangster. He wasn't close enough to ensure an accurate headshot. So, he ensured the gangster focused back on him.

"Jacobi, you know what? I'm fed up with you! You're nothing more than a paid stooge for Phillip Smyth," the shamus growled. "Some wise guy! Hell, you're not running the show now. And you're not getting the information if I'm dead. Your boys aren't good enough to wing me from here!"

"And you're not too smart," Jacobi smirked. "I've checked up on you, shamus. I know how you operate. My guys are ex-servicemen, so they won't miss you. I know you're bluffing."

He looked at Cat.

"I guess he wants to see my hand!"

He pulled the trigger.

The blast froze Irish. He stared in disbelief as Cat doubled over in pain. Then, he felt a sharp pain strike his leg along with the simultaneous sound of a gunshot from behind him. Irish fell against one of the support beams, grabbing the wood as he realized one of the thugs shot him.

Above Ray, a machine gun opened up, followed by a cry as a body fell from the second floor. The bloody corpse landed near him.

Arizona came into sight above the scene. He held a Thompson submachine gun in his hands. The cop saw Cat just when Jacobi's men started shooting up at him. His broad face turned red in a furious rage as he stood there and sprayed down a burst of lead. The hail of bullets immediately cut down one thug, who fell into his partner. The hoodlum quickly retreated out of the line of fire.

Amid the battle, Jacobi came toward Ray. However, the infuriated shamus pushed away from the beam and took a quick shot at the gangster. Disregarding the intense pain, Irish hobbled toward the Jacobi. With his .45 auto blasting away, Ray's first two shots missed. However, he saw the third bullet strike the thug leader in the upper shoulder.

Jacobi retreated, shooting wildly at Ray. Jacobi's two bodyguards joined in the fight, firing off wild shots to protect their boss. As his war experience kicked in, Irish took a limping zig-zag path between pieces of machinery.

He drew closer, and Ray felt an explosion of pain on his side. He twisted around just in time to shoot one of Jacobi's guards at point-blank range. The big thug's head whipped back from the force of the bullet before his body fell to the floor.

Ray's momentum sent him sliding into the floor, next to the pillar where the hostages were bound together. Orella yelled out a warning as Jacobi came out from the shadows. The shamus rolled away, and Jacobi's shot missed him. The second bodyguard for Jacobi stepped from behind a crate with his gun pointed toward Orella. He fired while Arizona let loose with another volley of rounds from his Tommy gun. Several rounds struck the thug in his back. He tried to rise, then got hammered by more slugs as the cop continued to shoot him. His dying body convulsed as the bullets smashed into him.

An eerie silence fell over the warehouse. Ray heard footsteps fading into the background. He lifted himself from the floor and staggered toward Cat, whose upper body remained pitched forward. She wasn't moving. When Irish reached out for her, his hand went numb. Then, blackness fell across his eyes like a curtain. He didn't feel the floor as he landed. Only the sensation of falling into an empty black pool went through his mind.

<p style="text-align: center;">~~~</p>

Irish woke when the sun struck his face. He found himself in a clean bed inside a hospital room. Everything was white, accented by the blinding sun coming through the window. As he groggily took in the surroundings, he realized there was a needle in one of his arms, hooked to a plasma bottle hanging by the bed.

In one corner of the room, Arizona sat asleep in a wooden chair which was propped back against the wall. The cop's suit had blood on it. Ray didn't remember much after passing out, just a whirl of red lights and the echo of a damn siren inside the ambulance.

He stared at the big cop who was dreaming. Ray watched him for a moment in fascination while he tried to shake off the effects of the drugs in him. There was an evil grimace that crossed Arizona's face before turning into a look of fear. In a stupor, Irish continued to stare, his brain telling him to ask questions.

Then, he remembered the image of Cat!

Ray tried to sit up. However, his movement sent a shock wave of pain through his ribs. He fell back, sucking in air as he waited for the waves of pain finally to recede. The shamus carefully pulled up his gown and saw the bandages where one bullet hit him.

He had to find out about Cat!

The shamus was about to call out to Arizona when he saw the door to the room open. A tall, thin nurse wearing horned-rimmed glasses entered the room. Her gray eyes widened when she realized her patient was awake. Orella walked in behind the nurse. Her tired face immediately brightened when she saw him. Orella went over to the sleeping policeman, and she shook him awake.

"How's Cat doing?" Ray groaned out.

His ribs still hurt. It reminded him of a hot poker going through his lungs. Ray saw Orella's reaction to his question. He knew something was wrong. Arizona's chair scraped as he stood. The policeman slowly walked to the bed as the nurse went to look at the glass holding the plasma. His face told Ray the answer that he didn't want to accept.

"Come on, how's Cat doing?" Ray's voice held on to hope.

"Ray, she didn't make it." Arizona's voice cracked, and he dropped his head.

A sorrow-filled silence filled the room.

"That son of a bitch killed her," Ray whispered.

Then his voice grew bitter.

"Is he dead yet?"

The detective shook his head.

"There was one of his men still there who helped him get out of there. The blood trail ran back to an alley. My best guess is that he left town. The state police are searching the roads back to Baltimore."

"No, not with that .45 hole in him," Ray insisted as the adrenalin surged. He looked at the nurse. "How long have I been out?"

"It's only been overnight," she told him. "The doctor operated on you as soon as you arrived. Mr. Irish. Your injuries are serious and you need to rest. I'll have these people leave."

Ray ignored her as he turned back to Arizona.

"I'll lay money that Jacobi's holed up somewhere close enough for a doc to get to him. And I bet I know where."

The cop's red eyes instantly turned cruel when he looked at Ray.

"Where?"

"The Camelot Motel! It's the place that Guy Young used for his prostitution ring."

Ray felt vertigo swarming through his head.

"How can you be so sure?" Arizona asked.

"The last I heard; some woman named Rosie came down from Baltimore. I didn't think about it at the time, but I heard she took over running the whores out of that place after Young died." Ray said. "I'll lay even odds she works for Jacobi."

He growled as he attempted to crawl out of his bed. The nurse insisted that he lay back.

"Shut up and get this damn tube out of my arm," Irish ordered.

"Mr. Irish, you can't leave the hospital," the nurse stated as she scrambled to stop him. Orella joined her while Arizona retrieved his bowler hat from the table by the bed.

"Ray, you can't go anywhere," she told him. "You just had two bullets removed from you. You're lucky they didn't hit any vital organs or bones. Now, please lay back and rest."

"They're right, shamus," Arizona interrupted.

He placed his hand on Ray's shoulder and pushed him back into the bed. Then, he started for the door.

"I'm handling Jacobi. This is personal."

"Damn it, Arizona; you can't go there alone. You're no longer a cop when you get out of the city. I'll help you!"

However, the detective paid no attention as he continued into the hallway.

Growing desperate, Ray reached over and suddenly pulled the needle out of his arm. The red fluid spilled across the white sheet. The nurse yelled for help as she scrambled to grab the tube. Ray slid out of bed, nearly falling from the agony of his ribs. That's when he felt his leg go wobbly, which threatened to drop him. Fortunately, Orella grabbed him by the arm before he fell on the floor.

"Ray, get back into bed," her voice was frantic.

"Like hell, I've seen that look in a guy before. I've gotta stop Arizona from getting killed. Where are my clothes?" he fumed.

Ray glanced over at the nurse.

"I swear that if you don't get my stuff right now, I'm gonna rip this damn place apart!"

Despite repeated attempts by the hospital staff to keep Irish from leaving, Ray finally limped out of the hospital. Partially dressed in a suit still caked in blood and grime, the shamus continued to fight vertigo and intense pain.

As he held on to Orella for support, Ray didn't see the hospital staff slowly follow him. They expected the wounded man to collapse at any moment. Irish's continued vicious curses spilled out when his reluctant body interfered with his slow progress. His gun holster dangled from his shoulder. Orella carried his socks and shoes in her hand, dropping them several times along the way. Ray leaned against the wall while she retrieved the clothing.

Finally reaching the entrance to the building, the odd-looking couple went down the steps to the waiting cab. Orella had the foresight to call while Ray dressed. When Ray got inside the backseat, he told the driver to take them to the motel.

"Mister, that's way out of town," the driver informed him. The sidelong glance from the cabbie told Ray that he was worried about payment from a dead man.

"Just get us out there as fast as you can," Ray growled out. "I'll pad your tip. Now move it!"

The trip to the Camelot Motel became an endurance test for the shamus. Between feeling each bump in the road, he also had to contend with an overwhelming weariness falling over him. His leg hurt, but that was manageable. However, the wound to his side limited him to slow and careful movements.

When images of Cat flashed through his mind, he adjusted. His memories immediately fell away with the surge of pain in his ribs. Orella put Ray's socks and shoes on him; then she helped him get his holster over his shoulder. When she finished, the woman remained quiet. She kept looking down at her clasped hands. An underlying fear filled her face.

"It's alright, Orella," he finally told her with a smile that looked more like a grimace. "I wounded Jacobi, and I don't think he'll have many men guarding him. While I appreciate your help to get me this far, I want you to stay in the cab when we get there."

"But you're taking a great risk," she reminded him. "And you can't even stand on your own."

Ray nodded; his eyes fixed on her finger.

"I'll make it. You're carrying around the damned ring that Jacobi wants," he explained. "I need you to stay away from him."

"But I don't understand what this is about. Even the policeman didn't know why Jacobi wanted the ring. Jacobi never explained why he kidnapped Cat and me. I just assumed it was to get you." She pulled off the ring. "I just feel better when I wear it."

"We'll talk about it later. Just remember what I said," Ray told her.

The turning car caused him to use her thigh to steady himself. When the pain finally subsided, he asked her why she came to Oyster City.

"Silly, I wanted to see you." She smiled, but he saw a shadow cross her face.

"What else brought you?" Ray finally asked after she remained quiet.

Orella took a deep breath, then explained.

"I saw us in a dream. I know it doesn't make sense. Something in my dreams led me back to this city. There's comfort by coming to you."

Ray grunted, unable to laugh at the absurdity.

"You're a sweet kid, but I wish you had stayed in New York," he told her.

When they arrived at the Camelot, Ray ordered the taxi to stop behind Arizona's car. He took a deep breath and steeled himself to get out of the cab. Orella placed his fedora on Ray's head.

"Stay here until I get back," he ordered the cabbie. Then he glared at Orella as she started to get out of the car.

"Stay with him and get to the state police if all hell breaks loose," Ray told her.

The shamus moved like a crippled old man as he hobbled to the building. He pulled out his gun when he reached the side door. When he entered the building, he looked down the hallway, which showed the lobby front desk. Standing at the counter was Arizona. He was looking through the guest registration book. The desk clerk kept glancing at the cop and the outside door. Ray moved to the stairway and leaned against the wall. He remained standing. Ray felt sweat break out on his forehead.

Arizona finally closed the register after questioning the desk clerk. Ray didn't hear the warning the cop told the pale man behind the counter. But he guessed it had something to do with not warning Jacobi. Arizona disappeared up the stairs. Ray turned and started up the steps. He prayed that the gangster's room wasn't on the next wing of the motel.

When he reached the next floor, Ray came around the corner into the hallway. He almost ran headlong into a man standing in front of the first room. The two men recognized each other instantly. Jacobi's thug swung out a fist and caught the shamus in his jaw. Ray fell to the floor. While pain overwhelmed him, he waited for the next strike.

However, when he looked up, the brute's jaw went slack, and his eyes glazed over. The man tumbled forward. Arizona stood behind him. The cop didn't look down at Ray. Instead, he turned and slammed through the door.

From his vantage point, Ray couldn't see much. He struggled to his knees as he heard Jacobi yell out. There was the familiar sound of a gunshot. Irish heard Jacobi scream in pain. He finally got to the door and saw the cop shoot Jacobi again. This time, the bullet struck his other knee. The gangster cried out.

"You can't do this," he pleaded with the detective.

Jacobi was on the floor in his pajama bottoms and no shirt. His bandaged shoulder wept blood.

"Like hell, you son of a bitch! This one's for Cat," Arizona said.

He calmly put a slug into Jacobi's belly. The gangster doubled up; his bulging eyes stared at Arizona.

As Ray watched, leaning against the doorframe, the policeman holstered his gun. He went to the edge of the bed. On top of the nightstand, Arizona picked up the gun lying there. Ray recognized it as the .38 revolver that Jacobi used to kill Catherine.

As the policeman walked by the groaning man on the floor, he shot him in the temple with Jacobi's revolver. Blood and brain tissue splattered across the floor. Arizona kneeled and placed the gun in the dead gangster's hand. He glanced over at the shamus.

"You shouldn't have come along, Irish. Thanks for distracting his bodyguard."

Ray nodded and carefully slid down to the floor. He tried to ignore a wave of sickening dizziness.

"There will be trouble," Ray panted out.

"No, the state police won't investigate this trash," Arizona replied as he kneeled next to the shamus. "He killed himself before I could cuff him. That's the story I'll tell them, and cops don't rat on other cops."

He pulled out a cigar and bit off the end. After spitting the piece of tobacco on the floor, he lit his stogie.

"That's not the trouble. You have Peter Smyth to worry about now."

"No, he has to worry about me now. I'm gonna take down every rotten son of a bitch who's involved," Arizona replied with a puff of smoke.

Ray laid his head back against the door frame.

"Not without me, you're not!"

~~~

Several days later. Orella escorted Ray Irish out of the hospital again. After additional stitches to fix his reopened wound, the shamus got another pint of blood and drugs to keep him in bed. Still, Ray finally convinced the doctor to release him. As the couple headed for his Nash. Orella's pretty smile dropped. Arizona waited for them by the car. The detective chewed on his unlit cigar while he leaned against the rear passenger door.

"Shamus, you look like death warmed over," he commented.

"Yeah, the doc would agree with you. He kept complaining about how I ripped out all of his great stitching." Ray recognized the cop had something on his mind.

"What is it?"

"Well, the prints on the dagger didn't match Henry La Spina. So, we've got nothing to pin on him." Arizona took out his cigar and spit. "Cat's funeral is tomorrow; Mrs. La Spina is in hiding. Plus, I haven't got a damn thing."

"You got that gangster Jacobi out of Oyster City," Orella offered.

She still held open the door, looking impatient as the men talked. Arizona gave her a smirk.

"There's always more of thugs like him who'll be happy to work for Peter Smyth."

"Then you're convinced that he's the cause of the problems in Oyster City?" Ray asked.

"Do I think Peter Smyth is a demon? Not likely," he replied. "But there's too much evidence that he and the rest of those old families are involved in something. Not that it matters, I guess. I'm off the Howard murder case."

"What do you mean? Did the DA pull you from the investigation?"

The big cop nodded.

"It's more than that. The chief called me into his office last night. He fired me from the Oyster City police department for my failure to apprehend a notorious
~~~

gangster, along with several charges of misconduct. It appears the police department frowns on using automatic weapons from the gun locker without the chief approving. I noticed a new sign on the locker stating that when I was clearing out."

Ray leaned against the car and removed his hat. Orella stepped next to him and opened the front door.

"So, what are you going to do?"

Arizona shrugged.

"I don't know. I've got a bit of savings, so I'll be looking for work." He spat again. "But they're not running me out of this city."

Ray turned to get in the car. Carefully, he slid into the seat.

"Then you need to follow us back to the office. We can discuss if my office has enough room for a partner."

~~~

The night before Catherine Bennett's funeral, the hot weather finally broke when a line of severe thunderstorms swept through the area. Inside the round room on the second floor of the Andras mansion, Peter Smyth looked over his small group of followers who restlessly waited. There were no masks on this night.

None of the Shadows knew about the next sacrifice. The last servant of Betty Andras died a month before, during the previous full moon. However, their master insisted there was no need to kidnap one of the drunken chattels of men or women who frequented the dock area of Oyster City.

Andras' servant, Wolfe, entered the room followed by his brother, the doctor in charge of the state asylum. The servant seated Dr. Wolfe between Marion Underwood and Henry La Spina. The exchange of concerned glances among the Shadows caught the eye of the demon, who calmly sat, sipping his glass of wine. After a long moment, he addressed the group.

"It is a memorable night for those who follow me. We will initiate a new member of our circle. The brother of my loyal servant, the doctor, will extend our reach into the circles of power beyond this city."

Polite applause came from those around the table. The short, plump doctor nodded grimly. Their clapping stopped when the demon rose. The tall man strolled around the table, his hands behind his back. His followers' heads turned and followed the progress of his journey behind them.

"As you know, there is a lunar eclipse tonight. It brings forth my harem of Lamia. These dark spirits will soon scatter on my command to seduce those men in power while sowing chaos and death within their families."

Andras stopped behind Julie Smyth and placed his hands on her shoulders. The woman, dressed in a low-cut red dress, looked down at his hands. Over the last few weeks, her husband's fingernails grew almost black with sharp points. She shivered at his touch. However, she forced herself to smile.
~~~

"Which brings me to our sacrifice for the night," Peter Smyth stated. He looked over at Bishop La Spina.

"Your wife has run from our circle. I hold you personally responsible for this incident."

"I told you she needed time," the priest reminded Smyth bitterly. "Besides, no one will believe…"

Suddenly, Henry La Spina grabbed his throat as his face went pale. He grabbed his neck. His mouth opened and closed like a fish gasping for air. The bishop stared into the demon's irises, his focus on the coal-black liquid pools of torment. After an eternal moment of choking, Andras released the bishop from his demonic spell. Henry retched out a spasm of coughs, trying to catch his breath.

"You will find her and return her to Oyster City. You have until the next moon to bring your wife back for our pleasure. Otherwise, you will take her place as our sacrifice. I don't care if you kill off her entire family to find her. I want her brought back to me. No one leaves my circle!"

The demon's long fingernails dug into Julia Smyth's shoulders, and she winced. While the Shadows stared at their still coughing companion, Peter Smyth turned to Phillip.

"Since Jacobi died, I will have our new contact inside the police department focus his attention on this private detective who continues to get in our way." The demon growled out the instruction. "I feel the spirits who block our path. We must know everything about the private detective's friends and family."

"Do you want him picked up by the police? They could be useful in retrieving the information. Then, he can hang himself in his cell, just like that racketeer, Guy Young." Phillip Smyth smiled at his suggestion.

"Not for the moment," the demon replied. "I sense a presence that may benefit us." Smyth stroked the hair of his wife thoughtfully. "There is a female with a strong attachment to the detective. She can benefit me."

Andras looked down at his human wife.

"That reminds me. Julie has shown a steadfast presence at the sacrifices held in my name. For this loyalty, I intend to give her the gift of everlasting service to my cause."

Julie's initial smile at the compliment quickly changed as the blood drained from her face.

"Wha—what do you mean?"

"It was a choice between you and Mrs. La Spina. With your competitor gone, you will have the honor of taking her place. I intended to give Myrna a child before her sacrifice. However, I must accommodate a new reality before those who oppose us," the demon stated.

"Over the years, I noticed how you were quite willing to enjoy the orgies before you bled the victims. You enjoy bringing torment and pain to your prisoners.

Bringing forth my harem requires your sex and your twisted soul," the demon stated. "What better way to prove your loyalty than to give yourself over to the Lamia?"

Julie tried to stand, but Andras pushed her down.

"But—my family is one of the original Shadows…"

Her eyes were wide with fear. She surveyed her friends who watched her. Their faces showed shock, but Julie also saw relief in their expression. They would live. She turned to look up at her master.

"I'm—not the one who deserves this honor," she insisted.

Andras gave her an icy grin.

"I insist you are the one. The family ties between the Shadows mean nothing anymore. I have arisen, and soon my realm will join me."

His voice echoed ominously. The smell of Sulphur surrounded the table. The demon's hand dug into Julie's shoulder again, and he lifted her from the chair as she yelled out in pain. Andras flung her to the floor.

"Take her to the crypt!" He ordered the others.

~~~

It was nearly midnight when Arizona finally left Ray's office. Irish stood looking out the window of his office. He glanced at Arizona, who walked to his car. The scrolling news ticker lit up the side of the Beacon building. Irish paid no attention. He remained lost in his memories of Catherine Bennett. She was the one who pushed him into becoming a private detective, even working out the details of his office with Gladys Peer, who owned the building. Now Cat was dead, killed because of him. The responsibility was his alone. Ray believed it in his soul.

He didn't hear the soft footsteps coming from the bedroom. Then, he felt Orella next to him.

"You can't blame yourself," her voice was soft like a whispering wind.

She slid her arms around Ray's waist. He brought his arm down to bring her closer. He winced from the soreness along his ribs.

"There's no one else to blame," he said. "If I take the shot, maybe Jacobi is dead and not her."

She leaned her head on his chest.

"And if you missed, you would still blame yourself," Orella told him. "That's not fair."

"Maybe not, but it's the truth," he replied softly.

Ray released her and limped over to his chair. While his leg didn't hurt from the wound as much, he still favored it when he walked. After sitting down, he pulled open the drawer and lifted out his flask of Irish whiskey along with a glass.

"Do you want one?"

Orella shook her head as she came around and sat on the top of the desk. She smoothed her dress as Ray gulped down a drink. He glanced at her crossed legs.
~~~

"How are you doing?" He asked. "I know you spent most of your time at the hospital."

There was a long pause as Orella watched him pour another glass.

"You know you can talk about Cat if it helps," she offered.

Ray shook his head. He let out a long sigh.

"That's not how it works with me. Catherine is not the first friend who got killed because of me. Tomorrow, I'll pay my respects, and that'll be the end of it."

"Cat told me you drink when you're hurting. Ray, I'm here for…"

Orella paused when they heard the rapid approach of footsteps ascending the stairs.

A few seconds later, there was a quick knocking on his door. A haggard-looking, middle-aged woman pushed through the door.

"Mr. Irish, I need your help!"

Her hand remained affixed to the doorknob. The woman's blonde graying hair kept falling into her broad face as she used her other hand to push it away. Her blue eyes glanced frantically between the man and the woman at the desk.

"Alright, calm down. What can I do for you?" Ray asked as he put his drink down.

"My husband is missing, and I can't find him. I think he'll hurt someone!" Her frantic tone verged on hysterical.

The shamus pushed back on his chair.

"Do I know your husband?"

"Yes, he's mentioned you often. My husband's name is J. Allan Dunn. I need your help to find him."

Irish immediately went to the woman and helped her to a chair by the desk. As the woman clutched at the arms of the chair, Ray closed the door. He noticed Orella went to the corner of the room.

"Mrs. Dunn, what makes you think he'll hurt someone?"

"He's not been the same since Catherine's death."

She fumbled around with her expensive leather purse before finally pulling out a delicate handkerchief.

"He's been drinking heavily, even at work. Allan came home this evening. He kept rambling about something he discovered, something about shadows. I'm not sure what he meant. But Allan claimed he knew the secret."

The woman's eyes teared up, and she dabbed at her nose. When she looked up, Mrs. Dunn noticed the expression on Ray's face.

"Do you know anything? I tried to ask him what he meant. All Allan told me was that he would fix them."

The shamus glanced over at Orella, who wrapped her arms together like she was cold.

"What did you do then?"

"I went downstairs and called my mother. As we were talking, Allan rushed out of the house. He nearly fell down the stairs. I tried to help. My husband was hysterical," she continued. "Mr. Irish, he's in no condition to be out on the streets. Will you help?"

"I'll try," he replied. "Tell me why you think he'll hurt someone?"

"He took the pistol that is in his dresser drawer. I discovered it was missing after he left."

"Do you have any idea where he might have gone?" The shamus asked as he limped over to get his coat and hat.

"No, not really," Mrs. Dunn shook her head. "He just kept talking about stopping the shadows and old families."

She hesitated, then suddenly sprung up from her chair. She followed Ray to the door.

"Maybe he went to see Mayor Hopely. I'm related to the Hopely's, and my cousin told me about their argument. You don't think he would harm the mayor, do you?"

Ray gave her a fake smile.

"I'm sure he's just sleeping it off by now if he was stumbling drunk. You go home and wait for him. I'll run by the mayor's house to make sure," he assured her, then opened the door.

"Now, you go home and stay there. I'll let you know what I find out. Your husband might already be back there."

Ray looked at Orella.

"Keep an eye on the place and get some sleep; I'll be back as soon as I can."

~~~

J. Allan Dunn watched in astonishment as a line of people in robes descended on Andras Hill. He could see some of them holding lanterns as they moved across the graveyard. The robed figures were crossing the narrow private driveway halfway up the hill. A wrought-iron gate which stood between two giant oaks barred cars from getting closer. However, Dunn knew the figures walking silently across the road were part of the Shadows. His discovery about Peter Smyth's association with the gangster Jacobi sent the man into several nights of continuous drinking. Sitting at the bar that night, J. Allan Dunn finally determined he would confront and shoot Peter Smyth.

The bastard killed my little girl!

Dunn rubbed his bleary, red-shot eyes and shook his head. Still intoxicated after his heavy afternoon drinking, he opened the door of his car and nearly fell out on the road. He'd parked the car at the gate to the Andras mansion with a single purpose in mind.

I'll make sure that Smyth and the rest of the Shadows pay!
~~~

Dunn heard the muffled scream and looked back along the path. He recognized the resisting woman as Julie Smyth. He also recognized the voice booming voice that came across the still night.

"Julie, we all have to submit! You should have made friends with Myrna to ensure she took your place."

"No! This isn't right!"

Julie tried to escape from the two rotund men holding her. She only took a couple of steps. A tall man in a black suit struck the woman in the head. She fell. The others quickly descended upon her. As Dunn slowly walked toward the gate, he felt like he was watching a movie. One of the robed figures promptly ripped off part of the woman's dress and shoved the cloth into her mouth. Holding her arms, two of the Shadows dragged her out of sight. The rest of the group quickly followed, the lantern lights appearing like flickering ghost orbs among the trees.

Hopely, you son of a whore, I knew that you're one of them!

Staggering to the gate, Dunn slipped through the opening and followed the narrow-paved road. As he walked along, the man shivered. He felt like the chateau was staring at him, despite the dark windows that filled the ornamented towers and spires of the building.

When Dunn reached a broken crypt under an enormous tree, he stopped. Despite the darkness, he noticed a trail leading from the mansion through the many tombstones of the Andras family. Before he took the path to follow the Shadows, he pulled out a nearly empty hip flask and took another drink.

The warmth of cheap whiskey filled him, and Dunn started along the trail. As he passed under trees, barely any ambient light got through. He repeatedly tripped over exposed roots sticking out from the ground. Several times, Dunn nearly fell before he ran into the low fence. Tumbling over the wall, he found himself next to a large white marble mausoleum.

As he struggled to stand, Dunn heard Julia's screams coming from inside the stone structure. The man pulled a pistol from his pocket and made his way around to the front entrance. As he eased his body around the corner, he saw the dim yellow light spilling out of the opened gate.

Dunn came closer to the light and peered inside. From his vantage point, he saw the naked woman lying on top of a wooden coffin. Dunn immediately recognized Julie Smyth when her face turned toward him. Her husband was on top of her, forcefully thrusting into her as she strained against the ropes that bound her to the casket.

Dunn's liquid courage suddenly drained away when he looked through the side glass of the ancient coffin. Inside was the desiccated corpse lying only a few inches below the struggling woman.

What the hell!

Almost immediately after his thought, Dunn heard an ominous voice rise from the mouth of Peter Smyth. He listened to the man he thought was the district attorney, chanted out words Dunn didn't understand. He watched with a mix of horror and fascination as Andras, the demon, summoned evil spirits from his hellish world. The voices of the robed followers inside the crypt echoed as they repeated words.

Just as the beast climaxed, Andras suddenly used his long fingernails to slice across Julie's neck. Blood immediately spurted across the woman's breasts and her face. Smyth lapped at the blood like a dog.

Dunn pulled back at the scene before him. His stomach twisted as he felt the dry heaves coming. He bent over, forcing himself to keep from throwing up. Then, he fell against the outside marble wall, trying to make sense of what he saw. Dunn heard the murmur of approval. Steeling himself, he looked back inside. Julie's severed windpipe gurgled as she died. Her eyes appeared to be staring at Dunn. The man felt her trying to make him intercede. He lowered his head in shame.

Andras finished licking the blood on his sacrifice's body and slid off the coffin. His voice rose again. This time, Dunn understood the words.

"Bring forth my harem! I give them this blood as nectar."

A gasp that came from one shadow forced Dunn to look up at the ceremony.

He noticed a dark wisp of smoke rising from the ground around the casket. Another wisp near the top of the coffin joined as the black smoke quickly filled the area near the body. Gradually, the mist transformed and darkened. The dark cloud grew more extensive, covering the coffin area. A moment later, the smoke turned into human-like figures.

Dunn lifted himself and stood by the doorway, his eyes transfixed by the sight. The drunken man saw three old women emerge from the smoke. Three naked hags looked like copies with black holes for eyes and hideous grins from their toothless mouths.

The creatures focused their attention on the corpse as they ran their long fingers across the gore covering the body.

One hag leaned over to suckle on the bloody breast while another licked on the dead woman's face. The third hag pulled herself on top of the coffin and lapped at the belly. The sight and sound reminded Dunn of dogs drinking.

Dunn's focus changed when he saw Mayor Hopely step toward Peter Smyth and hand the man a robe. It was the sight of two corrupt men in charge of Oyster City that suddenly pulled J. Allan Dunn from his trance. He remembered his daughter. While Smyth didn't pull the trigger, he was responsible for Cat's terrible death. He knew Jacobi came to Oyster City on the orders of Smyth. A burst of hatred swelled inside Dunn as he suddenly stepped into the mausoleum.

"You son of a bitch, I'll send you to hell!" Dunn raged as he pointed the gun at Peter Smyth.

The demon looked up at the stranger as the gun went off twice in rapid succession.

Smyth's body fell back into the coffin behind him. He slid to the floor.

The crypt remained in stunned silence for a split second. Then, Dunn fired his gun at the closest robed person, who attempted to flee. He saw Henry La Spina fall to the stone floor with a groan. Two shots later, the mayor went down. As he was about to shoot again, Dunn felt a presence behind him, then a sharp pain in his back. The man whipped around to see a tall man in a black suit holding a silver dagger. Dunn immediately shot Wolfe in the belly. However, Andras' servant came at Dunn again. The hammer of his revolver kept clicking on the empty cartridges twice. Dunn lashed out with his gun, striking the larger man in the temple with the butt of the pistol. However, Wolfe stabbed him in the shoulder before falling to the floor.

Amid the groans and panic of the remaining Shadows scattering around the small room, Dunn backed out of the entrance. Hopely silently lay next to the crypt while La Spina crawled away. As Dunn exited the mausoleum, he saw Peter Smyth staring at him from across the room. For a moment, Dunn thought Smyth remained alive until the man fell sideways and out of sight. Gun still in his hand, Dunn staggered away from the entrance.

"You bastards, I'm avenged!" he yelled back at the crypt. His body fueled by adrenaline; the killer limped along the path back to his car.

~~~

It was long after midnight when Irish got back to his office. He found only one light turned on in the bedroom: Orella was already asleep in his bed. He decided not to wake her. Instead, the shamus quietly went to his desk and called Mrs. Dunn. He gave her an update on his lack of success. The shamus tried to reassure her. However, Ray hung up the receiver; he knew Mrs. Dunn would be up all-night waiting.

As Ray leaned back in his creaking chair, he thought about Cat. Looking at his drawer, the shamus briefly considered getting a stiff drink. Then he remembered the look on Catherine's face when she told him about her nightmares. The image brought him out of his self-pity and back to the present.

He believed some sinister presence fell over Oyster City. She convinced him of that. Ray also thought that Jacobi might have killed her, but Smyth was the actual target for him. Having Arizona as his new partner might allow Ray to focus more of his energies on getting Smyth. Irish realized that he and Arizona were walking on a precarious cliff.

The wailing of a police car's siren as it sped down Peach Street broke his concentration. As he yawned, Ray thought about closing the open window, but he glanced over at the door to his office. He heard footsteps coming up his stairs.
~~~

However, there appeared to be hesitation in the person coming up. Then he heard a thud against the wall inside the stairwell.

Ray pulled his gun and carefully got up from his chair. Fortunately, his noisy chair only made a slight squeak. He worked his way over to the wall where his coat stand stood. Slowly, he edged to the door while listening to the sounds outside. The street noise coming from the open window made it difficult to hear anything. After a long moment of silence, Ray carefully took the handle and quietly opened the door. He glanced out, half expecting to see something horrible.

He was right!

J. Allan Dunn lay sprawled on the steps with his back against the wall. His head wobbled when he tried to look at Ray.

"I got him," the man croaked out.

That was when Irish noticed the blood on Dunn's coat at the shoulder. The man's pale face showed him the man was in bad shape. Ray hurried down several steps to Dunn's side.

"Are you hurt bad?" Ray asked.

He didn't need to bother with the question. The pale light of the single bulb showed a trail of blood on the steps below.

Dunn tried to nod. His strength gave out, and his head fell back to the wall with a thud.

Ray heard a surprised cry at the top of the stairs and glanced back to see Orella.

"Call the ambulance and tell the operator to get the cops here," he ordered.

As she stepped into the office, Ray scooped up the smaller man and carried him up the stairs. The shamus carefully laid Dunn on the floor just inside the office door when he felt the warm blood flowing through his fingers.

Dunn grimaced in pain and suddenly inhaled.

"Ray, I got the son of a bitch Smyth for killing Cat," he sputtered out. "You won't have to worry about him anymore. It was those damn Shadows working for him. I got a couple of them as well."

He coughed out blood. Ray told him to be quiet.

"Keep your strength for the docs," he said.

"Hell, I'm finished!" Dunn smiled. "If docs save me, I'm going to the gallows. But I don't care. I beat the bastards."

Orella hurriedly finished the call and rushed into the bathroom. She returned with a towel and kneeled next to the dying me. She cleaned his lips. Dunn coughed again. The blood on her hands suddenly reminded her of the nightmares.

"That damn Smyth hired Jacobi," Dunn continued. "I saw the contract come through my office. They set up a dummy company. After I checked it out, I went to the mayor about what I found. That son of a bitch threatened to fire me unless I kept quiet. I had to do something when Cat died." He voiced trailed away.

"I had to do some…"

Dunn went silent and Irish took the towel from Orella, who had tears welling in her eyes.

"He's had it," he told her gently as he wiped his hands. "But it appears that he stopped some of them."

~~~

It was past three when Sirk and his men finally arrived. The ambulance driver and Ray drank coffee at his desk. Orella stood by the window, staring at the news on the ticker across the street. A white sheet covered Dunn's body, that the ambulance driver retrieved from his vehicle.

Ray remained quiet as the cop investigated the scene. He listened to the uniformed men tell him about the trail of blood coming from the street into the building and up the stairs. Barely social, Sirk asked Irish why Dunn came to Ray's office.

"Hell, maybe because his daughter is dead and Cat and I were partners," Irish exclaimed. "He just kept saying he shot the bastards."

"Who was that?"

"He didn't say," Ray lied quickly.

Sirk looked at him for a moment.

"You know you could be an accessory?" The cop told him gruffly.

Ray had enough of the detective.

"Remember, I do everything on my own! Isn't that what you always accuse me of? Or better yet, why don't you check in with your boss, Devine from Baltimore. He can tell you what to do next!"

Sirk came at Ray, who stood his ground. A sergeant jumped between the two men and pushed the shamus away.

"You son of a bitch! You're damn lucky that the blood trail runs from Dunn's car up those stairs," Sirk yelled out. "I liked Cat, so I'm giving you a break. You keep your goddamn mouth shut!"

"Hey, don't give a witness a bunch of your malarkey." Arizona's voice boomed as he walked into the office.

"I thought you left town," Sirk glanced back with a scowl.

"Nope, Ray and I are now partners," Arizona responded with a grin. "I'll be getting my shamus license tomorrow. I heard you were running around looking for a killer tonight."

"Great, now I've got two hotshots who are gonna screw up everything," Sirk grumbled. "Alright, enough chatter. You stay out of the way Arizona. You got no pull in the force anymore."

The ex-cop grinned at Sirk, who turned his attention back to the body.

"Alright, haul him away. We've got nothing more to see here," he told the ambulance driver.
~~~

After a few more questions, which revealed nothing about what Dunn told Ray as he died, Sirk put his hands behind his back. He puffed out his belly with satisfaction.

"Well, we got the guy who killed the mayor and Julie Smyth tonight. The easiest case I've had in a while. Won't be any trial to worry about."

Ray glanced over at Orella, who looked like she was about to correct the detective.

"What are you talking about?" Ray interrupted. "Are you saying Dunn killed the mayor and the DA's wife?"

"No doubt about it! Hell, I expected it to be up on that ticker by now. There was a party at the Andras estate tonight. Dunn snuck in and shot the mayor down in cold blood before he killed Mrs. Smyth. Even Bishop La Spina got it in the back. He's at the hospital right now.

"What about Peter Smyth?" the shamus asked.

"He's fine! I guess his wife took the bullet for him," Sirk declared as they started carrying the body of J. Allan Dunn down the stairs.

He turned back to Ray.

"Don't worry, Smyth is still after your ass!"

No Remedy Against Death:

Ray Irish Occult Suspense Mystery Book 4

Chapter 1: Girl Trouble

"Listen, you clueless bitch! Leave or not, it's done. I won't talk about this anymore," Victor Dela Cruz hissed under his mask. He turned and rushed away as his bright jester clothes soon became lost in the rainbow sea of colored costumes.

Momentarily stunned by his vehement outburst, Yana stood in the ballroom's corner. Uncomfortably dressed like a countess from the 18th century, the woman no longer felt the itch of her wig or the mask slip from her fingers. A frigid blast of resignation left her staring at the spot where he disappeared.

The son of a bitch doesn't care anymore!

The haunting strains of a song rose from the front of the ballroom. Les Brown and the Band of Renown played *Confess*. The irony, along with her embarrassing night, became too much for Yana. She retreated toward the lobby doors. As she stepped past a row of colorful tents made to appear like a gypsy encampment, the woman felt someone grab her arm.

"You should have left that bastard years ago!"

It was Helen Day holding a flask in her other hand. She offered a drink to Yana, who shook her head.

"Come on, let's talk!"

As one of Yana's few friends in New York, Helen kept a close eye on her. The woman took Yana by the arm while directing her toward the nearest tent.

After taking a quick peek inside, Helen forced Yana to sit on the narrow bench. The woman adjusted her tight 1920s flapper dress before sliding in next to her. Helen placed her flask on the cheap table where a deck of cards lay. The heavy cloth curtains around them cut down the outside sounds, making the space refreshingly isolated.

"I need to leave," Yana insisted.

"No, you need to be with a friend. I watched what happened, and I know you. You shouldn't blame yourself." Helen opened her small handbag and pulled out a cigarette case and a handkerchief. She handed the cloth to Yana before lighting her smoke.

"No, I won't need this," Yana handed back the cloth. "I've seen it coming for a while now. I just didn't expect him to explode in public. Hell, am I the only one here who can act like the dutiful wife of a United Nations diplomat?"

"You need to get everything off your chest." Helen blew smoke into the air before tipping back her flask. "Trust me; it'll help. By the way, I know an excellent lawyer for you. He'll make sure that bastard loses his shirt."

"I don't want that. My family still holds the house and estate in Dagupan. Besides, Victor's a diplomat. The government gave him a post in Madrid. It makes things too difficult for such thoughts. He'll return to Spain soon."

She handed the handkerchief back with a troubled smile. Helen was on her third husband, so Yana trusted her advice on divorce lawyers.

"This just means I get away from him and return to my life. That's good. I have bigger problems."

"Orella?"

Yana nodded, then looked at the entrance as the curtain opened. A masked woman wearing the costume of a gypsy entered.

"I'm sorry I didn't realize that I have customers. Tonight's been slow."

The gypsy took a seat at the table, slopping her glass of champagne on the wood surface. She shuffled the deck of cards.

"I don't think…" Yana offered, but Helen cut her off.

"Yes, this is great. Can you give a reading to my friend?"

"Helen, I'm not in the mood." Yana tried again.

"Nonsense. You need to see the future." Helen merrily gave her a self-satisfied smile before turning back to the gypsy.

"How much?"

"It's a dollar for a reading. But one must reach out to the spirits."

The woman finished shuffling, then held out her hand.

"Oh, she's willing. She's going through a difficult time." Helen placed a bill in the gypsy's hand.

Yana let out a resigned sigh. Endearing, her friend's penchant for taking charge tonight annoyed her. Nevertheless, Yana moved closer to the table while the fortune teller laid out the cards.

"You'll notice that I lay out your cards in this Celtic cross spread. You must focus upon these, for each position within the spread has a meaning." The gypsy explained, then took another drink.

"The last cards are the staff. You can think of the two crosses where card one and two become nested within a larger cross in the middle. This situation represents the heart of the matter - what is most central to you at the reading time. Do you understand?"

Despite her reservations, Yana nodded.

"That's good. You see, this is the hub around which the wheel of your life is turning." The fortune-teller flipped a card.

"What about those cards?" Helen's wide-eyed interruption caused the gypsy to smile.

"I see you are helping your friend on her path of discovery. The staff is your consciousness, moving from your unconscious on the bottom to your conscious mind on the top. While the horizontal line of the cross shows time moving from your friend's past into her future."

The gypsy pointed at the first card. An angel holding a sword and scale stood out in the image.

"Justice stands with you, for you believe in fairness. You believe someone has done you wrong. If you put things right, then you'll find justice."

"See, I told you," Karen smirked as she lit another cigarette.

Yana glared at her, then waited for the next card.

Their hostess flipped over a card showing the sun.

"This is what you want most since you have been through a period of challenges. The Sun heralds an ending to your difficulties. Soon a time comes to celebrate with friends and loved ones, even the possibility of conception or birth."

"Ow, I didn't know you were expecting," Helen cooed and squeezed her friend's shoulder like they were sorority sisters. Yana smelled the liquor on the woman's breath and realized her friend was hiding her intoxication well.

"I'm not expecting," she replied through gritted teeth. "Can we get to the next one and get this over with?"

The fortune-teller scowled at them, then turned the next card.

"This concerns your fears, for the Moon shows you about the lies and insecurity that are prominent in your life at the moment. You are afraid of being deceived and misled."

"Wait, what are you telling me?" Yana's eyes widened as she gripped the table.

"The card is showing your turbulent emotions. It means you need to find clarity of mind and purpose, even when this seems difficult. While the Moon helps illuminate the way, it cannot show what hides in the shadows."

Yana backed away from the table.

"Helen, I've had enough of this." She stood up.

"Oh, are you afraid? Yana, every one of these cards is spot on so far. Do you want to know the truth?" She looked at the woman suspiciously. "Or maybe you want to go home and wait for Victor."

"Shut up!"

"Don't be like this. Sit down and let's get our money's worth." Helen offered her the flask again, but Yana ignored it as she returned to her seat.

"Get on with it!"

The gypsy woman stared at Yana for a moment, then she shrugged. When she turned over the next card, she immediately looked at Yana.

"It's not what it seems."

Without a word, Yana hurried out of the tent.

"Yana, come back." Helen tried to stop her, but her friend refused to respond.

When Helen peered out the open curtain flap, she watched Yana running away in a near sprint. The woman's tall, white wig danced precariously on her head as she burst through the exit doors. When she disappeared, Helen turned back to the table to retrieve her flask and cigarettes. The card image stared at her from the table, a grinning skull wearing a knight's armor.

"I certainly didn't expect that. What's that card mean?"

"That's what I wanted to explain. The symbol of death only means a time of endings and brand-new beginnings. Your friend will come to a new phase in your life."

The gypsy turned over the next card.

"Now, this is more of a warning about what is standing against her."

"Is that what I think it is?" Helen's voice was almost a whisper as she flicked the ash from her cigarette.

The gypsy nodded and took a cigarette from Helen's case.

"Someone, probably a male, finds little hope for the future because of this card. The creature on this card likes chaos in people's lives. Your friend needs to consider her friends because she will question the motives of everyone."

As the fortune-teller leaned forward to light her cigarette from the offered stub held by Helen, her expression showed concern.

"The devil's desire to control leaves her and her loved ones vulnerable."

~~~

A week after the burial of Katherine Bennett and J. Allan Dunn, Bishop Henry La Spina remained in the hospital. He looked out the open window, not noticing the trickle of sweat dripping on his chest. Below his chest, he felt next to nothing anymore, a permanent condition that Henry decided needed a resolution soon. For the moment, the man's thoughts returned to a woman that he could not get out of his mind.

Myrna!

He sighed, reconciled with the belief that she was safe.

Well, for the moment.

The bishop looked down at the passage inside a book he was reading. While he knew most, if not all, the Bible passages, Henry La Spina lived a life dedicated to mocking and scorning God. Before taking his vows as a priest, the man cut the throats of human sacrifices in tribute to his master, Andras. Since the beginning, he enjoyed his double life as a demon worshiper while acting as the leader of one of Oyster City's Protestant churches.

However, Henry quickly grew to regret the success of their endeavors to bring Andras from the depths of Hell. Among the privileged families who made up the Shadows, there was always an underlying expectation their group would remain in control. Andras quickly ensured such beliefs held no sway with him. The demon master abused, raped, and killed his followers with the same abandon as he
~~~

inflicted upon his sacrificial victims. Aside from his natural distaste for being bossed around by a bully, there was something that Henry found that he never expected.

He fell for a gawky woman!

A demon worshiper found love in a tender soul who remained untouched by the vile world.

Until she married me!

Henry's eyes went back to the book he received as a gift from a nurse. One passage inside the pages tore at him. It described the world he gave to Myrna.

Do not be afraid of those who kill the body but cannot kill the soul. Rather, be afraid of the One who can destroy both soul and body in hell.
Matthew 10:28

Henry did not hear the door open. But he suddenly felt fear across those parts of his body still capable of sensation.

"Andras, you've come." The bishop refused to look over at the demon that inhabited the body of Peter Smyth.

"Of course, you wouldn't expect me to send a messenger."

Peter Smyth took a seat across from the bed while his brother closed the door. Henry observed his master's act of social acceptance. As he looked the demon over, he remembered how Peter wore his middle age well with a lean body and chiseled porcelain facial features. However, something about the man's face looked different. His cheekbones were broader and pulled higher. The creature inside Smyth's body kept his mouth shut tightly as well. Only someone who knew him well would notice the change.

On the other hand, Phillip's heavily weathered face showed his years of excess and debauchery. He remained by the door with his hat in hand. However, he held the same piercing blue eyes as his brother.

"My condolences to your condition," the district attorney stated in his usual cold way.

"I was wondering if you've made any progress in finding your wife?"

Bishop La Spina glanced over.

"I woke up several days ago to find that I can no longer walk. But, I'm expecting Myrna to show up any day in her grief about my condition."

The gray-haired man with the face of a hawk gave Henry a silent smirk. The bishop decided his face looked more like a vulture.

"Henry, I believe you have access to a telephone," Phillip Smyth interceded, pushing his long silver hair back across his shoulders. "You could have called for help in finding Myrna. Our master stated that you have until the next moon to bring your wife back into our circle."

Phillip glanced at the man in the chair.

"Your condition does not withdrawal the order that I gave you. You know this festival will cement my rule over Oyster City. Those who follow me must make their vows upon that night. Loyalty to me is all that matters to mortals. Weakness is not something I tolerate."

"I'm quite sure of that," the bishop agreed.

"Good! There's a rumor that someone saw your wife around the *Beacon* with a columnist who works there. There is your clue to finding her. Bring that bitch to me on the night of slaughter. It is you or your wife that will hang over the pit of fire."

The ominous tone coming from Andras caused Henry to suppress a smile.

"Andras, I've had time to consider many things from this bed. My soul has been yours from the beginning of my life. However, I don't understand why you should worry about my wife. There's a whole town of people that we can use in the sacrifice. The night of slaughter will remove any interference to my plans."

The demon stared at him for a moment.

"If it provides you with an incentive, I'll expand my previous thoughts. Myrna is not a threat to me personally. However, her bloodline provides me with a means to bring more from my realm into the human world. We can breed her or sacrifice her. Like you and Phillip, even that foreigner who carries the Singsing ring, each person is marked by their ancestors' actions. I find them useful or an obstacle to my wishes."

Smyth stood from his chair, glancing out the open window.

"Which leads me to your interest in your wife's welfare. I took her on the day of your wedding. You resisted me. Yet, she's escaped your servants. Worse, you attempted to interfere with our inclusion of her into the circle. I'm wondering about your value."

LaSpina remained quiet, staring at his useless legs. He suddenly remembered Andras killing Julie Smyth to raise the harem of witches. The bishop looked at Smyth.

You find everyone temporary in value!

"As I've told you and the others from the beginning, family ties of Oyster City are not important," Andras continued. "The Shadows must follow my purpose; not shield those you wish to keep from a true calling as my servant."

Henry glimpsed Phillip's troubled expression at the demon's statement.

"As a cripple now, you cannot extend your bloodline," Smyth turned back to the bishop. "Let me be blunt. Your worth teeters between a painful death over a pit or your continued existence on this earth. Should you fail me, not only can I promise you terrible demise, but your anguish and torture will extend for eternity. Do I make myself clear?"

Henry slowly nodded.

"I'll make sure that I do what's best, just like my family has always done," the bishop told them. "We can't have any loose ends."

Peter Smyth walked to the door.

"I'm glad you understand. For a moment, you had Phillip concerned. I don't care if you kill off Myrna's entire family to get her back. I want her given to my supporters for entertainment before I break her. Her soul becomes my property that night. No one leaves my circle of friends!"

Phillip opened the door for the master. He looked back at his friend in the bed.

"Let me know if you need anything. We'll talk soon."

"Don't worry, I plan on fixing everything. You have my vow," Henry La Spina told the closing door.

~~~

The bastard doesn't even bother to come back to the house anymore!

Yana looked away from the untouched twin bed a few feet away. She glanced over at the clock on the nightstand. The harsh light coming from the lamp showed her it was just after four. Despite the uncomfortable feeling of sweat covering her body, Yana wrapped the covers around her tighter. It took away the heebie-jeebies that left her fully awake at the ungodly hour.

Orella is in danger!

Call it mother's intuition or, maybe, a wave of growing anger at the reason for her danger.

Ray Irish!

She could forgive her daughter's reckless and naïve rush back to the private detective. Orella still carried a crush on the man who saved her life. However, Yana focused her anger on Irish for his betrayal of their agreement. He knew her daughter remained vulnerable.

Yet, he let Orella stay with him in Oyster City. For all she knew, they were living together in his bedroom in the same dusty office where Irish scraped by as a shamus. Her daughter might not see the shame in the situation, but her mother certainly did.

Finally tired of the heat, Yana threw back the covers. As she let the still humid air try to cool her, the woman's mind came back to the reason for her early rise.

The nightmares are getting worse!

Her dream started in a field near Sorbonne University, a place that Yana enjoyed during her years in Paris as a student. Each May, she joined the girls in a ceremonial folk dance around a tall pole garlanded with greenery and flowers.

In the first part of her dream, she enjoyed reminiscing in her memories. The colorful streamers of ribbons hung from the top of the Maypole. Soon, dancers surrounded Yana, who stood by the pole. Amid the laughter, the young maidens took the cloth strips, and they wove intricate patterns around the woman. She smiled as they twisted and gyrated to the sound of a ceremonial drumbeat.
~~~

While Yana stood memorized by the dance, she first saw three beautiful women in the background. The colorful streamers partially hid them from Yana as the women joined in the merriment. Slowly, the scene changed as the dancers wrapped Yana to the pole. The woman's eyes followed the triplets so alike in every detail as her smile faded.

The sound stopped, and Yana looked up at the streams of bright ribbons flowing down like rain. Amid the display, Yana looked at the triplets who came close to her while shedding their clothes. The booming sound of a drum started again, and the three women began to dance. Unseen hands appeared to hold the ribbons, which whirled around them. After a moment, another woman joined them.

It was her daughter!

Orella danced with the same passionate expression on her face as the other women. Yana yelled out when her daughter stripped her clothes. The garments floated down as the girl danced. Despite the pleas, Orella grinned and continued her rhythmic dance with the other women. Slowly, the light around the scene grew dark, and the streamers grayed while the bindings around Yana tightened.

She saw a dark, slender man standing in the distance. While he never moved, his figure drew closer. Yana's arms and legs hurt as the ribbons holding her pulled tighter with each beat of the drums. She looked down to see blood oozed as the bindings cut into her.

While the drumbeat slowed, the dancers stopped their movement. Instead, the women went to their knees. They groveled before the dark stranger, now close enough for Yana to see. She screamed out in horror and revulsion when she recognized the person. Yet, no sound came from her lips.

The creature's hawk-like face turned skeletal while his pitch-black eyes looked upon Orella. She held out her hand with the Singing ring on her ring finger. The demon held her forearm while robed figures surrounded her daughter. Yana silently screamed again when she saw a dagger suddenly rise above the small crowd. She witnessed the weapon plunge into Orella's hand. However, her daughter did not react or even cry out. Instead, she offered her mangled hand to the triplets, who lapped at the blood like dogs.

Yana cried out in agony as she finally woke from the crushing nightmare. She shivered again while she tried to purge her mind of the images. The woman kept telling herself that she was a modern, rational person. Dreams and fortune-tellers were the stuff of legends from a primitive past.

Yet, something deep inside of the mother willed her to get out of bed. Resolved in her instant plan, Yana immediately went to the closet. She pulled out a leather suitcase and began to pack.

I've got to get her away!

~~~

"How dare you embarrass me like that! You take me back right now!"
~~~

The young girl's orders probably worked on her father's lackeys. However, Ray Irish did not bother to glance over.

"Girl, you're going home. Next time you run off, get a boyfriend without a glass jaw." The large man growled as he eased the girl's expensive Packard around the corner to reach the main highway back to Oyster City.

Irish remained annoyed at the fight, and his hand still hurt from the punch. Plus, he needed to take a taxi back to retrieve his car. On top of it all, the stitches from his bullet wound were itching again.

The woman leaned back in the seat, her eyes remaining on the shamus with an icy stare. He hoped that the woman would continue to give him the cold treatment at least until she returned to her plush bedroom on the expansive estate of her father.

Instead, Della Reece leaned over closer to him. The ploy gave him a delightful view of her cleavage that came with her tight blue dress. It was also so obvious that he nearly groaned in disbelief.

"How much is my father paying you? I can give you five hundred right now!" Her husky voice made him take another look.

Della immediately enjoyed the attention, giving him a bedroom smile. However, her gray eyes held little warmth. She was cute, but she wore too much makeup on her plump cheeks.

Another spoiled brat!

She liked suckers who gave in to her whims. Ray did not doubt that Della learned since puberty to get her way with the good smoldering look and a bit of cleavage.

"You should pull over on the next side road. I'll bet that we can make a deal," the woman continued. "Shamus, I'm great with men."

"Sister, I'll lay money that. I've followed you for the last three days. During that time, you've had this Packard in the back lots of five different clubs with four different guys. Hell, I've sat around watching you fog up backseat windows while you've been on your back. Daddy finally said enough of your game. It's time to go home."

His tone was for a child, but he glanced at the cleavage again. Irish was not above thinking about the possibilities. The girl noticed his peep. She opened her purse and pulled out cash, which she waved the bills at him.

"Come on; my father doesn't need to know a thing. Take the next turnoff. I can tell that you're the kind of guy who carries a flask in your hip pocket. We can have a few snorts and some fun." Her voice carried the throaty timbre of passion and experience. "You can just tell him I got away!"

Damn, women can be tough on a guy!

"Forget it! A guy working for a state senator doesn't take bribes from their daughter. Plus, your daddy has connections with certain people who'll put me in prison. Get yourself to twenty-one, then I'll consider it."

Ray explained the problem more to himself than to her.

"Now, just sit back and enjoy the night!"

Della huffed and slid back to the other side of the car.

"You're a bastard! You probably don't even like girls."

"Yeah, I'm no good, alright. Thing is that I like a woman who doesn't play around like a whore."

"You son of a bitch, you can't call me that! I'll have daddy break you!" The venom exploded from the other side of the seat.

"Sister, you're not doing anything. We both know that you're a spoiled girl from Miss Plummer's School of High Brow Ingrates. You get on the wrong side of me, and I'll pull over to spank your sweet little ass with a strap. Your daddy should have done that a long time ago."

He turned to her, his face dark with irritation.

"Now, shut the hell up!"

Still fuming, Ray turned on the car radio. He expected the girl to continue her rant, but she surprised him by stewing instead. He felt her angry stare from the darkened passenger side. A mile down the road, she finally spoke up.

"You should have been nice to me. I've decided that I'll tell my father that you hurt me. He won't pay you. I'll have the last laugh."

Her smug tone reminded Irish of why he hated people with more money than brains.

"Sister, I had Daddy already pay me upfront since I was trailing your ass across the state. Otherwise, your offer tonight might have worked on a poor shamus."

He gave her a cheesy grin with his lie.

"Take a bit of free advice. Get yourself married. Then, you can have all the fun on the side that you want. Daddy won't send a guy like me after you. Embarrassing your husband doesn't make your daddy politician look so bad."

This time, Della went quiet after crossing her arms in a show of defiance. While the money was good, Ray hated dealing with these cases. His mind immediately went to the far deadlier target that he needed to handle. The same guy who helped to put the itching stitches in his side and his leg. The bastard who killed his partner and friend.

It was near midnight when the Packard entered the estate of Walter Reece. Irish drove the large vehicle straight into the open garage. He got out and waited for the girl. She ignored him as she went toward the house. He quickly shut the garage door from the outside and hurried after her.

"All right, you bastard, I'm home! Now go away," she yelled.

"No, sweetie, your father needs to see you all safe and tucked into bed." Irish grinned at Della's glare. "I'd hate to see you make something up about how badly I treated you."

The odd couple took the path around the lawn, coming from behind the massive square house. Their passage through inky shadows of the narrow walk skirted the large formal garden. The moon pushed into the dark sky, highlighting the yellow feathers stuck on the woman's hat. The woman's heels clicked hollowly like a typewriter on the concrete, echoing out from the side of the structure. They swung around the corner and took the front steps, where dark shadows covered much of a large porch greeted them.

"You'd think they'd leave a light on for you," Irish grunted as he unbuttoned his coat. Even with the lack of rain or cold that evening, his trench coat remained comfortably handy, like his fedora. It also helped conceal his .45 auto resting in the holster under his left armpit.

Della stopped at the massive door.

"What, no key?" Irish reached over to press the doorbell.

"I don't need them." Her sarcastic reply brought another grunt from the shamus.

After several moments, the inside lights came on, and a haggardly looking woman opened the door. She wore a black maid's uniform.

"Ms. Della, I'm so glad you're back."

Della ignored her and brushed by the woman on her way inside. Ray followed them into a vestibule that displayed a grand staircase made of dark wood.

"Tell Walter Reece that Ray Irish brought his daughter back home," the shamus stated with a resigned sigh.

"Yes, sir, he's been in bed for a while. I'll direct you to his library, where you can wait."

"That's what I expected. I hope you have a cup of strong coffee hanging around here."

~~~

"I should have killed the bitch," Lance Carrol growled out as he took a sip from his silver flask.

As he sat in the front seat of his wrecked car, the young man still felt the stinging warmth where Victoria Owens slapped him. Still, he smirked at the fear he witnessed in her pretty eyes when he left his date in one of Oyster City's isolated make-out spots.

Damn whore put out for the other guys! The bitch can walk home!

Lance suddenly recognized the irony. After taking the turn past Andras Lane too fast, he drove his dad's Caddy into the deep ditch. Lifting himself from the driver's seat, Lance observed the damage to his front wheel. The tire was in shreds,
~~~

and the front wheel mount bent over. He smelled the odd acid sweet order coming from the steam that drifted from under the hood.

"Damn bitch caused that! By god, next time, she'll pay up!"

As Lance fantasied about the torturous ways he planned to inflict upon Victoria in the future, the tall, slender man looked over the quiet area. The lights of a few old mansions dotted the hillside.

"I'll go bang on some doors and wake up the dead!" Lance laughed before he took another sip of his drink.

The man stopped when he recognized the Andras mansion at the end of the lane. A light shining from the windows caught his eye. The dome on the roof looked like a beacon watching over Oyster City. Lance drunkenly considered his options, then peered at the next closest home. It remained dark.

Well, it looks like I'm going to the crazy lady's house!

Everyone knew the old Andras woman. She dressed like a gypsy, and she had a strange, old butler who looked like Abraham Lincoln. The lights showed him that servants were still awake. The servants would help him.

They always did!

He staggered out of the ditch, reaching the pavement, where he stopped to take another drink. He involuntarily shivered at the taste while trying to follow the paved road. Halfway to his destination, Lance began singing the only song that came to his mind.

When he found the stone and wrought iron gateway to the end of the lane, Lance stopped. Near the massive spread of an ancient oak, the man saw the gray stone crypts and headstones' rows. He licked his dry lips while a creeping chill covered him, while a beam of light dancing across the ground drew closer.

Lance noticed a long, lean woman holding the lantern in the hazy light of the dusky moon. Her unusual dark dress wrapped around her body, reminding him of a shroud or a type of toga. As she walked through the shadows, he stood transfixed. Her pale, almost ethereal face stood out under long, black hair, which appeared darker than the shadows that she walked through. She didn't seem to notice the man standing by the gate.

"Hey lady, can you take me to your house? I need to use your phone."

She slowed, then waved him over. He pushed open the gate and followed her. When he reached the first crypt, Lance stopped.

"Hey, wait a minute. The house is the other way!"

"Come with me. I know what you need!" The female voice filled his head. "I feel the lust coursing through your veins."

Lance watched her while feeling hairs on his neck standing on end. He glanced back at the Andras mansion, then slowly followed the strange woman. His nervousness suddenly changed to intrigue when he saw her unhook part of her dress. A long piece of cloth dropped to the ground. He picked it up. The delicate fabric smelled slightly of earthy, wet soil and mint.

When the man looked up, he saw the woman disappear around the corner of a large crypt. Still wary, he slowly followed the path. As Lance peered around the corner, he stopped.

The lantern sat on a stone ledge by the stone building. Partially hidden by the iron grate was the woman. He watched in fascination while she slowly disrobed as she hummed. Her skin took on a pale milky tone under the moonlight as she smiled at him.

"Are you one who's brave enough to enjoy my company?"

Lance wasn't sure if he heard the words in the still night air. However, she beckoned him with a finger. His eyes focused on her bare breasts. Thoroughly baffled by his experience, Lance dug into his coat and pulled out his flask.

He saw disappointment cross her face.

"I thought you like to take risks," she said, then disappeared into the crypt.

It took two quick drinks to stiffen his spine. Then he heard the woman call out to him again.

"Are you man enough to enter?"

"Sister, I'm all man," Lance called out. He frowned when he heard his voice crack, then hurried to the entrance. The young man glanced down at the discarded clothes before he investigated the dark opening.

"Lady, you're into some strange stuff," he moved inside as he saw her light a candle, then placed it on the bench beside a stone coffin. His eyes drank in her body as he drew close.

"I'm sure you'll approve," she laughed lightly.

Lance lifted the last shot from his flask before he slammed the silver object on the stone bench. A tinny echo filled the room. She turned to him; her brown eyes danced with delight. Lance pulled her close, roughly kissing her.

"Alright, baby, I'm here." He pushed her back against the coffin.

Her amused laugh caught him off-guard. Something in her demeanor made him pause.

"You're not playing with a full deck, are you, sister?"

"He's not very smart!" A voice came from the shadowed corner, forcing Lance to spin around.

Two women stepped into the light. Each wore similar dark shrouds as the naked woman discarded. However, wrinkles of age covered their thin faces while splotchy patches of gray hair trailed down on their stooped shoulders. Dark eyes set back in their pale faces; the women came closer as Lance stood there.

"Don't worry, my sisters and I will have you tonight," the naked woman whispered in his ear.

With surprising strength, she suddenly lifted him from the ground. As panic filled the young man, Lance kicked out. However, the old hags secured his feet. Soon, they dragged him across the top of the tomb while Lance futilely struggled.

Despite his resistance, the women tied his ankles with a length of rope to the handrails that ran along the side of the coffin. Cinching his wrist tight to the casket, the women cackled when Lance cried out in pain.

The naked woman crawled on top of the coffin, where she unbuttoned his pants. She pulled down his clothes to expose his semi-erect dick.

"Mortals make offerings of blood," the woman coldly stated with coal-black eyes. She glanced down at one of the old women.

"Panthia, hand me the dagger."

Her sister pulled an elaborately adorned dagger from the folds of her shroud. She handed the weapon to the naked woman.

"Psamathe, save some of him for your sisters."

"No, you can't!" Lanced screamed out and frantically tried to escape. The woman on top of his legs drew the blade close to his groin with an evil grin.

She straddled him. His inability to get leverage, combined with her weight, kept him pinned down. The witch ripped open his shirt.

"Your parts are safe!" The woman assured him before she slid the blade across the man's chest—her precision cut through his skin.

Lance screamed out in pain. Desperately, he twisted and turned, trying to lift the woman from him. She dug into him again as the blood trickled on the stone tomb top. Again, he cried out, unable to stop the torture.

One of the old sisters cackled as she began lapping the blood like a dog. The other hag stripped, then went to the other side of the tomb. The naked witch on top of Lance cut into his other side while the hag pushed her head close. She drank from his bleeding wound.

Finally, the witch stopped using the dagger on Lance. His agony filled brain suddenly heard whispering words from the naked woman on top of him. She leaned over him, forcing him to suckle her. Despite the searing discomfort of his chest, the man grew hard. Enjoyment filled the witch's face when she pushed his manhood into her.

"My sisters, keep him aroused!"

The old hags finished their blood ritual. Meroe and Panthia began chanting an ancient spell as they watched Psamathe rape the man. Their wrinkled faces slowly changed as they smeared the drying blood across their cheeks. Soon, the creature's skin tightened and smoothed across their bodies. When Psamathe finally finished, she slid down the crypt. One of her now beautiful sisters crawled on the man. She used the dagger to cut into Lance's flesh again. Despite his renewed struggles, Psamathe took her turn to lap at his warm blood. Lamia's identical-looking witches planned to enjoy themselves before following their master's instructions, the demon called Andras.

~~~

When Lance emerged from the tomb, he held no will of his own. He carried no conscience either as he followed the dictates of his masters. The man unconsciously cinched up his belt to keep his pants from falling. However, his coat remained inside the crypt. The tattered and bloody shirt barely hung on over his shoulders. In his head, his new master's voice sent Lance away from the cemetery.

The dawn barely lit the sky when Lance came to the backdoor of the large house near the bottom of Andras Lane. He was scarcely aware of his plodding walk to get there. The man felt no pain when the shards of glass cut into his skin after shattering the windowpane. As he entered the back room, he saw the light come on from the stairs leading to the next floor.

"Who's there?" The startled voice of a woman came into the room.

Lance went to the kitchen counter and opened a drawer. Then he moved into the shadows by the stairs. The soft creak of the stairs masked the man's breathing as he stood there.

"Mitzi, you darn cat, I better not find you down there getting into the cabinets again!"

Slowly, a barefoot appeared at the bottom of the back staircase. A fat lady in a robe turned on the light switch then entered the kitchen. Her gray hair was still in curlers, she nearly passed by the man standing at a statue.

Lance plunged the kitchen knife into her chest. Like a zombie, the slender man withdrew the blade, then proceeded to the main stairs. He paid no attention to the woman's dying pleas. As the man reached the master bedroom, a light appeared under the door.

~~~

Two weeks after his first run-in with Della Reece, the morning sun peered through the window of Ray's office. The detective sat at his desk with his feet propped up on the windowsill. Irish caught himself whistling again. Despite the long night tracking down Della a second time, his good mood came from the cabbage that Walter Reece paid him.

His latest overnight excursion brought Della back to her father's mansion again. The girl took off with another shady character she met at a nightclub. Since her daddy gave him standing orders to return her no matter the cost, Ray lost no time hunting her down. The woman made it so easy. The shamus debated if she wanted Ray to find her.

However, this time Della played nasty. She took his advice and got a tougher boyfriend. The guy still wore his ruptured duck on his lapel. He also made the mistake of telling Irish that he was an ex-Marine.

Irish's intentional smirk at the information started the fight on his terms. After the two big men damaged several chairs and a table, Ray's opponent finally went down hard. Della's new boyfriend forgot that a steel .45 auto pistol smacked across the head works just like brass knuckles. After cracking the guy's skull, Ray pulled a wallet out of his opponent's coat. He retrieved part of the money while the club owner and his bouncer came up.

"Tell Sleepy there that dating underage girls gets him a conversation with the cops the next time. I took my fee for keeping quiet."

Irish tossed the wallet to the club owner.

"He can pay for the damage to your place. A word of advice: don't allow this underage girl in your joint, or the cops will raid it next time. That's something I can promise you. Got it?"

Ray grabbed Della by the arm and hustled her out of the building. Fortunately, the warning about the police kept the owner and his bouncer at bay while they left.

While the woman resisted, he recognized it as halfhearted. This time, they took his old car. He saw her surprised and sour expression when he forced her inside the beat-up Nash. Ray learned from his mistake during their first encounter.

"What'd you think? That a shamus can live like the rich!" The man grumbled as he drove away.

During the long drive back, Della tried to engage in a conversation. He glanced over at her gray eyes, which still held her enamored view of the fight. Della liked the idea of two men fighting over her. It meant trouble down the line. He frowned at the thought and went silent.

Eventually, the girl grew sullen from Ray's attitude. When they reached Reece's estate, Della went back to her frosty ways. On his way out the door, he heard Della hurrying up the stairs.

Walking to his car, Irish glanced up at a shadow coming from an upstairs window. Della's unmistakable figure came through the sheer curtains as she watched him. He grinned.

She mentioned her twenty-first birthday was coming up soon!

Ray slid into his car, expecting that he and Della would continue their cat-and-mouse game.

The green ticker banner running on the *Beacon* building across the street suddenly caught his attention. The big headline flowing by on the large screen concerned the execution of General Hideki Tojo.

November 12—In Tokyo, an international war crimes tribunal sentenced seven Japanese military and government officials to death. Those condemned include General Hideki Tojo for his role in World War II atrocities.

Ray's memories returned for a moment to his time in the Pacific. The horrific slaughter and stench seared into his mind and his dreams. He'd seen the worst in men, and he also saw the best in people. Ray reminisced about the doctors and nurses who put him back together, as well as those who never came back.

Well, that execution couldn't have happened to a better guy! Ray thought with a grim, satisfied smile.

The next banner headline concerned the death of another gang member in Baltimore as part of an ongoing turf war among the gangs.

November 11—Suspected Jacobi gang member, Orville Hodge, found dead in a field of an apparent suicide.

Ray enjoyed the news.

"Not likely," the shamus told the window.

The ruthless gangster Johnny Jacobi killed Catherine Bennett in front of Irish only a few weeks before. Cat was Ray's partner and friend. While the entire plan to kill Irish blew up in the gangster's face, Jacobi still murdered Cat in sadistic revenge.

"I hope the bastard is burning in hell along with you, Jacobi!" The detective spoke the words aloud to the empty office.

November 12 - Another Smiling Lady murder in Oyster City! Missing husband suspected in the grisly crime.

The headline brought Ray's attention back to his new partner, Arizona. He frowned as he recalled the inside story from the ex-cop who kept in contact with his honest friends inside the police department.

The son of a wealthy Oyster City businessman wrecked his car and was still missing for a couple of weeks. The police believed that the young man entered a nearby house, then killed the family along with a female servant on Andras Lane. He recalled the two murdered women had their lips cut from the corner of the mouth back on the cheek, creating a hideous smile.

Ray frowned when he thought about the other strange part involving missing family members. The peculiar disappearances left the police and newspapers puzzled. No one knew if someone kidnapped the family members or where they involved in the murders in some bizarre way.

Of course, the wealthy society folks of the city insisted upon action. That meant the police increased their patrols around the mansions while rousting any thugs and junkies they came across in Oyster City. Part of the goal was reassuring the frightened citizen. Irish recognized that the other purpose focused on soothing those who put Peter Smyth in as the new mayor of Oyster City. The general election came in a few months.

The ticker continued with a headline from a local columnist's latest story.

Is anarchy coming? The number of murders and missing persons in Oyster City skyrockets!

Irish grunted as he unconsciously nodded in agreement with the glowing stream of lights. The grisly deaths among the wealthy estates brought the attention of large newspapers in Baltimore.

The creaking sound from the stairs outside his office forced Irish to look at his office door. A familiar hulking shadow came through the obscured glass that covered the top part of the door.

His partner entered, then took an unsteady route to the coat rack where he put his bowler hat. Irish scowled while he watched the former policeman, Lieutenant Arizona Charlie Campbell. His partner came in either hungover or drunk after drinking his breakfast. Irish let out a deep breath.

"Arizona, you told me once that I couldn't find solace at the bottom of the bottle. I'm telling you the same thing. Cat's dead and buried. Go get some coffee and sober up."

Arizona glared at him as he staggered to the other side of the room. He grumbled under his breath.

Ray looked at the small desk that came with his new partner as the big man took a seat. Immediately after Catherine Bennett's murder, Arizona tracked down the gangster who killed her. However, the man's vengeance left the detective unemployed and still hoping for revenge against the others involved. Irish agreed they should become partners; however, Arizona wasn't much good to him so far.

"I'm heading over to the cemetery. You want to come along? You keep your damn bottle here." Ray's chair squeaked like usual when he rose.

"Nah, I've got work to do," his partner replied.

"Right, you've got no clients, and I can't rely on you to keep an eye on Della Reece. I have to go handle that because I think you'll stop off at a bar and never get her."

Irish came over to the desk. Arizona's broad face, paler than average, held a pair of icy blue eyes that glared at him. His partner's brow furled.

"Get off my back, or we're going to have problems," the ex-cop growled.

"Part of the fee from last night's work, partner!" Ray smirked as he tossed a twenty down on the desk. "I told you to go get some coffee and breakfast. Damn it, do your job. Follow up with those records that Dunn told me about before he died."

Arizona gave him a blank stare.

"I told you that Dunn said Jacobi had a dummy company doing business with the city," the shamus reminded him through gritted teeth. "Maybe it ties back to Jacobi and Peter Smyth working together. When I got to this fair city, Dunn had files he stored offsite. It's a dingy office in the alley behind Chandler Avenue. You can't miss it. Go there and find evidence so we can nail the son of a bitch, Smyth. It's a start to pay him back for what happened to Cat. Or you can waste your time feeling sorry for yourself."

Arizona scowled.

"Alright, I'll go there, damn you. I'm still a decent detective."

Irish went to the door.

"Then prove it. I've not seen it so far, partner!"

He returned a glare before leaving the room.

~~~

The morning air struck him as pleasant, nearly spring-like. However, Ray didn't notice it. Instead, his mind was on Arizona, who surprised him with his breakdown about Cat's murder. He thought the cop would handle it better.

I guess he cared a lot more about the woman than Irish ever suspected!

He shoved his hands into his pocket as he walked along. Fortunately, Ray held his feelings about Cat in check. He was lucky. Orella Dela Cruz was still in town to keep him distracted. He did not have time to stew about it.

Hell, maybe I learned to bury my feelings now!

The image of Samantha Carter suddenly came rushing into his mind. He felt a knot in his stomach again.

Yeah, maybe not!

As he turned the corner to Cemetery Road, his thoughts went back to Orella. There was no doubt that her presence helped, but it also gave him things he didn't need. She smothered him with a need for constant attention. Worse, her possessive questions gnawed at him. Still, the shamus comforted himself in her need for him.

Hell, every time she's in Oyster City, some damn thug snatches her!

Kidnapped twice, the woman used Irish as her shield against the world in some ways. Ray recognized it, and he enjoyed feeling wanted. However, he knew Orella needed to get back to New York. Her life needed stability and a future. His life remained a twisted maze of apparent randomness. He struggled to know when his next paycheck might arrive.

On top of everything else, the shamus believed that Orella's staying kept her in danger. People died because of the damned thing on her finger. The Singsing ring was part of her family lineage, and, according to some people he knew, it was a powerful artifact for the occult.

Drawn out of his thoughts, Irish passed through the New Oyster City cemetery's wrought-iron gates. He paid no attention to the ancient gravestones. Instead, he went to reddish-brown mounds where two recent graves held the remains of Cat and her father, J. Allan Dunn.

Ray stood looking at the graves; his mind wandered back to the first day he met Cat. Her dancing eyes and a dazzling smile immediately intrigued him. At times, they worked well together, and she saved him from death on two occasions. While she always kept Irish at arm's length, they both realized an underlying attraction. Despite their disagreements, he eventually got past her mercenary ways to find a vulnerability that he understood.
~~~

"Well, Cat, I'm sorry that I couldn't make the shot," he told her grave. "I'll never forget that."

Or forgive myself!

The man turned around and barely noticed a woman in a green dress in the distance. As he walked past the row of bushes, he came into the next section of the graveyard. A movement made him glance over where he got a better view of the woman slowly walking. The lady in green looked at a crypt isolated away from the main cemetery. Her long, lean body remained turned away so he could only get a glimpse of the side of her face under a black-veiled cap.

His mind still focused on his memories; Ray glanced back at Cat's grave one last time. After a couple of steps, the man stopped in his tracks.

No, it can't be.

Greye?

Ray turned his attention to the isolated crypt. However, the woman was gone. As he looked around, the shamus hurried across the grass. He hurried to the place where he last saw the woman. The silence of the area greeted him when the man arrived. After several scans over the small field, Irish walked around the stone structure.

Where did she go?

The brick path led in two directions toward the back of the cemetery grounds. The iron gates he saw remained closed. Ray scowled, then pulled off his fedora. He looked over the line of brush, which obscured his initial view of the woman in green.

I would have seen her if she went back that way.

The man felt a chill on the back of this neck, and he unconsciously shivered. As Ray stood looking around the open area, his logical mind turned to the tangle of foliage that lined the brick path was only a few steps away.

No, a lady in a dress isn't likely to haul through a thicket!

When Irish turned back to the crypt, his eyes widened. He recognized the name engraved on the stone.

La Spina!

He leaned closer, but there was nothing else to indicate who was inside the chamber. The frigid chill of a foreboding curiosity filled him when he realized the crypt sat alone in the cemetery section, away from the others. The closest headstones were on another side of the thicket.

"Unconsecrated ground!" A man's voice startled Irish.

He glanced over to see a thin man, smoking a pipe while carrying a shovel over his shoulder. He pulled a cart that held several shrubs with canvas wrapped around their root balls. His weathered face looked over the detective with a bemused expression.

"What do you mean?" Irish asked as the man pushed the shovel blade into the ground with his foot.

"This area is for those who are unbaptized. I noticed you looking around like you were searching for someone. I get questions sometimes."

Ray looked around.

"I guess you know this place pretty well."

"That's right, I'm the groundskeeper and gravedigger. The names Harvey." He pulled a handkerchief, took off his sweat-stained hat, then wiped his balding head.

"Are you saying that nobody else is buried out here?" Irish turned back to the man.

"No, that's not what I said. None of the other graves have markers. Back in the day, they buried the infants out here. You know, those that died before they got baptized. Of course, nobody bothers much about such things now. From what I recall, this big ol' tomb is the last time that someone asked for burial here."

The detective's confused look remained.

"Wanted to be buried here. You mean they intentionally buried someone in this unconsecrated ground?

Harvey nodded as he put his hat back on. He went over to the crypt and knocked out the tobacco's remnants from his pipe on the stone.

"Yep, I remember when they put this thing up for Mrs. La Spina. She was the wife of the preacher, ya know. Died in childbirth. Didn't make any sense to me why they put this thing up out here. What that had to do with her soul is anyone's guess."

"I don't see any dates or names; I thought that was odd." Ray stared at the engraving.

Harvey came over to look as well.

"Yes, sir, never knew her but from stories, but they said Mrs. La Spina was a nice lady." He tipped back his hat. "Let's see, Nichol was her name. Mother of the current bishop."

"That's strange," the shamus observed. "By the way, you haven't seen a woman in a green dress and wearing a black-veiled cap over here this morning, have you?"

Harvey stopped filling his pipe briefly. His gaze remained on his pipe.

"Why do you ask?"

Something in the tone caused Ray to focus his attention on the gravedigger.

"I saw her by this crypt when I was leaving. When I got closer, I thought she looked familiar."

Harvey put his pipe in his mouth and patted his coveralls, looking for a match. As Irish waited, the man finally got his pipe lit. He glanced at the shamus.

"There's been talk that a woman stops here some days. But... well, you get people talking like that in a place like this."

"Meaning what?"

Harvey pulled his shovel out of the ground.

"Let's just say that normal women don't wear the same outfit each day."

"So, you've seen her. Do you know who she is?" Ray stepped next to the cart of plants.

Harvey glared at him.

"Don't you mean who she was?"

He turned away, pulling his cart.

"Well, you might not believe in such things, but I have my ideas. Now, I've wasted enough time gabbing."

"Come on; you can't leave me with that," Irish followed along.

When he realized Harvey wasn't going to give up the information, he hurried his pace to pull next to the gravedigger.

"Listen, I know what I saw. You can tell me anything. I won't mock you, alright?"

Harvey came to a stop. He glanced over.

"You mean it? It's bad enough when them spiritualists come through here, and I have to run them off."

"I swear it," Ray promised. "I just need to know I'm not crazy about what I saw."

"You ain't crazy, mister. Lest ways, not if you saw the woman in green. It's been going on for a while now. I came around that crypt one day, and she scared the bejeezus out of me." Harvey looked around. "There she was, those pretty eyes staring at me. She had such a sweet face all solid; then she was gone. I can tell you I hightailed it out of there."

"I'll bet," Irish agreed. "You say you got a good look at her. Was it Mrs. La Spina, the woman they buried there?"

The caretaker shook his head.

"No, not that one. The person was the La Spina woman that drowned overseas a few months back. I swore it was just like her picture in the newspaper. It was creepy. I went to the library just to make sure the sun wasn't playing tricks on me. I swear that I nearly shit my pants when I found that newspaper again."

"Greye!" Ray's voice croaked out the name.

"That's her name." Harvey pulled his cart away from Irish, who remained to stare at the crypt. "I guess she must want something. That's what they say about ghosts and unfinished business."

"Yeah, so I heard," the shamus dropped his head.

Chapter 2: Send Me an Angel

"I haven't seen you for a while," Pappy smiled as Ray Irish walked up.

"Yeah, about that." Ray went directly to the newsy's stand. He avoided looking at his friend for a moment while he scanned the new pulp magazines. Finally, he sighed.

"Listen, I want to apologize. I've been avoiding you since Cat's death. You warned me about the danger to people who were close to me. I'm sorry that I doubted you. I guess the idea you didn't warn me about Greye's death got to me when this unfolded. When you sit in a hospital bed, you get time to reflect. Truth be told, I wanted to blame you for my pigheadedness."

"Ray, we might come from different worlds, but you've never done me wrong." Pappy put his hand on the bigger man's shoulder. "You have my sympathy for Katherine. I realize she had a hard time accepting me—well, you know."

"Cat Bennett didn't trust you because she was racist as hell. She barely tolerated Orella. Mostly, Cat was a good egg, but that was the one thing she couldn't hide," the shamus grumbled.

"Yes, I know, but I believe she was a good person deep down."

"Well, you're a better man than I am," the shamus nodded as he picked up a magazine.

"Still, a lot of us never realize how stupid we can be at times. That means that I also need to apologize to Emma."

Pappy stopped his work and looked at Ray.

"I swear to God that I saw Greye La Spina this morning over at the cemetery. She was standing by the grave of the bishop's mother." Irish looked over with an embarrassed expression.

"I'll never doubt you or Emma again, my friend."

The newsy blinked several times as his eyes grew moist, then he went back to his work.

"Emma knows good people, and she tells me all the time that I need to look out for you. There's no need to apologize. You say that you saw her over at Henry's mother's grave?"

"Yeah, strange as hell. Did you know her grave is in the unconsecrated section of the cemetery?"

"No, but I guess I should expect that. I'll bet the old Andras graveyard is the same. Emma says the evil taking over this city comes from there."

It was Pappy's turn to avoid looking at Ray.

"Have you got anything new for me?" Irish turned back to the stand.

"Well, let's see. You know that we're in the worse drought since the 30s. The Farmer's Almanac expects it to continue for another month or so. Oh, they're moving that old cargo ship that's been sitting in the harbor. You know that spot where the *Stanley Rose* went down?"

Ray's puzzled look made his friend smile.

"You just don't look around. Don't you drive by the docks?"

"Yeah, I remember the Rose, alright. That's part of the reason they call me stubby?"

Ray held up his hand to show his missing part of a finger. Pappy chuckled at him.

"You use that all the time, and I recall your wound came from your run-in with Guy Young at the abandoned army base. How are the rest of your injuries?"

Ray frowned.

"Some better than others. There's been a few things on my mind," he explained.

"I remember a ship had to pull in there because the storm caused their load to shift, and they came up the Chesapeake. Sure, it's odd, but why's that news?"

"Well, after the crew abandoned it, the rumor is there are unstable explosives onboard. I guess the crew was hauling explosives left over from the war from Europe down to South America. The government threw them into jail over the whole thing. However, the Navy can't move it into the shipping lanes and, if there's an accident, it will wipe out Oyster City. That's why they're using tugs to anchor it in the middle of the bay until they can figure out what to do with it."

"Alright, that's news about the ship," Irish conceded. "But come on, give me something I can use. And not the latest fashion news from Paris."

It was a running joke between the men about Pappy's attempts to educate Ray on the finer things in life.

"Alright, here's something for your taste."

His friend went to the stand and pulled out a magazine from behind a shelf. He handed him the latest issue of *Weird Tales*.

"You better buy it before the kids come by after school."

Ray grunted as he thumbed through the magazine.

"So, what else has Emma been telling you?"

Pappy's silence made Ray look at him.

"Well, you remember when she said things would get worse? Emma's worried that you've got a lot of targets on your back."

The slender man paused, pulling off his newsboy cap. His gray hair shined in the sunlight as he scratched his head.

"Ray, you need to leave Oyster City. Terrible things are coming from that demon."

"Pappy, I know you mean well, but I need more than a warning. It's not like I can just leave. What's coming?"

He shook his head and put on his cap again.

"I'm not sure. I can't read the future like a fortune-teller. But I can read history and myths. I read a story a while back about this demon Andras coming to Earth several times. In every telling, a priest or sorcerer sends him back to Hell. Of course, that's along with massacring the demon's followers."

Ray glanced over at the news.

"Ah, for the good old days, where we killed everyone to fix the problem."

"Has it changed much? Remember that massacre in Italy last year?" Pappy pointed out. "That was over politics. But a demon is different. You have to find a way to protect yourself from their influence. Hold on."

The newsy handed a newspaper to a client who stopped and paid Pappy.

"Emma thinks you can protect yourself with religious relics. However, she says you can't just buy a crucifix. You need to have everything blessed by a genuine believer."

"Right, now do you know of anyone like that around this city?" Ray raised an eyebrow at the idea.

~~~

After Ray left the office, Arizona fumbled around his desk, trying to get the sticky top drawer opened. Frustrated, he slammed it shut and pinched his thumb.

"Son of a bitch, I hate this damn place!"

The man looked up to see Orella Dela Cruz standing at the open bedroom door. Surprised that he did not hear her moving around early, Arizona sometimes forgot that she stayed with Ray in the office's adjoining room. Her wide eyes watched him while she leaned against the door frame. He went back to his injury.

"Sorry!"

"It's alright. Do you want to talk about it?"

Arizona scowled as he waved his injured thumb in the air.

"There's nothing to talk about."

"You men are such fools," she sighed, then walked across the room to the office door.

"What's that supposed to mean?"

He continued to wave his hand around to ease the pain. Orella stopped at the door.

"It means that I'm going to get breakfast. You're welcome to join me, and we can talk about Cat. Or you can let it fester inside of you, eating you alive."

She walked into the hallway. Arizona listened to her heels clicking on the steps, then let out a deep sigh.

He did not have to walk far. *Frank's* diner sat in the building next to their office. The ex-cop pushed through the door to find Orella waiting in a booth. He slid into the seat across from her.

"Does this approach work with Irish?"

She shrugged.
~~~

"Perhaps, but I've never tried. I believe that you're both too stubborn to listen to reason without a little help."

Mildred came to their table. She gave a frosty stare at Orella, then turned her full attention to Arizona.

"What'll you have, sweetie?"

"Coffee and whatever she's having."

He held a hand up to shade his eyes in the morning glare coming in the large front window.

"Bacon and eggs with toast," Orella told the waitress, who quickly scribbled down the order before retreating to another customer who entered.

They sat quietly at the table until Mildred returned with the two plates. Orella took the toast and pushed her plate over next to Arizona's plate.

"You need it more than I do this morning. There's a lot of work to do."

"You overheard Ray's comments about me." He shrugged his broad shoulders.

"Every morning," she agreed. "But don't misunderstand why I gave you my plate. I don't like bacon or eggs."

"Then what do you prefer?" He picked up the plate and dumped contents on top of his food. Arizona realized he was hungrier than he thought.

"Well, I like bangsilog. It's a dish from my homeland. You can't find it in Oyster City." The woman explained the ingredients. She smiled at his nauseous expression.

"Ray told me you lived in the Philippines, but I'm not sure I could stomach some things there. My god, sour fish with a hangover."

He shook his head. Then he stopped and grinned to himself.

"I guess we have our tastes. When I was overseas, Spam was all the Army served along with powdered eggs when you came off the line. I swore I would kill the next cook who tried to serve me Spam again. The funny part is I see people eating it all the time after I got home."

"It's been a while since I saw you smile, even for a moment." Her comment made him stop with his fork almost in his mouth.

"Yeah, I suppose so! It's been hard to get this off my mind." The man laid the fork down on his plate.

"I know that you're not the only one. Ray thinks Cat died because of him," Orella told Arizona after a moment of silence between them.

"He lets it stew inside of him just like you do."

"That's nuts! He took a bullet to help her. I saw him weaving to avoid those bastards shooting at him. Hell, I had a better shot from where I was."

"Then why didn't you take it?" Her direct question surprised him.

The big man looked down at his plate.

"I keep asking myself the same question," he finally stated.

Orella nodded before she took a drink of her coffee. Her pretty face screwed up at the taste.

"Do you want to know why?" she quietly asked while leaning forward.

"How the hell would you know the answer?" Arizona stared at his plate.

"I was there, remember? Don't you think I haven't replayed everything in my head multiple times? Tied up with Catherine behind me, remember?"

She took a deep breath.

"You didn't shoot at Jacobi because you were afraid that you might kill one or both of us. I saw you looking down, trying to get the correct angle. That's the same reason that Ray couldn't shoot until he got closer."

She moved her hand toward him, displaying the Singsing ring that glittered in the light.

"You see that ring? In a way, it's the reason Jacobi kidnapped Cat and me. It's just the bastard just didn't realize it. I'm more responsible than either you or Ray for why Catherine died."

Orella leaned back and sighed.

"It's easy to second guess yourself after everything. If I just left Oyster City after what Maria Andras and Phillip Smyth did to me, then your friend would still be alive. You do not need to blame yourself for something that was out of your hands."

The ex-cop looked up at her as she watched him. Finally, he nodded.

"If you want to blame yourself, that's up to you. In my heart, I know that something evil put all of this in motion. Perhaps the devil wants you to feel sorry for yourself."

She paused, looking down at her hand again.

"And maybe this ring has something to do with it."

Silence fell over the table again as Arizona frowned at his plate. He glanced at Mildred, who came over to refill their coffee. He shook his head, and the waitress shrugged and went back to the counter.

"You know I still can't buy everything that you're selling. You and Ray can talk about this mumbo-jumbo supernatural stuff all you want, but it's good ol' fashioned detective work that'll take down that damn Smyth."

The man took to his plate with renewed frenzy.

"Anyway, I've got to finish up so I can get started on those records."

He stopped eating to look at her.

"Thanks!"

Arizona picked up his coffee cup as Orella smiled.

~~~

Pappy just finished rearranging his newspapers to display the latest shocking headlines of the morning. It was a learned trick to keep his circulation up despite
~~~

the downbeat atmosphere covering Oyster City recently. He stood back, looking admiringly at his work, when he sensed the presence behind him.

"Such a morbid headline. What's the world coming to?"

He turned to see a stunning woman staring at the display. Her pale face and long black hair stood out in the morning sun.

"Can I get you a copy?"

"No, thank you, darling," she shook her head as she drew closer.

Her expression momentarily hardened when she looked over his shoulder. The woman took a step back when Pappy turned to face her.

"Perhaps you can help me? I'm new here, and I wondered if you know of a man named Ray Irish. I understand he's some type of detective. Perhaps he might have a place nearby?"

"Well, yes, he's down a few blocks that way. Across from the *Beacon* newspaper building. There's a sign on the second-story window."

He nodded in the direction while his expression turned uneasy. Pappy fumbled with the newspapers in his arms.

"Oh, you're a doll." She ran a finger across his cheek.

The man frowned at the icy touch, rubbing his cheek as she walked away. He heard a whisper in his ear, and Pappy looked over at this stand.

"Why are you giving me that look, Emma? You heard her. All I did was explain where to find Ray. You never turn away a potential customer."

He paused and looked at the woman again.

"You know, something about her gives a guy the willies. I just didn't understand why she didn't go into the drugstore and look up the address in the phone book."

The man nodded while he listened to his dead wife for a moment. His eyes widened as he looked back at the tall woman nearly at the corner.

"Damn, I need to warn him."

"What's going on there, Pappy? You looking at white girls now?"

The familiar voice of Harvey Preston turned the newsy around.

"Although I can see the interest," the uniformed cop continued, then gave an appreciative whistle. Preston turned back to the older black man.

"Don't forget what you're thinking is against the law! I'd hate to run you in for that."

Pappy nodded absently at the unexpected warning. A bitter rage grew inside him while the policeman walked away. Pappy Washington knew Harvey Preston since the cop was a young snot-nosed kid who stopped by for his dad's newspaper and to look at the latest comics. The policeman helped him close his shop during storms frequently. He even stopped by to offer his condolences to Pappy when Emma died. Harvey never gave Pappy a reason to think that he was even a closet racist.

Emma's voice spoke to him.

Now you understand why Irish, and you must leave Oyster City. Evil is covering this city. There's something terrible heading this way!

~~~

Irish arrived back at his office, where Orella waited. When he walked in the door, the shamus frowned. She was sitting behind his desk and had already carefully placed all his files back in the drawer. His now tidy desk had several checks laid out for his signature.

"You need to sign these checks so I can drop them off. You don't want your electricity cut off." She smiled at him.

"I didn't know that you're my secretary," he said distractedly, as she rose from the squeaking chair.

Orella came over and hugged him while he put his fedora on the hat stand.

"You left early without getting breakfast," she said. "I talked to Arizona. He's going to that office to find the records that you spoke to him about."

Ray glanced down at her.

"You've been listening in on my conversations as well."

"Maybe you'll wait for me to get up with you next time." She saw his scowl.

"You should be happy," the woman told him. "I think Arizona will come out of it now. We had breakfast and talked about what he's going through."

Irish nodded while he took a seat at the desk. He looked over at his checks, already filled out.

"I take it you've looked into my account to verify that I can pay these?"

"Of course, I found your checkbook. Unfortunately, you haven't balanced it recently, so I called the bank. They were very helpful."

She went to the window and opened the blinds.

"Of course," he sighed, then glanced at Orella in the morning light.

A white blouse and blue skirt combined with her petite size gave her the look of a schoolgirl. So unlike Samantha or Greye in appearance or demeanor. Remembering their first encounter at the Canton Noodle Parlor, the shamus smiled. The black-haired cutie who had carried the same worried smile when she looked at him.

"Is there something wrong? You look pale," she turned to him and leaned against the wall.

"Just something I saw at the cemetery that's bothering me." He started signing his checks.

"You went to see her grave again. When will that stop?"

He looked up when he heard the tension behind her question.

"It will; I just can't say when. Last time I found a bottle that I tried to drown myself in," Ray glanced at Arizonan's empty desk.

"I've learned from that stupidity. However, it takes time to forget the ghosts."
~~~

Irish finished his task and slid the paper out of his way.

"You know that. It's not like I'm the only one with things we carry inside."

Orella unconsciously rubbed her abdomen.

"And outside as well," she agreed. "But I can help you if you let me."

The shamus leaned over his desk to look at the small brass calendar. He leaned back in his chair, avoiding her statement.

"I'm going to leave town as part of finishing up an old case. My stitches are coming out next week if I remember the doc's instructions. That means the healing is complete. When are you going back to New York?"

She frowned, then looked out the window.

"You don't want me here?"

Ray grimaced.

"Damn it, that's not what I said. But you have a family in New York. Besides, you're still in danger here. As long as Smyth runs things, there's a good chance that he'll find out about that damn thing."

He pointed to her hand.

"But we're both in danger. I can't run away."

She crossed her arms. Irish recognized the defiant look.

"We've talked about this too many times. They'll hurt you for that ring you're wearing. Oyster City isn't a good place. Do you really want more thugs like Jacobi after you?"

Orella looked down at her hand and nodded.

"I was just telling Arizona earlier," she turned back to him. "But that's not the question that I asked you. I want you with me. Can you tell me the same or not?"

"Orella, you're great to be around. I like…"

"You can't tell me, can you?" Her brown eyes expressed her heartache at his answer.

Orella turned away and returned to staring out the window. Irish watched her as the phone rang. He waited.

"It might be a client," Orella told him. "You need money."

He took a deep breath at her sarcasm; then he picked up the receiver.

"Ray, I've got it. Get down here right away!" Arizona's voice boomed across the line.

The shamus glanced over at Orella.

"I'll be right over."

~~~

After Irish left the office, Orella went down the staircase to the street. Still upset, she walked along Peach Street before crossing the road to get to Broadway. As Orella absently stared in the shop windows, her thoughts remained on her future with Ray.
~~~

Their latest spate confirmed an underlying suspicion. He would never let her inside. Irish always put up walls that Orella believed kept him from expressing any deep feelings concerning love and trust. While he never talked about it, she knew the suffering he encountered during the war contributed to his distance. Yet, she did not believe it was the sole cause.

The physical connection remained between them. However, Orella wanted more, and his emotional barrier was insurmountable. The woman held on to a vision that appeared to grow more unlikely each day. The realization nearly overwhelmed her.

Why can't he care as much as I do?

Still lost in thought, Orella stood looking inside a large window where an expensive jewelry piece caught her eye. An elaborate wedding ring glittered in the sunlight among several others in the case. The woman hesitated. The jewelry looked similar to the one she carried in her dreams. She glanced over at the entrance, then walked inside *Underhill's.*

Almost in a trance, Orella paid little attention to the woman standing by Marion Underhill at the back of the store. Her attention remained on the ring in the display case by the window. A whiff of chill filled her with nightmarish memories. She tried to dismiss the jewelry's similarity in front of her.

"Do you see anything that you like?" The woman's voice almost whispered in her ear.

Orella hastily turned, bumping into the counter.

"I'm sorry, dear. I didn't mean to surprise you. That is such a pretty ring."

Orella looked back at the display.

"No, I meant the one that you're wearing," the stranger said with an amused chuckle.

Orella looked down at her hand before taking another look at the stranger.

Tall and raven-haired, the woman held a haunting beauty with eyes that seemed to look inside of her. Orella stopped herself from smirking at the woman's long-black dress, which was ill-suited for the daytime, let alone clients.

"I'm Merle," the over-dressed woman grinned, appearing to read her mind. "By the way, I'm just another customer."

"Oh, I'm sorry, I didn't…"

"Don't worry about it," Merle replied airily.

She nodded to the ring in the case.

"You have great taste in diamonds, even if it's a bit splashy for my taste. I've been talking to my new friend, Marion, about his store. He carries such interesting items, but nothing that quite matches my taste. Then I saw you walk in, and I realized I have a kindred soul. That ring you wear proves it."

Flustered and overwhelmed by the sudden attention, Orella thanked her as she started for the door. However, Merle took her by the arm.

"I'm just leaving as well. Let's get some coffee. I know the perfect spot for outsiders like us."

She glanced back at the good-looking owner of the store.

"I'll see you tonight," Merle told him while she hustled Orella out the door.

As they got to the sidewalk, Orella stopped.

"I'm not trying to be rude, but what did you mean about outsiders?"

Merle smiled and placed her hands on the smaller woman's shoulders. Orella's expression showed her discomfort.

"You're a beautiful woman from a foreign land. I can hear it in your voice and see it in the pin you wear on your lapel. I'm a stranger to this city. Don't you feel the connection?"

Merle let go of her.

"I'm so sorry. I just thought I found a friend." The woman frowned.

"No, it's not that. It's just—well; you took me by surprise."

The frown remained on Merle's face.

"I suppose I'm forceful when I want something. Please forgive me."

Merle smiled at Orella when the woman finally nodded.

"Let me buy the coffee and make it up to you."

Orella glanced in the window of *Underhill's,* where Marion watched the ladies.

"Doesn't he look delicious?" Merle hooked her arm with Orella and led her down the sidewalk.

~~~

"I tell you we have enough evidence to put the heat on Smyth?" Arizona insisted as he opened the door to their office.

Ray went to his desk and opened the drawer to pull out a flash of Irish whiskey. He glanced out at the darkening streets.

"How? Do you think any of those newspaper reporters across the street will run with the story?"

The shamus went to the water cooler in the room's corner. When he glanced back into the bedroom, he saw Orella lying on the bed. Ray put his finger to his lips and nodded toward the room. Arizona went to the bedroom entrance and quietly shut the door.

"I agree that it's evidence," Irish offered the ex-cop a drink.

"Hear me out. It's like what Smyth did before when he had Cat and me put in jail. The bastard will make sure that he has people lined up against the evidence."

Arizona shook his head at Ray's offer, then went to the water cooler.

"As we were driving back from that storage office, I thought about Smyth's options," Irish continued. "If we're lucky, he can always claim it was Dunn who put his name on the contracts. You have the word of the mayor against a dead man. Who's going to win that one?"
~~~

"Yeah, I understand. That's if Smyth doesn't send his thugs after us. Damn, I hate it when you're right." Arizona went to his desk and tossed the file he carried on top.

"Anyway, we know that we're on the right track. That means I have to figure out what's next."

He glanced over at Irish.

"Maybe I can get into his bank account for checks that he signed?"

"Well, if you were still with the cops, maybe you can waltz into a bank without a warrant or a badge," Ray replied as his chair squeaked under his weight.

"Yeah, it's a tough nut to crack. Nothing I can do about it tonight."

Arizona put his glass on the desk and went to the door.

"Tell Orella thanks for this morning. I'll see you."

After his partner left, Irish quietly walked into the bedroom.

"I'm not asleep," her voice reached him.

"Sorry, I hope we didn't wake you."

The woman sat up and turned on the lamp next to the bed. Still fully clothed, Orella gave him a faint smile.

"I returned just before you did. I'm afraid I have a bit of a headache."

Orella got up and went into the bathroom. As she looked for the bottle of aspirin, Irish asked her about the day.

"I met a woman over at a jewelry store along Broadway. She and I just hit it off. We walked all over town."

Orella stepped back into the bedroom, where Ray was undressing.

"That's good. I think it's great that you are looking to meet people. Arizona had me rifling through boxes, but we found something."

"I'm glad," the woman sat on the edge of the bed. "I heard most of the conversation. What are you doing next?"

He yawned, then shook his head as he sat next to her.

"I think I'm letting Arizona lead on Cat's case. Like I said this morning, I need to put another case to rest first."

"That's not the only thing we discussed."

He frowned.

"That's correct," Ray agreed, then yawned again.

"I don't want to start another discussion right now. Let's call it a night."

He saw by her reaction that she disagreed.

Why do they want to get in your head when you're beat?

"I asked a simple question that you wouldn't answer," she started.

"That's not exactly how I recall it. I was trying to explain when you interrupted," Ray grumbled.

"Orella, we're both tired. An argument before going to sleep isn't going to do us any good. I promise we'll discuss whatever you want in the morning. We'll see how it goes from there."

He tried to read into her expression. All he got was frost burn and silence. The shamus stood and went to the bedroom door.

"I guess I'll make the call then," Ray stated before he closed the door behind him.

Orella heard the office chair squeak as Irish got comfortable for the night. Tears fell down her cheeks as she pulled the covers over her.

~~~

Ray sat at the counter of *Frank's* diner. His uncomfortable sleeping arrangement in a chair left him foggy enough. However, his nightmare forced him to wake up before sunrise.

Greye's ghost arrived in his mind again. Her familiar complaint about breaking his promise still replayed inside. Irish finally woke covered in sweat after experiencing her rotting corpse leaning close to kiss him.

Realizing he would never go back to sleep, Ray quietly went to the bedroom door. He peered inside to find Orella still asleep. The shamus watched her sleeping under the office light behind him that trickled into the room.

I can't catch a break!

Gathering his clothes and shoes, Ray silently dressed before he went downstairs to the diner. While his time at the counter spent analyzing his options didn't fix his problems, Ray made a decision.

Greye La Spina's dental files required his attention. Once he found those, Irish had his match to an unidentified body lying in a hole near the state capital. Then, maybe Greye's soul would finally rest.

"You seem lost in thought," Mildred told him as she refreshed his coffee.

"Yeah, you could say that. Rough night, I guess."

"I hear that all the time lately. It seems like we should sell coffee by the gallon with my customers."

Her sympathetic tone caught his attention.

"You too?"

"You bet. I swear I haven't heard anyone who doesn't have crazy dreams lately."

The skinny woman suppressed a yawn.

Ray looked up and noticed the dark rings under her eyes. She smiled at him.

"Where's your girlfriend?"

He looked back at his coffee.

"She's still asleep."

"That's too bad." he noticed that Mildred's reply carried a note of triumph.
~~~

He glanced back at the clock above the café door. Ray still had an hour, at least, before he could make his phone call. Cat gave him the name of a reporter in Boston not long before she died. He hoped that Charlie Greene at *The Boston Post* might have some answers about Greye for him.

"How about getting me a couple of donuts while I wait?" He asked Mildred after suppressing another yawn.

Orella emerged from the bedroom to find Ray on the phone. Unusually tired, she slipped into the chair by the window. The woman wore a silk robe that provided a beautiful portrait on the other side of the desk.

"Yeah, I'm still here. So, what'll it cost me for the info?" He finally got in a word to the fast-talking man. It took Ray a while to catch up with the thick Boston accent.

"I'm telling you that you don't have anything but an auld ghost story. Besides, I'm not familiah with noth side. There's plendee auf detectives here, so hire aune."

Irish sighed, trying to control his temper as the reporter continued his excuses.

"Alright, I get your point. Thanks for nothing!"

He hung up and stared at the telephone until Orella brought him out of his thoughts.

"Going to Boston?"

"It looks that way," he nodded.

"You told me that this woman never meant much to you. I don't understand why you're doing this, especially right now." Her brown eyes carried the hurt expression of a puppy.

He frowned and let out a breath.

"I know it sounds crazy! But you're not the one that keeps seeing her. What I saw at the cemetery yesterday hit me pretty hard." Ray paused and turned to look out the window.

"That's just it! You won't tell me the problem," she complained. "Maybe it'll help to tell me."

Ray looked at her.

She's got a point!

"Alright, I saw Greye at a tomb. It's the burial place for Bishop La Spina's mother. Something else keeps…," the shamus paused, unable to explain other parts of his nightmares to her.

"Well, I'm not sleeping because of it. It's time to lay the dead to rest."

Her expression remained distant.

"I see," she glanced out of the window. "When are you going?"

"I don't know, the next day or so. I'll have to track down the dental records for Greye La Spina. Probably be pretty boring for you, but do you want to come along?"

Orella's shocked look at the offer surprised the shamus.

"Ray, do you mean it?"

"I wouldn't make the offer if I didn't," he grumbled. "After all, I owe you a trip for some headaches. I do know that I'm difficult on my friends."

Suddenly excited, Orella jumped to her feet and came around the desk to hug him.

"Come on; it's not like we haven't done things together," he complained.

"That's true, but I think it'll do us both some good. Your nightmares wake me sometimes," the woman slid behind him.

She kissed him on his forehead.

"Like this morning. You were quiet when you left, but I heard you call out at one point."

The woman kneaded his broad shoulders.

"Dear, I'm sorry for pressing. You're right about Oyster City. But Merle pointed out that I'm an outsider. You are as well. We should both leave."

Irish patted her hand lightly.

"Merle sounds smart. Let me get Greye identified, and we'll go from there."

"You know, in my country, they call an unrested soul a *multo*. My mother told me it's good to help such a ghost rest before they come back to harm people."

Ray squeezed her hand.

"I'm glad you approve. Now…" The shamus stopped when he heard footsteps coming up the stairs.

The sound was lighter than Arizona's heavy tread. With a frown, the shamus glanced back at the door. A light knock followed.

"Come on in," he growled out.

A young man wearing the uniform of Western Union entered the office.

"I have a telegram for Miss Orella Dela Cruz," he announced.

"She's the only woman in here," Ray grumbled.

As Orella took the small envelope, the phone rang. Orella paid the messenger a tip, half-listening to Irish.

Damn, she's coming here.

Orella looked over when she heard Ray finally close out the call.

"I'll be right over, Senator."

~~~

As Irish left the state senator's estate, his mind was not on finding Della. Ray already guessed daddy's girl found a motel somewhere after her nightclub rounds. From his view, the woman wanted her independence. Her escapades into the arms of shady characters rubbed it in her father's face.

Ray wore a worried look as he turned his car onto the road back to Oyster City. He saw the telegram before he left the office. Yana Dela Cruz announced her upcoming arrival to see her daughter. Irish suspected the fireworks were coming, and he was about to get burned.
~~~

"Yeah, you're a damn fool," he announced to the empty Nash as he steered the path to Della's favorite club.

Irish made a promise to Yana before he left New York. He'd already broken that promise many times over once Orella arrived and stayed. To make matters worse, Orella did not know that he and Yana were lovers occasionally. Ray suspected Yana's motive was to remove her daughter from Oyster City. On that point, he agreed.

However, the shamus knew Yana's primary focus remained on getting Orella married to a suitable match back in New York. As the wife of a United Nations diplomat and part of an upstanding Philippine family, Yana could not have her only child hooked up with a two-bit gumshoe.

This whole affair is like a damn soap opera on the radio!

He scowled, knowing his reluctance to confront the problem came from his ego. Instead of drowning in a bottle, he let his libido think for him. When he left the hospital, it was a simple decision—no need to confront anything when the women lived in different cities.

"You're a coward for not just sending her back," he continued talking aloud.

Ray found the car made it easier to say what he needed to get off his chest.

"Sure, you've avoided hurting Orella, but that's the price she pays when she falls for a heel."

Ray didn't like how close the words hit home when he spoke them.

Truth hurts, you idiot!

As Irish turned into *The Pelican* parking lot, he saw Della's Packard sitting alone in the middle of the area. To make sure that she wasn't sleeping it off, the shamus drove next to the car. He noticed the moisture on the inside mohair roof covering and back window. She left the windows down all night.

Great, she's off in her boyfriend's car with several hours' head start!

Irish got back into his vehicle and drove up near the entrance of the club. While the sign in the window told him that the place was closed, he checked if anyone was around.

Pushing through the unlocked front door, Ray heard the noise of people moving tables and chairs. Passing by the hat-check stand, the shamus found arranging the furniture to finish cleaning the black and white checkerboard floor. The man in charge watched them work with his arms crossed.

"Hey, I'm looking for the girl who left her car out front last night. Is anyone around who might have seen her?"

After the glare for interrupting his duties, the man shook his head.

"Mister, this place is full of women at night. If they're a regular, Sam might know them. He owns the place."

He nodded toward the bar.

"His office is in back."

Ray found the owner, along with an aromatic stink of pipe smoke streaming from the office. When he got past the fog, he found a fat man with a bad attitude. At least until Irish pointed out that Della was underage.

"Plus, I'm sure the state senator isn't going to mind calling his friends with the governor who will enjoy closing this place."

"Now, let's not get hasty," the man puffed out. "I saw her last night, but she left early."

"Who with?" Irish growled. "Her car's still out there."

"Damn it; he wasn't any regular that I knew. But he flashed around enough dough and drinks to get the woman to leave. All I know is she comes in pretty regular. This dame used to like them with flashy clothes, but she's been going after big guys with attitude now."

"Did you get any name? Someone showing cabbage gets noticed, especially by the owner of a club."

Ray pushed back his hat.

Sam scowled, but he nodded.

"Yeah, Picket's the last name. I looked over his Lincoln after he paid for a couple of rounds. You can't tell if they're legit until you get the bill in the light. I overheard the woman call him Rusty. He's about your size with red hair."

Ray turned for the door.

"If you run into him, don't mention my place," Sam told him.

"Why not?"

"Because I get the feeling that he's not all there. I've seen them come in before, usually as toughs for their boss. He's the type that people hire for their dirty work, if you get my drift?"

The man streamed out a poof of smoke as Ray left.

<center>~~~</center>

After the third ring, Arizona picked up the phone at the office. He stubbed his toe, getting to the receiver.

"Campbell and Irish," he growled out.

To his surprise, the voice of Bishop Henry La Spina asked for Irish.

"Sorry, he's not around. Is there something I can help you with?"

After a moment's hesitation, La Spina's voice returned.

"Are you the police detective that I met before? The one that was recently involved in that gunfight with the gangster."

Campbell let out a breath, reminding himself to stay calm.

"Yes, I'm a partner in the agency now."

Again, the line fell silent.

"Detective, can you come to my room at the hospital? I need you to remain discrete, but there's information that you need to hear."

"Mr. La Spina, it might help if I knew what you needed to discuss."

"Not over the phone."

There was a click on the line as the bishop hung up.

Arizona glanced at the phone, then sat the receiver down. The brief conversation brought back grisly images of the bodies drained of blood. He debated the wisdom of becoming involved again. The murders were part of an active police investigation. However, Campbell recognized his departure left the cases in limbo.

With the new police chief coming in, the cops remained focused on the current killer making the headlines. Worse, Arizona heard that Andy Devine, a thug policeman who came from Baltimore, had the ear of the mayor. He was a favorite to become the new Oyster City chief of police.

They'd be happy to throw me in jail if word gets out about me poking my nose into this mess.

On the other hand, Arizona believed Myrna La Spina. When Arizona helped her escape from the bishop, she accused her husband of involvement with the murders. While he still did not think Peter Smyth was a demon, the ex-cop recognized that some of his leads pointed to Henry and others. His curiosity grew as he wondered about Henry La Spina's reasons for calling for Irish. Ray held the firm belief that the bishop's first wife died at the hands of her husband.

No, I'm not getting involved! Ray can see him.

With grim determination, Arizona went to his desk and looked over the papers on his desk. Letting out a whispered curse, he looked back at Ray's phone again. Then he picked up his bowler hat and headed for the door.

He found Bishop La Spina in his hospital room and nearly didn't recognize him. The large man he recalled appeared shriveled with a haunted expression as he looked up from the book he read.

"Thank you for coming so quickly, Lieutenant Campbell." Henry gestured for him to enter. "Do me a favor and put a chair in front of the door."

Arizona paused at the request, then did as La Spina asked.

"I'm not a lieutenant anymore. They fired me for insubordination, among other things."

"Please come closer to the bed. You have a loud voice, and our conversation would be dangerous."

Perplexed, Arizona took off his hat and wiped the leather band with a handkerchief from his vest pocket.

"I know all about your firing," the bishop pointed out. "You won't like to hear this, but I'm sure that I and others had something to do with it. I saw the newspapers about you. They told the story of a man who stands on the side of justice."

"I don't get it. Are you wanting help or just rub my face in it?"

Henry smirked, trying to suppress a laugh.

"Most assuredly, I'm not trying to hurt your feelings. On the contrary, I think you are much like Irish, persistent, and determined. What I intend to tell you puts you in a dangerous position."

He paused and looked at the door.

"Detective, before they dismissed you, I know you were on the trail of the persons who killed Detective Howard along with other similar murders. You worked with Irish occasionally, as I understand it."

"It appears you keep up with the papers," he scowled. "However, I said nothing about the killer or killers involved. Remember, it is still an open investigation, so anything you have to say, you should involve the police."

The bishop nodded, suppressing a grin.

"True; however, once I opened my mouth to the wrong person, I would be dead, and the police files would disappear. I take it you never really had an actual suspect for some of your murders. I'll add another puzzle that is related. There are many missing youngsters and servants over the years here in Oyster City."

Arizona frowned, then pulled his unlit cigar from his pocket.

"You appear knowledgeable about a lot of crime in our community. I don't get the connection you're trying to make. The way you speak, a cop might think you're doing a bit of confessing."

Henry leaned his head back on the rails of the bed. He watched a bird land on the ledge outside of his window.

"Once, I believed that the soul carried all the vices of mankind and that suffering, and death were as inevitable as birth. No soul rose and flew away like that innocent creature outside. In my childhood, the teachings explained that our present society shuns pride, arrogance, and sin to control people. Religion is a sham to hide us from the advantages inside the dark world. Those who cast off society's morals found refuge with our master. Andras turned us into creatures as powerful and invincible as a demon."

He looked over at Arizona.

"You probably don't expect such thinking from a man of the cloth. Well, I assure you others in positions of importance in this city follow the teachings of their master."

As Arizona chewed on his cigar end, he tried to decide if the man was insane.

"I'm trying to decide why you called me," he finally got out.

Henry's faint smile fell away.

"Myrna's in great danger. They're coming for her. You need to ensure she's far away from this place."

The ex-cop shook his head.

"I don't get it. Don't you want your wife back? I know she is terrified of you. But most men don't want their wives running off."

The bishop's expression fell.

"Yes, no doubt that's true. Myrna was not ready to become a Shadow. I told Smyth that. She witnessed and experienced every cruel thing that the Shadows are capable of doing. However, my one saving grace is that I will give my life for her."

He fumbled with the book in his hand.

"Listen, I understand that you're unsure of what I'm rambling about. My twisted thoughts become difficult to get across. I suspect the master has something to do with it. His powers are becoming too strong for us. He's in our minds and our dreams. No doubt, you're experiencing more nightmares recently."

Arizona exhaled with increasing frustration.

"Can you get to the point? You keep saying us and something about shadows. What are you talking about?"

Henry looked up at him.

"Please don't insult my intelligence, detective. You must realize that the people who control this city come from just a few families. I've seen the police file you submitted before they fired you. I'm a suspect in your investigation. As a member of this group who controls things, it's easy to receive the information from corrupt elements."

The surprise on Arizona's face caused the bishop to smirk.

"Use your brains, man. I knew either you or Irish had something to do with that missing dagger, which once rested on the display at my home. You're the lead detective on those strange murders of my chauffeur, a policeman, and other unrelated people. That the Jacobi gunfight did not get you fired, the police chief got rid of you over that dagger. You were close to finding out the reason for those people getting their throats cut and their blood drained."

The ex-cop glared at the bishop.

"No one knows about the lack of blood at the scene. Are you confessing to the murder of Detective Howard and the others?"

Henry hesitated; his eyes widened.

"I suppose, in a way, I am. However, should you go to the police, no one will believe you. Remember, I read your report. The dagger contained no fingerprints. You have no evidence to convict me or anyone else?"

Arizona frowned, still chewing on his cigar.

"Alright, I'll admit I have no concrete evidence concerning your guilt," he agreed.

"So, are you the killer?"

"I suspect Irish helped Myrna to escape," the bishop ignored the question. "The servant awoke confident that two men helped her. If you are the one involved, then you have my thanks."

"Listen, I still don't get what you're rambling about," Campbell's face grew red.

The bishop looked over at the door, then waved the shamus closer. He used his arms to steady himself as he leaned forward, and his voice lowered to a whisper.

"You said that you need evidence, correct? Well, I'm going to give you the keystone to the whole temple. It's inside the vaults on the Andras estate cemetery."

"What evidence are you talking about?" Arizona found himself whispering as well.

"That will become self-evident. They're running out of space. The Shadows were quite clever up to a point. Paperwork is easy to destroy. Sacrificed witnesses are different. In the end, the dead can stay hidden for only so long. Your elimination of Jacobi gives Smyth a colossal headache with his sacrifices."

The bishop pushed back with a grimace.

"And I'll wish you a good day, detective," Henry stated loudly.

"Wait a minute, is that it? By God, you can't expect me just to leave."

"As you stated, you have nothing on me. Besides, the death of this withering body won't bring anyone back. However, with the key I just gave you, the history of Oyster City returns. I suggest you learn how our forefathers handled this situation."

Henry closed his eyes and lowered his head. Arizona stared at him for a moment, then pushed his hat on his head. When he got to the door, he heard Henry's request.

"Please make sure that Myrna is far away from this place. It would be nice to know that I did one decent thing."

Chapter 3: Into the Devil's Lair

Inside the mayor's plush office, Peter Smyth observed his secretary as she read out his itinerary for the day. His piercing gray eyes observed the silent efficiency of the plump woman. Sally Clark served as Mayor Hopely's assistant for many years.

He read her thoughts, which betrayed a desperate need for her job. The demon recognized the hidden pain inside her green eyes that were mostly hidden by the woman's horned rimmed glasses. He smiled at the worried concerns the woman carried for her mother, who was dying of cancer. Smyth enjoyed his new employee's suffering while he made plans for her torment that evening. While he thought of the delicious abuse he planned to inflect, the monster missed the uncomfortable silence when Sally finished.

"Miss Clark, with the death of Hopely and changes going on within the various city departments, your position is being closely monitored. Do you realize that?"

Surprised filled her plain face. She glanced over at the silent man standing in the corner of the room. His pale face gave no sign he was listening to the conversation.

"No, sir, nothing showed there was a problem with my performance."

"Well, new guard coming in and all," he smiled coldly. "Anyway, I'll expect you at my estate tonight. I'm afraid that you'll be working late. We have much to work on."

She looked down at the notepad.

"I hope it's not something that will become a regular occurrence. You see, I'm at the hospital in the evenings."

"Yes, your poor mother." His indifferent tone sent shivers down her spine. "We'll see how things work out tonight. You may not have to worry about such things in the future. Now, send in my associates who are waiting in the lobby."

The flustered woman stood and hurried to the door.

"Also, make sure that you type up the documents that need my signature. I want Devine officially in place as my chief of police by the end of the day."

"Yes, sir!" She opened the door and waved the men to come inside.

The woman quietly slipped past Johann Weyer after he intentionally stood in front of her. Her face turned red as she went to her desk. Weyer watched her for a moment, then closed the door.

"Weyer, take a seat," Smyth ordered.

The short, plump man hurried over to take a seat next to Phillip Smyth. Weyer smiled, but Phillip ignored him. Instead, Phillip watched Andras. His brother's body still held the demon, but he recognized the changes as the body deteriorated. He speculated on what ultimate form the fiend would take.

Marion Underhill sat next to Dr. Miriam Wolfe. The jeweler exchanged pleasantries with the doctor for a moment. However, Miriam's eyes kept going to the corner of the room, where a distant relative silently stood. While his dark suit came from another era, and his top hat was almost comical, Mr. Wolfe carried no first name known to the others. As a psychiatrist, Dr. Wolfe knew the look of insanity, which he saw when his ancient lineage looked over. A detached evil remained in the tall man's stare. The doctor knew the man in black came from the pits of hell long before the demon behind the desk.

"Gentleman, the time draws close for our next celebration and the time of my final form. That's why you're here. As you're aware, the new full moon brings my next sacrifices and gives me to my return to this world. However, some of you don't realize that more of my brothers and sisters come into the mortal world on that night. When this happens, the true reign of Andras begins."

He looked over as Merle slipped into the room from a side door. She stood by the silent man in the corner. Her aloof beauty held the mortal's attention for a moment.

"Ah, perfect timing," Smyth continued. "My harem works to ensure the chaos inside Oyster City continues. They've also found sacrifices for me. However, Merle pointed out that the number of people attending the event grows larger. The need for a large pit makes the crypts of the Andras graveyard unsuitable."

Andras nodded to Merle. Relishing the mortal's attention to her, the witch stepped in front of the desk.

"The master believes an isolated place near the city is required. I've just returned from the spot that is perfect for our needs. The abandoned base outside of town is close to the clinic, which holds our victims. Plus, it gives us the isolation and control needed for the festival to our god, Andras. We'll use a field along the Chesapeake Bay to burn our victims and bring forth a new world."

The woman turned and bowed before Peter Smyth.

"Is that not risky?" Phillip spoke up. Instantly, he regretted the question when Andras glared at him.

"I mean, adding more people risks exposure from those who stand against you?"

"Do you think anyone in this place will come with their bibles and pitchforks against me?" Smyth smiled.

Weyer and Merle burst out laughing. They stopped when the demon lifted his hand.

"In fairness to Phillip, he has a point about exposing our plans to any potential opposition. The ring remains missing." Doctor Wolfe interceded.

Peter Smyth leaned back in his chair and rubbed his chin.

"Yes, if used by another with powers, it might hinder my progress. Once I have that ring in my possession, nothing can stop me from fully reading and controlling a mortal's mind."

He looked at Merle.

"What news have you concerning the Singsing?"

"I've seen it on the girl's hand. Orella will give you that ring," she told him confidently. "Her soul will be yours. My potions will soon have her crawling to you."

"I was there when she met Merle yesterday," Marion Underhill interjected. "This Dela Cruz seemed quite taken with your witch. Your harem will fight over her, I'm sure."

He only smiled at the laughter from his statement. Underhill surveyed the demon's reaction.

"Only after she gives me her soul," Smyth stated sternly. "Then they can use her for their entertainment. Merle, I'll have a visitor tonight. I want you and your sisters there to feed when I'm through with her."

"What a delicious idea, master."

The woman happily agreed with a smile. Peter Smyth gave a callous grin before turning his attention to the others.

"Now, what about other obstacles to my plans?"

Phillip spoke up, glancing around the room.

"I'll start with Irish and his new partner. Devine will arrest them once he takes over the police force. They will die of suicide in jail. That eliminates any potential problems that either man might know about some of our activities."

The demon nodded with approval.

"I enjoy the irony of Irish dying like that gangster he put in jail. I felt his anguish when Jacobi killed the little slut who was his partner. It's a delightful taste."

He licked his lips, then frowned.

"I'm interested in bringing her ghost into my realm, along with that La Spina soul that the Shadows killed. I can feel their presence in the mortal world."

Andras sighed.

"Their spirits will come when I eliminate this shamus."

"This brings the question of Myrna La Spina's whereabouts. Her husband's a weak imbecile. I want someone focused on finding her."

His eyes turned to Doctor Wolfe.

"This seems like something for your endeavors. I've put you in charge of those men who worked for those gangsters, Jacobi and Guy Young. Have those men find her. I want that bitch to burn in the pit."

The psychiatrist quickly nodded at the order.

"I'll make sure they get her."

"How are your efforts in the state capital going?"

"Not as smoothly as I hoped. My move here to Oyster City after the death of my partner, Doctor Horne, caused some delay. However, my contacts in the capital are spreading the word about your ambitions. I haven't told you, but those who meet a series of preliminary tests get an invitation to the Horne clinic. We slowly bring them into the fold using well-documented techniques of isolation, exhaustion, and control. It takes time, but I've achieved excellent results."

Wolfe clasped his hands together with obvious excitement in his eyes.

"A local banker passed my tests, and he offered his wife for your pit and brought her to the clinic. Our new member wants to replace his dear wife with his mistress. I have others like him who will attend your festival. At least one member of the governor's cabinet shows interest."

"It sounds promising. However, I'm hearing that some politicians have not agreed." The demon in Smyth's body leaned forward. "I cannot win the governor's seat without their support or, perhaps, an unforeseen death."

Andras tapped his knuckles on the desktop.

"While I might like to kill him, it's critical that the chaos and death that I bring to this world must have the veneer of democracy and hope as well."

The doctor smiled.

"Yes, there's one known for his pious family's ways along with fair dealings and an incorruptible past. I've persuaded a few of our allies in the senate to work on his vanity. He may come to believe that you'll support his efforts."

"And if that fails?" Smyth asked.

The psychiatrist rubbed his hands together.

"I'm already working on a plan to...well, let's just say that you'll have full sway over our main holdout within a week or so. He has a vulnerability which I plan on exploiting. I'm using a few of my men to spring a trap."

"Doctor, you impress me with your planning. I'll be interested in how this works out."

"If all goes well, I'll enjoy a little revenge." Wolfe nodded.

"Very good! In the meantime, you will find Myrna La Spina. I suggest you put out a bounty of ten thousand for her return within a week. Got it?"

Wolfe raised his eyebrow at the sum offered.

"What about me? Should I look for her as well?" Weyer asked the master.

"No, I have a special job for you."

~~~

While Irish and Arizona were away from the office, Orella impatiently paced between the bedroom and the office area. Her mother was due to arrive at the train station on the noon train. As the clock slowly ticked along, the woman stopped at the sound of footsteps coming up the stairs. When she heard the knock, Orella looked over at the shadow in the obscured glass on the door. There was a familiar outline, and she smiled. Orella opened the door to see Merle with a cigarette dangling from her lips.

"Well, I had to stop by and meet this boyfriend of yours," the woman entered the room. She wore a simple dark blue dress that tightly outlined her figure. Orella noticed her new friend wasn't wearing shoes again.

"Well, Ray's out on a case. But I'm glad you're here."

"Let me guess, you need a ride somewhere!" Merle stepped around Ray's desk. She ran her finger along the edge of the chair as she sniffed the air.

"How could you possibly know that I was going to ask you that?" Orella's shocked tone forced her friend to look over.

"Oh, I'm good at reading expressions." She bent down and looked out the window at the building across the street.

"And I'm extremely sensitive to smells. For example, I followed your scent up the stairs. I'm guessing you had breakfast at the diner next door. Your boyfriend's scent, on the other hand, smelled the strongest downstairs. So, I knew he must have left."

She turned and smiled at the shocked look on the woman's face.

"Is there a problem? Some people are more perceptive than others."

"No," Orella stammered out. "It's just the way you described it. I've heard of stories of witch doctors who followed their victims using their scent."

"Please, dear, don't be so morbid. I told you I'm especially sensitive. Now, where do you want to go? And the better question is, do they have cocktails for us?"

"Oh, you're unbelievable. Let me get ready. It'll only take a moment." Orella laughed as she hurried into the bedroom, leaving the door partly open.

Merle took a strategic angle near the door to observe Orella while she hurriedly changed her clothes. The witch enjoyed the view while she sniffed the other male's presence. Her smile returned as she glimpsed Orella's naked back.

Delicious!

A few minutes before the train arrived, Orella was back to pacing along the concrete platform. Merle glanced over as she leaned against the railing. She puffed out rings of cigarette smoke while watching the people with only a remote interest.
~~~

Uninteresting souls meant for the pit!

"To think so many people go about their day without a clue about what comes," Merle spoke her thoughts.

"What was that?" Orella broke from her thoughts.

"Oh, nothing. Just reflecting on the state of humanity. It seems not a lot has changed, just people moving faster to death."

The tall woman inhaled deeply.

"That's a rather morbid thought. I hope you won't talk that way around my mother."

"I'll be good, dear," Merle promised.

When Orella saw her mother step off the train, her expression remained impassive. She believed she knew the reason for the trip. Orella planned on making the conversation quick.

"Be careful!" The dark-haired woman standing next to her warned. "A telegram is never a good thing."

"Darn it, Merle. I've got enough on my mind. Don't make it worse."

"Look who's up at this ungodly hour with you? Certainly not your man."

Orella glared at her, but she missed Merle's approving smile as the woman stared at Yana.

"Yes, I know. And thanks again for driving me."

She stepped toward her mother, who waved.

"It's good to see you, mom." She gave Yana a quick hug, then took her mother's overnight case.

Orella took her mother by the arm, and she led her to Merle. When she introduced the ladies, Orella did not catch the momentary panic in her mother's eyes. Merle courteously nodded while Yana continued to stare. A burly porter in a black uniform standing behind them coughed, interrupting the scene.

"My car is right out front." Merle turned and led the two women through the lobby. As Yana looked over at the small station, she let Orella start the conversation.

"Mom, I know why you're here. I'm telling you right now that not going back to New York."

"Daughter, my trip here is not only about you. It also involves your father and me. Many things have happened since you left New York."

Yana stopped when her daughter stepped in front of her.

"Is dad alright?"

"Yes, it's nothing like that," Yana assured her. She glanced at Merle, who listened to the news with interest.

"Can you excuse us for a moment?" Orella noticed her mother's stern look. She took her friend by the arm.

"Can you show the porter where your car is? We'll be along in a minute. I promise!"

Merle's face turned dark, then she smiled.

"I'm sorry, you're right. I'll be waiting in the car."

Yana paid a tip to the relieved man carrying the baggage, and he followed the tall woman to the car. Then Yana turned back to Orella.

"Who is that?"

"I told you. Merle just got to Oyster City. She's a friend of mine."

"I don't trust her!" Yana replied, with her eyes focused on the stranger.

"You don't know her!" Orella snapped.

Yana glanced over.

"And neither do you. Not if she's new to this town, as you say."

The two women remained quiet for a moment.

"Alright, mom, I know you're upset. What's happened?"

Yana took a deep breath, then hooked her arm around her daughter's.

"I'm afraid that your father must return to Spain," she led Orella along the walkway. "He's getting a promotion, of sorts."

"That's great!" The girl replied with a smile. "He deserves it. You deserve it more. But you don't have to worry. I'm fine here."

Yana glanced away.

"You don't understand. I'm not going with your father. He and I—well, we're getting a divorce."

Orella went silent as they strolled together.

"I can't say that I'm surprised," she finally said. "What does this mean for you?"

"I still have a house in the Philippines. That where I want you to return with me."

Orella stopped.

"No, I belong here with Ray. He needs me!"

Yana frowned.

"Does he need you, or is it because you remain enamored with him as your hero?"

She watched her daughter's eyes widen at the suggestion. While Orella shook her head at the idea, she remained quiet.

"Orella, you're young. Many terrible things have happened to you in the last year. But you must realize that Ray Irish is not the man for you."

"How could you possibly know that? He's good to me," Orella countered.

Yana glanced at her daughter.

"But you didn't say that he loves you. I believe he's still a man of honor. That's why you must leave him."

"Mother, that's ridiculous."

"Is it? Tell me about the good times that you have together. Where has he taken you? Has he promised you marriage, or do you continue to live in sin?"

Orella went silent as they got to the car.

"Perhaps you don't want to hear it, but Ray and I talked about you when he returned the ring. He made a promise that I expect him to fulfill."

Yana put her hand on the door handle.

"What promise did Ray make?" Orella refused to move back from the door. Yana looked at her daughter.

"Ray and I agreed he must let you go."

The two women barely spoke on the ride to the Hotel Alexander despite Merle's attempts to lighten the mood. When she dropped them off at the front door, Orella thanked her friend and told her she would see her soon. As Merle's car drove away, Yana stepped next to her daughter.

"You should avoid her," she warned.

Orella turned to her.

"Why would you possibly say that?"

"Because I've seen her before. That woman is not who she pretends to be." Yana looked over at the disbelief on Orella's face.

"I'll explain when we get to my room."

~~~

Irish arrived back at an empty office and looked at his watch.

Damn, she went to get her mom by herself!

Ray hoped to get back sooner. He wanted to be there when Orella and Yana talked about the future. Instead, he heard Arizona's heavy footsteps as the man climb the steps to the office.

His partner entered the room and immediately went to his desk, saying nothing. As he rummaged through his drawers, he found a pair of gloves.

Damn, now I need to get a shovel.

"I just got back after speaking with Bishop La Spina," he suddenly told Irish. "I'm telling you, that bastard is as guilty as hell."

"Tell me something that I don't know," his partner said as he put his feet on the windowsill.

"I can tell you something that'll change your view. There are dead bodies in the Andras cemetery. I'm going to do some digging tonight."

"That's where bodies normally are. You don't mean you're digging in a graveyard?"

Ray looked back. Arizona shrugged.

"Listen, I'm not a cop, but that's a good way to get the wrong people's attention."
~~~

"It beats your wild ass theory's about a demon," the ex-cop shot back. "Think about it. What's a better way for a killer to dispose of bodies than a cemetery that only a select few ever use?"

"You're convinced that Henry is the killer of all those cases you've never solved." Irish shook his head at the idea.

Arizona slammed the desk drawer shut.

"He pretty much admitted it. The sick bastard claims that he's part of some group who call themselves the Shadows. I'm not stopping from putting him to the electric chair."

He stopped, then looked up at Irish.

"The Shadows! That explains a lot," Ray told him.

"You know what? I thought really hard about just killing him there in the bed. He's paralyzed, so I'm afraid that the bastard might get off by some damn sympathetic jury."

Irish shook his head, and his chair squeaked when he leaned forward to look out the window.

"You need to get that damn chair oiled. I can tell you don't believe me," Arizona complained.

"No, you're dead wrong. I was the one who came to you with La Spina's involvement. And I've told you he's not who he seems."

He glanced over.

"It explains how some killings happened when La Spina was somewhere else. Cat even pointed it out to me in her defense of the bishop. You tell me how a murderer leaves an event, then returns with no evidence of blood on his clothes, and no one notices that he's left for an extended time."

"Then you're convinced there's more than one. You believe in this idea of these Shadows."

Ray nodded.

"Yep, I've seen them in that alley across the street." He refused to back away at the skepticism on Arizona's face.

"Consider this idea. A gang could grab people and kill them. Leave a few bodies to make it appear random. Kind of like the Garrote Killer a few months back."

"And that's the flaw to your idea. You never explain how such a group would stay together. Gangs always have a squealer." Campbell pointed out. "Remember, one of Jacobi's hoodlums finally confessed he was the Garrote Killer."

"Not if your boss is the demon called Andras."

"And that's where you always lose me," Arizona grumbled.

"Oh, ye of little faith!" Irish replied under his breath.

~~~
~~~

Orella pushed through the doors of the hotel lobby, still upset at the argument with Yana.

I'm not a child! Mother has a stupid dream, and I'm in peril!

Her heels tapped rapidly on the concrete as she hurried on the sidewalk. An incessant honking finally caught her attention. She noticed a hand waving at her through the windshield.

It was Merle.

"Get in. You need a drink!"

After some persuasion, Orella got in the vehicle, and they drove along Peach Street. As they passed Ray's office, Merle smirked when she glanced over. Orella's refused to look at the building.

"I've got the perfect spot for us," she told her passenger.

At 22nd Street, they turned into an alley, following it past several small homes before stopping in a narrow parking lot between two red brick buildings. No sign showed there was anything inside the rusty metal door where Merle knocked. A thin metal plate slid open by the door, revealing two eyes, then the women heard the door unlock.

"Into paradise, my love." Merle cackled as she went through the entrance.

Orella hesitated, taking a deep breath before she followed. Inside, she found a dingy, smoke-filled dive bar. Only the bartender paid attention to them.

Orella followed her friend to the bar, where a woman dressed in a tuxedo and wearing a scarf looked them over. She nodded at Merle before setting out two apéritif glasses. She filled them with a green liquid. Merle downed her drink in one swift action, then asked for another.

"Make hers sweet," the woman ordered. The bartender pulled out a sugar cube and put it in Orella's glass.

"It's Absinthe," Merle explained as the woman sat next to her. "You'll find it's illegal and delicious."

She smacked her lips and blew a kiss at the bartender, whose eyes remained on Orella.

"Now, you've had your disagreement with mother. Drink up."

"How did you know?" Orella frowned as she sniffed the liquid.

"Do I have to keep telling you I'm sensitive to things? It's like your ring gives off your moods. Right now, you're upset and still wondering why you came in here. But you don't want to return to that office."

Orella nodded and took a sip of the drink. The taste reminded her of licorice, which she enjoyed. The woman looked around the room.

In a nearby booth, she saw two women and an older man with a white beard. They smoked hand-rolled cigarettes while making crude jokes. Two women necked in another corner while a man leaned back against their table with a pipe dangling from his lips. He's paid no attention to the women behind him. Instead, he started reading a poem aloud to the room.

"He's a terrible poet," Merle leaned over to Orella. Her hot breath is close to her ear.

"But he looks delicious," she stated loudly.

Orella looked down in embarrassment, again noticing that the woman wore no shoes. She asked her the reason.

"I find shoes too constrictive, much like those who run the world." Merle downed her third shot of absinthe.

"Why did you bring me here? I don't drink when I'm upset."

"Oh, I know that. You're uncomfortable here. That's because you're a bit of a prissy girl. Probably comes from your religious schools," Merle told her.

Then the woman put her arm over Orella's shoulder.

"Yes, I can smell it on you. You enjoy the sensations of life and sex. You want to break away from all the things that keep you pinned down. It's like you want to break out of the very skin that surrounds you. People like your mother and your current lover restrict what you do. They force you to follow their misguided rules."

Orella frowned.

"You don't know me well enough to say that."

"Maybe I know you better than you think?" The woman replied airily. "I noticed you didn't say that my observations were wrong."

"I just want to be happy," Orella shot back. "Are you happy in a place like this?"

The tall woman's expression changed, and she removed her arm. For a moment, Orella saw confusion. Then Merle's smiled sadly.

"Happy? What is happiness? Isn't it enjoyment and comfort? These people make me comfortable. There, take a look at those two women."

She pointed to the lesbian couple near them.

"I've seen them in here before. Forced by society to hide in this bar, they find pleasure in their forbidden lust. Comfort comes from hiding in the shadows. But I can tell that they are ready to seek new worlds and meet with new friends. It'll come sooner than they expect!"

She laughed to herself before she took another drink.

"Soon, I'll introduce them to my friends. They'll exist in a world that they cannot imagine. Dragged from the shadows to become toys of the powerful."

The woman looked over at Orella with a shark smile as her friend continued to watch the couple who were feeling the effects of their smoke.

"I wish I knew what you're talking about," Orella went back to her drink. "But I can't figure it out. You act like you're involved with a secret joke, laughing at us who don't understand it."

Merle snorted.

"My dear sweet friend. A whole new world is opening up soon. You just need to stick with me. You see, I find that you're an outsider like me. Soon, I'll introduce you to my sisters."

"I thought you were in Oyster City alone," Orella shook her head as the effect of the drink hit her.

"Oh, you'll like my sisters. They're a lot like I am. We enjoy all the things people fear trying."

Merle's eyes went to the Singsing ring.

"You keep staring at my ring. It's a family heirloom."

The witch nodded, taking Orella's hand. Her soft fingers sparked excitement that Orella felt a ripple through her body.

"I can feel the power emanating from it. Limahon once used the Singsing of Multo in countless sacrifices." Her eyes were alight with the spark of fascination.

Orella frowned, then laughed.

"You're making a joke. I can never tell when you're serious."

"Oh, I'm quite serious when it comes to power. Your family probably never encouraged you to see the truth about that ring. Limahon stole it from the Spanish when he invaded Luzon in 1574."

"He was a Chinese pirate with an evil side. When he took his prisoners to the beach, the sharks waited offshore while he butchered thousands to summon the master for the first time."

Merle smiled while Orella stared at the ring.

"How could you know such things?"

The mortal's attention broke away from the Singsing when a woman in a brown dress stepped next to Merle. She looked like a carbon copy of Merle.

"Orella, this is Pas, which is short for Psamathe. As you can see, we have a lot in common."

Both women laughed at Orella's shocked expression.

How could my mother know Merle had a sister?

Pas slid her arm around Orella's shoulders as she came around on the other side of the stunned woman.

"I'll have what they're drinking," she told the bartender.

Pas stared into Orella's eyes as the mortal felt the ripple of excitement fill her.

"What are we drinking to?" The sister smiled.

~~~

On the other side of town, Ray paced back and forth behind his chair. Arizona left earlier, and he did not know where his partner went.
~~~

Ray's calls to track down Della were bearing no fruit so far. Plus, he expected to hear from Orella at some point. However, the ticking clock and traffic noise from the street below managed to increase his frustration with the day. Finally, Irish picked up the phone and called the Hotel Alexander. The hotel operator answered, and when he asked for Yana's room. Ray only got out a hello when the woman asked him to come over.

"I suppose we should talk," he agreed.

"Yes, I would think you owe me that much. Orella left a few minutes ago."

"I'll be there in ten minutes," he told her, then hung up.

Ray arrived with butterflies in his stomach.

"This is almost as bad as hitting the beach." He whispered before knocking on the hotel door.

When Yana opened the door, he saw the sparkle in her eyes. However, her expression immediately turned cold.

"Thanks for coming here. You know why I called."

Irish nodded as he entered. Her perfume immediately brought back images and feelings from their intimate times together.

"Yeah, I have a pretty good idea that it's about your daughter." He tried to remain jovial, but her deadpan expression remained.

"Don't give me that look," he grumbled. "Alright, maybe I screwed up when she showed up out of the blue."

"Then when are you letting her go?"

Irish glared at her.

"Did you see a collar around her neck? She knows that we're not in love."

The man looked away, knowing it was a lie.

"Does she? Have you told her that?"

Yana's bitter tone caused Ray to turn back.

"In a way, probably not as I should have. Damn it; I like her. Believe it or not, I don't want to hurt her."

"Don't give me that! You took advantage of her innocence." Yana crossed her arms as she stood there.

"No, don't try that with me. I felt bad enough when Orella showed up and nearly got killed because of this job. But I won't apologize for her help in getting me through the last month. We needed each other, whether or not you like the idea!"

Yana turned away, stepping next to the bed. Ray watched her, unable to think of anything comforting to say.

"She needs to get out of this city. We both know you are wrong for Orella."

She finally told him. The shamus nodded.

"I'm not arguing about that. But you're her mother. As far as I know, you've had no communication with her since she arrived on my doorstep."

He partially regretted his statement when Yana turned around. Her eyes narrowed, and her face grew livid.

"You son of a bitch don't throw this back at me. Are you not a man who lives by his word?"

"Fine, it's my fault if it lets you sleep at night," he spat out. "But I'm not big on casting someone to the curb. Unless maybe you were afraid to come here."

The room went silent as they stared at each other.

"Don't talk rubbish. This is about Orella."

Ray refused to believe her.

"Is it? Have you told her about us? Of course not!"

The room went silent again.

"Listen, I know Orella wants more than I can give her. Believe it or not, I've tried to get her to return to New York. That damn thing on her finger is too risky. But she seems to find excuses for not returning."

Yana turned away. She went over to the window and looked out at the busy street below. Finally, the woman looked over at him.

"Perhaps I bear some of the blame in this. One reason I didn't come here was because of my problems in New York. Victor and I are getting divorced. But that's not what brought me here."

Fear showed on her face.

"I've also had a scare today that forces me to insist that Orella leave this godforsaken city."

"What happened?"

After taking a deep breath, Yana explained her dream and the fortune teller. Then she told him about seeing Merle in her nightmare. To her surprise, he didn't laugh. Instead, his expression turned dark.

"It reminds me of things in my nightmares as well. What about this gypsy? You say she was using tarot cards?"

The woman nodded.

"Do you believe me?"

"Of course! I've had strange nightmares that show me things. You know, Pappy told me I should see a fortune teller. He mentioned tarot cards when I first got to know him."

Ray pulled out a whiskey flask from his coat. He walked over to the console and poured a shot into a water glass.

"Do you want one?" He glanced over at Yana, who shook her head.

After adding water to the drink, he came back to the woman.

"Now, some people think Pappy's strange because his dead wife, Emma, talks to him. But I have to give him credit. He's had a knack for knowing when something bad is going to happen." He paused, looking at his drink. Then he downed it.

"Pappy wants me to leave town. So, that's the reason I think you're on to something about your nightmare. It was strange, but I never had them when I was out of town. It's when I return to Oyster City that these damn visions seem to come alive."

"Would you believe me when I tell you I saw a demon, and I'm sure it was Peter Smyth? He was the one who sent Orella home with Victor. I saw his picture in the newspaper about the murders in Oyster City."

Surprised at her calm observation, Ray nodded.

"Then what you're feeling is not a coincidence. While I can't prove that Peter Smyth is the devil, he's been behind many of the problems here. Hell, we can't be sure who is an ally in this place. There are only a few we can trust. Where's Orella now?"

Fear filled Yana's face at a sudden thought.

"I'm not sure. She should go back to your office. I'm afraid we argued. Orella didn't like my thoughts about you and Merle."

"Well, I'd like to think I rate a little better than that." He joked as he put down his glass on the nightstand by the bed.

When he saw Yana trying to compose herself, tears were in her eyes. Ray reached over to hug her, and the woman pushed him away.

"No, never again!"

Irish stared at her.

"Fine, I'm the bad guy. But, for the record, that was nothing but sympathy for your problems."

He turned and went to the door. Ray stopped as he took the handle in his hand.

"By the way, I mentioned taking Orella to Boston for one of my cases. Your daughter was pretty excited by the idea. I'll make this easy for you. We get train tickets, and I'll leave you both in Boston with a farewell letter to Orella. That should stop her from returning to Oyster City."

He did not look back.

"Satisfied?"

Irish left the room.

~~~

Still fuming at the bitter reaction from Yana, Irish stopped by his office. However, no one was there. He took a run by the *Del Rio* club before returning to the office. He still needed money for his trip, and Della remained missing. Irish followed Broadway out to 33rd Street.
~~~

When he arrived at the club, Ray found the place nearly full. After he checked out the tables with no luck, he went to the bar. To his surprise, the bartender told him that Rusty had just left.

"He's kind of a loudmouth, telling everyone his name like it meant something."

"Was he with anyone?"

"Yeah, some blonde was hanging on his arm. She carried an attitude along with a nice figure. Every time I tried to serve my customers; they kept calling me over. Picket pushed me to call his place for him. I told him to use the payphone outside the front door, but he insisted he couldn't leave the girl on her own. She was a cute dish, but not like a hundred others that come through a week. Anyway, the girl got upset, saying she deserved better for the money they were spending. Anyway, I dialed the number and gave him the phone, just to shut her up."

"Do you remember the number?" Irish grew excited.

"Nah, but I know it was the Whitehaven Loft. The building operator answered the phone." The man picked up Ray's greenback with a smile.

Irish hurried toward the door, stepping past a man who appeared interested in his conversation. Ray stopped by the hat check booth and started chatting with the girl as the stranger passed by him.

Still suspicious, the shamus kept his eye on the stranger as he went to the payphone booth. After a minute, the man walked back inside and went to the bar.

Irish quickly left, looking for anyone trailing him, but he saw nothing out of the ordinary. During his drive back downtown, he had a gut feeling that Della was still playing her game.

Well, the game ends tonight!

Ray arrived at the five-story tower with the blue neon sign and parked. He walked inside the lonely lobby to find there was no one behind the front desk. Looking around, Irish soon discovered the name of Picket on the wall of mailboxes.

Room 4B!

The shamus took the stairs, despite the pain in his rebuilt legs when he climbed the steps. Ray found the door, carefully drawing close to listen inside. He heard music before Della's voice came through. Ray tried the doorknob, finding it unlocked. As he stepped into the shadow-filled room, his hand searched for the light switch.

Click!

A yellow glow bathed the spacious, luxuriously furnished room.

Standing in the far corner of the room was Della.

"Alright, time to..."

Ray did not finish the sentence. The blackjack glanced from the side of his head, and he stumbled as he reached for his gun.

From behind the door, Irish caught movement. A thin, pasty-faced man with a pointed nose slapped his blackjack against his palm. Irish moved sideways away from that wall. A burly figure hurled into him on his left and knocked Irish to the floor while his partner slammed the door shut. A third man standing near Della yanked the protesting woman back as she tried to leave.

"Hey, leave me alone. You're not supposed to hurt him bad."

"Shut up, bitch!" He slapped her across the face. Della fell back into the corner.

Irish rolled to his knees, glimpsing her shocked expression as he drew his automatic. He slugged the pasty-faced man with his free hand, but the burly man with auburn hair clung to Ray's gun wrist. Irish struggled to his feet when the thug lowered his head and charged. Irish backed two steps and fell over a chair. His gun bounced with a clatter across the floor. Then, four hands jerked Irish to his feet and slammed the shamus back against the wall.

Standing there, Irish saw his attackers. The thin man with the blackjack glared at him as he helped pin Ray's arm. The burly man on the other side carried a grin. His thick muscles tightened the sleeves and shoulders of his suit.

"Finish him, Tony," a voice called out. "The little girl's just waiting for us to get to the action."

"Yeah, Rusty, I'll give him a beating he won't forget."

Irish's left lashed out, caught the burly man on the cheekbone. The thin man swung the blackjack. Irish took the weapon's blow on the shoulder while he smashed his fist into the man's face. The thug sputtered curses as he fell back. However, his partner slammed Ray's body hard into the frame of the door.

Stunned, Irish smacked weak, short-arm jabs into the body of the beefy guy. As he tried to pull away, the thin man caught Ray with the blackjack again. This time, it struck home.

Irish went to his knees.

"Lemme polish him off now."

"Don't be silly, Slick. This guy enjoys taking a beating." Tony pushed Slick to one side, reached down, and jerked Irish to his feet.

"Don't you like it, little man?" The big man put all his weight behind the next blow when he smashed his fist into Irish's mouth. Blood splattered into the wall along with Ray's head.

Irish somehow kept his feet, but his right fist lacked any power when he swung. Then, the shamus dropped to a knee.

"Ok, you get to finish him," Rusty gleamed with satisfaction at the beating.

Through a swelling eyelid, Irish glimpsed Rusty, a thickset thug with a sappy grin on his face, as he brought Della close to him. The white-faced, wide-eyed girl stared at him; her expression varied between shock and confusion.

But Slick, bleeding from the lips after Irish striking him, swung his blackjack first. The weapon connected to the back of Irish's head, sending Ray face down on the floor.

"You're a heel. Now I only get one shot," the big man grumbled. He bent over, grabbed Irish by the lapels, and yanked him to his knees. Holding him upright with his left, he smashed his fist into Irish's face.

Ray's head bounced back against the wall. By the time the shamus fell over on his side, he was unconscious.

~~~

Orella felt the effects of the booze when she nearly stumbled while shifting her weight on the barstool. When she looked at her watch, her vision blurred. The woman believed it was still mid-afternoon. Orella looked up to see another bartender behind the counter. It was a tall man, his features delicate, and his skin pale as the moon. She smiled as his green eyes studied her. He did not return the smile. Instead, he returned to cleaning glasses stacked up at the end of the bar.

When Orella glanced at Pas, she tried to remember the dozens of questions. At first, their insights about Irish and her annoyed the woman. However, her concerns about their relationship eased as the women grew supportive of her. Then Merle told her that the future was never as dark or bright as she saw in her dreams.

Orella laughed at the thought. Her nervous tension stopped when she leaned against Merle.

"Being with you helps. At least I'm not having my nightmares," Orella shook her head.

"And what nightmares are those?" Merle put her arm around the woman's shoulders.

"Oh, they're terrible. It's always about me handing this ring to some devil guy."

She looked up. Merle's face was close to hers, and Orella suddenly felt an urge to kiss the woman.

I'm not a kiki!

Her mind rebelled when she remembered what Maria Andras had tried to do to her.

"Is there something wrong?"

Orella felt Pas touch her knee. And she reacted with a start.

"No, it's just. Well, I'm not like those women in the corner."

She glanced over, but the two women were gone. Orella shook her head.
~~~

"When did they leave?" Orella wondered aloud.

"Don't you remember, dear? I introduced you. I was getting jealous when they started pawing at you. They left you their number on that piece of paper in your hand. Don't worry; they'll see you again at the party I'm organizing."

Shocked, Orella looked down at the paper in her hand. She looked at her watch again, then put it close to her ear. It wasn't ticking.

"I can't believe I've been here this long. I guess my watch stopped."

She looked at Merle, asking for the time. Merle glanced at the woman's wrist and smiled.

"Sorry, love, but I don't wear such modern contraptions."

The woman leaned over the bar and asked the bartender.

"It's almost eleven," he replied.

"Oh, my God, I've been here all this time!"

Pas and Merle scowled at the suddenly frantic woman.

"I'm sorry if I've bored you with my problems, but I've got to go!"

"Nonsense. Everyone has problems. Friends like us will listen." Merle tried to get Orella's attention as the woman slid her pocketbook into her purse.

"Well, you've been patient." Orella slurred her words. "I'll talk to you later."

She tried to stand, and her knees almost gave out.

"You know what—I've had too many of those drinks." She looked sheepishly at Pas.

"But I've got to leave. My mother will be worried. I should have called her!"

"Nonsense! You're a big girl now!" Merle grabbed Orella and forced her to look into her dark eyes. The frantic woman suddenly calmed.

"You're right; it's just rude of her not to wait on me!" Orella's voice turned mild again.

"Come on; we'll take you home." Pas smiled at her sister.

Despite the number of drinks, Merle and Pas appeared unaffected as they helped their new friend leave the underground bar. With Orella between them, the two women guided her into the back seat. Merle sat next to the drunken woman. She laughed as Orella fell forward while trying to remain upright.

"Lay her head on Merle's lap," Pas ordered as she slid into the front seat.

"Give me some time before you drive," Merle said as she stroked Orella's hair.

When she was confident the woman remained unconscious, Merle pulled a bottle from her purse. The witch stuck her finger in the clear bottle and removed a small helping of a dark powder with her fingernail. Merle sprinkled the substance inside the lips of Orella. The intoxicated woman attempted to spit it out.

"No, take it all in," Merle ordered.

Orella unconsciously licked her lips. Then Merle leaned over and forced her tongue into the woman's mouth. Orella responded. Soon, the two women locked in an embrace, their heavy breathing filling the car.

"I wish the master would let us have this one," Pas told her sister as she watched Merle kiss Orella.

"Oh, stop it, Merle. You keep going, and I'm coming back there as well, master or no master."

The witch reluctantly broke away from Orella.

"Her passion will soon serve us. Even better, her blood will nourish us for years." Merle slowly placed Orella's head on her lap again. "My potion will give her interesting dreams tonight. Soon, she'll hate her boyfriend. By the time Andras takes her, Orella will be our eternal slave."

"Sister, she's already becoming one with our minds." The driver observed.

The cackled laugh from Pas caused Orella to grimace as her nightmare started.

"No, don't go in there!" The sleeping woman called out.

"Hush, my little slave!" Merle placed her finger on Orella's lips. "Let's go. Did I tell you that her mother looks like an older sister? Maybe we'll have her until her daughter is ready."

"Delicious!" Pas chuckled as she drove away.

When the car arrived at Ray's office, the two women woke Orella. They helped the unsteady woman out of the vehicle. Laughing at their victim, the sisters helped her up the stairs and into the office.

Arizona watched in amazement as the trio entered the room. At first glance, the women appeared unhappy to see him sitting there.

"Is everything alright? What happened to Orella?" He rose from behind the desk.

"I'm afraid our friend went overboard. I don't believe she's been drunk before. We brought her home." Pas beamed a smile at Arizona. "Where is her bed?"

The big man went over and opened the bedroom door.

"Arizona, don't be giving away my secrets," Orella told him happily as she passed the big man. "My friends had nothing to do with it."

"You just lay back and get some rest. We'll talk about it later."

He watched the woman flop back on the bed when the sisters let go over her.

"Oh, I don't like the spinning," Orella complained as Arizona motioned the woman into the office.

After he closed the door, his perplexed look caused the women to laugh.

"I'm Merle, and this is Pas. I guess we're a terrible influence on your girlfriend. It's nice to meet you, Mr. Irish."

"I'm afraid you've got the wrong guy; I'm Arizona Campbell, Ray's partner."

"Oh, how stupid of us," Pas told him. "I'm afraid that I need to powder my nose. Is the restroom in there?"

Arizona automatically nodded in the direction, and then he went back to his desk. Merle followed him, taking up a position next to the wall so she could look inside the partially opened door of the bedroom.

"You know, we're new to Oyster City. We don't get opportunities to meet with private detectives," Merle purred as she glanced over to see Pas walking to the closet on the other side of the door.

With a smile, Merle leaned close, her cleavage near the ex-cop's face.

"I hope you don't think we're causing problems. Orella's upset with her boyfriend. I suspect that she'll need a couple of aspirin and strong coffee in the morning."

Arizona nodded as he moved back to his chair. He tried to avoid staring at the woman's breasts.

"I'll make sure that Ray apologizes to her," he agreed. The man glanced over at the clock on the desk.

Come on; I need to stake out the Andras cemetery!

"That's good," Pas replied when she entered the office again. She closed the bedroom door.

"You know we need to get home," she told Merle while winking at the shamus.

"Darn, just when the conversation was getting started," Merle pouted as she looked down at the man. "One of these nights, I'm sure we'll meet your partner. In the meantime, don't be a stranger. It's difficult for newcomers to meet people."

Arizona watched the women as they leave.

I doubt either of those ladies has a problem meeting people!

The ringing of the phone jolted the man from his thoughts. When he picked up the receiver, he heard a familiar voice on the other end of the line.

"I'm afraid I need help, or I'm going to end up as a sacrifice hanging upside down with no blood left in me," Bishop La Spina told him.

"I'm on my way," Arizona stated, then slammed down the receiver.

~~~

It was long past sundown when Sally Clark frantically hurried from the Andres' house. The woman carried most of her clothes in her arms. Her skin tone appeared nearly luminous in the moonlight sheen covering the open yard when she reached her car. The woman opened the door, but someone pushed
~~~

her away. The door handle slipped from her hand as she tripped to the ground. Sally heard the car door slam shut, and she looked up into the darkness. A tall man in an old-fashioned suit and tall hat stood ominously over her.

"You shouldn't have run away. Please come with me."

"Mr. Wolfe, please let me go. I'll say nothing about what I saw, I promise. He's crazy."

The man bent over and grabbed her. His vice-like grip dug into her arm, causing Sally to cry out. Dropping her clothes during her struggle, the woman noticed car lights suddenly cover the driveway. Encouraged, Sally found the strength to pull away. She ran to the vehicle as it stopped. Sally waved her arms, yelling for help. When Pas and Merle emerged from the car, the woman halted.

"Please help me," she cried out.

"Come along." Wolfe grabbed Sally's arm and pulled her along the drive.

"No, let me go. Please help me," the woman pleaded as the two witches drew closer.

"Oh, look at this. Finally, we have one to please us for the night," Pas stated.

Merle laughed as she hurried over to help the man subdue the woman.

"Ouch, let go of my arm." The woman's pleading grew desperate as she continued to resist. She swung at his hand, but the man's grip tightened. Soon, the pain became unbearable. Then Merle grabbed the woman's breast.

"Please, you're hurting me. Stop!" Tears filled Sally's eyes when she slid onto the gravel.

"Come on, my dear. The master must want you." Merle ordered. The pain forced Sally to stand.

"Please help me!" Sally pleaded again.

"I'm helping myself," the witch replied. "Come, time to enjoy the night."

Wolfe's eyes remained hidden in the shadows of his hat brim.

"Come along," he repeated.

"You heard him!" Pas grabbed the frantic woman by her butt.

Sally's resistance faded when the two women took her by the arms. The trio led her along the gravel road to the cemetery. When they entered through the gates, she suddenly wrenched away. However, the women's grip remained too strong. Wolfe grabbed her by her hair, forcing her back on the path.

"Save your strength! We have plenty of night left," Pas laughed as they forced their victim deeper into the graveyard.

When they reached a large crypt, Sally attempted to hold on to the iron grate before the witches painfully pried her fingers off. Nearly exhausted, the woman observed the glow of a lamp. They pushed Sally to the floor by a casket. The woman cried out to a young man in tattered clothing who quietly stood in the light near the corner. The man remained unmoved.

"It's too bad. You might have lived to a ripe old age by serving my desires and needs." The demon's ominous voice filled the stone chamber.

"I'm afraid that you made the incorrect choice."

Peter Smyth stood nude next to the crypt. His harem quickly gathered around Sally.

"No, don't hurt me. My mother needs me."

"Well, that's too bad. But we're going to enjoy you." Merle gleefully unhooked Sally's bra. Sally tried to retreat, but the other sisters grabbed her by the arms.

"You'll submit and learn that pleasure and pain are the same."

Sally screamed when she glimpsed the desiccated corpse on the other side of the glass on the side of the tomb. Sally's renewed burst of frenzy came as they tried to place her on top of the dark brown bloodstains covering the top of the stone slab over the coffin. The witches finally tied her arms and splayed legs to the coffin rails.

"Why are you doing this?"

Sally screamed out in desperation. The female creatures laughed.

"To satisfy the master and ourselves. You will feed us to keep our beautiful forms," Merle explained as she ran her hands through her graying hair. Merle picked up a jewel-encrusted dagger while Smyth climbed on top of the woman.

Sally's shrieking eventually stopped, replaced by the animal grunts of the creature thrusting into her. She only cried out when the witches cut into her. Finally, her begging pleas fell silent. Semi-conscious, the victim barely heard the lapping noise of the monsters filling themselves with her blood.

As the night went on, her horror continued as another witch joined them. Sally tried to blink away the images and sensations while the creatures defiled her in ways she never imagined. She prayed aloud for her release from life. The witches laughed at her pleas while the demon left the crypt.

~~~

When Ray Irish recovered consciousness, he stared at the white light coming from the lamp by the wall. He rolled over on his knees, groaning at the effort. Finally, the man crawled to the couch. When he finally drew himself erect, Irish used the arm of the sofa and top of the end table to steady himself. He looked around for his gun, then stumbled to the wall where it still lay. Using the wall as a brace, he retrieved the weapon.

For some moments, he stood there, gathering his thoughts. Staggering past the small kitchen, he went into the bathroom. As he walked into the small room, he nearly slipped on the wet tile. Looking into the mirror, Irish saw the lump on his forehead, and he felt the other behind his ear. One eye had a cut over it while his other eye remained swollen partly shut. There was a gash on one cheekbone, along with a lip covered with blood taste.
~~~

Irish went back into the hallway. At the end of the hall, behind a closed door, he heard muffled yells. He stood there, weaving back and forth on his feet like a punch-drunk fighter, then started down the hall, his hand feeling along the wall for support.

From behind the panels, the muffled tones sounded again. The shamus swung into the room and groped for the light switch. Inside the bedroom, the yellow walls hurt his eyes. The dainty, feminine hangings and pale green furniture explained the female on the bed.

A girl in a wet bathrobe struggled to look over at him. Her wet blond hair hung out from under the damp towel, still partially wrapped around her head. With hands and feet securely bound, the woman's pale blue eyes, wide and angry, stared out of a flushed face. A twisted towel dug into her opened mouth, tied off around her neck.

Irish lurched to the bed, picked at the cord binding the girl. After fumbling around, he thrust his hand into his trouser pocket, retrieving a penknife. Shaking his head, he opened the blade and cut the ropes.

The girl sat upright after he untied the towel around her face. She began rubbing her wrists as Irish dropped on the bed beside her.

"Go got any Irish whiskey around this place?"

The girl's eyes never left his face as she carefully got up from the bed. She continued staring at him for a second, the look in her eyes a mixture of pity and disgust.

"Yes, I have some in the liquor cabinet," she said. "Who are you?"

"I'm the idiot who walked into a trap. The better question is, who are you?"

"My name is Edna. Are you a shamus named Irish?"

He nodded.

"I'm a friend of Della," she told him. "She's been staying with me. She told me you were after her."

He glared at the woman.

"Is your last name Picket?"

Her pretty eyes widen.

"No, it's Ackroyd. Why did you think it was Picket?"

"I told the wrong people that I was looking for Picket. Your mailbox downstairs had the name Picket on it. The bastards set me up for this reception. I think Della was in on it."

He stared at her for a moment.

"In fact, you might be part of this."

He watched her face pale, then grow angry.

"You don't think I had anything to do with this? Two men dragged me out of the shower. I tried to yell out, but one of them gagged me. I thought they were going to rape me when they brought me in here."

Irish listened while she vented with frustrated rage.

"Sorry, I had to be sure." He explained, but she still kept her glare on him.

"You're a son of a bitch if you think I enjoy getting groped while they tied me up."

The woman went toward the door.

"Listen, I took a beating, so I'm not in a mood for a lecture on my manners," he shot back. "Della hooked up with a guy named Rusty Picket; that's the reason I'm here. Daddy doesn't want her daughter hanging out with the rift raft."

The woman stopped and looked back.

"Yeah, Della's been finding some real losers. She called Rusty this morning. Right before I got in the shower, she told me he would come by and get her."

Edna turned back to him.

"Do you think she's in trouble?"

"Could be," he dabbed at his eye, then Ray noticed she walked down the hall.

"At first, Della acted as if she wanted my beating," he got louder. "But just before the lights went out, I think she was trying to get away from them. I can't imagine your friend wanted you groped by Rusty's thugs."

Irish was still sitting upright on the bed, bracing himself with his hands, when Edna returned. She carried a glass and a square brown bottle. She drew the cork and poured an inch of whiskey into the glass. Irish tossed it off in one gulp. He coughed once, then reached for the bottle. The girl gave it to him, and he poured another third of a glassful. The shamus drew back his lips as the alcohol burned the cuts.

"Thanks, Edna. You're off my suspect list." He tried to grin, but it hurt too much.

The woman's face remained stone cold as she sat in the straight-backed chair across from him. Her eyes studied Irish. The man returned the gaze, looking through the bloodied eyebrow without lifting his head.

He liked what he saw. With her hair now hidden inside the towel wrapped around her head, he got a good view of her face. Despite her ordeal, she recovered nicely—no tears, just straight and honest concern.

"How long have you been tied up here?"

She looked over at the clock sitting on the cabinet by the bed.

"Over an hour."

She leaned forward in the chair, rubbing her wrists absently. Her robe opened up, and Ray looked away despite the view. Edna sheepishly grinned and rearranged her robe.

"Well, at least I know that you're not a pervert."

"Don't bet on it," Irish absently said.

After he gave her a brief rundown on what had happened, the woman asked him a question.

"Shouldn't we call the cops? I heard Della's voice as they took her away. As you said, she didn't have those men tie me up."

He shook his head.

"No, I'm not on good terms with most of the police. Plus, the senator won't want publicity. This will get out in a big way. I've got to think this through."

The shamus filled the glass again and offered her the bottle.

"I'm trying to figure out why they took Della along. She could have stayed and called the cops. Her boyfriend could claim I started the whole thing."

"I don't like drinking alone," he told her, forcing the woman to take the bottle.

"You look like you can use it. Do you have any idea where this Picket might live? Anything that Della told you about him?"

Edna poured herself a drink, then shook her head.

"Not really. I think Della picked him because he was tough. She mentioned that was something she had to have in her boyfriend's now."

"Yeah, I guess she listened to me too closely. You need to pick your friends better. Della's got a warped mind. I thought she was enjoying the cat and mouse with guys fighting over her."

Ray carefully touched his brow.

"I think she got in with the wrong crowd."

"Where was she sleeping?"

"In the next bedroom. Why?"

Irish slowly got to his feet.

"I never considered your friend to be a genius. Maybe she left me a clue or two. If she's in trouble like I imagine, then I need something to track her down."

After a painful short walk made by the shamus, Edna impatiently walked past him and opened the door while trying to hold her bathrobe closed.

"I'll help you if you let me know what you're looking for."

"I appreciate the offer," Ray held on to the door frame. "Take a look in the living room for anything that catches your eye, something that appears out of place. Then, get your clothes on. It's distracting!"

He walked into the bedroom. There was a wastebasket at the foot of the bed, nearly hidden by the frilly bedspread. He stepped to it, pulled out a newspaper, picked up the crushed paper that lay beneath. It was a receipt from *Underhills* for a necklace.

Irish looked over the paper carefully before he stuffed it into his pocket. Her boyfriend had some money, and Della was willing to spend it. From her reaction, Della set this whole thing up, but what was the endgame? The way the thug struck the woman told Ray that he was not playing the same game. The shamus came back to the receipt in his pocket. Maybe it was a coincidence about the name of Marion Underhill.

Then again, probably not!

Chapter 4: Running Out of Time

The lights were off at the office of Irish and Campbell when Yana reached the door. Repeated unanswered phone calls finally became too much, and the woman arrived by taxi. She knocked several times, but no one answered. Frustrated by the lack of response, she kicked the door bottom. The action hurt her toe. Then, she saw the light finally come on. After another round of knocking, she saw the figure of her daughter approaching through the obscured glass.

"It's nice to know that you're still alive," Yana told her as she pushed into the office.

"Nice to see you again, mother. Why are you here?"

"We were supposed to have dinner, but it's a little late for that now. Where have you been? I've been calling all evening."

The woman surveyed the office. It was not as she expected.

"I'm sorry, but I'm not feeling well," Orella told her. "I should have called you."

"Well, where were you?"

Orella suddenly felt a wave of anger wash over her.

"Damn it; I'm old enough to make my own decisions. I don't need you trying to pry into my life."

The anger surprised Yana.

"I do not mean to…" She turned and looked into her daughter's face.

"It was that woman, Merle. You were with her!"

"Yes, we went out for a few drinks, and it got out of hand. When I got back, I was in no shape to meet you. Alright, are you happy now?"

Orella's face grew red at her admission.

"Mother, I'm tired, and my head is about to explode. Can we discuss this tomorrow? Please!"

They heard footsteps on the stairs and looked over to see the sizeable frame of Irish at the door. When the shamus stepped inside, both women immediately noticed the damage to his face.

"What happened to you?" Orella got the words out first.

Irish just shook his head and went to his desk. He pulled open the drawer and got out a small bottle of his favorite whiskey after sitting down.

"Do you want one?" he asked while pouring a drink.

The woman came closer.

"Alright, out with it," Orella told him.

He shrugged.

"Not much to tell. I walked into a setup. Three goons used me for their punching bag. Della took off with them."

He downed the whiskey. He leaned back in his chair.

"I got nothing to show my client, the senator. Great way to finish an evening."

Then, Irish noticed the pale look of sickness on Orella's face.

"Are you alright?"

The woman nodded and took a seat.

"She's fine. Orella's deciding to act like you and go get plastered."

Yana's condescending tone struck her daughter hard.

"Oh, shut up!" She snapped with her head in her hands. "I've never had absinthe before."

"I'll bet," Ray observed. "Listen, you must feel like hell. Go to bed. We can have this big conversation in the morning. We're heading to Boston."

Yana was about to say something when she saw the glare that Ray gave her.

"Orella, he's right. This can wait."

The woman looked up at her mother, then glanced over at Irish.

"Well, I'm not going to argue with either of you." She got up and went into the bedroom.

After the door closed, an awkward silence fell in the office. Finally, Ray leaned back in his squeaky chair and pointed to the bottle.

"Have a snort. It looks like you can use it."

Yana looked at the door to the stairs, then she silently sighed. The woman took the chair next to the desk and sat down. Her eyes stayed on his profile while the shamus stared out the window. The bulge on his cheek already darkened, with his eye nearly closed.

"I'm sorry for earlier," Yana finally told him.

"Forget it," Ray stiffened. "You're right. I'm a damn coward sometimes. I was too willing to forget our agreement when it suited me."

"No, you're not a coward. As much as it pains me, you had a point. I should have come here sooner. But I couldn't."

He looked at Yana. In the shadowed light, he remained amazed at how much she and her daughter looked like twins.

"Why not? Nothing is holding you in New York, is there?"

Silence fell between them.

"No, you and I had delightful times together. However, I realized you're not going to let people inside. I've lived with that for my entire marriage."

Ray nodded in agreement.

"I'm going back to the Philippines, back to my home," Yana told him.

"A new start is always good," he remained diplomatic as he sipped on his drink. "Let's see about making your plan happen in the morning."

~~~

Della was shaking when she noticed the unoccupied guard shack and the open gate that their car passed going into the compound. They stopped in front of the central building of three.

"Rusty, where are we?"
~~~

"Oh, it's a place for nut jobs, but they closed it when one owner got offed by a patient."

"Why are you taking me here?"

"Don't worry, sweetie; you're going to love this place," Rusty told her after an unnerving laugh.

He took her by the arm, then hauled her with him toward the building. The lights inside showed yellow through two dirty windows on the side of the front wall. The remaining windows remained dark.

Della looked over the compound at the other dark buildings as a chilling feeling came over her.

"I don't like here!" she announced.

"Nobody gives a damn," Rusty growled back. "Come on!"

Della looked back at the callow smirks coming from the two men following the couple. Rusty took her through the double doors into a long hallway. The blast of stale, musty air struck her.

At the end of the corridor, they pushed through a door, where they found several people milling around the nearly empty room. Della clutched at Rusty's elbow when she saw each person wearing creepy looking paper Halloween masks covering their faces.

"I want to leave," she said while she watched one man on a ladder was just finishing testing spotlights.

The beams focused on the center of the linoleum floor, where several chairs sat in a large circle.

"Shut up," he hissed, then grabbed the woman by the collar of her shirt.

He presented her to a man wearing a pirate mask.

"Doc, here she is. Our new movie star." Rusty announced.

"Any problems?"

"Nah, that shamus is suffering a headache. We waited like you said. He'll get it worse when he calls the cops about a false report of a missing lady. Funny thing, everyone knows Della was with us the whole night at the club. I paid off the owner."

"Very good. Now take a seat, my dear." The man behind a savage-looking mask ordered Della.

The woman appeared confused at the request; then, she drew up her courage.

"Listen, my father is an important person. He'll have you thrown in jail, and they'll throw away..."

"Quiet!" The pirate slapped her.

A wounded, fearful expression covered Della's face as she felt Rusty push her into a seat.

"Don't bother telling us what we know. You're a senator's underage daughter that likes to frequent clubs and lay in the back seat with the wrong men. You're about to help us with your father's reluctance to play ball."

The psychiatrist turned to Slick.

"Give Miss Reece a drink from your flask. I think she'll need a few drinks while I explain her upcoming task tonight."

He saw the man frown as he pulled out a glass flask from his coat. Slick held it out, but Della refused the offer.

"I don't want it. Listen, I'm twenty-one now, and I do what I want. I want to leave here!"

The man slapped her again. Shocked at the abuse, Della tried to suppress the tears as she rubbed her cheek. Slick held out his flask, and the woman refused.

"Drink it or suffer more pain," Wolfe ordered.

This time, she took the container. The harsh rotgut whiskey burned going down. She coughed and sputtered while the pirate waved over a blonde female dressed in a nurse's uniform. She began petting the captive's head. When Della tried to talk, the nurse wrenched the woman's hair back.

"Listen to the good doctor. He likes to inflict pain on his patients."

"Because your father wishes to become governor, your performance tonight determines his fate."

The masked doctor looked over at Della.

"Don't worry; it'll be just another exercise to show the public the disregard that you hold for your family. It will cement your rapidly deteriorating reputation."

"Rusty, bring in the remaining equipment."

The woman watched as one of the masked men brought in a movie camera on a tripod. Another man worked on other photography equipment. Rusty and his comrade left the room. When they returned, the two men dragged in two dirty mattresses they placed on the floor by the woman's feet.

As the man with the camera pulled out a reel of film from a box, his comrade focused on the beams of the bright lights on the mattresses. The nurse standing next to the woman began to disrobe. Rusty whistled while he took off his suit coat.

"It's going to get hot under those lights. Get your clothes off, baby." Rusty gave Della an evil smile.

"Never!"

She dashed to the door. However, Slick caught her before the panic-stricken woman made it. He lifted Della from the ground; then he hauled her to the middle of the room. Rusty grabbed her and forced the screaming woman down on the mattress.

Amid the cries, brutal laughter, and shredding of clothes, the cameramen stopped their work momentarily. They restarted once Della lay naked and pinned to the floor.

"Film's ready to roll." The man setting up the tripod stated to the pirate. He turned to the man who set up the lighting. "You take the stills. I'll roll the camera."

"I need negatives as soon as you can get them done." The pirate told the cameramen before turning to the thugs gathered around the mattress.

"No permanent damage; I'd hate to see my golden goose get too injured. Give Della more of that rotgut. Vera, give her some pills."

The nurse joined the trio on the mattress as Della continued to struggle. Eventually, the winded woman could not fight anymore. Tears of rage flowed down her cheeks as she pleaded with the woman to help her.

"You just stick with me, sweetie. Here you go," the naked nurse cooed as she forced her to drink more from the flask.

Her blue eyes held on to Della's. The blond woman placed her finger on her captive's lips, then forced a bitter pill into her mouth. Della tried to spit out.

"No, trust me, it'll help." She assured her. The woman gripped Della's jaw and forced the pill back in her mouth.

"Don't make them punch you to force it down," the nurse told her with a grin.

She poured the whiskey into the woman's open mouth. Della sputtered, then had to swallow. After slowly consuming most of the flask, Della felt the nurse release her jaw.

"There you go, sweetie. Soon, you'll be in another world." She kissed the captive on her forehead.

"You just follow my lead!"

Not long after, the nurse recognized the dilation in her victim's eyes.

"Lean back!" she stated, then ordered Della to be released.

"You and I will give the boys a show. They look eager to start."

The snap of flashbulbs followed as the nurse started nuzzling on Della's neck. Their captive no longer resisted as Vera worked her way down to the woman's breasts. The men watching made crude remarks while they undressed to join them.

Vera glanced back at the man in the pirate mask.

"Make sure shots don't have my face. I don't want this guy after me." Then she returned to kissing her victim.

Doctor Wolfe nodded while he smoked a cigarette through the uncomfortable mask. As expected by the psychologist, his nurse's proclivity for sexual exhibitionism, along with her need to dominate other women, made her the centerpiece of his show.

Vera had a natural ability in front of the camera!

The doctor enjoyed his new position as an ad hoc movie director. He recognized the opportunities for him to fleece other people in power from this experience. He needed her father to believe his daughter willingly had the movie filmed. Rape and violence might turn Reece into an implacable foe instead of the malleable politician that Wolfe wanted. It was a risk, but, in the end, Andras could remove his enemies.

Doctor Wolfe reached out to the man holding the still camera.

"Remember to focus your pictures on the girl's face and body," he whispered. "I want the bitch to look like she's enjoying herself. Especially with the other woman. Her father needs to see the negatives first thing in the morning."

"The only thing is, I may not have enough time if this session takes too long. That movie reel takes some time to process."

He stopped, then took a picture when one thug crawled on top of Della. The prisoner no longer resisted as she sank into an abyss from the combined effects of the drug and whiskey. Immediately, Vera encouraged Della to think of fun things in her past. Before long, a strained smile showed on their victim's inebriated face.

"The master only needs those negative stills to lay everything out for her father. The movie is to ensure cooperation in the future. You'll soon be making other movies like this. I can ensure this lucrative business will soon make us rich, so don't disappoint me."

"Alright, alright, I'm your new partner," the man agreed. "When I get finished with the edits, her father will publicly disown her."

The cameraman moved to another angle and set up for the next round of pictures. While he didn't like where his business was going, the money for this job was too good to pass up. He waited for a moment, then got a money shot of Della's unfolding nightmare.

~~~

Campbell pulled into the quiet hospital parking lot. When he turned off the motor, he surveyed the building. Going to the front door would invite more questions than the man cared to explain. He took the side stairs instead. When he reached the top of the stairs, the shamus looked down the long corridor. The nurse's station was empty.

As he drew close to the bishop's room, the detective heard a menacing voice inside. Then, the sounds of a struggle started. Arizona burst into the room and saw a short, fat man struggling with La Spina. Weyer held a bloody scalpel in one hand that the bishop away by grasping the attacker's wrist. Arizona pulled his gun. The shamus smashed the pistol butt into the fat man's head. Weyer fell to the floor, and the deadly weapon skittered across the tile.

"What the hell's going on?"

"That's Johann Weyer," Henry finally got out between heaving breaths. "He is a cousin of Maria Andras. He's also a member of the Shadows. Andras is making his move to kill me."

Arizona went to the phone.

"Who are you calling?" Henry asked.

"The cops, we need to get this bastard put in jail, and a guard posted."
~~~

The bishop reached over and pushed down on the receiver handle, disconnecting the call.

"That just gets me killed sooner."

Arizona looked at the man, amazed at the indifference that he displayed.

"I'm going to get the night shift nurse in here."

"Don't bother. Just before you arrived, Weyer told me he killed her. He boasted about putting her body in the closet by the nurse's station. That little bastard always was a toady among the Andras family."

Arizona looked at him suspiciously. He walked to the door, then went down the hallway. When he reached the nurses' duty station in the middle of the building, he called out. Only silence came back to him. Keeping his revolver at the ready, the detective went to the door of the door marked closet. He didn't bother opening the door when he noticed the drying blood flowing on the tile near his shoes.

That son of a bitch!

When the shamus got back to the room, he looked down at Weyer, who remained out.

"I suspected Andras would do this, so I've been staying up most of the night, learning the staff's schedules. The next shift will come in at six."

The bishop handed Arizona a book. It was the same one that he saw Henry reading the day before.

"Since I couldn't be sure who might come for me, you'll notice my inscription to you inside the cover. I've been making notes for you in the margins. It's a compressed version of my damned life starting halfway through the book."

He shrugged.

"When you read it, you'll probably dismiss the passages as those from a lunatic mind. But you need to look at how much my memory matches up with those files you remember during your time with the police department. Each one of those deaths that my group used to bring evil into this world."

The ex-cop looked at the book, then put it into his pocket. His expression caused the bishop to chuckle.

"You'll die a skeptic unless you open your mind to the possibility that I'm not crazy. I'd advise you to tie up Weyer before you go. I don't want to die by his hand."

"What about you?"

Arizona went over to the blinds. He cut off two lengths of cord, which he brought back to the unconscious man. The detective looked up at the bishop as he worked.

"Well?"

"I'll be fine," he assured Arizona. "I've just passed the danger to you in that book I gave you. It gives you a way to remove the demon. But you'll need to read it."

"Damn it, that's not an answer."

Henry La Spina chuckled again.

"My life was forfeit once Dunn got me with the bullet in my spine. Peter Smyth doesn't allow for weakness in his group of followers. Besides, your concern is misguided. I have more deaths on my hands than your worst serial killers."

Arizona finished hogtying Weyer.

"Listen, detective. You have everything you need. But I need you to ensure that you've protected Myrna."

"She's fine. No one knows where she is," the shamus assured him.

"No, you need to get to her and move her quickly. They want her for the festival during the next full moon. Andras wants her for his next sacrifice. She escaped, and it bruised that bastard's ego."

"What festival?"

The bishop looked at him.

"You don't believe me, but I'll tell you, anyway. In a few days, the full moon returns. We've already brought forth his witches. Now, Andras is inviting over those who will remain his loyal subject. Once he's made living sacrifices of people cast into a fire pit, it will ensure his hold over the city. I suspect it will soon extend over the rest of the state. People he considers unworthy have already died. That's why the police cannot save the people despite all the patrols around Andras Hill. Andras sends one of his witches out with Lance Carrol, that missing murderer. A simple spell puts the people in the squad car into a trance."

The bishop saw Arizona didn't believe him.

"Fine, you don't have to believe me. But get Myrna out of harm's way. Weyer bragged that her death was coming. He said Smyth has a ten thousand dollar bounty on her whereabouts. Doctor Wolfe is using his contacts to get the word out. They even have Jacobi's old gang working for Smyth."

"You mean that bastard Wolfe is one of your group? I should have known."

"It's worse than that," Henry replied. "Andras has people up to the governor's office and a few in DC, as well. Now, do you understand the danger to you? The Shadows looked at everyone who might be a threat to our power in Oyster City. That's how I know you have no family here. It's the same with your partner. It also means you're both easy to dispose of because no one will come looking for you."

The silence told La Spina that Arizona remained skeptical but overwhelmed by the information.

"I'm sure it sounds crazy to a rational person who has no spiritual beliefs. Read the book and remember that this demon came to our world before. Now, bring me that scalpel. We can't have that murder weapon skipping out when the police finally arrive." He grinned. "It's easy to lose the evidence. Remember those daggers on my wall that you and Irish kept trying to match with murders? Would you believe that Detective Howard actually brought me the dagger used in a ritual killing? My notes will tell you about that as well.”

Arizona stopped and turned back with the bloody weapon, holding it with his handkerchief.

“So, Howard got caught up in this? I don’t get it. He was as corrupt as hell.”

“Of course, we needed him to get in your way on an investigation. Why do you think so much evidence ended up missing? Howard made his mistake by trying to extort the Shadows. We couldn’t have that.”

Henry pointed to the table next to him.

“Leave it there. I want plenty of witnesses to see it with Weyer’s fingerprints on it.”

Almost in a daze at the thought of helping a confessed murderer, Arizona placed the scalpel on the table.

“Please go help my wife. You know Jacobi’s men will find her. She’ll never believe it, but you can tell her how sorry I am for betraying her,” the bishop told him.

Arizona slowly backed out of the room, looking at the man who should pay for his crimes. The ex-cop wanted to involve his friends and cohorts in the bloody affair. He desperately wanted the bastard in the hospital bed to die for the things he’d done. Yet Arizona recognized that too many corrupt people remained involved. The man stared at his prime suspect for a moment.

I hope he pays soon!

Then Arizona glanced down the hallway before he took the side stairs back to his car.

After he was sure that the ex-policeman was gone, Henry picked up the phone. The hospital operator finally picked up. She asked him for the destination.

“This is Bishop La Spina. Please bring the police to my room. There’s been a murder committed by Johann Weyer. One of your nurses is dead by his hand.”

He heard her voice asking for him to repeat it when he hung up the phone. Henry used his top sheet to pick up the weapon.

“Well, Bacchus, let’s see if Andras gets you out of this. I bet that he just lets you hang. I’ll see you in Hell.”

Then, Bishop La Spina, the last heir to one of the founding families of Oyster City, plunged the scalpel into his throat. Blood shot across his chest. Then the memory of Myrna in her wedding dress came to him before the dying man’s images faded to black.

~~~

It was early the next morning when Ray felt the hand across his face. Tuned by his two years in the jungle, Irish shot up fully awake. In the bed beside him, he heard Orella call out.

“No, I don’t want this. Get away!” Panic filled her voice. “Damn it; I don’t like it.” Then the woman groaned and trembled. Sweat covered her chest as her
~~~

pert nipples showed through her satin pajamas. She licked her lips as she started panting.

As Ray watched, he recognized the sounds and the movement. His lover had an organism. His fascination turned to amusement. Then he heard the name come from her lips.

Andras!

Before he could react, Orella screamed. However, it wasn't the scream of a human. Instead, it was a terrifying and gut-wrenching sound that seemed to fill the room. Instantly, he reached over for her. Orella began punching and thrashing when Ray tried to hold her. Then the woman woke. Immediately, Orella started crying. Shuddering in pain and agony, the woman sobbed as she emerged from her terrifying nightmare.

Her arms wrapped around him, squeezing him so hard he had a hard time breathing for a moment. As the small woman shivered and wept, Irish vowed Orella would leave Oyster City forever. He held her until she finally went back to sleep, then he rose quietly from the bed.

Going to the closet, Irish found a clean suit and got dressed. As he put on his shirt, the man felt Orella standing next to him.

She put her arms around his waist.

"I'm scared! Something's not right."

"I know. Now, get dressed. We've got a big morning ahead of us."

She frowned.

"What's this about?"

"It's about getting you back to your old self. I told you we're going to Boston. I meant it!"

When Orella stepped into the office, she had on a white dress. He noticed that, while she was hungover, Orella put up a decent front.

"You look great. We'll get breakfast on the way. That'll help with the hangover."

Her excited smile made him feel like a louse. But he went to the door.

As the couple left the station with their tickets in hand, Orella could barely contain her excitement. The hangover effects from the night before disappeared. She had her arm hooked with his as she thought over the places she wanted to see. Orella suggested they meet Yana to let her know.

"You're the boss," he told her as he held the passenger door open for the woman.

~~~

Irish arrived back at the office in a good mood. He didn't bother with looking at the headlines across the street. He would save the problems of the world for later. Orella and Yana were making amends when he left them at the Hotel Alexander.
~~~

As he was leaving, Yana squeezed Ray's arm, which he took as a thank you. Orella was already making plans for the sights in the city. The two women then went shopping for clothes. To Ray's relief, they let him return to his office to prepare for his time away.

After setting up an answering service to take his calls, Irish wrote a quick note to Arizona. He couldn't reach his partner at his house. Ray also called Senator Reece's home about Della, but the servant told him Reece was out. A few phone calls later, Irish had a hotel reservation in Boston and a private investigator who would check on Greye La Spina's past. He frowned when he heard the cost, but the shamus decided he needed to put Greye's ghost to rest.

After getting his clothes gathered and laid across the only suitcase he owned, Ray noticed the white powder-like substance covering his clothes. He looked for the cause, thinking a mouse might have come through the ceiling. Finding nothing to show the source, he shrugged, then brushed the powder off his clothes with his hat brush.

When he finished, Ray heard his phone ringing in the office. He picked up the receiver.

"Della's at my apartment." Edna's frantic voice came through the line. "She's locked herself in her room, and I can't get her to talk to me. I think she may do something to herself!"

"Alright, I'm on my way!"

It took Irish twenty minutes to get his old heap over to Edna's place. Ray discovered he was already too late when he got to the lobby.

Edna stood there waiting. She already had her hat on and was holding her purse.

"I'm sorry I couldn't keep her there. The sneak got me to come down to the lobby to mail a letter for her. Then she snuck out. I think she heard me call you. I think I know where she's going."

The two hurried back to his car, and she directed Irish out of town. Ray nursed his old jalopy along Peach Drive until he reached Dock Ave. He followed it out until the road turned into Coastal.

"Damn, I wish I could have made more progress yesterday trying to find her. The only clue I found was this handwritten receipt for jewelry, but it doesn't say what type."

Ray handed Edna the piece of paper.

"Did she have any new jewelry on?"

"No, not that I recall," she replied. "Why?"

"Well, if it's a ring needing fitting, they'd have an address for sure. It might lead me back to those characters that used me as a punching bag. When I stopped by, *Underhill's* was closed."

"I don't get why a ring. Why not a necklace?"

"A guy will claim he wants marriage will go for a ring. Then they can put a deposit down on a Friday." He glanced over. "They give her ring back to the jeweler to pick up on Monday. He's gone after his weekend stand, making sure to get his deposit back on Monday morning."

"Are you always so cynical?" She continued to look at the receipt.

"I've been through the school of hard knocks. Tell me what happened at your place."

"She got to my apartment a little after nine. Her clothes were a mess, ripped, and torn. She'd been drinking and still kind of out of it. When I went to help her, Della just went to her bedroom and locked herself inside. I tried talking with her through the door, but I could only hear her sobbing."

As they followed the road that ran parallel with the Chesapeake Bay, Edna explained she wanted to call the police.

"Those bastards raped her, I'm sure of it. She could barely hold her clothes on when she knocked at the apartment door. She didn't have her shoes or her purse. You should have let me call the cops last night."

Ray looked over.

"And how would this be different? Hindsight is easy. Let's stay on Della. I know this is the road back to her family's house. Is that where she's going?"

The woman shook her head.

"There's a turnoff next to the bay. She talks about it a lot."

"Why go there?"

"I think she's going to jump off. When I looked in Della's room after she left, I saw a line of razor blades laid out on the dresser. I think she got scared. She hates blood. Now, she's thought of another way."

"Damn it!" Ray pushed the accelerator to the floor.

"At one point, Della asked me what the worst thing that could happen to me. I told her that my parents and my friends dying were the worst things I could imagine."

Edna's voice broke.

"She laughed at me. Can you believe it? Then she said that living through a nightmare that will go on and on is worse than death. I tried to talk with her, but I couldn't get much more out of her. I feel like such a fool."

"Don't blame yourself. Others are responsible for this mess." He had to slow to take a sharp curve. The woman slid next to him on the slick leather bench seat.

"Sorry, what else makes you think she's going this way?" Ray glanced over at her worried expression.

"She said that she'd miss the view in the mornings. That's why I believe she'll go to that point between Oyster City and her dad's house. Della told me once that it has the most beautiful sunsets in the world."

"Well, you'd make a good detective," Irish said when he saw the flashy car ahead. "That looks like her Packard."

The shamus didn't see Della as he pulled near the car. However, Edna did. She jumped out of Ray's car and hurried toward the front of the Packard. Della wore a white blouse with slacks. She dangled her legs off a precarious ledge that overlooked the waves below.

"Oh, it's you," Della glanced over at her friend, then at Irish.

"Edna, you shouldn't have brought him along. Irish will just rub my face in this mess. He never liked me!"

Ray carefully went to the edge while remaining several steps away from Della. He noticed her puffy cheek carried a blue mark near the temple as her dulled eyes turned back to the water.

"Della, I'm not here for anything like that. Edna was concerned, and so am I."

"Sure, you are. You just want my father's money. That's the thing about men, isn't it? It's always about money and power."

Irish grimaced as he kneeled.

"Look, I don't have any idea what happened. But I've seen enough to know that someone hurt you. Maybe I can help fix the problem."

Della's laugh was sour and short. She looked over at Edna.

"Do you remember Paul Grey?"

"Sure, he was in your class. You told me that picked on him a lot during your senior year."

Della shrugged, kicking her feet out in the air like a young child.

"Yeah, I guess I did. I do that with people I like."

Her deadpan face looked down at the crashing waves.

"Paul and I made out one night right over there. After the senior dance, I got him to stop here before he took me home. The poor sap got all hot and bothered; then, he asked me to marry him."

The woman sighed.

"Of course, I laughed in his face! Like I was better than him."

"I never knew that," Edna replied.

"Of course you didn't. Nobody knows what's inside of me." Her harsh tone surprised her friend. Della saw the reaction and paused.

"Problem was that I was afraid. I liked him so much, yet I hurt him. I saw how much I crushed him when I laughed. It's like that. I hurt everyone."

She glanced over at Irish, her heels kicking off several pieces of the cliff face.

"You told me I should have married, so my father would quit worrying about me. I was going to do that with that bastard. That's what got me a night in a warehouse. Now, I have a better idea. It's right below me."

"Then you're a coward," Irish told her coldly.

His expression turned dark.

"Shut up," Edna hissed.

"No!" Ray stood up.

"Lady, you've made some bad decisions. But that doesn't make it right for others to hurt you. But if you think knocking yourself off helps, then you're a damn fool. Stop and think about it. Doing that allows the bastards to beat you!"

He calmed down.

"What kind of pain do you want your friends to endure? Those who care about you, like Edna, they have to live with knowing what you did."

The flash in Della's eyes caused him to lower his voice.

"Della, I've seen some of the worst things people can do to each other, so I know about a few things. First, you're not alone."

Irish kneeled again.

"Let tell you about the pain and suffering that others feel. Some nightmares rattle your brain every night. You see kids who should still be in high school, screaming for their mothers while they try to stuff their guts back inside their ripped-out belly. You wake up with the smell of burning flesh filling the air around you. It's so foul that you can't get the taste out of your mouth."

The man hesitated as he looked down to stop his swelling emotions. He didn't see Edna do the same thing as the glint of tears welled up in her eyes.

"You remember the faces of friends while you bury their bodies. I'll tell you God's truth that I thought about throwing myself in front of a train to stop it! I swear I fight through every damn nightmare that returns."

Della's glistening eyes stared at the water.

"You're alive, and that's the start to fixing the problem. The truth is that you were set up just like me. They played us for saps."

The shamus tried to estimate his distance from her. He didn't like the odds.

"Della, I know they must have hurt you in ways that I can't understand. But I know about pain and suffering. Don't let them win!"

"Listen to him; you know he's right! We'll help you." Edna pleaded as she came next to Ray.

"That's what a good friend does. I'm with you all the way!"

For the first time, Della looked over at Irish. Her expression carried an agony that reminded him of when Orella recounted her experiences with Maria Andras and the Shadows.

"Tell me you forget," she pleaded with him.

"Della, I won't lie to you. I still remember things I don't want to. But the pain and hurt fade away. I can guarantee that much. Edna's right! It's your friends that help you through it."

The distraught woman closed her eyes, not seeing the pieces of ground next to her break away. A few seconds later, they heard the splash below.

"Don't move," Edna warned.

"What hurts the most is I can't erase any of the memories. It's all recorded for history. They have everything on film for my father. Each time they…" Tears filled Della's eyes as she paid no attention to the warning.

Ray held out his hand to her.

"Then we have to get it back. I'll let you destroy whatever they have on you. You need someone to help you fight them. I can do that."

Della glanced over, then shook her head.

"No, you can't! He had money and power. I could tell by the way he ordered the men around."

"Then that's a way to discover the bastard and make him pay. You heard him, and you've heard names," Edna interjected.

"He can't hide when you have that. Rusty knows who the bastard is. I promise that I'll make him talk. Your father has the power to help us make him pay for what you're going through."

Her glance told Ray that they were slowly getting through.

"Della, you're strong enough to help Irish find this person and make him pay for what he's done," Edna promised.

"How can I be sure? My father's going to disown me when they show him the pictures."

Ray edged closer to the woman when he saw more of the embankment slid off.

She's got to get out of there!

"He's your father. He'll know that they forced you into this if you tell him the truth," Edna replied. "I know it hurts, but you need to tell us everything. Then I'll take you to your father and support you all the way."

Della stared at her friend.

"You promise?"

"You bet. Now come with me, and let's get the bastards that did this."

Della sighed, then looked over at the water.

"It's a lovely day," she said.

As the woman rose, the soil beneath her feet suddenly gave way. Della yelled out as she fell back on her back. Her body started to slide off the edge. Half expecting the event, Irish jumped across the remaining steps and caught her by her blouse at the shoulder. More of the cliff face dropped away, and the woman wildly grabbed at anything. Her hands frantically gripped around his wrist when her blouse ripped away. Ray felt himself slowly sliding forward as most of Della's body now dangled in the air.

"Hold on, I'm getting help," Edna saw a car driving up, and she stood. As she waved and yelled for them to stop, Ray felt his weight shifting.

"Grab my leg!" he cried out.

Edna turned and saw the struggling pair slipping along. The woman grabbed

Irish by the belt.

"Help us!" she cried out to the road.

As Edna tugged on Ray's belt, Della lost her grip with one hand. She dangled precariously while her fingers dug into Ray's leather wristwatch band. Blood dripped from his wrist.

"Just stay with me!" Ray stared into Della's eyes.

They heard people running over. Hands grabbed Ray's ankles.

"Hold on, lady. We'll get you."

"Ray, I...you..," Della said.

Then, the leather band of Ray's watch broke.

~~~

Senator Reece arrived with the state police an hour after it happened. While the gray-haired man stared out at the water where a boat looked for his daughter's body. Irish watched several troopers pushing photographers away. He asked the state policeman if he could leave. The man nodded, and Ray went to his car.

Edna was waiting for him. She sat on the passenger side, and her puffy eyes looked over at his bandaged wrist when he slid inside. They remained silent for a moment. She wanted to ask if he was alright, but Edna realized how stupid the question sounded.

"Can you drive me home?"

Without a word, Ray started the car and drove away. Except for the road noise, they remained silent back to Whitehaven Loft. When he stopped, she remained in the vehicle.

"I want to hire you to find her killer." Edna suddenly announced.

"You're looking at him," he stared straight ahead. "I marched right into a baited trap like an imbecile. Then I let her slide off my arm. She wanted to live."

She reached over and squeezed his arm.

"Don't do that. I was there, and you did everything you could do. Della was as responsible as anyone for how this turned out. You were only searching for her, as her father asked."

"Thanks. If you don't mind, I need to catch a train."

With a shrug, Edna released his arm and got out of the car. Suddenly, she turned back. Her face was furious.

"Does it make you feel better to take the weight of the world on your shoulders while you reject those around you? Did you not hear a damn thing you told Della?"

The woman slammed the door. Ray glanced over, then drove away. Edna remained there, watching his vehicle go out of sight.

~~~

The sun was dropping from the sky as Ray drove his car to the train station. In the seat next to him was Orella, who kept quiet as well. She recognized something was wrong with Ray. Over the last weeks together, she understood when to press him. It was not the right time.

While he gave her an update on his day, Orella recognized he wasn't telling her everything. When she asked about his arm, he remained annoyingly vague.

"My work for the senator finished today. So, let's get to Boston. I have a case to solve."

She looked at the big man next to her. His face still held the bruising and puffiness from his beating. His rugged looks used to make her heart flutter. However, when she looked at him now, the woman wondered how many sleepless nights came from staying with him.

Orella sighed as she debated whether to bring up her encounter with Merle earlier. Ray hadn't met the woman yet. However, he was usually a pretty good judge of people. Orella carried doubts from her last conversation with Merle.

After she left Yana at the hotel, Orella took a taxi back to Ray's office. When she got out of the cab and began unloading her packages, Merle was waiting for her.

"I'm just checking in to see how you're doing. I called, but nobody's in the office."

"That's very nice. But I'm fine, better than fine. I'm packing."

Merle looked puzzled by the statement.

"You're going somewhere?"

"Yes, Irish and I are on the 8 o'clock train to Boston. He's finishing up a case there.

"But you can't leave," Merle told her as Orella lifted the packages.

"Why not? I'll be back before you know it."

The tall woman grew furious.

"No, I need you here. You'll never return to Oyster City. He's fooling you."

Nearly dropping her packages, Orella stopped.

"Merle, I can't understand why you're acting this way. Now, I've got to get ready."

The tall woman came at Orella and pushed her against the building. Some packages fell on the concrete sidewalk.

"You're mine, pet. Don't ever forget it!" Her savage expression scared the smaller woman.

"Lady, are you alright?" The taxi driver was out of his car, staring at the two women.

Merle looked back at him, realizing others were watching them.

"We're fine! You should mind your own business." She turned back to Orella and released her.

"Isn't that right, my love?"

Orella hesitated, then nodded.

"It's nothing," the woman lost her will momentarily.

The driver frowned as he scooped up the boxes on the sidewalk.

"I'm sorry, I should have helped you with those packages," he told his customer.

When Orella looked at him, her mind cleared.

"Thanks, I appreciate the help."

Orella refused to look at Merle when she retreated into the stairwell.

"I'll see you soon. My pet!"

Merle's voice followed her up the stairs.

"Are you alright?" Ray's voice brought her back into the present as he turned the car into the parking lot.

"Yes, just excited," Orella told him.

"We'll soon be off, and you can forget about Oyster City," he replied.

~~~

Several miles away, Arizona drove along the coastal road on the way to Myrna La Spina's hideout. He wanted to ensure that her husband told him the truth about her danger. He yawned, then glanced at his watch. Arizona had another hour to reach Bayport.

The ex-cop spent part of the day with Lieutenant Montgomery Sirk, a former colleague, who told him about the bishop's suicide. Sirk remained the one cop he trusted. No one found a way to corrupt his friend.

At least, not yet!

"Damn it; you're acting like that crazy Irish." Sirk told him after the first terrible cup of coffee at *Vinnies* down by the docks. The cops stayed away because of the appalling food, which made it a perfect spot.

"Listen, Bishop Henry La Spina was part of a group killing people for years. That bastard practically gloated over it to me in person about Howard's murder. I'm not crying over his death. But you and I both know that the police won't investigate that angle. Do you think that Don Devine is the right guy to get the force back in shape?"

Sirk looked around.

"No, but I need my pension."

"Alright, I'll keep you out of his sights. All I ask is that you keep Irish and me out of his crosshairs, or at least give us a heads up when you hear something. In the meantime, I'll keep you in the loop as we figure things out."

Arizona leaned forward.

"I can tell you that La Spina left me notes. It was about the missing people. He also claimed we could find the evidence inside the Andras cemetery."

"The guy committed suicide. He must have been unstable. That means you can't depend on his word," the detective leaned back. "Again, you've been hanging around Irish too long."

"Maybe, but tell me again, how many of those murders and missing persons
~~~

have the police force actually solved?"

Sirk scowled at the question.

"Don't think like an old cop," Campbell told him. "Think like you're a rookie. All wet behind the ears. Would you think that something is wrong with this place?"

After a moment, the lieutenant nodded.

"Alright, I've turned a blind eye to this crap for a while. But I'm not joking about my pension. I can't afford to hang around with you."

As Sirk slid out of the booth, Arizona chuckled under his breath.

I thought the same way once!

Then, Arizona ran into Irish. The shamus kept leading him into one crazy case after another. Every time, luck kept them alive. Sometimes, Arizona believed his partner carried a curse that caused him to stumble into every screwy situation imaginable. And now, his partner left for Boston.

Arizona got back to the office as Irish packed the rest of his clothes. While Ray was pleased when hearing about Henry La Spina's death, he reminded Arizona that he had debts to honor.

"I'm going to finish my work on proving Greye died before she left Oyster City."

While Arizona thought the idea was nuts, he suspected Ray planned on the trip to get Orella out of Oyster City. When he asked Irish if he was popping the question of marriage with the woman, Ray shook his head and went quiet again.

Arizona glanced over at the setting sun as he drove along the narrow highway. It was a picture-perfect evening. Then he thought of Cat and frowned.

It reminded him he wanted to ask her on a date, but he never got the chance. His idea was to grab a picnic basket, take her on a ride along the road, and then stop at an overlook to enjoy her company. Sure, it was hokey and old-fashioned like the bowler hat he wore. But, somehow, Arizona figured Cat would appreciate a simple date.

He sighed.

Forty minutes later, the ex-cop arrived in Bayport. As he drove through the single paved street of the old fishing village along the Chesapeake Bay, he passed the general store with a couple of gas pumps out front. The boarded-up windows on the building across the highway reminded him of his turn. A sandy road led to Myrna's hideout, where small homes lined either side of the path. Most of the tidy homes didn't have cars in front. Those in the village who worked took the bus to the cannery a mile further down the highway.

Arizona stopped in front of a small white cottage with blue shutters and trim. It was a rental that he got for Myrna La Spina when he helped her escape her husband.

When the big man knocked at the door, he noticed the blinds move, then a moment later, the deadbolt unlocked. Myrna's worried green eyes looked at him before she opened the door.

"How are you doing?" he asked as he took off his hat and entered.

"Fine, but I'm worried. The neighbors told me that a stranger had stopped by the general store. He didn't ask for me by name, but they said the description he gave them pointed to me."

The thin woman pointed to the small brown couch. She took a rocker next to it that faced a fireplace.

Henry was telling me the truth!

"I've been in this chair a lot," she explained. "It's kind of comforting to rock your troubles away. It's nice to have you here. I've been jumpy since the neighbors told me about the stranger. I have the pistol you left with me on my dresser."

She glanced over at him.

"Then, I'll need to get you to another place," he gave her a comforting smile, then looked at the sparse accommodations in the room.

"Maybe a few books as well. The store doesn't have much of a selection," she told him. "I was thinking about doing a garden. I've never tried that before."

He remained standing as he watched her. Her brief stay agreed with her. Her skin was darker, while her blonde hair no longer had a platinum tone. The woman's side profile showed her hook nose. Still, Arizona considered her quite stunning. He fiddled with his hat, trying to determine how to let her know her husband was dead.

"Things are still hot back in Oyster City." He felt the heaviness of the book that her husband gave him in his suit coat as he looked down. "I think you'll be safer out of state."

"I'm already packed!"

He reacted with surprise.

"When you live thinking that the next ring of the doorbell could be someone trying to kill you, you learn to be prepared."

Her thin smile failed to hide her nerves.

Arizona took a deep breath when an idea came to him.

"It'll be a long drive, but I have an idea where you can get a garden started. It's isolated. Plus, only I know the location."

"Then, let's get going!" She rose from the chair.

He looked out the window.

"Are you up for it? It'll be all night."

"Give me five minutes," Myrna paused, then looked at the rocker.

"Go get your stuff," Campbell told her.

When Myrna stepped out of the house, she saw Arizona finishing tying the rocking chair to the roof of his car.

"Where I'm taking you doesn't have a rocker," he glanced over. "I'll let the owner know I bought it from him."

Myrna stood there, unable to say anything, as he slid down from the trunk of his car.

"Don't just stand there, bring over your bags. We have a lot of miles to cover." He grumbled.

Myrna smiled and carried her two bags to the trunk. When he turned around, she kissed him on the cheek.

"Thank you for everything."

~~~

Ray Irish remained lost in another world. He was sitting in the club car with Orella in the seat next to him. She watched the streetlights passing by as the train sped toward their destination. However, Irish kept seeing a face desperately staring at him for help. He downed the drink in one shot and called over the bartender for another.

"We should have dinner," Orella reminded him.

"Probably," he absently agreed as he retreated to his thoughts.

The afternoon back with Orella had been a blur. On the way out of town, they stopped by Pappy's newsstand. He let his friend know that he'd be gone for a few days. The man looked inside the car and waved back to Orella.

"I'm trying to tie up loose ends with Greye La Spina," Ray explained.

"That's fine. I've got something in that might help with your other problem." Pappy looked around.

"Andras again," Ray sighed after the man nodded in agreement.

He slid back into the car. The shamus glanced at Pappy, who appeared interested in telling him something more. But his friend just nodded as Irish drove away.

"What's wrong?" Orella's voice brought Irish back to the moment.

"You've been holding in something since you finished with Senator Reece. Did he do something wrong?"

"Yeah, he hired the wrong guy! Let's skip it." Ray grumbled. He glanced over at her pained expression. Then, he went back to staring out the window.

"Is this seat taken?" a familiar voice asked.

"Mother, what are you doing here?"

"Didn't Ray tell you? I'm coming to Boston with you."

Yana explained, as Irish looked at her.

Orella glared at him.

"No, he did not!"

"Thanks," he sneered at Yana. Then he turned to Orella.

"Your mom thought I wouldn't spend enough time with you, so she wanted to come along to keep you company. I should have said something."

He looked over at Yana.

"It slipped my mind."
~~~

Yana pressed on her daughter's arm.

"My dear, is it so bad that I took a trip with my daughter?"

"No, I guess not," Orella looked over at Irish. "I just wasn't expecting it. I kind of hope we'd have some time together."

"Listen, I won't get in your way. Ray told me he's going to wrap up a case. How many times has he left you alone for hours on end? In those few letters you sent me, you mentioned it several times. We can see the sights while he's not around."

"Yeah, she's got a point," Ray hastily agreed.

Damn, Yana sure knows how to make a guy feel like a heel.

Orella picked up her whiskey sour and leaned back in her chair. When she looked at it, she smiled.

"Right now, I wish this was absinthe!"

Chapter 5: Chasing Ghosts

After feeding on Sally for the last time, the three witches of Andras finally untied the mangled corpse. Sally's days of agony and torment laying atop the tomb ended when they cut her throat. Pas directed Lance to pick up the mutilated corpse after they filled a bottle with her remaining blood. However, Panthia stopped him and then used the sacrificial dagger to make the final desecration to Sally's body. She cut off Sally's right hand. Chuckling, she turned to her sisters.

"Merle, we'll use this to create a hand of glory. Then you can find your little pet."

"The woman was no murderer, just our victim," the sister replied.

"It'll still work with dead man's candles that I've created," she insisted. "I used the body fat from the remains of Maria Andras to create the wax. She murdered many before they sacrificed her to Andras. The Shadows believe she betrayed them."

"How would you know that?" Merle cocked her head.

"I encountered her soul when she hung in front of Malphas while he tortured her." The witch glanced over at Psamathe, who continued to lick the blood on her fingers.

"Wait, why were you with Malphas? He's a rival of Andras. You must want our master to flay you alive when he finds out." Merle cocked her head at the news.

"Don't think you can use that against me. The master knows. Besides, you have your own problem." Panthia chuckled. "Let's get back to finding Orella. My incantation on the dead woman's hand will direct you to your prey. Do you still have your pet's hair?"

Her sister nodded.

"And her mother's hair as well." Merle warmed to the idea.

"You know Panthia; your idea should work. We'll follow them and finish our job. The master will forgive us."

Panthia glared at Merle.

"You mean he might forgive you. Perhaps you can bring back the mother as well as an offering for Andras. Whatever you do, it's better to have the ring for Andras than nothing at all."

"Yes, yes," her sister agreed. "I know that you're becoming his favorite."

"I please him as a servant must. But you know that my help comes at a cost," Panthia glanced over.

"And what do you want?" Suspicion filled Merle's face.

"I'll determine that when you return. Perhaps I'll suckle on your blood to drain you of power; just a bit, mind you. Then again, I might want a finger or a toe. Andras wants to control minds. It's better to take the flesh of a witch for such spells."

"You would do that to me?" Merle growled. "I taught you those rites to become nearly immortal and powerful as your sister or me."

"And you would take something from me or Psamathe should the need arise," the woman stated with glee. "Don't worry; it's a small price to pay for serving our master."

Merle turned away, upset at the idea, but she realized her sister was correct.

"Put that body into the tomb with the others," Merle yelled at Lance. She hated the idea of giving in to extortion.

"You'll pay for this," she looked back at Panthia, who cackled at the threat.

Her sister wiped the blood from her mouth and looked down at the bloodstains on her only dress.

"I can't go to the mayor's office like this."

"Take the dress that our girl wore. She does not need it now." Pas licked her lips with a dreamy expression.

Her sister went to the corner of the crypt and picked up Sally's clothes. She held them up to her figure.

"The dress is big for me, but I'll make it work."

The trio of lookalikes paid no attention to the wasted husk of the young man while he slowly carried the body to a rusty door on the side of the crypt. Lance opened the door before he brought the body into the foul room. He remained obvious to the nauseating odors of the decomposing bodies that lined the floor to the vault.

"I'm afraid we'll need a new servant soon. That one won't last much longer." Pas told the others when Lance returned. "Andras has another task coming that Panthia is working on."

"Then, we'll let Panthia find us this servant," Merle grumbled, then looked at her sisters. "She can do that when she works for the master. I'll go after Orella and the ring. I have many things planned for my pet for leaving me."

~~~

Arizona Campbell and his passenger arrived in Short Corner, West Virginia, about noon the next day. He looked over at Myrna. Her head rested on his curled-up coat. When he slowed the car to a stop in front of a small hotel, she opened her eyes.

"I've got to get some sleep," he explained. "I know this might be poor form, but I'm getting a room here. My parent's farm is a few miles out of town, but no
~~~

one's lived in the house for years." He rubbed his eyes before looking around the familiar street.

"Just a word of caution. It'll take some fixing to make it ready for guests. It doesn't have a bed."

Myrna scanned Main Street with an excited expression.

"Don't worry; nothing has been proper since I got married." She handed him his coat.

"Let's check-in."

They entered the two-story building with Campbell carrying Myrna's luggage. A ceiling fan slowly pushed around the warm air inside the small lobby, where a large woman stood behind the counter.

"How y'all doin'?"

"Doin' well, and I hope you're not full up."

She laughed and turned the resister book to face them.

"I've got a real quiet spot for you and the missus."

Before Arizona could respond, Myrna spoke up.

"We appreciate it. I'm Myrna Campbell. Arizona is taking me out to his parent's farm. His family's lived in the area for years."

"Aw, bless your heart. I knew the Campbells." She looked over at the man, trying to keep the shock off his face.

"I must say, I'd never recognized you. It's been a long time. I'm Carolyn Menyes. Y'll sign in while I get your key."

Myrna smiled sweetly at Campbell, then pulled in front of the man to sign the register. The hotel owner went to the stairs waiting while Arizona dumbly followed the two ladies to the next floor. After Carolyn left the couple in the room, Myrna went to the window and looked at a couple standing by Arizona's vehicle.

"We've got the locals talking."

Arizona sat the luggage on the single bed. He looked at her, then at the comfortable-looking bed.

"Yes, and I'll have a heck of a time explaining how I'm suddenly married. Plus, we have to figure out the sleeping arrangements."

"It was a great idea," she insisted. "It'll be harder to track me under another name. Just stay on your side of the bed, and there are no problems with the sleeping arrangements."

Arizona looked perplexed as he stepped next to her.

"I don't know how, given the size of the bed. Anyway, you've got a bit of deviousness in you."

She grinned.

"You look worn out; get some sleep. I want to see this town."

Nodding, he turned back to the bed while she went to the door.

"Don't get lost," he warned.

Myrna opened the door and looked back. Her protector had his bowler hat covering his face as he lay on the bed. Smiling at the sight, Myrna quietly closed the door.

Amid the fond memories as a child on the farm, Arizona Campbell smelled bacon. He sniffed the air again.

Yes, it's bacon!

He opened his eyes. At first, the man didn't recognize the ceiling. He saw Myrna sitting by the window. She looked up from her book at his movement.

"You better eat your food before it gets cold!"

Arizona sat up to see the small table next to Myrna's chair had two plates filled with eggs, biscuits, and bacon, along with two cups. There was even an enamel pot sitting on an iron trivet in the middle of the table. He glanced at the darkening sky outside the window as he got out of bed.

"How did you come up with this?"

"Oh, a little horse-trading, I think you farmers call it," she grinned while the big man pulled up a chair.

"When I went into the shops, it was already common knowledge that we're newlyweds. So, I took advantage of their hospitality. The diner cooked those up when I explained we drove all night to get here."

She put her book down and poured coffee for both of them.

"Oh, and we have a mattress for the farm now. The dealer will bring out the bed in the morning."

Arizona nearly choked on the eggs. Then, he burned his tongue while trying to down the hot coffee to stop his choking.

"I thought a cop could handle unexpected situations." She gave him a wry smile, then continued to sip on her coffee.

"I can, but you got to give a guy a head's up on certain things."

She nodded absently.

"I'll remember that. The good news is that people remember you. I met an old classmate who runs the drugstore. Also, the butcher told me a charming story about you and little Mary Joe."

Arizona glared at her.

"Don't believe everything you hear in a small town."

The woman smiled.

"Just eat your food. We're invited over to the parson's house after dinner. He was a little perturbed that we didn't get married here. I guess you'll have to explain that."

The shamus stopped in mid-bite with part of the bacon still hanging from his mouth. After he quickly stuffed the meat down, his face was red.

"Lady, I take back what I said earlier. You've got a real mean streak in you!"

He grinned at her laughter.

~~~

When Orella woke the next morning, she turned over to see the sleeper car's wall next to her. The woman yawned, then smiled. For the first time in many days, she had no memory of dreaming. No nightmare woke her. Orella stretched and turned over. She leaned over the edge of the bed to see Ray still asleep on the bed below hers. Frowning, the woman remembered Ray did not make love with her when they came back to the room after dinner.

As she thought about it, the distance between them increased lately. Even when he held Orella after her nightmares, they seldom felt the need to turn the closeness into something physical. Orella remembered something he told her when they first met.

"Babe, you don't deserve the cruel fate of staying around me."

At the time, she laughed it off to his modesty. However, it was during the quiet times when the words came back to her.

Orella watched his feet moving, and then one leg kicked out from under the covers. The red scars covering his leg showed under the sunlight coming through the window. A familiar sensation of goose flesh prickled along her arm. The woman rolled over on her back.

Even after all this time, I still can't look at his horrible scars!

She let her hands run across her stomach. The burn scars from her torture remained. Orella felt the slight bumps of skin growth in the three lines that ran from her hip to just under her breasts.

I wonder if Ray feels the same revulsion when he sees these.

Self-conscious of the wounds, Orella also vividly remembered the pain. She welcomed her lover's killing of the bastard who carried out the torture. Still, it was challenging to believe Ray's assurances.

Below her, the woman heard Irish rousing. Orella smiled when he yawned. The nightmares stayed away from his night as well. For that, she was grateful. Maybe he was right to tell her to forget about Oyster City. Her mother would agree with him.

Orella looked over as the man stood by the bed. He didn't turn her way. Instead, he went to the sink.

I wish he would forget about Oyster City!

After the first real night's rest in many days, Irish was actually in a good mood. He joined Orella and Yana in the diner car for breakfast. The women wore
~~~

similar-looking white summer dresses and looked like sisters. He noticed their attitudes were upbeat as well. He pointed it out to Orella.

"It's strange, but I feel like a strange weight lifted from my shoulders," she looked at Yana. "Mother, I must apologize to you. I've felt darkness inside me lately. I believe that's what caused me to lash out."

For a moment, Yana appeared confused. Then, her smile beamed at the admission. She peeked over at Ray before she thanked her daughter.

"I'm so glad. I admit that I felt a heaviness when I arrived."

Irish listened to the women as the waiter brought them their food. He didn't bother to interrupt since he enjoyed the lack of tension. Then, he remembered the tragedy the day before.

When he finished his plate, Ray noticed his companions had barely started eating. The waiter stopped by and whispered in his ear.

"Let them know we'll be at the train station in less than an hour."

Ray nodded and thanked him.

"Ladies, you better finish your breakfast and get ready for Boston. I don't want to leave you with the check."

His cheesy grin made Orella laugh. Yana smiled as well.

After arriving at Boston's North Station, the trio pushed through the pedestrian traffic. As they followed the corridor leading toward their destination, the trio passed an advertising poster on the wall about the Hotel Manger.

A Tower of Hospitality, With a Radio in Every Room!

Ray and Orella entered a room on the 10th floor that held refinements of the past and the push into the modern era. The French telephone sat on a Scandinavian style desk. A carved headboard of the bed had buttons and a dial for the radio, which gave only three stations. Ray took a seat on the edge of the mattress after sitting his suitcase in the closet. Orella watched him playing with the radio like it was the first time he'd seen such a thing.

"Get over here and pay the man," she ordered after pointing the bellhop to the closet with his cart holding suitcases and hatboxes.

Irish went to the door and gave the man his tip. He didn't get the door closed when he felt Orella's arms around him. He turned and looked down at her.

"What brought this on?"

"In a way, I feel like I'm free again," she said, then reached up and kissed him.

He felt the passion of the moment and held her tight for a longer kiss. Then the woman led him to the bed. Orella playfully pushed him on the mattress. Ray watched her slowly unbutton the front of her dress with a devious smile as he laid back. When her dress slid off the woman's shoulders, she stopped the dress from showing her stomach. Then, Orella let the dress fall while studying his reaction. She smiled as he did.

"Mother will be over before too long so that we can start the day," she told him as she crawled on top of Irish. He nodded in agreement.

"Then we'll need to hurry!"

"Tomorrow, you'll be hard at work. I want to enjoy every minute I have." the woman helped unbuckle his pants.

Yana finished touching up her makeup after hanging her clothes. She smiled while looking out the window from her room. She looked over the Charles River and parts of the city, which reminded her of how much she disliked the drab views of Oyster City.

While the woman stood there, she felt the relief filling her. Yana was confident that the dream and tarot cards she believed sent her to Oyster City would never happen. One last task remained. However, she recognized her daughter now held doubts about Irish.

Once the shamus left, Yana would put a bevy of good-looking suitors in front of Orella. Then, her daughter would have the excellent family needed for Yana to return to the Philippines to start her new life. She grabbed her purse from the bed.

When Yana reached the door to Orella and Ray's room, she heard the squeaking sounds of a mattress through the cracked door. Despite the alarms going off in her head, Yanna slowly pushed open the door and looked in. The woman couldn't believe it was her daughter sprawled on top of Irish. Then she saw the familiar scars on Ray's legs amid the lover's heavy breathing. With his pants dropped around his ankles, the man had his hands cradled around Orella's buttocks.

After a moment of observing her daughter's uninhibited passion on top of her lover, Yana quietly closed the door. The sounds of Orella's moaning and Ray's groans remained in her head when Yana got back to her room. The upset woman threw her purse down on the mattress. When she looked into the mirror by the bed, she saw the tears streaming down her cheeks. She fell into the bed and buried her face in the pillow.

~~~

Phillip Smyth's tall shadow overlooked the new secretary who sat behind the desk in the mayor's office's front lobby. Dressed in a white blouse that still enhanced her cleavage, Panthia looked up with a semi-civil smile. The woman's attempt to project a professional image included a dark ribbon to tie her long black hair back. The change in clothes surprised the man. Then he remembered that Mayor Hopely's secretary wore a similar blouse and plaid skirt when he last saw the woman.
~~~

Andras and his harem had another sacrifice.

Years of killing turned Phillip into a man incapable of empathy for those slaughtered as a sacrifice. He barely remembered the faces of those killed. However, Phillip remembered his friends.

As he waited, the man thought about the Shadows, his friends and colleagues who came from the most powerful families of Oyster City. Throughout history, many of the city's original founding families made up the group. Now, many of his comrades were dead or nothing more than errand boys for Andras. At one point, Phillip believed his closeness to his brother, Peter, would give him an inside role when Andras took over Peter's body.

Phillip scowled as he looked at the dozens of small boxes on the desk. The witch put a tiny bottle inside each package.

Just another plan that Andras keeps secret!

A buzzer sound came from the box on Panthia's desk.

"You can go in now!"

He nodded and took a deep breath before entering the office. Behind the massive desk, Andras stared out the window with his back toward the entrance. Mr. Wolfe stood in his customary position in the room's corner.

"A man is interfering with my plans!" The demon growled.

Surprised, Phillip stood there in silence.

"It's a man who owns the newsstand on Broadway," Peter Smyth turned in his chair.

The demon's face showed the effects of his body's deterioration.

"You mean Pappy? He's been selling papers for years down there. How can he interfere with your power?"

"My witch claims this Negro escapes my nightmares. My harem cannot go against him. He carries the cross of the fisherman. He's a friend of Irish. I want this man arrested and killed."

Phillip hesitated.

"Did you not hear me?"

"Speaking as the district attorney, sending the cops after him will cause problems, especially on the Southside of the city. He's a fixture among those who go by his newsstand daily. Plus, he's too well known to disappear." Philip explained.

"If he dies in police custody, those agitators in the capital will raise a fuss. We don't want publicity like those Chicago race riots last year. It might impede your goals in the capital. After all, you're the mayor of Oyster City with larger plans than this one person."

Andras leaned back in his leather chair, his eyes turning dark as night. For a moment, Phillip wondered if he had overstepped the master's invisible line.

"Perhaps you're correct. Do you have another idea?"

"The doctor controls men who'll be eager to run him out of town," he assured Andras. "More and more of those gangsters come to Oyster City each day. I believe they come to the dark that emanates from this city now. Soon, you can flex your rule without worrying about such minor details."

"Very well, make sure these criminals understand that anyone who is a friend of Ray Irish is on the list of people I want gone or dead. Is that understood?" Smyth told him.

Phillip nodded, and his onetime brother turned back to the view from the window.

"What about Weyer?" Phillip asked.

"As I read the papers, the Oyster City police have his prints on the murder weapon of the nurse," Andres replied. "You're the district attorney, don't you prosecute such people?"

"This is true! However, we've lost evidence before. I'm afraid that Henry La Spina set Weyer up to take this public fall. Aside from that, I'm still not sure who helped Henry." Phillip pushed aside strands of long hair from his face. "I suspect maybe the detective, Irish."

"Then I suggest you arrest him." Andres sighed. "I'll use him for a sacrifice."

"I've already had the police chief check on it. Irish left town last night with his girlfriend and her mother. I'm still waiting to hear where they went and when they return. You might have finally scared him away."

The demon turned around at the news. Phillip realized what he said was a surprise. He had a feeling of vindication at the reaction. The demon pressed the intercom button.

"Get in here," Peter Smyth's gravelly voice ordered Panthia.

When the witch entered, she glanced at Phillip, who revealed nothing in his expression.

"Does the harem know that the Singsing ring left Oyster City?"

She glanced over at Phillip again.

"Foul bitch, I'm talking to you."

The woman's face suddenly twisted in pain as she flopped to the floor. The mental hold the demon had on the witch continued while she kicked out, sending her shoes across the room. When the gasping woman's hair changed to gray, Andras released her. Panthia lay in a heap, coughing and retching.

"Your lack of an answer tells me I have fools in my circle. Attempt to deceive me, and I'll rip your flesh from your temporary body. Have the harem waiting for me when I return tonight."

He turned his back on the woman, lifting herself from the carpet. When she finally got her voice back, Panthia begged for the master's forgiveness.

"Hell doesn't forgive, and neither do I. Leave now before I decide I need one less creature in my harem."

Visibly older, the woman hurried from the room, nearly tripping on one of her shoes, which remained on the floor. Phillip slowly followed her to the door.

"Throw the book at Weyer," Peter Smyth ordered. "He failed by not killing La Spina. My demon brothers and sisters reach out and tell me that the bishop's soul enjoys a special brand of torment right now. Weyer will join him. I reserve places in my realm for failures."

Phillip scowled at the comment.

~~~

For Myrna La Spina, the rutted drive to Arizona's family farm made her wonder how far away they were from civilization since the last crossroads. She looked over green fields in the valley between two ridges on either side of a meandering stream they crossed at least two times. After one last jolt, the car turned between two trees. That's when she finally saw the little white farmhouse hidden behind several overgrown apple trees.

"Well, that road is certainly worse than I recall," the shamus told her when he brought his vehicle to a stop.

He paused, looking out of the windshield that held the splattered remains of bugs from their long journey.

"From the way you talked, I didn't expect much," she confessed, while leaning forward to get a better view of the roof.

"It's cute!"

He smiled at the statement.

"I come out once a year to make sure that storms haven't damaged the house and barn." He pointed to a stump several yards away. "That tree went down after a storm a couple of years back. It took me a week to get it cut and hauled out of here. The neighbor keeps the grass down since I let him cut and bale the hay to use for his stock."

Arizona opened the car door.

The quiet immediately struck Myrna as she followed the man toward the house. He moved the rock doorstop, used for the screen door, to expose the house key.

"Not much security but, then again, there's not much need out here. The
~~~

nearest neighbor is Hank Williams, who has a couple of young boys. They have a hundred and sixty acres further up the road."

The front door creaked as he opened it. A blast of stale air struck them.

"Time to air out the place," he stated, while heading to the closest window.

With a couple of tugs, he lifted the sash to open the window while Myrna looked around. The walls had wallpaper with images of golden leaves of wheat, with outdated curtains covering the windows. An old couch, along with an Eastman style chair, were on one side near the fireplace. On the other side was the dining room, which led back through an open door toward the kitchen.

Arizona opened the door that led into a hallway.

"Back here is the bedroom. There's another upstairs. The bathroom is over here."

He wandered into the bedroom and opened the window as she followed him. She noticed the small twin bed.

"I thought you said there wasn't a bed out here."

He glanced over.

"Well, not big enough for a married couple," he grinned. "Anyway, I'll move that upstairs. There's no furniture up there. My parents got rid of it when my youngest brother went out on his own. I guess they wanted to make sure we didn't come running back home."

"So, you have brothers?" she asked, while checking out the small bathroom. It needed cleaning, along with a fresh coat of paint.

Nodding, he passed her on the way to the kitchen.

"I warned you it needed work."

"It'll be fine," she told him. As she entered the kitchen, the woman frowned at the wallpaper.

"I must admit, it's a bit overwhelming. I grew up where people served me. You know that in the last couple of months, living on my own. I've enjoyed it."

Ray finally got the window over the sink unstuck, and the breeze rushed into the room.

"Well, I hope you're not too bored out here. I have to say; there's not much to do. I'm sure that your presence is spreading like wildfire. Hank will come by once I leave. Watch out; he's known to get handsy with the pretty ladies."

"Alright, consider me warned." She chuckled.

"Now, let's go unload the car," he went toward the front door.

The new bed didn't arrive until mid-afternoon. When the men left in their truck, Arizona watched the vehicle's dust as they headed into town. He entered the house to find Myrna was sitting by the window in her stolen rocker. It reminded him he should have called the guy who owned the cottage back at

Bayport.

The shamus stood looking out the open door. Memories stormed back of running through the apple trees as he hurried to the one-room schoolhouse down the road.

"A penny for your thoughts," she looked over.

He shook his head.

"Memories," he told her as he pulled a cigar from his shirt pocket. He chomped down on it, then went to his father's Eastlake chair.

Arizona noticed she was watching him.

"What?"

"Nothing. I just haven't seen you relaxed before. You're not wearing your coat and hat." Myrna looked out the window. "I forgot how peaceful the country is."

"Yeah, I always knew coming out here when I got to retirement." The man stared out the window. "Put in a few peach trees for canning and get a chicken pen in the back. A guy could learn to forget."

"Do you mind a question?"

Arizona looked over with a puzzled look.

"Not at all."

"Have you gotten over Katherine?"

His face darkened for a moment while he groped a bit for the answer.

"Yeah, I've had to learn I held more for her than she ever could for me. I guess that made it harder to let go."

"Why do you say that? From what Gladys Peer told me, Katherine liked you."

A faint smile crossed his lips.

"Cat had one major weakness that she couldn't get over. She saw money as the way to happiness. I'm a little too simple for that."

When Arizona looked over, he noticed how the woman's green eyes glinted. When he first met the woman in the bishop's grand house, those same eyes had the haunted look of a dying person.

"It's interesting that you say that." She replied. "I was just thinking about a simple life. You're right. Sometimes you need to just forget about things."

The ex-cop chewed on his cigar for a moment as he considered the idea.

"Well, you're in the right spot. They might be poor dirt farmers around here, but they'll treat you like royalty if you give them a chance."

He observed the open field across the road from his seat. The tobacco crop looked in good shape.

"I'm going back to Oyster City tomorrow. I want you to stay there until I come for you. That's when you know you'll have no more worries coming from that place.”

“Are you sure?”

Arizona shrugged. He didn’t bother to explain that he might never show up again.

~~~

The exhausted screams finally stopped when Andras finished punishing the witches of Lamia. The women lay in sobbing while the winded body of Peter Smyth finally dropped his whip to the floor.

“Get up and kneel before I decide you’re not worth my time,” he ordered.

The witches struggled to kneel before their master. The backs of each woman held long, bloody trails of shredded flesh that painfully mixed with their sweat. However, the injuries were only a last part of the cruelty that he inflicted upon them that evening.

“Had I more time, I’d hang you by your toes for a week,” his ominous, deep voice explained. “However, your screams of torment warmed me enough to let you try one more time.”

“Yes, master,” they agreed in unison.

He looked down at the witches, his dark eyes looking for any hint of rebellion. His cruel smile at the subservient creatures revealed the enjoyment Andras found in torture. Finally, he took a seat next to the fireplace, where he stoked the fire with the poker that he used on their flesh earlier.

As he considered his options, Andras glanced over at Sally’s severed hand that lay on his nightstand. The demon stared at the blue flame on the candle set in the palm. The demonstration provided by Panthia gave him some confidence they would succeed.

“Psamathe and Meroe, you will take the Hand of Glory and track down the Singsing ring. There is no excuse for your failure to bring it to me. Is that understood?”

“Yes, great Andras,” the women replied. They painfully rose from a kneeling position to face him. The candle’s glow showed the damage the demon inflicted upon their chest, abdomen, and legs with the red-hot poker. The witches’ faces held streaks of tears as they endured the hours of agony. While they controlled the power of enchantment and powerful spells, their twisted souls were owned by the demon for an eternity of torment. Andras did as he wanted with those from his realm. Subservience came unless they wished for more suffering and pain.

Merle glanced at her arm. Her skin was already turning back to the petrified skin of the corpse that she occupied. Her own body turned to dust centuries before her release into the mortal world again. The demon’s terrible temper left the
~~~

witches depleted. Incantations and blood sacrifice brought them into the world of the living. They were also necessary to maintain their bodies.

"Great master, we must have blood to stop our return to dust after your punishment," she gently reminded him.

"Then get out of my sight and find a sacrifice to bring your beauty back. I'm tired of looking at you."

The women struggled to their feet and went to the door. As Panthia followed her sisters, Andras ordered her back.

"Your sisters will complete the task. I have work for you."

The aging woman avoided frowning at the thought of continuing to age. However, she dutifully came back into the sweltering room.

"You will go to the man we hold in the crypt. Use the list I gave you and lead him to the houses. I want more sacrifices for our upcoming festival."

The witch's eyes danced in hope.

"May I have the blood of them? I need to replenish my looks to serve you."

He stared at the fire before he finally nodded.

"Very well. You may have a daughter or son to slaughter." He smiled to himself. "It'll keep the newspapers happy with another missing person. Now go bring me, Mr. Wolfe."

Panthia left the room with a puzzled look. She found the silent assistant standing at the end of the hallway. He nodded at her request and followed her back to the room. The demon pulled his attention from the fire.

"I need trusted followers who obey without thought or pity. When I arrived here, it was clear that the Shadows were a club for vainglorious families to maintain their hold over Oyster City. Such limited thinking must stop. The goal is to spread my reign."

He poked the fire with the iron rod he still held.

"Raising twisted souls like the Harem takes time. It will come as I spread my power across the lands. However, I must leave my mark on the young ones. They're the ones who'll turn into the next powerful families who'll sacrifice their babies to follow me into Hell."

"Wolfe, you'll gather boys and girls from the reform school to become my junior servants for this house. I've already contacted the head of the school, who's happy to oblige. Panthia, you'll enchant them to be my entertainment at night. Our experience will return to their nightmares while they gradually become my loyal and brutal followers."

Andras rested his head on the chair back.

"I so enjoy the taste of the fear in the mortals while I rape them," he sighed. "We'll call it their rehabilitation. After all, I'm teaching them to be my servants for eternity. They will become my shock troops of anarchy and discontent, that will lead the sheep into following me once I become governor."

His servants bowed, then walked out of the bedroom while Andras smiled to himself.

~~~

Marion Underhill paid no attention to the bell ringing when the door to his jewelry store opened. His eyes focused on morning headlines in the paper as the footsteps approached.

"It appears another one of the Shadows is no longer needed."

Underhill looked up to see Phillip Smyth standing there. He glanced around the empty shop.

"Yes, and I'm wondering how long I have left among our dwindling group."

Phillip nodded as he leaned over the counter. He rested his elbows on the counter.

"I have been thinking along a similar line when Henry did himself in."

A thin smile came to his lips.

"Henry never liked Weyer, so it's strangely ironic."

"I don't find it that amusing that the master would let us hang like that. The Shadows covered for our friends."

Underhill rolled up the paper noisily and threw it in the trash.

"Really! I seem to recall losing Marie and Betty when Andras came forth."

"That was different. Marie thought everything we did was for her amusement. Betty was the leader. We both know that Andras couldn't allow someone who disagreed with him. Everything is contrary now. We used to run the damn city. We could take any woman and man we wanted to enjoy and kill. Now, Andras uses us as his personal chattel." He spat out.

"The harem is his advisers. Do you want to bet on those roasted alive for his damn festival won't include us?"

Phillip gave him a faint smile.

"I won't take that bet. You never complained before."

He waited for the man's glare.

"Listen, I agree with you. You saw the headline this morning. Another prominent family of Oyster City is missing, and the police believe Lance Carrol remains involved. Andras appears intent upon remaking this city as a living hell on earth. But he tells us nothing. He doesn't want to listen when I tell him that this chaos makes us no friends in the capital."

He scratched at his temple thoughtfully.
~~~

"It reminds me of what Henry La Spina told me about the first time Andras rose. He said the state militia overran Oyster City and executed everyone involved. The governor feared the citizens would match on the capital."

Underhill shook his head.

"That's not something told to me."

"But think about why our parents never discussed it. It shows a weakness in Andras. He loves using fear and intimidation in his torment. He doesn't understand that people will resist if they can. You can see it's not something our ancestors wanted to bring up. It was only about power and control."

Phillip replied as he started tapping his finger on the counter.

"I wonder if this is a repeat like last time. Andras admitted to rising from his world before. He's not the type to return to Hell on his own. We know the faithful who follow him remained limited in numbers. We can't take over the state."

"Do you really believe it?" There was a trace of hope in Marion's question.

Phillip shrugged.

"Who knows? It just struck me when I remembered a conversation between Andras and Doctor Wolfe. Some politicians in the capital are nervous about the events in this city. Maybe they'll send the troops if this place gets bad enough. They did it once before. It allowed our families to survive."

"No, you're reaching." Marion shook his head. "Andras brought out his Witches of Lamia. The next sacrifice in the moonlight will bring more evil into the world. You heard him; the burning of victims brings him a new form. He'll no longer need your brother's body to exist. It means he'll become immortal among us. It's past our ability to stop it."

Underhill looked up as the bell rang. It was the postman. He automatically waved as the man dropped off the mail.

"These witches are not infallible," Smyth continued. "They let the Singsing ring leave town. Now, they must scramble to find it. There's always the possibility he'll never get it."

"What does that matter to us? We'll end up like Weyer. Reviled by our family and awaiting execution. If we don't end up as a blood sacrifice."

Underhill's continued complaints irritated Phillip.

"Then what do you propose? Do you want to stand up to Andras? The witches would use our blood to stay young, as Andras slowly killed us by torture."

Smyth glanced over. Marion's expression told him the answer.

"You'd think we no longer believed in self-preservation since our souls are already damned. Damned by our parents and their ancestors who now drown in his world of pain and agony."

Phillip sighed.

"If Henry were still alive, I'd ask him. I know he felt as we do."

"What about his estate? Maybe he left papers or a journal?" Underhill suggested. "He was kind of the historian among us. Henry liked to talk about our ancestors and the past of Oyster City. You saw his reaction after Henry got married this last time. Peter Smyth helped kill the bishop's first wife, and then Henry stood up to Andras about that ugly woman he married. It was unbelievable."

"Yeah, the irony isn't lost on me. But it didn't do him much good. Andras raped him, along with his bride. The master's intent always includes humiliation as part of his control."

Phillip reminded him of the events during the day of the wedding.

"Hell, we took turns with Myrna that day," Underhill agreed. "Just did as our master commanded. It wasn't just to humiliate her. It was to save our skin. We've changed from masters of this city to the mice working for Andras."

Phillip reluctantly nodded at the idea.

"Henry was the type who didn't like being pushed around. Something he said the last time I saw him strikes me. He vowed to Andras that he'd make things right. I wonder if he made a deal with someone up in the capital to look at our city?"

The man slapped the counter lightly.

"Damn it; I think that makes sense. Henry recognized Andras would not let him live as a cripple. And we know Henry helped to capture Weyer. Someone tied him up. They didn't kill him. It sounds like his ally is a person who believes in justice."

Smyth paused at his thought.

"Henry was pretty devious in his way. If he were afraid of the Shadows coming for him, he would probably go to the one person we'd never expect."

Phillip glanced over at Marion.

"Who was the one man Henry feared the most?"

"You mean that detective, ah, Irish?" Underhill shook his head. "I don't know about that. La Spina knew Andras wanted that detective dead."

"Maybe you're right," Phillip agreed with a shrug. "I'll check Henry's stuff, then go over to the hospital. Maybe someone went to see La Spina before he killed himself."

"What will you do if you find out?" Underhill's eyes widened at the idea.

"Maybe a way to keep Andras under our control?" Phillip started for the door.

"You know there's always another option according to the myths of Henry's church," the jeweler reminded his friend.

Phillip turned back from the door.

"No, it can't happen. Remember that the foul Almighty struck down our families with blindness on the way from Sodom. We must bring this world down."

He opened the door.

"Our lot has always been to serve those from Hell. We must find a better demon as an ally, not a master."

~~~

As Phillip Smyth left, he paid no attention to the pretty lady who walked past him to enter the jewelry store. Edna Ackroyd pushed through the door, where she saw a good-looking man standing at the back. She casually looked over the items in the display cases.

"May I help you?"

Marion Underhill came over to the display. She looked at his rehearsed smile and returned it.

"Yes, I'm helping a friend."

The woman pulled the receipt that Ray had left with her on the day of Della's death. She handed the paper to Underhill.

"My friend was with a gentleman who purchased a piece of jewelry for her. However, she tells me she never received it. I was wondering if you could tell me more about the item."

His puzzled expression slowly changed as he looked over the receipt.

"I'm afraid it was a ring that this person ordered. He put a down payment on it, then returned the next day and canceled the order." He handed the paper back to Edna.

"You see, he paid in full. On the back, you can see the terms for our special designs."

Edna feigned a look of confusion.

"Oh, yes. How stupid of me not to look closer. I'm afraid my friend is distraught over this."

Underhill nodded sympathetically.

"I'm afraid people are not always as they seem. I recall them coming into the store. They spent a while picking out an engagement ring."

He let out a sigh.

"Such people waste everyone's time."

"It just makes a person angry," Edna confided.

"Did you know the gentleman?"

"Most certainly not!" He looked offended.

She smiled sweetly.
~~~

"I'm sorry, of course not. What I meant was this receipt had no address. I would like to get this person a piece of my mind. You wouldn't have his address, would you?"

Marion shook his head.

"I'd love to help, but the customer didn't leave it."

Disappointed, Edna thanked the man for his help. She turned for the door.

"Miss, what's your name? I'm happy to call you if I see him again. Or perhaps we could get together for drinks."

Edna glanced back with a grin.

"The name's Reece. Thanks for the offer. Maybe I'll stop in again sometime with my boyfriend."

As the woman walked down the street, she enjoyed the perplexed expression that she left on Marion's face.

~~~

It was on the second day in Boston that Irish finally got the dental records of Greye La Spina. The bulk of his information came from a private detective that had the unenviable name of Phillip Dick. Irish showed up at the detective's rundown office only a few blocks from his hotel earlier that morning.

Dick's eyes lit up like a green Christmas tree when Irish laid out the money he owed for the work. The short man with a belly and chubby cheeks quickly rolled up the bills and stuffed them in his pocket.

"This Greye woman was some dame," Dick told him. "As you told me in your letter, she barely stayed ahead of the law with her scams and cons. The last partner was Sydney Green, but you knew that."

The shamus leaned over and rubbed his feet as Ray stood by the dust-covered window.

"I looked for your woman by her maiden name of Pendexter, but that didn't pan out. I don't know if you heard that Greye used a lot of aliases as she ran with her partner."

"Yeah, some of it. Cat looked her up using some reporter friends out here." Ray momentarily saw the image of his dead partner in the window.

"You could have saved yourself some cash if you used her for this." Dick put his shoe back on.

"She's dead. What about Greye!"

The fat man glanced over, then picked up a file that he flipped across his desk.

"You can see her trail here. Her last address was over in East Boston. I couldn't find anything under her maiden name or the aliases you gave me. Then, I got an idea. She was trying to look like a big shot for that church scam. Why not
~~~

act like a married teetotaler who never misses church on Sundays? People are less likely to consider you're a grifter when you have a married name."

The detective leaned back in his chair with a sense of triumph. Irish nodded and glanced over.

"Not a bad idea. What did you get?"

"Green was the name that worked! They got simple and just used her partner's last name. I found out that she and her partner went down to city records and pulled the marriage certificate of a dead couple with the same last name. A couple of changes to the dates, and they made the swindle work for them."

Ray went to the desk and picked up the folder.

"Yeah, it looks like you got it."

"Now all you got to do is find a dentist," Phillip Dick grinned as he put his hands behind his head. "I'd suggest a few blocks around her old address."

Dick had it right. Irish found the dentist late in the day as he walked along Bennington Street.

Dr. Aleksander Khrkhryan's office was close to where Greye stayed in the low-rent district of East Boston. It took twenty dollars to get the aging dentist to retrieve the files for a Greye Green. However, it beat trying to get a court order on a hunch and no official police investigation. The brief conversation between the two men confirmed that Irish finally found what he sought. His key to proving Greye La Spina died in Oyster City, most probably at her husband's hands.

As Ray walked to the subway, that would take him back to the North End. He passed the diverse shops run by new immigrants, combined with the older waves of people arriving in the country. The wafting aroma of various restaurants got his belly to rumble. However, a smile crossed his face.

Maybe now, Greye can get some rest!

Then, his next steps concerning Orella came to his mind, and his expression turned dark.

<div style="text-align:center">~~~</div>

When they finished their day of sightseeing in downtown Boston, Orella and her mother returned to Hotel Manger. They stopped by the desk for messages, but there were none for them.

"You know he's not likely to let you know what he's doing." Yana led them to the elevators.

"Mother, it's been a great day," Orella let out a sigh. "Why do you have to spoil it? Ray's here on business. We'll see him for dinner."

"Perhaps, but do you like what he does? Be honest, dear. Can you enjoy being left alone, knowing nothing until he comes back either beat up or with another bullet in him?"

"Of course not," the girl snapped, then hesitated. "It's not like it happens all the time. His job can turn dangerous."

"Yes, we both know that. But it doesn't make you happy. You've had one day with him, and he's already hard at work on a case that's he's already blown the money he received. Think about it! He's solving the case of a woman who's dead and her husband committed suicide. Ray told us that. While it appears admirable, it's not smart for his business. But that's who he is."

"You don't know that!"

Yana smiled at her daughter as the elevator opened.

"Orella, I know more than you think. Can you see yourself back in Oyster City in that shack of an office? Two years from now, he'll still be there. You know Ray will never give it up."

"Yes, he will for me," Orella confidently stated as she entered the empty compartment.

"And what's Ray supposed to do then? He's found something he's good at, but we both understand that it's not right for you. He's not right for you."

Yana pressed the button to their floor. Orella faced her mother.

"Alright, we're not a perfect match. We have our problems. Maybe I'm not happy with him all the time. But why do you keep trying to get me away from him?"

She looked at Yana's face. There was something in the back of Orella's mind that bothered her.

"I'd think you're jealous if I didn't know better."

"Orella, I'm your mother. I'm trying to ensure your happiness."

However, Yana's eyes betrayed her, and Orella recognized it. They went quiet, then the doors of the elevator opened.

"It's alright. I understand." Orella said.

~~~

Well before dawn, Irish quietly knocked on the hotel door of Yana Dela Cruz. She opened the door, surprising Irish with her dress instead of nightclothes. She scrutinized the man dressed in his suit, reaching up to adjust his fedora.

"Do you want me to explain?" she asked when she glanced down at the suitcase in his hand.

"No need. I left her a note."

"I'll go with you to the terminal." Yana stepped into the hallway.

"Suit yourself," Ray told her, then went to the elevator.

On the silent ride to the lobby, neither person looked at each other. It wasn't until they were in the open concourse of the terminal that Yana finally spoke.

"What time's your train?"
~~~

"6 am," he replied.

"You'll have a long wait. That's over an hour."

"Yeah, I woke up for the dog watch, I guess." He yawned. "I figured since I'm the cad, I might as well go out with a bang. Besides, she's an early riser."

"You don't need to hate me," Yana told him.

"Why? Does it matter?" Irish glanced over.

He shrugged at her silence.

"It's the right decision. Orella needs to find a place in the world that doesn't have this shamus tied to her."

"She told me you'd quit such work for her."

She looked over for his response.

"No, she's wrong. I'm not cut out for a 9 to 5 job. It's been tried." Ray recognized the satisfaction in his statement.

"Besides, you're not happy with me being around her. There's always another danger if you stay around me too long," Irish continued as they came to a stop at the junction into the massive open lobby of the terminal.

"I don't know what you mean." Yana looked up at him.

"Really?"

Ray sat his suitcase down; then, he came close to her. Yana let him pull her close. When he kissed her, instead of resisting, she wrapped her arms around his neck and kissed him back. When they pulled away, the man and woman kept their gaze.

"Don't ever kid yourself. We would want this every time we meet. It's a shame that you know me too well."

He gave her a smug grin.

"It's not love!" Yana insisted through moist eyes that glinted in the terminal light.

"Maybe not. Maybe it could be, but it can't happen."

His tone lowered as he turned away.

"We have tickets to different destinations. Yana, you take care of yourself."

After taking a step, he looked back.

"Please help Orella understand it was my fault that it came to this point."

Yana watched the one man she cared for walk out of sight. She turned and went back to the hotel.

~~~

"Come on, my pet. It's time to leave with me!"

"No!"
~~~

Orella woke up, unable to move. Her eyes shifted to the left, and she saw Merle lying next to her. Then she felt a hand on her left breast. Pas caressed her with a smile.

Orella tried to yell, but only a pathetic grunt sound escaped her mouth.

"Oh, I can smell the man who took you earlier. Where is he? I want to kill him slowly."

Merle looked at her sister. Pas went to the open closet door.

"He must have left before we arrived. There are no men's clothes in here," Pas replied.

She looked back at Orella. The woman wore a long black dress like Merle, with a rope tied around her waist. Leather bags hung from her belt.

"Oh, you're surprised to see us." Merle turned her prisoner's head back to her. "This is your new world. A sprinkle of the right things will hold a mortal under my power. Soon, we'll turn you into our loyal servant."

Her evil smile turned into a frown.

"Unfortunately, Andras wants you to serve him first. But when he's finished with you, we'll have an eternity to enjoy ourselves."

Orella's panicked expression caused the witch to chuckle. Merle ran her finger around the prisoner's lips.

"With this spell, you become the grunting beast of your nature. Notice the sudden sensation in your loins when I do this."

The witch leaned over and gave the captive woman a deep, probing kiss. To Orella's shock, she responded as their tongues met. The prisoner arched her hips into the air.

"You see, a world of unbridled lust without restrictions. Mortals please us and die for our beauty. You will soon think of nothing more than pleasing me. And we have another hour before we must go."

"The master wants her first," Pas warned her sister. "He'll not accept another error on our part. We should prepare her to glide with us into the night."

Merle frowned, then nodded.

"Sister, you're correct. Hand me the flask, and you get the mother. He didn't say that we couldn't have her for our pleasure. Orella can watch and learn."

Merle chanted as she unbuttoned the woman's pajama top. Pas watched as her sister spread the liquid across the victim's breasts. Orella reacted, her breathing coming in spasms. Merle pulled a jeweled dagger from the belt around her waist. She made a series of cuts into the chest of her prisoner. Each cut sent Orella into ecstasy. Tears flowed from her eyes while her hips jerked into the air.

"Oh, she'll do fine," Pas agreed.

The witch suppressed the urge to lick the flowing blood. Instead, he looked at the scars on their captive's abdomen.

"My, our little girl's already experienced the exquisite taste of pain," she told Merle.

The twin witch picked up Sally's severed hand, which held a burning candle in the palm. She looked over as Merle ran her fingers along Orella's scars.

"We'll bring more of this to you for your pleasure," she purred as the creature enjoyed the tears flowing along her victim's cheeks.

"Relax, you'll think you have the wings of an angel in your temporary form. Only the memories of what we do to your mother will follow."

After leaving the room, Pas followed the blue flame's direction as it led her to the place of her prey. When she got to the door, her face dropped. The blaze turned black. Perplexed, the witch lightly knocked on the door. No sound came from inside the room. The witch found an unlocked door before she stepped inside the lit room.

The bitch is gone!

Pas went back to the hallway, where she noticed the flame pointed toward the elevator. She went to the closed doors and heard the machinery kick on when the elevator started its ascent. Pas paused for a moment before returning to Orella's room.

As Yana stepped off the elevator, she turned to her room, and movement near the end of the hallway caught her eye. The woman stopped in disbelief. For a moment, Yana thought she saw Merle. She shook her head and went to the door of her room.

It was open.

Fear and panic filled Yana as she started toward Orella's room.

"I know you're fighting me inside," Merle told Orella as she ordered to sit in an upright position.

"But you see how much your body enjoys the potion. Before long, you'll lose any will. I told you, pet, you're mine to do as I please. I have so many delicious things you'll do for me.

"Sister, transform her to leave with us," Pas said as she entered the room. "The mother is not there. The hand pointed me to the elevator. It's impossible to go to each floor to search for her."

Merle sighed.

"That's too bad. She would be a nice sacrifice."

She turned back to Orella.

"Isn't that interesting? Your mother went to another room. I wonder if she's a whore like her daughter?" The woman cackled.

"Now rise, my lovely. We'll fly home so you can meet Andras and bleed for us."

Orella obediently rose from the bed. Tears streamed down her cheeks as she felt her satin pajama shirt drop to the floor. The warm blood trickled from her wounded breast, and she felt a strange sensation in her bones and muscles.

"Yes, that's right, my pet. We'll go into the roof for the night sky to envelop us."

Then Orella saw Yana walk into the room. Unable to do anything, she could only watch her mother's expression of shock, that quickly changed into horror.

Without hesitation, Yana stepped next to the bar console as the witch's remained focused on her daughter. She picked up the heavy liquor decanter, then slammed the glass container into the back of the witch's head.

The sound of an audible thud followed the noise of shattering glassware. Pas made no sound when she collapsed to the floor.

"Oh, mother's here to play!" Merle cooed when she turned.

"Get away from my girl, you filthy bitch!" Yana yelled out while still holding the neck of the crystal glass out.

Merle started toward the mother, glancing down at her sister. She hesitated, and her shocked reaction made Yana look down.

Instead of a young woman at her feet, the creature had gray hair, and a face filled with deepening wrinkles. Her open eyes stared in disbelief at Yana.

With a raging howl, Merle attacked Yana. She whipped out a dagger, and the blade sliced into the woman's side. Yana held her ground. The broken glass in her hand missed Merle's neck, but it gouged a deep wound into the witch's shoulder.

Merle's scream pulled Orella from her trance. Able to move, the woman immediately jumped on Merle's back to protect her mother. The witch screeched at the assault. Orella's scratching fingers ripped at her face as Merle grabbed Orella's hair. With a sudden flip, Merle sent the woman over her shoulder like a rag doll. Orella's body sailed past Yana, landing hard against the open door, slamming it shut.

Grabbing the silver tray from the table with both hands, Yana whipped around and struck Merle in the back. The glancing blow failed to stop the witch. She came around with her knife and caught Yana in the arm. As the two women looked for an advantage, Merle glanced over at a dazed Orella. Her daughter struggled to get on her feet while using the door frame for support.

Sensing an opportunity, Merle lunged. Yana backed away. However, the witch went after Orella. The creature pushed up against the young woman and plunged her knife blade into Orella's ring hand. Orella's agonized scream filled the room while she watched two of her fingers flip across the floor. The dagger remained embedded in the door frame. After Orella pushed her attacker away, she grabbed her mangled hand.

Merle went after her again. This time, Yana slammed the heavy tray in the back of the head. The witch fell face-first onto the floor. Yana hurried to her daughter, pulling her away. They fell on the bed. Then Yana grabbed the phone.

As Yana pounded on the switch, shouting for help, Merle slowly rose to her feet. Her bloody face showed her desperation as the skin quickly aged. The witch clutched at the bag tied to her belt while desperately glancing at the embedded dagger. Yana dropped the phone, retrieving the silver platter. She stood in front of her moaning daughter. Outside the room's door, they heard shouts and murmurs in the hallway.

Knowing she lost her advantage, Merle reacted. She scooped up the Singsing ring along with Yana's fingers before flinging open the room door. When the blood-covered witch burst into the hallway, the shocked onlookers quickly moved aside.

Halfway to the exit, one man stepped in front of the witch to stop her. Merle pitched a white powder into his face. Instantly, the man screamed as he grabbed his face. Merle's wild cackles filled the air as she escaped through the door leading to the stairwell.

The dying man's screams turned to death gurgles as his body writhed across the carpet. The incredulous onlookers turned away, some growing sick from the stinking smoke that lifted from the man's burning flesh.

Inside the room, Yana dropped the platter. She held her side, suddenly noticing the amount of blood covering her blouse. Then, Yana collapsed next to her daughter.

"Someone, please get a doctor!" Orella desperately cried out.

As she tried to wrap her satin robe around her bleeding hand, the bloody, half-naked woman glanced up. She noticed no one moved among the curious onlookers, who peeked into the room from the hallway.

"Damn it, get a doctor!" Orella screamed at them.

Chapter 6: Turn of the Screws

Boston Detective Barry Ryan arrived on the 10th floor of the Hotel Manger just after sunrise.

"What have we got?" the detective yawned at the patrolman. He saw the body in the hallway covered with a sheet. It was a couple of doors down from the open door where the policeman stood.

"You're gonna love this one. When our first men arrived, we had guests in a panic, a lot of them hiding in their rooms. The hotel detective was the first one on the scene. He found that body over there; then, he finds the room where the whole thing started. Two women with multiple stab wounds."

The policeman pointed his thumb behind him.

"A guest who is a physician on vacation treated the women before the ambulance arrived."

He looked up from his notes before he followed the detective over to the body. Ryan sniffed the air.

"Is that white phosphorus?"

The policeman shrugged as Ryan kneeled and pulled back the sheet of the body. Then the detective covered his mouth. Mostly blackened, burned muscle stretched tight over the skull remained.

"Damn, his face is gone." he put the sheet back over the head. He looked up at the policemen, who was taking notes.

"Phosphorus never did that in Tarawa. It looks more like napalm to me. Poor bastard! You say he was a guest?"

"Yeah, Room 1009. Salesman out of Detroit by the name of Pepper."

Ryan nodded as he stood and looked around. Bits of white powder on the floor around the victim remained. The detective stooped over and touched the residue.

"Son of a bitch," he yelled out while wiping his injured index finger on his coat.

Ryan hurried over to the water fountain and ran water over the blistering area. After a moment, he inspected the blistering area.

"Get the lab boys down here and find out what the hell that is," he ordered his partner. "And keep people away from this area."

Tenderly wiping his finger with his handkerchief, the detective came back to the body.

"Where's the medical examiner?"

"He's on the way. I have some men taking statements from the guest. You need to see the room where they found the women. You're not going to believe it."

The detective waved his finger in the air, trying to cool down the burn as he walked back to Orella's room.

"Alright, when doc gets here, find out what his thoughts are about the guy with no face."

Ryan avoided the bloodstains on the floor and carpet as he walked into the bloody room and stopped in his tracks. By the bed was a desiccated corpse. He guessed it was a woman in an advanced state of decomposition.

"It looks like a damn slaughterhouse in here. What the hell is this?"

"The two women in the hospital claim this corpse walked in with her identical sister and attacked them," the policeman explained. "The mother used that shattered decanter to kill this one. It seems to match up with the evidence here."

Ryan barely listened as he carefully approached the nightstand, where a severed hand still held the remains of a burned-out candle.

"Oh, that's another crazy part of this. The young woman claims the old ladies brought that thing with them to find her."

"I take it you've already got them scheduled for a head shrink?" Ryan looked at his fellow cop.

"I thought that at first. According to witnesses, after they heard the women screaming, they witness a woman who appeared to turn older as she ran down the hall. They also claim that she threw a white powder into the face of the dead man when he tried to stop her."

The patrolman looked up from his notes to move away from the evidence on the floor.

"Do you believe them?"

Detective Ryan looked down at his throbbing finger.

"Son of a bitch, what the hell is going on?"

He lifted his hat and looked over the scene.

"We'll need lab guys looking over the splatter details. Maybe this is some damn cult thing."

"Oh, yeah, that reminds me. Take a look over by the door," the policeman pointed at the entrance to the room.

Orella's dried blood revealed where she slid down. The jeweled dagger remained embedded in the frame.

"One victim is missing two fingers, and the evidence here matches her description of the events. These old ladies wanted the ring the woman wore. She claimed the woman that escaped stole the ring along with the fingers. You can see where the fingers were, and they're missing."

"Are you kidding me?" Ryan went to the door and looked around the floor.

He saw the bloodstained bare footprint on the tile by the door.

"Where did this person escape to?"

The man with the notes frowned and shook his head.

"I'll have to show you this."

The two men cautiously stepped out of the room and went down the hall to the stairwell.

"She went upstairs," the patrolman stated. "We've checked every room from this floor to the roof. There's no sign she went down. I don't know how you can fake what I'm going to show you."

"And you haven't found her yet?" The detective grumbled, as the case was already giving him a headache.

"You can follow the footprints and blood trail yourself," the patrolman went up the stairs.

When they reached the Hotel Manger roof, the morning light fully revealed the trail to the side of the building. The faint outline of a bloodstained handprint showed on the ledge. Detective Ryan looked down at the busy street below.

"I thought they burned all the witches in Salem a couple of hundred years ago," the patrolman stated.

"Don't joke about this."

"Who's joking? I heard a call from dispatch earlier tonight with some lady in the building a few blocks away claiming to see human bats flying by. I figured it was just some crazy with too much hooch. Now..."

Ryan looked over at his comrade's serious expression. He glanced at the blister on his fingertip, then looked over the area one more time. He took a deep breath as he made a decision.

"The official report will state that a woman killed the man after attacking three women in the room. One old woman died of her injuries. The fugitive escaped down the fire ladder from the roof. Get your ass back down there and make sure we cover those bodies and remain that way. None of this gets out to the damn newspapers. I'll make sure the coroner's report matches the story."

~~~

When Arizona finished his drive into Oyster City, it was late in the afternoon. The long journey meant he had plenty of time to think. To his surprise, his thoughts kept coming back to a skinny blonde who remained on his farm back in West Virginia. In some way, he felt a sense of betrayal to Cat's memory.

However, when he reached the state line, Arizona buried any thoughts he once had for Cat as nothing more than a pipe dream. Instead, he focused on his future. When he saw the welcome sign on the outskirts of Oyster City, the ex-cop realized how much he hated the city. Thoughts of a simple life crowded out a need to avenge Cat.

I've already taken out her killer.

When Arizona passed the police station and saw Oyster City Hall, he remembered.

Peter Smyth! The bastard who set the whole damn thing in motion.
~~~

He drove straight to his apartment. The shamus thought about checking in with the answering service, then shook off the road weariness. The shamus leaned back in his favorite chair with his last beer.

Arizona jolted went the phone rang. He looked over with a scowl. On the third ring, he picked up.

"Rumor has it that anyone who's friends of Irish are on the hot seat with the police," a familiar voice told him.

"What else is news?" He replied with a yawn.

"It's worse, like the old west now. Even the criminals have a bounty on you and your friend."

There was a click in his ear.

"Son of a bitch," Arizona thought as he immediately went to the window and looked out. He saw nothing unusual, but his tiredness evaporated.

The old west? That means dead or alive!

Less than fifteen minutes later, the ex-cop drove out of the parking lot. He kept a careful eye on the lookout for someone tailing him. After a couple of quick turns down alleys, Arizona determined he was clear. He kept trying to think of a place where he could lie low until Irish returned. Anything outside of town would be a long drive, but it might work. However, he needed to warn Ray.

The motel outside of town was close, but he instantly dismissed the idea. It was a known hot spot for prostitutes and members of Jacobi's old gang. Too many people would recognize him.

They'd just as soon put a bullet in me! The question is, where can I hide in plain sight?

As he drove along Chandler Avenue, a grin suddenly crossed his face. He drove past a familiar rundown building with a faded sign above the door before turning into a side street. After coming to a dead-end, Arizona backed his car into a spot between buildings. The police were unlikely to come down the alley, and his vehicle remained out of sight from the street.

Arizona carried his suitcase to the white door of an office. After unlocking the door with Ray's key, the shamus entered the office owned by Oyster City. The former Director of Public Works, J. Allan Dunn, used the place for storage. Shelves filled with boxes of municipal codes and legal documents needed to construct public projects within the city. He also used it as a second office to store all the illegal activities he coordinated with the former mayor. With the death of Dunn, only Ray and Arizona knew about the place.

"What better place to hide than a place owned by this corrupt city?" he said aloud in the dingy room as he went to the large desk.

As he sat his suitcase on the desk next to the phone, he picked up the receiver. The buzzing confirmed the line still worked.

More taxpayer money spent by Dunn!

He glanced back at the tiny restroom.

Too bad he didn't think to put in a shower.

Arizona tapped his fingers on the desktop, yawning as he looked around. The size of the room was sufficient, but the number of boxes was nearly overwhelming. After deciding on the best way to fit a cot into the room, the man pulled down the dusty boxes. When he reached the second box, he glanced down at the receipts from dummy accounts that Dunn set up for the mayor and Peter Smyth as the district attorney. The evidence remained neatly stacked on the desk where the ex-cop left them. Then another idea struck him, and the grin returned.

I can wait to clean this place up!

Arizona dumped out a box of papers related to old municipal codes and put the evidence inside the box. For the next hour, he went through other packages, which showed evidence of the scandal going on within Oyster City. The detective soon needed another box to put all the contracts with dummy companies and the handwritten ledgers that Dunn kept. As he quickly reviewed the material, Arizona realized that the Director of Public Works intended to have an escape clause to keep going to jail. The shamus held enough information to bring in state auditors. That would lead the Attorney General to clean house in Oyster City.

Sometimes, payback is hell!

After hauling the boxes to his car, Arizona went back to the office and called Ray's office. The messaging service picked up, and he left a warning for Irish. Then Arizona locked the door to the office before he drove away.

~~~

It was after dinner time when the Boston train stopped at the station in Oyster City. Ray stepped off the train from the opposite side of the terminal. Then he walked around the back of the passenger rail line with a suitcase in hand. By the time he reached his car, the shamus was confident no one followed him.

The reason for his caution came from information gained when he changed trains in Baltimore. He spent the rest of his spare cash calling the office for messages. The woman on the end of the line carried a voice that reminded him of nails on a chalkboard.

The first message came from Pappy, who stated he had something important for Ray. The fact that his friend had never called his office before left Irish with concern. His other messages did not get better.

Senator Reece asked Ray to meet with him at his estate upon his return. Also, he received a call from Edna, but there was no message. According to the woman reading her notes, his last call came from Gladys Peer. She insisted on his immediate attention.

The yellow flames caught his attention as he turned the corner to Pappy's newsstand. Standing outside of the stone facade of the Farmer's Trust building, the burning structure carried no danger to the other building. Irish pulled to a stop near
~~~

the flames. He saw men running away when he got out of the car. While Pappy's life's work went up in flames, Ray yelled out for his friend.

Irish saw a body on the ground near the corner of the Farmer's Trust. He ran over to find his friend groaning. As he helped Pappy turn over to his back, Irish didn't recognize his badly beaten friend. Then the man beamed a smile.

"I gave them some of it back!"

"Damn right you did. Stay still; I'll get you an ambulance."

Pappy grabbed Ray's coat.

"No! That'll make it worse. Get me to your car."

Irish paused at the idea.

"Come on, Ray. I'll be alright."

The sound of approaching sirens reached Irish as he practically carried his friend to the car. Ray helped him into the passenger seat.

"We'll find a doctor for you," the shamus told him as he got in the car.

However, Pappy refused.

"Just take me to my place. The cops will grab you if you hang around here."

With a scowl, Irish drove away. The fire truck passed them as Ray turned down the street toward his friend's apartment.

"Who did this to you?"

"They looked like they came from the docks. Maybe longshoremen, by the way they talked. They called me names and all, but I've dealt with real racists before. I think someone paid them to run me off." Pappy lightly dabbed at his cheek, then grimaced.

"Still, a few didn't like the color of my skin."

"Who the hell would pay people to burn your place and beat you? You've been there for years. That makes no sense."

"I agree; it's not like another newsstand is going up across the street," his friend stated. "This is about you."

Irish glanced over.

"You mean Andras?"

Pappy's silence confirmed his suspicion.

When they got to his apartment, Ray helped Pappy to the building. A gray-haired black lady in a floral pattern dress saw them. She hurried to the door and opened it for them.

"What have they done?" she asked before turning her glare on Irish.

"Maggie, don't you fret now. I'm alright. Some punks didn't like my newsstand. Ray's my good friend, and he's helping me."

Still suspicious, the woman put her hand on the injured man's shoulder.

"Alright, Pappy, you just let me know if you need anything. We can return the favor to those white devils, by God!"

As the woman walked away, Irish noticed her words sounded similar to those who beat Pappy because of his color.

"Don't pay her no mind. They beat up her boy a few months back for being in the wrong neighborhood."

"Damn place," Irish fumed as they trudged to the elevator.

Inside Pappy's apartment, Ray carefully put iodine on the worst scrapes. The patient sucked in breaths from the stinging pain. When he finished, Irish looked him over.

"I still say you need a doctor. They might have done some damage inside your belly."

Pappy nodded.

"If I promise to have my nephew, Joshua, take me, will you quit acting like my Emma?"

"It's a deal," the shamus growled.

He helped Pappy to the couch and ordered him to rest. Ray took a seat near him and leaned back in the chair. Irish pulled the manila envelope that contained the evidence that he collected during his trip to Boston. He laid it on the coffee table like a trophy.

"Well, here it is, the evidence to put Greye's ghost to rest and her husband in jail. I guess it was worth the trip, but I'm down to my last dollar," Ray told his friend.

Pappy frowned when he looked over at Ray.

"You don't know. Bishop La Spina's dead. He committed suicide the night before you left."

Irish stared in disbelief.

"Is that what you didn't tell me before I left?"

Pappy nodded.

"Damn it, just when I had his ass in a sling," Ray complained. "Why didn't you say something?"

"Did you get Orella away from Oyster City for good?"

"How did you know I did that?"

The shamus carried the expression of a kid with a hand caught in the cookie jar.

"I'm no detective, but I didn't see her or the luggage in the car when you helped me to your car. You were leaving with her, so I put that together with the things you told me before."

He noticed Ray look the other way. Pappy carefully pulled a wooden cross from his coat. It had a leather strap attached to a necklace that dangled when he held it out to Irish.

"Don't fret; it was for the best," Pappy assured him.

"Yeah, I know, but it still makes me a heel how it came out."

"Well, that's the least of your problems. Andras is coming for you now. Take this! The pastor at my old church blessed it. Joshua brought it to me yesterday. I haven't introduced my nephew since he's staying with some friends. You know, he thinks his uncle's a bit strange since I talk with Emma."

Ray looked it over.

"Ah…thanks. But I'm not the church type."

"Hell, you think I don't know that?" Pappy scoffed. "Now, this is to keep you from those nightmares. In my reading about the first time Andras came to earth, thousands of people perished before they could drive him back to Hell. He controlled people to kill others, a kind of mind control. That's how he influences people. Comes in through their nightmares."

"Wait a minute; you told me that militia came to Oyster City and wiped out his followers before he could rise here."

"Yes, but it's a demon. Andras has risen many times. I found that out just before you left town. There was an ancient Chinese text by a guy name Ji Lin that Crowley had translated. *Broad Histories of Cursed Dynasties* only exists at the Smithsonian, and the only microfilm copy is hard to get. Believe it or not, Cat had your landlord call in a favor. They lent out the microfilm to the Oyster City library. However, I could only have it for a week."

Pappy saw the shadow cross Ray's face at the mention of his ex-partner.

"Anyway, I read through the darn manuscript, but I had to hurry. The text mentioned that hé lā sī, as Ji Lin called Andras, rose several times before. One time, it was in a land called Lusòng. That's the Philippines in Chinese. Isn't that where Orella is from?"

Irish dumbly nodded while he tried to comprehend the news.

"You mean—damn, that must explain why the Shadows were looking for the Singsing ring." Ray slammed his hand on the chair arm. "They must need it for Andras."

"It's as good an idea as any," Pappy conceded.

Irish stretched and looked down at the cross necklace.

"What about this thing?"

"Emma tells me it's quite powerful. A lot like the Singsing ring. Pastor Adam fought demons before and cast them out of possessed people. He knows what's going on, but I'm afraid that he's too old and frail to travel here. He made sure to bless these with holy water and words from the good book."

Almost disregarding the idea, Irish put it in his coat pocket. Then he saw the expression on Pappy's face. He pulled the cross back out, took off his hat to slide the jewelry around his neck. He wasn't sure if it was the cross, but his downbeat mood improved.

"Sorry, I guess I need to remember my manners," he apologized.

"Ray, I know you've seen and done bad things. But don't think that there's not someone above trying to guide you in the right direction. You still believe Peter Smyth is Andras, don't you?"

Irish nodded.

"It's the only logical thing left in this whole crazy city. Too many things always point back to him. Still, it's hard to wrap my head around the idea of demons and such."

"Then, believe in the good to help you. And don't take that cross off." Pappy insisted.

His friend pulled out a duplicate that he wore under his shirt.

"Besides, I might write a column about how it's a great fashion accessory for Oyster City.

Ray grunted out a laugh, then stopped.

"What about your stand? What are you going to do?"

Pappy tried to smile through his bruised face.

"My Emma told me to quit this town. I guess I need to listen to her. Tonight proved I'm not as young as I remembered."

He looked around the apartment. His mind focused on all the memories that it held.

"Or maybe I'm not as brave as I pretend."

Both men jerked in their seats from the suddenly knocking at the door. They glanced at each other. Another knock came.

"Pappy, are you there? It's Arizona."

Irish rose to let the ex-cop into the apartment. Arizona went to the table and looked over the injured man.

"I drove by to warn you about things that were coming. Then, I saw your stand was gone. The fire truck was just leaving."

He placed his hand on the man's shoulder.

"I'm sorry."

He looked at Irish.

"I got a call when I got back to my place today. The warning came from Sirk. The way I took it, there are no rules now. Cops or thugs can kill you or me. Hell, it's what happened to Pappy as well. Friends caught in the crossfire as well."

Pappy nodded and thanked the man. Then he handed Arizona a copy of the necklace that he gave Irish.

"I'll tell you the same as Ray. Put this on to protect yourself from the evil in this city."

"I've got half a mind to drive over to Peter Smyth's home and put a bullet between his eyes," Ray fumed. "I'd like to see a demon get out of that one."

Arizona grinned at Pappy, whose expression remained serious.

"Ray, that's not how this will work. An evil sweeps across the city like a fire, cleansed, just like the Old Testament says."

"Well, not before I put some things to rest. Demon or not, I've already got wheels in motion. That'll put some heat on Peter Smyth and the rest of the city staff."

Arizona explained what he found at J. Allan Dunn's old office.

"Yeah, I remember those boxes of files. So what? Everybody knows most of the mayor's office is corrupt." Irish replied.

Arizona took off his hat and placed it on the coffee table. With a devious smile, he took a seat.

"Everybody except those at the top political offices in the state. You don't think like a cop. I just sent evidence to the Attorney General. He's as straight as they come. Plus, I hear that he's planning on running for governor in the future. Can you imagine the publicity that he'll stir up with taking down the corrupt city members of Oyster City, including the new Mayor and his cronies?"

Ray glanced at Pappy, who looked just as surprised.

"Then you expect the state officials to come into town pretty soon?" Irish slapped his leg. "I would love to see Smyth's expression when a bunch of coppers hauls him away."

"That means we need to lie low until this whole thing blows over," Arizona beamed. "I took up residence at Dunn's old office. The phone still works, and the electricity is on. I'm betting the city doesn't even know they're paying for it each month."

"What makes you think it's blowing over?"

Pappy suddenly interrupted.

The two men looked at him.

"What makes you think a demon cares about the police hauling him away? Andras seeks total control of Oyster City. The way my body feels tonight, I bet he's pretty close to achieving it. You said it yourself when you have to hide from the cops. Who are the good guys now?"

"Now, Pappy…"

"Stop this dream, Ray. You and Arizona don't understand. This creature lives for power and blood. I just told you that Andras rose into this world multiple times. Each time they've had to destroy Andras along with his followers. They don't care about life or death, so they will break those who try to stop him."

He looked at them.

"Do you really believe that such a creature will stop by someone arresting it?"

The room went silent at the newsy suggestion. As Pappy looked back and forth between the detectives, he recognized the disbelief in the ex-cop's eyes. It didn't surprise him. However, the struggle inside Irish was apparent. His friend didn't want to believe it. The newsy shook his head.

"Please leave," he told them. "I need to get some rest. I have to pack tomorrow."

The two men rose from the chairs and collected their hats. Ray picked up the packet holding Greye La Spina's identity.

"Alright, we're leaving. Pappy, call me if you need anything," Irish told him. "We'll keep the answering service through the end of the month."

The man absently nodded, his focus on the coffee table. After Arizona and Irish left, Pappy looked over at the empty chair across from him.

"I know Emma. They needed a kick in the butt. I just don't want them to get hurt. Andras has harmed so many."

He looked back at yesterday's newspaper lying on the couch.

"He's even hurt me in a way that I didn't think he could."

~~~

"I'm going to swing by the office and get some things," Ray told Arizona as they stood by the Nash. "Plus, I like your idea of hiding. I don't think anyone spotted me coming into town, but staying in another place should be safer."

"Alright, I'll see you there," Arizona walked over to his vehicle.

Irish watch him drive away, then glanced up at Pappy's apartment. After a deep breath, he got in his car and went back toward downtown Oyster City.

As Ray drove by his building on Peach Street, he saw a dark car parked across the street. The oncoming car headlights silhouetted the two men inside. Irish continued down the road. He looked in the mirror, but the car didn't try to follow him.

They're staking out my place now!

After taking a few extra blocks and doubling back to Chandler Ave, he turned into the alley that led to Dunn's office. He pulled in behind Arizona's car. As Ray got out, he saw the blinds moving from inside the office.

I guess we're all getting nervous!

Irish reached up and unscrewed the light bulb above the door until it went out before entering the office. Arizona was sitting behind the desk with an unlit Perfecto in his mouth. He had his feet up on an old army cot that was only partially assembled.

"Something wrong at our office?"

Ray nodded as he took off his hat and put it on a hook by the door.

"Yeah, a couple of toughs sitting in a car across the street. Can't tell if they're cops or thugs."

"Does it matter?"

"Not anymore, I guess," Irish replied with a growl. He pulled up a chair by the desk.

"Damn shame I had a good bottle of Irish whiskey in the office. I could use a snort."
~~~

Arizona pulled opened the drawer and pulled out a flask of rye. He handed the bottle to his partner.

"Why are we still here?"

Ray took the bottle and leaned back.

"Hell if I know, but it's a damn good question. I'm the one with the target more than anyone." He looked across the desk. Ray saw the man chomping on his cigar, which always showed Arizona was deep in thought.

"Did you take care of Myrna La Spina?" Ray asked.

His partner nodded.

"Yeah, nobody's going to find her. I left her on my family's farm. How did your trip go? I noticed Orella didn't come back with you. That was a smart move. She's a good kid. Maybe it'll help those nightmares she was having."

"Let's skip it," Ray took another drink. "We got enough problems in the daylight."

"Alright, I understand. I tell you; I'm getting jumpy. On the radio coming back, I heard a news report about some strange deaths in a Boston hotel. I immediately thought of you. Kind of trouble follows you."

Arizona's smile faded at the troubled expression on his partner's face.

"Why, what's up?"

Irish pulled back the bottle, then shook his head.

"Oh, nothing. You've got me jumpy. Are you planning on staying?" Ray asked.

Arizona stared at him for a moment. The same question he mulled over for a couple of days. Finally, he nodded.

"Yeah, I owe it to someone."

"You're a brave man, lieutenant."

Ray hoisted the bottle before taking a drink.

"No, but I don't see another option."

Irish sat the bottle on the desk.

"Like hell! Do you have any friends or family here? You're just like me. The only friends I have are you and Pappy. And I expect Pappy to be gone soon."

Arizona frowned at the comment.

"Yeah, I suppose. But I'm not the type to leave."

Ray nodded.

"That's the problem. Neither of us is going to take the sucker punch and walk away."

The ex-cop looked at him.

"Do you think Pappy's right? That evil is spreading over the town?"

"You wouldn't ask me unless you feel it as well," Irish observed, then picked up the bottle again. After a snort, he placed it on the desk.

"Listen, I'm mad about what this city has done to Pappy, Cat, Greye, Samantha, and all the rest. It comes down to one guy at the top who seems to manipulate it all, like he holds the strings to a puppet. I think we have to go straight after Peter Smyth. I wasn't joking when I want to see a bullet in his head."

"That's murder." Arizona reminded him.

"Is it? I call it self-defense."

He stared at his partner, who slowly shook his head.

"Oh, all right, I'm not a damn killer. But do you think your push to get the state investigators in here is going to work? Pappy was right about one thing. A demon won't play by our rules. I think it's just going to piss Smyth off. You can bet he's not stopping until we're out of here or dead."

"Well, maybe what I did might help. Someone who's getting hit from multiple angles doesn't think as clearly." Arizona said. "I say we keep up the pressure. Hell, we're doing that just by him putting people out to find us."

Ray frowned.

"You know, that's something I hadn't thought about. Kind of like we're the bait, and he can't be sure what we'll do next."

He looked down at the cross around his neck.

"If Pappy's right, Andras can't get inside our heads to figure out our next move."

"Yeah, I suppose that's correct. I'm not sure about this hocus-pocus stuff. Anyway, I still want to see what evidence I can turn up on the Andras estate. Assuming Bishop La Spina's book was honest, there's a lot of bodies stacked up around there."

The ex-cop leaned back in his chair.

"That's an angle that keeps the police hopping around. Maybe it keeps them out of our hair. The problem is the police know our cars, and they'll be looking for them. Nobody's sneaking up Andras Hill with the cops keeping a close eye on it."

The room went quiet as the men thought about their problems. Ray slid the bottle over to Arizona. Finally, Irish looked at his watch, then picked up the phone.

"I might as well see what Gladys Peer called me about."

His landlord picked up on the third ring.

"Thank you for returning my call, Mr. Irish," her nasal voice grated on his nerves. "I'm afraid to inform you that you must vacate your office by the end of the week!"

"What are you talking about? I've paid up through the next month."

"Well, I'm afraid that Mrs. Purvey requires a new tenant. Your reputation in Oyster City is unsuitable for the building."

Anger filled Irish at the news.

"Cut out using this pen name crap, Gladys. I write the rent checks to you. Are you saying someone is pointing heat in your direction?"

There was silence on the line, and then he heard her whispered voice.

"It's getting out of hand, Ray. Rumors fill the newspaper building. Even the reporters can't do stories about certain people now. Do you understand what I mean? Watch your back and get out of there. I'd hate to see you end up like Cat."

The woman hung up before he could reply. He looked at the handset before he placed it back on the base.

"The office and apartment are off-limits to us now," Irish looked over at his partner. "You know what? That son of a bitch Smyth is really getting me steamed."

~~~

Ray drove out of town in his Nash the next morning after an uncomfortable night sleeping in the chair. Worse, his new roommate had a terrible snore. The noise finally forced Irish out to his car, where he got a couple of hours of sleep.

When he called Reece, the servant told Ray that the politician would return home from the club around lunchtime. The shamus replied that he'd be there.

Before he left, Irish dropped Arizona off near Cat Bennett's apartment. The woman's gray Olds coupe remained in the parking lot since her death and burial. Ray watched as the ex-cop pulled down the visor before picking up the key that dropped in his lap. It took his partner a couple of minutes before he started the vehicle and then drove away.

Irish stopped off at a roadside diner at the edge of town for a cheap meal of toast and coffee. The owner behind the counter looked at him suspiciously, causing Ray to rub on his day-old beard. He realized his clothes showed he slept in them.

At least, I'm not back to being a bum yet.

The shamus took the morning paper off the counter and scanned the front page. The only items of local interest were the ammo ship's movement, along with a tidbit about Mrs. Purvey's last column for the *Beacon* would run on Friday.

Gladys Peer is leaving this damn place as well!

However, the story on page three nearly caused Irish to drop his coffee. The incident in Boston happened at the Hotel Manger on the morning he left town. His scowl deepened as Ray read the description of the attack on two females who went to the hospital by ambulance. Their names did not show in the story, but he knew. Irish carried no doubt in his heart that Andras or someone working for him went after Orella and Yana. The shamus did not bother to finish his toast. Instead, he left in shame and growing anger.

I'll get that son of a bitch Smyth or whatever he's called!

Ray sat in his car, staring out the window while his hands tightly gripped the steering wheel. He kept thinking about leaving Boston like a coward. His mind raced with self-doubt and second thoughts while he tried to think of a way to find out what had happened. The paper mentioned two deaths, a man and a woman.

Was it Yana or Orella? All I had to do was wait for another day to leave! Just one more day!
~~~

When the sweat dripping from his brow landed in his eye, the shamus finally came out of his trance. Rapidly blinking from the salt sting, Ray swiped his sleeve across his face. After seeing the time, Irish started his Nash.

On the way to Reece's house, he drove past the scenic overlook where Della had died. However, he refused to look over where she slipped off into the Chesapeake Bay. Instead, Irish looked over at the browning fields on the other side of the road. The heat of the morning coincided with the drought effects once he left Oyster City.

The sight bothered him as well. It reminded him of death. He tried to push away his guilt by focusing on his meeting with State Senator Reece. He wanted to know the purpose. As far as Ray was concerned, their business deal stopped when Della died.

A butler named Jensen answered the doorbell, then escorted the shamus to the library. As he approached the dark walnut desk, the servant closed the paneled doors.

"I got here as soon as I could, Senator. I apologize for the appearance."

The silver-haired man behind the desk came out of his thoughts. He looked tired and troubled. The man's gray eyes had dark rings, and his cheeks were pale. He glanced to his right by the window.

"Miss Ackroyd asked that I bring you into our conversation."

Ray's surprised expression when he glanced over at Edna caused her to smile at him.

"Hello, Mr. Irish. I'm glad you're back. The senator and I have an interesting idea that you might agree with."

Curiosity filled Ray as he looked at her walk over to the plush red velvet chair in front of the desk. Her white floral dress showed off her long, lean body. The woman removed her matching white gloves after she sat. He removed his hat and leaned on the back of the chair a few feet away.

"Well, you've got me here. However, I'm not sure what I can bring to your conversation."

Reece stood and went back to the shelves that lined the wall. He retrieved a leather-covered hardback. When he came to the desk, he opened the book to a page and pulled back the silk bookmark left between the pages.

"Yesterday, I buried my daughter. Despite our problems, Della meant the world to me," he told them as he scanned the page with his finger.

Reece glanced up at Irish.

"You know, of course, that I'm a widower. I have no one now. That's part of the reason I employed you to get my daughter."

"Listen, if…" Ray stood, frowning at the conversation.

"No, Ray," Edna interjected. "Please listen."

"Mr. Irish, I've spoken with Miss Ackroyd every night since…" He looked away to compose himself.

"Anyway, I don't hold you personally responsible for my daughter's death. Miss Ackroyd explained all that you did. You did as much as humanly possible."

He recognized Ray's skepticism.

"No, I mean that. I hold others responsible for what they did to my girl. I invited you here today because I have an idea."

He lifted his hand to silence Ray before he could reply.

"I came upon this passage the night that Della died. I don't know why I picked up a work of fiction." His face showed a hint of shame. "I suppose a good person might pick up the Bible."

Reece paused for a moment.

"Nevertheless, I read a few pages of Dumas, just to stop my thinking. You understand how easy it is to recriminate yourself when you have such heartache." The man wandered around the desk on Edna's side. "That's when I read this. I would like you to hear it."

"Life is a storm, my young friend. You will bask in the sunlight one moment, be shattered on the rocks the next. What makes you a man is what you do when that storm comes. You must look into that storm and shout as you did in Rome. Do your worst, for I will do mine!"

Della's father closed the book and handed it to Edna.

"How do those words strike you, Mr. Irish?"

With a perplexed expression filling his broad face, Ray came around the chair.

"I agree with the sentiments," he told the man as he slowly sat in the chair. "It's something that I understand."

"Of course you do! I didn't hire you from the phone book. I had an agency check into your background before you came into my home."

"But where are you leading? I'm not good with puzzles," Irish told him.

The politician laughed.

"I don't believe that. However, you're entitled to know what Miss Ackroyd and I were talking about."

He patted the woman on the arm, then stepped to the window.

"Ray, it's like this. That morning, a messenger dropped off pictures showing Della… well, you know what those images contained. The envelope had a note for the senator to call a telephone number."

"Which I did," the man interrupted. "And the smug bastard who answered told me he made a film of the entire night. I'd killed him if he were standing in front of me."

"Did you get any name or contact?" Ray asked.

Reece shook his head. The room went silent for a moment as they watched Reece staring out the window.

"I'm sorry, my dear. Please continue."

She turned to Ray.

"You see what's happening? Those responsible for Della's death threatened to turn over these pictures and film to ruin Mr. Reece. He's the leader of his party, so you can see where this is leading. It could ruin the senator."

Her expression turned bitter.

"What they did to Della and now this. They're truly evil men!"

Irish looked at her; his jaw muscle twitched from clenching his teeth. The men who beat him were the toughs, not the leader. Like those in the room, he wanted the leader.

"The senator is between the devil and the deep blue sea," Irish glanced at the man, still staring out the window.

"He gives in, and they own him. Tell him how to vote and all that stuff. If not, he's a political disaster for the party. They'll run like rats from any associations with him."

"I see you know popular music. It's a correct and concise way of laying out my dilemma. At one point, I considered a run to become governor. I suspect this has something to do with it."

"Why?" Irish watched the man. He felt a sense of the man's rage that he tried to bury.

"Because the person I spoke with showed that my bonus was becoming the Lieutenant Governor."

He turned around. His eyes were bright with a burning flash.

"I bury my only child, and that bastard calls it a bonus. I don't give a damn about a political office."

"You want revenge. That's the reason you quoted from the book."

"Correct, Mr. Irish. I want every single one of those bastards to pay for what they've done!"

"Well, I'm game to track them down," he nodded as he played with his fedora. "I'd love to see a little payback as well."

"Payback in blood," Reece told him.

Irish glanced at Edna. Her face showed her agreement. The shamus looked back at the man seeking revenge as he stood silhouetted by the light of the window. He understood what the man really wanted.

"I have a feeling that you're asking for something that gangs and thugs handle. The police…"

"Don't give me the police," Reece exploded. "The Oyster City department carries its corruption as a badge of honor. Everyone in the state knows it. On top of that, some crazy murderer is killing the wealthiest families in town. That damned new mayor is smack dab in the middle of it and can't stop it. What makes you think my Della doesn't deserve retribution?"

He walked closer.

"I told you I've looked into your background. Are you telling me you could walk into the police station today? The way I've heard it, you're number one on their list. I'm offering you a way to get back at these people."

Ray leaned back and took a deep breath.

"I agree that there's no justice in Oyster City. The good cops are leaving or stay low."

Irish saw the rage in Reece's face, and he suddenly stood, throwing his hat on the chair.

"Look, the city is worse than I think even you can imagine. But the fact is, I'm not some slimeball that knocks off people, even when they deserve it."

He started pacing with his chin down in his chest. He glanced over at them.

"I want the people that hurt Della. I'm just not cut out to kill them."

"You've killed before. Twice you've taken on gangs…" Reece pointed out.

"In self-defense, damn it!" He absently felt the missing part of his finger. "Hell, I'm still carrying the stitches from the last time I tried to stop the damn criminals. All it got me was a dead friend."

Irish turned back to them.

"I wanted revenge almost as much as you do. That night, I might have walked up to Jacobi and blown his brains out. But that's in the heat of the moment. Whatever you two think of me, I'm not a butcher."

Irish walked away, stopping in front of the fireplace.

Edna stood and went to him.

"Ray, Mr. Reece is speaking out of his anger and frustration. We're not asking you to assassinate anyone."

She glanced back at Reece, who nodded.

"She's correct, young man. You understand my emotions are running high right now."

"I don't believe you're a hired killer," she stepped toward Irish. "But you're good at finding these people. How else could you take down those gangsters? That's why I came to the senator to hire you. He has the power in the capital to back you in your work to get these men."

Irish turned back to her. He glanced back at Reece as he tried to get a read on the man. The silence fell across the room for a moment.

"Say that I track them down," the shamus bit into the idea. "Then what? Hell, I could tie them up with a bow. The cops would drag me into jail and release them for lack of evidence."

"What we want is to identify these people and get information from them," Edna explained. "Once we have what we need, Mr. Reece can get the resources of the state attorney general involved. Racketeering and such are state crimes. I'm sure there are a hundred charges they can throw at them. That's justice, isn't it?"

The shamus stared at her.

"That's not getting anyone the death penalty. I can see it in your eyes. Ultimately, that's what you want."

He turned to Reece when the woman looked down.

"If I find them for the state police, it's going to bring all of this out," Ray warned. "It will not matter how much you cared for Della; once the press gets it, they'll drag her through the mud. They sell newspapers. They don't tell you the news."

The politician nodded in agreement as he came next to Edna.

"Mr. Irish, that doesn't matter now. You forget that this will come to a head within a few days, one way or another. I damn well don't want my daughter's legacy to be her rape and humiliation shown in back-alley theaters for perverts. I'm playing for time so that you can discover the identity of everyone involved."

He looked over at the woman.

"Fortunately, Edna discovered that this man, Rusty, remains in Oyster City. I want you to get him and find out the truth about that night. You can do whatever you need to do. I want the name of the person who controls these bastards, and we won't have much time. Once you tell me who did this, then the scandal is no longer about Della. She'll truly be the victim. It's about those who did it. Now, you just name your price!"

Irish looked back at the fireplace, placing his hand on the mantle. He recognized lies mixed in with the man's grief. As his fingers tapped the cold marble, the shamus kept remembering the look that Della gave him when his watch band broke.

"Mr. Reece, I'm telling you that this is a risky plan. In the end, you know that this might bring more than just heartache. It's bad enough that the damn news people will stand out by your gates, then throw all sorts of trash all over the place with your name on it. This is how I see it. The person responsible for this blackmail was smart enough to set you up with hardly any options. That means that they've probably looked over ways to stop you beyond blackmail. Are you prepared to handle that threat?"

Reece's eyes widened at the warning.

"Earlier, I said it doesn't matter now."

He turned away.

"How about you?" Ray looked at Edna. "You'll find nothing pleasant about what's coming once this thing starts."

"I'm tougher than I look," she replied.

Irish looked them over again, contemplating his decision.

"Alright, I'll get to the bottom of it. Senator, you know my rate. How do you want to handle my progress updates? I suggest the phone is not the best option.

People are watching me, and probably you. That means they're probably listening in as well."

Reece stepped to his desk. He pulled out a signed check and handed it to Irish.

"You're correct; I don't trust anyone at this point. For as long as possible, I want this kept quiet. Please come here to update me each evening. If you run into problems, you may use the servant quarters above the garage for a place to stay."

He sighed.

"Funny, a lifetime of service to the community and known for…" He shook his head.

"Anyway, I'll make the arrangements with my staff to let you in day or night. You have carte blanche protection where I have influence."

Reece walked back to the window; his eyes focused on the large tree in the yard. He quietly remembered the swing under one limb that his daughter loved to play on in the summer.

"There's one more thing for you, Ray. There's another passage in the book in which a character asks Edmond Dantes about his mercy?" He turned back. "Do you know how he responded?"

Irish shook his head.

"Dantes replied that I'm a count, not a saint," the senator told him as he turned back.

"That's exactly my view of the matter. I ask that you not risk your life to save the vermin who did this. Not when there are other options. I hope you understand what I mean."

Chapter 7: Time to Dance

"Alright, give me your story!" Ray told the woman as they walked across the circle drive to the place where he parked.

"What do you mean? I told you I need a ride back to Oyster City."

Irish stopped and glared at her.

"Why are you so angry?" Edna pulled on her gloves.

"Don't play me for a fool," he snapped. "You orchestrated this whole thing. Chummy up with a grieving father for the last few evenings and point him in the direction that you wanted. You worked him like a damn violin. This whole thing is as much about your revenge as his. And you're both heading into something neither of you will like."

He headed to his car.

"I thought I'd seen it all with women!"

He continued to rage. Edna hurried after him when she heard his comment.

"Damn it; you can't treat me that way after I helped you."

Ray suddenly stopped, and the woman nearly barreled into him.

"Help! Is that what you call it? I might be an idiot for agreeing to this setup, but I'm not that stupid. Do you think I'm such a fool? What options do you think he just gave me? Reece wants blood! I could hire killers tomorrow, and he would not bat an eye about it. I only agreed because of this damn place and the bastards who make it happen. What's your excuse to lose your soul?"

He took off again. This time Edna grabbed him by the arm.

"Stop and talk to me!"

Ray turned back as she drew close. Her eyes betrayed her turmoil.

"Yes, I want blood. But this has always been about justice for Della. I want that for any woman who's gone through what she did. Does that make me evil like the ones that did it to her?"

His fury subsided only slightly.

"Yeah, let's turn this into that comparison. I'm telling you right now that I don't trust you because you set this up!"

Her blue eyes widened at the comment, then narrowed.

"Alright, that's fair. Now, tell me something. What were you going to do for Della? Did you owe her anything? Or did you just plan to sit on your ass while her tormentors walked away?"

For a moment, she thought he might lash out when she saw his barely suppressed temper.

"Yeah, I owe her," he growled. "Just like the others, including the two I left in Boston to come back to this hellhole."

He turned back to the car, placing his hand on the door handle. The shamus stopped suddenly.

"I'll tell you something. Yeah, I wanted revenge, retribution. I saw Cat die while I was only a few feet from her. I found Samantha's body in a filthy basement. Hell, I wanted to pull out the bastard's beating hearts with my hands."

His shoulders slightly sagged as he looked over his car at the large tree. The peaceful scene got to him.

"Yes, I had something to do with avenging my friend's deaths. Believe me when I tell you it doesn't help. Damn it; nothing stops eating you alive with what might have been. It's because you know deep down that just one decision caused their deaths."

The shamus tried to force the memories away.

"I made the mistake of not seeing the obvious, which got Samantha murdered in the first place. Cat got it because she was in my office when Jacobi came looking for me. Revenge is a fancy word for not seeing your own damn stupidity."

Surprised by his statement, Edna watched him open the car door.

"Ray, I'm sorry!"

He paused.

"For what?" Irish didn't look back.

"For putting you in the middle of this. I should have talked to you. I didn't realize—well, I didn't know, alright!"

"Forget it. I've got a job to do." He slid into the front seat.

"You son of a bitch, you're doing it again!"

Edna ran forward and slammed the car door shut, nearly pinning his leg.

"Don't you dare walk away like that when I'm apologizing to you," the woman yelled at him through the closed-door window. Then she finished her tantrum with a string of colorful curses.

Irish stared at her with an expression of dumbfounded shock while she regaled him with her salty language. Finally, he rolled down the window. Her exasperation and pain showed through as she tried to stifle the inner turmoil. She went quiet, leaning over as her hands shook. He let her rage subside. When the woman turned away, an idea came to him.

"Maybe a drive will help us both."

Edna stared at him for a long moment, and then she stepped around the front of the Nash. After she got inside, the woman remained quiet for a moment. She fiddled with the pleats of her dress.

"Let's go to the point of land that Della liked. I think I need to see it again."

A few minutes later, they were standing near the cliff face overlooking the bay. It took a long time before either of them spoke.

"Tell me about Boston."

He shook his head.

"I can't tell you much because I just don't know yet. I guess it doesn't matter to this case because it has nothing to do with Della's death."

"Please don't do that," she frowned at him, then took a deep breath.

"What I was trying to tell you back at Reece's house is that I made a mistake. It was unfair for me to assume I understood you. I guessed that a big guy carrying a gun, along with a cocky attitude, would jump at the chance at payback. All I remembered was your reaction to Della's pain that day. I know you cared. However, I didn't realize how much more there was to it."

Edna sat on the bumper of his car.

"I guess I was so desperately in love with my plan that I forgot to consider anyone else. You saw how Mr. Reece would do anything now. I'm truly sorry for the squeeze play. You can back out. Maybe you should."

Ray looked over. Her profile showed him a tired and hurt woman.

"No reason to apologize. As stupid as I look, I knew what I was doing. I'm the guy that gets paid to do dirty work. Since I've been a shamus, many of my cases turn into revenge and retribution. That includes some things I've done. I understand how it changes a person."

He stared at his shoe, then kicked at the ground.

"I believe you said that I put the world on my shoulders. It's true. I guess I can't shake the responsibility for the many awful things that come directly from my decisions."

"Then, you do listen!" She softly chuckled.

"Occasionally," he admitted. "But it doesn't mean I'll always agree."

"Ray, I don't know every detail of what happened, but I know situations call for making a call. It's not any different from those things I'm sure you dealt with during the war."

The woman looked out at the bay.

"I understand what happened to Katherine and Samantha. But you can't put it back on everything you've done," she observed. "Cruel people killed them, not you. However, I can see things differently when you think about all the other things that have happened to you."

She saw his glance.

"Remember, Mr. Reece showed me the information he had on you. A rich man can find out a lot about people."

The woman took in a deep breath, glancing at his legs.

I don't know how he learned how to walk again after the injuries he received!

"Anyway, you're right about some of my actions with the senator. I guess I'm as stubborn as you are."

Several minutes passed as they felt the wind on their faces and listened to the crash of waves. Edna glanced over at a passing car. The driver paid no attention.

"You know what? Della was right about this place."

She leaned back. The woman didn't care that her white dress pressed against his dusty car. He remained quiet, listening to the sound of the waves below them.

"Tell me, what do you want to know, Ray? I can feel the questions running around inside of your head."

The shamus looked down at her. He liked how she got to the point.

"Alright, I'll outline what I see." He pushed back his fedora. "You're living alone in a swanky apartment with no job that I'm aware of. It suggests that you have the means to enjoy life without worrying about your next meal."

"Is that bad?"

Ray shook his head.

"No, but it's puzzling when I add in other parts that I've seen. You're tough, and you don't easily rattle. It tells me you've experienced tough situations at some point. And you swear like a sailor, so that didn't come from you hanging around the social club playing bridge with the ladies."

He sat next to her on the bumper.

"Somehow, I'm having problems reconciling the woman I see for the one who's inside. It doesn't help that I find most women are first-rate actors."

Edna frowned.

"Don't you mean liars?"

"No, I mean what I say. Everyone lies at some point. However, the women I've known have a natural ability to keep a guy off balance while they're playing footsies with you. That's the acting part."

"Oh, you're certainly a cynic when it comes to women." She grinned smugly. "Perhaps a girl likes a little mystery."

He scowled at the suggestion.

"At this point, we can't have mysteries between us. I'm telling right now, trust is everything, or you're dead. If you hang with me, we're taking on people that hurt people. You've already seen how bad things turn out for those around me."

"Ray, I don't think you're cursed. Your luck had nothing to do with Della's death. Shouldn't we get back to Oyster City so we can find Rusty?"

She smiled.

Slowly, her grin faded when he kept his stubborn scowl directed at her.

"Alright, I suppose you should know more," she stood and turned to him. "Lord knows what you'll think of me afterward. Let's head back to my apartment. I wasn't lying when I said that I needed a ride."

Less than a mile down the road, Edna hit him with the broadside.

"You ever hear of the name Henry Beloumant?"

He hesitated for a moment.

"You mean that gangster out of LA or someplace west? I remember reading something about his death. It made the *Stars and Stripes*."

"It was San Francisco, and he was my father," she admitted. "A rival gangster killed him in 1944. It became a bloody battle between gangs."

She watched his reaction. Interestingly, his eyes revealed only curiosity.

"The man I knew was a kind and caring father. He shielded us from how bad he truly was. It's strange how naïve a young person is when you look back. I mean, we had bodyguards and took different routes to school, for Christ's sake. Anyway,

Pop controlled a gang involved in everything along the waterfront. They killed and maimed people."

Edna shook her head.

"I tried to live down his legacy in a lot of ways. That's one reason I go by my mother's maiden name."

"Make sense to me. Were you living with your family when he died?"

"No, I was in France as a nurse. I was in college back east when the war started," she paused.

Ray noticed her face darken at a memory. Edna immediately masked the expression.

"Of course, I learned a lot during that time. One day I was walking along the street, feeling pretty low, and I saw the patriotic posters. Something inside me thought helping the war effort would fix things, you know?"

The woman looked at Irish like he understood. He nodded.

"Maybe it would stop some of the pain—you know, remove the stain of my father's past. Anyway, I joined the army nursing corps. It was following the 10th Armored Division that I finally came to terms with my father's legacy, along with a whole lot of rage."

Her head dropped for a moment, and Ray saw her suppressing the tears.

"I guess you got inside of me when you mentioned your experience to Della. I knew everything about what you were saying. For a long time, I could block out those boys dying so horribly. But when I lost my best friend during an air attack, I almost lost it."

She composed herself.

"You know about those nightmares. You're the first person I've met who knows what went on inside of me."

Ray quietly nodded as he kept sneaking peeks at Edna. The woman looked out the window of the car while she rubbed her hand absently across her thigh.

"Mom lived on my father's money until she died a couple of years ago. You were right that I don't have to worry about money. I guess I should feel bad about it, but I can't. I'm not the same person as my father was. Besides, I won't live my life apologizing for his flaws, despite how terrible they were."

She turned to him.

"Does that make me a horrible person?"

"Hell, no!" he growled out, then paused. "It makes you human. You have to go on living. It beats the alternative."

Edna nodded, her eyes betraying relief at his statement.

"In college…" she paused. "Well, I shut out people from getting close to me. When I got here after the war, I took a job at the base until it shut down, just to keep busy. One of the bad things about living alone is you do a lot of thinking and reading. But it's helped me understand that pushing people away can't get you through forever. How can you have something like love without heartache? It's always been that way. There must be good with the bad."

Ray's eyes remained on the road. His jaw muscle twitched from his clenched teeth. Much of what the woman told him passed through his mind over the years. He understood her pain and disappointment.

"I think you're right, but it's hard to tell people who've never seen or experienced the terrible things that people do," he finally told her. "I guess it's good to meet someone who does."

The shamus smiled to himself.

"You know that's what struck me that night that I came into your room?"

He glanced over at her curious expression.

"When I saw you tied up like that, I expected tears and fear. But you weren't afraid. No, you were hopping mad at what those men did. They say the eyes are a window to the soul."

She smirked at the comment.

"You can bet that sounds like me. So, what do you think now?"

Ray glanced over.

"You're human with your flaws like the rest of us," he tugged at his ear.

"Hell, I've never been very good at reading people. Time will tell."

"That's grudging acceptance," she stated.

The shamus looked over and saw her playful grin.

"Well, I've always had a soft spot for nurses." He stated. "But cursed or not, just remember it's dangerous hanging around me."

"Ray, I told you. I'm tougher than that, so let's focus on the next steps. Let me tell you what I've found out so far. We can go from there."

By the time they reached Edna's apartment, they had a plan for that evening to catch their first target. The woman suggested that they change vehicles as Ray came to a stop by the front door of her building.

"There's no need for that. You don't need to go with me. I'm stopping by my temporary office before I head over to see the state coroner. It's only an hour away. I'll be back to get you."

His reluctance made her grin.

"You mentioned the cops are looking for you here. That makes my car perfect. Besides, you're not going anywhere in this heap. You can't be sure you'll be back in time."

"Betsy doesn't like to hear that," he grumbled as he patted the dash of his Nash.

He turned his gaze to her.

"Tell me why you're sticking your nose into my business. It's an old case that I'm trying to set right."

"Curiosity. Besides, I'm going to be your driver," Edna replied airily. "The clubs don't open for several hours, and I'll go crazy just waiting around my apartment."

"You know what they say about the curious cat. Trust me; I'll come back to pick you up."

"Yeah, yeah, save it. You have a driver today, buster!"

Irish grunted when she smiled at him. He pulled his Nash over to a parking space. When Ray got out, the man watched her walking to her car for a moment before he followed her. Her perseverance and sudden breezy charm reminded him of several recent women.

Damn, it's like the nightmare is starting all over!

~~~

Inside the Andras mansion that morning, the last screams of Merle suddenly stopped. Her bulging eyes stared in disbelief as her bluish face withered. A naked Panthia held a thin piece of wire around her sister's neck, twisting the wire so tight that Merle's drying flesh still bled. While Andras put the poker into the fireplace that burned on that summer day, Panthia smiled triumphantly. She enjoyed feeling the life force draining from her victim.

"You knew there could only be one to serve the master," she cooed to Merle. "It was the unspoken agreement from the start. I'll see you back in Hell when my long reign in this realm finally ends, my dear sister."

The choking crack of Merle's larynx finished the witch's life among the humans. Panthia released the wire and stared at the dilated eyes of the person she knew before the time of Christ. Then the witch turned back to her master.

"I've finished your task," she announced.

Andras came back to the woman. He turned her around before he pulled back his robe.

"Bend over so you can receive my blessing," he ordered.

Panthia did as commanded. The demon growled like an animal when he forced himself into the witch. Her howling enjoyment was immediate each time the demon thrust into her. Panthia cried out her obedience to him. Peter Smyth's open mouth held crooked and elongated teeth that were more suitable for a shark. The creature commanded a rotting body that could no longer hide the demon. Drool from the beast spilled out on the back of the woman, burning Panthia like boiling water. She screamed out in pain as the black claws of the inhuman hands cut into her. When Andras finished, he pushed the witch to the floor. The woman remained there in a submissive position, waiting for his next move.

Andras tied his robe while he looked over at the remains of the witch that he initially expected to finish as the sole survivor. Now, Merle was nothing more than a desiccated corpse. Her facial features were becoming unrecognizable.

"Get rid of that thing," he told Panthia.

He stepped next to the bed.
~~~

"Over the next few days, your sole attention with Mr. Wolfe is to prepare our festival. Dr. Wolfe has already found several of our sacrifices. They'll be with him until the night of the full moon. Then we'll place them over the fire pit. Their dying screams will bring forth more of my kind and return my form to its rightful state. This mortal coil grows useless."

The woman rose and went to her dress.

"Do we have enough people?"

She glanced over at the demon staring at the Singsing ring on the bed with the two fingers of Orella. The final witch of his harem found it strange such a powerful creature could not lift the object from the mattress.

"No, but I expect more who will join us that night. There are always those who balk at the terror they see in the pit. They'll join the others unworthy of living in my new world."

An evil frown came to his face.

"I see it in your eyes, witch. You believe I have a weakness with this body's inability to take the Singsing in my hand."

His guttural roar forced the woman to turn to him.

"I trust you no more than your sister. You know that I never accepted her excuse for not returning with my prey. Remember the punishments that I'll inflict upon you if you make a mistake. While I can't touch that Singsing in this form, I received a vision while I tortured Merle. I saw childlike blue eyes looking at me when the woman gave me the Singsing. In the background, a parade ground. Since I don't have enough time for a journey to Boston for that ancestor of my first rising, we'll use my vision for my return to his world."

"Isn't such a thing unusual for you? I thought that was the reason for you to wear the ring?"

Distracted, he waved his hand.

"All demons can see into the future, although it's limited unless we possess an item like the Singsing. Now, I need a simple person from this city. They will present me the Singsing on the night of my ultimate form before I cut their throat. I'll let you have their blood."

"Should I find one suitable for you?"

She grew excited at the offer.

"Perhaps a young maid who works for Phillip? She's got the bluest eyes that I've seen. She's not smart at all, barely able to clean. But Phillip says she'll follow any command given."

Andras continued looking at the ring, then he nodded.

"Yes, that will work. Have Mr. Wolfe take that ring and put it in a safe place for the moment. You'll put a spell on the maid to come here, then take the ring and deliver it to me on the night of the festival."

Panthia nodded in obedience, relieved the demon remained unable to read her mind.

~~~

Edna introduced Ray to a new driving experience without regard to the speed limits and most traffic rules. By the time they reached J. Allan Dunn's old office, Edna had convinced him she learned her driving skills from the cabbies in New York.

Her expensive two-toned Frazer Manhattan handled the abuse with reluctance. When the woman took the turns, her action forced Ray to dig his feet into the floorboard.

"It's amazing what you can get away with when you bat your eyes at a policeman," Edna smirked when she saw his pale face.

She rolled to a stop a few feet from the office door.

"Yeah, some ladies have all the luck." He glanced over at his partner's car in its hiding place, next to the building.

The couple entered the office to discover Arizona lying back on an old army cot. His bowler hat hung over the top of his face.

"Some good you'll be if the bad guys come looking for you," Ray announced.

The ex-cop didn't move.

"I could hear your car a mile away."

"Then you need to check your hearing. Miss Edna Ackroyd drove me." Ray glanced at the woman while he waved his arm toward Arizona.

"Edna, meet Arizona Charlie Campbell!"

His partner's introduction forced the man in the cot to look from under his hat. Edna's bemused smile sent Arizona scrambling to his feet.

How does he find them?

"I'm sorry for the rudeness, ma'am," Campbell stuck out his meaty hand. "They call me Arizona."

"That name sounds familiar. I think I read about you in the paper." She shook his hand.

Perplexed about how to respond, Arizona just stared. Ray stepped between them to get to the desk.

"Well, since Edna plans on hanging out with me, she might as well get both barrels about us. We'll start with reality inside Oyster City. The Oyster City police fired my partner because he took down the Jacobi gang. That tells you all you need to know about our relationship with city officials."

"In fairness, Irish was there as well," the ex-cop smiled. "His relationship with the city bureaucrats is worse than mine."

"Yes, I remember. It was headline news for a couple of days. You even killed the head of the gang at a motel outside of town."

She saw the glance between the two men at her statement.

"I always thought they rewarded the police who took down gangsters." Edna bit her lower lip, puzzled at the news. She looked over at Irish as he hunted for something inside the desk.
~~~

"Apparently, Edna doesn't get out of her apartment much," the shamus replied.

"Yeah, I expected better," Arizona smiled at the woman's glare toward his partner for his comment.

"But the truth of the matter is the people in this city are happy to keep things in the shadows. They deal themselves into schemes involving crooks and killers. Unfortunately, they've used the police to shield them from exposure as well."

"Don't forget that our new mayor isn't quite what he seems! I'll let Arizona explain what he's doing." He played with a fountain pen that didn't work. "Damn, doesn't this office have a pen?"

Arizona shook his head as he pulled one from his pocket, which he gave to the shamus.

"Are you sure you can handle this guy? He's got a temper." He asked Edna.

"Yeah, but nothing on hers," Ray grinned to himself as he continued to rummage through the drawer. "Now tell her about your warning. I don't think she really believes me."

Arizona frowned, then took a deep breath.

"Ray's right. It's extremely dangerous to hang around us. Those in the know told me to leave town. Men are watching our office; that's why we're here. Otherwise, we're considered fair game to cop or thug."

"I didn't realize everyone that's friends with Mr. Irish are under such threats."

Ray glanced up at Edna.

"Now, maybe you'll get some sense and go back to your apartment."

He pulled out a few sheets of paper, then sat down.

"Not a chance, mister. You're stuck with me until we get those bastards who hurt Della."

Arizona raised an eyebrow at the woman's underlying anger in her expression. She was not the type to back down any more than Irish. The big man shook his head.

"Yeah, you and he will make a good team if you don't come to blows."

The scribbling caused both of them to watch the shamus sitting at the desk.

"What are you writing?" She finally asked.

"A note to Yana and Orella, telling them about Pappy's warning." He looked up at Edna. "I think they ran into something in Boston. I feel like a damn heel for leaving them there. There's a church I noticed on the way to Salisbury. Can I get a ride there?"

Puzzled, the woman nodded.

"What's this about? I thought you wanted to go see the state coroner?"

"I don't think we'll have time." He kept writing as Edna glared at him.

"You son of a gun, you were lying about driving to see the coroner."

Irish peeked up.

"Well, not exactly a lie. I was planning on it, but I changed my mind when I read the paper this morning. My enemy is only a few blocks away."

She waited, but he continued scribbling his note.

"What does that mean?"

"It means that Irish can be a pain in the rear," Arizona rejoined the conversation.

"What I'm going to tell you will probably make you reconsider some of your ideas about this city and the people in charge. Or maybe you'll reconsider your thoughts about Irish and me. It's kind of hard to tell about people."

A few minutes later, Edna remained silent. Her mind reeled at some ideas Arizona gave her in his overview of Peter Smyth and his control of Oyster City. She glanced over at Ray, who leaned back in the chair, watching her reaction.

"Good ol' Ray here still thinks a demon's involved, maybe even taken over Smyth. He's even convinced his one friend about it. That's why we wear these things. Of course, it didn't seem to work last night," the ex-cop grinned at Irish.

"Well, if someone didn't snore so loud, I might find out if it works, Ray grumbled.

"He gets cranky when he doesn't get enough sleep," Arizona winked at the woman, then yawned.

"I'm not sure how much of what you told me is a joke," Edna finally confessed.

Confused and suddenly leery of the men, she wanted to dismiss the idea. However, their lighthearted banter reminded her of the gallows humor she recognized from men facing death.

From cops and thugs!

"We're the most serious when we're joking," Irish told her. "Anyway, we have evidence that this group called the Shadows is genuine enough. Arizona's been reading the late Bishop La Spina's notebook. I believe it confirms much of what you just heard."

"Oh, don't let him fool you. He's correct that I've been reading those notes from this book the man left me. If La Spina's not one of the craziest bastards who lived, I'll eat my hat."

Suddenly embarrassed at his curse, he apologized to Edna. She laughed.

"I've heard worse. Are you talking about the man who committed suicide?"

"Yes, and it's a darn good thing for him. If his notes are true, he's already down burning in Hell."

Arizona turned back to Irish.

"Listen, I'm staking out that the graveyard on the Andras hill. Do you want to come along?"

Irish glanced over at Edna.

"No, my temporary shadow has me keeping an eye on a club. One thug that did a number on me has his eyes on Edna. He also has information about Della and what happened to her."

The ex-cop looked at the woman.

"You be careful!"

She smiled, but Arizona's expression hardened. The man quickly glanced at Irish, who returned to his writing.

"I mean it when I say, be careful," Arizona repeated.

Edna nodded, surprised by the exchange. Her curiosity heightened; she was about to ask more when Irish suddenly spoke.

"It's not going to do much good now, but I planned on going to the state morgue with those dental files I have on the bishop's first wife."

He finished up with the letter and put it in an envelope. Ray looked at his watch. Then he turned his gaze to Edna.

"Edna, are you ready for a trip to that church?"

The shamus stuffed the envelope in the breast pocket of his jacket as he headed to the door. Edna followed him. As she pulled the door shut, Arizona called out to her. The woman stuck her head back at the entrance, and she noticed the big man's serious expression.

"Remember what I said about being careful when you're with him."

~~~

Marion Underhill took a seat on the hard wooden pew inside the United Church. He looked up at the pulpit of Bishop La Spina's church, trying to imagine the big man's sermons. Marion seldom stepped inside the unholy facade that some Shadows used as their cover for years. Despite the wicked duplicity of La Spina, who preached at the pulpit over the years, the faithful still entered the building. They read from their bibles, sang their hymns, and prayed to their god from the pews. It was the reason that Underhill was just as confident that Andras would never step inside.

Phillip Smyth's lanky form slid in next to him. Both men glanced around the abandoned-looking facility.

"I finally got away from that Beacon reporter concerning the recovery of the Singsing ring. Why did you want to meet?"

"I've got some news," Underhill told him. "There's only one witch left. Wolfe called me this morning. He went by the house, and he saw Panthia leading Mr. Wolfe into the cemetery. When he investigated, he found them dumping the body. He asked about it, and the woman told him she's the last of the harem."

Smyth went quiet, pushing away several wayward strands of hair near his face.

"I guess that explains Mr. Wolfe coming by with the ring this morning. Andras can't touch it."
~~~

"How do you know that?" Underhill looked back over his shoulder at a sound. Smyth glanced around as well before he leaned closer.

"Because I've been reading those notes from Henry. He knew of the master's weakness until he came to his last form. I believe he was going to let the rest of us know this before that madman tried to kill all of us in the crypt."

"Do you think Henry intended to betray Andras?"

"I'm not sure," Phillip admitted. "When he started resisting the master, he told me that things were spiraling out of hand. He asked for my help."

"What about Doctor Wolfe? Would he help us?" Underhill lowered his voice. "I mean, if we're thinking the same thing."

Smyth shook his head.

"No, he's living it up as a gangster. All of those hoodlums who worked for Guy Young and Jacobi now come to him. He's resigned from his state job at the asylum and hangs out at that old clinic on the base. Andras had him pegged right."

The man leaned back and sighed.

"All I know is that we have a few days before we are nothing more than any other citizen of this town. Money and influence will mean nothing. Only the dictates of Andras."

"You should learn to keep your voices down. I could hear you from the back pew."

Panthia suddenly appeared in the aisle next to the men. Both of them sprang up in her presence. The witch laughed at their glances for Andras.

"You needn't worry. Andras won't bother sneaking up on you. He's taking up a new hobby of watching his victims suffer while he burns them with hot pokers inside his bedroom."

Her face fell momentarily, and then she twirled around in the aisle. Her skin-tight dress showed off her curvaceous body.

"Fortunately, mortal blood can fix almost any problems with my body."

As the woman watched the men, a mischievous grin took over.

"You wish to keep Andras from achieving his ultimate form. However, you're afraid. I can smell the fear on you. It's delightful."

"Alright, whatever witch you are, you've made your point. Now, keep your voice down. What do you want?" Phillip's attempt to glare failed to impress her when she saw the fear still on his face.

"Oh, I'm Panthia, the winner over my sisters for the right to sit next to the master. However, I believe that we have a common foe, and I'm willing to help you." She turned to look at the stained-glass windows.

"You know, I had that saint at one time." The woman's voice grew remorseful. "His concubine threw him out for it. It's too bad he ended up on the wrong side. He wasn't a poor lover."

While Underhill looked up at the image of Saint Augustine, Phillip stepped next to her.

"Get to the point!"

Panthia sighed and shook her head.

"I just told you. You and I wish Andras would return to his domain. I can make that happen with a little help. That's why I'm here."

Marion came next to her.

"How can you do that? He's your master as much as ours."

"Oh, even more so in some ways," the witch agreed. "However, his human body is failing quickly. That's why the time is right to return him to his home."

She turned to him and ran her finger across his lips.

"As for how, it couldn't be simpler. We push the living body of Peter Smyth into the pit of fire. Who do you think suggested the new method of sacrifice for the ritual? Letting of blood would work, but Andras so enjoyed the idea of torturous death that he was putty in my hands. Once Andras cannot take his form, the demon falls back into his realm. However, the monsters I've summoned that night will remain under my control."

"Then you're planning on taking over for Andras," Phillip scoffed. "What's the difference?"

Panthia smiled like a salesman.

"Yes, I see great opportunities for those who join me. I will not cast you aside like garbage. The Shadows will become my closest and most loyal advisers."

"Why should we trust you? This could be a setup," Marion interjected.

"Please, attempt to use a bit of your brain. Why would I go to this trouble? I can simply tell Andras about the conversations you've been having, and you'll join the other prisoners to die in a few days."

Panthia gave them an evil smile.

"The modern world forgets simple things that a witch can do. With the right spells, the papers you touch, or the clothes you wear can inform me of your conversations. In some ways, it's better than reading the minds of mortals."

The two men cast uncomfortable glances at each other, and the woman smiled.

"Now, I use such information for my benefit, not Andras. However, that can change."

"This doesn't make sense. You're part of the Harem of Lamia." Smyth objected.

"That's a term used by Andras, not me," she flashed, then turned on her charm again.

"It's true that I'm a Lamia with an evil soul held by him. However, he cannot breed more of us. That is for mortals only. Now our so-called master wishes to replace the Shadows with those he'll mark."

"I don't get your change of heart with the master," Underhill looked about ready to puke.

"There's nothing to understand. But if it helps, I'm the last witch in the land of the living. Andras will tire of me, just like he did with the Shadows. Then he'll cast me aside, after sufficient torture, of course. However, I like it among the living. Plus, I'm tired of his incompetent ways. You've seen how he blames others for his failures. Unlike me, he does not understand the mortal mind."

The woman saw the silent agreement in their eyes.

"Plus, I have something that Andras does not."

"What's that?" Phillip asked.

"I lack the master's overpowering ambition! I don't need the world. Why bother with such things? I'm content to rule, say, a city. Pulling strings from my perch while the mortals continue their dance with inevitable death."

Panthia leaned against the wall and crossed her arms. The pose emphasized her breasts for the men.

"You see, that makes my desires less of a risk for everyone involved. I carry simple yearnings, the lust for power along with the lust for flesh. You enjoy this mortal coil I wear. You lust for flesh as I do. Men or women, child or old, I don't care as long my servants please me."

The woman sprang away from the wall, coming close to Marion. He backed into Phillip.

"I'm quite candid with both of you because your choices grow limited with each tick of the clock. From Hell, I witnessed how the mortals rose and drove Andras back to his domain. So, it's quite possible to help you and myself."

"You'd kill anyone on a whim. I still don't know how we can trust you." Marion tried to keep his mind off the woman's scent so close.

"Trust is an overrated concept," she told him with a touch of her finger on his lips.

"I feel your desires. And I enjoy the pleasure it brings me. I intend to go on savoring it for centuries. In the past, a Lamia abducted human males to mate with them. However, in the modern world, I don't believe I need to worry about such things. Those who support me and bring me my victims will benefit. For such work, I can give a substantial fortune to you and your family." The woman smiled.

"With the right spell, I can give you anything that your heart desires. Think about it. Or would you have the world you know slip away where you remain servants to please demons? More of them are coming, I assure you!"

Panthia backed away, radiating confidence.

"Has Andras offered you anything but groveling and worshiping him? Perhaps you enjoy letting him rape you. I will come to you with much more. Yes, so much more for your loyalty."

Their silence confirmed she was winning their hearts.

"You can control those demons who rise in place of Andras?" Phillip warmed to the idea with a nod to his friend.

"Everything has a weakness," she assured them with a smile. "The demons require blood and souls. Properly managed, it gives me power over them. You saw what happened to the boy who wanted to be a killer. I've kept him alive for these weeks with nothing but my spell."

"And the flesh of corpses," Phillip reminded her. "Still, we need to know that you're not leaving us to demons once Andras is gone."

Panthia walked past them and toward the back of the store. She glanced back with an enticing smile. The woman curled up her index finger and motioned for them to follow. Slowly, the men entered the aisle, trying to understand how smoothly the witch ensnared them.

"I believe there's a dressing room in the basement. I'm sure it smells of the bishop's many conquests. Should we not consummate our new agreement with a little pleasure and blood for me to taste? I'll let you do anything that you wish to this body. I ask for your loyalty in return."

She walked down the inclined path to the sanctuary area. The woman stopped at the drawn curtain and looked back. Panthia frowned at the hesitation.

"Gentleman, you have no choice," her whispered voice chilled them. "Andras will never believe that I would betray him after killing my sister. Now, come along before I change my mind. The spell I conjure between us will ensure your pleasure and loyalty for an eternity."

Marion took the first step toward the witch when she disappeared behind the curtain. Then Phillip slowly followed, his mind reeling as he accepted his new fate.

Blood and pain are two things I can understand!

~~~

Edna's Frazer pulled up in front of the tiny white church in the middle of the farmland on the way to the small town of Princess Anne. She looked over at her companion. The woman was still trying to understand how her search for Della's rapists turned into a side journey to have three necklaces blessed. Ray did his best to explain, but she recognized he did not tell her everything. Edna already knew when the man glanced away that he was already keeping parts of his story to himself. The woman thought about the nightmares she continued to have since arriving in town. However, Edna could not bring herself to believe in some supernatural evil.

It's only humans that are evil and without conscience!

Ray looked around before he slid out of the car.

"Well, I'll be right back," he announced.

"You didn't explain why this place?"

He stuck his head back in the open window.

"I told you we need to have these blessed. Plus, I can't believe that there's a church in Oyster City that's not corrupted to its core in some manner. I'm convinced that years of dealing with people like the Shadows force them to look away."
~~~

Edna stared at him for a moment.

"You know, you sound a bit like those crazy people that they lock away. Next thing, you'll be telling me you want me to drive you to a monastery."

Her expression revealed she was only half-joking.

"Well, that's highly doubtful. You should know that I like women too much," he grinned. "I won't be too long."

He walked away.

"Besides, I need all the help I can get," he said under his breath.

Edna overheard the remark, and she stared at his unusual gait until he went into the building. Turning to look over a nearby open field of hay, the woman recalled similar-looking areas in France as her unit got closer to Paris. Assigned to the 104th Evacuation Hospital mobile unit, she recalled unending horror and destruction. Each mile closer to the end, her work as a nurse became a bloody treadmill. By the time she closed out the war near Munich, Edna doubted everything she once held dear. Her religious belief changed.

The woman found the idea of a supreme being guiding her through the hell that she experienced almost nauseating. In her mind, the overwhelming stench of death and misery wiped away any random acts of kindness she witnessed.

I've had nightmares before I left Europe.

The bitterness of the thought surprised her. As she looked over the dry and dying brush near the parking lot, the scorched grass appeared ready to burst into flame after so many rainless days.

"Perfect for a demon," she smirked.

When Irish finally emerged from the church, she decided Ray held on to the concept of a demon as his defense. With the recent deaths of people close to him, the shamus needed a way to fight on. Battling an evil entity from hell gave him a reason to get up every day. She remembered Ray's words to Della.

I fight through every damn nightmare that returns.

"Well, driver, lead us to the post office," Irish interrupted her thoughts when he opened the car door.

"I'm getting the idea that you're enjoying my work as a chauffeur a little too much," she shot back.

"You're the one that wanted to be my partner today." His cocky smirk forced a grin from her.

"Alright, you're off the clock now. Let's find a place for lunch as we go to mail this letter."

He gave her one of the blessed necklaces. The woman absently stuffed the cross into her purse, and then she turned the long car around.

~~~

It was late in the evening when Arizona Campbell finally arrived outside of the Andras estate. Peter Smyth now made his home there, which left the ex-cop curious.
~~~

Why would he move into this place?

Smyth had his own expensive home just down the road. He passed it on the way there. Still driving Cat's car, Arizona also passed several police cars along the route. Fortunately, the uniformed men's indifference to his vehicle allowed Arizona to come to the end of Andras Lane without a problem. The dark mansion sitting on the hill looked abandoned as he backed the car near the open entrance. Arizona pulled the sedan in close to the dense tangle of brush lined the old fence line, keeping it out of sight from the road.

After turning off the motor and the lights, he rolled down the window and listened to the stillness descend over the area. The shamus waited several minutes, his eyes adjusting to the darkness. Hazy cloudiness socked in the city all day, leaving the night particularly dark.

So, the cemetery is the keystone! We'll see about that.

Arizona pulled the mostly chewed cigar from his mouth and threw it out the window. The noise of Cat's car door opening filled the air as he crawled out. He quietly pushed the door nearly closed before he pulled down his bowler hat. He scanned the area, then brought out his flashlight from his suit coat pocket. The man followed the two-lane path into the cemetery. Coming to the massive tree near a shattered tomb, he paused to shine the beam of light on the broken marble.

Curious, he went over. Arizona noticed dark splotches across the top of the stone top. Then, a sweep of his flashlight caught something moving above the tomb.

A rope with a small noose hung down from the large limb above!

Then the ex-cop felt his skin crawl. He remembered finding a dead ex-con named Ulysses hanging by one leg with his body drained of blood. Bishop La Spina's voice came back to him.

Each one of those deaths brought evil into this world.

Trying to the heebie-jeebies he felt, Arizona continued on the path. Eventually, the shamus came upon a footpath. He flashed his beam on the weathered tombstones, which showed him the city's founders' last names. In the background, he saw the outline of a stone structure.

As he got closer, Arizona twisted off his flashlight when he saw movement near the crypt. Taking a roundabout path, he stepped closer to the structure. He saw the name Andras on the partially opened door. Quietly, the man pulled his revolver from his shoulder holster when he spotted the light.

Somebody's up to no good!

Campbell carefully went down the steps and slid next to the entrance. The cold air coming from the crypt reeked of musty death. The detective grimaced at the stench of rotting flesh in the blast. His obscured view showed him a candle sitting on a mourner's bench. He also saw shadows on the far wall of tombs as another light source moved around. The ex-cop pulled open the door after taking a deep breath. The high-pitched groan of rusty hinges gave away his advantage as the shamus rushed inside.

An emasculated man stood like a zombie in front of him. The creature reeked of body odor, and his thin beard barely hid the waxy pallor to this skin.

"Don't move," Arizona ordered as the vague recollection of the staring face came back to him.

With a smile, Lance stepped toward the shamus, who backed up.

"Damn it, don't!"

After the man took another step, Arizona pointed the revolver down and fired. The bullet struck Lance in the leg. Still, he came at the ex-cop.

Another shot exploded, and this time, Lance fell back while holding his belly.

"Thank you!" the injured man croaked out as he fell to the stone floor.

The shamus kneeled next to the dying man, who pointed at the corner of the crypt.

"Terrible things! Forced me to put bodies over there. Bitches kept bleeding me." He shuddered and his head lulled momentarily.

With a burst of energy, Lance grabbed Arizona's coat with frantic, wide eyes.

"Tell me I'm not going to the master's home because I did this. God knows I had no choice. It was the only way to survive."

"No, son. Just lay still," the shamus told him softly as he pulled the man's hand from his coat. "We'll get you to a doc."

The young man slipped back to the floor. His laugh was nothing more than a whisper.

"Doctors can't stop witches! You'll see over there."

Nodding, Arizona rose and walked to the dimly outlined door. He picked up one of the burning candles on the way. As he got closer, Arizona wrinkled his nose at the familiar smile. He suspected he would not like what was behind the door.

He was correct!

Nausea almost got to him when he pulled back on the latch as the grating steel sound filled the chamber. He looked in and stood in disbelief for a moment. It took all of his willpower not to puke at what he saw. Bodies stack up on top of each other. Worse, some corpses showed missing skin and flesh.

"What the hell is happening here?"

Arizona heard a nearly silent footstep behind him. He instinctively took a sidestep while grabbing for his gun. A tall man came around with an iron bar as the shamus turned. Fortunately, Arizona's reaction caught his opponent off-guard. The bar just glanced off the detective's head, sending his bowler hat into the air.

The shamus immediately fired into the tall man with the cragged face. Despite the bullet striking him, his adversary swung again. The pain swept across Arizona's arm, but he hung on to the gun. Another two shots rang out, causing the tall man to drop the metal rod. However, he was close enough to grab the shamus by his coat sleeve. The fabric tore away when the ex-cop pulled away.

"I should warn you that Mr. Wolfe worked for generations of the Andras family, and, of course, our master. He's beyond a mere mortal now." Panthia announced as she walked in.

The witch looked down at Lance's dead body, then turned back to the deadly struggle between the two men. Her smile showed her enjoyment of the battle.

Arizona had his hands full with Wolfe's overpowering strength. The bullet wound barely fazed the man. Wolfe's fingers gripping the shamus around the throat with one hand and his gun wrist with the others. Arizona struggled to bring around his revolver. However, Wolfe's tight grip increased on the ex-cop's throat, immediately choking him.

Desperately, Arizona suddenly kicked up like he was a punter. His foot landed square in his opponent's groin. Feeling the loosening grip on his wrist, Arizona swung around with his gun, placing the barrel against the side of Wolfe's head. When the shot fired, the servant's skull nearly exploded. Gore showered Arizona as he fell back into the wall.

Choking and coughing, the shamus leaned over with his hands on his thighs. He ripped off the remaining sleeve of his coat while he stared down at the body, trying to recover. Then he heard two hands clapping.

"Such a fine performance from two evenly matched opponents. I didn't suspect a mortal could do that. You've proven me wrong, my hero!"

Panthia stepped over Lance's body, not bothering to lift her tight dress.

"Now, let's get you out of those clothes. Come to the house; there's a shower waiting for us." She shifted the small bag that hung from her belt.

He looked up at the woman. His bloody face could not hide the disbelief in his expression.

"Merle, what kind of a nut job are you?"

He finally stammered out.

"Oh, that's right, you've met my sister. Unfortunately, she's unavailable to you now. I'm the ultimate victor, just like you."

The witch drew closer.

"This is so exciting. It reminds me of the old days when men fought for the right to seduce a woman. Panthia enjoys the winner."

To his amazement, Arizona found himself strangely enchanted with the woman. Despite the smell of the death and blood around him, her eyes held his as the man stood erect. He felt an eerie sense enveloping him as she smiled.

"You smell of heartbreak and triumph. You're experiencing those things that a conqueror feels when he destroys a city and brings the noblewomen before him. I require someone with your skills."

She came around him, sliding her fingers along his neck. The tingling sensation was cold and clammy, like a corpse. Yet her blatant seduction overpowered his growing need to run away from the tomb. When she came in front of him, he suddenly saw Cat Bennett's face and blonde hair.

"I can be anyone you want me to be. You long for someone you called Katherine. I can see inside your wretched heart." She cooed at him.

There was a tug in his mind to put his gun away. Automatically, he opened his coat and slid the revolver into the shoulder harness. Then, Arizona saw her eyes widen, and she took a step back. He looked down at the cross hanging from his neck.

"He carries no authority here!" The witch told him. "Remove it from my presence."

With her spell broken, the shamus shook his head and came toward her. Panthia did not expect the man's answer. He smashed his fist into her jaw. The woman staggered back, then fell between two coffins.

Arizona went over to verify if Lance still lived. However, he found no pulse as he leaned over.

Well, no more answers from him!

Arizona turned back to the coffins to retrieve the woman when she came at him. Panthia sent a shower of white powder in the air, and the man instinctively lifted his arm while ducking to the side. Immediately, the shamus felt his forearm burning.

Still coming around to her side, he saw the woman going for another bag hanging on her belt. Arizona stepped close and belted her as hard as he could in the face. The witch went down like a rock. The white powder fell from the bag she held, spilling across her legs.

Arizona had no time to gloat, as the pain in his arm became unbearable. Blisters covered his skin from the elbow down. He staggered out of the crypt, not hearing his own voice moaning at the agony. When he reached the night air, he heard screams erupt from Panthia that followed him into the night.

With only one thought in his mind, the shamus lumbered through the graveyard in his frantic escape. He fell at one point, then got up in the darkness. Soon, he stumbled to the path back to the car. Nearly out of breath, he fumbled with the car door. In the dim light coming from a streetlamp down the road, Arizona stubbornly shook his head. He refused to accept what his eyes saw. Some of the skin on his arm fell away when he fell into the vehicle.

Barely able to function between his agony and fear, Arizona sped down Andras Hill. He looked for the police car that was no longer there.

Hospital!

Barely able to shift the car gears, the man nearly drove off the road several times. His glance down at his arm almost caused him to throw up. Finally, Arizona refused to look at the damage.

No, it can't be!

After an eternity of suffering trying to push the vehicle beyond its limits, Arizona's eyes went out of focus. He recognized his limit was close. Then he saw Cat's face again. He could hear her voice urging him on.

The shamus fell into the car door as he turned into the parking lot of the hospital. His head nearly hanging out of the window, he tried to steer past the row of cars near the entrance. The ex-cop felt nothing as his sedan slammed into the backs of two vehicles, then glanced off to stop in a line of flower bushes near the walkway to the building.

Falling out of the car, Arizona saw the unfocused image of a woman in white running toward him. When she kneeled next to him, he grabbed her arm.

"Call Lieutenant Montgomery Sirk with Oyster City Homicide," he begged her. "It's important that you talk only with him. Tell him the cowboy knows everything about the Andras Crypt. He needs to go there now!"

Chapter 8: A Time for Regrets

Andy Devine paced back and forth in the library as he waited on Senator Reece. He wore a green trench coat, and his brown pork-pie hat dripped from the brief shower outside that evening. The new chief of police for Oyster City kept his hands behind his back to keep his boss from showing his nervousness. He occasionally glanced over at Peter Smyth, who quietly sat in a chair. Despite his boss's daily meetings, Devine still felt a wave of icy dread cover him when he looked at the man. It came from the fact that Andras appeared less and less human. Even the shadow that covered his face made it difficult to hide. He also knew the demon underneath gave no tolerance to mistakes. Devine had no intention of becoming a sacrifice.

That damn tip better be correct!

An ornate door behind the desk opened, and Reece entered the room. His eyes widened when he saw Smyth remaining in the shadows.

"My butler told me you have an interest in Della's recent death."

"Yes, that's true in a way," Devine spoke as he took off his hat. "I've received information that you've engaged a private detective name Ray Irish to look into your daughter's death. I'm here to warn you that this shamus is a known criminal. We're concerned that he might try to fleece you during this time of grief."

"And why would the Oyster City Chief of Police and the mayor have concerns about such an arrangement?"

The politician's eyes focused on the quiet man in the wing-back chair.

"So, it's true!" Devine sounded relieved.

"Senator, you're interfering in business you should stay out of," Smyth suddenly spoke. "The pictures we enjoyed showed that your daughter was simply doing what came naturally to her. Engaging Irish is a grave mistake."

Reece jumped out of his chair.

"You're the one behind this! I suspected that I'd bring the cockroaches from out of the shadows when I went after those thugs."

Suddenly, the senator's eyes went black, and his movements became stiff. Andras stood and walked closer to the desk. The demon's elongated jaw opened to reveal his now jagged teeth.

"You might sleep under the cross to ward off my dreams, but I can see inside your memories when I stand this close."

Smyth's gravelly voice filled the room. After a moment, he turned to Devine.

"He's got two people searching for Doctor Wolfe. Both of them are outside of my influence for the moment. I want your men to hunt them down."

The chief of police nodded; his eyes focused on Reece. Fear and torment covered the spellbound man on the other side of the desk. Devine slowly backed away and went to the phone. He glanced over at Andras, who stepped around the desk next to his victim.

"Now, senator, have a seat. You have a .32 caliber revolver in the right-hand drawer. You're thinking of using it on me. I'm afraid that it'll do you no good. Instead, you'll pull a piece of paper and write out your suicide note."

~~~

The car door slamming across the seat surprised Irish from his nap in the front seat of Edna's car.

"Do you want a piece of Rusty Picket?" Edna Ackroyd asked.

"Of course," he growled back.

"Then pull the car around to the alley."

Ray slid over as she got in on the passenger side, and he started the vehicle. The shamus steered the Frazer Manhattan around the club and into the nearly pitch-black narrow drive behind the building.

"Careful, don't run him over!" She grabbed his arm, then pointed toward a line of bushes.

"You got a cigarette?" She asked.

"No, I don't smoke. Where is he?"

"Damn, I deserve one. The idiot's behind those bushes. I dragged him out of the alley when he finally passed out. The bastard had his hands all over me, then tried to puke when his mickey took effect."

Ray got out of the car and went over to the shadowed area. He found the unconscious man, then struggled to lift him over his shoulders. Finally, he carried him to the car where Edna held open the trunk. Irish got him inside, then took a piece of rope to hog-tie their prisoner.

"There's an advantage to being a nurse. I can find ways to pay back jerks trying to put the moves on me," she boasted, then slammed the trunk lid closed.

"I'll remember that." He replied while looking around.

They got into the car, and Ray drove the vehicle through the alley and onto the street.

"Listen, what I'm going to do with this guy to make him talk will not be something to watch. Let me drop you off somewhere, and I can handle it from here."

"No, I brought him, and I'll finish it."

Ray stopped the car next to the curb, then turned to her.

"I've seen and been through my fair share of brutal beatings. Listen to what I'm telling you. You're not going to like this once we get started. I can't have you suddenly get squeamish. It'll kill the pressure on our prisoner. He can use any sympathy you give him to hang on."

She returned an icy stare.

"He's gonna pay for what he did. You can do this, or I will."
~~~

The shamus paused, rubbing the day-old growth of beard on his cheek.

"Alright, let's have it. You're not telling me something. Della was your friend. But this is a personal vendetta right now. I can see it in your eyes!"

The car remained quiet except for the engine humming. Edna stared out the window, refusing to look at him.

"Remember when I told you about my dad?" Her hands fumbled around in her purse; then she clasped it shut again.

Ray remained quiet as he nodded.

"Well, I didn't tell you about what happened in college. One of my dad's rivals sent his hoods to my apartment."

Irish put the car into gear when he saw her hands shake. Her lower lip trembled as well.

"Listen, you don't need to tell me. It's none of my business. You just confirmed my suspicion. A shamus gets a feeling around people and their reactions."

Ray glanced out the rear-view mirror before he turned the car into the street. They remained silent as the car continued along the side street for several blocks. As he drove along Broadway, heading to the city limits, Edna finally spoke.

"You should know, since we're in this thing together. In a way, they used me like Della. I found out later that the men who broke into my apartment were only supposed to scare me. It was to get my father to back off some petty territory dispute. It started the turf war that led to his death. I guess my dad didn't believe they'd go across the country after me. That's the other reason I joined up to be a nurse, to run away from the memories."

She went quiet for a moment.

"Like that didn't make it worse when I returned home. Anyway, some bastards who forced their way into my apartment were pretty drunk. They started with beating me, then…well, you can guess the rest."

Edna stared out the window at the passing lights.

"When they finally left, they bumped into a patrolman as they were leaving my building. I guess they panicked because one of them shot the cop."

The woman looked over at Ray.

"You see, that's why three men ended their miserable lives at the end of a rope. It was because they killed a cop. It had nothing to do with what they did to me! The police never asked me why the men were there in the first place. Like I was those bastard's moll or something. No, they liked the headlines of getting the cop killers off the street."

Ray let out a deep breath at the information. He stopped at the blinking red light, then turned on to the state highway.

"You won't like this question. Do you think what we're doing will change what happened to you?"

Edna remained silent for a while.

"No, of course not. Maybe it doesn't make sense, but I feel like I need to try. Besides, what other options do we have? Nobody's going to do anything about Della, except for us. Certainly, nobody's going to talk, and the police have no interest. I still say Della deserves justice. Just like I do!"

He watched her expression harden in the light coming from the dashboard.

"No, there are no other options," he agreed.

"Damn, I wish I had a cigarette!" Edna complained, then sighed.

Ray nodded.

"Alright, we're heading to a quiet spot where he can scream. Nobody will hear a thing." He grumbled as he glanced back in the rear-view mirror.

"Just remember, this isn't going to make you sleep better at night!"

~~~

The man in the trunk was just coming around when they opened the back lid. Ray half-dragged Rusty out of the dark hole, forcing face-first into the gravel path. When the prisoner struggled and mumbled, the shamus smacked him in the back of the head with his gun butt.

"Come on. It's time to wake up!"

He pulled Rusty to his feet and forced him toward a concrete structure that looked out over the Chesapeake Bay's edge. With his .45 auto pushed into the prisoner's back, Ray led them into the old artillery battery. The car headlights' yellow beam pointed at the narrow entrance, allowing Ray to see a thick steel pole where the large caliber gun once sat.

Irish stopped the groggy man in front of the pole, and then he tied his prisoner's wrists together. With Rusty's arms wrapped around the steel rod in the middle of the room, the thug shook his head.

"Wha'cha trying to do, scare me!" He mumbled out the words as his eyes watched Irish.

The shamus ignored him as he came around behind the prisoner.

"Here's how we're playing the game. You're going to tell me everything about your involvement with Della Reece."

"I remember you. You followed that no good tramp around for her daddy."

His smug grin lasted only a second when Irish threw a punch into the captive's exposed rib cage.

"Christ!" The man finally puffed out after sliding to his knees. He was still recovering when Edna came inside the concrete structure.

"That's your first and last warning. I'll ask the questions, and you will tell me the answers. Otherwise, more pain comes. It's simple, even for you!"

"Yeah, you're a hard flatfoot. Except you're too stupid to realize there's nothing you can get out of me."

"Like hell," Irish lashed out with his fist into the man's back.
~~~

Rusty groaned as Edna stepped closer. She waited until Ray came around in front of the man.

"Listen, you dumb hick. Della was my friend, and I'm going to enjoy my revenge. You'd better tell him everything," the woman told him.

Her vicious tone surprised Irish.

"You're too stupid to realize that I'm the same woman that you and your bastard friends hauled out of the shower that night."

Rusty grunted out a laugh at her.

"You're a whore like your friend! I should have done you that night. You enjoyed me feeling you up!"

The thug looked back and puckered his lips in a kiss.

Before Edna could say anything, Ray grabbed the man's pinky finger, then snapped it back. Edna winced at the sound of Rusty's scream. As the man slowly recovered with his panting breaths' echoes filling the area, the woman came around next to Irish.

"You can start cutting off parts of him anytime," she told Ray coldly.

This time, her tone got to the prisoner.

"Damn it; I didn't kill her! You can't do this!"

Ray crouched next to Rusty, taking his hair into his fingers.

"We can do anything we want tonight. Nobody's coming to save you. I remember you telling your buddies that I enjoyed taking a beating. I still got a couple of scars from that time. Isn't payback hell?"

Then he slammed Rusty's head into the pole. Irish followed with a backhand. Blood trickled from Rusty's nose while the prisoner shook his head.

"Just remember that you'll talk eventually. Maybe I'll need to cut off some fingers if breaking them don't do it. It's up to you."

Irish stood and grabbed the man's other pinky finger.

"No, don't! I swear I was only following orders for a guy. You can blame that senator. He didn't listen to reason. That's why we did it! There was no great harm to her. You followed her. Everyone knows she was a tramp. I swear she enjoyed every minute."

"Just like you'll enjoy this!" Irish growled at the thug.

Rusty's cries of agony echoed with the snap of the second finger.

"You've only got eight fingers to go before the pain becomes unbearable," Edna told him. Her chilling reminder slowly cut through the howling man's fog of pain.

"I know you can hold out for only so long. Everyone has a breaking point. And we have all night. When you finally break, I'll laugh in your face."

Sucking in the breaths, Rusty shook his head, and tears streamed down his cheeks.

"Son of a bitch, I can't. He'll kill me. The bastard is crazy, and he's got too many guys working for him. He rules Jacobi's men!"

"Well, you can die in agony here instead," Ray barked. "I don't care anymore. The only hope for you is to bare your soul."

He slowly walked around the prisoner. Then Irish appeared to hesitate.

"Alright, maybe I'll turn reasonable. Let's say that I'll give you an out. Might be that I drop you off on some lonely road heading out of town before I go after your boss. Otherwise, you can die for him."

Irish grabbed another finger. As he pulled back, Rusty pleaded.

"I haven't heard a name yet," the shamus calmly replied as he kept up the pressure.

"Wolfe! It was Doctor Wolfe who hired us. He used to run the state asylum."

Rusty's head dropped. Irish stood, his face darkened at the news.

"Do you know him?" Edna noticed his change.

"Yeah, I've dealt with the son of a bitch before!"

Irish grabbed the captive by the hair, wrenching back his head. After a couple of backhands on the man, Ray ordered him to tell them everything.

Slowly, the story of Della's nightmare of organized rape came out. The beaten captive gave them the names that he knew. Irish immediately recognized them.

"Yeah, some of us worked for Jacobi until he got knocked off. The gang kinda split off. Then, the doc came along, you know, paying us to do odd jobs for him."

"I'll bet!" Ray grunted. "What types of jobs?"

"Simple stuff. Get tough with people who weren't playing ball. Roust a store owner into insurance. Come on. You know how it works in this place. That's why Wolfe wanted me to get Della. Hell, it didn't take much, just buy her drinks, and she'd…"

Rusty's eyes widened, and he immediately shut up as he glanced over at Edna.

"I already know those two that help you kidnap Della. Keep going with names that night." Irish pulled up on the man's finger.

"Alright, some guy that Wolfe called Jack filmed the whole thing. Well, him and his assistant. I don't know the other guy's name. Wolfe also had some little tramp along to spice everything up. She called herself Velma."

"What a minute! Is Velma a platinum blonde?"

The prisoner nodded, sweat dripping from his brow.

"Yeah, she was wearing a nurse's uniform. Some wild broad. She took charge like it wasn't her first time. Velma got Della calmed down after giving her a pill, along with Slim's rotgut. That woman took the lead on everything for the rest of the night."

"You know that woman as well. How many evil people do you know?" Edna glared at Ray.

"Too damn many!"

He turned back to Rusty.

"You said everything happened out at the clinic. What happened to the patients out there?"

"Hell, I don't know. They closed the place, but Wolfe still hangs out there. I've only been in his office a couple of times. The place gives me the creeps with the screams and all!"

Rusty suddenly went quiet. The shamus realized the man said something he wanted to take back.

"Wait, you just said they closed down the place. Keep talking!"

Their prisoner shook his head stubbornly.

Irish pulled out his penknife. Then he placed the blade on top of the man's pinky finger. The prisoner's sweaty hand shook from the pain.

"Now, little man, you're telling me every detail. I want to know about what's going on out there and those jobs you've done for him. If I'm not happy with any of your answers, you lose this broken finger."

~~~

Lieutenant Sirk paced the floor inside the waiting room. He glanced down the hall, half-expecting police officers to show up. While the nurse kept her word to Arizona Campbell by calling Sirk at home, the cop knew his friend's whereabouts would soon get around.

When he arrived at the hospital, the nurse who called him took him aside for a moment to explain the patient's baffling injuries. She also told him that Arizona's arm required amputation.

"I'm afraid there's nothing the doctors could do. His flesh and tissue were almost gone when he fell out of the car," she explained after several glances around the quiet room.

"I've seen nothing like it before. All he kept saying was to call Lieutenant Sirk; I'm the cowboy. And that you need to go to the Andras Crypt. Do you know what that means?"

That news struck Sirk like a bullet, and he absently nodded.

How does a guy get burned so badly that they have to cut off his arm?

He pulled off his hat and scratched at his bald spot before putting the cover back on. Sirk's potbelly extended from his brown suit coat when he placed his hands behind his back. He continued his circular pace.

He did not like how the police department treated Campbell when he and Irish took down Jacobi's gang. However, Sirk never believed in getting involved in others' business. Campbell surprised him and the rest of the police force by becoming partners with Irish. Sirk considered Irish too headstrong and fixated on the strange things occurring in Oyster City. Now, Sirk wondered if Campbell got caught up inside a hair-brained scheme of Irish.
~~~

He carried worry for his friend in surgery, along with a desire to see what lay on Andras Hill. For the moment, Sirk recognized he had to keep things quiet. Running up to the estate where the mayor now lived made him think twice. He certainly knew that sending a police car up there to snoop around would have repercussions. That might create questions for which he had no answers. Still, he needed to find the evidence. The cop stopped and looked up at the clock, then went to the nurse's lounge again.

I need to speak with Arizona. It couldn't have happened in the cemetery!

~~~

Weary and still sick to his stomach, Irish pulled Edna's car into the back alley. His hands still shook from the brutality he inflicted upon his prisoner. The shamus refused to look in the rearview mirror during the drive. He half-expected to see Jacobi's torturer, Butcher Max, looking back at him.

The car sat behind the home of Vera. On their way around the block, he noticed a limousine in front of the house. A tough-looking man inside the car casually glanced at their vehicle as they drove by. Irish continued done the block and turned back up the alley to reach the back of Vera's house. After coming to a stop, the silent couple stared ahead. Finally, Edna spoke.

"You're right; I didn't like you when you started torturing him. Worse, I didn't like myself after that. I feel corrupt, like it ripped out a piece of me."

"You lost a bit of your soul,"nod. "Even if you decided he deserved it."

The woman turned her head and stared at the blackness outside the window.

"Do you think that they have people locked inside that clinic?" She finally composed herself. "Who could they be?"

Ray dropped his hands from the steering wheel and leaned back.

"I'm not sure."

The shamus looked at the silhouette of Doctor Wolfe in the closed curtain. His prey was talking on the phone. He saw Velma walk by on her way to a couch. The radio voices came through the open window—characters in the latest episode of Fibber McGee and Molly.

"But you think those people have something to do with this demon you told me about," the woman finished the thought for him.

He glanced over and noticed her unconvinced expression.

"Something wasn't right about that clinic and Wolfe's position at the state asylum. You never saw what Wolfe and Horne did to Florence Rice, one of my clients. There's also the fact that I know beyond doubt the Shadows kidnapped two high school kids and raped them. The police only found the boy, and he ended up under the care of Doctor Wolfe. That's more than a coincidence in my book. Wolfe, Smyth, La Spina, and the rest of these bastards come together to control and kill."

He let out a deep breath.
~~~

"Add to that, Wolfe had a psychopath torturer coming after me at one point with the help of a gangster. The guy inside that house is as dirty as you can get. Worse, he's got connections in the capital. We might go down a hole that might be impossible to get out of, but I'm going to find out the truth."

He quietly opened the car door. Edna hesitated, trying to grasp everything that he had just told her. Then she followed him into the darkness.

Irish found the backdoor unlocked. He stepped inside while pulling his .45 auto from under his coat. The shamus felt Edna on his heels as they eased their way through the kitchen. Ray heard the doctor hang up the phone and walk over to Velma. The sound of his leather shoes carried into the small hallway, where Irish peeked out. Just as Wolfe took a seat next to the blonde, Ray stepped out with his gun leveled at the couch.

"Alright, Wolfe, it's time for a ride. Keep your mouth shut, and nobody dies tonight!"

The psychiatrist didn't move. Unexpectedly, he smiled. On the other hand, Velma's initial surprise turned to fear when she looked at the gun.

"Of course, I should have known you'd find me." He glanced over at the woman next to him. "My dear, I believe Mr. Irish and his pretty friend have something in mind for us."

"You've got that right! Now, cut the talk and step over here. No need to attract the attention of your bull out front. Get cute, and you get hurt."

Wolfe glanced back at the curtain in front of the window.

"I see you've done your homework. Very well, it appears I don't have any choice. But I should warn you that you're making a terrible mistake. You really should leave and drive as fast as you can away from this city."

Ray waved his pistol toward the kitchen, and Wolfe's grin disappeared.

"Yes, well, you can't say that I didn't advise you. Come on, Velma. I don't believe he'll let you stay here."

"Not without a bullet in her head," Irish growled.

He enjoyed the panic that crossed the woman's face at his threat.

"I'm glad you're willing to see it my way."

"Go to the back door and make sure there's no one waiting out there!" The shamus ordered Edna.

She hurried through the kitchen while Wolfe and his companion carefully came toward Irish. He backed through the kitchen to the back door.

"No one's out there," Edna whispered. He saw a mix of excitement and nervousness in her expression.

"Alright, you head to the car and start it up. I'll escort our guests to the car."

Ray looked back at the couple.

"You heard the plan. Now follow the lady."

A minute later, Edna drove her car through the alley with the prisoners in the backseat and Irish holding his gun on them from the front.

"Where are you taking us?" Velma suddenly asked, her wide eyes remaining on the blued steel weapon in Ray's hand.

"To meet your fate! Shut up and enjoy the drive!" He growled.

"But mister, you don't need me along. I haven't done anything wrong."

"Velma, let the man have his hour of glory." Doctor Wolfe leaned back in the seat.

The man's confident, relaxed manner tore into Irish.

"Don't push too far, doc. A couple of bullets in the knees won't kill you, but you'll wish you were dead," Irish warned, then he turned his focus on Velma.

"As for you, bitch, there's a guy named Rusty in the trunk with a few busted fingers for lying to me. He told me everything about the things you and your friends did to Della Reece. You're on my hit list right with the good doctor here."

Velma slid back into the seat.

"You haven't introduced us to your partner in crime," Wolfe pointed out. "I mean, after all, shouldn't we know who else is going to die for kidnapping us, Mr. Irish?"

"I can talk for myself, you son of a bitch," the driver announced. "The name's Edna Ackroyd, a friend of Della Reece. I'm here to make sure that you're going to pay!"

Wolfe nodded.

"I see you want revenge. It's too bad that Rusty didn't bring you along as well that night. You know, you've got a certain pretty innocence about you. I'd enjoy watching Velma and you. Have no fear; I'm sure the master has plans for you shortly."

The man in the back seat smiled at the glare that Edna gave him through the rearview mirror.

"What the hell are you talking about?" Irish growled out.

"You'll learn soon enough," the man replied smugly. "Once we get to my clinic. That's where you're taking us, correct?"

Ray scowled. Wolfe appeared to know each step before they took it.

"You know what? My one mistake was not putting a bullet between your eyes the first time I met you. You keep pushing, and I'll damn well fix that."

"Detective, if you think I'll scare, then you're quite mistaken," Wolfe told him. "You see, it's easy to imagine what you think will happen. You want a film that I have. And you believe it's at my office. It's a simple deduction. You know, after Della played her role so well that night, I invited her to return. It's too bad she killed herself."

"Shut up!" Edna snapped.

"Ah, yes, Miss Ackroyd's involvement in this sorted affair," he ignored her. "What if I told you that the master already knew that you went to Senator Reece to involve Mister Irish? He expected your need for revenge would involve the shamus. The master probably implanted thoughts into your dreams for vengeance. He's quite capable of that."

The doctor put his arm around Velma.

"You know, dear, I've decided to have the master bring Irish and his girlfriend out to the clinic when the police capture them. We can use them for those experiments we discussed the other day. Would you like that?"

Velma glanced at Irish, then looked at Wolfe.

"Are you sure they can't do anything to hurt us?"

The doctor nodded.

"Of course I am; this is all for show. I've studied this detective. He talks a big game, but even this brute is timid with the action of murdering someone in cold blood. He can't! Remember what happened before when he entered the clinic? He couldn't even kill Horne for what he did."

"You're just asking me to beat you into a pulp," the shamus warned.

"That's not going to do you much good, but please continue this little charade." The man looked over the seat out the front windshield.

"Ah, there's our turn off now!" He smiled at Irish.

While Irish ground his teeth in frustration and worry, the conversation stopped for the last minutes of the drive. Still perturbed by the doctor's smugness, Ray manhandled the psychiatrist as he got them out of the car. Edna opened the trunk and helped the thug out of the vehicle. Rusty complained and yowled with his hands bound behind his back with each bump into his broken fingers. When he saw Wolfe, his face went pale.

"Alright, to those negatives and film," Ray ordered with a wave of his gun.

As Wolfe and Velma led the way across the gravel drive, Rusty followed behind them while staying quiet. Irish saw how the thug kept glancing around with thoughts of escape. Then Ray heard a pathetic cry. He stopped the group.

"Did you hear it?" He asked Edna, who nodded.

"Your man told me you had prisoners out here. Which building are they in?" Irish demanded.

In the dim light, he saw the man's frown.

"Do I need to break some of your fingers?"

"Alright, they're in Building 2." Wolfe let his calm demeanor slip. "But you're wasting your time. They're mentally unstable leftovers from Doctor Horne's work here."

"How dare you call people leftovers, you son of a bitch," Edna fumed.

She headed for the dark building. Irish glanced over at Wolfe's expression of hate.

"Looks like we'll start with that building first! Get going!" He ordered the trio.

Entering the building, Edna found the light switch. At the end of the corridor, they came upon an unattended desk. Edna saw a string of keys on the desk and picked them up.

"Show me where you've got them locked in!"

Wolfe refused until Ray struck him in the back of the head with his gun barrel. After a glare, then rubbing his scalp, Wolfe led them down another passage. Edna remained back with Irish as they took a flight of stairs to the next floor.

Halfway down the next hallway, Wolfe stopped them in front of a door that appeared more like a vault. The man hesitated after he placed his hand on the handle.

"You know you can't just release them into the world again. They convicted some of these people of murderer."

"What do you think?" Edna asked Ray. She frowned when she noticed his eyes were on the blonde woman standing next to her lover.

"I think that this lying son of a bitch doesn't want us to see inside." The shamus stated. "Velma is about to jump out of her skin. What about it? Are there only crazies in there?"

The nurse looked over at Wolfe, then slowly nodded.

He turned to Rusty.

"What about you, tough guy? Are you curious?"

With his eyes about to bulge out of his head with fear, the thug backed away, shaking his head. Ray went over and pushed him back to the door.

"Wolfe, prove it to us!"

The doctor opened the door, and the foul odor of sewage struck everyone, followed by pathetic moans and cries.

"Get the light on!" Edna grabbed Velma and sent her through the entrance.

When the blinding light came on, screams erupted. Ray pushed the two prisoners into the deep room. They nearly fell over the row of chairs moved into the middle of the area.

Inside the first section on their right, they found a line of people with their wrists handcuffed to a chain running along the wall. Only partially dressed in a wide variety of clothing, the prisoners attempted to shield their eyes from the lights' glare. Feces and urine covered the floor around their feet.

"You bastard!" Ray told Wolfe as he forced his three prisoners to the spot where the chain hooked into the wall. Their chains looked welded to the steel pillar running through the building.

"They're badly dehydrated," the woman quickly inspected the first woman before she went to the next prisoner.

"They've been beaten as well!"

He watched Edna work her way through the line. Irish recalled similar scenes many times before when the nurses and corpsmen worked their way through the dead and dying on the battlefield. Then Ray did a double-take, and he stepped down the line to an overweight woman partially hanging by her wrists.

Dressed in silk pajamas, the woman kneeled with her head thrust back with her mouth open. He recognized her dead, bloated face despite the mascara streaks running down her cheeks.

Pearl!

Ray recalled the banker's wife, who liked to be in the middle of the social circles of Oyster City. As he took a quick count of the other prisoners, he didn't see Pearl's husband.

The bastard is on the demon's side!

Rage filled him when he went back to Wolfe.

"You chained up nine people in this hellhole! And that woman's dead!" Irish pulled him from his comrades. "What kind of sick bastard are you?"

"Orders of the master," the psychiatrist's replied. "You'll soon find yourself with them. Their temporary suffering is nothing to their ultimate sacrifice, I assure you."

The man's disinterested tone finally got to the shamus. Enraged, Irish swung his fist. The satisfying sensation of Wolfe's breaking nose came and went too quickly.

The man cried out in pain as he fell to the floor of filth. Velma went to him, but Irish slapped her away.

"Touch him, and you get the same, you worthless bitch!"

He watched with satisfaction as blood poured from Wolfe's nose. The doctor pulled a handkerchief from his pocket and moaned while trying to staunch the flow.

"Ray, I need help here," Edna called out from the other side of the room. "Unlock these handcuffs."

Slowly backing away, the shamus glanced over. His partner was comforting a hysterical man in a tuxedo. Irish joined her, and she handed him the keys. As the shamus unlocked the first prisoner, he heard Wolfe speak up.

"You're wasting your time, you fool. Andras holds the trump card. I didn't tell you I received a phone call before you arrived. Do you realize that you longer have an employer?"

"What the hell are you talking about?" Edna looked over.

"Senator Reece is dead! I'm afraid that he took his own life less than an hour ago."

Wolfe rose while holding the bloody cloth over his nose.

"You're lying?" She stood up from the last captive, who was trying to thank the woman.

"My dear, I have no reason to lie. The master can make a mortal do anything. It was the Oyster City Chief of Police on the telephone line just before you and Irish came into the house. Devine was there when the senator blew his brains out. It seems your powerful ally named the two of you as the reason for his suicide. I think the DA will soon have warrants out for both of you for various felonies. The poor grieving senator tricked by those who failed to protect his daughter."

Irish went after the doctor again, but Edna stopped him.

"Ray, get the rest of these people out of the handcuffs. We'll deal with him later."

Anger made the shamus hesitate before he worked to release the captives. The first two captives went over by the door, where they halted. Edna went over to them. Despite the open door, the prisoners refused to move.

"You need to leave," she told them.

Irish finished unlocking the third prisoner when he noticed Wolfe moving from his position. The doctor's face showed his excitement while staring at the entrance to the room.

"Get your ass back," the shamus pointed his gun.

"Your weapon is useless against Andras," Wolfe boasted. "Before long, Mr. Irish, you'll be begging me for mercy. I'll ensure that your pretty accomplice enjoys all the pleasures and pain of the flesh while you die watching."

Ray glanced over at the entrance, and he saw Edna staring as well. Then, her attention turned to him while fear covered her face. She started toward Irish with halting, unnatural steps. Then the two prisoners next followed. Their expressions slowly twisted into a crazy mania. An icy fear enveloped him as he watched the group move toward him.

"Yes, it won't be too long now. Come, Velma, you must meet the master!"

Wolfe's awed tone carried over the surreal atmosphere.

"Stop this now, you damned psycho!"

The shamus rushed over to Wolfe.

"You should turn to meet me, mortal!"

A menacing chuckle came from the entrance to the room. Irish turned to see Peter Smyth. At first, Irish didn't recognize the silver-haired man. His grotesque looking face looked more like a deformed troll than a living human.

"Take his gun! I want that detective to roast upon my open flames."

The demon's voice growled out his order to Devine as the police chief stopped by his side. Ray sensed somebody coming up behind him.

Rusty!

Instantly, Irish slid over next to Wolfe, intentionally slamming the man into Velma. Taking advantage of the chaos, the shamus swung around with his .45. Despite his bound wrists, Rusty rushed headlong at the shamus. Irish fired his automatic, and the bullet struck the man in the middle of his chest. Rusty's body slid face-first onto the floor.

Immediately, Devine fired from the other side of the room. The bullet missed Irish, who moved in behind the doctor and his nurse. The shamus kept Wolfe between him and the cop.

"Kill Wolfe if you need to, but I want Irish alive!" Smyth stated as he stepped next to Devine.

The demon nodded to the people under his control. Again, they started their awkward push toward Irish.

"Wolfe, you're still my shield," the shamus told the man in front of him as he pressed his gun barrel into the doctor's back.

Irish saw Edna continued to come closer. Her face held no recognition of him; only raging hate showed in her eyes. He realized Pappy's cross was keeping him safe from the demon. Ray scanned the floor.

She needs her purse!

Velma turned on the shamus. Her sudden attack surprised Ray as he tried to hold his ground by throwing up his forearm. She bit into flesh through his coat with a snarling growl. Irish yelled out while he pulled away.

Devine pointed his revolver and fired. Irish heard the bullet strike the concrete pillar next to him, just missing his leg. Then the police chief fired again while Ray and Velma struggled. The nurse's attack suddenly weakened, and Irish shook her off of his arm. She looked down at the spreading red on the side of her robe. Then Irish struck her in the face with his fist.

Freed from the gun pointed in the back, Wolfe hurried forward to his master. However, the three prisoners under the control of Andras got in his way. He stopped in front of Edna with Irish on the man's heels. Ray got to the doctor, then pushed the smaller man into the two male prisoners coming at him. The line broke. Edna fell to her knee, while another spellbound captive fell backward.

Devine saw his chance. He fired several times at the moving shamus. This time, the bullets slammed into Wolfe, along with one prisoner. Screaming, the doctor fell to the floor, opening up a shot for Irish. The detective turned his .45 on Andras just when Edna attacked him. The demon fell back from the impact of the .45 bullet. However, Edna's fingernails raked across Ray's cheek. Animal-like, the woman sank her teeth into his shoulder with a snarl.

"Stop it!"

Ray punched his female partner in the stomach. When she fell into him again, Enda's face landed against the cross hanging down from his neck. Instantly, she screamed while backing away. The woman tripped over Wolfe as he lifted himself from the floor.

Edna came out of her blackness as the psychiatrist screamed for his master to save him. Then she rose to see the cross dangling under Ray's coat. Edna immediately hurried to her purse. As she drew close, the blast of more gunfire filled the room.

As they moved for better angles, Irish and Devine simultaneously fired their weapons. This time, the chief of police staggered when Ray's slug caught him in the shoulder. Fortunately for Irish, Devine's bullet struck Wolfe's arm first. The deflected lead cut across Ray's ear lobe.

Irish turned his pistol at Andras while the creature smiled at him. The body of Peter Smyth walked toward him with red stains covering parts of his expensive suit.

"Time to finish this!" the shamus cried out.

"Mortal, you cannot harm with such weapons," Andras growled.

"Time to find out!" Irish pulled the trigger.

His last bullet exploded through Smyth's head. As the demon's head whipped back from the lead that struck his forehead, his body fell back into the wall. Slowly, the Oyster City mayor slid down to the floor while blood spilled across his face. His wide-open eyes showed surprise, and Irish watched the unfolding scene with a sense of satisfaction.

Glancing over as Edna joined him, Ray was about to say something when he saw the horror on her face. He turned to see the dead man's eyes alive again with recognition, and his growling laugh filled the room. In disbelief, they watched the demon gradually lifted himself from his sitting position. Despite the massive wound in his head, Peter Smyth staggered to a standing position.

"Mortal, all the demons of my realm will feast on your flesh!"

The room filled with the stench of sulfur as the growling voice echoed in their heads.

"Let's see how you handle this weapon." Edna lifted her crucifix, and Smyth hesitated. His hideous face no longer smiled as he took a step back.

Ray noticed movement on his left. He kicked the woman away. Devine shot at Edna just as the shamus got there. Irish felt fire across his back as he fell on top of the woman. The shamus rolled over and stumbled to his feet with his empty gun in hand. All he saw was the blackness of the corridor, along with the sound of footsteps leaving. Immediately, Ray popped out the magazine and started fishing for cartridges in his coat pocket.

"Christ Almighty, what have you gotten me into?" Edna's voice trembled with fear and anguish.

The man remained focus on destroying his enemy. He started for the door to follow.

"Ray, that's not going to work. Stay here and help me."

Irish looked over to see the pain on Edna's face as she tried to get to her feet.

"Did you get a bullet?" Irish kneeled by her.

She glared at him; her face covered in filth and gore, then Edna groaned.

"No, you fathead, you twisted my ankle."

She held up her hand, and he helped the woman to her feet.

"You're not going to stop him with your damn gun," she told him, looking around. "Let's figure out who we can help and get them out of here."

~~~

True to her training and resolve, Edna cared for the wounded while Ray went over to unlock the remaining prisoners. They reminded him of shell-shock victims covered in their filth. He directed them to the door, telling them to get outside. Then the shamus heard Velma call out to Edna. The ex-nurse paid her no attention as she watched a prisoner shot by Devine gasp his final breaths. Ray looked at the dead captives on the floor.

Devine better hope I don't find him!

Irish stepped over to Velma. She held her hand over her liver. But the shamus had no sympathy as she pleaded for a doctor.

"You're done for!" He told her. "These prisoners are leaving! We'll send the state police when they are safe."

Velma's eyes widened at the news.

"No, you can't. I'm too young."

"So was Della!"

He left her crying, then went over to Wolfe.

Blood covered the floor from the doctor's frantic attempts to staunch his wound. His labored breathing told Irish that the man wouldn't last long. The man did not appear to know that Ray was standing next to him.

"What was that thing? He took over my mind!"

Velma cried out to Edna, who arrived and kneeled beside her.

"You understand, don't you?" she continued her confession while staring at Edna.

"I saw how that creep controlled you as well. I never expected Wolfe was crazy enough to get involved with something like this."

Edna remained silent, her expression cold even as she looked over the woman's mortal wound.

"I won't forgive you for what you did to my friend. As far as I'm concerned, you deserve everything that bastard Wolfe gets. It all comes back in the end."

"You join me in hell, whore!" the dying doctor suddenly cried out. "The master will come back. After he finishes ripping you apart, he'll give you to his demons for their fun."

"Shut up and enjoy the pain of death." Irish sneered at him.

"Have your fun now, shamus. Your days are numbered. You'll beg for death over a pit of fire!"

Ray spat on the ground, then kicked him.

"Burn in Hell, you insane son of a bitch!"
~~~

Irish waited for the psychiatrist to give his final breaths when Edna tugged at his arm.

"Come on; we need to get those prisoners out of this place!"

With a reluctant grimace, he followed her from the building.

~~~

It took a while to leave the compound. While Irish gathered everyone near Edna's car, the ex-nurse ran inside the other building. When she finally returned, Edna carried a small box of film and negatives. Then she drove the ragtag group into Oyster City.

The ex-nurse had the two women survivors sitting next to her in the front seat. One woman kept talking to Edna, but Ray couldn't hear the conversation. Squeezed in with the four males in the back seat, the wind rushing by the side of his face made it difficult to hear much. However, even with the windows rolled down, the shamus found the stench coming from the captives to be gut-wrenching.

As they rode into the town, Irish recognized the man next to him from the papers. Thompson Hunter sat on the city council, and he ran several successful businesses.

"The women in the front seat saw their husbands murdered. I think it had something to do with the *Smiling Lady murders.* Some kid broke in and killed them, but when the women tried to escape, they found men were waiting outside the house."

"It's the same twisted diversion. That explains why no one understood where the women went," Irish growled. "Thing is, I didn't even know you were missing. You're pretty prominent in Oyster City."

"It's my wife who's involved somehow as well! She was with me when several thugs grabbed me. I'll bet that bitch didn't call the cops. She didn't even bother to yell as they hauled me away in the back of a car. As I was in those handcuffs, I kept hoping it was about the money. Now, I..." He stopped and shook his head before turning back to Ray.

"What the hell is going on? I thought my wife wanted her youth again when Underhill got friendly with her."

"Are you talking about Marion Underhill?" Ray's interest grew at the news.

"Yeah, the jeweler. He's young and a lady's man, but I never for a moment thought that Rita was capable of this. It's like a damn movie. I saw you shoot the mayor in the head, and he got up and walked away."

Hunter shook his head, still trying to comprehend it.

"Yeah, this place is going crazy," Irish told him. "Don't think about it; just tell me what happened with all of you in the clinic."

Hunter explained what little he understood after being kidnapped. Most of the prisoners came into the facility over several weeks. The men who captured them gave the captives little water or food.
~~~

"That guy named Wolfe came in to look at us each day. I overheard him say something about a sacrifice on the next full moon, somewhere close to the clinic. I guess that was to be us."

Irish looked over at the other men's reactions to Hunter's story. Their dull, passive stares revealed hurt people lost in their own world of betrayal.

"Edna, we can't take them to the hospital or the police," Ray raised his voice over the wind noise.

She glanced back.

"Well, what do you suggest? We can't just take them home."

"Take us to my shop," Hunter spoke up. "We have showers and lockers in the shipping warehouse I own. I'll have my foreman bring clothes along for us."

"You're sure you can trust him?" Irish looked over.

"I'd trust him with my life," the man said. "We were in England with the 918th bomber group. Seventeen missions without a scratch, and now I have to worry about being some damned sacrifice."

Hunter laid his head back on the seat.

"You know you can't go to the police. Too many of the cops who work for Smyth or others might talk." Ray insisted. "Hell, the bastards might take you back to that damn place."

"I understand. I can't trust anyone. We'll get cleaned up and food, then figure out how to get the hell out of this goddamn city! I know people who'll fight this creature we saw tonight. By God, I'll get the governor in here with the National Guard troops!"

"That's the most sensible thing that I've heard all night. To your warehouse, we go." Edna stated as she looked in the rear-view mirror.

She glanced at the captives in the backseat. Their haunted expressions reminded her of a war that the woman wanted to forget.

~~~

It was nearly dawn, and Irish wasn't paying attention. He sat in the front seat as Edna drove. Bone crushingly tired, the shamus kept going over the events of the last few hours. When the car came to a stop, he looked up and noticed their location back at her apartment building. Ray got out and started toward his vehicle.

"Where are you going?"

"My office is back downtown."

"No, you're shot, mister. We both desperately need showers. You can use my spare bedroom to sleep in."

He turned around.

"No, I should go to Dunn's old office." He shoved his hands into his pockets.

"Don't be a fool. There's nothing but a cot there and no place to bathe. That's assuming that your partner hasn't already taken the only place to sleep. Nobody knows about my place in this crazy mess."
~~~

Edna's voice was tired, but firm.

"You're wrong! Andras and Devine know. That could mean the cops will come for you, even if that bastard police chief finally dies. You need to stay out of this case from now on."

The woman came around the front of the car. Her bloodshot eyes and pale face showed her exhaustion as well.

"Damn it, stop trying to play the martyr? They won't come to arrest me unless it's to get at you. Like it or not, we're in this together."

He recognized the apprehension on her face.

"You saw the creature had a way to control me. It scared the hell out of me, Ray. Stay with me."

His weary mind tried to put a plan together for her to stay away from him. Then a surprising thought crossed the man's mind. He wanted to go over and hold her.

I'll take you away and just let this place fall to the ground!

"Alright, let's get a couple of hours of rest and figure out our next steps," Irish told her instead.

He shook his head, trying to understand the reason behind his reluctance to act on his thoughts. He glanced at her building.

"But what'll your neighbors think?"

He was too tired to grin at his joke.

"You need to work on your lines. Let's get out of these stinking clothes and get some sleep."

Irish followed her into the building.

~~~

Lieutenant Sirk came out of the crypt inside the Andras cemetery with an expression of horror as a photographer's lightbulb flashed in his face.

"Get him out of my face," he growled at the *Beacon's* leg man, Seymour Trike.

"Come on, Sirk, you promised me an exclusive," the man replied.

"Alright, hotshot, go on in and get a picture. I'll have your hide if you touch anything."

He watched the reporter hurry inside with the photographer. As he waited, Sirk watched the rookie uniformed policeman coming back from the other end of the stone building. Neddly sheepish expression caused Sirk to grunt. Then he heard footsteps running from the crypt. Trike rushed by, nearly making it a tree before he threw up.

"You're a son of a bitch!" Neddly told him as he looked over at the reporter. "You didn't bother to warn either of us."

Sirk nodded.

"I suppose, but he wanted that exclusive. And as for you, I expected you saw
~~~

worse than that in combat.”

“You know I never saw action. I was stateside when the war ended,” the young cop complained.

The detective wasn’t listening. He realized he was breaking every rule in the book. That was his intent after he finally listened to the voices in his head. The cop couldn’t see Arizona, and his waiting finally got to Sirk. He saw the truth.

Once he discovered the corpses, the detective called it in to the police headquarters as a murder investigation and took charge. He wanted to shine a light on the grisly scene out to the world. With the chief of police nowhere to be found and the new district attorney coming to the cemetery, Sirk intended to play the dumb flatfoot for all it was worth.

Arizona found the gateway to hell!

“What are we doing next? I’ve got the medical examiner coming.”

“Standard procedure, rope off this place for the coming crowd of reporters and curious onlookers. Then you coordinate with the DA who’s on his way.” Sirk put his arms behind his back and started pacing.

“You don’t act surprised by this. How did you know that kid we were looking for was hanging out here?”

Lieutenant Sirk glanced back at him in the growing sunlight.

“It was a tip. I can’t tell you the source yet.”

“The mayor’s going to have kittens when he sees all cops and reporters running around on this estate. Didn’t he just move out here?”

The detective nodded, suppressing a grin.

“That’s what I hear! But this is a murder investigation. We have two men shot, probably by each other. Plus, another room full of corpses. I’m laying odds; they’re some of the missing people that we’re looking for.”

“I didn’t see any weapons,” Neddly told him. “But I didn’t stay long enough to look.”

“Don’t sweat it, I’ve got the weapon right here,” Sirk patted his trench coat pocket. “They were fighting for it.”

That’s how it will go in the report!

“So, those two men were working together on this. But why would they do store bodies in there?” The uniformed policeman watched as the reporter wobbled while walking toward them.

“Your guess is as good as mine right now. That’s why I’m investigating.”

Sirk smiled at Trike.

“Did you get your story?”

The man glared at him, then noticed his photographer leaving the crypt. Trike started pressing his partner about the photos. Sirk listened in on the conversation between the men as they hurried away.

“Well, that’ll make the front page in a few hours,” he told Neddly. “Now, nobody goes inside the crypt, and those men got in without my authorization. Understand?"

The policeman slowly nodded, unsure what the detective wanted. Sirk turned and walked away.

"Wait, what about the DA?" Neddly asked.

"Just tell him I'm following up on a lead. You do as I told you, and I'll be back. Remember, nobody goes inside the crypt but the DA and medical examiner. And the mayor if he leaves his house."

Chapter 9: Sow the Land with Salt

Two crucifixes fell into Yana's lap when she opened the airmail letter that arrived that morning inside the Boston General Hospital.

Yana,

I can't begin to express my many regrets for leaving you and Orella that morning. The news doesn't give many details, but I can only imagine it had something to do with Oyster City. Please make sure that you and Orella wear these for your safety. A priest from outside of Oyster City blessed them. You must understand that all Hell is breaking loose soon, and no one ever associated with me is safe.

I know you'll probably never forgive me for my failure to protect you and your daughter from harm. Take these as my small way to make amends.

Ray

Yana lifted the silver items the danced in the sunlight. Then, she carefully laid back in her bed. Her muscles still rebelled at specific movements near her stitches.

"What did you get?" Orella looked over after pushing away her tray in frustration.

Her mother showed her.

"It's from a friend."

"That bastard is no friend. I hope he burns in Hell for what he did," Orella said as he looked down at her bandaged hand.

Her index finger, like her injured hand, remained swollen from the damage and the surgery. Using only one hand made her life difficult. Orella also hated how the injury would look in the future.

I'm scarred for life!

"Don't say that. He helped us leave that place. There's no way that Ray knew they would come for you."

"How can you defend him? He left us when I needed him most. We nearly died while he's enjoying a train ride back to his lousy office. Then, the son of a bitch didn't bother to come back."

Orella's face turned ugly at her fury.

"You read the damn letter he left. He didn't even bother to wake me. He intended to leave me the moment that we left Oyster City."

Yana looked over, tired of the same conversation. Yet she still refused to explain her role in helping Irish leave her in Boston.

Maybe when she's married with children, then I can explain, and she'll understand.

"Yes, dear, he was an ass for doing such a thing. But he could have never known the morning he left that those evil women would find you."

"I don't care! No man is worth this suffering!" She held up her mangled hand. "On top of it, I'll bet the bastard won't even get our family's ring back unless we pay him for it!"

"That's not fair. Ray didn't do that to you. And I had to force him to take money from us after he brought back that cursed Singsing ring. Have you forgotten that? Why must you remain ungrateful to the person who saved your life?"

Yana grimaced when she turned her body to face her daughter.

"No man is perfect, most certainly not Ray Irish. Still, he doesn't deserve your scorn. And, for your information, that ring isn't coming back. I won't allow it!"

The stares between the women continued until Orella looked away. Then Yana picked up the letter and read it aloud to Orella.

"Does that sound like someone who left us high and dry? My god, he's all alone in that filthy city, and you want to blame him for trying to get you away from the danger."

"I just heard him admit he deserves my anger. I'm not going to forget that. Every time that I look at this hand, I'll know who did this to me," Orella grumbled.

She looked over at her mother, who angrily rummaged through her purse by the bedside. Then Yana used the back of the letter to write her response. Orella looked away in sullen silence. After a while, the grating noise of the fountain pen on the table got to her.

"Mother, maybe you can forgive him, but I can't. I won't!" Orella lashed out.

"Now you won't explain why you don't want our family heirloom returned. The Singsing's been part of us for generations. We deserve it back."

Yana paused her writing and looked out the window.

"You're correct; we do deserve what came from that ring," she agreed after a long sigh.

"Have you stopped to ponder that since we found the Singsing again, evil things came after us? It's not a coincidence. You and I've seen it in our dreams."

Her daughter flopped her head back on the pillow. Her expression betrayed her confusion and bitterness. However, Orella remained quiet.

"You've been hurt in so many ways. As your mother, each time I think of what you've gone through, I die a little inside. That's why it's time we let it go. I'm telling Ray just to throw it in the sea."

She wiped her eyes while the tension remained in the quiet room. Finally, Yana broke the silence.

"Orella, I'm going to tell you a story. It concerns your grandmother. She first revealed the truth about the Singsing. At the time, I didn't believe her. I couldn't believe something so fascinating carried a curse. Now, I do!"

A scowl came to Orella's face.

"What are you talking about? You've always told me that the ring brings our family good fortune."

"It was a lie handed down over the generations. Unfortunately, traditions die hard in our family." The woman laid back her head, remembering the experience.

"When I turned sixteen, my mother was in the kitchen, making me a special *dinuguanone* when I stopped to look at the Singsing inside that case. It sat by my father's dresser. For some reason, the ring seemed to call me. My father never believed in superstitions, so he insisted we display it. However, they warned us never to touch the Singsing. I remember how thrilled and terrified I was when I took it from its case. After I got it, I hurried to my room and put on the ring. I planned to wear it at my birthday party that evening."

Yana smiled briefly at the memory.

"I heard my mother calling me, and when I went into the kitchen, I never saw my mother so upset when she saw what I was wearing. No, that's the wrong description. Your grandmother was terrified. She slapped me, almost as a reaction."

The mother looked over at Orella.

"That was the only time my mother did that. Anyway, she made me remove the Singsing immediately. The whole incident terrified me, and I ran out of the house."

Yana paused, looking at the crucifix in her hand.

"Later on, after I returned, your grandmother came to my room and explained. I'll never forget the worry in her eyes when she told me that the Singsing came into existence from the blood of innocents. I asked for the reason, but my mother just shook her head. She refused to say anything more about it."

The woman sighed.

"Of course, I couldn't believe such things. Later on, when my mother grew old and forgetful, she insisted on telling me the story behind the Singsing. It was the first time I heard our ancestors worshiped a Wakwak."

"What's a Wakwak?"

Despite her initial skepticism, Orella found herself drawn into the tale.

Yana shook her head.

"It depends on the family tradition."

She looked over.

"But consider how similar the story is to what we just went through. Some say it's a bird-like monster that snatches people at night to drink their blood. My mother claimed it was a witch who worked for demons."

Orella looked at her hand.

"That man in the hallway. I heard people screaming that his face was burning. Merle must have done that," her reply was breathless. "But no one believed me."

"Orella, this is a modern time," Yana explained. "People can't believe it. That's why I told Detective Ryan that the women put some type of drugs in that drink they gave you. Otherwise, they'd put us in an asylum. Honestly, the policeman believes something supernatural happened, but what's he supposed to do? You must learn to forget that night."

She pitched the second crucifix to her daughter.

"Now, put that on and sleep peacefully at night. It's my mistake to let you wear the Singsing after you came back to New York. It's strange, but at the time, I hesitated. I should have listened to my fear. If you want to blame anyone, then blame me. I thought it was just a legend. When you went to stay with Ray, that's when the ring showed in my nightmares."

Her mother sniffed, forcing herself to hold back the tears.

"But Merle took my fingers. We know she must have some evil powers. Isn't it possible she could put a spell on me?" Orella's face drained as she spoke about her fear.

"Ray had these crosses blessed; it will protect you," Yana reassured her. "Well, go to church when we leave this hospital and give confession as well. You said that the main thing that those women wanted was the Singsing. But, to make sure, I'm asking Ray to destroy Merle and throw that damned ring into the sea."

Yana looked down at the letter that she started.

And ask his forgiveness for not telling him everything!

Orella stared at the item in her hand for a long time as her mother wrote. She thought about Ray's violent temper once he knew details of what happened after he left. At first, the woman wanted to forgive him. She delighted in the fantasy of Irish killing Merle. However, her anger about Ray's betrayal of her soon returned when she tried to use her maimed hand again.

Every time I think of him, I'll see this hand!

The nurse's soft footsteps entering the room caused Orella to look over as the woman approached with her medicine.

"Could I get you to help me put this on?" Orella asked the woman as she held out the dangling silver cross.

"Sure," the woman told her. "My, that's a pretty necklace. Is it from a boyfriend?"

"Hardly! I think it's a way for a bastard to soothe his conscience," Orella sneered.

She could not see her mother's reaction to the statement. Yana glanced over at the other bed, then returned to her letter and penned a quick postscript.

Ray, one last thing I must ask. Please forgive me for how things have turned out! You deserved a better explanation than this brief letter.

~~~

Irish only got a couple of hours of unrestful sleep as he lay on Della's bed. Every sound from the hallway kept waking him as the building tenants went about their daily routines. The sunlight coming through the open curtains caused him to lift into a sitting position. He heard the mantle clock strike out the time.

Damn, already noon!

Then he paused.

No nightmares!

For the first time since he left Boston, Ray came into the moment without the terrifying images still in his head when he rose. Clutching the blanket around him, he went to the open window. His suit remained filthy with stains and blood spots, despite his attempts at cleaning with Edna's naphtha. At least the fumes from the cleaning fluid knocked back the worst of the smell. He dropped the blanket and started to get dressed when Edna quietly entered the room.

She watched him for a moment, embarrassed for him yet strangely fascinated by the long scars that ran along his legs. The woman stared, then cleared her throat.

"Those doctors did a hell of a job on your legs."

The shamus glanced back with one foot in his pants. He continued dressing.

"Yeah, I'm a regular Frankenstein."

"I see you didn't sleep any better than I did." She looked at the door of her apartment. "Too many sounds in this building."

Ray nodded as he buckled his belt.

"Yeah, but no nightmares. Pappy's remedy appears to work. What about you?"

Her eyes widened.

"You know, I didn't think about it, but you might be right." She saw he wasn't listening.

"Is there something wrong?"

Irish looked back at her; disbelief filled his face at her statement.

"I mean, you're acting distracted. Is it your partner?"

"Yeah, Arizona didn't pick up when I called last night, either." Ray pulled his suit coat from the back of the chair.

"You'd make a good mother hen. I'll make us a pot of coffee. Are you hungry?" Edna called out as she went to the kitchen.

"Starved, but need the coffee more," Ray followed her.

He went over to the counter and picked up the phone. After trying Dunn's office again, the shamus called into the message service. The lady who answered told him there was only one message.
~~~

"It's a strange one with no return name or telephone number given. The message states the cowboy is in the hospital emergency room. I'm keeping him company."

Ray hung up, and Edna looked over at him.

"Forget the coffee. I'm heading to the hospital."

Thirty minutes later, Irish pulled up to the three-story building in his car, with Edna beside him.

"Alright, I'm going up the back way since I do not know what the cops might do. There's a visitor's room on the second floor. You find out where they have Arizona, and we'll meet on the second floor."

The woman nodded as Ray got out of the car. He walked along the front of the building before following the sidewalk around to the back. He found the back entrance to the stairs that Arizona had mentioned and went inside.

Edna entered the main lobby and went to the desk to find out more about Arizona. The woman wearing a nurse's uniform told her that Campbell was in critical care.

"I'm afraid that no one could see him at the moment. You can wait in the visitor's area on the second floor," the nurse suggested.

Edna thanked her, then went to the stairs. When she reached the room, the woman found Irish standing by the door. After she told him the news, they heard footsteps hurrying toward them.

"Irish, you damned fool. Are you looking to get arrested?"

"You don't think I give a damn about that right now, Sirk? How's Arizona doing, and what happened?"

Ray stood his ground as the detective looked him over. Then his eyes took the full measure of Edna as well. The cop's face softened slightly.

"Yeah, I get it," he grumbled as he directed them back to the stairway. After the cop scanned the hallway, he turned to Ray.

"Listen, I haven't got a lot. Doctors just got out of surgery for the second time. They told me they had to remove his arm. I overheard them say he'd never seen burns like that except from a steam explosion."

"Son of a bitch."

Ray's face paled at the thought; then he looked down the hall.

"What room?"

Sirk shook his enormous head.

"Won't do you no good. You can't see him yet. He's still under the drugs, and the doctors are in the room." He glanced at Edna again, and then the cop returned his focus to Ray.

"Can you tell me anything about what happened? When I got here, Arizona's car was halfway up the lawn. I don't know how he drove Cat's old car in his condition. What was he up to?"

"Hell, it was a simple stakeout job. Arizona had a tip that something was going on at the old Andras family cemetery."

"You're talking about the old graveyard on their estate up the hill, right?" Sirk insisted.

"Yeah, that's the one. Arizona told me it had something to do with those missing people," his curiosity grew. "Why, do you know something?"

"You can say that. Arizona told the nurse that discovered him to give me a message. I went up to that graveyard around sunrise. Our missing killer, Lance Carrol, was in the main crypt with a couple of bullet holes in his body, along with another guy who looked as old as Moses. We haven't identified him yet."

He glanced around before continuing.

"The whole damn place held recent bodies. I think those bastards used that family crypt for storing their murder victims. Hell, maybe even some damned occult stuff was going on from the candles and white powder I spotted, along with a half-filled leather pouch."

Sirk frowned and pulled his hat back.

"Where did Arizona get his tip?"

"That's the crazy part as well. Bishop La Spina told Arizona. He said the guy practically bragged about it. The bishop was in a group called the Shadows that—well, they worked for Smyth."

The shamus refused to tell the cop everything. Sirk was too stubborn to believe in demons.

"Are you serious?" The detective growled at Irish.

"Damn it, Sirk. I'm not a liar. I've got a partner who's hurt, and I'm telling you what I know."

"But if La Spina committed suicide after that guy tried to kill him, then I guess someone needed to follow up, even if it's a crazy idea."

The cop stared at Irish.

"He should have told me. That was not a shamus job."

"Sirk, don't point at me. You discovered Arizona was right. Let me turn it back to you. How could Smyth and his people inside the house not know about something going on in that graveyard?"

The cop scowled at him.

"I'll add another thing for you. Remember Detective Howard's death? Arizona told me that Howard died just like that ex-con Ulysses Davis that he and I found. You remember that—kind of the same as that chauffeur who worked for the bishop. I'm telling you that the same group worked to kill and kidnap people in this town. I'll make you even more uncomfortable. The whole thing's coming from the top!"

Irish looked at Edna, who listened with interest. Understandably, her skepticism had vanished. However, Sirk remained unconvinced.

"Are you telling me that the mayor and others are involved in the kidnapping and murders occurring for the last several years?"

The detective grew nervous as he glanced around the area.

"I'll admit that what I saw is unbelievable, but I got a different idea. What I found were two fresh bodies who lost in a shootout with Arizona."

"They shoot it out with him, then somehow Arizona gets burned bad enough to lose an arm. Come on, Sirk. Not even a dunce will buy that."

The cop screwed up his face in frustration, but the shamus continued.

"Get a grip on this as well. I had the chief of police and the mayor trying to kill me last night. Your boss, Devine, shot down several people in cold blood. They just got in the way. That includes Doctor Wolfe and his nurse. Their bodies are out at the Horne Clinic."

Sirk's shocked expression at the news might have made Irish laugh, but he heard a door open.

"Sirk, quit trying to save your pension, or you'll..." Irish stopped, then looked over when he heard voices in the hallway.

"You're off your rocker," the cop started.

Irish didn't say anything; instead, he pushed past the cop. The shamus went to the small group of doctors and nurses who emerged from a room.

Edna grabbed Sirk's arm when the detective tried to follow Ray.

"Mister, I think you should listen to him. I'm a witness to the whole thing. I've seen a picture of Andy Devine in the newspaper. Will you believe me when I tell you that your boss shot several people in cold blood? Irish didn't tell you he put a bullet into the man's shoulder."

Sirk remained rooted to his spot in stunned disbelief.

"I didn't believe any of this until I saw it with my own eyes," she continued. "Irish told me you're one of the good cops left in Oyster City. If you don't believe us, then take a trip to that clinic outside of town. The bodies are still there! Get Devine's gun, and you have your killer along with a lot of information about everything in this city."

The woman left Sirk in silence. Shaking his head, the detective slowly followed her for several steps. Everything he heard and what he already knew caused the policeman to go into the visitor's room. Sirk picked up the phone while he watched Irish talking with the small group of hospital staff.

"Are you his next of kin?"

"No, and there's none around. Now, how's my partner doing?" Ray repeated with an exasperated growl in his tone.

The doctor had the freckled face and blue eyes of a kid just out of high school. However, his expression darkened as he laid out the injuries.

"My colleagues and I are having a hard time trying to determine what happened. His flesh carried injuries that appeared similar to acid burns. However, the damage to the tissue also carried signs of napalm-like substance."

He shook his head.

"I'm sorry, but the trauma was widespread, and we had to remove his arm. His condition is stable but weak because of the extensive loss of blood and the injury."

Edna asked for more details. The man hesitated before explaining what Ray didn't want to remember from his time spent in too many hospitals. Then he heard a remark about Arizona's head wound.

"Wait, you mean someone tried to cave in his head?"

The doctor frowned.

"The injury was similar to that. However, it's possible that the trauma came from his crash out front."

"That's doubtful," Sirk declared as he arrived. "I found the damn bowler hat back in the crypt. It had a crease in it. There was a piece of iron lying nearby. My bet is someone struck him!"

The cop's expression changed when he realized his observation went against his theory of a shootout.

"How soon before we can move him?" Ray's question caused the doctor and nurse to stare in bewilderment for a second.

"Well, the patient just came out of surgery, and he's only been stable for a short amount of time. He could go into shock."

"Irish, what are you fishing at?" Sirk pulled his handkerchief and dabbed at his bulbous nose.

"Damn it, detective, how long do you think Arizona will last without a guard at the door? That wasn't a bullet that got his arm. Remember Wilber, who tried to kill the bishop? I think it's the same group."

He ran his hand through his hair.

"Think about it. Either Arizona's injuries are part of your mystery in the crypt, or he plays with napalm as a hobby. Those are your options. There are no others."

"Always a wise guy," the cop let out an exasperated grumble. He slowly nodded as he glanced at Edna.

"Alright, I'll figure something out to keep him safe. You and the lady follow me."

Sirk led them to the stairway.

"Both of you need to leave here. I just called the county sheriff to do a drive-by at that clinic. Right now, it's just a tip. But if it's as bad as you say out there, then I suspect all hell will break loose. The press will make it out as another Saint Valentine's massacre. Many people will be interested, including my boss. You understand that there's no one to protect you in Oyster City."

He turned to Edna.

"A word of warning, I'd get out of sight," the cop let out a frustrated breath. "I don't know what's going on between you and Irish, but you should find the first train out of town. Got it!"

"I forgot to tell you that Devine and Smyth had captives handcuffed inside the room where you'll find the bodies. Building 2…"

Ray interrupted as he pushed Edna through the open door into the stairwell.

"Yeah, we get it. We'll call you later," the shamus told Sirk.

He paused.

"Lieutenant, I know it doesn't mean much coming from me, but thanks. Keep Arizona safe."

"Get out of here!" Sirk told him gruffly.

He scratched his head as he watched the couple going down the stairs. Sirk wondered what Edna was trying to tell him.

Ray's not a liar, but he's not telling me something!

Then, the detective saw the freckled-faced doc standing by himself at the nursing station. He hurried over.

"Say, doc, that man you just worked on might be an important witness for me." Sirk looked around. "Problem is that I need to protect him without a lot of guards, and, for that matter, nobody knowing his location."

"That's why your friend talked about moving him so soon," the doctor smiled.

"Well, we're not buddies," Sirk grumbled. "But he's got the right idea. It could be nothing, but I got to make sure that someone can't slip into Arizona's room when no one's around. Do you have any way that we can kind of put him on ice so nobody would know what room he's in? I know it's some trouble for you, but I can't think of a better way. I can't get a policeman to hang around just because I have a hunch."

The doctor looked around, then slowly nodded.

"I think I understand. I'll set up something with his nurses, at least until you can move him. If someone asks for him downstairs, I'll make sure that we contact you. How does that sound?"

"That's better than I hoped. Thanks, doc. You're the tops!"

As the policeman walked back to the patient's room, the doctor smiled to himself.

I haven't heard that expression since my pop used to say it!

~~~

Andras stood in front of the dressing mirror. His body was already suffering the effects of the wounds caused by the bullets. His brain injury made it difficult to move and control the dead body. The flesh covering him already smelled of rot, so there was little use in trying to hide the injuries. He glanced back at his bed, where the last of his witches watched over a sleeping Devine. She tended to his
~~~

arm and put the man asleep with one of her spells when they arrived at the mansion. Andras observed Panthia running her fingers across the naked man's chest.

"I have a use for this mortal's body if you don't need him," she told Andras without looking up. "He's not a loyal follower, and he serves for an opportunity."

"He's just another sacrifice," the demon told her in a gasping voice. "Like the rest of those who attend my festival, we'll use him to feed my brother demons when they arise tomorrow night."

Smyth hobbled over to his window and stared down at the activity on the lawn.

"You were fortunate the police did not arrive on this estate when that detective killed Wolfe. It is not as I've foreseen."

Andras frowned as he looked back from the curtain.

"I don't understand why that man looked into the crypt."

"He's the partner of Ray Irish, the one who continues to get in your way. Perhaps he sent that detective?"

She walked to the end of the bed.

"Yes, it's possible. Irish remains protected by the wretched son from Nazareth," the demon looked over at the man in the bed. "And Devin failed to kill him. Another mortal who cannot do the job."

He looked back at the window.

"I must know what they are saying about this discovery on the estate. Yet, I can't go out of this house to find the truth. I'm trapped for the moment. It reminds me of..."

The creature whipped the curtain closed. He remained silent in thought, then turned to the witch.

"After you encountered that ex-policeman, you fixed your flesh. Can you do such a conjuring for this body?"

Panthia looked over at Andras, surprised at the question. She felt a moment of weakness in the demon. The woman frowned as she stood to show her long legs, which carried no scars from her injuries that came a few hours before.

"I've only barely managed to fix my injuries. Unfortunately, you've waited too long," the witch lied. "However, it's only one more day for you in that shell."

Andras acted like he did not hear her when he crossed the room.

"Mr. Wolfe is dead, along with the doctor. I don't like this," the creature fumed.

"Well, I have an idea that can help you," she suggested.

The demon glanced back.

"What is on your mind, woman? You're growing confidence makes me suspicious."

"You have two mortals who remain dedicated to your cause. I suspect you wish to bring back the Shadows for your work. They carry influence for you."

She watched his expression turn foul at the idea.

"It's only advice, but if you order Devine to rein in the police who remain on the estate, then send me after those two detectives who remain alive. I want revenge on the ex-policeman who tried to hurt this body."

His silence told the witch that he was interested. Andras slowly walked back to the bed, and his head dropped as he considered the idea. She noticed the corpse's hair pulling away from his scalp. The demon looked more and more like a cadaver each hour.

"Alright, Panthia, you'll have your revenge. But first, take those men who worked for Wolfe and get me my sacrifices for tomorrow night. We've lost our prisoners. Grab whoever you can from the streets, but one of them must be Irish. I want him to roast over the pit. It is the last time he gets in my way!"

The creature looked down at Devine. Immediately, the sleeping man's eyes opened. He stared at Andras, his eyes blinking lazily.

"You go back to your office," the demon told him. "I want your policemen sent away from this estate immediately. You can make any excuse to get your detectives to look for someone else. Then you will wait for my next instructions."

Like a drunken man, the chief of police tumbled out of bed. He stiffly pulled on his shirt in a trance while Panthia went to the room's entrance.

"Woman, don't disappoint me!" Andras growled out as she held the door for Devine, who slowly stumbled along.

The witch looked back with a stunning smile.

"I'll have everything prepared. I'm taking this mortal to his office. After that, I can assure you everything that we've planned will go off without a hitch, my master."

~~~

"Aright, now you know as much as I do," Ray told Edna. "Somehow, a demon took over Peter Smyth. Probably as part of the Shadow cult that La Spina worked with. I know that the surviving members are Underhill and Phillip Smyth. Oh, and now Devine, of course. Other than that, I'm not sure who we're up against."

He put his fork down on the plate before leaning back against the chair. He refused to look down at the unappetizing meal that was nearly as bad as boot camp chow. While the shamus regretted coming back to *Vinnies*, he believed it was the safest place, since the police never stopped at the diner. It had lousy coffee to go along with terrible meals. He swore it only stayed in business as a front for something else. Given the looks he saw from the few patrons, he suddenly believed it might have been a mistake to come here.

"You know, if you'd told me this at the beginning, we could have saved a lot of time." She pushed her plate away with a grimace. "I could have just told Reece that you were a nut job, and I would have gone my merry way."

Edna tried to make light of the situation, but Ray saw through it. He made a
~~~

feeble attempt at a grin.

"And you would miss these high-class places I take you to." The shamus said as the waitress approached. Her sour expression showed that she didn't appreciate Ray's humor.

"Are you done?" She picked up the plates before they could answer.

"Yeah, how about a refill on that coffee when you get back?"

The waitress nodded before hustling away. She walked past the counter toward the back of the diner.

"How did you find this place?" Edna's tune was more shocked than amused.

"The cops won't come by. I think someone at City Hall looks the other way at some crooks that come here. At one point, the gangsters ran it. Anyway, it's the only place where I could meet Arizona. On a good day, you can look across the street and see the same empty harbor as you can from on the hill."

He leaned on his elbows as two hobos sitting at the counter started to argue about how they would split the single sandwich they ordered.

"Listen, let's get to the point. You know what I'm up against. There's nothing here for you. Take Sirk's advice, pack your bags, and get yourself to a nice place without this?"

Ray gestured to the room.

Edna glanced over at the squabble, which died down when the overweight cook came out of the kitchen. He called for the waitress, then went back through the double doors as he cursed.

"Ray, I'm not going to lie to you. After the other night and reading about the death of Senator Reece, I'm scared beyond belief. I'm not joking when I tell you I want to leave Oyster City."

He looked at her trembling lower lip and nodded in agreement.

"Then, go! Nobody will come after you."

The woman stared at him, then shook her head.

"Are you that dense?" Edna stopped, her troubled expression catching Ray off-guard.

"No, that's not what I should say."

Her hand shook as she tried to maintain her composure.

"You once asked me a tough question about Della. Now I have one for you. I'm curious how much do you care for Orella, or for that matter, Yana? Or did you leave them both, so you didn't have to decide?"

The big man's eyes narrowed, and she recognized his anger building inside.

"No, it's a fair question, given what I've seen so far," she stated calmly. "Why must you return to Oyster City? Would you rather face that bastard Smyth instead of people who?" She paused. "Well, those who find a way to care about you?"

Irish got up from the table and threw down two dollars.

"That's for the meal. I'll be damned if I answer such stupid questions."

Ray told her as he left.

The shamus was outside at the next building, walking along the sidewalk, when he heard Edna's voice again.

"Stop, you asshole!"

When Irish turned, Edna was in his face with a furious anger that matched his growing temper. Her blue eyes were almost gray as she started cursing at him like a sailor.

After the initial shock of seeing her rage at him again, Irish suddenly smiled. He couldn't help it. The sight of the slender woman raging at him along Dock Street in broad daylight struck him as hilarious.

Then Edna punched him in the jaw.

It hurt!

It also wiped away his silly grin.

"You thick-headed bastard!" The woman twirled around in pain while grabbing her injured hand with the other.

"Damn, that hurt!"

Ray stared at her, rubbing his jaw.

"Enough, Edna! You win, alright!"

His large hands stopped her from moving away as he gripped her shoulders tightly. She quit resisting when he apologized.

"I'm sorry for being a jackass. You're right, I should answer."

Her shoulders slumped.

"You damn fool, you won't go!"

He let out a long breath as he looked across the street at the dock. The shamus saw the spot where the *Stanley Rose* remained in a watery grave about a mile offshore. He let go of her shoulders and stepped into the street. Ray got halfway across and stopped to look back at her.

"You want to know, then follow me!"

As he waited for an opening to cross the oncoming traffic, a curious Edna joined him.

"You know, they placed all the dead and injured from the *Stanley Rose* disaster on this dock."

He glanced over at her nod, and then he hurried across the road.

"I was right in the middle of that," he told her when they reached the sidewalk. "I walked away without a scratch, just covered in cold water. Out there is the spot where the ship sank."

Puzzled at where he was leading, Edna followed him as they wandered along the mostly unused rail tracks before turning to the pier.

While they slowly walked, Ray told Edna about the night of the sinking ship. He explained his complicated relationship with Katherine and her father, J. Allen Dunn. Silently, she listened to the man's meeting with Greye La Spina and their affair. After a while, they came to one piling at the edge of the dock. They sat on the piling and looked at the scummy water below.

"You want to know about Ray Irish? Here's a startling fact for you. I arrived in Oyster City on the top of a train car, nearly frozen to death. Half drunk, I watched people inside the diner car eating while I debated just sliding off the top each time the train came to a river."

"At the end of the day, I'm nothing more than another one of those nameless tramps you saw in *Vinnies*. Some will tell you I'll do almost anything to make a buck. I damn well have in the past to get my booze. Now, I'm making a living playing a shamus, but it's because I don't know what else to do. That's the truth about Ray Irish."

"That doesn't tell me anything about why you can't answer the questions," she continued to stare at the water.

"What I've just told you is more than anyone else knows about me. I'm not a good person, probably a bastard in a lot of ways. Still, I won't make excuses for my past. The one thing that this city hasn't done to me yet is to turn me into a liar. You asked about leaving, and here's the truth. It would be really easy for me to run away with you, Edna. Hell, of course, I'm scared like you. Who wouldn't be when you got something you don't know how to stop?"

Ray looked over at the woman. Her profile held a serene expression. Edna would have been a superb model for an artist, he decided.

"Yeah, I could say hell with it and follow your smile anywhere. That's what you really wanted to know, isn't it?"

He grunted, and he looked over at a security officer wandering along two piers over from their location.

"It wouldn't be good for you, but I could do it," Ray continued. "Lord knows I had thoughts about Grey and getting her to leave her husband. But she was a grifter, in a way, probably too much like me. To answer your question, I was never in love with Orella. The truth is, she fell for me because I was the hero in her mind. I could never live up to what she saw inside of me."

The man turned away again.

"Yana's smart like you. She pointed out that her daughter was too young and naïve. Of course, I ended up with Yana as well. Felt like a damn fool later, but it didn't matter at the time."

Ray shrugged his shoulders.

"Anyway, Yana came here to get her daughter out of Oyster City. Yana told me about the nightmares, and that was happening in New York. I saw what Orella was facing each night with her dreams as well. So, I concocted a plan for them to go to Boston with me. The intent was to leave them there. That damn Singsing ring had more to do with me getting them out of here than anything else. If Andras wants it, it needs to go far away from here as possible."

Irish paused, looking down.

"Now, you know the truth about those women and me. I agreed with the decision because it was right for everyone involved. I even reminded myself how much the whole thing turned into a soap opera."

He stood and scuffed his leather sole on the pavement, then shoved his hands into his pants.

"Part of being a jackass is stubbornness. This damn city tried to kill me coming in. I'll be damned if I let it force me out without my agreement."

Edna remained silent, listening to his reasoning and surprised that she didn't walk away in disgust at some things he told her. She reasoned that asking for the truth and not listening to his unpleasant tale made her a hypocrite. In the end, she felt terrible at the situation, not at him. He was no different in his attempts to survive bitter experiences and to make sense of life.

"Maybe, I'm damned anyway."

Ray's words came through her thoughts.

"I can't answer a simple question that's been going through my head for a while now."

He stared at the spot where the ship went down. Edna crooked her head to look at him. Her demeanor remained distant but thoughtful.

"What is your question?"

"Who else is going to stop Andras?" He glanced over when he told her.

"Have you considered that maybe you can't stop that thing? Why are you playing the hero this time?"

Ray's immediate glare softened when he saw her expression.

"I'm certainly not trying to play a hero." Ray pulled on his earlobe. "It's hard to explain, but I feel like I have ghosts tugging at my sleeve. They're pushing me along this path to fix things. I swear I can almost feel it."

The shamus shook his head. Irish glanced back at the road.

"You wrapped your pain around an idea of justice for your friend. Hell, maybe I'm doing the same thing in some strange way with those that died because of this demon. There's a trail of bodies from here to the capital coming from Andras."

Their eyes met again.

"As to stopping the son of a bitch, well, I do not know. All I know is Pappy said they drove the bastard back to Hell before. I have faith in that. I thought about what happened last night, and I've seen how the crosses protected us. Maybe it's part of the plan."

The man smiled to himself.

"Maybe it's someone's way of turning me into a monk!"

Edna didn't laugh. She only nodded and turned back to the harbor. They were quiet for a while, each left to their thoughts.

Unable to shake the feeling that someone was staring at them, Ray looked back at the row of buildings behind them again. Only a few dock workers, most in dungarees and caps, were on the other side of the road. They were standing in line outside of the Union Hall, talking among themselves while they smoked their cigarettes and pipes.

Edna rose. She stepped closer to the man. He smelled the scent of her perfume, and Ray grew tense.

"I keep thinking about the danger we face. Honestly, I don't think this place is worth it."

The woman's pretty eyes expressed her feelings.

"But there's something else. You're still in love with ghosts. Do you know how creepy that appears?"

"I suppose it might appear that way." The shamus nodded, trying to remain detached from the rising emotion he felt inside.

"If I told you I'm leaving, how would you feel deep down inside of you?"

Ray looked away, but she put her hand on his cheek and forced him to remain focused on her.

"I need an honest answer."

"Well, my first thought is that it proves you're a smart lady. In one way, I'd be relieved."

He put his hands on her shoulders and drew her close. Then Ray kissed her on the lips. When he pulled back, he smiled at her surprised expression.

"That's also how I feel. As crazy as it sounds, I think you're one hell of a woman, Edna Ackroyd. Far better than a guy like me can hope for. Now, be that smart girl, and get the hell out of here."

Her stunned expression quickly faded, and she smiled.

"Well, you're a flatterer, that's for sure. But I won't chase you. You need to remember that. Now, come on."

Edna started back to Dock Street.

"I'm not making any promises that I'll stay here. But why don't you talk with Pappy again? Maybe he can come up with a way for us to leave this place. Hopefully, walking on our own two feet and not in a pine box."

~~~

When Irish arrived at the apartment building with Edna, the sun was alright close to the horizon. Ray told her about Pappy's ghost wife as they took the elevator. Her expression remained strangely serene at the news.

"I've come to expect it with you." She announced when they stepped into the hallway. Black men carried boxes toward the elevator and suspiciously eyed the two strangers who passed them.

"I wasn't expecting you," Pappy told Ray when they walked past the opening into the nearly empty apartment.

"You weren't lying about leaving." Irish looked around. "It's strange to not
~~~

see all of your bookshelves and furniture." He glanced over. "I'm disappointed that you didn't bother to ask for my help."

Pappy absently nodded as he looked at the woman with him.

"Oh, I'm sorry. Edna, this is Pappy. He's probably the best friend I've got in this place."

She shook hands with Pappy. They glanced over as a man entered the room.

"Uncle, we're almost done. We need…," the young black man stopped. His expression immediately turned hostile when he saw Irish.

"What's this whitey doing here? Isn't it enough that he's involved in what you've already been through?"

"Ray, this is Joshua Johnson. He's the nephew I'm always talking about."

The man scowled at his young relation.

"He's not normally so rude to my friends. Now you get the packing done. I have important things to discuss with my friend."

Pappy's nephew looked over at the couple, then went into the bedroom in a huff. Pappy waved them into the kitchen.

"I have a pot of coffee on the stove. Let's talk about why you're here. My Emma told me you'd be dropping by."

The man pulled two coffee cups from a mostly packed box sitting on the counter as Irish followed Edna into the room. It was the only box left in the kitchen. Everything that Ray remembered about the apartment was gone, replaced by the empty feeling of open space. As Pappy poured the coffee, he apologized.

"After that beating that I took the other night, he and his friends don't trust the white folk."

He turned and handed them a cup.

"Well, there's been other things as well. Bad people are coming into Oyster City. They don't like the colored folk either. This demon likes chaos and destruction."

After he looked them over, the newsy shook his head.

"So, you're still going to stop Andras. I should have known you'd be foolish enough." The man looked at Edna.

"What about you?"

"I'm just a fool, like this dope." She smiled momentarily, but Pappy failed to laugh. His serious expression remained.

"As soon as they know you're with him, they'll come for you."

"They already have," Ray interrupted before he took a sip of coffee.

Pappy shook his head as he poured a cup for himself.

"No, as I said, Emma had a feeling. Now, she agrees that you're both fools."

He paused after he poured his coffee.

"By the way, I heard Arizona was in the hospital. One newsie stopped by and told me he had a shootout with a couple of killers.”

He turned with a frown.

“Darn, I’m already missing my newsstand.”

“Well, the cops don’t know what happened. The problem is that Arizona came out of the Andras crypt with his arm so mangled with burns that they had to amputate it.” Ray downed the rest of the hot liquid.

“No, you don’t say. That’s a damn shame. Oops, sorry young lady. I didn’t mean to curse like that,” Pappy told Edna, who smiled back.

“Don’t worry, he’s said a lot worse,” she nodded to Irish as he poured more coffee for himself.

“And she’s not quite what she seems either,” the shamus retorted. “Anyway, why would a demon do that to Arizona? I’ve only heard of this thing getting into our minds. Sirk mentioned they found a white powder. I don’t know what that can mean.”

Ray shrugged when he looked over at his friend.

“Seems more like witchcraft to me,” their host speculated.

“Maybe his followers are coming home to help him. All I know is we need to get out of Oyster City before tomorrow night.”

“Wait, why do you say that?”

Edna’s eyes widened, and she glanced at Irish.

“Emma tells me the next full moon means the demons will rise. That’s tomorrow at 11:59 PM. Oyster City will not be a place to stay when the demons come to feed on the living.” Pappy told her. “Those who stay can expect Hell on earth that night. Like I always say, when ghosts are afraid, you’d better listen.”

His warning caused the conversation to stop with an uneasy air hanging over them.

“I know that these crosses around our necks help ward this damn thing away. Yet, you and your wife won’t believe that someone can stop this Andras. They sent him back before.”

Ray reminded him.

“After hundreds, maybe thousands of deaths,” Pappy quickly replied. “Look, everything I’ve read tells me that people can stop a demon. But many people die when it comes to Andras. Plus, it’s not clear the best way to remove his presence. The first time, his advisers betrayed him, chopping his body apart. During the last time the Shadows brought him to Oyster City, I discovered they used a cannon. Before they left, the militia buried that same cannon. It doesn’t make much sense, does it?”

“No, that’s strange, alright. But you must have a theory.” Irish watched his friend closely.

“Well, it’s just as strange. I believe the military might have strapped the demon on the cannon barrel and overstuffed the barrel. It blew Andras and the cannon apart. That helps explain why the troops buried that cannon under the light of a full moon.”

“You’re kidding!” Edna interjected.

Pappy shook his head.

“No, the common thread in the stories is a full moon or a special moon phase. Every story shows the body inhabited by Andras is his weak spot. They must destroy the human body before Andras does some ritual at the time of a full moon. After that, then Andras might exist here forever. That’s my other guess from researching this. My wife tells me that the full moon renews the spirits.”

The kitchen remained quiet as they sipped on the coffee.

“You know, Smyth’s body didn’t look right before I blasted him. I wonder if that’s what others noticed. Your story shows he’s vulnerable until tomorrow night. I might not kill him with bullets, but it gives me an idea if we can get him isolated. Maybe we finish the demon in some other way.”

“How’s that?” Edna sat her cup on the counter.

“If he’s sporting those wounds still, I can’t imagine he’s going to be running around in public. It appears we have to isolate him or kidnap him somehow. And how do you destroy him? It’s not like we can just find dynamite to blow him up.”

“You can’t forget that he has allies. We don’t know how many, but I have the bruises to prove there are more than a few.”

“But we have something he wants,” Ray told them with a frown. “He’s still looking for me! I’m the bait for any trap that we come up with.”

~~~

“That’s correct. Irish will come to me. Use Slim and his friends for help in tracking him,” Panthia told Phillip Smyth as she slid away from him. “Have them readied to help when the detective comes to you.”

The witch rolled off the enormous bed and picked up her clothing from the floor. Smyth held a piece of gauze compress on his arm to staunch the blood where the witch bled him and drank her fill. Since he made his deal with Panthia, she came to him and Underhill for sex and blood, along with assurances they would become immortal soon. The mortal man still had his doubts while he tried to shake off his lightheaded feelings.

“Irish will come to you since he’s dealt with you before. He’ll know where his partner is. I want that ex-cop, and Andras wants Irish for this sacrifice. It was my idea, of course,” she slid her black dress over her voluptuous body that carried a sheen of sweat.

“What about this man named Slim? Can I trust these gangsters? After all, they worked for Wolfe, and you said he’s dead.”

“Most certainly, no one trusts him!” the witch laughed. “He’s been on his way to hell for a while. His sister works at the diner, where she overheard the shamus and his girlfriend’s plans. Slim and his friends want revenge. They haven’t
~~~

forgotten that Irish and Campbell killed their boss, Jacobi. I made sure they knew he killed Rusty as well. These gangsters are perfect for my plans, and you'll now lead them."

The woman looked over and beamed a false smile.

"Of course, you'll need to dangle money in front of them to keep them on your side. Just wait for this detective to come to you. The spells left by my sister in his clothes let me know his thoughts during moments of weakness. Then, I want to see him die in some delightful way."

She glanced over at Phillip, who remained silent.

"By the way, these gangsters will join us to ensure that our guests run away from the festival once it gets going. We must provide a proper greeting for the demons when they arrive."

Phillip Smyth stared at her self-satisfied expression.

"You're using these thugs as your muscle to deal with anyone who gets out of line when we remove Andras, is that it?"

"I guess you might say that." she paused at the thought. "They'll soon know the real master of this world." The woman tied the rope, holding her leather bags around her waist as Smyth watched her.

"Phillip, I like you. Your devious thoughts are so similar to my own." she looked in the mirror.

"Underhill is more attractive and a better lover, but you know how to peer inside a person. I can sense your thoughts about removing Andras. You think why should I bother to sacrifice people if we destroy this creature?"

Panthia watched his expression from the mirror. Phillip nodded, remaining silent while he buried his growing resentment.

"You see, Malphas will accept our offerings on that night. His crow form will enjoy the eyes of the dead as his snack. The rest of those who remain alive will feed his legion of damned when they come through."

"I guess that I'm a little slow. You're removing Andras and giving his followers to Malphas as a sacrifice. How does that put you in charge?"

Smyth stood; his anxiety at her idea grew.

"Oh, you let me deal with Maphas. We made our deal long before you and your group brought Andras from the pit. He's not coming through into this world," she assured him.

"I have plans to stop that. Only a few incubi and succubi will remain to seduce and feed on the living with the right spell. They'll be useful in my plans to secure Oyster City forever."

The witch glared when she saw the man's doubts.

"You don't need to trust me. I only require your obedience. Now, put on your pants. You are the replacement for Doctor Wolfe with our new enforcers."

"Why not just use the police?" Phillip grumbled as he grabbed his clothes.

"As the district attorney, I can control them."

He felt her stare. Finally, the man glanced over.

"Even a corrupt police force will have fools who believe in justice and the city's respectability," she growled out in the same way as Andras did.

"Devine hasn't been able to remove all of them."

She came closer to him, running her icy fingers along his shoulder.

"I will use those destined for hell to ensure the cooperation we need and to remove those for any reason. My plans ensure success over the failed ideas of the past. This is just another example that shows why I'm superior to Andras. Even his past followers should see that by now."

Panthia walked past him and opened the door. The witch didn't see the foul expression on the man's face at her slight.

~~~

Late that night, tension immediately filled the hospital room when Irish entered to see his partner. The shamus ignored the icy stare coming from Arizona.

"I had a heck of a time trying to find your room. Off-hours nurses didn't want to give me the information. I thought I'd check in with you to see how you're holding up," Ray offered.

Arizona continued his stare at his partner while refusing to reply. Edna entered the room, forcing the ex-cop to turn his attention toward her.

"I see you're still around as well. You haven't dumped him yet. You should follow Pappy's example."

She smiled, then glanced at Ray. She held a newspaper under her arm.

"I can't get rid of him yet. I need protection. Did he tell you that Pappy's hightailing it out of Oyster City?" Edna paused. "I know it's a bad way to ask, but how are you doing?"

"You need to dump this guy who can't protect himself."

"That's good coming from you," Ray grumbled. Then, the shamus came to the foot of the bed.

"Enough with the attitude, Arizona. You got it bad, and you didn't deserve it. But it finishes nothing. We've had our run-in with Andras and his minions over at Wolfe's clinic when you got it. We barely got out of there alive, and some of those we tried to help died."

"Yeah, you still got your damn Irish luck, don't you?" the man shot back. "What's the real reason you're here? It's a little late for reinforcements."

Irish glanced at Edna, then let out a breath.

"Look, Sirk told me something about a shootout in the graveyard, which I know is bullshit. Tell me, what really happened? Give me the truth, not Sirk's version."

"Can't you figure it out? I'm missing my arm!" Campbell lashed out, then refused to look at his friend.
~~~

"You want to mope or..." Ray stopped when he saw Edna shake her head.

"Arizona, we're still trying to stop Smyth or whatever you call that thing. We can't have you give up." The woman implored. "I know you're tougher than that."

His angry face turned to her.

"What the hell do you know about me? You know no more than that idiot there. Maybe some of us are tired of following Irish around like he's got a damn clue. Take your fake sympathy out the door!"

"Fine, I don't have a clue, but I'm not going down without a fight! So, get over this crap and get back in the game," Irish fumed, then turned away and stared out the window into the night sky.

"Quit the coach nonsense! Maybe I'd fight too if I still had my arm to fight with!" his partner shouted.

The room went quiet while both men refused to look at each other. Edna stepped away from the bed and paced slowly. Arizona pulled at the bedsheet with his left arm.

"Damn, I wish someone around here smoked. I need a cigarette."

The woman sighed as she leaned against the wall. She glanced at both men while growing angry. Finally, she turned to Campbell.

"Arizona, the cold hard truth is that neither of us can bring back your arm. You've got every right to yell to the sky about it. Maybe Irish is a stubborn ass, but damn it, so are you."

She waited for the glare from the ex-cop. When Campbell looked up, Edna stepped toward him.

"It's up to you to decide whether you walk away or continue to fight. You went up to the cemetery and dealt with something evil. It's alright if you want to quit. We'll leave you alone. But we need to know what we're up against. Fair is fair."

Arizona glanced at Ray, then stared down at his stump of an arm, wrapped to just above where his elbow once extended. Finally, the silence got to him. He took a deep breath.

"The truth is, I don't know what I ran into. Some of it's seared in my mind, but other parts are hazy."

He stared at Edna as her expression softened.

"Maybe talking it over might bring it back?"

"Hell, maybe I don't want to remember some of it." his sarcasm dripped out, followed by a resigned laugh.

Edna patiently waited.

"Oh, alright. I got there, and it was quiet. I took a look into that crypt and saw the light coming from inside. That's where I found that kid, Lance. He looked like one of those concentration camp survivors. He wouldn't stop coming at me, and I had to shoot him."

Campbell stopped and looked away, and his face screwed up at the image inside his head.

"The son of a bitch thanked me for it."

Ray turned to look over at his friend. After a moment, Arizona continued.

"When I went to check out the room Lance pointed to, I found the bodies. I'm sure it was the missing people that the police were looking for. At least that's what Sirk told me. Someone skinned some bodies. Hell, I think I saw bite marks as well."

Arizona shook his head.

"That's one damn memory I don't want to stick inside my head."

"What happened then?" Edna's voice remained calm, almost soothing.

After another awkward silence, he replied.

"I heard something, and when I turned around, some ass tried to take off my head with an iron rod. As we were fighting, that bitch Merle started making crazy comments about how it was like some gladiator show to her. That's something I'll never forget. That insane laugh that she had."

As he recalled the encounter, the man looked out of the window and went silent for a moment.

"When I finally blew the brains out of the guy trying to strangle me, then Merle attacked me. I laid her out with a punch, but when I went to check on Lance, the bitch flung some type of powder at me. The pain was like nothing I had ever felt before. I can still feel it. I should have killed her."

Campbell glanced over at Irish.

"As I tried to get out of that place, I heard the woman screaming in pain. That's why I think some of the stuff flew back on her. After that, it gets really fuzzy. I remember telling myself repeatedly that I had to get to the hospital and tell someone about the crypt. Somehow, I got the car into gear to take it down the hill."

Arizona grimaced.

"That's the last I remember until I woke up here."

"This Merle, is it the same woman that came to the office with Orella and her sister?"

Ray pushed away from the window.

"No, well, the two women I saw were twins, so I can't be sure who it was," he frowned. "Pan, something or another, was the name of the other one. All I know is that the stuff she got me with is worse than anything I've ever seen or heard of before. It makes me think she comes from hell with Smyth."

"No more doubting my crazy idea?"

Arizona shook his head.

"Listen, I tried to doubt this stuff just to keep my sanity. After Cat got it, also knowing what happened to Orella after they kidnapped her—well, it was easier to remember that people did that to them, not some demon. But there's no doubt that something evil is out there in that cemetery. Who knows, maybe the whole worthless town.”

He looked at Irish.

“After seeing those bodies, I believe alright. I also think you’re a damn fool for hanging around here. It’s not your battle; it’s the good people in this town. And they’ll never do a thing!”

Arizona slammed his fist into his leg.

“Nobody is going to stop what’s coming. You understand that, don’t you? Whatever that demon is, he’ll do to you, just like the others piled up in that crypt. Hell, I’m lucky this is all I got.”

Silence filled the room, and Irish turned back to the window. Edna shrugged and stood by the door.

“I told him the same thing.” The woman agreed.

“And I see where it got you with him,” Arizona nodded.

After a moment, Ray turned back to them.

“You know, a question just came to me.”

They watched him, waiting as he gathered his thoughts.

“First, let me lay out what we know,” he started. “Tomorrow night, something big is happening. Based upon previous experience, it’ll involve Andras and all of his cronies. According to Pappy, the time will be during the full moon. Before we broke up their party, the bastards held nine people to sacrifice. That makes me believe Smyth will need a quiet place and won’t attract attention in the middle of the night.”

His eyes glanced between them.

“Is there a spot where you can kill that many people in Oyster City at one time?”

Following a long silence, Arizona reached over and picked up a small book from the nightstand.

“Why don’t you ask Bishop La Spina?” He tossed it to the foot of the bed.

Irish glanced at it.

“Given the fact that he’s dead, what is the answer?”

The ex-cop scowled at Ray.

“The bastard explains that the Shadows normally hung their sacrifices over trees in the cemetery and inside the dome of Andras’ estate. All the people in the Shadows were there for the ceremony. Pretty much everything in the margins of that book ties to something we know in our murder investigations. That’s why he told me that the crypt was the keystone to everything. Like I said before, that bastard was proud in some ways about his work.”

“Ok, then we should expect them to be at the estate,” Ray smiled. “That’s a start.”

Edna picked up the leather-covered volume.

"You forget something," Arizona told them. "Sirk came by and told me about the murder investigation on the Andras estate. They pulled the cops off of the grounds, but they're still hanging around Andras Lane. I don't think anybody uses that place again. Not with a lot of people watching this thing."

Edna looked up after perusing through the pages.

"It seems likely that someone would have heard about the murders before. I don't know how they did it with just one person in the Andras cemetery. You'd think the servants would say something."

"Yeah, except they even killed their servants," Arizona agreed as his demeanor slowly turned to thoughtfulness.

"Somebody will notice a lot of people gathering at night. If those men working for Andras find more prisoners, they'll need a place to hold them."

"They certainly don't have that clinic anymore." Edna stepped over to pick up the newspaper she left on top of a cart. "I just saw the headlines before I walked in here. Look for yourself. Sirk had it correct. State troopers are calling it a massacre."

She laid the paper out on the bed as Ray came around to look at it with Arizona.

After they scanned the news and the photos, Irish began his pacing. Arizona laid back, and his face showed his weariness. Edna took Ray by the arm.

"You need to rest," she told Campbell. "We'll come by tomorrow morning."

"Between now and then, seriously consider leaving Oyster City for good," Arizona warned her as Irish got his hat. "I have my place to go when I can walk out of this hospital. I damn well won't ever come back here!"

"Edna, before you go. Open the drawer of this nightstand."

She went to the piece of furniture, glanced at him before she pulled open the drawer. Inside was a revolver.

"Sirk returned my gun earlier. I want you to have it for protection."

Hesitating at first until he encouraged her, Edna picked up the weapon.

"Irish can't be around all the time," Campbell told her.

"What about you?"

Arizona grunted.

"Hell, it'll take me forever to get the darn thing out of the stand. Go on, keep it. I'm sure that Sirk's got me covered. He's been here every night."

Edna thanked him and left the room. Ray was almost out of the door when the ex-cop called out.

"Irish, why don't you ask one shadow where they're going to be tomorrow night? I believe you know some of them, and you don't need to be nice about asking them."

The shamus stopped, then he glanced back with a determined scowl before nodding as he shut the door.

It was nearly dark on the night of the full moon when Edna brought her car to a stop under the streetlight. A couple of parked cars were down the block. Ray watched the car behind them pull into the long driveway across the road and continued toward the dark house behind a line of trees.

"I think we're clear," he let out a breath.

Both of them remained frustrated after wasting much of the day trying to find Marion Underhill. Following a quick breakfast, they started by staking out Underhill's jewelry shop, which gave them nothing. The young woman who opened the business told Edna that Marion wasn't coming in that day. The couple spent the rest of the morning at Underhill's residence. Eventually, they determined his car was gone. Ray's inquiry with the man who answered the door got him nothing concerning the jeweler's whereabouts.

The shamus his attention to Phillip Smyth. Ray explained that Smyth's place held too many servants to get to their quarry quickly.

"I guess that we're running out of time," he said before directing his driver to the parking spot on Andras Lane.

They took a long route through the city, stopping at the train station on the way. He had Edna drive through the full hospital parking lot as one last measure to avoid being trailed.

From their spot outside the fence that separated the estate of Phillip Smyth from the public, they looked up at the grand house. All the lights appeared on, giving the structure a shimmering effect from all three floors.

"Impressive!" Edna whistled.

"Yeah, but the rat who lives there deserves to die. You wait here," Ray told her when he opened the car door.

"What are you doing?" She replied with an annoyed stare.

"I'm going to visit this old friend. I know the layout of his place so that I can get in without a problem."

"That's not what I meant!"

"Alright, I plan on bluffing this bastard using the worst hand imaginable. I remember you telling me that La Spina knew the only real weakness for Andras was his rented body. We only have this shot tonight. The one thing I have going for me is most of the Shadows are dead. Phillip was Henry's friend, so I think he'll play ball now. If not, I'll bring him down here, and we can give him the same treatment as Rusty."

Edna saw through his overconfident grin.

"What about that woman that got Arizona?"

"You heard my partner. He said he should have killed her. Witch or not, she won't stop me with a bullet in her chest!"

"That's what you said about Andras," she replied.

Edna frowned at the way the words came out. Irish grimly nodded, then walked away from the car.

"I'll keep the engine warm," she called out.

He doesn't believe it! He's trying to keep me away!

Irish remembered the route he got in to find Orella as he pushed through the hedge near the end of the fence line. The shamus walked across the broad expanse of brown grass, which crackled under his feet. Using the occasional large tree to shield his outline from the house, he felt confident that no one would look out at the dark lawn. Ray realized he was out of options. Andras was running out the clock on him.

I have to make Smyth talk!

Drawing near the house's side, Irish waited in the shadows before he slowly eased up to the first window. As he peeked inside, he recognized the small, narrow hallway outside the room. It led to the kitchen, where he saw the cook and several servants who sat around a table. Their attention focused on a card game.

Ray started toward the front of the house, peering inside the window that had light streaming out. He saw the dining room. The shamus continued until he came upon a set of French doors between a columned portico above him. Unable to get a good view, Irish saw a chair moving behind a desk. He carefully tried one of the French doors.

Unlocked!

With an inaudible sigh of relief, Ray quietly pulled his .45 auto and slipped inside.

Across the room, the movement of the drapery swaying from the door caused Phillip Smyth to look up from his work. He tilted his head; then, his eyes widened when Irish stepped from behind the curtain panel with the gun pointed at him.

"Don't get stupid! We're going to have a little talk about Peter Smyth." Ray told him quietly.

Phillip's eyes glanced over at the chair near the desk. Yet, he did not show fear.

"I suppose I should have expected this visit. However foolishly misplaced, I must give you credit for your bravery. I take it you know Marion Underhill?"

Ray looked over to see Marion lean forward to stare at Irish. He sat in a leather wingback chair with a glass of red wine in his hand.

"So, she was right! The famous detective came to us."

"Stow it," the shamus growled. "I don't plan on wasting a good bullet on either of you unless you force my hand. But you're going to tell me what I want to know."

Phillip slowly leaned back in his chair. His expression turned bland. He tossed the gold dagger he was cleaning up on the desk.

"You see, you'll get to meet Andras soon. He has a special thirst to watch you die."

He nodded at his desk.

"That is the weapon which will cut your throat if you're still a lucky man. Otherwise, you'll burn in a pit. It's a quite nasty death, I'm sure."

"Your friends tried to plant me several times. It hasn't happened yet. I've been on the receiving end of torture and pain caused by you and your sick Shadow friends. That makes me your worst enemy. You call out, and I kill you without a thought. I'm past caring about the rules. Do I make myself clear?"

Smyth visibly suppressed a grin.

"Oh, quite clear. I will happily tell you what you want to know. But I'm afraid that you've chosen the wrong side."

"I'm on the side that's going to remove Andras, you son of a bitch!" Irish grunted out. "Now, you're going to tell me where he's going to be near midnight."

"Do you think you can scare me with a gun? After all, I have a demon on my side.

"The last son of a bitch who thought he was tough cried like a baby when I broke his fingers for information. Get the drift now."

"My servants…"

"Don't matter to me!"

Ray took a step forward and pistol-whipped Smyth across the head. While his victim hunched over his desk, his hands covered his bleeding wound. Underhill rose from the chair, but he froze when Irish pointed his gun at him. No sound came from the hallway. Irish returned his focus to Phillip.

"I shot your brother in the head, and the bastard still got up and walked away. Now, I'm betting you can't do the same thing. I asked you a question, and your time's running out!"

"That's not my brother!" the man shot back. "Peter died on the night Andras took his body."

The outburst caught Irish off guard. It gave him an idea. He reached into his coat pocket and pulled out Henry La Spina's book. Ray tossed it to Philip.

"Then you need to read this. Your old buddy knew what you idiots didn't.

That's why he offed himself. Read it and know there's only one chance. Where is Andras going to be in a few hours? He has to be stopped."

"Oh, there's no need for that. I'll take you to him!" A feminine voice came from behind Irish.

As Ray turned, he felt a jab in his neck. He saw a woman in a black dress staring at him when he backed away. The creature's eyes were alight with delight, but she appeared older than Arizona described.

"You're that woman! The bitch Merle that works for the demon," he grunted out.

Then, the convulsions started. Irish dropped to the floor. Unable to control the painful spasms that shot through him, the shamus could only listen to the creature gloating.

"I'm Panthia, the greatest of the Thessaly witches! Don't insult me, you pathetic mortal. I killed my sisters to take this world."

She picked up the dagger from the desk and bent over to stab Irish in his shoulder as he writhed in pain. She brought the blade up to lick his blood several times. Her lined complexion immediately softened, and the wrinkles disappeared.

"You'll remember me when I flay your skin from you," the witch cackled.

Then Panthia looked at Phillip.

"You see, I've already captured the man who kept thwarting your last master. He'll remain alive to watch the demons entering his world. The last insult to his worthless life when we kill him."

The witch licked the blood from the tip of the dagger blade one last time while she looked down at the suffering prisoner. Ray started puking from the effects of the woman's poisoned fingernail.

"I expected you could handle my potion better. Mr. Detective, remember this suffering. It'll soon become worse. Then you'll tell me where your partner is." Panthia slid the dagger into her belt as she looked over at the French doors where she came in.

"I was expecting his girlfriend to come in with him." She shrugged. "I guess I'll have her later during the orgy of flesh."

"Get your men in here and take him to the barracks," Panthia commanded Phillip as she left the room.

Phillip looked at the book that Irish tossed to him and put it in his coat.

~~~

Edna Ackroyd ran in a panic through the brush, tripping at one point and losing one of her leather pumps. She immediately pitched the other shoe and pushed herself to reach the road. She ran across the lawn, not feeling the occasional limb that caught her in the face. The image of Arizona's missing arm kept her moving.

When Panthia took down Irish with just a scratch of her nail on his neck,
~~~

Edna moved closer to help him. She even put her hand around the grip of the revolver in her purse. But she froze at the sight of the woman licking the blood and growing younger. Even when the witch stabbed Ray, again and again, the woman slowly backed away. But when the witch looked out the door, saying she expected Edna to come inside, the woman panicked.

Winded, Edna tried to catch her breath after running across the estate to the car. As she pulled back on the car door handle, the woman felt like she was about to heave.

"Where'd you think you're going, babe?"

Edna turned at the voice.

"I—I need your…" She stopped when he stepped into the light coming from the streetlamp above her.

She recognized that man who helped kidnapped Della. Edna turned back and hurriedly pulled at the handle.

Locked!

She heard the thin man laugh. The jingle of her keys came to her as he twirled them around his finger.

"Dumb broad, it's not too smart to leave your keys in the car. From the look on your face, you met our boss. I guess your boyfriend won't be coming back."

The man behind Edna whistled.

"Slim, this one's got a sweet body. We'll enjoy our time with her. Right, cutie? You keep us happy, and we don't have to hurt you."

The woman glanced back at the larger man as he stepped from the shadows. His brutish face looked uglier under the highlights of the match-light when he lit his cigarette.

"Tony, she's got no choice." Slim shook his head as he closed on her.

"But don't worry, we'll keep your ass busy. Talk is that the boss wants an orgy tonight. You'll be our main course." He chuckled, but his face remained deadpan. "When we're done, we'll kill you."

Edna kept watching them close on her while she slid her hand into her purse.

"What'cha gonna do, sweetheart? That shamus isn't around to protect you. Our boss knew he was coming to see Smyth. She had a trap just waiting for you both. I'm telling you, she's amazing. Our boss can tell what you're gonna do before you can figure it out. Plus, we get a bonus. There's five hundred on your head, me and Tony can collect cash as well when you came running back. She must have scared the hell out of you!"

The big man coming around the front of her car suddenly rushed her, forcing Edna to pull the gun from her purse.

The trigger hooked the bag!

While she fought to release the weapon, Slim came up from the other side. He caught her by the forearm before Edna could fire. His backhand sent her against the car. Tony, the hulking brute, wrapped his massive arms around her body and lifted her from the ground. She screamed out before the man got his hand over her mouth. Slim punched Edna in the belly. Unable to breathe, she collapsed in Tony's arms. Slim ripped the weapon out of her hand along with the purse. Then he kicked it away.

"Little girl needs a lesson. Throw her in the back seat."

The thug told Tony as he unlocked the car door.

"Work her over until she begs, then we'll tear off a piece of ass for ourselves."

With a lecherous grunt, the big man forced the struggling Edna into the car. When his first punch hit the woman, Slim laughed.

"Teach this high-class tramp what pain means!"

On the second blow, the woman heard in her skull crack from Tony's fist striking her. Stars flickered in her eyes. Stunned, her arms went weak. Only her brain continued to work. Memories of her rape flooded through her mind when she heard her blouse rip as the man tugged at her bra. When Edna clawed at his face, he punched her again. The woman tasted the blood in her mouth before the pain spread across her face. She barely heard the voice of a man outside the car.

"Alright, you assholes, get away from the woman!"

Slim turned around to see a slim black man standing there with Edna's revolver in his hand. Pappy's hand trembled as he pulled back the trigger.

"Boy, mind your own business and get out of here," the thug told him.

"Don't call me, boy, you white piece of garbage!" Pappy snarled. "I'm not telling you again."

Slim suddenly rushed Pappy, who pulled the trigger. The bullet struck the gangster in the belly. Shocked, Slim clutched his middle as Pappy pulled the trigger a second time. The thug fell to the pavement.

When he heard the first shot, Tony scrambled to pull his weapon. When he left the backseat, Edna instantly grabbed his arm. She fell out of the car while hanging on to the brute. As they rolled on the brick street, Pappy stepped closer. The woman held on to Tony's wrist with both hands.

"Shoot him," Joshua insisted as he came by his uncle's side.

"I can't; she's in the way! Get him off of her."

Joshua rushed forward to help as Edna bit into Tony's shoulder. He howled, pushing her away. The thug tried to turn his head, but Joshua got there first. His savage kick caused the thug's head to snap back. Tony convulsed once before he died.

"Come on, we've got to get out of here," Pappy helped Edna to her feet.

Blood covered her lips as the woman held on to Pappy's shoulder. They went over to Joshua, who picked up the keys to Edna's Frazer.

"Call an ambulance!" Slim spit blood on the pavement a few feet away.

"Tell me what they're doing with Irish?" Edna demanded.

Slim shook his head as the woman went over to him.

"Go to hell, bitch. I ain't no squealer."

"Come on; we need to go!" Joshua insisted as he took his uncle's arm.

"You take your car and get out of town," Pappy told him. "I'll take Edna home in her car."

Joshua refused to move.

"Don't go crazy, uncle. They'll string you up if they catch you with a white woman."

"I know what I'm doing. Now get out of here." Pappy insisted as he whispered in his nephew's ear. He took the car keys.

"Take the road back home and wait for us at the city limits sign."

As Joshua slowly started back to his car, Edna stared down at the Slim.

"You're going to die in the street, you rat! Too bad I don't get to watch."

The thug violently coughed as he rolled over on his side.

"Damn, I didn't want to die tonight! She promised me." Slim's voice weakened after he caught his breath. "Wanted Irish for information, but you're— in the way."

The distant sound of a police siren came to them.

"Tell me what they'll do!" There was desperation in her plea as she came closer to him.

He smiled, blood tricking down his lips. His eyes looked Edna over.

"She'll burn 'em. You've got…"

Edna didn't hear the last. She sprinted to her car and jumped in the passenger side while Pappy sped away. The newsy drove to the first turn, then continued taking the side streets until he came out on Cherry Street.

"I don't know how you found me, but I'm thanking my lucky stars for it," Edna finally spoke after tense moments of staring out the back window. "But you can't take me to my apartment!"

"Don't worry, that was in case the bastard lives long enough for the cops. We're going to the city line to meet up with Joshua," her driver explained.

Edna turned back to Pappy as he continued.

"Emma told me you and Ray were in trouble. Joshua and I drove by your place, but no one answered the door. Then, we went to the hospital, thinking that you were checking on Arizona. That's where my nephew recognized your car. It's a good thing you like a fancy car in a two-tone color. It stands out. As Joshua turned through the parking lot, he noticed those hoodlums following you. They were so interested in you and Ray that tagged along."

Edna went quiet again.

"What happened to Ray?"

Pappy glanced at her before turning the car on to Dock Ave.

"I don't know. I needed to know why Ray didn't want me to come with him, so I followed him. As I got close, I saw someone in the shadows following him around the side of the house," the woman recalled.

"When I got closer, I could hear him talking with a guy; I think it was Smyth. I crept around to look inside, and I saw a woman sneak in behind Ray.

She swept her hand across the back of his neck, and he dropped like a rock. At first, I thought he was dead when he started convulsing. I heard her say she was Panthia, the greatest of the Thessaly witches. I don't even know what that's about."

She stopped, then Edna dropped her face into her hands. Pappy glanced over.

"I think it has something to do with the Greeks if I remember my mythology correctly," he told her. "That explains what you and Irish told me about the items in the crypt."

The woman felt the cross hanging around her neck. It weighed down on her neck while she leaned over. Edna told him that the witch had transformed when she licked Ray's blood.

"I think that's what got to me. I saw what Andras could do, and this witch has the power to grow younger with blood. Irish was lying there, convulsing in pain, and all I could do was think of escape. Even when I felt for that gun in my purse, I stopped. I just took off and left him there. I felt so helpless and alone. Now..."

"Don't blame yourself for being human. None of us can take on such things," Pappy told her. "I would have probably done the same thing."

"Thanks for that, but I've seen terrible things before," she lifted her head. "I can't believe I panicked like that."

"If she's a witch from the time of the Greeks, nobody in our lifetime has seen such things. Did you hear anything else that might help us? We don't have much time left to decide where they are going."

Edna shook her head, then looked over.

"I'm not sure what it means. I remember that bitch saying something about how she wanted to torture Ray."

Her eyes widened when she recalled.

"She said barracks! That must mean that they're going to use that abandoned army base outside of Oyster City! That's the isolated location that we were trying to figure out. It's the only logical spot. They had those people held captive in Wolfe's clinic, and it's not far down the same road."

Pappy nodded in agreement.

"Yes, I suppose that makes sense. Nobody goes out there except the occasional security guard."

The newsy glanced over, but Edna remained lost in her thoughts. After a few moments, they came upon a car parked at the city line. Pappy pulled in behind his nephew.

"I'm sending my nephew back home. You should go with him." He told the woman.

"What are you going to do?"

Her expression showed relief as she glanced out the windshield.

Pappy shook his head.

"My Emma told me I should help. Truth is, I'm not sure what I can do. But I'm not going to let Ray die without a chance. If it goes wrong, I know I'll get to see my wife soon," he sighed.

"I guess there's some comfort in the idea. I can't go to Hell for battling a demon, can I?"

After a moment, Edna shook her head.

"No, I guess not." The woman looked out the window for a moment, then she made up her mind.

"Alright, I'm going with you."

"You shouldn't," Pappy told her. "You have to realize that there will be no escape for you this time. If they get us, we have no hope!"

He paused and looked in the rearview mirror.

"No, Emma, that's not what I meant."

The man shook his head before he glanced sheepishly at Edna.

"She didn't like me saying it that way. What I mean is, there's only death and the afterlife if they catch us. You can count on that."

Edna glanced at the empty backseat.

"I wish I had your faith, Pappy." She took a deep breath. "But what options do I have? If nobody can stop this, will I really be safe, even if I leave this place? I keep thinking about how many more people might end up like Arizona or those prisoners we found."

"Well, I don't know what to tell you," Pappy admitted. "But I have a friend in need. I nearly forgot that when they came after me."

Edna forced a grin.

"I know. I just needed to hear this unbelievable stuff coming out of my mouth. If the best we can accomplish is to get Irish and leave, then so be it! The devil can have this town."

"I hope we're right." Pappy nodded and got out of the car. As Edna watched him talking to Joshua, the woman kept wondering how she got to the moment.

Am I just a crazy as Pappy and Irish?

"Everyone's got some crazy in their soul!"

The woman looked around for the source of the female voice she knew she heard. Goosebumps covered her arms as she glanced at the back seat again and then slid over into the driver's side. Pappy came back to the car. He went to the passenger door and got in.

"Are you alright?"

Edna nodded as she put her vehicle into gear and turned it around on the highway.

"I'm going to stop on the way and make a phone call. There's at least one other person who can still help us."

<center>~~~</center>

Inside the trunk of Smyth's limousine, Irish finally shook off Panthia's potion's worst effects. He had no concept of time, only the sense of dull pain from the bindings tied around his wrists and the tremendous aching of his muscles. After the distraction from his agony finally receded enough to think, the shamus hoped Edna would follow the vehicle he was inside.

Otherwise, I'm dead!

The drive went on longer than he expected. One bounce on the rutted road sent him into the trunk lib. When he landed against the cross still inside of his jacket, the sensation reminded him he carried a shield of sorts. While he did not accept Pappy's faith, Irish remembered back to the stories of his youth when the knights of old traveled the lands in their armor.

For some strange reason, the ridiculous flashback comforted him. Then, the shamus thought of Greye and the others who died from the demon and his Shadows. Painfully sliding into the backseat, Irish suddenly recalled an experience on the island of Guadalcanal.

Amid the bodies that covered a shattered airfield, Ray cleaned his rifle during a lull in the fighting. As he complained to a Marine across from him, telling him that he was a dozer operator, not a rifleman. The man gave Irish a thousand-yard stare before he replied. His words remained embedded in Ray's memory.

Hell, everything good inside died once we got off that LCM. With no future, there's only payback left. You have to kill the bastards!

~~~

Phillip Smyth brought the limousine to a stop outside a row of weathered green barracks. A long row of expensive cars ran along one side. Tents protected the guests who were already there. When he got out of the vehicle, the district attorney looked over at the large tent amid the sound of merriment and laughter. Car lights pointing at the tent showed the outline forms of naked people.

Drunken fools!

While the guests enjoyed themselves, several from Jacobi's gang walked the perimeter. They carried rifles and shotguns. It was Panthia's way of ensuring the guests stayed for the coming events.

One light-post near the edge of the former parade ground cast a yellow glow over the car. Marion Underhill got out of the passenger side. He hurried back to the rear door and opened it for Panthia. The witch went to the entrance of the barracks with Marion while Phillip opened the trunk. He pulled Irish out of the vehicle. It took a moment for Ray to recognize the location.

It's the same place where Guy Young and his gang tried to kill me!

"Yeah, I read about your shootout with that gangster on this base. Get a good look since you'll die here," Phillip told him as if he could read Ray's thoughts.

He pushed the shamus forward near the front of the car.

"Where's your funny uniform?" Irish smirked. "It's amusing to see the old
~~~

families of Oyster City are servants to a witch and a demon. You're no different from a chauffeur now!"

"Shut your mouth!"

"You don't like it knowing that you're no better than me. I'll give you odds that she's planning on sacrificing you the next full moon." Ray kept up his goading.

He recognized the man's annoyance.

"Or is your demon brother going to order it?"

"You'll never know since you die tonight." Smyth shot back.

Their conversation stopped when Panthia led three captives from the building. They stumbled along with their hands tied in front of them, and their mouths gagged. The first two were women with their clothes ripped and partially torn away. The man in the back staggered like a drunk while one of Panthia's henchmen pushed him forward.

Panthia stopped them in front of Irish. An evil grin spread across her face. Her face reminded him of a grotesque mask under the pale light from the nearby pole to Irish.

"You get to see who dies with you tonight!"

Panthia waved one thug forward with a young woman who looked barely out of school. Stripped naked, the girl visibly shook with fear. The witch frowned at the lashes on her prisoner's back.

"I brought this one in. She came to the store after you sent her that note. I showed her the special place I have in the back." Underhill boasted to Panthia.

"Yes, the servant girl that I wanted. Why did you beat her?"

"She tried to bite me," he explained. "I made her pay for it."

"Oh, I'm going to enjoy you tonight," Panthia stated. "Put her in the car."

She waved the next prisoner to her.

Phillip heard Underhill complain under his breath as he pushed the young woman past him.

"Watch it, or Panthia will make room for another sacrifice if you keep it up."

Irish overheard Phillip's warning. He saw Underhill's face turn pale while Smyth went over next to the witch.

The next woman prisoner brought to Panthia mumbled to Phillip through her gag. Her green eyes widened with terror when the witch ran her fingers along the back of the woman's expensive dress.

"This is Rachel, a friend of the family," Phillip informed Panthia. "I volunteered her services for tonight. I remember how she so loved to humiliate my physical looks during the dinner parties."

He turned to the prisoner.

"I guess you'll learn about humiliation now."

His satisfied enjoyment at the terrified captive's reaction caught the witch's notice.

"You bring your motives to sacrifices," Panthia told him approvingly. "It makes it difficult to read your thoughts when you're so bold. Strip her, then put her in the car. She'll entertain our guests before she dies."

"Boss lady, she's wearing an expensive ring. Can we have it?" One henchman suddenly asked.

Panthia nodded.

"Sure, she doesn't need it."

The henchman smiled as he helped Phillip rip the struggling woman's dress away. The thug tugged on Rachel's ring finger, slapping the crying woman who struggled to stop him.

Irish felt Underhill's presence as he struggled to loosen his own bindings. Rage began to fill him at the deliberate, humiliating show Panthia was putting on for him.

"You should see the look on your face. Panthia knows what you're thinking." Marion chuckled.

"Then she better get used to seeing how I'm going to kill her!" Ray lashed out.

The witch didn't look over. The drunk middle-aged prisoner occupied her as he kept trying to shout muffled curses. She ripped open the back of his shirt with a laugh.

"This one's got spirit. Where did you find him?"

"He's a salesman we found at a bar," one thug explained. "We fed him some hooch and brought him. I didn't have much choice since it was getting dark, and you wanted three people. No one will miss him."

"Let's see how much fire he'll have for the ceremony. Strip this drunk down and give him some lashes before you put him with the others."

Panthia felt Ray's stare even from a distance. She slowly started back to him while her henchmen immediately whipped the businessman with a belt. His muffled howls caused the witch to smile while she stared back at the shamus.

Then, her attention went back to Rachel. The burly thug still fought to remove the ring from the captive's finger. Anger filled her face as she pulled his dagger from the sheath she had tied around her waist.

"This is how you do it!" the creature cried. With incredible speed, she struck Rachel in the head with the pommel of her dagger. Then Panthia grabbed the dazed woman's finger. She cut her victim's ring finger off at the knuckle with practiced skill in one quick motion. The hideous cracking sound was immediately followed by the woman's muffled scream.

"Pick up your payment, then put our sacrifices in the car's backseat," the witch ordered the stunned henchman.

Rachel slid to her knees, her hand gushing blood.

"Andras will be here," Panthia looked up at the rising moon. Then the creature casually licked the blade of her weapon.

"We'll soon start the ceremony to bring in a new era," she told Underhill. "Go over to the tent and get our guests into their cars. Have them drive into the field. Make sure you order them to direct their car lights to the burn pit we've made. Tell them we'll start the orgy of blood and lust soon."

When she turned toward the car, a raging Irish rushed toward her. His building anger at the mistreatment he witnessed overcame any thoughts of safety. With a picture-perfect blocking move, Ray got his shoulder under the woman's chest when he struck at full speed. The force of his gigantic frame sent Panthia into the side of the car. He heard a satisfying crunch of her bones breaking when they struck the door together. The dagger skittered across the gravel to the feet of Underhill. Even during his attack, the shamus felt an incredible burning sensation in his chest when his body pressed against Panthia. The woman cried out briefly while Irish bounced away. Somehow remaining on his feet, he briefly relished her horrified look of dismay and shock.

"I'm going to finish you here!" Ray screamed as he attacked again.

Before he could bring his foot down on her head to finish her, the shamus took a blow from a pistol butt to his skull. Irish staggered, then a fist smashed into his face as the closest henchman jumped him. Ray nearly blacked out as the thug pounded his face into the hard ground. Phillip grabbed his man and pulled him off of Irish.

"Let me kill him for you," Smyth offered Panthia.

The woman angrily shook her head as she favored one leg. Surprised at her careful reaction, Phillip stared at her for a moment before he pushed Ray over onto his back. The dazed detective looked around and glimpsed something unexpected in Panthia's blazing eyes. He swore he saw fear as he felt the heat on the left side of his chest again.

The cross inside my jacket!

"Tie him to the back of the car. That will scourge him before the real fun begins."

The witch limped over to open the front door of the limousine.

"I'll slowly flay and bleed him after we remove Andras!"

~~~

Hidden behind the nearby line of overgrown trees, Pappy and Edna watched the events unfold. They could only hear some conversations, and the darkness made it difficult to see much of it. But they saw enough to recognize the difficulty they faced.

When they witnessed Irish attack Panthia, Pappy grabbed Edna, stopping her from rising. He forced her to wait, even when they overheard the vicious order from the witch about tying him to the back of the car.

"You're not going to do him any good getting yourself killed."

As they waited, the guests in the large tent happily made their way to their cars. Pappy watched in stunned disbelief as one middle-aged man led a naked young man on a leash, who willingly accepted his subservient role. Nearby, two
~~~

women, partially dressed in men's clothing, were enticing one guard to join them.

"Hell on earth is already here," Pappy stated with a scowl. "I hope your cavalry is coming! I just don't know how they'll find us."

"I'm working on it," Edna grumbled.

She focused on Underhill as he yelled out orders to some thugs. They hurried to one car to lead the line of vehicles into the field behind the barracks. As one car passed by their position, the swirling particles of dirt and debris made her turn her head away. Then she felt the breeze coming from the beach, which quickly cleared away the dust.

"Come on; I have an idea. We'll follow them to get to a safe place."

Edna hurried away before Pappy replied. Shaking his head, he followed the woman through the undergrowth to her Frazer.

"There are artillery emplacements near the beach that's on the other side of the field," she breathlessly explained when Pappy got in the car.

"They'll never know that we're not in that line of cars."

Edna hit the accelerator and used the headlights coming through trees to find a path. Edna's sedan came out just as one car passed them. Keeping her lights off, she guided her vehicle just behind a large black Cadillac. The lead car had trouble keeping a straight line behind the other motor vehicles. They saw the man who was driving had a woman practically in his lap in front of them. Every time the man took a drink, the large car swerved.

The woman smiled at her luck and stayed close to the Cadillac's rear. When they reached the open field, Edna immediately took a hard right and floored the car. The moonlight gave her enough light to stay on what looked like a trail. Looking over her shoulder, she saw the other vehicles' car lights slowly making a circle near the middle of the field. That's when she turned her car toward the first large concrete structure she saw in the moonlight.

~~~

Panthia's limousine sped through the courtyard, kicking up gravel as the vehicle followed the caravan. Irish struggled to keep his body from dragging, but his wrists burned from the rope wrapped around the bumper. Pieces of the ground bit into his flesh when the vehicle swerved along the old trail. Thick dust made it impossible to breathe when the tires kicked up debris from the parched field. After his muscles tired, the first pothole the car struck sent Irish into the ground hard. Then, the driver turned hard to the left, which sent the shamus into a twisting spin. Unable to control his movements, he soon felt the burns and welts as the debris tore through his clothes. Pieces of cloth cut away along with part of his flesh when they came back over the gravel. Finally, the limo came to a stop.

As the man lay there in pain, catching his breath, he heard the doors open. He looked up to see the prisoners' bare feet as men in scuffed leather shoes herded them away.
~~~

Ray could only see parts of the circular area where parked cars had their front lights aimed at four poles coming up from the ground at an angle. Surreal sounds of laughter and excited screams came from the people getting out of the cars. Some spectators hardly bothered to pay attention to the places of sacrifice. Instead, they were having sex in pairs or small groups. Ray caught a glimpse of some people he recognized as members of banks and businesses. He even saw the Banner's news editor groping another man along with his drunken wife.

Irish heard the footsteps come next to him. Immediately, two of Panthia's men lifted him to his feet as the witch came closer. Still tied to the bumper of the car, Ray hunched over while he watched her. She pulled her dagger.

"I'll take care of this one," she waved the men away. "You entertain yourselves with our sacrifices until Andras arrives. Then be ready for my signal. Do you understand?"

After the men quickly agreed, they hurried over to the naked captives standing near the poles. Ray watched them grab the young girl and throw her to the ground. He glanced over at Panthia, who dangled two severed fingers attached to a crude leather necklace.

"I thought you might recognize my sister's trophy. She came back from Boston with them along with the Singsing. Your bitch fought and lost. Merle wanted her here for the festival. But you can't have everything, can you?"

She held out her hand with the ring on the index finger.

"I can feel the power of the night coming!" The witch declared. Suddenly, she screamed at a nearby man holding a shotgun.

"You get the fire in the pit going. We need it burning, you fool!"

Irish kept pulling at his bindings, realizing he had little hope of releasing himself. However, the pain coming from his bleeding wrists kept him focused on ideas for getting at Panthia. He wanted to beat her lovely face into an unrecognizable pulp.

The witch frowned when she noticed him not paying attention to her. She came over and suddenly embedded the blade into his thigh. The shamus cried out, cursing her while holding the bumper to remain standing. Panthia licked the knife again.

"You know, I could let you burn on those stakes over there. I wanted painful revenge for when you attacked me. However, I've realized that I'll have more fun draining you of life. Your blood will energize me while you die, knowing there's nothing you can do."

She stepped around behind him, then stabbed him in the back of his thigh.

"You worthless whore!"

The witch laughed with a cackle that reminded him of old radio programs.

"You see, I know just where to stab you—missing your vital organs and arteries. Before coming to this world, I mastered ways to keep my victims alive while slowly killing them. I might not read your mind or touch that cursed object you have on your clothes, but it can't stop me from cutting you."

"You bitch, it doesn't matter. You'll never survive what's coming," he growled out.

The witch smiled as Panthia focused on her victim. She overlooked Phillip Smyth, who carefully watched her tormenting the shamus as he stood by the front bumper.

"Oh, your trap to remove Andras? It's too bad; I've known about that for a while. But it's all for naught. So foolish to think a few of you thought you could defeat a demon," the creature purred triumphantly.

"A little of my special dust on your partner's clothes told me everything. Just like those fools who call themselves the Shadows. I'm the one who'll send Andras back and usher in my new world."

Irish noticed Smyth's reaction when he looked through the windshield.

"You talk pretty big for a bitch who can only order people around. The demon still rules you, and when he's gone, you'll be kissing his ass in Hell still."

The detective tried to think of anything to keep the woman talking and play for time.

Panthia stabbed him again. This time, high on the shoulder. She came around as Irish groaned at the pain. Sweat poured down his forehead.

"You don't still believe that your friends will get to Andras. I'm afraid the woman, what was her name, Edna, that's it! Well, she has other plans tonight. I sent a few men to make sure that she'd pay for helping you. I'm sure she is in the backseat of her car, keeping those grunting men happy. They were distraught that you killed their friend Rusty. I think they'll take out all of their frustration on her."

Panthia leaned close to whisper in his ear.

"It's humiliating for you to know that you led another woman to her death. Andras told me all about your fears and dreams before you blocked his influence. Now, this is the world that is coming!"

She grabbed him by the hair, forcing him to look at a group of naked women and men. One thug stood over a protesting male on the ground while others held him down.

"Tonight, we get to screw the banker," he boasted, as his victim kept begging for release.

Those around the scene laughed and started chanting for Andras.

"Now, look over there in that group. You see that little blonde maid, fresh off the streets? You can barely see her under all those men. Soon, we'll roast her alive, and you can die knowing it. Andras told me about a knight on a tarot card foretold to the Shadows. The funny part is he believed it was a premonition."

"You God damn spawn of hell," Irish raged as he forced her away with his body.

Furious at his resistance, Panthia stabbed him deep in the thigh. Ray collapsed to his knee while the witch licked his blood from the weapon.

"You should be happy that I'm letting you watch this. Now you know the innocent are weak. Mortals are nothing but toys for the demons of the night. I'll go to your detective with some of my demon friends so he can feed them."

"What about your Shadow friends? They are your servants. Don't you trust them?"

Ray mocked her through his grimace. He saw Marion Underhill join Smyth on the other side of the limousine.

"You act like you have everything. You don't have the genuine power, just a whore for another demon."

"You know nothing, a big man with a small mind. Andras will cease to bother the world when I remove him. But Malphas is coming," Panthia boasted.

"You see, we have an agreement."

"You stupid bitch, no one can control a demon. La Spina knew what was coming when Andras brought forth the witches of Lamia. He wrote about it." Ray spat out through his clenched teeth as he still struggled to free his raw and bleeding wrists in their bindings.

"I read about you. You exist only to serve demons, condemned from the start of time. Kind of like some of those families who run Oyster City. Nothing more than a servant!"

Panthia lashed out with her dagger, slicing his cheek. Before she could do more, car lights spilled over them. She turned to see a black car speeding toward the area. The witch called out to her henchman.

"The master is coming! Make way for Andras!"

Phillip immediately came over next to her.

"Devine is driving him. Let me take the sacrificial dagger. I wish to make that police chief a sacrifice. Otherwise, he might cause problems."

"You're becoming bold," Panthia smiled, handing him the weapon. "Here, you may stand ready when we go to him. Use one guard to help you."

Ray watched as the car came to a stop. There was no mistaking the creature sitting on the passenger side, Peter Smyth's rotting corpse. Devine stopped the vehicle a few yards away. The chief of police got out of the car, then opened the door on the other side. Andras emerged, his movements frail and jerky.

Weakened, Ray frantically pulled on his bindings. Another pair of headlights suddenly came to life from the direction of the beach. He watched the car driving toward the circle, and then he noticed smaller yellow circles emerge in a line. While he stared hypnotically at the flickering string of lights, they suddenly spread across the field.

Fire!

The sight almost made him scream out in happiness. Ray smiled at the growing line of flames heading for them.

Someone up there is helping!

He turned back to the unholy circle of activity around the fire pit. Smoke bellowed from the hole that was blazing. Irish watched the evil going on around the area. Combined with the yells and moans of the upper class of Oyster City, he decided it was as close to hell as he wanted to get.

When he glanced over at Panthia meeting with her master, Ray saw the evil leaders focused on the firepit. Underhill stepped over to Irish with one of Jacobi's thugs. The jeweler put his hand in his coat pocket, then pulled out a gun.

It was Ray's .45 auto that he pointed at the shamus.

"Panthia says it's time for you to meet Andras."

"Go kiss your ass!" Ray told him.

Underhill nodded to the henchman, who immediately punched Irish in the back. While the prisoner got his wind, the thug popped open his switchblade and cut the rope holding Ray's wrists to the bumper. The man grabbed Irish by the collar and lifted him from his knees.

"Come on!"

A bright light suddenly covered the trio. They looked at the vehicle barreling headlong at them. Ray recognized the Frazer as Edna barreled toward them. The thug holding onto Ray released him, and they dove out of the way when Edna's car nearly hit Underhill. Irish turned in time to watch in stunned fascination as the woman steered right into the small crowd standing around Andras.

The demon barely had time to react when the front end slammed into him and another man. Her Frazer finally stopped when it crashed into Devine's car, crushing Andras and one other in the wreckage.

The dull roar of steel smashing into steel stopped, leaving a stunned hush along with the roaring crackle of wood from the nearby fire-pit. An inhuman roar suddenly filled the air, combining with the delayed screams and yells from the crowd as they hurried toward the wreck.

Ray lifted himself from the ground as sparks of small flames erupted from the front of Edna's car. He glanced over at Underhill, who remained standing and in a stunned daze. Irish immediately grabbed his gun from the jeweler's hand. Simultaneously, he slammed his right fist into Underhill's face. With a groan from the pain of his wobbly legs, Irish went over toward Frazer. Edna remained slumped over the steering wheel. When he reached the car, flames were shooting up around the front of the hood.

Inside, Edna finally moved. She lifted her hand to her forehead in a delayed reaction to the wetness she felt. After observing the blood where the woman hit the steering wheel, the woman stared at the flames in a stupor. Then, the bodies of the trapped men amid the growing fire a few feet away finally jolted her. The pitiful screams finally made her pull on the door handle. As she pushed on the jammed door, she grew more frantic.

"Look away," Irish yelled at her as he tugged on the door as well.

When she did, the glass exploded next to her when Ray smashed the window. He kept striking at it with the butt of his .45 auto until most of the window was gone. The shamus reached inside, and Irish tugged on her arm. His sleeve ripped from the glass, and he felt a stabbing pain. As she implored him to hurry, Edna twisted her body to help Ray get her through the window. Despite the cuts she received, the woman kicked away from the car as flames shot up over the car's front.

The agonized shrieks of the burning man forced Edna to look back. She saw the body of Andras pushing against the car, and the vehicle moved. However, the intensity of the fire built, and the demon let out an ominous roar.

As Irish half-carried Edna away from the burning cars, she immediately pulled him down.

"No!"

Devine stood there with his gun pointed at Ray. Then a look of shock crossed his face, and the chief of police slowly fell forward. Behind him stood Phillip Smyth. Holding the sacrificial dagger that he killed Devine with the district attorney looked at Irish and Edna for a moment. Ray lifted his gun, expecting him to attack.

"Get him!" Panthia came up next to Phillip.

"Get him yourself, you lying bitch."

He turned away, going back to the limousine.

The witch glanced at Ray and Edna; her twisted face furious. She raced after Phillip, crashing headlong into his back. The impact sent them both to the ground. Panthia scratched into Phillip's eyes with her fingernails as he screamed out in terror and pain.

As Irish and Edna lifted themselves from the ground, Underhill stumbled over to the fight to help his friend. With a shrieking curse, Panthia pointed her hand at the jeweler. He immediately went to his knees, screaming in agony.

With the witch appearing close to winning the battle, Ray told Edna to get into the limousine.

"Get the car started. I have to get the Singsing," he hurried toward the two men struggling with Panthia.

As the detective got close, he saw Phillip's face covered in blood. Irish pointed his weapon at the witch, but Smyth stabbed the witch just as he was about to shoot. Even with one eye missing, the man pushed the sacrificial blade into her again as she groaned and fell back. Her injury immediately released Underhill from her spell.

"Marion, get to her belt—dust!" Phillip called out as he collapsed on top of the witch.

Underhill scrambled over to grab one of the bags hanging from the cord around her waist.

"No, get that away!" Panthia tried to push Phillip's dead weight off her as the jeweler tugged open the leather pouch.

Then Underhill swiped the contents at Panthia. The woman shrieked as the man kept whipping the bag over her. The two men soon joined her high-pitched screaming when the whipping wind sent the fine particles across their bodies. Underhill dropped the leather pouch, holding his hands over his eyes while Smyth rolled away.

Seeing his chance, Ray went after Panthia. He pulled out the cross that hung under his ragged shirt. The shamus found the creature rolling on the ground. He kicked the witch, and Panthia looked up at him. He no longer recognized the woman's face, that smoldered and bubbled from the dust. Paying no attention to Panthia's agonized groans, Ray kneeled, then shoved the cross into her mouth.

"Swallow this, bitch!"

While the creature gargled out frenzied screams, the flesh on the witch's once beautiful face slid away from the bones. Ray grabbed Panthia's finger with the Singsing ring and ripped off the finger from the woman's decaying hand. Out of breath, he rose in triumph.

"It's a grass fire! Get out of here!"

The panicked cries filled the air around the circle of vehicles. A line of growing flames coming from the beach swept toward their side of the field—the crowd who watched the carnage amid the burning cars suddenly panicked.

"Ray, come on!" Edna cried out.

Irish hurried back. He passed Underhill, who pitifully reached up, trying to mumble something with most of his cheek flesh missing. The shamus continued without another glance. His focus was on the oncoming flames and people rushing toward the limousine.

Ray's legs weakened with each step until he saw two burly men trying to pull Edna out of the limo. Rage took over as he came around the car; he fired his .45 auto twice at their exposed backs. As the two thugs went down, he rushed to the other side of the vehicle and fell over a girl curled up by the front tire.

Getting back to his feet, the shamus recognized the naked victim of Panthia's debauchery. He yelled at her to join him, but she refused to move.

"Damn it, get in here!"

He barely heard Edna's voice as two screaming half-naked women ran by him. Ray pulled up on the sobbing woman by her arm. The woman immediately clawed at his face as she shrieked in terror. Irish punched her before he swept her into his arms. Her resistance quickly faded when he shoved her into the moving limousine.

"Don't stop!" He cried while their new passenger slid into a curled position between Edna and Ray.

Embers of smoking debris rained down on them when Edna floored the accelerator. She swung the large vehicle away from the oncoming wall of flames. Frantic people bounced off the fenders while the acrid smell of smoke filled the car. The woman slowed to avoid a speeding car trying to leave the area. She glimpsed the vehicle slamming headlong into another car amid the waves of smoke.

Ray watched with growing anxiety from his side of the car as the fire rose high into the night sky. When they turned to avoid a group of people, an older couple threw themselves on the vehicle's front hood.

"Keep moving!" Ray ordered.

"What do you think I'm doing?" Edna growled back as she tried to look over the woman hanging on the hood in front of her.

A frantic driver in front of them spun out, trying to gain speed in the dirt. The vehicle turned into the back passenger side of the limousine. Edna hit the gas and steered away from another car that almost struck them at the same time. Her quick reaction sent the couple on the hood into the air. Ray got a glimpse of them falling in front of another car that drove over the couple. Then he stared as a wall of flames swept over the car when it slowed.

"Head to your left and stay on the gas! It's almost on us!"

Despite his adrenaline surge, Ray shook his head at the dizzy feeling threatening to overtake him. She glanced over with a determined expression.

"We just have to make it to the barracks."

"Babe, do whatever it takes!" Ray felt lightheadedness sweep over him. He looked down at the bloodstains on his torn pant legs, wondering how much blood he had lost.

When Ray looked over at the woman, her eyes were closed. Her lips, covered with soot and dried blood, moved. Irish barely heard the girl's words over the noise inside the car. Then it came to him. She kept reciting the Lord's Prayer.

"Keep praying, sister."

He gave her a wink when she glanced at him.

The car hurtled into the air over a large mound in the field. The woman next to him suddenly grabbed his arm, her fingers painfully digging into his bicep. Irish saw fresh blood covering her hands and his sleeve. He felt lightheaded again.

Not good!

The light of the fire suddenly grew intense, forcing Irish to turn back at the scene so close to them. In awe and fear, he saw the flames shooting up into the night sky as a fire tornado twirled right through the few cars left near the fire pit. Fuel from the cars sparked the intensity of the flames behind them. Just as he witnessed another speeding car overtaken by the fire, a gray veil fell across his eyes.

With another sliding turn, Edna found the old gravel path to the barracks. Her foot kept the accelerator on the floor as the woman willed the heavy vehicle to move faster. She glanced in the mirror, partially seeing witness the fire tornado, and thought about Pappy.

I hope he didn't follow me!

A glance in the mirror showed her that the tornado of flames transformed into a blazing line, veering away from their path. A hopeful smile slowly crept across her face when she recognized the shadows of the old army camp. Edna slowed to make the turn behind the barracks when she heard the siren. She immediately saw the flashing red light on top of a gray and black car and swerved to avoid the onrushing vehicle. Of the long line of automobiles that initially entered the field, only a couple followed her. The driver saw more cars with flashing red lights speeding past the limousine.

Sirk got the state police here!

She breathed a sigh of relief.

"Ray, we're alright now!"

She glanced over, then immediately hit the brakes when she saw his closed eyes.

"He needs a doctor!" The naked woman's pale face held no emotion. However, she continued to hold on to Ray's bloody arm.

~~~

Several weeks after the destruction of Andras, Arizona Campbell arrived by train at the small depot in Short Corner, West Virginia. As he stepped from the last iron step onto the brick pavement, he waited for the porter to hand him his bag. Awkwardly, he got the strap over his shoulder and turned to the small depot building.

Myrna was standing there, along with a small crowd of curious onlookers. Embarrassed by the attention which he knew focused on his missing arm, the man looked like an animal trying to escape his cell. Myrna suppressed a laugh as she walked over to him.

"I thought you'd remember that interesting news spreads like wildfire in a small town."

She hugged the startled man.

"Remember, we're married in their eyes," she whispered in his ear.

She took him by the elbow and led Arizona through the gawking people. Some of the townspeople expressed their welcome, but the vast majority stared at his missing arm.

"A ticket purchased from Maryland meant everyone had to see who got off the train. It's big news when the husband returns," she grinned, then thanked a woman who held the door open for them.

"You know, I kind of expected you to show up," Myrna continued talking.

While the big man walked with her, his smile and greetings to people he barely knew were automatic. Arizona's emotions swirled through him, switching between fear, dread, excitement, and happiness. Some struck him at the same time when he glanced over at Myrna.

"You're going to be surprised at some changes out on the farm."

"Wait a minute," he hesitated. "I have some luggage that I got from my old office."

"It's already taken care of," Myrna assured him as they walked through the
~~~

lobby. "The porter's taking it to our car."

Our car!

A uniformed doorman smiled as he opened the door for them. Myrna led him to a new car parked along the street.

"I got that from Morgantown. I told him you'd need an automatic transmission."

The man frowned at her.

"How did you know about this?"

Before she replied, he instantly spat out his thought.

"Ray told you!"

She nodded and slid into the driver's side. Arizona fumbled around with his bag after opening the door, then tossed it into the back seat. The porter closed the trunk, and Arizona paid him a tip from the spare change in his pocket. After he got in the car, the big man looked over at Myrna.

"You know this will never work!"

Her expression soured briefly. Then Myrna smiled at him.

"I don't know what you're talking about. I'm taking you to your home. What happens after that is up to you."

She started the car.

They drove away to the waves of the curious townsfolk. When they passed the small hotel where they spent their first night together, Arizona stared at the window. It was the place that he decided he could fall for Myrna. Then he looked down at his stub of an arm.

"Tell me, does this thing bother you? I need the truth."

The woman looked over.

"Arizona, I've thought about this a lot since Irish let me know what happened. No, the condition of your arm doesn't bother me."

She noticed his expression of doubt.

"Let me explain why. I saw the worst when I lived in Oyster City. Since I've been here, I've met some of the nicest people on earth." She sighed.

"I've also realized that I missed you. That farm needs more than I can do alone. We'll make it work if you want it."

Arizona nodded and took a deep breath.

"Then, I'm right. This will never work. You and I need to go to Morgantown and make this marriage official."

~~~

As Arizona drove toward his farm, Yana Dela Cruz stepped out into the sunlight from her cabin on the *SS President Cleveland*. It was early morning as the ship traveled from San Francisco to Manila.

As the woman inhaled the ocean breeze, she wished her daughter did not want to remain in New York. However, Orella appeared intent upon using her friends to become a steady patron of the city's diverse nightlife.

For Yana, the lonely trip across the country gave her time to reflect upon
~~~

her life and choices. It also allowed her to think about the man who sent her another letter. Ray's last note explained that she and Orella were free. The Singsing would no longer follow them.

When she read the newspaper accounts of the disastrous fire, it was difficult not to sympathize with those who died on the field of the abandoned army post. The governor called out the National Guard to help in the aftermath of identifying and burying the bodies. While Ray didn't elaborate about the carnage, his comment at the end of his message gave her pause.

When you hear the reports of those poor souls who died, just remember that I'm confident that I'll meet them in Hell.

She prayed for Ray's soul during her last night in New York.

In her hand, she held a picture of a smiling trio at the dinner table in a New York nightclub. Yana glanced at the photograph, and a realization came to her. She'd not seen Orella's beaming smile much during their time together in New York. Her daughter attended all the right events and still held little interest in the men her friends introduced. However, Yana understood the reason for the invisible barrier Orella automatically put up with men now. It would take time for her daughter to trust anyone again, even her mother.

She'll hate me for the things I did to protect her!

Yana stared at her smile in the photo. She remembered the night vividly. It was the night she fell for a rugged shamus who had none of the charm and gentle demeanor of her ex-husband. Yet, his simple belief in trying to do right, along with his cynical view of the world, captivated her. In the end, she understood Irish was just another beat-up soul wandering the world to find his place.

You had no room for me!

She looked over the image of Ray Irish with his uncomfortable smile. He remained a fixture inside of her heart. With a sigh, Yana let the letter drop from her hand. Then, the woman dropped the photograph as well. She watched the square image land in the waves, and soon it was out of sight. Yana turned and strolled the deck to the ship's bow.

~~~

"Well, you do like your cars fancy! Wood trim and all!" Irish exclaimed as Edna drove up next to him.

The shamus stood by the entrance to his office. When he stepped toward the car, she saw his painful limp.

"You like it? I decided to try out a Nash since you loved yours so much. It's the Ambassador model they called the Suburban. Only one on the lot."

Her grin dropped when she saw his suitcases sitting by the building.

"Are you going somewhere?"

"Yeah, I closed the office. I don't plan on returning. I'm heading up to the capital to settle my last open case. Then—well, I've got to go see Pappy say goodbye."
~~~

Edna nodded.

"Get in, and I'll drive you. I need to test this thing out on the highway."

"Are you sure? It's a long drive. I can get the train." He glanced around for a taxi.

"Just get in," she ordered.

With feigned reluctance, Ray hobbled over to get his suitcases. After he put them in the backseat, he slid in next to her. Edna kept waiting for him to say something as she drove through the city. However, after he asked a couple of questions about her car, the man remained quiet.

"How are your stitches doing? Did you get them out yet?" She broke the ice.

"Yeah, it sure helped with all the itching." Ray unconsciously rubbed his arm, where the glass shard punctured a central vein.

"I had to fight like hell so they would release me from the hospital. By the way, I never got to thank you for saving my hide that night. A nurse told me you stopped by while I was still out of it."

"Yeah, the state police kept bothering me for my story. And you pulled me from a burning car, so we're even!"

She paused, thinking back.

"You and I went through a lot over that week. I can't believe we were together for only a week. Heck, Pappy saved us both by starting that grass fire."

"And nearly got us killed in the process," he grinned. "You can bet I'll let him know about that."

"Don't be like that," Edna glanced over. "If anyone knew, he'd make the perfect scapegoat for those bastards looking for answers. He was supposed to drive in with me and get you."

Ray's expression turned to disbelief.

"Do you mean you left him there on purpose?"

She nodded.

"I didn't want him to meet Emma. To be honest, I thought you were dead after we saw them dragging you behind the car. Pappy and I came up with the plan to light the fire and send them to Hell. Pappy insisted we speed through and grab you. He was sure you were still alive."

Edna paused when she noticed Ray's perplexed expression.

"Anyway, I took off while he was lighting fires. When I got close enough to see you were still moving, I noticed Andras. I remembered those images he placed inside my head. That's why I went after him!"

Irish stared at her. The cold-blooded thoughts did not surprise him. However, her belief in his demise bothered him.

Logically, it makes sense. Still…

"Just remember that Pappy will probably complain that he had to walk several miles to make a phone call," she continued. "I decided that whatever happened to me, he needed to survive. After all, I owed him that much after he and his nephew stopped those goons who got me.”

“I’m certainly glad about that.”

He leaned back in the seat.

“You overlooked a couple of things. First, as you told me once, I’m tougher than you think! Plus, you forgot about my Irish luck.”

“Touche!” Edna’s surprised glance made him grin.

~~~

The manila folder slid across the green desktop.

“What the hell is this?” The state coroner looked up at the couple with part of his sandwich hanging out of his mouth.

“Remember me? I came up a year ago concerning that Jane Doe you had in storage that your boys brought in from the Chesapeake.”

Ray sniffed the air, hating the smell of disinfectant and death inside the cold room.

The gray-haired man shook his head while he finished chewing on his meal.

“I get a lot of Doe’s,” he finally replied after opening the front of the folder.

“How many do you get that are missing the ring finger?

The man’s expression showed Ray that he remembered.

“The dentist’s records are proof of who the woman was and her true cause of death. They declared Greye La Spina missing off the coast of Italy. Her husband, the bishop of Oyster City, killed her and his friends dumped the body in the bay as he left town.”

The man leaned back in his chair with his sandwich in one hand and the folder in the other. He scanned it briefly.

“Yeah, I remember,” he frowned.

“Besides, the body is in a pauper grave. Digging her up to match these records on a hunch costs money.”

The coroner took another bite of his lunch.

“And a court order!” the man stated, although it was hard to understand through his munching.

Ray glanced over at Edna.

“Wait a minute, you mean you just let her remain there? The woman was a murder victim,” she jumped into the conversation. “Don’t you have any respect for that?”

“She’s buried. There’s no need to bother. None of you are kin, are you? It doesn’t matter.”

“Like hell. She was a friend.”

Ray shoved his hand into the breast pocket of his coat. He tossed the folded paper on the desk.

“There’s your court order. I figured you pencil necks would drag your feet. Inspector Sirk will call for a positive id. I wouldn’t upset him. There’s talk. He’ll
~~~

be the next chief of police in Oyster City.”

As Edna and Ray left the morgue, she looked over at him. His expression held a sense of relief.

“Is it over?”

He nodded.

“What’s this information about Sirk? I thought he was retiring soon.” She walked around to the driver’s side.

“Oh, that’s what he told me as well. But the pencil neck doesn’t know that.”

He grinned smugly. Edna laughed as she opened her door.

“Only one more stop,” he told her as he slid into the car.

Edna’s smile fell away, and she nodded. As she pulled into traffic, she looked over.

“Where are you heading to in Wyoming?”

“I’m not sure of the exact place yet. But I’ve got two suitcases of clothes, which is more than when I arrived at Oyster City. The only difference is that I’m riding on the inside of the train this time. I sold ol’ Betsy for the ticket.”

He paused.

“Damn thing is that I’ve left a lot of graves here as well.”

After a long silence, he looked over at the woman.

“Did you know that Arizona’s heading back to his family farm? He’ll need a lot of time to recover.”

“No, I didn’t. It sounds like you have the voice of experience,” Edna replied.

Irish nodded.

“Yeah, I tried doing it as a drunk and a hobo riding the rails across the country. Still, Arizona got me to thinking about home. I never told you I grew up on a ranch in Wyoming. Lots of open space and nobody to bother you. You can go for miles and not see another person.”

Edna’s eyes lit up at the description.

“Sounds like you’ve got a dream. That’s nice. It sounds wonderful.”

Irish leaned back in the seat, staring out the window.

“Yeah, it should be nice. I have to stop by Baltimore since I owe Pappy a goodbye.” He smiled to himself. “I must see if he’ll part with more of those magazines I like from his new stand for the long ride. Then it’s on to Laramie, where I’ll find a plot of land somewhere.”

Edna remained silent; her blue eyes kept glancing at him. The man continued staring at the road in front of them.

“You make sure to thank Pappy for me again. I don’t think we’d be talking if he and Joshua hadn’t followed us that night.”

She finally offered after growing tired of listening to the hum of her car motor.

“Yeah, I’m glad to tell him. I’ve grown to trust his Emma.” Ray glanced over.

“So, what are you going to do?”

She shrugged her shoulders.

"My apartment was in shambles when the cops broke in to find me. The manager saved what he could. I need to go by and get what I can carry in this fancy new car. All I know is I can't stay in Oyster City. Too many memories, I guess."

Edna glanced at him as Ray absently nodded. He sat up when he saw the terminal building.

"I guess that's best for you. Are you thinking about going back to California?

"Actually, I have," Edna lied. "It's been a while, and I'm sure I can find something to do. You can say that I'm footloose and fancy-free."

Ray glimpsed her blue eyes, then pointed to the curb.

"You can drop me off here."

Edna brought the car to a stop, and he opened the car door. Ray looked at the stairs leading to the red brick building. Then he turned back.

"I know I told you this before, but you're quite a woman, Edna Ackroyd." Ray leaned over and kissed her.

"You're a rare bird. Please, take care of yourself."

After Ray pulled out his suitcases, he waved to her and went inside the building. Edna waited for a moment. She looked over at the door, half expecting to see the man walking back to her car with that same cheesy smile.

The bastard is leaving!

She pulled her new vehicle down to a parking spot. After hurrying along the sidewalk, Edna entered the building. Crossing the marble-floored lobby, she found a porter. He pointed her to the gate, and the woman hurried to the iron bars separating the ticketed passengers. She spotted the large man by his unique walk as he stood in front of a newsstand. At first, Edna wanted to call out, and then she changed her mind. Instead, she went to the ticket counter while glancing back at the train schedule on the board.

"How much for a ticket to Wyoming with a sleeper car? Make it through Baltimore."

The mustached clerk ran his hand through a booklet, finally stopping at the cost of a ticket.

"That's the only way to get there from here. Price is $72.32 for one person," he told her. "I've got one spot available."

The woman opened her purse. Then she hesitated. After a moment, she put her wallet away.

"Ah, Ma'am, do you want the ticket?"

"No thanks, I told him I'm not running after him!"

Edna walked away from the ticket counter as the clerk shrugged.

~~~

Ray took a seat at the counter bar as the train left the station. He turned to
~~~

look out the window as the terminal building slowly left his sight.

That was damn hard, but she doesn't need to hang around me!

Irish heard the hints and felt her look. He came close to turning around and insisting that Edna drop everything and join him.

No, I'm not what she needs! Too many scars remain.

"Can I get you something, mister?"

Ray looked up to see a hulking black bartender waiting patiently. He noticed the ruptured duck on the man's white shirt.

"Yeah, do you have a good Irish whiskey for a fellow vet?"

The bartender grinned.

"I might have something to suit you. Not many people ask for the good stuff. Give me a minute." He winked before turning back and opening the doors to his stock in a cabinet.

As he worked, Ray got a glimpse of a familiar red dress. He turned to see a woman standing with her back to him, then walk out of his sight in the next train car. Shaking his head, he looked back at the bartender pulling bottles from the cabinet.

It can't be!

Ray rose and walked to the dining car.

"I'll be right back!"

The shamus quickly opened the doors and stepped across the coupler platform to get into the next car. Only a few diners sat at the tables, and no one wore red. A steward came to him.

"Did that woman in a red dress pass to the next car?" Ray hurriedly asked.

Instantly, he knew the answer from the man's baffled expression.

"No one in red came through here recently," the steward replied.

After he inspected the diners, the shamus nodded and backed away. When he got to the door, Ray stopped. A familiar scent hung in the air that he recognized with the same certainty as the red dress he witnessed earlier. Greye wore the same expensive and exclusive perfume from Paris.

What the hell is going on?

Still mystified, Irish made his way back to the bar. He walked to the back door, watching the rail ties speeding away. No other passengers were in the train car. Finally, he shrugged and went to the same chair he had left earlier. The bartender held a bottle in his hand, along with a smile on his face.

"I found a bottle of Jameson Green Seal that I keep out of sight from the other stewards. Truth be told, I'm partial to it myself."

"You have great taste," Irish told him with an approving nod. "Set me up a tumbler."

As he waited, Ray noticed what appeared to be a small invitation card sitting on the counter. He did not recall seeing it earlier. Glancing around with a puzzled look, the man picked it up. It smelled of the same perfume he noticed in the other train car.

Thank you!

He flipped the card over and stared in disbelief.

"Mister, are you alright?"

Clumsily, Ray looked up at the bartender, not seeing him. He nodded automatically, turning his attention back to the card. The memory of his cold first day in Oyster City flooded into his mind. He saw Greye sitting next to him on the pavement after they ran into each other. The shamus would never forget the uncertain grin that caused her slightly upturned nose to wiggle. He adored that image.

Still, the card he held in his hand sent a chill down his spine. He picked up the tumbler of liquid and glanced at the lines again.

Mrs. Henry La Spina
Terrace Court

"Here's to the memories!"

"Excuse me?" The bartender asked as he turned back to his customer.

"It's nothing, just talking out loud."

Ray shook his head as he looked at his glass.

The dark amber color reminded him of Samantha Carter's hair, another love. He pictured her twinkling eyes when she wanted to discuss something interesting. The whiskey glass was in the same hand he used to stroke her hair when he found her body.

All because I was too damn slow to solve the case!

Edna could never understand that Ray never forgave himself for his mistakes that got people killed. He recognized he needed to learn how to forget and maybe forgive himself. Dragging Edna along to find that out was not fair.

"Here's to the others who never made it home," he quietly toasted the bartender, then he finished his drink.

The shamus laid down his money and left the bar. As he walked toward the passenger car, Ray Irish held the perfumed card to his nose and smiled.

About the Author

Gordon Brewer is the pseudonym for a professional geek, history buff, and full-time dad who took up a challenge from his son to finish his first novel. As the author of over ten books, Gordon believes he's met his son's challenge in the world of writing.

Raised on a farm in Kansas, the author spent nearly five years in the US Navy, traveling to 12 different countries during this time. After his discharge, he received his BS degree with double majors in History and Political Science.

Over the next 20 years, Gordon focused on the business and IT world. His experiences left him with a need to explore wide-ranging interests in multiple genres, each with historical consideration given to the characters and settings.

Residing in Tennessee, he often uses his family and friends as unfortunate guinea pigs where they endure his tales, no matter how poorly conceived they may be.

You can find out more about the author, his upcoming books, and novellas at his website, www.gordonbrewer.com.

www.ingramcontent.com/pod-product-compliance
Lightning Source LLC
Chambersburg PA
CBHW070226200726
48293CB00005B/1478